Black Fox
&
Outlaw Kingdom

NOVELS BY MATT BRAUN

WYATT EARP
BLACK FOX
OUTLAW KINGDOM
LORDS OF THE LAND
CIMARRON JORDAN
BLOODY HAND
NOBLE OUTLAW
TEXAS EMPIRE
THE SAVAGE LAND
RIO HONDO
THE GAMBLERS
DOC HOLLIDAY
YOU KNOW MY NAME
THE BRANNOCKS
THE LAST STAND
RIO GRANDE
GENTLEMAN ROGUE
THE KINCAIDS
EL PASO
INDIAN TERRITORY
BLOODSPORT
SHADOW KILLERS
BUCK COLTER
KINCH RILEY
DEATHWALK
HICKOK & CODY
THE WILD ONES
HANGMAN'S CREEK
JURY OF SIX
THE SPOILERS TOMBSTONE
THE OVERLORDS

Black Fox
&
Outlaw Kingdom

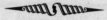

St. Martin's Paperbacks

These are works of fiction. All of the characters, organizations, and events portrayed in them are either products of the author's imagination or are used fictitiously.

Published in the United States by St. Martin's Paperbacks, an imprint of St. Martin's Publishing Group.

BLACK FOX / OUTLAW KINGDOM

Black Fox copyright © 1972 by Matt Braun.
Outlaw Kingdom copyright © 1995 by Matthew Braun.

For information address St. Martin's Publishing Group, 120 Broadway, New York, NY 10271.

www.stmartins.com

ISBN: 978-1-250-23416-2

Our books may be purchased in bulk for promotional, educational, or business use. Please contact your local bookseller or the Macmillan Corporate and Premium Sales Department at 1-800-221-7945, ext. 5442, or by e-mail at MacmillanSpecialMarkets@macmillan.com.

Printed in the United States of America

Black Fox St. Martin's Paperbacks edition / July 1994
Outlaw Kingdom St. Martin's Paperbacks edition / January 1996

10 9 8 7 6 5 4 3 2 1

Black Fox

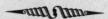

**THE THUNDEROUS SAGA OF
WEST TEXAS IN FLAMES,
WHEN MEN AND WOMEN FOUGHT
AGAINST ALL ODDS . . .**

ALLAN JOHNSON:
On his twenty-first birthday he had inherited a manservant on his family's Louisiana plantation. Now he was fighting for his land—with his former slave by his side.

BRITT JOHNSON:
To his fellow settlers he was an outcast. To his closest friend he was a man of wisdom and courage. To the Comanche he was the most dangerous warrior of all.

MARY JOHNSON:
A Comanche raiding party seized her and her children as slaves. But she never gave up hope—or lost sight of her family's future in the rolling Texas hills.

TOM FITZPATRICK:
His hatred for a black man threatened to splinter the Texans. But when fighting began he would either see beyond his prejudice—or die because of it.

LITTLE BUFFALO:
He united the Comanche and Kiowa for a war against the Texans. Along the way he would come face-to-face with a man unlike any other—an enemy who would fight hand-to-hand for his life.

To
Bettiane
The unwavering one

AUTHOR'S NOTE

The saga of Britt Johnson is not a myth. Black men seldom became legends on the frontier, and this former slave proved no exception. Yet the story of his audacity and fearlessness is as real as any to emerge from Western folklore. While his name appears only briefly in the historical chronicles of Young County, Texas, the daring task he undertook ranks high among the boldest deeds recorded in the annals of the West.

Though events depicted in *Black Fox* are historically accurate, certain liberties have been taken regarding time and place. Something over seven hundred Comanches and Kiowas did join forces to raid Young County for the very reasons described in this book. However, the unusual magnitude of this raid has tended to overshadow the awesome courage of a lone black man who risked his life to ransom the women and children taken captive by the hostiles.

Britt Johnson actually made four trips into Indian Territory, each time unaccompanied and with nothing more than his own cunning to protect him from the hazards involved. These daring sorties were not prompted by thought of reward or fame, but rather by the black man's love for his own family and an enduring compassion for the plight of his white neighbors. And the hazards were very real indeed.

Many historians credit the Comanches and Kiowas with killing more settlers, particularly Texans, than any of the southern Plains tribes. They were a proud, fierce people, closely allied for more than a century, and they bitterly resented the white man's encroachment on their ancestral hunting grounds. For any tejano (Texan), black or white, to venture north of the Red River in that day and time was considered both foolhardy and tantamount to suicide. Yet this was exactly what Britt Johnson did *not once but four times*. Had he not been a black man, his name would have undoubtedly become as renowned as the most legendary of frontier scouts.

The saga of Britt Johnson's courage and ultimate death at the hands of the Kiowas actually encompassed seven years. For the purposes of this narrative, his harrowing adventures have been compressed into a single year. While certain aspects of *Black Fox* are pure invention, the story is essentially true and accurate in detail. Possibly even more astounding than the tale itself is the fact that this black man's singular exploits have remained nothing more than a footnote to history for over a century.

MATTHEW BRAUN

❦ CHAPTER ONE ❦

One

THE WAGON LURCHED ALONG a rutted trail, from a distance its swaying motion a mere wavering speck in the vastness of the rolling plains. Stretching to the horizon, the unbroken terrain shimmered hypnotically in the heat waves from the sun. Low hills obscured broad valleys beyond, and from the crest of any given hilltop the viewer observed nothing more startling than an identical series of stunted elevations. Three days' journey to the west lay the trackless reaches of the true Plains, a barren waste devoid of trees or vegetation. Once a man had sampled the inhospitality of that land, the undulating landscape of north-central Texas came almost as a relief. Still there was a stark emptiness to the rolling plains, which made the occasional creek or shallow-bottomed river all the more appreciated. Here a man could rest in the shade of the massive oaks and willowy cottonwoods fringing the prairie tributaries and escape the relentless heat.

Two

Braced against the jarring impact of the wagon, Allan and Britt Johnson clung precariously to their seats as the team of sorrels gingerly traversed the pitted track which skirted the Brazos River. Roads were as yet a luxury in the frontier regions of Texas, and when traveling by wagon, the choice between trails or cross-country was determined more by habit then any real sense of convenience. Shifting in their seats as the wagon wheels struck a solid bed of rock, the two men stared wordlessly at the twisting track unraveling before them. Since they had been traveling steadily for two hours, conversation had gradually given way to the resigned silence of those who prefer to endure a jolting wagon without complaint. Occasionally they sighted a house set back away from the river, but the ramshackle dwellings hardly seemed worthy of comment. Neither of the men was especially garrulous, at any rate, sharing a somewhat taciturn disposition. Behind them a distance of some ten miles lay the juncture of Elm Creek and the Brazos, and after an uneventful morning on the trail it seemed apparent that nothing remarkable had happened to the settlers along the way during the winter. Lacking anything of significance to discuss, they both felt more comfortable with the silence; the quiet of strong men whose companionship had withstood the test of time and no longer required the crutch of idle conversation.

Although Allan and Britt bore the same surname and both dressed in the coarse linsey of frontiersmen, the similarity between them ended there. Allan was of medium height and rawhide lean, with the sandy hair and

deepset eyes which instantly marked unbroken generations of Anglo-Saxon heritage. When he spoke, his
voice betrayed the soft inflections of a native-born
Southerner, and something about his manner evoked
the cultured gentry of magnolia-studded cotton plantations. While strangers could only surmise, those who
knew Allan intimately were well aware that his family
had once belonged to the southern aristocracy. The dissipations of a wastrel father, who subscribed to the theory that gaming rooms and bordellos presented a
greater challenge than the pastoral life, ultimately
brought the family to ruin. Shortly afterward, the elder
Johnson died from the residual effects of his debauchery, and Allan resolutely determined to seek a new start
for the family on the frontier. En route, his mother also
died, and with her passing an era had ended for the
once distinguished family.

Of all the Johnsons, Britt's life was least affected by
the sudden change in fortune. For Britt was black, a
former slave. And what a man had never possessed
could hardly be wrested from him by the caprice of
fate. Born to parents who were themselves the children
of slaves, his heritage was a curious blend of savage
courage fused with docile servitude. As if a predator cat
had been crossed with a cream-fed tabby, the mutation
that resulted was neither wild nor tame. Much like
trained tigers who have surrendered their freedom for
a warm cage and full belly, what was once a race of
warriors had grown obedient to the lash and humble
beyond all understanding.

But unlike his fellow blacks Britt had been graced
with a master of enormous compassion. Opposed to
slavery solely on the basis of its essential inhumanity,

Allan found the degrading of another human being the most repugnant aspect of plantation life. On his twenty-first birthday Allan inherited Britt as a manservant; he immediately renounced the legacy by declaring his newly acquired slave a freedman. But the bond between them remained impervious to a mere declaration of freedom. They had been raised together, separated only by a year in age, and the difference in their color had never proved a deterrent to the closeness they shared. Allan's rashness had marked him as a rebel among the gentry, and those in the slave compounds were equally astounded when word spread that Britt had elected to remain in the service of his former master.

When the Johnson fortune crumbled and Allan turned his eyes to the frontier, Britt once again chose to accompany his lifelong friend. Privately they made a pact that everything acquired on the Texas plains, be it land or wealth, would be held jointly. And in Allan's brassbound strongbox there resided a document of incontrovertible legality which provided Britt and his heirs a full share in all future holdings.

Accompanied by their wives and children, Allan and Britt arrived in Texas only four short years after the battle at San Jacinto. Wandering ever westward, they had searched for land that would lend itself to both farming and cattle raising and had finally homesteaded on Elm Creek a few miles east of the Brazos.

Over the ensuing decade the fertile bottomland proved exceptionally bountiful, and with each passing year their herd of rangy longhorns required more space on the open grazing lands to the west. Prosperity and good fortune had once more returned to the Johnsons, and their decade of toil on the merciless plains had drawn the two men even closer. Seated before the fireplace during the winter of 1860, Allan and Britt had listened to the howling blizzards beating at the door and remarked that the last ten years had indeed been a time of plenty for the Johnsons of Elm Creek.

Spring had come early that year, with the chill winds giving way to warm breezes almost overnight. Where ravaged clumps of brown grass struggled for existence only a fortnight ago, there now flourished a succulent green sea of knee-high graze. Brilliant colors sparkled throughout the gently rolling grasslands, as if nature had robbed from every hue in the spectrum. Absorbed in nature's handiwork as the wagon jolted along the river trail, Britt felt a renewed sense of awe that a stark and ofttimes hostile land could produce such lurid beauty. Bluebonnets spread widely across the plains like deep cerulean pools, and on the hillsides mountain pinks flamed as if the earth had burst forth in molten greeting to the warming rays of spring. Sunflowers reached skyward with tawny, golden delicacy, and like spots of melting snow on the prairie, daisies wove a hoary carpet through the lush green grasses.

Britt was suddenly struck by the deceptive contradictions of the Plains, the awesome spectacle of its vast, serene beauty that, as easily as not, could conceal any number of dreadful fates just over the next rise.

Three

While his mind was preoccupied with such thoughts, the wagon crested a slight knoll, and Fort Belknap came into view. A sense of relief swept over him as it had many times in the past; the instinctive waning of tenseness experienced by any man once the ever constant dangers of the Plains are left behind. Although Britt frequently chided himself for this wary attitude, he realized it was a carry-over from a decade of ceaseless raiding by the Indians and would doubtless remain a habit for the rest of his life. Indian Territory lay only a day's ride north of the Elm Creek settlement, and almost from the moment the first homesteader broke ground, the Comanches and Kiowas had retaliated with a prolonged nightmare of bloody raids.

The rolling terrain of north-central Texas had once been the prime hunting grounds of the southern Plains tribes. Until the arrival of the first settlers in the 1830s the prairie lands west of Fort Worth had teemed with game of every description, particularly with immense herds of buffalo. Since the Indians depended on this shaggy-coated beast for their very existence, they were understandably enraged that the white-eyes had violated their sacred hunting preserve. With the appearance of plowed fields and herds of longhorn cattle, the game animals were driven even farther west, and the Indians reacted with savage violence.

Each spring brought a resurgence of the terrible raids, leaving the Plains strewn with scalped settlers and burning homesteads. Only with the first frost and the blinding fury of winter's blizzards did the Comanches and Kiowas halt their bloody depredations. Wintering in the sheltered valleys of the Wichita Mountains, they patiently endured the swirling storms, awaiting only the first signs of spring to resume their war against the hated tejanos.

With characteristic sluggishness the government finally acted to save the settlers of its newest state. Troops poured into Texas at an accelerated pace, establishing a chain of forts across the western Plains. Fort Belknap became a pivotal command post for the army, with Fort Richardson located twenty miles to the east and Fort Griffin an equal distance to the southwest. Situated on the Brazos, approximately ten miles below Elm Creek, Fort Belknap's cantonment area rapidly spread across the irregular terrain, eventually housing close to a regiment of troops. As if to compensate for their past indifference, the army took the field with a vengeance and carried the war to the Indians. Striking with unrelenting ferocity, their campaign forced the Plains tribes ever backward. Step by step the Indians retreated, until ultimately they were driven to sanctuary in the vast, unmapped wilderness of Indian Territory. Retaliation was swift and final whenever the Indians dared even a token raid, and by the close of the 1850s the Comanches and Kiowas seldom ventured below the south bank of the Red River.

Peace had come at last to the western Plains, and the unyielding encroachment of the whites now seemed complete. As Allan and Britt rolled through the front gate of Fort Belknap in their wagon that cloudless spring morning, there had not been an Indian raid on the Elm Creek settlement in over two years.

Four

The fort was a beehive of activity that morning, swarming with knots of soldiers, freighters, and meat hunters.

Spring had arrived, and every man on the post was eager to shake the enforced lethargy of winter with a furious burst of energy. Nonetheless, they each paused in their work, nodding and smirking as the wagon moved onto the road which skirted the parade ground. Allan Johnson and his freed slave were well known in and around Fort Belknap. Over the years, they had become a subject of curiosity, if not outright envy, due to their rapidly expanding ranch on Elm Creek. Although few men dared to cross the Johnsons openly, they looked on Allan with studied contempt for having so casually freed a black man. For the most part, soldiers and settlers alike would never accumulate the necessary wealth to invest in slaves. Owning another human being was a godlike pursuit seldom attempted by any except gentry. And they deeply resented a man who displayed such offhanded indifference to the principal status symbol of the day.

Envy, of course, was an emotion that no white man would admit regarding the black half of the Johnson family. Nevertheless, there was undisguised bitterness toward Britt, often of a more overt nature than that expressed for Allan. Within the compound and throughout the various settlements of the area he was known simply as Nigger Britt, which identified him in terms of both name and rank in the social order of the white man's newly acquired Plains kingdom. While the name was rarely used more than once in Allan's presence, it was in common usage among the settlers themselves. Circumstances being what they were, Britt had finally learned to grit his teeth and hear only that part of the derisive appellation which he wished to hear. But there were still times when he would have liked to ram the white man's mockery back down his throat with a meaty fist.

Ignoring the stares, Britt jumped lightly to the ground as Allan brought the wagon to a halt before the sutler's store. For a big man he moved with uncommon litheness, betraying a deceptive speed and agility beneath the corded bulk of his shoulders. Although he was raised to be a manservant and never experienced the back-breaking labors of a field hand, Britt had still inherited the towering stance and awesome bulk of his primeval ancestors.

Regardless of their superior attitude and patronizing smirks, no white man had ever risked provoking Britt to the point of physical confrontation. And even in the provincial outcountry of the Plains, it seemed that intolerance and malice had been tempered with equal parts of discretion. The fact that Britt confidently wore a Colt Navy .36 was also a matter of some conjecture among the white community. On more than one occasion he had used it with indisputable results against the Comanches, which doubtless gave pause for thought to those who had been reared in the belief that black men rarely possessed the backbone for a fight to the finish.

Side by side, Allan and Britt mounted the creaky stairs and entered the sutler's store. Stony faced, they ignored the loafers on the front porch, who had stopped talking and were watching their progress with amused winks at one another.

Sutler's stores normally restricted their trade to army personnel. But since the nearest civilian merchant was in Weatherford, some fifty miles distant, the post commander allowed settlers to replenish staples on a limited basis. Colonel Jason McKensie had proven to be a friend to the homesteaders in many ways during his tour of duty, not the least of which was permitting them to purchase necessities whenever weather or events prevented the long trip back to civilization. Passing barrels of dried fruit and an ancient potbellied stove, the two men crossed the dimly lighted store and stopped before the counter.

"Morning, Mr. Phillips," Allan said, leaning across the counter to look down the aisle where the sutler was seated at a makeshift desk.

Turning from his preoccupation with a set of ledgers, the storekeeper smiled broadly and walked toward them. "Good morning, Mr. Johnson. Haven't seen you since that last big storm." Glancing over the counter at Britt, he nodded. "Britt, see you made it through the winter."

"Nothin' to it, Mr. John," Britt responded with a faint grin. "All you've got to do is breathe in more than you breathe out."

Unsure if the black man's remark wasn't slightly mocking, the merchant ignored him and looked back to Allan. "Well, what can we do for you this fine spring day, Mr. Johnson?"

"Got a list all made out," Allan replied, tossing a battered scrap of paper on the counter. "Hope you can get to it right away. We'd like to make it back to the place before dark."

"Certainly, no problem at all. Just make yourself to home while I start gathering these things."

The sutler began moving from shelf to shelf, selecting items as he glanced at the list. Allan and Britt wandered casually through the store, pausing to inspect goods they had seen many times before. Like most back country people, they never quite lost their fascination for the profusion of items stocked by merchants, almost as if they were overawed by the sheer abundance lining the bins and shelves. Moving quickly from counter to shelf and back again, the sutler began a none-too-subtle probe for the latest gossip as the pile of goods started to accumulate.

"How's everyone over Elm Creek way? Haven't heard much from you folks most of the winter."

"Getting along just fine," Allan said, absorbed in reading the label on a bottle of patent medicine. "Old man Whittiker passed away, and there's two new babies, but nothing of any real consequence, I guess you'd say."

"That's a shame," Phillips commented. Without clarifying whether he meant the death or the births, he resumed without pause. "What do you folks over there think of this new President we've got?"

"Mr. Lincoln?" Allan asked. "Oh, I guess most of our people aren't too happy with a Northern Republican in office. Course, some folks have trouble seeing the good in anything if it's not just according to their own ways." Allan and Britt exchanged glances, and the black man cut his eyes at the sutler, shaking his head in amusement.

"Well, it takes all kinds," the merchant replied cryptically. "On the other hand, though, I hear lots of people saying he's going to split this country right down the middle. And if it comes to that, then we all might as well pack it in."

"Maybe," Allan said. "But it's always been my experience that most fights are started by hot air more than anything else."

"Well, you never know, do you, Mr. Johnson?" Phillips huffed. "You just never know."

Grunting, the sutler began searching through a bin for a spool of thread, and they could hear him mumbling fitfully to himself. Britt smiled fully at Allan, delighted that his friend had gigged the busybody on the prongs of his own shaft. Without further attempt at conversation the merchant toted up the charge and sacked their provisions in burlap bags. The Johnsons hefted their sacks, nodded to Phillips' curt thanks, and strolled unhurriedly through the front door. Both of them were well pleased with the way the morning had started. Crossing the porch they again chose to ignore the loafers' sudden lapse in conversation. Heaving the bags over the side of the wagon, they walked forward and climbed onto the seat.

Suddenly there was a commotion at the front gate, and a sentry's urgent shout carried across the cantonment, "Corporal of the guard!" That instant a mounted courier raced through the gate at a full gallop, sending chunks of turf flying as he bypassed the road and thundered straight across the parade ground. Reining his lathered horse to a halt before headquarters, the trooper dismounted and darted inside, leaving the wind-blown animal heaving and gasping for breath.

Five

Allan and Britt remained in their seats for a moment, watching curiously. Then settlers and freighters started streaming toward headquarters from every part of the post, and within minutes a large crowd had assembled in front of the building. Dismounting, the two men hurried across the parade ground and joined the excited crowd. Speculation was rife, and as the murmuring voices swelled in volume, it seemed that each man present had a different opinion as to the courier's dramatic arrival.

At that moment the headquarters' door flew open, and several regimental officers rushed from the building, moving grim faced and purposefully toward the barracks areas. Close on their heels, Colonel McKensie appeared in the doorway and stepped to the edge of the porch. The crowd grew silent as they noted his foreboding expression, and he observed them closely for a moment, as if collecting his thoughts. Then he seemed to straighten slightly, and the impassive mask of a professional soldier covered his features once more.

"Men, I've got some bad news," McKensie called in a grave voice. "The Southern states have seceded from the Union, and civil war has broken out."

Bedlam swept over the crowd as several men began shouting questions at the officer while others stared at one another with stunned disbelief. Many of those with Southern sympathies were elated beyond words, slapping each other on the back; laughing and yelling like schoolboys who had just been challenged to a snowball fight. Raising his arms for quiet, Colonel McKensie's voice carried over the steady din of the gathering.

"Quiet! Let me have your attention! Now all the details will be posted later, but for the moment you should know that both the North and South are mobilizing armies, and it appears there will be a major battle sometime soon. Since Texas no longer considers itself a member of the Union, we are in effect standing on foreign soil. My command has been ordered east to Fort Leavenworth, and we will depart within forty-eight hours. In the meantime, if further information becomes available, I will see that it is passed on to you immediately."

With that McKensie turned to enter the building. The roar of the crowd once more swelled to a fever pitch, and already the two factions which now comprised their severed ranks were eyeing one another with undisguised hostility. Suddenly, like the popper of a bullwhip, the sharp crack of Allan Johnson's voice sliced across the cantonment area.

"Colonel McKensie!"

The crowd fell silent and turned to stare, puzzled by the rage so apparent in Allan's harsh tone. McKensie halted in his tracks as if stung by the command, and then spun about, sweeping the men with a piercing glare in an effort to locate the one who had shouted. Allan separated from the crowd and moved forward, halting a few paces from McKensie.

"Colonel, if I understand you right, you and your men are pulling out, which means the settlement people are left to fend for themselves. Have you got any idea what'll happen when the Comanches and Kiowas get wind of that?"

"Mr. Johnson, soldiers don't make wars, they only fight them," McKensie snapped, his voice tight and strained. "This command is under orders, and whether it suits you or not, that's how it stands."

"Orders be damned!" Allan shouted. "The minute you ride out that gate the Indian raids will start all over again, and this country will be knee deep in dead ba-

bies and raped women. Do you want that on your conscience?"

"Lower your voice, sir, unless you want to spend the
night in the guard house. You seem to have forgotten
that the South started this war. Texas is the one that seceded from the Union, and I suggest you look to Texas
for protection!"

Turning on his heels, McKensie marched into the
headquarters building and slammed the door with rattling force. For a moment the crowd stood silent, eyeing Allan uncertainly. Then the Union men began
drifting toward the sutler's store, declaring raucously
that the occasion called for drinks all around.

Sobered by Allan's brutal statements, the settlers
gathered in a somber knot. Glancing at one another
with apprehension, the men shuffled from foot to foot
and pondered the dismal situation. Finally a leathery-
faced homesteader from the Graham settlement spoke
what was in the mind of every man present.

"Johnson, it appears to me you done hit the nail
square on the head. Come summer, this here country's
gonna be crawlin' with Injuns, and a white man won't
have no more chance'n a woodpecker in a rock quarry.
I don't know about you boys, but I'm gonna load up
my family and git the hell back to civilization."

"Mister, if you're bent on running, then you'd best get
started," Allan growled. "Personally I didn't break my
back for ten years just to let a bunch of scraggly-assed
Indians send me down the road."

Glancing around, Allan caught sight of Britt, and the
black man smiled shallowly, nodding his head with approval. Allan's mind stopped whirling for just a moment, and it occurred to him that with a score of men

like Britt he'd take on the whole damn Comanche nation. Suddenly it dawned on him what must be done, and he signaled for Britt to follow as he strode rapidly toward the hitching rack in front of the sutler's store.

Six

The horse felt good under Britt. The smooth, rocking motion of the animal's steady lope seemed to stimulate both his mind and his body. Watching the countryside rush by as they pounded north along the Brazos, he realized that since settling in Texas, he had become a real Plainsman. The manner by which a person traveled from one point to another had once been a matter of complete insignificance. But the vast, hostile distances of the Plains quickly reshaped a man's attitudes. After a decade on the frontier he now found himself openly scornful of anything less reliable than a fleet, sure-footed cow pony. The horse he was now astride, while adequate and certainly not a crowbait, was a far cry from the powerful mustangs he and Allan had broken to saddle. But then, under the circumstances, he really had no leeway to be critical of another man's horse.

Allan had stormed into the sutler's store and offered a hundred dollars to the first man who laid the reins of a horse in his hand. That amount of money represented three or four months wages to most men, double the value of an ordinary horse, and when the dust settled, a grizzled meat hunter had led the rush to accept Allan's startling offer. Within moments Britt was mounted and galloping through the front gate. Allan's plan was simple and direct, and unless the situation changed drastically, it was the only way left open to the settlers. A meeting must be called among the Elm Creek homesteaders, and before the night was out, they would have to organize in some manner to protect their settlement.

The army had abandoned them, and with Texas mobilizing troops to fight a civil war, it seemed obvious that the settlers must look to their own defenses. Otherwise, their only alternative was to forsake the land and homes they had struggled so hard to wrest from the wilderness. Britt was to alert the settlers to the outbreak of war, emphasizing the strong likelihood of renewed Indian raids, and to urge everyone to attend a meeting at the Johnson ranch that night.

Slowing the horse to allow him a breather, Britt's thoughts focused on this unforeseen and now imminent danger to his family and the bountiful life they had found in the West. From the day Allan freed him and their immigration to Texas shortly thereafter, Britt had known a serenity which rarely came to those of his race. With Allan's steadfast patronage he was building a secure and substantial future for his children. A legacy bequeathing not only legal freedom but, equally significant, the material independence that would allow them to deal with their white neighbors on a basis of live and let live. Certainly a black man was still a nigger, even in the West, but somehow it was different from the South. Perhaps frontiersmen had all they could do just to stay alive and, as a result, had neither the time nor the energy for preoccupation with fine caste distinctions. Whatever the reason, it was a damn sight more gratifying to be a nigger on the Brazos than it was to have been a liveried manservant back on the plantation.

Not that the frontier didn't have its share of bigots and fiery-eyed racists. Farther south, in the fertile Blacklands of central Texas, there were any number of cotton plantations. And in every sense of the word, a black man's life there was undiluted old South nigger from dawn to dusk. But on the outer reaches of the frontier, where life was an unrelenting struggle for mere survival, there was a tolerant outlook about the time-honored prejudices of civilized men. Certainly the whites of Elm Creek displayed a superior attitude around Britt, and there were many who even evidenced something akin to loathing or hate. But in the main, they were willing to accept him as a freedman and a member of the settlement, albeit one of a peculiar and somewhat ill-defined station.

Of course, he had often mused on the fact that his family comprised the only blacks in Elm Creek, and it was an interesting pastime to speculate on the marked change that would occur should every family suddenly acquire their own resident nigger. Still, it was doubtless more pleasant to remain the community freak, and it had never especially bothered him to be surrounded by a sea of curious, if somewhat aloof, white faces.

Rounding a bend in the river, Britt sighted the juncture with Elm Creek, and his thoughts were once more wrenched back to the more immediate problem. Although he was a long way from gaining the spontaneous acceptance of his white neighbors, there were more pressing concerns on the not-too-distant horizon. For the moment he would have to remain content with the fact that he and his family were allowed to live in peace. Chuckling to himself, Britt momentarily pondered the irony of having won a niche in the white man's world only to find that it was now being threatened by a race for whom he instinctively felt great empathy. The Indians were just beginning to experience the calculated ruthlessness of the white man. His people had trudged through two centuries with that yoke of oppression shackled around their necks, and without probing the thought too deeply, he sensed that the blacks and the Indians were only shortly removed from sharing a bitter repugnance for the white man's callous superiority. Spurring the horse, Britt turned onto the trail bordering Elm Creek and tried to convince himself that the warning he carried was still an alarm against the true enemy.

Seven

The boundless prairie sky seemed cluttered with a profusion of stars as the men began arriving on horseback. Creaking saddle leather and voices raised in sober greeting shattered the stillness of the night, and within an hour after dusk the yard was filled with settlers. Standing in small groups or squatting down with their backs against the house, they spoke in muted tones, and the intensity of the words laid bare the depth of their concern.

While they would hardly have thought of themselves as frontiersmen, there was a distinct, roughhewn sameness to their appearance. They were dressed in coarse clothing with pants stuffed in cowhide boots and worn pistols strapped around their waists. Their features were windburned and wrinkled beyond their years from constant exposure to the relentless Plains sun. Although the majority had not yet reached forty, their faces seemed leathery, with the grainy surface of poorly tanned rawhide, and the visage of each man reflected the deprivation and hardship they had endured. Their eyes were the eyes of old men, wary and passionless, cold pools mirroring the death and suffering they had outlived to wrench an existence from the hostile plains.

Many were the descendants of men who had once challenged the frontiers of Kentucky and Tennessee, and rather than social position or wealth, their legacy was the irresistible urge to follow the sun and take root where few men dared to linger. They were hard men, accustomed to death in its multiplicity of forms, and in the face of threat they could display the brutal savagery of those who have come to grips with the compromise between conscience and survival. On this still, starlit night, however, their thoughts dwelt not on the danger to themselves, but rather on the unspeakable horrors which awaited their loved ones at the hands of the Comanches and Kiowas.

The conversation ceased, and a silence fell over the men as the rattling sounds of a wagon approached from the darkness. Moments later the wagon came to a halt before the house and Tom Fitzpatrick, the Johnsons' closest neighbor, leaped to the ground. Nodding to the curious men, he helped his wife and two children to dismount, and the family walked slowly toward the house. Fitzpatrick was a man of formidable bulk, strapping and husky, with pugnacious features and hands scarred from a lifetime of meaningless brawls. His sandy hair and flashing blue eyes were in keeping with an ungovernable Irish temper, and more than one man in the group had reason to respect the deadliness of his sledgehammer fists.

Fitzpatrick was generally liked and even admired by some, but for the most part men moved cautiously around him, as they would a surly dog or a temperamental stallion. There hovered about him the unpredictability of a wild beast. As he approached the house, the men remained silent, having long since learned that the wisest course was to fathom his mood before testing his humor.

Soft light spilling through the open door created a distorted shadow as Allan stepped into the yard. The men gathered closer, some greeting him by name, and it was readily apparent that the gravity of the meeting had dissipated the jocular manner which they normally enjoyed. Allan glanced around the group, nodding solemnly to the grim faces, quickly satisfying himself that the men of the Elm Creek settlement were present.

Before him stood eighteen men and three boys.

"Glad you could all make it," he announced. "We've got a lot to settle tonight, so why don't you come inside and find a seat while the women serve coffee."

Quietly the men trooped into the house and took seats around the large main room. Sarah Johnson bustled about the kitchen area, busily filling crockery mugs with steaming coffee. Mary, Britt's wife, moved around the room with a tray, serving the men as quickly as they found seats. The Johnson children, Allan's two girls and Britt's two boys and a daughter, stared round-eyed from a corner in the dining area, completely overawed by the presence of so many men. Elizabeth Fitzpatrick quickly seated her own children, a boy and a girl, with the Johnson children and then joined Mary in serving coffee. Within minutes the room was settled, and the somber group sat clutching their mugs, waiting expectantly for Allan to begin. Standing near the fireplace, he stooped to light his pipe with a stick of kindling, then turned to face the men.

"By now you all know the situation. The army is pulling out, and we're faced with the choice of defending ourselves or running. Not a man in this room doubts that the Indians will start raiding as soon as the troops are gone, and I expect everyone here still remembers what that means." Allan paused as the men shifted in their seats and glanced apprehensively at one another, all too clearly aware of what they could expect from the Kiowas and Comanches. "Just so you won't be grasping at straws, I'll tell you now that I spent the afternoon raisin' hell with Colonel McKensie, and there's not even an outside chance he'll give us any help. He's leaving day after tomorrow, and when he goes, every last trooper goes with him. I suppose the first thing we've got to decide is how many of you are going to stay and how many plan on leaving. After we know that, then we can figure out what has to be done next."

Many of the men dropped their heads, wrestling with conflicting emotions as they stared at the floor. Their dreams and years of sacrifice were weighed against the devastation they knew would come. The choice to stand and possibly die or run and start over again now forced each man to search the depths of his own soul. Jonathan Hamby, a thin, ferret-faced man of outspoken views, slowly rose to his feet when it became clear that no one wanted to be the first to speak.

"Seems to me we're losin' sight of the main issue,"

Hamby said. "Whether your loyalties are North or South, this country's at war, and our first responsibility is to take part in that fight."

"Jonathan, every man has to do what he thinks is right," Allan replied. "If a man feels he has to take part in the war, then that's what he'd best do. Personally I don't feel like I owe the government a thing. North or South. I figure we're going to have all the fight we can handle right here, and if somebody doesn't hold the frontier, then this country will be set back a hundred years by the time the war's over in the East. Britt's staying, and Tom Fitzpatrick is moving his family in with mine for added protection, but it's going to take more than three men to hold the settlement. Right now the only thing I'm interested in is how many of you are going to stay with us."

"Well, I don't know how the rest of you feel, but what Allan says makes sense to me." Grady Bragg spoke from his chair without rising. Somewhat older than the others, normally reserved and slow to take the lead, he was a rotund little man who somehow always managed to look ill at ease on a horse. "We took this country, and the Indians weren't able to drive us off even before the army came. So I reckon it's like Allan says, we don't owe the government a damn thing. But we sure as hell owe it to ourselves and our families to hold onto what we've grubbed and rooted to make out of this country."

There was a murmur of assent from some of the group. Joel Meyer and Bud Williams nodded emphatically and voiced their determination to stand and fight. But others were either skeptical of the settlement's chances against overpowering Indian forces, or else felt that their main obligation was to Texas and the South.

Within moments a heated argument broke out amongst the group, and as the acrimony swelled in volume, Tom Fitzpatrick's voice could be heard denouncing the holdouts as a bunch of "chicken-gutted pig farmers." Finally, just as the meeting was on the verge of being transformed into a bareknuckled donnybrook, Allan was able to quiet Fitzpatrick, and an uneasy silence fell over the room. Disgusted by their antics and yet needing their support, Allan stared the men down and waited for their anger to subside.

"It appears to me we've got too many talkers and not enough thinkers in this group," Allan finally informed them. "While you gents have been spewing hot air all over each other, I noticed that one of us has been doing some thinking. And he might just have some answers worth hearing. How about it, Britt, you got any suggestions?"

As a body, they turned to stare at Britt, who was leaning against the back wall and thus far had not uttered a sound during the entire meeting. The expressions on their faces ranged from puzzled amazement to undisguised resentment. The furthest thought from their mind was to seek the advice of a black man, even if he was Allan's pet nigger. But at the same time, their attitude evidenced a faint trace of amused curiosity as to what Britt might say. Watching them, Britt was instinctively aware of their patronizing air, and for a moment he thought to tactfully avoid speaking. Then he glanced at Allan, and as their eyes met, Britt realized that his friend was purposely using him as one would use a hickory switch: stinging the men with their own childishness so as to shock them into rational thought.

"Seems to me you got to decide what comes first,"

Britt commented frankly, "your families or some war
we don't know nothing about. Allan's daddy used to
say that wars was made by old men too dried out to
fight and all lathered up to get their names down in the
history books. I'm not real anxious to fight anybody,
but I mean to protect what's mine. So if it was me, I'd
let the folks back East fight their war, and I'd look to
my own. The only other thing I'd say is that I haven't
heard anyone mention asking Austin for help. Even if
they don't act like it sometimes, we are part of Texas,
and they might just have a few men they could spare."

The simple eloquence of Britt's incisive speech had a
stunning effect on the men. With a few words he had
cut away the useless gristle and penetrated to the very
marrow of their divisive attitudes. Moreover, he had
suggested an obvious and yet seemingly elusive solution
to the problem of the settlement's defense, one which
might easily resolve the threat of Indian attack long before the first raid could even be mounted. But if the
men were taken aback by the clarity and directness of
Britt's logic, they were also openly affronted that a
black would presume to give them a lesson in disci-
plined thinking. They avoided looking directly at Britt,
but sharp, darting glances left no illusion as to the extent of their resentment, and while the solution lay exposed for anyone to grasp, the room grew thick and
oppressive with a hostile silence. Somewhat disconcert-
ed himself, Allan finally recovered from the impact of
Britt's words and jumped into the breach.

"Something else my daddy always said was that when
a man gives you a good idea, you should do something
about it. I propose that we form a delegation and send
them to Austin with a request that state troops be sent

to garrison Fort Belknap. Seems to me they could protect us from the Indians at the same time they're
guarding this area for the South."

Allan's assured manner galvanized the men to action.
No sooner had he stopped talking than Fitzpatrick and
Bragg volunteered to beard the Austin politicians in
their own den. Suddenly everyone in the room was
shouting, demanding that they also be considered for
the honor, and before it was over, Allan was forced to
organize an election to choose the delegates. When
calm once more settled over the group, Joel Meyer and
Grady Bragg had been selected to leave at sunrise for
the state capitol. And without actually realizing how it
came about, the men of Elm Creek settlement had
elected to stand and fight.

Eight

As Allan closed the door, after bidding the settlers
goodnight, the muffled sounds of their horses began
fading in the distance. For a moment he paused, reflecting on the events of the evening, then turned back to
the room with a relieved smile. Britt and Tom and the
three women were watching him closely, anxious for
his reaction to the meeting, and his obvious good spirits quickly eased their minds.

With the first crisis behind them Allan's thoughts
shifted to more mundane problems, such as where everyone was going to sleep. Britt had his own cabin less
than fifty yards south along the creek, but even with
imminent threat of an Indian raid, he knew that Mary
would never consider moving. So that aspect of their

situation seemed to take care of itself. But the main house had only one bedroom, and the sudden addition of the Fitzpatrick family definitely posed a problem.

"If you're worrying about where everyone is going to sleep," Sarah advised, "don't bother." After twelve years of marriage she had developed an eerie faculty for anticipating his thoughts, and on occasion it had proved downright embarrassing. "Tom and Elizabeth can take the loft, and we'll make pallets for the children in the parlor."

"Good idea," he agreed. Moving to the fireplace, Allan scraped the bowl of his pipe and began tamping in a fresh load of tobacco. "Before we all get off to bed, I want to caution everybody about what we're facing. The Indians might well come raiding before we get any state troops, and I don't have to draw pictures for you women about what they've got in mind." The women glanced at one another, and the fright on their faces made it evident that no further warning was necessary. "The men will never be far enough away that we can't hear a gunshot, and I'll leave my pistol hanging beside the door just in case we do have visitors. And Mary, until things get a bit safer I think it would be a good idea for you and the children to spend your days here in the main house."

Mary looked at Britt, and his quick affirmative nod convinced her that their own home would have to remain neglected until the danger had passed. Allan paused to light his pipe and in that moment of distraction failed to see the frown that crossed Tom's face.

Fitzpatrick had never owned any slaves or even had any dealings with blacks, much less being thrust into a situation where he was forced to live with them. But he was second generation Tennessee, having been raised like his father before him in the foothills of the Smokies, and in his scheme of things there were few creatures lower than a black man. Generations of prejudice and envenomed bigotry had been transfused from father to son, and although there was no rational foundation for his hate, Fitzpatrick was fond of declaring that he'd sooner own a good horse than a lazy nigger. The thought of his children being forced to spend their days playing with three woolheads was more than he could swallow gracefully. Still, he was in Allan's house, and as he glanced around the room, it occurred to him that it might be best to take things slow.

"Them goddamn Indians better take care none of 'em fall into my hands," Tom snarled. The savagery in his voice brought everyone's head around, and his wife peered at him quizzically. Hesitant to vent his anger concerning the blacks, Fitzpatrick's wrath had quickly spilled over onto the Indians. "By Jesus, I'll teach 'em not to mess around with white women."

If Tom was aware of his insult by omission, he portrayed no outward indication. But the others found themselves unable to look at Britt or Mary. The black woman's face blanched perceptibly, and her eyes sought sanctuary in the floor. The momentary void in the conversation made the slur all the more inescapable, but before anyone could move or change the subject, Fitzpatrick's rancorous voice again broke the stillness.

"I don't know about the rest of those fainthearts that was here tonight but if any of them red devils come raidin' my land, they'll get more than they bargained for." Gesturing toward Allan, his tone seemed puzzled, as if he were seeking the answer to some profound riddle. "Lousy Indians aren't good for nothing anyhow. Why didn't the army just kill 'em off so they wouldn't come down here huntin' our women and burnin' our homes?"

"Maybe the Comanches and Kiowas figure this land is still theirs, even if we are living on it." Britt's sharp reply startled no one more than himself. Fitzpatrick had obviously intended his remark for Allan, but the black man found himself unable to hold his peace any longer in the face of such a crude affront to his wife.

Tom's head jerked around, and he stared at Britt with open animosity for a moment. Then he relaxed and glanced at Allan, shaking his head with a patronizing smirk. "I suppose you couldn't expect anything else from a nigger. If a man's got any sense at all, he knows we drove 'em out of this country, and that makes it ours."

"What if they drive us off?" Britt responded mockingly. "Does that make it theirs again?"

"Boy, you'd best watch that smart mouth while I'm around here," Tom growled, "or I'll peel a few strips off your black hide."

"Mr. Tom, you're a good man in lots of ways, and I've always admired the way you work your place, but don't crowd me." A sardonic smile played across the corner of Britt's mouth. "More than one man's tried, and I ain't lost any skin yet."

Fitzpatrick's features contorted with rage as his temper came unhinged, and he shifted as if to move toward Britt. The women stared incredulously at the scene before them, unable to grasp how the situation had become so tense in only a few moments. While Britt was

slightly taller than the Irishman, it was clear that the
two men were evenly matched, and no one had the
slightest doubt that a fight would end with one of them
being killed. Suddenly Allan leaped forward, blocking
Tom's path, and restrained him with a none-too-gentle
shove.

"Tom, let's get something straight right from the
start. While you're under my roof, you'll behave accordingly, and in this house Britt is one of the family. If
there's any argument on that score, you'd best pack up
and move on back to your own place."

Fitzpatrick's anger was replaced with a deep scowl,
but his eyes remained on Britt, and the look clearly
conveyed the surly emotions he was struggling to control. Allan was the only man in the settlement who had
won Tom's respect, and even then it was grudgingly
given. Fitzpatrick sensed in Allan the inborn qualities of
leadership, integrity, and force of character, all of the
traits he secretly longed to possess. And for reasons unfathomable even to himself, he had extended loyalty
to another man for the first time in his life. Unable to
withstand the force of Allan's stare, Tom's eyes fell to
the floor, and then he turned away. Moving to the fireplace, he leaned against the mantel on outstretched
arms, stiff and charged with tension, staring sightlessly
into the flames.

The room grew hushed and still, as if the others
dared not speak for fear of rupturing the fragile truce
which Allan's intervention had brought about. Finally
Britt broke the spell with a nod to Mary. Gathering the
children, she followed him to the front door, where
they were joined by Allan. A disquieting influence
had entered their lives, and as the men spoke their

goodnights, they each felt a strain which had never before existed. When Allan closed the door and threw the bolt for the night, it was as if Britt had been locked out from their home, and he suddenly was overcome with a premonition of unalterable disaster. Some malevolent force was at work, unseen but not unfelt, driving a wedge between him and Britt. And for the first time in his life Allan sensed that he was powerless to forestall what must come.

〰 Chapter Two 〰

One

SEATED ON A HIGH MESA with sheer red cliffs of sandstone dropping off before him, Little Buffalo stoically kept watch on the distant figures approaching across the plains below. The corners of his eyes wrinkled with concentration, and yet there was a certain impassiveness to his gaze. Broad shouldered and unusually deep chested, with the lithe suppleness of a wary mountain cat, he seemed tensed and poised on the verge of springing at some unseen threat. Still, his sharp, angular features remained frozen in a cryptic mask, and only the slight movement of his eyes betrayed the fact that he was watching the scene below.

Actually his mind was occupied with matters which lay heavily on his shoulders, troublesome thoughts that distracted his senses from the reality unfolding around him. But his eyes beheld the dust trails and the tiny antlike figures moving fatefully across the open grasslands, and in some dim recess of his consciousness there was an awareness that his time had grown short. How could the days have passed so rapidly and without recognition, he pondered. Only yesterday, or so it seemed to him now, he had come to this same spot, alone and somewhat fearful of what he was about to do. Then there had been no distracting movements on the plains below, and he had passed four days and four nights without awareness of anything save the vision which would preserve the tomorrows of his people. Now the Moon of Deer Horns Dropping Off was all but past, and the path over which he would soon lead two nations yawned before him with unsettling finality.

"Little Buffalo greets his warriors in a strange manner." Shaken from his reverie, Little Buffalo turned to find Ten Bears, elder chief of all Comanches, watching him with a concerned expression.

"*Hao*, Ten Bears," he greeted the older man. "Would you have me stand beside the trail and welcome them with the hollow flattery of a Ute dog?" Staring off into the flatlands below, his features grew even grimmer. "Many of those men will not return from the path we are to take, and when a man is rubbed out, his leader must ask himself if the path chosen was one of wisdom and purpose. Have I not seen Ten Bears mourn his brothers and ask himself these same questions when war parties returned with empty horses?"

"Your tongue is sharp," Ten Bears grunted, "and yet it bites to the heart of this thing we do. When there is war, men are rubbed out, and maybe it is the ones who remain behind that suffer the most. And yet a leader must never forget that when a warrior crosses to that other life, he does so willingly. Whether for personal glory or to hold the land for his children's children, he makes that crossing without regret. For are we not men and unlike beasts, who pass over without choice or reason?"

"Yes, that is so. We are the True People, and we decide the fate of our enemies according to our own needs. I have followed you on raids since boyhood and never once questioned your right to lead. Still, now that it is I who am about to become the leader, I cannot shake the thought that no man has the right to decide the fate of his own brother." Looking out over the vast grasslands and the river below, Little Buffalo's eyes narrowed, and he once again fell silent, watching with misgiving as the erratic form of the distant specks drew nearer and took shape.

Stretched across the plains to the south, large bands of Indians moved steadily northward, evoking a spectacle seen by few men on the Western Frontier. On and on they came, weary and trail worn, their scattered columns visible for miles in every direction. Like swirling plumes of discolored smoke, the dust cloud from their horse herds drifted skyward with unbroken symmetry, ending only on the outer rim of the distant horizon. Comprised of countless bands, both Comanche and Kiowa, they came from the barren isolation of the Staked Plains, the craggy slopes of the Wichita Mountains, and from every remote valley and rushing stream in the western reaches of Indian Territory. With the homing instinct of a nomadic race they came onward without deviation or pause, guided solely by the stars and a primitive cunning for recognizing every landmark encountered since childhood. Their destination was the land of Red Bluffs on the Canadian River, and in late September they assembled to hold council. And make war.

Shortly after the snows had melted and the wild flowers bloomed in the Leaf Moon, runners arrived from a band of Kiowas encamped on the Red River with an astounding message. The pony soldiers were deserting the string of forts which for years had desecrated the sacred hunting grounds, and from all that could be learned, they had no intention of returning. Moreover—and this the Indians found all but incomprehensible—word had spread across the Plains that the white-eyes had split into two warring tribes, with one of the tribes disavowing the Great White Father in Washington. Even now the white-eyes were battling each other on the distant side of the Great River to the east, and from the fragments of information available it seems entirely possible that they might annihilate one another before the fighting was finished.

But greater than all this was a disclosure that made the white-eyes' puzzling war seem pale by comparison. With the pony soldiers gone, the hated tejanos were left defenseless; having grown soft like women, they no longer had the long-knives to cower behind, and now at last their immunity from attack had vanished like a puff weed in a strong wind.

Elation ran rampant through the Indian camps. Warriors fired their muskets into the sky and dashed around the villages lashing their horses to a frenzy; the women sang and cried with joy and prepared great mountains of food in thanksgiving, while the children watched with growing awe and dreamed of returning to the ancient tribal lands spoken of so often by their fathers. The pony soldiers were gone, faded away like the morning mist on a sunny day, and soon their beloved Plains would grow fertile from the moldering bones of the helpless tejanos.

After their original excitement had run its course, many of the warriors spoke of striking the white-eyes while the pony soldiers were absorbed in preparations for war. Still others advocated patience, suggesting that it was wiser to allow the long-knives to weaken themselves fighting one another and then attack the tejanos. The debates ranged far into the night, often provoking harsh words and animosity, for within the social order of the Plains tribes each warrior had an equal voice, and few were noted for any reluctance to speak their mind in matters concerning war. According to tribal custom, any warrior could raise a war party simply by announcing his intention and extending a ceremonial pipe to anyone willing to listen. Those who accepted the pipe and smoked with him thereby committed themselves to the raid, and when an imposing number of braves had been recruited, the *to-yop-ke*, or leader, was then recognized as the sole authority during the expedition.

In the weeks following the pony soldiers' sudden departure a number of war parties were organized and rode out to seek vengeance on the hated tejanos. But these were minor raids, affairs of no consequence, and the great body of warriors were clearly awaiting some sign; the appearance of a *to-yop-ke* whose wisdom and foresight would lead them to a victory overshadowing anything previously known by the Plains tribes. While the preeminent chiefs of the two tribes, Ten Bears of the Comanches and Santana of the Kiowas, were as anxious as any to deal a death blow to the white-eyes, they too felt that an opportunity of such extraordinary magnitude required a war chief of invincible character. Thus, as the Leaf Moon drew to a close, the Comanches and Kiowas girded themselves for a fight to the death with the tejanos and impassively awaited the coming of their *to-yop-ke*.

Two

Tilted backward in a chair, with his head resting against the wall of the cabin, Britt puffed contentedly on his pipe. Through a haze of blue smoke hanging softly in the still air, he watched the sun merge slowly with the western horizon. He was bone-tired from a grueling day in the saddle, but with Mary's fried steak and milk gravy now on the backside of his belt, the weariness had taken on a pleasant glow. This was his favorite moment of the day; a good pipe, a sense of peace with all around him, and shortly, the soft warmth of Mary snuggled close in the intimacy of their bed. Faintly he heard the children talking inside the house, and as on other nights, it occurred to him again that he had been blessed with about all a man could ask from life.

Frank, his oldest boy, was growing tall and strong, now approaching thirteen, and already there was a quiet steadiness about him which hinted at the man he would become. Young George, on the other hand, was a mischievous hellion, full of fire and spirit even at eight, and it seemed fairly obvious that nothing short of manhood would ever calm his rowdy nature. And then there was Sue Ellen, his favorite simply because she was a tiny replica of her mother. Bright and gay, eternally smiling and asking endless questions, she was the culmination of all his hopes for the new land. Listening now to their distant laughter, Britt was filled with a sense of well-being and fulfillment, if only for a moment.

Then, as frequently happened these days, his mind whipsawed from thoughts of the good life shared by his family to the horrors they would surely face in days to come. Already word had drifted back of sporadic raids on settlements to the northeast; hit-and-run affairs which exacted small toll in lives. But a portent none-theless of the savage atrocities soon to be inflicted on the entire frontier. Before he had time to become deeply engrossed in worry, however, the thud of hooves sounded on the south trail, and two riders approached the main house. His fears of a moment ago were even further stilled when he noted that the mounted men were Joel Meyer and Grady Bragg, evidently returned from their mission to the state capitol.

Walking toward the main house, Britt saw Allan and Tom rush out the front door. The four men shook hands all around and were excitedly questioning one another as Britt reached them. Meyer and Hamby greeted him with casual nods, but their attention was quickly diverted by Fitzpatrick's bellowed demand.

"Goddammit, boys, are you gonna make us wait all night? What happened in Austin?"

Bragg and Meyer glanced at one another sheepishly, their faces suddenly gone solemn, both of them clearly reluctant to speak. Britt's eyes narrowed as he observed their hesitant manner, and the thought suddenly sped through his mind that the news they carried for the Elm Creek settlement was going to be ominous indeed. Allan and Tom were also watching the two delegates,

and their jocular attitude of a moment ago had been replaced by looks of dour apprehension.

Grady Bragg finally broke under the combined
weight of their eyes and in a wavering voice confirmed
the worst of their fears. "Allan, we did our best. Our
dead-level best. But those bastards in Austin don't give
a damn for anything right now except fightin' Yankees."
Bragg's eyes fell to the ground, and his mumbled tone
was barely audible. "They did promise to send us
twenty men and an officer."

"Twenty men!" Fitzpatrick roared hoarsely. "Christ,
they might as well not send anybody."

"Now wait a minute, Tom," Allan interjected. "Maybe
there's more to this than we've heard." The evenness of
his tone hardly compensated for the shock written
across his face, and the others were only too well
aware that their predicament was growing more acute
by the moment. Allan's voice remained calm, despite
the funereal atmosphere. "Joel, haven't you got anything to add to that?"

Haggard from the long trip and far too little sleep,
Meyer's waspish reply inferred that he clearly wasn't
about to play whipping-boy for their frustration. "Not
much. The governor same as told us to go shit in our
hats, and the way I've got it figured, none of you boys
could of done any better."

"That's right," Bragg confirmed anxiously. "The governor's got Yankee on his mind, and he just flat out told
us that the settlements would have to give ground or
else fend for themselves. We finally got to the general
in charge of the state militia and damn near had to put
a gun on him just to get twenty men."

"Twenty men," Britt repeated dully. "That's like trying

to put out a brushfire with spit." The men turned to look at him, slightly startled by his unsolicited remark, and there was a moment of stillness as they digested the full significance of the statement.

"By God, he's right for once," Tom grunted. "Twenty men are worthless as tits on a boar hog. Those Comanches will level this whole settlement, and there won't be a man, woman, or child left alive."

"Don't be too sure," Allan mused aloud. "If we can get everyone to the fort before the attack really gets started, we might just give those Indians more than they bargained for. When you come right down to it, they haven't got much stomach for a head-on fight with forty or fifty well-armed white men." Allan glanced sharply at Britt, suddenly aware of the unconscious slur and sorely embarrassed by the prejudice implicit in his comment. Britt's understanding smile relieved the tension, however, and Allan resumed hurriedly. "There's one thing for certain, though. If any of us start spreading scare talk, we'll end up with half the people on Elm Creek running so fast you won't even see their dust."

Grady Bragg chewed thoughtfully for a moment and then squirted a nearby rock with a juicy stream of amber sputum. "Maybe, maybe not. But if you're looking for a cinch bet, you just wait and see if those same fainthearts don't high-ass it into the fort when word gets around about what happened in Austin."

The other men looked at him quizzically, wondering just how many of the settlers would move into the fort and silently debated the wisdom of such a move for their own families. Shortly afterward, Meyer and Bragg mounted and rode into the dusk toward their own homesteads. Britt discussed the situation briefly with

Allan, aware that Fitzpatrick was purposely withholding comment, then walked slowly in the direction of his own cabin. Tom's bigotry had manifested itself in subtle ways since Allan's blunt warning. His latest ploy was to withdraw from any conversation which included the black man: an insidious expression of his bitter contempt for the resident nigger. Approaching the cabin, Britt once again caught the sound of children's laughter, and abruptly he decided that there were far greater dangers afoot than Tom Fitzpatrick's childish prejudice.

Three

Among the Comanche there was one warrior who stood out above all others. Since the days of ancient times, when the True People had ridden out to conquer the Plains, there had never been another who fought with such disregard for his own life or struck such fear in the hearts of his enemies. Squatted around their fires during the long months of winter, the Comanches never tired of recounting his deeds in battle. His daring and utter fearlessness in the face of death were known throughout the Plains, and even as a young man his fame spread to the camps of their ancestral enemies, the Utes and the Crow. Although it shattered centuries of precedent, it was nonetheless understandable when, as a mere boy, he was initiated into the *ko-eet-senko*, the warrior society comprised of the tribe's ten bravest men. And yet, even as a man, recognized as the most formidable warrior on the Plains, he had refused time and again to accept the mantle of war chief. Little Buffalo lived to fight, glorying in the crunch of the ax and the muted thud of an arrow as it struck home, but never once had he sought to lead his brothers to tempt the fate he himself defiantly challenged.

When runners had arrived during the Leaf Moon and word spread that the pony soldiers had retreated from Texas, there was much speculation among the tribe as to who would lead them in a war which was taken for granted. Many names were discussed, among them warriors who had previously displayed remarkable skill in organizing raids on the tejano settlements. But this was to be no mere horse-stealing expedition, one which concerned itself more with adroit theft than with devastation of the settlements. Instead, it would be a full-scale war, a fight to the finish, one last chance to drive the hated white-eyes from Indian land for all time. And an undertaking of such far-reaching significance demanded the leadership of a master warrior: a tactical genius who would provide the vision and audacity essential to a conquest of such immense proportions. A name frequently heard in these fireside discussions was that of Little Buffalo, but then everyone knew of his aversion to personal power, and they just as quickly passed on to more likely candidates.

Secretly, after it became apparent that the tribe had reached an impasse in selecting a leader, Ten Bears sought out Little Buffalo and urged him to reconsider his lofty views concerning the role of *to-yop-ke*. Far into the night they debated the authority that godlike men arrogated to themselves over other men, but Little Buffalo remained unshakable in his rigid beliefs. Finally, as the last embers of the fire began to dim, Ten Bears lost patience and for the first time in memory spoke harshly to the man he admired above all others.

"We struggle back and forth like two dogs gnawing on the same bone, while our people grow weary seeking a leader. Now you force me to speak of a matter which comes hard to my tongue. You are as my son, and it is not easy to admit that one's son is a coward. But from your own mouth you have condemned yourself, showing the skulking manner of a Crow who fights only women."

Little Buffalo stiffened, his eyes registering both anger and shock at the older man's tongue lashing. Observing him closely, Ten Bears pressed on, elated that he had at last shaken the obdurate warrior. "There are many men who are brave in battle. That is a simple thing, even enjoyable, to risk one's life with the lance or warclub against another man. But there is a higher form of bravery which few men dare to attempt, and so it becomes the test of courage for those who have left all fear behind them. My son, if you learn nothing else this night, then take away the truth that it demands greater courage to send one's brother to his death than it does to count coup on some whining Ute. One is the courage of a man who fights for his people, while the other is the courage of a boy who merely fights for himself. The man who possesses this higher courage and refuses to test it is little better than a coward, for he fears failure as surely as some men fear the knife. Until you have placed the good of your people above yourself and set aside your fears for the cause of your brothers, you must live with the thought that you were found wanting when your courage was brought to the test."

Little Buffalo stared at the chief through a haze of fury, outraged that any man would dare to speak to him in this manner. His hands clenched, and his throat tightened as he fought to control the mounting indignation which swept over him. But the ring of truth had sounded undeniably in Ten Bears' words, and even as he smoldered, he knew that for the first time in his life he must come to grips with this haunting fear of leading other men to their doom. Slowly Little Buffalo lowered his head, focusing his eyes in the dull embers of the fire, and within moments his mind cleared. Gradually he became aware of what must be done, and with a fleeting moment of regret for the carefree days now gone forever, he looked once more at the chief.

"My father, you have spoken wisely, and while it is bitter to swallow, I must accept what you have said. In the past I have fought for myself, vainly and without thought to the common good. Now I will set those childish ways aside and attempt to be the man you thought me to be. But I must do it in my own way and without promise as to what might come. With the sun I will go alone to the red cliffs and fast while I await a vision from *Tai-me*. Should He speak to me and open my mind to what lies ahead for the True People, then I will know what must be done. If the vision is a good one, I will seek the honor of *to-yop-ke* and lead the warriors south. Only thus will I dare this higher courage of which you speak and risk lives other than my own. Should the vision be bad or refuse to come at all, then I will ride south alone and fight my last fight in the only way I have known."

Ten Bears nodded solemnly and silently made a prayer to *Tai-me* for a vision of the highest order. Both the life of Little Buffalo and the tomorrows of their children's children clearly demanded a vision which ordained the wholesale slaughter of the miserable tejanos.

Four

Britt shifted uneasily in the saddle as they approached Fort Belknap, silently wondering what kind of reception they would be accorded by the new commander. Riding beside Allan and Grady Bragg, he passed through the front gate, nodded casually to the lone sentry, and proceeded toward headquarters.

Only that morning a messenger had arrived with word that the state troops had reached the fort. Captain Buck Barry, the militia commander, requested a meeting with the Elm Creek leaders just as quickly as practical. Leaving Tom to guard the homestead, Allan sent Britt to fetch Grady Bragg, and within the hour they were riding south along the Brazos.

Britt's presence was something of a ruse on Allan's part; a minor deception to placate Fitzpatrick for having been left behind. Ostensibly Britt was along to serve as a messenger back to the settlement should the need arise. Allan's guile didn't extend to himself, however, and he was distinctly aware that he wanted the black man present during the forthcoming conclave with Captain Barry. After years of observing Britt's instinctive cunning for the right decision in a tight spot, Allan readily admitted to himself that he preferred to have his own judgment supported by the black man's counsel. Not that he would admit it to anyone else, for other people would have scoffed openly at the thought. But both he and Britt were aware of it, and within the

very personal bonds of their friendship the fact alone
remained sufficient.

Glancing around the cantonment, Britt noticed that a
number of settlers had already moved into the fort, oc-
cupying buildings recently vacated by the federal army.
Most of these were families from the settlements south
and northeast of the fort, but here and there he spotted
a few familiar faces from Elm Creek. Thinking back to
the near panic which followed the governor's haughty
dismissal of the settlements, he found himself pleasantly surprised that such a small number had deserted
their homes from along the upper Brazos.

Dismounting in front of headquarters, they entered
the orderly room and were immediately ushered into the
inner office. Captain Barry rose from behind a littered
desk and came forward to greet them as they stopped
inside the door. Britt smiled inwardly at the puzzled
glance the officer darted in his direction and wasn't in
the least surprised when Barry failed to extend his hand.
Accustomed to being ignored in any white gathering, almost as if he were an inanimate black shadow, Britt
studied the new commander and quickly discerned that
his extraordinary size had left Allan and Grady somewhat overawed.

Buck Barry was a burly giant of a man, not so much
in height as in sheer girth. While an inch or so shorter
than Britt, his thick bull's neck stuck atop massive
shoulders, and the heavily muscled immensity of his
arms more than made up the difference. On first glance
he resembled a sour-tempered grizzly bear, and the assured movements of his waddling gait betrayed the
enormous power concealed beneath his hulking frame.
Lumbering toward the desk, he invited the white men

to sit with the wave of a bristling paw, then slowly eased his ponderous weight into a groaning chair.

"Appreciate you men comin' in right away," Barry rumbled amiably. "From all we've heard about you folks at Elm Creek, I sort of expected we'd have to drag you in."

Allan exchanged perplexed glances with Grady and decided to proceed cautiously. "I'm not quite sure we follow you, Captain. Exactly what was it you heard?"

"Why, that you're a bunch of thick-heads," he snorted. Barry's face split in a good-natured grin, and he leaned back in the creaking chair, which threatened to collapse at any moment under the strain. "Some of your friends have already relocated to the fort, and they claimed wild horses couldn't get you to move. I'm glad to see their judgment was misplaced."

Britt observed the heavy frown that appeared over Allan's features and wondered if his friend would see through the officer's rather crude attempt to badger them into relocating within the fort. Allan watched Barry stolidly for a moment, much as a fighter sizing up an unexpected adversary, and a tense stillness settled over the room.

"Captain, do I understand that you intend to order the settlers to leave their homes and occupy the fort?"

"Hell yes, that's what I intend," Barry rejoined. "That's the only way I can keep you people from getting scalped." The wide grin had been replaced with a surly scowl, and all pretense of bonhomie rapidly evaporated. The mercurial transformation in his manner seemed to unsettle Allan and Grady, and they stared at him uncertainly. "You didn't seriously think I was going to ride north and engage the Comanches with twenty men?"

"No, I didn't," Allan said. "But if you expect the people at Elm Creek to just walk away and leave their homes to Indians, you're in for a shock. Sooner than do that, they'd burn 'em down themselves and move back East."

"No two ways about it," Brady interjected, somewhat recovered from his awe of the officer's intimidating size. "And mister, if you were to go over there and tell them what you just told us, they'd more'n likely laugh you all the way back to Austin."

"By Christ, that's just the kind of stubbornness that gets people killed!" Barry leaned forward, slamming his meaty paw on the desk. Startled, Allan and Grady winced slightly as the desk shuddered from the impact. "Either you move those people over here—every man, woman and child—or goddammit, I won't be responsible for what happens to them."

The room bristled with hostility as Barry finished speaking and glared sullenly at the two settlers. Still standing by the door, removed from the arena itself, Britt suddenly realized that what the captain had failed to obtain with rough cajolery, he now hoped to win through outright bullying. Although Allan didn't turn to look at him, Britt could feel the unspoken convergence of their thoughts, and he willed the white man to hold his ground. The silence lengthened, and just when Britt began to doubt the staunchness of his friend's resolve, Allan spoke.

"Captain Barry, you were sent here to protect the settlements, not to dictate conditions. The people of Elm Creek need your help desperately, and we'll cooperate gladly in organizing a defense. But if your only solution is to try to browbeat us, then we'll just have to look after ourselves. Further than that, I have nothing more to say."

Barry's heavy features reddened at Allan's tone, and he seemed on the verge of lashing out. Then he appeared to gain control of himself, and his rigid tenseness of a moment past settled into a phlegmatic mask of resignation. "So be it, Mr. Johnson. But don't come crying to me when the Comanches get through amusing themselves with your women."

Five

Four days after his fateful discussion with Ten Bears, Little Buffalo returned from the standstone cliffs east of the village. Hollow eyed and gaunt, he nevertheless walked with the erect stoicism of a warrior, and his countenance gave no hint as to what he had seen on the mountainside. The vision had been slow in coming, even though he prayed and made repeated offering to *Tai-me*. Only after fasting and denying himself sleep for three full days was he able to summon forth the netherworld images, and what he saw drained his spirit of all power to resist further. The vision prophesied the bloody decimation of the tejanos with stark clarity, and Little Buffalo knew at last that some power greater than himself had decreed that he lead the Plains tribes in their war on the white-eyes. Reconciled, he quickly called a council meeting with Ten Bears and the village elders and related the vision in its entirety. After a moment of stunned silence, the elders confirmed the enor-

mity of the revelation, and Little Buffalo reluctantly
became the *to-yop-ke*. Now all that remained was to obtain the sanction of the nomadic bands scattered
throughout the wilderness, and the Plains tribes would
have at last found their leader.

With the passing of the Leaf Moon, Little Buffalo sent
couriers galloping across the Plains in every direction.
Lashing their horses to the point of exhaustion, they
rode with the determination of fanatics, and within a
fortnight word had spread throughout the Wichita
Mountains and across the Staked Plains that the famed
Comanche warrior was raising a war party. At each village the riders called a hurried meeting and related the
vision word for word as he had described it to them.
When discussion ceased as to the vision's significance
and the full import of its interpretation, the couriers
then delivered Little Buffalo's appeal for all True People
to join in driving the hated tejanos from their sacred
hunting grounds. The message was direct and without
adornment: united under one banner, combining both
their might and a concerted will to avenge past indignities, the True People could humble the white-eyes for
all time. But if the tribes chose to make war with isolated raids, rather than massing for a cohesive assault
on the enemy, the Comanches and Kiowas must then
resign themselves to the fact that their children's children would forever bear the stigma of defeat at the tejanos' hands.

Over the summer months Little Buffalo also sent a
steady stream of scouts riding into Texas, maintaining a
close surveillance on both the settlers and the now-
abandoned forts. As reports drifted back and a clear
picture of the tejanos' defenses began to form, it be-

came apparent to the new *to-yop-ke* that his best chance for an opening blow of crushing impact lay in attacking the remote settlements along the Brazos River. Located on the outer fringe of the white-eyes' westward expansion, as well as being a half-day's journey removed from one another, these settlements were uniquely vulnerable to a sudden, overwhelming assault by mounted warriors. Within the bounds of a two-day march along the Brazos, a fast-moving war party could strike ten or more settlements, leaving in their wake a swath of desolation and carnage unlike anything ever visited on the tejanos in the past.

Fixing in his own mind the most favorable target for the first massive raid, Little Buffalo next sent messengers calling for the True People to assemble at Red Bluffs no later than the passing of the Moon of Deer Horns Dropping Off. But while the objective was firm, his own inner resolution never ceased to waver, and his sleep was haunted with terrifying images of a lone warrior leading the True People into a holocaust of destruction.

Gathering the tribes at one location was a tedious process, at best, and seldom without a host of attending frustrations. Warriors were obliged to hunt far in advance of the gathering, drying thin strips of buffalo meat into jerky for the lean days ahead. Once the combined villages descended on a given area, the game animals quickly took flight, and a shortsighted man might easily find himself with a ravenous family and no meat in his lodge. Moreover, the Plains tribes were a leisurely people who rarely allowed the future to take precedent over the moment. After all, the white-eyes weren't going anywhere, and if the council should decide to follow Little Buffalo, then the tejanos would still be holed up in those airless, suffocating log huts they used as lodges.

But as the leaves slowly turned from green to hues of gold and the mellow warmth of summer's end gave way to the first crisp nights of autumn, the banks of the Canadian River began to fill with a vast array of brightly decorated tepees. By the time of the Yellow Leaves Moon the prairie west of Red Bluffs was swarming with Comanches and Kiowas from every band on the Plains. While young boys tended a horse herd of six thousand head on the grasslands to the west, the warriors spent their days thrusting jibes at the latest arrivals or whooping with delight at the antics of a small army of children roving mischievously through the village. A medicine lodge was erected in the center of the village to house the sacred gods, and the preparations were at last completed for the council meeting. Observing the comings and goings of so many holy men, the more cynical warriors were prompted to speculate that the war on the white-eyes might easily be waged with nothing more than magic potions and a few well-placed curses.

Finally, as the Yellow Leaves Moon relinquished the night's skies to the Geese Going Moon, the assembled might of the Plains tribes was gathered on the Canadian, and more than three thousand Indians waited for Little Buffalo to speak.

Six

"Well, from where I stand, it seems to me that we might—and I stress the word *might*—just be out of danger." Bud Williams' pronouncement carried across the cantonment as he addressed himself to the crowd of settlers lounging before headquarters.

"Bud, you might not be far wrong at that," Joel Meyer agreed. "If the Indians meant to attack, it seems like they'd have done it before now. I mean, who ever heard of Indians raiding after first frost?"

"By God, he's got a point there, boys." Jonathan Hamby's nasal twang seemed all the more offensive because of the pompous tone he consistently employed. "Anybody that's got anything besides mush between his ears knows that Comanches just don't have a taste for fightin' in cold weather. If they let a whole summer go by without a full-scale raid, you can mark it down that we're not likely to see 'em till spring."

Leaning against a post at the side of the porch, Britt glanced skeptically at Allan and shook his head with a slight, barely perceptible motion. Only last night they had discussed this same subject and concluded that the Indians might very well have delayed a mass raid in the hope that the settlers would grow careless. Second-guessing a Comanche was a hazardous game at best, and it was entirely possible that the Indians had deliberately lulled hem into a false sense of security. The Plains tribes held the element of surprise in high regard, seldom attacking without a distinct advantage. And should the settlers become reckless at this juncture, it might well precipitate the raid they had dreaded throughout the summer.

"You fellows sound like you got it all figured out. But it appears to me you've still got a hell of a lot to learn about Indian fightin'." The crowd turned to find Captain Barry gazing at them from the doorway. Although no one had noticed his silent appearance from the orderly room, it was obvious he had been eavesdropping on their conversation. The mocking grin twisting his features made it even more clear that he felt they were misguided amateurs, if not outright fools.

"Just for openers, you're apt to learn the hard way that a little frost has about as much effect on a Comanche as it does a grizzly bear." Pausing, he looked directly at Hamby, shaking his head ruefully, as if correcting an inept pupil. "Matter of fact, bears and Indians have a lot in common. Neither of 'em quits hunting and goes into hibernation till the first snow flies. Only in this case, what the Comanche is hunting is people."

The settlers' muttered comments were unintelligible for the most part, but they were clearly impressed by the harsh candor of Barry's statement. Each Sunday since the militia's arrival in May, the settlements had alternated in sending crews of men to work on the fortifications. Slowly, week by week, trees were hauled from groves along the river, and a chain of log walls began to interconnect the fort's buildings. When the stockade was at last shored and timbered to Barry's satisfaction, it appeared all but impregnable to the weary settlers. As the summer months passed and the dreaded attack failed to materialize, the men grew increasingly restless and balked at further strengthening the walls. Gradually the Sunday sojourns to the fort deteriorated into brief spurts of work interspersed with lengthy bull sessions, the main topic invariably centering around the Indians' curious disappearance. Toward the latter part of May the hit-and-run raids had ceased abruptly, and for the next four months it was as if the Comanche and

Kiowa nations had vanished from the face of the earth. Now on the first Sunday in October, the air was brisk and chill, and the settlers found it extremely difficult to convince themselves that a major raid was still imminent.

Still pondering Barry's remarks and slightly nettled by his partonizing tone, the crowd came alert as Tom Fitzpatrick sardonically voiced their own thoughts.

"Captain, none of us would think of disputing an ol' Injun fighter like yourself, but we just find it damn hard to believe that those redsticks are going to let the summer go by and then start raidin' just as winter sets in." Unable to resist the temptation to show off, Fitzpatrick hitched up his pants in a cocky manner and glanced around the crowd with a smirking grin. "Course, most of us only been fightin' 'em ten years or so, and what with you being the big expert and all that, why I guess we better just go right on sleepin' with one eye open and the hammer cocked."

Buck Barry's features knotted with cold fury and the hair bristled on the back of his massive neck: The settlers were hushed, their faces charged with tension as they waited to see how the officer would handle the Irishman's calculated insolence.

Barry shoved away from the door jamb and a looseness came over his body; the ease of a tested fighter who has steadied himself to meet the likely rush of an antagonist.

"Fitzpatrick, it's thickheaded micks like you that get other people killed. You're so goddamn sure you've got all the answers that you just can't resist flapping your tongue. But when push comes to shove, your kind is always standing around with his thumb up his ass, trying to figure out which way to run."

Tom stiffened and took a step forward, so enraged by the insult that he was blinded to the militiaman's obvious advantage in a rough and tumble encounter. Barry's hand dropped to his side, casually brushing a holstered pistol, and his eyes took on the icy glaze of a seasoned executioner.

"Don't move or, by Christ, I'll dust you on both sides." The rumbling voice had assumed a cold ferocity which jerked Fitzpatrick up short. "I ought to beat the livin' crap out of you, but you're really not worth skinning my knuckles on. Now the rest of you men pay attention. Just so you won't be taken in by this flannel-mouth's big talk, I'm going to give you a little lesson in Indian customs. Some of you have probably been wondering why I take such a peculiar pleasure in fighting redskins. Well, I used to be just like Hamby and Meyer and *Mr. Fitzpatrick*—thought I knew all there was to know about Indians. So one day about thirteen years ago, when there was a heavy frost on the ground and I was dead certain the Comanches were holed up for the winter, I left my wife and three kids at home and went into Fort Worth for supplies."

The burly captain paused and looked around the crowd. Later men would tell of having seen his eyes mist over, and when he spoke, his voice cracked. "I'll leave it to your imagination what I found when I got home."

The settlers remained deathly quiet as his words faded, and their faces were etched with shame. Barry stood sightlessly for a moment, seemingly gripped by some inner torment, then turned and disappeared through the door. Fitzpatrick was unable to look the other men in the eye, and he was the first to walk away, his head bowed in self-disgust. Slowly the others followed, singly and in small groups, unwillingly to speak of what they had witnessed and yet filled with re-kindled concern for their own families. Within minutes everyone had returned to work except Allan and Britt.

Allan glanced at the black man and silently jerked his head toward the orderly room. Once inside, Allan knocked on the office door, and they heard the captain's gruff voice bid them enter. When they stepped through the door, Barry was in the process of filling a whiskey tumbler. Without looking in their direction, he downed the drink in one neat gulp.

Turning toward them, his face remained impassive, but Britt was slightly taken aback by the curious twinkle so clearly evident in the officer's eyes.

Allan hardly knew how to start, and his words came in a halting, awkward manner. "Captain, I want to apologize for everyone involved. The people of Elm Creek have always insisted that I act as their spokesman, and I'm sure they would want me to say how very much we regret what happened."

"Well, Mr. Johnson, that's real charitable of you, I'm sure," Barry responded, unable to keep a slight smile from playing across the corners of his mouth. "But as one leader to another I feel obliged to let you in on a little secret. I've never been married, and while I've probably sired a few kids in my day, I sure as hell never bothered to keep count." Allan's incredulous expression caused the officer to falter momentarily, then he rushed on. "Now don't get your hackles up. Maybe it was sort of a tricky dodge to pull on those men, but it's a cinch they won't be so careless from now on. And you'll have to admit, it was one hell of a lie."

Allan glanced at Britt, and they both started chuckling at the same moment. Barry's broad face dissolved in a huge grin, and like three partners in some highly amusing conspiracy, they shushed one another lest their laughter be overheard by the humbled settlers. Later that night Britt awakened Mary with bed-rocking guffaws as he recalled the crestfallen expression on Tom Fitzpatrick's face.

Seven

Flickering shadows of light spilled across Little Buffalo's face from the small fire in his lodge. With a buffalo robe thrown loosely over his shoulders, he stared vacantly into the flames, absorbed in reflection on what he was about to do. Never before had any single warrior united the full power of the Comanches and Kiowas in a common cause, and at times the weight of this responsibility seemed all but unendurable. Dating from the Year of the Stars, when the sky had filled with flashing meteors, the two tribes had steadfastly remained allies for seventy winters. On occasion they had joined ranks in fragmented alliances while fighting the Crows or Utes, but not once had the scattered bands comprising the tribes come together as a single, unified force. Little Buffalo's vision had led him to this moment in time as if he were but the instrument of some greater power, the means by which the Plains tribes' destiny would be charted on an irreversible course. And in retrospect, he wasn't at all sure that Ten Bears had done the right thing in forcing him to seek a vision.

There was no doubt in his mind that tonight the assembled warriors would proclaim him *to-yop-ke*, war leader of the combined forces. Already *ko-eet-senko*, the elite warrior society, had announced their support of his plan. Now it was a foregone conclusion that the *t'ai-peko*, the broad spectrum of braves forming the six lesser warrior societies, would unanimously affirm his leadership. Tonight he would be proclaimed the bearer of the sacred pipe: the sign of office of the one chosen both for tactical wisdom and personal bravery to lead the warrior societies into battle. Of these things he was certain, filled with an overwhelming confidence.

He would lead the warriors across the River of Red Waters to the south, and the despicable tejanos would die as if consumed by a relentlessly advancing prairie fire. That much was clear in his vision, and the images revealed on the mountaintop affirmed that his medicine would be strong enough to drive the white-eyes back beyond the eastern perimeter of the Brazos. But what happened afterward remained unclear, shadowed in the mists of his vision, which did not extend past that point in time. And it was the uncertainty of this longer perspective which led to his present ambivalence.

Lost in a maze of introspection, he stared into the fire without seeing the flames, certain beyond doubt of the victory to come and yet apprehensive about the obscure and darkened path which that same victory would set his people upon. Years of slowly retreating before the white-eyes' greedy encroachments had taught him that they were a formidable enemy. Not the least of their strengths being that no matter how many were killed, they seemed to spring anew, performing some miracle of self-regeneration as did the buffalo clover tenaciously clinging to life beneath the wintry snows. Still, his vision had revealed a conquest of overwhelming proportions, one which would leave the tejanos utterly desolate in their defeat. And it was difficult to imagine that a victory of such magnitude could be meant as nothing more than a prelude to the destruction of his own people.

Suddenly a fleeting chill settled over him, and he shivered imperceptibly. Hunching nearer to the flames, he drew the warmth to his body, wondering if this were some further omen of the impending fate which awaited those he was to lead. Slowly his mind surfaced from such ominous thoughts, and he became aware that his *paraibvo*, Morning Star, was standing just inside the lodge entrance. With her presence came the realization that it was a draft of crisp night air through the open flap which had chilled him. And then it flashed through his mind that the fears conjured forth by seemingly grown men are sometimes childlike in their absurdity.

Morning Star watched him silently, her face etched with pride at the honor which was about to be bestowed on her man. Glancing at her, Little Buffalo's eyes softened, remembering both the comforting laughter and selfless love she had brought to his life. For a moment the tenderness in their eyes held, and they shared a wordless communion of all that had passed between them. Then her expression changed to one of somber expectancy, and he knew that the moment for the council meeting had arrived. Standing erect, Little Buffalo filled his lungs and then exhaled deeply, as if to force from his mind all but the significance of what must now be done. With his face frozen in the resolute stoicism befitting a Comanche *to-yop-ke*, he moved forward and stepped confidently through the lodge entrance.

Eight

Arrayed before the medicine lodge in the center of the village were the warriors who had journeyed vast distances to witness the most momentous event in the recorded history of their people. Crowded behind them, jostling for position, were the women and children. War would be declared on the white-eyes this night, and everyone present intended to carry away an indelible image of what transpired on this occasion. Seated around a fire directly in front of the medicine lodge were the many chiefs who bore responsibility for the nine bands of the two tribes. As befitted their position of preeminence, Ten Bears of the Comanches and Santana of the Kiowas were seated at the head of the chiefs' council.

Excited murmuring arose from the spectators as Little Buffalo strode through the crowd and without hesitation took a seat on the ground between Ten Bears and Santana. Within moments the crowd grew silent, and as was the custom, the assemblage waited patiently for the host to begin the council meeting. After letting the tension build for a few moments longer, Ten Bears rose and swept his arms outward in a dramatic, all-encompassing gesture. Wrinkled beyond his years, the sinew of youth bloated with age, he focused on the crowd and squinted slightly to bring them into sharper focus. Then the wily old politician drew his bent frame erect, and his rasping voice sounded across the deathly stillness of the council grounds.

"Brothers, we come together in this council to decide what must be done about the tejanos, who have taken our lands below the River of Red Waters. When I was young, I walked all over this land and saw none other than the True People. After many winters I walked again and found another people had come to take it away. How is it that we have allowed this to happen?

"The Comanches were once a great nation, but before the white-eyes they have grown as skulking dogs and carry their lives on their fingernails. Should we all put our heads together and cover them with a blanket like squaws and mourn the loss of our lands? *Brothers, are not women and children more timid than men?*"

Ten Bears paused to gauge the effect of his goading challenge, and in that moment of silence a wave of outrage swept through the crowd. They had come to be lauded and cajoled, to be told the manner and variety of ways in which they would strip the tejanos of their manhood. And now this wobbly old man with the croaking voice stood hurling insults at them. Glaring defiantly at the massed warriors, Ten Bears flung his final mandate in their faces.

"Little Buffalo has seen a vision, and his medicine is strong. We have smoked the war pipe. In the days to come, hail him as *to-yop-ke*. When Little Buffalo rides against the white-eyes, the Comanches will ride beside him, and once more the scalp sticks will stand before our lodges as befits a nation of warriors. I have spoken, and my voice is but an echo of the Comanches' will."

The fire held in the old chief's eyes for a moment, and then with a disdainful snort he resumed his seat before the council. An undercurrent of approval moved through the ranks of the Comanches, and it was obvious to the other chiefs that Ten Bears' words had struck a spark which might easily ignite both nations. Now the warriors awaited the voice of Santana, chief of the Kiowas, for Ten Bears' challenge had clearly been directed as much to them as to his own tribe. The Comanches openly referred to themselves as the Lords of the Plains and made no secret of the fact that they looked upon the Kiowas as an inferior people. While the two nations were bound together by ancient tradition, the Comanches nevertheless considered the Kiowas a weaker, somewhat backward tribe and over the generations had eased their adopted brothers into the role of tolerated vassals.

Slowly rising to his feet, Santana glanced at Ten Bears and smiled sardonically, as if amused by an old man's toothless rantings. The Kiowa chief was a man of brutish stature, towering over his brothers; a warrior of enormous gusto, he loved a savage fight or a hearty meal and could never really decide which he enjoyed more. His face was an open reflection of his emotions, hiding nothing, and the jet black hair flowing over thickly muscled shoulders somehow reinforced his evil visage. Arrogantly he waited for the warriors to cease their mumbled conversations, watching them with a churlish expression which was clearly meant to intimidate those still speaking. Finally the crowd grew still and his penetrating gaze briefly crossed the faces of those nearest the council fire. Then he began to speak, the ferocity and hate of his words rolling across the clearing, frightening the children and causing them to clutch at their mother's legs.

"The white-eyes swam across our land as maggots on a rotting buffalo carcass. Before these people ever crossed the great water to come to this land, the plains and rivers belonged to our fathers. But when I cross the river now, I see the lodges of tejanos who turn the soil to the sun. They cut down our timber; they kill the buffalo and drive all game from our sacred lands. And when I see that, my heart feels like bursting.

"When the prairie is on fire and the animals are surrounded by flames, you see them run and hide themselves so that they will not burn. That is the way we are here. The tejanos surround us, destroying the buffalo and our lands, until now we have nothing left except this wilderness to which they have driven us.

"I love to roam the plains; there I feel free and happy. I never wanted to leave that land; all my ancestors are lying there in the ground, and I say to you that when I too fall to pieces, I will fall to pieces there.

"The Kiowas do not cower before a fight, for of the True People none are braver. We too will follow Little Buffalo as *to-yop-ke*, and before the Plains are ours once more, the Kiowa will match the Comanche blow for blow in making the land run red with the blood of tejanos."

Santana remained standing as the Kiowa braves howled and brandished their weapons, excitedly voicing their delight with the contemptuous tone of his closing remarks. Satisfied that the honor of his tribe had been preserved in the face of the Comanche chal-

lenge, Santana eased himself to the ground and cast a
mocking stare at Ten Bears. The old man met his gaze,
and a cryptic smile broke shallowly across the Comanche's face, almost as if he were congratulating himself
on having ensnared the Kiowas in some murky subter-
fuge. For a fleeting moment it occurred to Santana that
the wily old man had purposely baited him into accept-
ing Little Buffalo as *to-yop-ke*, and he returned Ten
Bears' amused look with cold distaste.

This pungent exchange was lost on the crowd, however, for all eyes were quickly drawn to Little Buffalo.
As a warrior and a man of undisputed bravery, he was
known throughout the Plains, and his daring in battle
had long made him the envy of lesser men. But as *to-
yop-ke*, war leader of both nations, there was little on
which to base a judgment. The Kiowas, as well as the
Comanches, had come solely to hear this man speak; to
listen as he revealed his vision so that they might decide for themselves the wisdom of the one who would
lead them against the tejanos. Although the council had
committed both tribes to war, tribal law decreed that
each warrior remained exempt from obligation, free to
determine for himself whether or not the elected *to-
yop-ke* was a man he chose to follow into battle.

As Little Buffalo came erect, the assembled warriors
edged closer, watching him expectantly. And no man
present was more aware than the *to-yop-ke* himself that
the next few minutes would decide both the size and
the spirit of the war party he was to lead. Revealed
by the bronze glow of the fire, Little Buffalo's face radiated the determination and force of character which
had brought him unscathed through a hundred separate battles. As if gathering himself for yet another test

of combat, the *to-yop-ke* stood motionless, appraising the temper of the curious faces before him. Then without any trace of apprehension, the quiet intensity of his voice spread throughout the packed ranks of the spectators.

"Two summers ago I rode with many whose faces I see here this night, following the buffalo below the River of Red Waters. I did this as my father had done before me, so that my wives and children might have plump cheeks and warm bodies. But the pony soldiers fired on us and since that time have driven us ever backwards, so that as in a thunderstorm we have not known which way to go.

"The pony soldiers came from out of the night when it was dark and still, and for campfires they lit our lodges. Instead of hunting game, they killed our warriors, and our women cut short their hair for the dead. So it was in the south, and so it will be in this place unless we dare more now than we have dared in times past.

"During the Leaf Moon, I fasted and sought guidance from *Tai-me* as to the path we must take with the white-eyes. And a vision was granted to me, the same vision of which you were informed in the Summer Moon. In this vision I saw the Great White Father fighting for his life against men of his own tribe. White-eyes fighting white-eyes for seasons beyond counting, and all around them the land lay in desolation.

"All that is except the Plains, the land that was once ours. And presently it became clear to me that on that land there were no longer any forts and the land was no longer scarred by the white-eyes' plows. The grass was once again high, and as far as the eye could see, the buffalo browsed undisturbed, waiting as in days past for the True People to feed and clothe themselves as the need arose. And on the edge of the herd, distant farther than three days' sleeps, the white-eyes' women and children wailed into the night, mourning the loss of their men, their lodges, and all that they had once stolen from the True People."

Little Buffalo paused, as much to collect his own thoughts as to await a reaction among his listeners. But the response of the warriors was one of stunned silence, for as a body they recognized the enormity of his vision, instantly grasping the significance of each symbolic revelation in his graphic account. Watching them intently, Little Buffalo instinctively sensed the awe that had been kindled in their minds. Without hesitation he resumed speaking while they were still under the spell of his astounding vision.

"I was born on the Plains, where the wind blew free, and there was nothing to break the light of the sun. I know every stream and wood between the Rio Grande and the Arkansas. I lived happily like my fathers before me, and like them, I will die there. The white-eyes hold that land now, but for those who ride with me, we will roam there once more.

"The tejanos made sorrow come into our camps, and like buffalo bulls when their cows are attacked, we must drive them into retreat. Where we find them, we must kill them, and their scalps will hang in our lodges. The Comanches and Kiowas are not weak and blind, like pups of a dog when seven sleeps' old. They are strong and farsighted like the gray wolf. The white-eyes have led us on the path to war, and as we are not less than men, we must accept it.

"Now it will be the tejano women who cry and cut short their hair, and our lodges will know laughter once more. From this day forward, until the stones melt and the rivers run dry, I live only to kill tejanos. *And this I vow: those who ride with me will once again call themselves warriors.*"

A moment of silence ensued as the beguiled Indians strained for a better look at this man who would lead them back to the old life. Then the warriors went wild as Little Buffalo's seductive promise resounded across the council ground. The tightly packed braves pushed closer, splitting the night with frenzied yelps. Those with muskets thrust them skyward, firing into the darkness, while others brandished axes and war clubs, screaming vile threats of mutilation and death for the cursed white-eyes. Within moments the council ground had been transformed into a scene of insane blood lust, almost as if the earth's creatures had gone berserk and the people in it were running amok with some virulent madness.

There was a long night of celebration ahead, however, and Ten Bears moved to quell the explosive situation before it got out of hand. Coming erect, he stood beside Little Buffalo, arms swept outward and face raised to the stars in symbolic supplication to the gods. Slowly the nearer ranks of warriors began to calm as they observed his solemn entreaty, and a gradual hush drifted back through the crowd until a reverent quiet at last settled over the council ground. Without lowering his eyes from the heavens, Ten Bears nodded slightly, and an elderly man detached himself from the spectators.

Sky Walker moved with great dignity, as befitted the

foremost *puhaket* of the Comanches. Oblivious to anything save the gravity of his mission, the prophet and holy man strode purposefully to the medicine lodge and entered. Moments later he reappeared with a large rawhide bundle and placed it on the ground before the fire.

Worshipfully Sky Walker removed a smaller bundle from the first and unwrapped it, revealing a large, carefully crafted idol. He then held *Tai-me* aloft for all to see, and at the sight of the Grandfather God a moaning sigh swept over the crowd. Carved from obscure green stone in ancient times, *Tai-me* was fashioned in the image of man and bore a distinct resemblance to the angular-faced warriors. Arrayed in a resplendent robe of white feathers, with a headdress of ermine skin and blue beads around its neck, the idol somehow seemed charged with life. In the flickering shadows of the council fire it was as though Sky Walker held a shrunken, finely garbed old man above his head, and the assembled might of two savage nations bowed their heads in homage. Later they would dance to the beat of throbbing drums and gorge themselves on buffalo hump and boiled dog, but for the moment the fiercest warriors on the plains groveled before their god and prayed that they might acquit themselves as men in the bloody days ahead.

Nine

As dawn broke over the Plains, a shimmering glaze of frost cloaked the autumn grasses. Shortly the sun eased over the sandstone cliffs to the east, and there was a crisp bite to the chill morning air. A slight breeze carried the discordant strains of barking dogs, and in the village, women stood with their eyes shaded against the sun, anxiously scanning the grasslands for one last glimpse of their men. On the prairie south of the river seven hundred mounted warriors were massed, silently awaiting their leader. The Comanches and their Kiowa brothers were riding to war, and the spectacle of the formidable host presented by their milling ranks was one which even the tribal ancients had never before witnessed.

Suddenly a small party of horsemen rode from the village, and an expectant stir swept through the massed warriors. Little Buffalo led the riders, flanked on either side by Ten Bears and Santana, and in their wake rode the holy man, Sky Walker. Little Buffalo had decorated himself in the garish heraldry favored by the Plains tribes, and he rode astride a barrel-chested *ehkasunaro*, a magnificent, fiery-eyed pinto. Little Buffalo's face was painted the blue of the sky, with an irregular pattern of large red spots, and his war shield was decorated as a brilliant orange sun with showers of flame arching outward. Atop his head was the war bonnet of the *to-yop-ke*, streaming a coveted train of eagle feathers in the brisk wind. The fabled headdress had been a gift from Ten Bears, who had worn it without mishap or defeat for four decades, and its presence on the new *to-yop-ke* was taken as a sign of strong medicine by the superstitious tribesmen. The overall effect of the *to-yop-ke*'s appearance was startling and somewhat bizarre; there would be no doubt among friend or foe as to who commanded the war party. And that was exactly what he intended.

Little Buffalo brought his horse to a halt before the vast array of mounted warriors. The *ehkasunaro* pranced sideways, snorting frosty clouds through its nostrils, and the only sound across the wide prairie was the muffled stamping of thousands of hooves. The *to-yop-ke*'s wrenching concern for the lifeblood of his nation was now a thing of the past, and as he stared across the sea of painted faces, Little Buffalo realized that from this day forward, the fate of the Plains tribes was sealed beyond the hand of man or God. Before first light he had received Ten Bears' blessing and embraced the aged warrior in final farewell. Now even the thoughts of his tearful wives and the plump children asleep in his lodge departed his mind, and he turned his face to the south. Toward the sacred land. And the tejanos.

Wheeling the skittish pinto to the front, Little Buffalo raised his clenched fist and roared the ancient war cry. *"Ah-ko!"* The stillness of the moment was instantly charged with tension, and the valley suddenly reverberated with the rumbling thunder of the warriors' frenzied reply. *"Ah-ko!"* Little Buffalo kicked the *ehkasunaro* into a scrambling lope, and the warriors parted as he passed through their ranks to the plains below. Santana and Sky Walker fell in behind him, then the warriors closed ranks once more. To a man the Comanche and Kiowa nations had extended an oath of fealty to their reluctant *to-yop-ke*.

Without a backward glance or a thought for the carefree life now left behind, Little Buffalo led the True People to war.

𝗪 CHAPTER THREE 𝗪

One

Britt stepped through the cabin door and buckled his gunbelt in place. Tugging at the holster, he settled the Colt over his hip, then glanced automatically at the sky. Methodically scanning the northern horizon, he noted the absence of any darkening clouds, and his brow wrinkled with a slight frown. Glancing at the trees along the creek, his frown deepened as the stillness of their branches confirmed another windless day. Within the past two weeks this had become his morning ritual, hopefully searching the skies and the silent trees for some sign of oncoming winter.

While mid-October was too early for a storm of any consequence, he still woke each morning hoping to find the ground blanketed with snow. The depth of the snowfall, or the fact that it might melt within a few hours, was incidental. What mattered was some indication that winter had finally arrived; a threat of impending storm, regardless of its intensity. For only then would there by any certainty that the Indians had abandoned all thought of raiding the settlements.

But the skies remained clear and bright, obstinately sunny. Soon great gusts of wind would come sweeping down out of the northern Plains, the temperature would drop with lightning speed, and within a matter of hours a swirling blizzard would have covered the landscape. But prairie storms were capricious, rarely breaking when expected or hoped for. And the nagging thought that left Britt uneasy and even a little frightened was that the first snow might not come soon enough.

Absorbed in his grisly thoughts, Britt was startled by Mary's gentle teasing. "Whatever you're lookin' for must be mighty important to make you forget this."

Turning, he found Mary smiling at him from the doorway, with his rifle cradled across her arm. "Woman, what would I do without you?" Grinning, he jumped to the doorstep and lifted her easily, holding her a few inches off the floor. Playfully jiggling her from side to side, his eyes came alive with laughter. "Keeps my feet warm and my belly full and she's even got time to chase around remindin' me what a forgetful no-account I am!"

"Lordy, just listen to that man talk," she said. Squirming, Mary tried to free herself, but his grip grew firmer with each wiggle. "Now, Britt, you set me down before them big hands of yours pock me all up with bruises."

Suddenly the doorway was filled with dancing, screaming children as the three youngsters crowded around to watch their mother's predicament. Gently Britt eased Mary to the floor and, before anyone could move, scooped George and Sue Ellen up in his arms. Squealing with delight, the children struggled to break loose, their tiny voices shrill with mock terror. Frank, who had only recently grown too serious for such horseplay, watched on with the detached amusement of an elder brother. Releasing the children, Britt snatched the rifle from Mary's arms, kissed her soundly on the mouth, and leaped from the doorstep to the yard before anyone knew what had happened.

"Now that's enough funnin' for one day," he called back, still chuckling. "This man's got work to do. And, woman, when I get back for dinner, I want to find all of you over at the big house just like you're supposed to be."

Mary frowned, still reluctant to spend her days in the main house, even though it had become a routine after so many months. But beneath the humor in Britt's voice there was a stern note which made his statement more a demand than a request. With a saucy shake of her head Mary smiled and nodded just as Britt knew she would, and he walked lightly on toward the corral.

Hearing voices, he looked around and saw Allan and Tom Fitzpatrick leaving the main house, also headed for the corral. Situated west of the cabins, the corral was a crude affair of split logs. Hastily thrown together after the first Indian scare, it formed a rough square with two sides butted against a steep hill which overlooked the homestead. With the Comanches on the loose, herding cattle in the normal manner had become risky as well as time consuming, and the men were fearful of staying away from the house any longer than necessary. After discussing it, they had decided to corral the herd at night and drive them to the grazing lands each morning.

Though nocturnal by nature, the longhorns quickly adapted to the new scheme of things. Famished after a night in the corral, they were content to graze throughout the day, and soon it required only one man to herd them once they reached the grasslands. The log enclosure now held over a hundred head, including Fitzpatrick's small herd. Milling about expectantly, the cantankerous beasts began crowding against the gate as the three men entered an adjoining corral and set about roping their mounts for the day.

As they saddled their horses, Britt noticed that Allan was quieter than usual, seemingly preoccupied with some troublesome thought. Fitzpatrick rarely extended anything more than a perfunctory nod each morning, and his withdrawn attitude was to be expected. But from Allan it was out of character, and therefore, something to think about. Shrugging it off as a passing mood, Britt kneed his horse in the belly, and when the rangy chestnut released a whoosh of air, he jerked the cinch tight. Still bothered by Allan's distant manner, he decided to take a shot at lightening the mood.

"Boss man, I sure could use a good rest today. Don't you think it's about my turn to play drover and catch a few naps?"

Allan's head jerked around, and from the severe expression on his face, it was clear that the black man's humor had missed the mark. "No, I've already asked Tom to herd the cattle. Once we haze 'em out to graze, you and me will come on back here and work on the new well." Britt's smile faded with the sharp tone, and Allan sensed that his dark mood could stand some airing. "Didn't mean to growl at you. I've got a low feeling today and can't seem to shake it. Probably just a touch of the ague."

"Hell, who wouldn't be feeling poorly," Tom cracked,

"playin' shit kicker to them steers night and day. What we need is a little excitement around here for a change."

As if the thought left nothing unsaid, the men silently mounted and rode toward the log corral. Once the bars on the gate were dropped, the longhorns made a rush for the creek and began swizzling greedily after a night without water. When the steers' thirst had been slaked, the men started popping their backsides with rawhide lariats, hazing them toward the grasslands to the north-west. Within a few minutes the herd disappeared over a slight knoll in the distance, and the gritty dust from their passing settled once more to the ground.

Two

Squatted beside the creek, the scout washed his face in the cold rushing water, then paused to scan the open countryside. The brittle stillness of early morning lay unbroken over the land, and except for a crescent-shaped hill to the north, the bleak terrain seemed desolate in its flatness. Satisfied that nothing unusual was afoot, the scout dipped a tin cup full of water and moved back up the bank to a grove of cottonwoods.

Moments later he reached a small clearing in the trees which was littered with blankets, saddles, and assorted gear. Two horses, munching grain, were tied to a picket line, and a second scout was engaged in splashing a rock at the far edge of the clearing. Easing himself to the ground, the first man dug jerky and hard-tack from a saddlebag and began eating with an indifference matched only by the stolid chomping of the horses. Chewing a mouthful of stringy meat, he twisted around and watched as the second man finished relieving himself.

"Damn if you ain't the pissingest man I ever seen. You must of woke me up ten times last night splatterin' that rock."

"It's all this infernal waitin'," the second scout grumbled. "Makes me nervous. Besides, there ain't nothin' else to do anyhow, 'cept freeze our asses off waitin' on Injuns that won't never come."

"Yeah. Sorta buggers me too that the cap'n wouldn't let us build no fire out here." The longer he chewed, the larger the wad of jerky became, and he stubbornly ground on it for a few moments. "Do you reckon the cap'n really believes the Comanch is still gonna come raidin', what with cold weather already settin' in?"

"Who the hell knows what Barry's got spinnin' around in his head? That man's the most untalkative bastard I ever run across." Dropping to the ground, he pulled a hunk of jerky from the saddlebag and regarded it with disgust. "I'll tell you one thing, though. When my time's up, they couldn't get me back in the militia if they greased a brass cannon and jammed it straight up my ass."

"Oh, it ain't all that bad. Not near as bad as fightin' Yankees. And anyway, we only got one day to go till the cap'n sends our relief up."

The two men lapsed into silence, occasionally scanning the empty countryside as they finished a cold breakfast. Since assuming command of Fort Belknap, Buck Barry had been sending teams of scouts to guard the upper end of Elm Creek, and the assignment had long since become a grim joke among the militiamen.

Barry had speculated that in the event of a raid the scouts could forewarn the settlers, thereby allowing them to reach the fort with a margin of safety. But as autumn passed, and the ground grew hard with morning frost, the militiamen came to resent Barry's undiminished fear of attack. As far as they were concerned, the Indian threat had come and gone, and their surly attitude was evident in the laxness with which they guarded Elm Creek.

The scouts on duty at the outpost that morning were cold and bored and somewhat irritated with themselves for having overslept. But though the sun had risen, there was nothing about to cause alarm, and they leaned back against their saddles, absorbing the warming rays that filtered through the tree tops.

Since chiding the other man about his overactive bladder, the first scout had been resisting a similar urge with gritted teeth. Finally he decided that a bit of teasing was preferable to the discomfort, and he stepped to the edge of the clearing. The second man was about to make a sarcastic comment when he noticed that his partner's back and chest were pierced clean through by an arrow. Blinking, he stared incredulously as the first scout tottered and began to fall. Still confused, it flashed through his mind that this was either a damn poor joke or one hell of a bad dream. Then as he lurched erect, an arrow ripped through his throat and all doubt was suddenly dispelled. His legs collapsed, and he sank to the ground, vaguely aware that blood was gushing down over his shirt front. His eyes clouded over, and through a haze he saw three Comanche warriors step from the trees behind the clearing. Blackness closed in over him, obscuring all vision, and his last sensation was the tingling sweep of a scalping knife around his hairline.

After mutilating the dead scouts, the three warriors trotted across the creek onto the open plain. Facing north, the Comanches thrust their bows overhead in a rapid up and down motion, then waited passively for some unseen response to their signal.

As they watched, a horseman crested the bald hill and kneed his spotted *ehkasunaro* down the forward slope. Behind him the knoll filled with riders until the skyline was an indistinct blur of war shields and prancing buffalo ponies. Trailing their leader, the loosely massed warriors then advanced down the hill, and the muted rumble of pounding hooves shook the earth as they crossed the open plain.

Little Buffalo reined to a halt at the headwaters of Elm Creek and whirled the pinto to face his followers. Seven hundred strong, they halted before him, holding a tight rein on their ponies as the excited animals reared and tossed their heads in milling confusion. Waiting for the warriors to calm their mounts, Little Buffalo's face settled on Sky Walker, and he nodded firmly.

The elderly prophet kicked his horse forward in a scrambling lope and then spun him about to face the war party. Holding an ornate buckskin bag aloft, he thrust his hand deep inside and groped for something which seemed to resist being caught. With an air of mystery and omnipotence, Sky Walker slowly withdrew his hand to reveal an owl sitting on the end of his arm. The bird ruffled its wings, and its great yellow eyes flashed ominously in the early morning sun. From a distance it looked real, as if it might leap from Sky Walker's arm at any moment and dart into the grove of trees.

The warriors suddenly grew deathly still, waiting with edgy tenseness for the *puhaket* to invoke a blessing through the sacred owl. While everyone knew that the bird was nothing more than a superbly skinned owl, with Sky Walker's nimble hand providing the lifelike motions, they nonetheless regarded it as strong medicine. Even the bravest of warriors feared the ancient prophet's supernatural powers, and to ride into battle without the blessing of the owl was considered the act of a *pawsa*, a crazy man.

Sky Walker thrust the owl even higher in the air, and the bird cocked its head from side to side as if gazing upon the warriors. Magically the enormous yellowed eyes blinked with casual disdain and across the stillness of the plain came the twittering screech of a swooping, predatory owl. Smiling enigmatically, the prophet returned the sacred owl to its buckskin sack and withdrew his hand as if it were in no way connected with the godlike creature.

Little Buffalo spun his horse abruptly, reining the *ehkasunaro* with a cruel jerk, so that it reared high as he thrust his war lance toward the sky. Supremely confident that his orders would be carried out to the last man, the *to-yop-ke* kicked the pinto into a gallop and led the Comanches down the north bank of Elm Creek. Without looking back, he knew that Santana was already fording the stream with his Kiowas to attack along the opposite shore.

Three

Joel Meyer kicked the stump a solid whack. Off and on
he had been working at this stump for close to a year,
and he had slowly come to feel a very personal animosity toward its gnarled and battered form. Like some
men, the stump clung tenaciously to life, clutching at
the earth's moist warmth long after hope had vanished.
Shortly after the tree had been struck by lightning,
Meyer chopped it down and began hacking at its
deeply imbedded roots in what now seemed a never-
ending contest of wills.

While he held no firm convictions regarding the soul
of man, it seemed to Meyer that this stump possessed
some power beyond mere bark and life-sustaining
juices. Often he had sat outside the cabin in the evening, watching it with a burning sense of frustration as
he sought to discover some previously undetected
weakness. And on this bright, crisp morning it was still
there, scarred but unconquered.

Meyer glanced around to find his son eyeing him curiously, and the boy quickly resumed digging with a
spade at the twisted roots. Without turning, he knew
that his wife was also watching from near the house,
and the thought fanned his determination all the more.
Hettie derived a perverse sense of amusement from seeing him thwarted by a grubby stump, and he refused to
increase her pleasure by acknowledging that he was
aware of her scrutiny.

Removing his coat, Meyer dropped it to the ground
and shivered slightly as the chill morning air penetrated
his shirt. This was a good time of year for stump clearing, he thought. Once a man worked up a good sweat,

the cold disappeared, and he could keep chopping all
day without tiring. Spitting on his palm, he rubbed his
hands together briskly, then hefted the ax and swung it
in a high overhead arc.

The glistening blade hung in midair and failed to de-
scend, as if frozen in a moment of time. From the distance came a deepening roar unlike anything Meyer
had ever heard, and with the ax poised to strike, he
stopped to listen. Puzzled, he slowly lowered the ax
and turned toward the northeast, in the direction of the
strange noise. For a moment it sounded like the rumble
of thunder from a great distance, and then it occurred
to him that thunder lasts only briefly, ending as quickly
as it has begun. This was a constant drumming roar,
and whatever it was, it was rapidly approaching the
stunted knoll less than a quarter-mile away.

Suddenly hundreds of mounted warriors spilled over
the low hogback, and Meyer gaped in disbelief as they
thundered toward him at a full gallop. His first instinct
was to run for the cabin, where his guns hung on the
wall; to bolt the door and hold off the red savages until
help arrived. But within that same instinctual urge
came the realization that it was useless to run. He and
his family were doomed as surely as hogs in a charnel
house, and if a man was to die, it should be attended
to with dignity.

Grasping the ax, he stepped forward and swung as a
howling Comanche outraced his brothers to count the
first coup. Unaware that his son had just been impaled
on a lance or that Hettie had been borne to the ground
by a horde of yelping braves, Meyer reeled backward as
his head was squashed from the impact of a war club.
Staggering blindly, he disappeared beneath an ava-

lanche of hooves, and his last thought was to curse the stump that had defeated him after all.

Little Buffalo circled the pinto to the front of his warriors, urging them forward lest the element of surprise be lost. Through the milling swirl of ponies, he saw Hettie Meyer thrashing naked beneath one brave, while another impassively ripped her scalp away. Rising, the warrior vaulted onto his pony and held the thatch of wavy hair aloft, loosing a blood-curdling scream of jubilation. Little Buffalo drove the barrel-chested *ehkasunaro* through the tangled horses, forcing the warriors' attention away from Hettie's gory struggle. Laughing and shouting, offering vile suggestions to the braves who swarmed over the hysterical woman, the mounted warriors finally heeded Little Buffalo's scathing exhortations.

Wheeling their horses, the war party followed their *to-yop-ke* from the carnage that was once the homestead of Joel Meyer.

Within the next ten minutes, striking almost simultaneously, the Comanches attacked the Hambys while the Kiowas besieged the Williams family. The two homesteads were situated on opposite sides of Elm Creek, only a few hundred yards apart, and the war parties stormed the cabins in a fanatic craze, each determined to outdo the other.

Jonathan Hamby had been mending harness when he heard gunfire from the direction of the Meyer homestead. Without bothering to ponder it, he knew exactly what had happened. Racing to the creek, he emptied his pistol into the air as a warning to the Williamses, then turned to the escape of his own family. This moment of selfless concern sealed their doom, however, for as Jonathan was harnessing a team of horses, Comanches appeared along the creek bank a short distance to the east. Escape was now out of the question, and Hamby quickly forted up inside the cabin with his family. Reloading his pistol, he watched with mounting terror as the warriors galloped forward and resolved to make the Indians pay dearly for the lives of his loved ones.

Bud Williams' luck took an even grimmer turn, despite Hamby's warning shots. The fear that gripped his insides was somehow sensed by the horses as he attempted to rope them, and the normally gentle animals fought like cornered wolves. Feverishly chasing the team from one end of the corral to the other, he failed to see the Kiowas until they were pounding into the front yard. And by then it was too late.

Running toward the cabin, blindly determined to reach his trapped family, he went down under the first wave of warriors and was hacked to pieces in a matter of moments. Had he lived, there would have been small consolation in the knowledge that his wife and two children were taken captive even as a screeching Kiowa lifted his scalp.

Across the creek Little Buffalo was infuriated by Hamby's stubborn defense. Already he had lost five braves, and precious time was being wasted on one insignificant cabin. Patience exhausted, the *to-yop-ke* finally ordered a small band of warriors to burn the cabin along with its occupants. While the buffalo medicine men lashed the dead and wounded to their horses, the rest of the war party thundered south beside the winding creek. Little Buffalo whipped the pinto to a faster pace, cursing the reckless, headstrong warriors. Should they persist in treating each cabin as the sole target of the raid, his plan to annihilate the tejanos would surely fail.

Four

Alerted by the sounds of distant gunfire, the three women on the Johnson homestead knew immediately what to expect. They were each veterans of countless Indian raids and the sight of a painted Kiowa or a blood-thirsty Comanche was nothing unique in their lives. Still, this was the first time any of them had been confronted with the prospect of facing red savages without their men. Standing in the yard, huddled together with their children, they attempted to sort out the alternatives and decide what must be done.

"We've still got time to hitch up the wagon and make a run for the fort," Elizabeth Fitzpatrick suggested. Glancing toward a bend in the creek to make sure the Indians hadn't already removed that option, she turned back to Sarah Johnson. "After all, that's what Allan has been talking about all these months. Getting to the fort before those red devils have a chance to trap us in the cabins."

"I know," Sarah replied indecisively. "But what if we left and the men came back? They'd get trapped trying to save us." Hugging her children close, she looked on the verge of tears. "And we wouldn't even be here."

"If the Comanches were already here, the men couldn't get to us anyway." Elizabeth darted another glance up the creek, certain their time was growing short. "Besides, we've got these kids to think about.

The men can look after themselves. Leastways, that's what they generally do anyhow."

"Beth, that's not fair," Sarah cried. "You know the men will come back. And even if the Indians are already here, they'll try to fight their way into the house."

Mary had been listening to this exchange without comment. But her eyes were also on the bend in the creek, and she suddenly became aware that the gunfire in the distance had ceased. Survival was an instinct one acquired shortly after weaning in the slave quarters, and she sensed that if the argument went much further, they would likely die where they stood. "Miz Sarah. Miz Beth. I'm takin' my children in that house and boltin' the door. That's what Mr. Allan told us to do, and I don't reckon I'm smart enough to outguess him just cause this raid came along different'n he expected. Whatever you're gonna do, you'd better do it quick, cause them Comanche are headed this way right now."

Startled by Mary's outburst, the two white women stared at her for a moment and then turned to listen. The gunfire had been replaced by a strange rumbling sound, and while they had no way of knowing what it meant, they felt the earth shimmer beneath their feet and realized that something ominous was rapidly approaching.

"Beth, she's right," Sarah announced firmly. "We're going to fort up just like Allan said, and if you've got any sense, you'll do the same thing."

Elizabeth Fitzpatrick regarded Mary with a vexed expression as the black woman moved toward the house, then she gathered her children with a sigh and followed. Entering the cabin, they bolted the door with three massive cross bars and quickly shuttered the windows. The children were herded into a corner and admonished to remain still. Mary instructed Frank, who was the oldest, to keep the other children quiet and to make sure that no one left the corner, regardless of what might happen. Turning, she saw Sarah pull Allan's pistol from a holster beside the door.

"My God," Sarah moaned. Her lip quivered, and large tears spilled down over her cheeks. "Oh, my God. We forgot to fire the gun, and the men are too far away. They'll never hear the shooting over at the Hambys'." Hysterically she began to tear at the cross bars, obsessed with the urgency of warning her man.

Striding swiftly across the room, Elizabeth jerked her away from the door and slapped her squarely in the face. "Gimme that gun. Right now I'm the best shot in this house anyway." Wrenching the pistol from Sarah's hand, she took the sobbing woman by the shoulders and shook her forcefully. "Now you listen to me. Those boys are going to hear plenty of shooting any minute now, and they'll be headed this way before you can say scat." Glaring around at Mary, her voice took on a harsh edge. "You two talked me into staying here, so by merciful Jesus, you just keep your heads. If any of them red devils come through that door before our men get here, I know just what to do with this popgun."

Only minutes had passed since the women entered the house, and outside, the distant rumble had now given way to the staccato beat of pounding hooves. Little Buffalo rounded the bend at a steady lope and led the Comanches across the plowed-under field bordering the homestead. Within the span of a deep breath the cabin was encircled by howling warriors, and the

Johnson *remuda* had been added to the herd of captured horses now trailing the war party.

Still smarting at the delays which threatened to offset
his tactical advantage, Little Buffalo merely glanced at
the shuttered house and ordered it burned immediately.
If the tejanos were to be outgeneraled and outfought,
then the red man's war must be conducted according
to plan. And if that deprived the warriors of their lusty
pleasures, it was unfortunate but no less essential. Little
Buffalo fully intended that tribal history would record
him as the *to-yop-ke* who had utterly desolated the
white-eyes, and on this raid at least, the braves would
have to be content with victory rather than a carnal display of their manhood.

The barn went first. Filled with hay, it became a raging inferno within seconds, and curiously enough, the
Comanches' passions seemed momentarily slaked by
the roaring flames. The warriors quickly fashioned fire-
brands, circling the cabin with yipping war cries as
they tossed the torches on the roof. The shingles flared
instantly, and within minutes of Little Buffalo's order
the homestead was wreathed in a cloud of billowing
smoke.

Still intent on taking captives, a group of warriors
then wrenched a log from the corral fence and converted it into a battering ram against the front door.
Granted, the *to-yop-ke* had ordered the buildings fired,
they shouted gleefully, but that didn't obstruct men of
cunning from collecting a few of the white-eyes'
women before they roasted alive.

Inside the house the women huddled in a corner,
clutching their children as flames slowly ate through
the underside of the roof. The room was filled with ac-

rid smoke, stinging their eyes and throats with a biting rawness. Gasping for a breath of untainted air, their faces streaked with soot and tears, the terror-stricken women watched in horror as the door shuddered from the impact of the battering log. Elizabeth Fitzpatrick slowly cocked the pistol, rising to shield her children's bodies with her own. Sarah and Mary also stood, brandishing common butcher knives they had snatched from the kitchen, forming a human barrier before the whimpering youngsters.

Suddenly the door splintered and slowly caved inward with a wrenching groan as the log penetrated the room. Guttural voices filtered into the cabin, and hands began tearing at the shattered door. To the women it sounded as if a pack of wild animals was clawing at the entrance, snarling and slashing with bared fangs as they fought to be the first to reach the helpless prey. With one last blow the sharded door disintegrated completely and collapsed on the floor.

Gouging and kicking, a dozen warriors jammed the breached entryway and tumbled into the smoky cabin. Through the haze the Comanches and the paralyzed women stared at one another for a moment. Then the center beam in the roof cracked with an explosive report, and Elizabeth Fitzpatrick was jarred into action. Leveling the pistol, she fired and a brave dropped to the floor clutching his groin. Before she could cock the hammer and fire again, a musket belched flame from the doorway, and the top of her head disappeared in a bloody froth. As she toppled forward, the gun clattered to the floor.

Without a moment's pause young Frank leaped from behind his mother, scooping the pistol up as he moved toward the Indians. Thumbing the hammer back, as he had seen Britt do many times in the past, the boy thrust the revolver to arm's length and fired into the mass of red bodies. Another Comanche pitched to the floor. But before the youngster could cock the gun again, a warrior hurtled across the room and buried a war ax in his forehead. In the same moment an arrow meant for Frank pinned Tom Fitzpatrick's daughter to the back wall, where she hung briefly before slumping forward in death.

Screaming, Mary dropped the butcher knife and threw herself across young Frank's inert form. Howling triumphantly, the warriors leaped on their wild-eyed captives and began dragging them toward the door as a section of the roof collapsed in a shower of sparks and flame. Struggling with all her might as a paint-smeared Comanche hauled her through the door, Mary looked back in time to see a grinning warrior rip away the scalp of her oldest son.

Five

The longhorns ambled along with bovine listlessness, raising a rooster tail of dust in their wake. The herd had grazed steadily westward throughout the summer, and the men were now pushing them toward a wide valley enclosed by a series of low hills. Slightly more than a mile from the homestead, the bowl-shaped terrain formed a natural amphitheater which made it easier for one man to control the intractable animals. Along the way steers occasionally fell behind as they spotted a particularly tempting clump of grass and drifted off to investigate.

Riding drag, Britt had been kept busy hazing the stragglers back into line. He had just finished chasing a stubborn old cow and her knobby-kneed calf when the muffled crack of gunshots sounded from the rear. Reining his pony about, he stared in disbelief as a thick column of smoke rose skyward in the east. For a moment his mind resisted what his eyes beheld, unwilling to comprehend that the dreaded day had at last arrived. It just wasn't possible, he raged inwardly, not with winter about to break. And yet, there was no denying the chilling implications of smoke mixed with gunfire.

Wheeling the chestnut around, he noticed that Allan and Tom remained unaware of the drastic turn of events. Riding flank near the front of the herd, they were unable to hear the shots and hadn't the slightest idea that anything was amiss. Raking the pony with his spurs, Britt circled the herd at a gallop and overtook Allan. "Indians," he yelled, pointing frantically to the rear. "They're burning the house!"

With a single backward glance Allan grasped the situation and began motioning to Tom, who had already turned in the saddle to stare eastward. Looking around, Allan saw that Britt had spurred his horse back down the trail, and he viciously kicked his own mount into a startled lope. Tom was only a moment behind, ramming his horse through the now-forgotten longhorns. Forcing their minds away from the certain horror that awaited them, the three men raced across the prairie, flogging their horses unmercifully.

Minutes later Britt skidded to a halt in a stand of trees on the knoll overlooking their homestead. Leaping from the saddle, he flung himself to the ground and crawled to the forward edge of the tree line. Allan and Tom followed close on his heels, and the sight they beheld made each man gasp with terror.

Hundreds of screaming, battle-crazed Comanches were massed in the clearing that only hours before had represented a decade of labor for the Johnsons of Elm Creek. The barn had been reduced to glowing ashes, and the house was a blazing inferno which was slowly collapsing wall by wall into a fiery rubble. Britt's cabin was also burning, with flames leaping skyward in great orange fountains, and even as they watched, the roof caved in with a molten roar. Billowing clouds of smoke swirled across the clearing, momentarily obscuring knots of Indians as hot wind eddied to and fro off the creek.

Suddenly the wind shifted, and the three men strained forward, their faces gone cold as death itself. Squinting past the murky haze, they saw a string of captives being dragged through the swarming Comanches, and the horror so long anticipated had now come full circle. Sarah and Mary stumbled forward with their arms cruelly lashed behind their backs, and the wide-eyed children cowered around them in a whimpering huddle. Surrounded by a small band of warriors, the women were being jerked along by rawhide thongs tied around their necks. Abruptly the women were brought to a halt and forced to their knees before a garishly painted Indian on a huge pinto. Even from the hilltop the three men could tell he was a chief, for the eagle war bonnet clearly separated him from the maelstrom of frenzied braves.

Stepping forward, one of the warriors guarding the

captives began a loud harangue, gesturing wildly at the
women as he addressed the chief. While the three settlers couldn't understand the guttural ranting, the warrior's meaning was all too clear, and their throats went
dry with fear. Whether the aroused Comanche was demanding death or the rights of conquest, the ultimate
fate of the women was beyond question, and the
watchful men stared at the scene below with mounting
revulsion. Without warning, Tom Fitzpatrick suddenly
leaped to his feet, muttering hoarse curses as his glazed
eyes swept madly across the clearing.

"Beth's not down there! Allan, she ain't there. Oh, Jesus, Jesus! Them murderin' sonsabitches have done
something to her."

Later he would remember that his daughter was also
missing from the nightmarish scene below, but for now
his tortured mind could focus only on the hideous, unspeakable things the Comanches might have done to
his wife. Crazed with shock and grief, his reaction was
that of a wounded animal. Fumbling aside his coat, Tom
snatched his pistol from its holster and with trembling
hands brought it to bear on the howling savages.

Bounding to his feet, Britt swung with every ounce
of strength in his body. His fist landed against Fitzpatrick's jaw with a mushy splat and the Irishman staggered drunkenly, then pitched to the earth with the
chalky pallor of a bled-out corpse. For a moment Britt
thought he had killed him, but slowly the color returned to Tom's face, and his labored breathing grew
more regular. Crouching beside the unconscious man,
Britt's eyes turned once more to the grisly scene in the
clearing.

The chief on the spotted pinto was now speaking, rebuking the defiant warrior in cold, merciless tones. The braves surrounding the captives hung their heads, shamed before their brothers by the scathing attack. The chief's voice ended with a harsh command, and the crestfallen warriors meekly turned their captives about and marched them toward the rear of the war party. Never losing sight of the women and children, Britt and Allan watched closely while they were hoisted aboard ponies near the prisoners taken earlier in the morning.

Satisfied that the Indians meant no harm to Mary and the children for the moment, Britt turned back to the fallen Irishman. As he did so, a searing, white-hot stab of pain gripped his insides. *Frank wasn't among the captives!* Maybe the boy escaped or is hiding along the creekbank, he thought, desperately grasping for some ray of hope. Then with the fatalism of all black men he knew that the boy was dead, more than likely buried in the smoldering ashes of the main house. His face hardened, and his eyes grew cold with a rage like a wild thing that has seen its young hunted and killed. Kneeling on the ground, he savagely drove his fist time after time into the frost-hardened earth.

Tom Fitzpatrick moaned and rolled over, coming to his hands and knees as the film of senselessness slowly retreated from his eyes. Braced against a tree, he hauled himself erect and stood glaring at the other two men. Slobber stained his chin a burnt red, and he thoughtlessly spit a broken tooth out onto the ground. Blinking his eyes, he fixed Britt with a malevolent expression, but his words were directed at Allan.

"Johnson, you better lock your nigger up and throw away the key, cause the first time I catch him runnin' loose, I'm gonna cut his heart out and feed it to the hogs."

Hurtling up from the ground, Britt threw Fitzpatrick against the tree and rammed his forearm across the Irishman's throat. Tom's eyes bulged, and he gasped for breath as the pressure on his Adam's apple became excruciating. In Britt's murderous gaze he saw death staring him in the face, and he ceased to struggle.

"White man, I'd just as soon kill you as not. But right now I need you. All three of us has family down there, and the only chance they've got of stayin' alive is if we stay alive. If you'd fired that gun, they'd have had their throats cut like winter shoats." Jerking Fitzpatrick away from the tree, Britt gave him a violent shove toward the backside of the hill. "Now get your ass on that horse and start actin' like a man. We've got things to do."

Six

Grady Bragg sucked air into his lungs and ran a little faster. His short, paunchy frame wasn't suited to quick movements, especially when the excitement had his heart beating faster than his stubby legs could run. His face was flushed, like a plump child choking on a fish bone, and with each frantic step his breath came in great sobbing gasps. Staggering under the load, he tossed a huge trunk into the wagon, then turned for a hurried look at the columns of smoke along the upper creek.

"Maggie, for God's sake, haven't we got enough?" Leaning against the tailgate of the wagon, Bragg marveled at the cowlike composure of his wife. Then, pa-

tience exhausted, his voice rose in a harried screech.
"Woman, you're gonna get us scalped trying to save this
tacky pile of shit!"

Turning as she was about to enter the cabin,
Maggie's pinched, tight-lipped face was a portrait of
righteous indignation. "Grady Bragg, if you insist on using filthy language in front of women and children,
then you can just leave us here, and we'll find our own
way to the fort." Spinning on her heel, she stormed into
the cabin and in calm, measured tones instructed the
children to ignore their father's vile manner.

Bragg was dumbstruck, completely unnerved by a
feminine viewpoint which took offense at a man's cursing when only a mile away the Comanches were probably mounting everything in skirts. Upon sighting the
pillars of smoke less than an hour ago, he had immediately hitched the team and saddled his best horse. But
Maggie was not about to be rushed, even by the Comanches. If their home was going to be burned, then
she was determined to save the accumulated treasures
of a lifetime, and she methodically set about loading
the wagon. Grady had urged, cajoled, and finally resorted to curses, all to no avail.

Bragg glanced upstream once more, fully expecting
to see the raiders come boiling over the distant hills at
any moment. Goddamn women just aren't human, he
fumed, worried about saving a wagonload of doodads
when we're only a short hair away from gettin' roasted
alive. Then his body stiffened, eyes wide with alarm as
he sighted riders cresting the stumpy knolls to the
northeast. Grabbing his rifle, he ordered Maggie and
the children into the wagon, never taking his eyes from
the approaching riders. Surprisingly his heartbeat had

calmed, and with a touch of pride he realized that his earlier panic had now been replaced with steady coolness.

The horsemen drew nearer, gradually assuming distinct form, and Grady suddenly sensed that they were white men. Squinting, he looked closer. No, two white men and a nigger! By God, it was the Johnsons and Tom Fitzpatrick! Overcome with relief, Bragg waddled forward with a sudden burst of energy, shouting and waving them on.

The three men rode into the yard at a full gallop, reining the horses back on their haunches in a blinding cloud of dust. Without asking, Bragg knew that they would never have come alone unless their women and children were beyond hope. Allan leaned across the saddle, his voice tight and strained, gesturing in the direction they had come.

"Comanches! No more than a mile back. If you want to keep your hair, you'd better get that team movin' now!"

Before the words were out, Maggie cracked her whip with the deftness of a muleskinner, and the team broke into a headlong lope. Grady ran to his horse and mounted clumsily, listing in the saddle like a corpulent bulldog unaccustomed to great heights. The men reined their horses after the wagon and pounded out of the yard.

Glancing back over his shoulder, Britt saw the war party top the rolling hills behind them, and he shouted a warning to the others. Slowed by the pace of the wagon, the four men checked the loads in their pistols and watched the dust cloud to their rear with a growing sense of alarm.

After what seemed a small lifetime they reached the wider banks of the Brazos and thundered south along the river trail. Ahead of them the rutted track was cloaked with the dust of a dozen wagons racing for the fort, and it suddenly dawned on them that they were the last to escape Elm Creek alive. Turning in the saddle, Britt's eyes narrowed as he saw two columns of Indians converge where the stream joined the Brazos. Astounded by what appeared to be upward of a thousand warriors, he realized for the first time that what had taken place since daylight was something more than a mere raid. The Comanches were bad enough, but if they had joined forces with the Kiowas, then it might just be that even Fort Belknap would go up in flames.

Abruptly it flashed through his mind that Mary and the children now rode with that same war party. Willing himself to live, regardless of the cost to those around him, Britt rammed the chestnut in the sides and concentrated on reaching the fort in one piece.

Seven

Earlier that morning, shortly after Jonathan Hamby's cabin was put to the torch, a sentry at Fort Belknap spotted a thin wisp of smoke far across the plains. For a moment he watched it uncertainly, hesitant to sound a false alarm in the event it was nothing more than an illusion evoked by the glare of sunrise. Then, even though he remained skeptical, the sentry decided to play it safe by calling the corporal of the guard. If he had learned anything after six months in the militia, it was that a smart

soldier always hedged his bet; survival in the army, as seasoned campaigners had demonstrated, was simply a matter of passing the buck upward until some hero made
the decision.

Within a quarter-hour the amused sentry was congratulating himself as he watched first a corporal, then
a sergeant, and finally a grumbling, sleepy-eyed lieutenant confound themselves staring at his discovery. The
lieutenant was also well versed in passing the buck,
and with some misgiving he in turn sent an orderly to
fetch Captain Barry.

Unlike his subordinates, Barry had never lost belief
that the Comanches would ride south before the first
snow. When he lumbered up the stockade ladder to the
catwalk a short time later, the raid was already well
under way, and the distant pall of smoke removed any
doubt as to what was happening on Elm Creek. The
prospect of a good scrap instantly aroused him, and
with the surly disposition of a grizzly in mating season,
he ordered the militia saddled and held ready for a sortie.

Quickly assembling the settlers quartered in the fort,
he advised them of the situation and outlined his plan
to ride against the Comanches. After informing them
that the responsibility for manning the stockade had
now fallen on their shoulders, the commander turned
and marched brusquely toward headquarters, leaving
the gaping civilians to stare after him. Still somewhat
incredulous, they watched in numbed silence as Barry
led the troop of militiamen through the front gate and
galloped north along the river trail.

Less than a half-hour later Barry began meeting settlers as their wagons rumbled toward the fort. Con-

cealing his troops in a shallow depression behind a hill, he stationed himself in a stand of cottonwoods near the trail. With his combative nature at full pitch he relished the idea of ambushing a pack of howling savages, gloating already over the shocked confusion that was sure to result when the trap was sprung. As yet, none of the settlers could actually say they had seen the Indians, and his hurried questioning had yielded nothing firm regarding the war party's size. But Buck Barry was a man of supreme confidence, if not outright arrogance, and he was satisfied that the Texas militia could handle anything the Comanches were able to raise with winter so near.

Shortly afterward Barry saw Grady Bragg's wagon careening down the trail with four horsemen bringing up the rear. Reining his mount out of the cottonwoods, he waved the wagon on and held up his hand to halt the riders. The four men jerked their winded ponies up short and crowded around the burly officer. Exhilarated by the imminence of a fight, Barry greeted them with a huge grin, failing to notice the utter despair written across their faces.

"Boys, here's where you quit running. I've got my troops back over that hill, and we're fixin' to bushwhack ourselves a few redsticks. Care to join us?"

The four men looked at one another with amazement, slowly comprehending that the captain was ignorant of what it was chasing them. Then Tom Fitzpatrick's sardonic voice broke the silence. "Mister, in about five minutes everyone of your soldier boys is gonna be standin' in a puddle full of piss. There's enough Comanches coming down that road to eat your bunch alive and spit out the seeds."

Buck Barry's grin dissolved into a churlish scowl, but before he could reply, Allan confirmed the odds they faced. "Captain Barry, you'd better set aside your personal feelings about Tom and listen. Otherwise, you'll likely lose your whole command before the fight even gets started. There's somewhere around a thousand Indians headed this way, and nothing this side of the swivel guns at the fort is about to stop them. The only reason we got this far is because they couldn't resist burning the cabins along the river trail."

"Johnson, you must have been drinkin' too much popskull," Barry growled. "And the rest of you must need spectacles. The Comanches couldn't raise a thousand braves if they had Jesus H. Christ beatin' the drum."

"Cap'n, it's not just Comanches," Britt retorted heatedly. "I've lived through enough raids to know what kind of Indian I'm lookin' at. And about half that war party is Kiowa." The other men looked at him in bewilderment, unaware that he had observed the two tribes regrouping forces on the Brazos. "I'm not real set on losing my hair today either, so I think I'll just get this horse headed in the right direction." Nodding upstream, the black man smiled at Barry. "I got a feelin' you won't be far behind."

Without another word Britt spun the chestnut about and headed toward the fort at a fast lope. Barry and the three settlers glanced north along the trail, and Britt's cryptic remark needed no explanation. Less than a half-mile distant the vanguard of the Comanche and Kiowa nations surged forward at a thundering trot. Barry's features blanched noticeably, and his eyes took on the glassy vagueness of one who has just looked into an open grave and seen his own face. The homesteaders spurred after Britt, and the captain hesitated only briefly before plunging back over the hill.

Gathering the puzzled militiamen, he led them in headlong flight toward the south. Once the soldiers got a look at what was chasing them, they needed no urging. Long before the column reached the fort, Buck Barry found himself overtaken and outdistanced by at least half the troop. When fighting Comanches, stragglers rarely stood to for the next mess call, and among the Fort Belknap complement there was an obvious reluctance to be the last man through the gate.

Toward midmorning Little Buffalo brought the *ehkasunaro* to a halt just out of rifle range on a hill overlooking the fort. Swarmed around him, spilling out over the plains below, the warriors hooted contemptuously as the last rider raced through the stockade gate. Their mocking chant floated eerily across the open ground, filling the air like an ominous hot wind, and those inside the fort knew they were listening to the voice of death.

But their day of judgment was postponed by the wily young *to-yop-ke* who watched from the hill. Little Buffalo had no intention of losing both warriors and precious time by laying siege to a fortified position. Such an attack would be lengthy, as well as costly, and a poor exchange for the lives of a mere forty or fifty whiteeyes. Below Fort Belknap lay a multitude of unsuspecting tejanos, and the shrewd tactician always struck first at the weak underbelly of his enemy. Besides, his warriors were interested in scalps and fair-haired captives, and they would quickly grow bored with the childish white-eyes cowering behind wooden walls. Men fought openly, testing their courage face to face, and how was a brave expected to count coup on a race that scampered to their hole like a timorous rabbit?

Reining the pinto downhill, Little Buffalo forded the Brazos and led his warriors south. Death had paid a brief call at Fort Belknap and, finding it wanting, moved on to more receptive company.

Eight

The brilliant, starlit sky seemed wholly at odds with the mood of the settlers. Ominous black clouds, with an oppressive dirge and tolling bells, would have been more appropriate to their glum silence. Gathered along the stockade catwalk, they solemnly stared at the distant glow which illuminated the southern horizon. Throughout the long afternoon and early hours of darkness they had observed an advancing chain of smoke and flame as one settlement after another was put to the torch. And from the fort it appeared likely that every homestead along the Brazos had been reduced to ashes. Drained of emotion, they simply stood and watched as the holocaust spread through the night. Remorse for neighbors and loved ones lost in the raid left them overcome with grief, and they could only hope that the families farther south had fared better at the hands of the Comanches. Prayers they reserved for their own dead.

Suddenly the stillness was broken by the sound of a horse being pushed hard, and a rider appeared from the darkness. Rifles came to bear over the stockade wall, and there was the unmistakable click of hammers being thumbed back. Then, as fingers tightened nervously on triggers, a voice from below calmed the jumpy settlers.

"Hold your fire! Scout coming in!"

The gate swung open with a creaking groan, and the rider galloped through on a lathered horse. Clambering down from the walls, settlers and militia alike ran after the scout as he reined to a halt before headquarters and dismounted. Buck Barry filled the doorway in the same moment and stepped forward to greet the man. Observing his haggard appearance, the captain called for whiskey, and the gathering crowd waited tensely as the scout drained a brimming glass with obvious relish. Smacking his lips, the man wiped his mouth with a grimy sleeve and slowly looked around the curious faces.

"Goddammit, man, tell us!" Barry roared. "Or are you waitin' for somebody to start pitching coins?"

"No, Cap'n, I ain't. It's just that I don't rightly know where to start. Whatever you expected, it's about ten times worse'n you thought."

"Well, I don't see anybody here crying for a sugar tit, so suppose you just give it to us like we was full-grown."

The scout nodded, glancing around the somber crowd. "It ain't exactly pretty. I done just like you told me and snuck around Elm Creek first. Then I cut cross-country and hung behind the redsticks down the lower Brazos. Cap'n, the easiest way to say it is that there ain't a building left standin' within twenty miles of this fort. What they couldn't burn or carry, they killed. They're trailin' a herd of about a hundred horses, and they slaughtered enough stock to feed an army." Then his eyes wavered, unable to meet the settlers' frozen stares as he voiced their innermost fears. "I couldn't get too close, you understand, but near as I could figure, they've got somewheres around ten women and eighteen kids."

There was a moment of deathly silence, then settlers throughout the crowd began pushing forward to inquire of wives or children missing since the raid. The scout shook his head in response to the anxious shouts, repeating over and over again that he had never gotten close enough to actually see the captives' faces. Suddenly the man noticed Britt among the crowd, and his face took on the look of one who has just recalled a minor but salient detail.

"Say, there's one thing I thought of," he said, quieting the settlers as he nodded directly at Britt. "And it might just interest this man. Even as far away as I was, I could tell there was a black woman and two black young'uns mixed in with them taken prisoner."

The crowd turned to look at Britt, and for an instant in time the separation between black and white became an unbridgeable chasm. Their faces reflected anger and resentment, and about them clung the unspoken thought that a nigger had been singled out over God's own. While each would have given his life for the knowledge that friends and loved ones were at least alive and uninjured, this coveted solace had been granted solely to a black man. And in that they beheld a highly profound injustice.

Watching their faces, Barry sensed the temper of the crowd and quickly diverted their attention back to the scout. "Which way were the Indians heading when you left them?"

"Cap'n, I stuck with 'em till they turned sorta north-east after raidin' Mineral Wells. Appears to me they're gonna circle Fort Richardson and hit the settlements up that way. Ain't nobody chasin' them, but they seemed just a mite anxious to get back across the Red." When the officer failed to respond, apparently digesting what he had just heard, the scout ventured a shrewd judgment. "You know how Injuns is. Once they get enough horses and scalps, there ain't nobody this side of Lucifer himself could talk 'em into more fightin'."

"Why don't you go sample that jug sittin' on my desk?" The man scampered through the door before the unexpected offer could be withdrawn, and Barry turned to the crowd. "You all heard the report, and you know as much as I do at this point. So why don't you turn in and get some sleep just in case the Comanches decide to surprise us again in the morning."

As the captain turned to the door, the crowd broke up and began drifting toward the old federal barracks, where they had been quartered. Their movements were slow and dispirited, characteristic of those who have seen a lifetime's dreams suddenly go up in smoke. Shoulders slouched, their features blank and forlorn, they seemed bereft of hope. And beneath their hollow stares waited the tears that would come in the solitary night. For while the dead could be buried and done with, there would be no end to mourning the women and children now consigned to a living death.

Britt walked beside Allan and Tom, seeing in his mind's eye the picture briefly described by the scout. Hundreds of leering warriors surrounding an island of white captives. And within that vast, hostile throng three tiny black faces searching desperately for some end to their terror.

It was like a grotesque nightmare, clawing its way up from the slimy depths of a man's secret furies. But it was no dream, and where death had a finality to it, the thoughts of Mary and the children being enslaved by the Comanches tormented Britt all the more. Slowly his mind surfaced from such thoughts, unable to cope with the odious specter they conjured up, and he became aware of the white men's strained conversation.

"Tom, I don't give a damn what you say, it was all my fault," Allan snapped. "I took it upon myself to give the orders, and if I'd just left one man at the house, none of this might have happened."

"Hindsight ain't no better than hind tit," Tom replied. "Even if a man could see every little thing that's going to happen down the road, he'd still make mistakes, maybe more." His voice broke, and they walked a few steps farther in silence. "We just got careless. Lazy, goddamn careless! And we're all gonna live with that for a long time."

"You won't get any argument there." Allan's voice was barely audible, filled with loathing for his own short-sightedness. "I had a feeling this morning something was wrong. But I put it off. Just put it out of my mind. And instead of being concerned with the women and kids, I was worrying about getting those steers out to graze. By God, if I had the mangy bastards here, I'd shoot everyone of 'em right between the eyes!"

"Who gives a shit about cows!" Tom exploded. "You wanna know what sticks in my craw? I lost my whole family and ended up not even killin' *one* of those red sonsabitches!"

"You didn't lose your son," Britt suggested. The two white men glanced around sharply at his unexpected comment. "Leastways, he's not dead. And there's just a chance him and the others might be gotten back."

Fitzpatrick glared at him suspiciously, still rankled by the incident on the hillside that morning. Allan knew the black man well enough to grasp that there was something tangible beneath his matter-of-fact attitude, and a stirring of hope echoed in his insistent demand. "Britt, I'd move heaven and earth if there's even the slightest chance we could get them back. Now don't come at it sideways. Whatever you're scheming on, let's hear it straight out."

The white men halted, facing him, and Britt searched their faces for a moment. When he spoke, his tone was calm and understated, without a trace of bravado. "I'm going to cross the Red River and see if I can find the village where they're being held. Ever since we settled here, I've been hearing stories about people ransomed back from the Comanches. And the way things are, I reckon that's the only chance our women and kids have of not being camp slaves the rest of their lives."

Silence mounted as the two men stared at him incredulously. Many Texans had been ransomed from the Comanches over the years, but always with the army or unscrupulous Indian traders acting as intermediaries. Never had an individual negotiated the release of captives, regardless of the price offered. And for a lone man to cross the Red River was tantamount to suicide. Not as quick, perhaps, for being roasted head down over a slow fire was a prolonged death. But just as final.

"Britt, you're overwrought, or you wouldn't even consider such a plan." Allan's tone was solicitous, slightly indulgent. "Even if you could find where they're being held, the Comanches would more than likely kill you anyway. And what good would it do Mary and the children if you're dead?"

"If you're talking about a white man, I might agree with you," Britt said. "But we both know the Comanches don't feel the same way about blacks. They think we've got good juju, or whatever it is they call their brand of voodoo. I've always heard they're real curious about blacks, and I'm willing to risk it if it means getting our families back."

"Risk is the right word. You'll be staking your life that they won't lift your hair just because it's not straight and blond."

"By God, I hate to say it, Allan, but I think he's got the right idea for a change." Fitzpatrick's support came as a surprise to Britt, and he eyed the Irishman skeptically. "There's only one thing wrong. He needs someone to show him how to outsmart those stinkin' bastards. So, Britt, boy, I just declared myself in on your little expedition."

The black man's cold eyes bored a hole in Fitzpatrick, recalling his hysteria and muddled thinking on the hillside. "Sorry, this is a one-man show. If two of us ride in there, the Comanches will start thinking about scalps instead of how good a deal they can make."

"Slow down, highstepper," Tom cautioned with a patronizing smirk. "Your stride's getting too long for your britches. Maybe it slipped your mind that I got a son up there too. So what the hell gives you the right to say whether or not I come along?"

"Mister, you've got things a little confused," Britt replied stonily. "I didn't say you couldn't go. I just said you couldn't go with me. If you're itching to get killed, do it on your own time."

"You goddamn smart-mouth coon!" Tom flared. "Got your black ass perched up there on some kind of throne and sit around snickering at us dumb white folks!" Heads began appearing in windows and doorways as his strident voice carried throughout the fort. Observing the spectators, Fitzpatrick took courage, ignoring his narrow escape at the black man's hands just that very morning. "You better listen to me good, boy. The day ain't arrived that a uppity nigger can start tellin' white men where to head in! And if you don't want your balls nailed to a tree, you'd best start planning on some company when you ride north."

Britt started forward, determined to still the Irishman once and for all. Their brief encounter on the hillside flashed through his mind and with it came regret that he hadn't killed the bigoted loudmouth when he'd had the chance. But Allan quickly moved to block the black man's path, voicing an unspoken warning as he jerked his head in the direction of the barracks.

Shadowed forms were running across the parade grounds, attracted by an argument that unmistakably involved a white man and the Johnson nigger. More settlers were pouring out of the barracks each moment, and an icy chill suddenly settled over Britt. Earlier their eyes had filled with hate simply because the scout had observed only his family among the captives, and if he read the signs right, they were spoiling for an excuse to vent their anger over the raid—the same anger that had turned to jelly before the Comanches. Black men had died before with even less reason, and Britt had no illusions about his chances now if the crowd suddenly turned ugly.

Nine

Buck Barry broke off interrogating the scout when he heard angry shouting from outside. Barreling through the orderly room, he reached the porch in time to see men running toward the parade ground. Even in the starlight their forms were indistinct, and it was difficult to make out the exact nature of the commotion. But harsh words were being exchanged, and Barry was in no mood to tolerate dissension among the fort's defenders. Not with the Comanches still ravaging the countryside.

Striding swiftly in the direction of the gathering mob, Barry reflected on the absurdities practiced by seemingly reasonable men once they came under great stress. God knows they've got good cause, he thought, what with their homes being burnt and their women carted off to share some Comanche's blankets. But he had spent most of his life among fighting men, and instinctively he knew that their curious antics after a defeat sprang from a far deeper source. Once he had heard a brimstone preacher rant about a man being a soul concealed in an animal, and after twenty years on the frontier he found it to be a fair judgment. Men could withstand danger and hardship as a matter of course; they could even face death with the civilized veneer intact. But when their manhood was threatened, some strange, atavistic force seized them, and the animal inside was quickly unleashed.

The crowning humiliation, as he had often noticed, was not that their women were raped or that they themselves had been forced to run. Rather it was the fact that these things had happened without any retal-

iation from them. Almost anything could be endured,
but how could a man live with himself if he failed to
strike back and in the process lost his own manhood?
Curiously this impotent rage was more often than not
turned back on a man's own comrades, and as Barry approached the crowd, it occurred to him that a mob of
overgrown little boys seeking to regain their virility was
no joking matter.

"You men are letting personal feelings get in the way
of your judgment." Shouldering his way through the
crowd, Barry could detect in Allan's voice the urgency
of a man with his back to the wall. "Britt's the one man
who has a chance of crossing the Red and coming back
alive. And that's only because the Indians have always
been friendly toward blacks."

"Johnson, we're sick to death of you and your smart-
aleck nigger." The crowd muttered with approval as a
settler from below the fort lashed out angrily. "Lots of
us here lost women and kids today, and before we'd let
some numbskull coon go up there and get 'em killed,
we'd just as soon cut his throat. Yours too if you don't
back off."

The mob edged closer around Allan and Britt as an
undertone of hostility swept through their ranks.
Clearly they were bent on avenging the frustrations of
a long, disastrous day, and an uppity nigger sounded
like a good substitute for the red bastards that had gotten away. Knocking settlers aside none too gently, Barry
sensed the swelling of their hoarse threats as he
reached the center of the pack. The men were eyeing
Britt menacingly, waiting for someone to make the first
grab, and it seemed unlikely that even the militia commander could stay their wrath.

"Now let's don't go off half-cocked, boys." Tom Fitzpatrick's joshing tone made them hesitate. Surprised, they turned to look at him with some bewilderment, since it was his truculent outburst that had started the trouble in the first place. "I think we got us a coon that's about to see the light. Aren't you, boy?" Tom grinned crookedly at the black man, but Britt returned his stare with cold insolence. "See there, he's already learnin' to put a damper on that smart mouth! And I got an idea him and me will get along real fine while we're up there talkin' the Comanche out of all them women and kids."

"Fitzpatrick, you're living proof that there are more horses' asses than there are horses!" Buck Barry's malevolent snarl rocked the crowd back on their heels. "You're the one that's got a smart mouth. And the only thing you'd accomplish talkin' to the Comanches is to get yourself *and* Britt staked out on an anthill."

"Soldier boy, I've had about all of you one man can take," Fitzpatrick grated as his face purpled with rage. "This here's civilian business, and we don't need some rumpot muckin' it up. If you're so all-fired concerned you should of done a little more Injun fightin' this morning, 'stead of running back here like a gelded hog."

Almost before the words were out of his mouth, Fitzpatrick felt something explode in his brain, and the whole left side of his head suddenly went numb. Through a red, star-shot haze he saw Barry standing over him, and as a swirling darkness sucked him under, he faintly realized that he was flat on his back.

Barry gingerly rubbed the knuckles of his bruised fist, staring thoughtfully at the fallen Irishman. The grizzled officer's very appearance was enough to halt most antagonists in their tracks, for no man knew his full strength. And he was always curious about anyone with the audacity to crowd him. Dismissing Fitzpatrick as a reckless hothead, he glowered around at the settlers, amused by their reluctance to meet his eye.

"You men seem to have forgotten who runs this fort. I'd advise you not to listen to blowhards like Fitzpatrick in the future." Pausing, he waited to see if anyone was inclined to pursue the matter, but the men again avoided his gaze. "Now if Britt Johnson wants to cross the river, that's his business, and I don't want to hear any more about it. And just in case any of you are still skeptical, I'll guaran-damn-tee you he's the only man on the Brazos that's got a chance in hell of bringing those women and kids back alive. This meeting stands adjourned. Some of you men drag that thick-headed mick back to the barracks and let him sleep it off." Turning away, he called over his shoulder, "Britt, I want to see you in my office."

Ten

The three men stood near the front gate, talking quietly in the predawn darkness. Their words hung in the chill air, wreathed in puffs of frost, lingering eerily even after the sound had drifted off. About them there was a sense of grave finality, as if only the moment existed and their tomorrows were obscured by some impenetrable veil. Moments of stillness followed each taciturn flurry of words, and their reluctance to evoke a final parting formed an unspoken bond between them. Finally the larger of the three men shook hands, then turned, and lumbered wearily toward headquarters.

Britt and Allan remained silent for a moment, lost in their own thoughts as they watched Buck Barry trudge slowly across the parade ground. The night had been long and grueling, and their eyes were etched with the tenseness of men embarked on a hazardous undertaking. Less than six hours had passed since their meeting with Barry in the commander's office. After confirming Britt's resolve to ride north, the captain had advised him to leave the fort before dawn. The settlers were in an ugly mood, and if Barry was any judge of men, they wouldn't rest until their own guilt had been absolved in some violent manner. Right now Britt looked to be the most likely prospect for the sacrificial goat, and before the situation worsened, Barry wanted him long gone from the fort's volatile atmosphere. Allan concurred, though not without some misgiving as to the black man's chances north of the Red River.

The rest of the night had been spent in outfitting Britt for the journey. Barry loaned him a sturdy pack horse from the government mounts and opened the fort's storeroom for food and gear. That left only the matter of presents, and Allan quietly roamed the barracks gathering trinkets and household items which might appeal to savage curiosity. When he returned and the three men stood gazing at the assortment of paraphernalia, it became obvious that they lacked anything sufficiently ostentatious with which to honor a proud, and quite probably antagonistic war chief. The problem was one of acute significance, for the chief must be won over before the issue of ransom was ever broached.

Then, in a tone of mock disgust Barry cursed his
own weakness and stepped to a gunrack on the wall.
From it he jerked a highly prized Belgium Over and
Under rifle/shotgun and handed it to Britt with the
awkward stiffness of one who finds selfless acts intensely embarrassing. Gratitude among such men came
equally hard, and without a word they began packing
the goods and provisions for the long trek northward.

The time to depart had come. The first, diffused rays
of light were beginning to break in the east, and the
two men could faintly make out one another's features
in the dusky glow. Loath to part, they had been
avoiding this last moment with idle conversation. But
the words seemed forced, hollow of meaning. And they
were both aware that Britt had best be gone while the
fort still slumbered.

Clasping the black man's hand, Allan's voice was
husky and strained. "Britt, we've never been much for
words. Seems like there wasn't any need. And I can't
think of a hell of a lot to say now, except that I want
you back here in one piece. No matter what happens
up there. Sleep light and keep your dobber dry."

Britt smiled tightly, sensing the emotion behind his
friend's laconic manner. "That's a promise. And I'll stay
downwind too, like your daddy taught us." The words
came harder now, and he paused. "I'm not plannin' on
staying up north, but just in case I don't get back, I
want you to know I went under trying to save yours
just like I would my own. Even then I reckon I'd still
owe you. Watch after yourself, Allan."

Mounting quickly, Britt reined the chestnut around
and led the heavily laden pack horse through the front
gate. The sentry glanced curiously at him, and he nod-

ded in silent reply, certain that word of his departure would be all over the fort before breakfast. Glancing back, he saw Allan standing just outside the gate, and he waved. Then he put the chestnut into a trot, and the rushing waters of the Brazos were soon left behind.

Presently he crested a knobby hogback and reined to a halt. The sun had now scaled the horizon, casting golden shafts of light across the plains. Far in the distance he could make out the shapeless mass of Fort Belknap, and it occurred to him that the settlers would probably spend the day swilling whiskey and damning his black soul. Then Buck Barry's gruff voice came back to him, and in his mind he again heard the words that had startled him so last night.

"Britt, I wouldn't defend Fitzpatrick if his granddaddy was Jesus H. Christ. He's a loudmouth and a trouble-maker, and if he doesn't force me to kill him, it'll be nothing short of a goddamn miracle. But even the devil deserves his due, and the next time you get to thinkin' about how much fun it'd be to bust him up, you ought to recollect a couple of things about Fitzpatrick. For openers, he was the only man in this fort with guts enough to try and join your little expedition. None of the rest of 'em wanted anywhere near it. Now the other part of it has still got me bumfuzzled, and I don't pretend to understand why he did it. But whatever his reasons, he stopped the mob just when they were about to jump you. If he hadn't of spoke up when he did, they'd have left you stone cold faster'n a horse turd draws flies." Then Barry had slowly shaken his head, like a man confronted by some unfathomable riddle. "Maybe you can figure it out."

Britt mulled the words around in his head, trying to

find some clue to a man who would sic a mob on a lone adversary and then call them off just as if they were a pack of bear hounds. Thoroughly at a loss, he pushed the thought from his mind, determined to settle with Fitzpatrick one way or another when he returned. Then his great, booming laugh echoed across the rolling hills. *When I return!* Hell, black boy, you best start worryin' about *if you return*!

Still chuckling, he pointed the chestnut north and gently nudged him in the ribs. Ahead lay the Red River and a wilderness crawling with Comanches. And that, my friend, he chortled, is enough for any smartass nigger to take on at one time.

⚜ CHAPTER FOUR ⚜

One

CHILDREN ROAMED THROUGH THE VILLAGE in small, predatory bands, their chubby coppery faces twisted with mock ferocity. Even the young warriors needed to practice their trade, and the air was filled with squealing howls as they gleefully savaged one another in the never-ending war games. A bountiful summer had left their bellies plumply taut, and their spirited laughter bespoke the sense of well-being which permeated the village. The grove of trees bordering the Canadian was now bare of leaves, making the ground crackly and alive with sound underfoot as they stalked each other through the brush. Gray-barked cottonwoods and amber scrub oaks stood out in bold relief against the bronzed earth and the vermilion bluffs rising to the east. And as the Geese Going Moon approached, the lodges were warm and filled with the happy chatter of women preparing pemmican for the long winter ahead.

The chill wind had fallen away, as it did each evening when the sun retreated westward. Dusk came earlier now, casting dim blue shadows across the sluggish Canadian, and smoke from the cooking fires hung undisturbed in the dry, still air. Later the breeze would come again, crisp and more biting in the clear darkness, and before morning the trees would moan in creaking anguish as the rising wind whistled through their stark crowns. But the last rays of sunlight faded slowly, and old men who squatted before their lodges watched the prairie to the south with patient, watery eyes.

Since early morning an air of expectancy had hovered over the village, causing women to pause in their work and stare hopefully across the shimmering plains. Somehow, in ways which they neither understood nor questioned, they sensed that their men were close, and the long hours of the day had dragged by with unbearable slowness. Now as dusk resolutely settled over the village, each woman stood alone in her mounting concern. The forces of darkness were evil and pitiless, and for the men to return now might be a bad sign indeed. But it was always like this when the men returned from a raid. Whether they rode in with the break of dawn or the shadows of dusk, fear gnawed at the insides of every woman: the instinctive dread that the face she sought would be missing from their ranks.

When the war party finally appeared on the plains to the south, most of the people were in their tepees. The distant thud of hoofbeats brought their heads around, making them pause as they cocked their ears to the swelling rumble. Then the lodges emptied, cooking pots forgotten, as lighthearted villagers and a chorus of barking dogs streamed toward the edge of camp. Far away they could see a rolling wave of horsemen advancing steadily across the flaxen grasslands. As they watched, the bobbing mass slowly separated into distinct forms, and yipping cries of victory floated in on the south wind. Muttering among themselves, the toothless elders shook their fists to the sky, proclaiming deliriously that the tejanos had been devastated beyond all belief. Clearly it must be so, they jabbered, for had not Little Buffalo chosen to ignore the night devils and bring his war party home as the last faint glow of light slipped over the horizon?

Suddenly the warriors thundered into camp, laughing, shouting at friends and loved ones, howling the ritual chants of blooded victors. Reining their ponies tightly, they never once broke ranks, according their stern-faced *to-yop-ke* the honor of leading them on an exultant march through the village. Little Buffalo stared straight ahead, closing his mind to the hysterical cries of the villagers who ran alongside the skittish ponies. His manner was proud and yet filled with humility, somehow above the petty arrogance that such adulation might have exposed in lesser men. As befitted the leader of a conquering nation, he sat the *ehkasunaro* with lordly bearing, aware of nothing save the glory his warriors had brought to the True People.

Before the medicine lodge, he brought the horsemen to a milling halt and spun the pinto around to face them. The villagers fanned out around the war party, jostling and shoving as they sought a better look at the man who had avenged two decades of humiliation and defeat. Little Buffalo thrust his lance to the sky so that all might see the gory, light-haired scalps which festooned its shaft. Then he plunged the lance into the ground, jangling the crusted scalps as they flapped against one another, and raised his voice in savage exultation. *"Ah-ko!"*

Three thousand voices split the night as villagers and warriors alike echoed the war cry with a crazed roar. While the howling braves worked themselves into a frenzy, Little Buffalo cast a searching gaze through their ranks, smiling faintly as Ten Bears stepped forward. Their eyes locked, and for a moment the two men were alone, isolated in a soundless void that excluded all but the force of their own thoughts. The old chief's grizzled features were flushed, buoyant; the face of a man who has lived to see his uttermost prayers answered in full. And the clenched fist he extended in salute came almost as a benediction for the triumphant son. Then the shrill clamor of the spectators broke the momentary spell, and Little Buffalo again became the *to-yop-ke*. The stoic mask fell into place, and his hooded eyes once more swept the crowd. Raising his arm, he commanded silence, and within the space of a heartbeat the screeching voices fell still.

"What was promised has been fulfilled! The tejanos along the Brazos are rubbed out, no more! Their lodges are now ashes in the wind, and behind us comes a herd of horses that will make every man here a person of wealth!" The spectators roared their jubilation, laughing and slapping one another on the back as they congratulated themselves on the good fortune of the True People.

"No more will the white-eyes desecrate our sacred hunting grounds, for they have been left desolate, without the means of food or life in that land. And as their horses and cattle have been sacrificed, so have we taken away the tomorrows of their children. *There before you stand the tomorrows of the tejanos!*"

Little Buffalo's arm slashed in a violent arc, coming to

rest on the band of terror-stricken captives. Jerked from their horses, they had been kicked to the ground and huddled there in a filthy, shivering heap. Again the crowd howled with delight, gesturing derisively at the wide-eyed captives as they cowered even closer together. Then the *to-yop-ke*'s strident voice sliced across the village, stilling their jeering taunts.

"But we return with more than this! Something that was promised and a thing of far greater meaning to the True People. For what are horses and white-eyed bitches with their pups when stood against the honor of our nations? When we rode from this camp, we were men in name only, cringing in our lodges before the white-eyes' greed. But this night you will hear of the scalps and coup taken from the tejanos. We have come home, brothers, and this time we return as did our fathers and their fathers before them. Once again we rule the Plains, and wherever men gather, they will point to these lands and say, *'There live the warriors!'* "

Little Buffalo kneed the pinto forward, and the spectators' ranks silently opened before him. For a moment they watched in awe as he rode through their midst, and then the warriors' thunderous chant lifted to the sky in acclamation. *"TO-YOP-KE! TO-YOP-KE! TO-YOP-KE!"*

Without a flicker of acknowledgment Little Buffalo rode toward his lodge. *Tai-me* had guided his hand, and only something less than a man would accept credit for what the Grandfather God had ordained. Right now he would settle for the tender rewards that awaited any returning warrior, and they had nothing to do with either immortality or gods. Urging the *ehkasunaro* forward with a lusty kick in the ribs, he briefly wondered if Morning Star was already waiting beneath the robes.

Two

Mary staggered under the load of brush wood and braced herself for the blow that was sure to come. When the supple oak switch struck her thigh, she ignored the stinging pain, dimly aware that the squaw behind her had muttered a guttural curse. Gritting her teeth, she straightened under the load and lurched forward. Whatever happened, she was determined that these savages wouldn't force as much as a moan from her lips. Already she had seen Sarah Johnson and some of the other white women beaten to the ground simply because the squaws enjoyed hearing them scream. And it had quickly become apparent that the only way to survive was to accept their cruelty without flinching or crying out.

Grasping the rawhide straps holding the branches atop her back, Mary struggled on toward the medicine lodge. Great stacks of wood were being gathered there, and it seemed evident that some sort of ceremonial meeting would take place later in the night. She had heard of people being burned at the stake, and as the wood pile grew, she idly wondered if such a fate awaited her bedraggled group. While it wasn't entirely unlikely, she somehow just didn't care anymore. Weary and sore from five grueling days astride a barebacked horse, she only wanted a place to flop down and submerge her tortured mind in the refuge of sleep. The horror of watching her oldest son killed had slowly given way to the deeper anguish of knowing that she would never again see Britt. And with that realization came a numb insensibility that was not unlike death itself.

Her only other reason to live was to protect George and Sue Ellen. But they had been taken away from her shortly after arriving in camp and put out to play with the Indian children. From the start it was obvious that the two little blacks were a source of curiosity and amazement to every Indian in the village, and they had been readily adopted by their red playmates. As she stumbled back and forth with loads of wood, Mary glimpsed them shyly but eagerly joining in the games around the campfires. At first she was offended and hurt, almost as if they had forsaken her when some better diversion presented itself. Then she recalled that little children are all but immune to the sorrow of adults, especially when their grief is shunted aside by interacting new playmates.

Abruptly she decided she was wallowing in her own self-pity. Instead of resentment, she should be thankful that the children were being treated kindly. Whatever happened to her, they would be cared for, and for the moment that was all she could ask.

When the chief on the big pinto had ridden away, Mary and the other prisoners had been turned over to the squaws. The captive youngsters were treated with the same gentleness that Indians showed all children, regardless of their race. Within the hour they had been drawn into the games and were soon busily engaged in learning the ways of their new companions. But the women were a different matter entirely, and the squaws were quick to demonstrate that even the slightest hesitation in obeying an order would result in a severe beating. Before the women had time to gather their wits, they were pressed into service packing food and wood to the council grounds, and as the night wore on, their spirits sank lower with each back-breaking load. Children might be revered and coddled, but to the women it seemed abundantly clear that their lot was to be that of slaves, harnessed for life to the drudgery of menial camp chores.

While Mary and the white women had no way of knowing it at that moment, their status was about to undergo an abrupt change.

Trudging wearily toward the medicine lodge with another load of wood, Mary became aware that her gloomy thoughts had been penetrated by a mournful wailing unlike anything she had ever heard. Passing near a tepee, she saw the shrouded body of a warrior being loaded on a travois behind a horse. Earlier she had seen the Indian wounded being carried to their lodges, and quite obviously this one was destined for the burial grounds. But it was the woman seated before the lodge who left Mary gripped with fascinated horror.

Slowing her pace, the black woman watched with growing revulsion as the squaw calmly hefted a knife and slashed deep furrows along her forehead and cheeks. Bright rivulets of blood welled up from the wounds and splashed down over the squaw's face, burying her features beneath a bubbling crimson mask. Then she placed her forefinger on a log near the fire and lifted the heavy skinning knife high overhead. Mary gasped, unable to believe what she was witnessing. With only a moment's hesitation the squaw swung the knife in a downward arc, loping the finger off just below the knuckle. Suddenly another squaw appeared from the shadows, wrapped the grieving woman's hand in a rabbit skin and tossed the severed finger into the fire.

The switch flicked against Mary's legs, warning her that it was time to move on. Perversely she welcomed the pain, for it distracted her mind from her churning stomach. As she passed by, the blood-splattered squaw resumed her wailing chant and followed the burial party toward the plains to the west.

Somehow it had never occurred to Mary that a savage could grieve as deeply as other people, and she was astonished to find her heart reaching out to the mutilated squaw. White people, and blacks too, bottled their grief inside, distilling it into self-pity. Their sorrow was for their own loss, rather than for the soul of the departed. And rarely was there a tear shed or a moan uttered that the dead could rightfully claim as their own. Suddenly Mary's own grief seemed diminished, somehow spent, and as her pace quickened, there was a new awareness for the brutal but strangely tender people among whom she had been cast.

Later that night a huge fire was kindled in front of the medicine lodge, and warriors stepped forth to reenact gallant deeds performed during the raid. While these heroic tales were being related, the women served a feast of buffalo meat and boiled dog, and before long the entire assemblage lay back in a glutted stupor. Afterward, Little Buffalo rose to stand before the towering flames, and in a ringing, impassioned voice honored the most valiant among them with awards of extra horses and captive women. Then four elders seated themselves around a large drum, and the haunt-

ing throb of the victor dance floated out over the village.

As the howling warriors began leaping around the
fire, the forlorn settler women clutched their children
tighter and huddled together in the flickering shadows.
Their faces were grim, seemingly destitute of hope, and
more than one stared into the night and wondered if
the flames might not be a better fate than the one that
awaited them.

Three

Leaden clouds covered the sky, and a bitter wind
gusted across the prairie. Britt hunched forward, pulling the heavy coat up around his neck, and mechani-
cally scanned the bleak countryside. The north fork of
the Red crooked and twisted off to his left, generally
paralleling his northerly course. Sprawling elms, tupelo,
and blackjack lined its erratic banks, and from a distance the leafless trees rose from the earth like the towering spine of some ancient behemoth. Gently rising
away from the river, a deep carpet of bluestem and buffalo grass moved constantly beneath the crisp breeze,
and for the lone rider there seemed no respite from the
chill bite of the probing cold. With one last glance at
the trees he reluctantly turned the chestnut northeast
and rode toward the faintly ominous mountains.

After fording the Red five days past, Britt had followed the winding bank in a westerly direction, hoping
to cut the trail of the war party. But the ground remained barren of sign, and each night as he camped
along the shallow waters his spirits had sunk a bit

lower. Upon reaching the juncture of the south and north forks, it became apparent that the raiders had crossed somewhere far to the east. Retracing his steps would take days, with no assurance that a sudden rain squall wouldn't obliterate the already moldering trail. Suddenly the enormity of the task confronting him seemed all but insurmountable. The vast, uncharted wilderness beyond the Red was a formidable and grudging adversary. Desolate plains, broken occasionally by streams and impenetrable tangles of dense undergrowth, stretched endlessly for hundreds of square miles. And with but a few exceptions, no white man, or black either, had ever returned to wipe away the mystery shrouding this hostile and uncompromising land.

Buck Barry had mentioned that the Kiowas were reported to have their camps in the Wichita Mountains, which weren't especially hard to find if a man was foolish enough to try. But the whereabouts of the Comanches within those trackless reaches remained an enigma to all save a few renegade traders. With Barry's obscure comment as his only lead, Britt decided to follow the north fork on the off-chance he would encounter a friendly hunting party. Failing that, his only alternative was to enter the mountains and take his chances with the Kiowas.

Now almost a fortnight after departing Fort Belknap, he was nearing the foothills bordering the craggy, unexplored mountains. Rising abruptly from the prairie, the sheer granite outcroppings of the Wichitas dominated the landscape for a hundred miles in every direction. Visible from the Washita River in the north to the Red in the south, they seemed cloaked in a bluish mist, veiled by an eerie haze which seldom varied from one season to the next. From afar the mountains appeared mottled in tone, but as Britt drew nearer, the soaring palisades broke clear, and he could make out formations of jagged granite boulders delicately splotched with moss. Centuries of erosion had cleaved steep gorges through the massive outcroppings, and the walls of these uninviting corridors were covered with gaunt, drab underbrush.

Viewed from the distant Plains, the Wichitas had only looked faintly ominous. Up close they looked downright deadly.

Slumped in the saddle, weary and somewhat disheartened, Britt passed through the blackjack-studded foothills as the shadows of late afternoon lengthened across the countryside. Though he had crossed the tracks of unshod ponies twice that morning, there had been no sign indicating a village of any size. And the futility of wandering aimlessly over this dismal landscape was slowly beginning to sap his spirit. Reflecting on the turn of events, it occurred to him that while he hadn't found any Indians, there was every likelihood that they would find him once he entered the mountains. But that wasn't quite the same thing. Grimly he recalled once having heard an army scout snort that any man who strayed north of the Red was fool enough to go hunting grizzlies with a switch.

Cresting a small knoll, he suddenly jerked upright in the saddle. Below him stretched a sheltered valley, and grazing contentedly on the wide expanse of grass was a herd of buffalo ponies. But the horses were only of passing interest, for across the way, on the opposite side of the herd were two mounted Indians. Their relaxed, slightly indolent manner confirmed that they were guarding the horses, and Britt's heart quickened at the significance of his blundering discovery. Such a large herd meant there was a substantial village nearby, and if he could somehow befriend these horse guards, there was a fair chance he could enter the camp with his hair still in place. Still somewhat hidden where he had come to a halt in a scrubby stand of blackjack, Britt sensed that he must make some gesture before the braves spotted him and took alarm.

Quickly he tied the packhorse to a tree and kneed the chestnut over the forward slope. Halfway down the hill he saw the Indians snap erect and knew they had sighted him. Holding to a steady trot as he reached the bottom of the hill, he reined the chestnut into a series of tight, jogging circles. He had been told somewhere, by someone long since forgotten, that this was the Plains Indians' signal of peaceful intent, and he could only hope that the custom was still honored.

Alert and cautious, the warriors held their position, scanning the brush-covered hills behind him for any sign of reinforcements. Clearly they were suspicious of a strange black man suddenly appearing from nowhere, and they weren't about to be sucked into a trap. Still they both had rifles and thus far had made no threatening moves, so there was an outside chance they might let him approach closer. With the reins in his left hand and his right thrust outward, Britt circled the herd and rode toward them.

Drawing closer, he saw that they were quite young and growing more apprehensive by the moment. Both were chunky and heavy chested, which was characteristic of most Kiowas, and even from a distance Britt could see that the taller of the braves was watching him with a cold, predatory look. The smaller one seemed curious more than anything else and kept nodding his head with a faint, nervous smile. Britt knew that most Plains tribes spoke a smattering of Mexican, and as he reined to a halt some twenty yards out, the black man offered a silent prayer that his broken Spanish would ring true on a Kiowa ear.

"Buenos días, amigos." Wrapping the reins around the saddle horn, he folded his arms across his chest. "I enter your land in peace for the purpose of speaking with your chief."

The Indians eyed him warily, still unconvinced that this black apparition wasn't in some way dangerous. There was no sign of warmth in the wide, dour face of the taller youth, and the menace in his gaze was clearly noticeable. Pursing his lips, he spat on the ground, jerking his neck forward like a snake striking. "The Kiowa have no business with tejano *Negritos.* Lay down your guns and we will then decide if you are to enter our village with your buffalo wool uncropped."

"Young friend, I come in peace," Britt said, forcing a smile. "But only a fool would set aside his guns when his good will is questioned." His confidence rose as the burly youth mulled the thought over, now somewhat uncertain. "I come offering gifts and ransom. My family was taken in your raid on the Brazos, and I am prepared to pay many horses to buy them back."

"Eeh-yah! This man's words are coated with honey, my brother." The smaller brave spoke for the first time, glancing at his companion with a toothy grin. Horses were the only recognized measure of true wealth among the Plains tribes, and when a man spoke of such matters, he deserved to be taken seriously. The other warrior watched Britt sullenly, obviously thrown offstride by the black man's unexpected proposal. Santana was an ambitious man, and it passed through the boy's mind that the chief wouldn't look kindly on a young upstart who carelessly rubbed out a new source of wealth.

"I can offer horses to match even these you guard, young warriors," Britt said. Alert to the slightest reaction, he caught the flicker of greed growing brighter in their eyes. "Can you tell me if I have come to the right village? Are there women and children taken in the raid being held here?"

The warriors looked quickly at one another, again wary and uncertain as to how much they should reveal. But youthful enthusiasm won out over caution, and the smaller brave couldn't resist a manly boast. "Would you insult the Kiowa, buffalo man? There are many white-eyed slaves in our village. More than you have horses, I would wager." Then he paused, regarding Britt speculatively for a moment. "But now that I think on it, there are none as black as you."

Britt's soaring spirits plummeted back to harsh reality. The Kiowas and Comanches roamed this vast wilderness in many bands, and it surpassed belief that he could have found Mary and the children on the very first try. But the odds were good that he could learn of their whereabouts from these Kiowas, if he could somehow manage to keep from losing his own hair in the process. And that was a damn sight closer than he had been since crossing the Red. Smiling warmly at the two young warriors, he motioned back across the valley.

"Let me catch up my packhorse, for I have many gifts to please your people. Then as you escort me to your village, you can tell me more of these tejanos you have broken to halter."

Four

Santana sat alone on the side of a hill overlooking the village. Often he came to this peaceful spot to meditate and thrash out within himself the festering anger which dominated his moods these days. But somehow he hadn't been able to reconcile the malign thoughts crowding his head with the triumphs and good fortune of his people. His gaze shifted down over the village, observing squaws busily engaged in tanning hides for the winter and warriors seated before their lodges gambling with the bones. There was an obvious sense of prosperity about the camp, for each lodge was well stocked with meat and many of the braves had gained added wealth from the recent raid. Their camp was ideally situated in a snug, sheltered valley which would protect them from the blizzards to come. The mountains around them teemed with deer and elk, should their stores dwindle before the snows melted. Being entirely pragmatic about it, as the people themselves generally were, the Kiowa were better off this winter than they had been for many snows past. And that was the thing Santana couldn't bring to light within himself.

Sighing pensively, he lay back under the pines and watched the grass-sweetened wind stir the treetops above him. This thing ate at his bowels like a nest full of worms and, try as he might, he couldn't set it aside.

While he hesitated to put a word to it, in the secrecy of his own thoughts he could admit that it was nothing more than simple jealousy. He was a proud man, vain and ambitious in his ways, and it was a bitter thing to know that he harbored envy for such dogs as the Comanches. But there it was, and no matter how he skirted around the feeling, there was no way of dodging it.

They were such arrogant scum, those Comanche. Forever scoffing at the Kiowa, ridiculing the ways and customs of a people even more ancient than they themselves. And their audacity knew no bounds, for only a misbegotten Comanche would have claimed that the Kiowa had hung back during the raid on the Brazos. Only with the threat of an open break had Little Buffalo been coerced into awarding horses and captives to the Kiowa braves.

Perhaps respect was too much to hope for from an ignorant Comanche. Certainly they would never admit it, but their uncivilized behavior regarding the bear was what started the trouble in the first place. They knew that the Kiowa worshipped the bear as a medicine animal; a shaggy reincarnation of ancestors from the unknown of ancient days. Yet they still persisted in killing a bear on the march to the Brazos. But the unforgivable abomination was that they actually *ate the sacred one*, taunting the Kiowas with mocking jeers as the grease dripped down over their chins.

They were barbarians, these Comanches. Backward, ignorant, uncivilized in both manner and speech. For only a barbarian could have eaten the sacred one and laughed at the Kiowas' fears that the raid would be plagued by misfortune. Even to speak the name of the sacred one was bad medicine; to eat one was to invite the wrath of all holy things, who stood united in the face of such vulgarity. Santana's ears still burned when he remembered Little Buffalo's derisive jest on the trail home.

"Brother, your people twist their necks to the rear like a limbful of sick turkeys. Do the Kiowa also hunt for lice behind their wings, or is it that they fear what sniffs at our trail?"

If only he could humble the Comanche in some way. Bring them to their knees and make them cringe with shame at their own ignorance, just as they made the Kiowa slink away like scalded dogs whenever they felt in need of sport. Stretched out under the pines, he looked peaceful and serene, a wise chief musing on the tomorrows of his people. But within him the seed of envy smoldered corrosively, tainting his every thought with the fetid shadow of insults long past.

Shouts from below suddenly snapped him out of his malignant reverie, and he rose to his feet in a quick, fluid motion. Looking out over the valley, he observed a crowd gathering at the far edge of camp. As he peered closer, it became clear that the villagers there thronged around three horsemen. And one of those horsemen wore the garb of a tejano. Galvanized by the thought that a cringing white-eye might just divert his loathsome mood, Santana exuberantly leaped a boulder and bounded down the hill.

Breathing only slightly heavier from the run, Santana cut across the camp and arrived in front of his lodge moments before the two horseguards rode up with Britt. Back stiffened, chin outthrust, the chief drew himself into a dignified pose, determined not to betray his surprise at the sight of a black man. He had seen *Negritos* before, of course, and like all of his people, found them objects of great curiosity. But to have one materialize in your own camp was another matter entirely, and something to be considered without haste. Besides, this man had the look of a warrior about him, and it was just possible that keeping him alive might be more amusing than killing him. Watching the black man dismount, Santana was again struck by the similarity between *Negritos*, with their woolly-fuzz hair, and the buffalo with their equally curly topknot.

"*Hao*, Santana," the taller young brave said. "We bring you a tejano *Negrito* who claims he has come to make the Kiowa rich with horses."

Santana ignored the boy, having always considered him a loutish bumbler. Instead, he gazed aloofly at the black man, his features cold and tight lipped. After a moment he spoke, resorting to Mexican, even though he found it a frail, distasteful language. "Only a brave man or a fool rides alone into a Kiowa camp. Which are you, *Negrito*?"

"Neither," Britt responded, meeting the chief's eyes with a level stare. "I am a man who seeks his family and is willing to pay generously to have them returned."

The crowd drew closer, their interest sharpened by this talk of gifts and wealth. A murmur lapped back over their ranks as word spread that the tejano *Negrito* was offering horses for captives.

"Well spoken. A man's affection for his family is a good thing." Santana casually waved his hand around the throng of onlookers. "But as you can see, we have no buffalo people here."

"I have observed as much," Britt agreed reluctantly.

But he had seen something else riding into the village.
Sarah Johnson and her children, along with the Fitzpatrick boy, standing forlornly beside a lodge. He had
nodded in recognition and then hurriedly looked away,
not wanting the Indians to know that he would pay as
dearly for some whites as he would blacks. Now he
gently baited the hook as Santana eyed him speculatively. "But if the leader of the Kiowa is agreeable, we
might still make a trade. The tejanos have empowered
me to bargain for white-eyes also. That is, if they are
unharmed and able to travel."

"Hah! The buffalo man sets an inviting snare,"
Santana snorted. His stony face cracked with a slight
smile as he nodded knowingly. "But where are your
horses? Are you a *shaman* that you can blink your eyes
and a fine herd of ponies will suddenly appear?"

"Hardly that, great chief. But the horses are waiting
for those who wish to trade. Before we haggle like
tradesmen, though, let me first honor you and your
people with a few tokens from those who seek your favor."

Striding to the pack horse, Britt loosened the rawhide thongs and removed a bulky canvas packet.
Spreading it on the ground, he threw the flaps back to
reveal an assortment of mirrors, knives, cloth goods,
and various foodstuffs. As the Indians crowded around
to examine the curious treasures, he stepped back to
the horse and withdrew a long object wrapped in soft
cloth. Unwrapping it, he heard a sharp intake of breath
as the nearer warriors caught sight of the rifle/shotgun.
Without undue fuss he casually loaded both barrels and
checked the caps. Searching the ground for a moment,
he selected a fist-sized rock and tossed it high into the

air. Throwing the weapon to his shoulder, he triggered the shotgun and saw the rock disintegrate in a cloud of pebbly dust. Instantly he turned, sighted on the lodge pole of a distant tepee, and fired the rifle. As the top of the lodge pole disappeared in a shower of splinters, the crowd began chattering excitedly, overawed by a gun which spoke with two voices.

Britt walked directly to Santana and extended the gun. "This is for the leader of the Kiowa. When it speaks, his enemies will know that wherever they stand, their name has been called."

Santana accepted the gun hungrily, caressing its surfaces tenderly as an old warrior would fondle a nubile young wife. His eyes glowed, and when at last he looked at Britt, there was a spark of undisguised admiration in his gaze. "The buffalo man causes me to think that we have underestimated some of those who walk among the tejanos. My braves will show you a lodge where you can rest and think about how you will make those horses appear. Tonight we will feast and talk of the value you place on white-eyed slaves."

Stroking the gleaming walnut and steel of the gun, the leader of the Kiowas nodded with a crooked, enigmatic grin, then turned and entered his lodge.

Five

Santana belched appreciatively and tossed a gnawed rib onto a pile of bones near the fire. Soon the buffalo would disappear for the winter, secreting themselves from the red man as they had for a thousand snows, and fresh meat was a thing to be relished fully. Britt pat-

ted his distended stomach and managed a respectable
burp. He had eaten till his jaws ached, determined to
honor Santana's hospitality with a properly ravenous
appetite. Now he felt sated, drowsy from a full belly
and the cloyed warmth of the chief's lodge.

Upon entering the tepee, his nostrils had rebelled at
the curious stench of an Indian lodge. The odor was a
potent blend of sweaty bodies, rank buffalo hides, tobacco, rancid grease, and campfire smoke. Separately
the smells might have been acceptable, if not agreeable. But together they formed a pungent, highly seasoned aroma which left his stomach churning and his
appetite numb. Nevertheless, diplomacy demanded a
hearty eater, and he laid to with gusto, breathing
through his mouth whenever possible.

As Santana's wives served them, the chief's reserve
lessened with each greasy mouthful, and he steadily
grew more talkative. Before the last bone had been
sucked clean of marrow, Britt's silence was rewarded
with a casual disclosure of his family's whereabout.
While Santana couldn't remember the warrior's name,
he did recall that the black woman and her two little
Negritos had become the property of a Comanche. After the victory celebration the Kiowas had returned to
their mountains, and presumably the Comanches had
split once more into their five nomadic bands. Which
band Mary and the children had accompanied and
where they would winter on the Plains were matters
beyond Santana. And quite obviously one which left
him coolly indifferent. The Kiowas had only white-eyes
to trade, and these incessant questions about *Negritos*
wearied him.

"Enough of this idle chatter." Santana lay back on a

buffalo robe and casually picked his teeth with a grimy fingernail. "Let us talk of horses. Or of more importance, how you intend to make these imaginary horses appear in the Kiowa camp."

Britt eyed the red man cautiously. What he must now attempt was a delicate thing, and unless the words were chosen carefully, there were many white families who would never again see Texas. "Santana is a wise chief, for only the far-sighted man perceives that a horse is of more lasting value than a feeble tejano woman. And in that wisdom he will also see that in order for a man to grow wealthy, he must place a certain trust in those with whom he trades."

"What you say is true. How could I deny my own wisdom?" Santana's bronzed features twisted in a wolfish grin, and his hooded eyes regarded Britt curiously. "But I tire of this game we play. While I wish only to hear of horses, you talk in circles, like a slippery-tongued medicine man."

"Sadly, I must, for it is necessary that you believe what is behind my words." Britt's throat went dry even as his brow grew damp with cold sweat. "I have no horses nearby, nor can I make them appear. What I propose is that your warriors return the captives to the Brazos and exchange them for horses at that time."

Santana's eyes went cold, and there was a deadly chill to his voice. "You are a brave man, and for that I can respect you. But you are a fool. When you rode into camp, I took you to be a warrior, and we may yet test your courage. But even a warrior can be a *pawsa*, a crazy man."

His face remained hard, and a tense stillness settled over the lodge. Clearly he was torn between greed and

caution, for his stoic expression couldn't entirely mask
the inner conflict. Finally he spoke in a guarded tone,
seemingly resolved on which path to explore. "If I am
as wise as you say, then how could I trust the white-
eyes to honor your word? What is to stop them from
killing my warriors instead of handing over the horses?"

"That is a thing to consider, I grant you." The black
man's heart quickened as he realized that an opening
wedge had been driven into Santana's sullen wariness.
Now for the ticklish part, and he had the feeling it
would require all the tact he could muster. "While it
shames me, I cannot deny that the tejanos are incapable of trusting even one another. And as wise men
know, cynics are rarely a trustworthy breed. But
Santana must remember that he holds a mighty club
over the tejanos' heads. For if they attempt to betray
the trust, your warriors can easily kill the women and
children. And that is a threat which even the white-eyes
will respect."

"Maybe. Who knows the mind of the white-eyes?"
Shaking his head doubtfully, the chief stared into the
fire for a moment. "And what is to stop them from killing my warriors after the exchange is made? A herd of
horses will slow the march, and they could easily over-
take my people."

"There is no need to concern yourself with that,"
Britt said. "The army no longer patrols the Brazos, and
after our exchange the tejanos won't have enough
horses left to pull even a wagon. Thus, there will be no
one to pursue your warriors when they travel north
again."

"That is true," Santana chortled. "After all the horses
we took on the raid, such an exchange as this would

leave the tejanos afoot like squaws." The thought seemed to please him immensely, and he toyed with it for a moment. "Your words have a certain wisdom, *Negrito*. Still, I'm not sure my warriors would undertake such a hazardous venture. After all, if they had the foresight of which you spoke, then it is they who would sit as chief."

Suddenly Britt sensed that beneath Santana's chiseled mask lurked a vain and ambitious man. The chief had no intention of joining in the exchange himself. He meant to send only the warriors and rely on their wary cunning to make him a wealthy man. Just possibly this deal wasn't as difficult as he had thought. Scenting blood, he decided to strike for the jugular.

"Who is to say that the warriors are not justified in turning their backs on such a risky undertaking? Certainly not I. But from what I have seen, the leader of the Kiowa is not a man whose wishes are treated lightly by his people. When Santana speaks, his warriors listen. This I have witnessed for myself. Of course, like your braves, I am but a common man, and my mind has difficulty in grasping what is right or wrong for the good of all. This is a thing which must be left to the leaders." Britt paused, steadying himself for the final thrust, and then plunged on. "But I have served under many leaders in my life, and there is one thing I have learned above all else. Honor and fame go to the bold, and the meek are left to haggle over the scraps."

Santana blinked owlishly, studying the black man with a puzzled frown. For a moment he couldn't decide whether he had been insulted or praised. But he hadn't survived over forty snows without acquiring some instinct for men's motives, and it slowly dawned on him

that he had just been treated to a wily and highly subtle
challenge. There was more to this strange tejano than
he had thought, and just as he admired a brave man, so
did he respect an artful intriguer.

"*Waugh!* My warriors will follow you to the Brazos,
Negrito. But for the sake of your throat, let us hope
that your tongue is not forked." His forehead wrinkled
with concentration, and he regarded Britt with a
searching gaze for what seemed like a full minute to
the anxious black man. "You are a slippery man, not
like the white-eyes at all. Just when I think I have hold
of what you are, you slide away and show me something else. It pains me to say it of a tejano, but you put
me in mind of a fox. For they too are shrewd and
crafty, and just as you have done, they employ cunning
to see them through."

Suddenly his eyes blazed with amusement, and he
leaned across the fire to slap Britt's shoulder. "Hah! I
have just decided to rename you, *Negrito.* A good Kiowa name. From this night forward you will be known
as Black Fox." Then his voice dropped to a hoarse, conspiratorial whisper. "But if you ever let it be known that
you came to this name by outfoxing Santana, I will slice
off your manhood and feed it to the dogs."

"And what of the horses, my chief?" Britt inquired
with a smile.

"Your white-eyed brothers will pay three horses for
each woman and one for each child. That is my final
word, so let us hear no more of it."

"Santana makes a just trade, and it is agreed. But do
not call the tejanos my brothers. As you have said, they
are simply a people who I walk among."

Santana's belly rumbled with laughter, and his great

black mane shook with the force of his mirth. "You are a man who bears watching, Black Fox. Your tongue is oily, and it rushes to fill each crevice in a man's doubts. But the Comanches are not wily like the Kiowa. They are blunt and lacking in wit. And it occurs to me that they might mistake your cunning for trickery. Knowing this, I think I might do well to protect the Kiowas' interests by having certain warriors escort you to the Canadian."

"A fine idea, great chief." Britt's teeth flashed in a mocking smile. "For if I am unable to return to the Brazos, how would we obtain your horses?"

"Enough! Your tongue flays me with my own words." Santana rose effortlessly to his feet, and the black man also stood. Glancing through the lodge entrance, the chief lowered his voice and threw an arm around Britt's shoulders. "Come, Black Fox. The warriors await us before the medicine lodge. We will speak to them with solemn words, and for the good of the Kiowa nation I will allow them to convince me that certain of their number should guard your return to the Brazos."

Chuckling like a thief in the night, the leader of the Kiowa led the black man outside and walked with somber dignity toward the expectant warriors.

Six

Mary squeezed her eyes tightly and tried to close out the whimpering cries. Then there was a quick, strangled yelp, and she knew it was over. Talking Raven was very good at killing dogs, cutting the throat deeply and fast, so that the animal suffered only a moment's pain.

Among themselves the squaws joked that when Talking Raven's cooking pots came out, the wise dogs disappeared in the willows along the river bank. Tonight was a special occasion, and Standing Bear had ordered boiled dog along with the ever-present buffalo meat. Two Moons, his youngest wife, was already in labor with her first child. And since he had paid the *puhaket* a fine roan mare to guarantee a man-child, Standing Bear was preparing to celebrate the arrival of his son.

Talking Raven came around the lodge with the bloody carcass in her hands. Though it was skinned and gutted, she always left it up to Mary to chop it into pot-sized chunks. Mary's throat clogged with bile, but she accepted the still-warm carcass and began cutting it with sickened resignation. All her life she had assisted at slaughter time with pigs and cattle, and she certainly wasn't squeamish. But a dog that had licked your hand and sidled up to be petted was somehow different. It was almost like eating a member of the family, and Mary's stomach churned as the knife grated against bone.

Still, Talking Raven was a harsh disciplinarian, and she allowed no malingering in her lodge. As Standing Bear's first wife, and therefore the oldest, she ran the lodge with firm, gruff-voiced benevolence. She brooked no nonsense and whipped Mary repeatedly for refusing to kill the dogs. But finally she had conceded to Mary's queasy stomach, and the matter rested there. In all other things the black woman was a strong, willing worker, and Talking Raven had never been one to beat a good horse to the ground.

Little Buffalo had honored Standing Bear's courage in the Brazos raid by sending Mary and the children to his lodge. This was a signal honor, attesting to Standing Bear's ferocity and prowess as a warrior. For of all the captives taken in the raid, the black family had been coveted most by the warriors and their squaws. Many lodges had white-eyed slaves, but the blacks were different, special somehow, and therefore prized above all others. Blacks were believed to possess a strange, mystical kind of medicine, and it seemed reasonable that the power of this medicine would attach itself to the master of their new lodge.

The Comanches also felt some distant kinship with the blacks, the brotherhood of underdogs and outcasts who had fallen before the oppressive cruelty of the white-eyes. Over the weeks of her captivity Mary had noticed that while Talking Raven was rarely hesitant to use the switch, she never struck with the fury that other squaws used on the white women. Slowly she came to realize that because she and the children were black, they had been accorded a dubious honor: they were slaves, but they were treated with a harsh affection which would never be extended to the whites. The children in particular were cuddled and spoiled unmercifully, and it soon became apparent that it was only a matter of time until Standing Bear adopted them as his own.

As she was to discover, Standing Bear had other ideas too. She frequently caught him watching her, and the look was not that of a master inspecting his slave. It was the look of raw, animal lust, the same look she had seen in white men's eyes when Britt wasn't around. But never had she felt so naked or defenseless as when Standing Bear's hungry eyes followed her about the lodge.

She had the feeling he would have bedded her long before this if it hadn't been for Talking Raven. The squaw bullied him just as she did the women, and while he sometimes beat her savagely, her sharp tongue was never still for long. Whenever she caught him watching the black woman, her voice rose in a shrewish screech, and even though Mary didn't understand all of the words, she knew a shamed husband when she saw one.

But these thoughts were far from her mind as she finished butchering the steaming carcass and dropped chunks of meat into a kettle of boiling water. All she could think of was that frisky little brown dog with its waggly tail. Only that morning it had followed her to gather wood, barking and scampering about playfully as she collected branches. And now it was nothing but greasy chunks bubbling away in the smoke-blackened kettle. She grimaced as the odor of stewed dog wafted out from the pot and fought to swallow the sour gorge that flooded her throat. Damning Standing Bear for the inhuman brute he was, she made a mental note to invent some story for the children when they began searching for their curly-tailed playmate. Thank God they had been off in the woods when Talking Raven went to work with her knife.

Suddenly the lodge flap was thrown open, and Standing Bear came through the entrance. Jerking his head back toward the tepee, he uttered a guttural command, then seated himself before the small cooking fire. Mary could understand a few of the simpler Comanche words by now, and she knew from his curt order that Talking Raven wanted her in the lodge. Obviously Two

Moons' time had come, and the older squaw wanted her inside in case there was trouble with the delivery.

After setting the kettle to one side, Mary rinsed her hands in a water skin and entered the lodge. Two Moons was stretched out on her side near the fire. With the weather so cold and the skies threatening snow, the cooking would normally have been done inside. But Talking Raven didn't want Two Moons sickened by the odors of cooking. Delivering women of their first born was bad enough, but to have a young mother retching and gagging at the same time was more than she could abide.

Two Moons' eyes were glazed with pain, but like all Comanche women when their time came, she remained stoic and silent, never once uttering so much as a moan or a whimpering cry. Talking Raven was busily applying warm stones to the girl's stomach and back to relieve the pain. Though all of her own babies had been stillborn, the squaw remembered the pains vividly and knew what Two Moons was going through. Glancing around, she signed to Mary to heat more stones at the fire. Cooing softly, as one would gentle a hurt child, she then wiped the girl's feverish brow and combed the matted hair back from her face.

Watching raptly, Mary was again astounded by the conflicting aspects of Indian temperament. Only minutes before, this grim-faced squaw had pitilessly killed a dog which she had raised from a puppy, and now she was tenderly working over a young mother to bring new life forth. Shaking her head in dismay, Mary wondered how long she would have to live among the Comanche to comprehend their savage and yet somehow childlike minds.

The baby was slow and uncooperative. When it finally began to show, Talking Raven got the girl up on her hands and knees and coaxed her to strain harder. To Mary the older woman's insistent tone sounded exactly like the squaws when they urged the warriors onward in stickball games. Mary decided that Talking Raven was well named. Never slackening her demanding chatter, she knelt behind the straining girl and to all appearances literally talked the baby into joining the human race. The lusty squall he loosed when Talking Raven eased him out onto a doeskin made it plain that the cold world seemed a bad trade for the snug womb. His indignant cries seemed to berate her for having advised him wrongly, and he fought like a little warrior as she briskly rubbed him dry with the soft skin and knotted the cord.

Standing Bear would be proud. His man-child had come into the world like a true Comanche.

Two Moons remained on her knees, panting and arching her back as if she were about to drop another baby. Mary watched with breathless fascination, thoroughly bewildered by the girl's strange behavior. Abruptly Talking Raven shoved the screaming baby in Mary's arms, snatched up another doeskin, and knelt once more behind the straining girl. Suddenly there was a gush of blood and the afterbirth plopped in a steaming heap on the skin. With a shuddering sigh Two Moons eased forward and dropped in a quivering, exhausted lump.

Talking Raven quickly wrapped the afterbirth, bound it tightly with rawhide thongs, and scuttled from the lodge without a backward glance. Later Mary would learn that the afterbirth was bad medicine, a thing which could bring misfortune and grief to all who came in contact with it. Talking Raven would bury it deep, where even the coyotes couldn't find it, and in a place where no Comanche would ever go near it. Even walking across the spot where it had been buried was bad medicine, which was all right if it happened to a Ute or some dumb Kiowa. But a decent, thoughtful person made very sure that it would never bring disaster down on the head of a brother Comanche.

When Talking Raven returned, she washed the baby, wrapped him in a fresh doeskin, and placed him in Two Moons' arms. Only then did she call Standing Bear. Entering the lodge, he stood for a moment gazing with fierce pride upon his warrior son. Two Moons' face radiated the joy of a mother who has presented her husband with his first male child, and she searched Standing Bear's solemn visage for some sign of praise. But he had eyes only for the boy, and as he knelt, watching the baby suckle greedily, his features softened in a moment of guileless humility.

Then the stern hauteur once more masked his face, and he stalked from the tepee. This was a day for a man to sit in front of his lodge and bask in the adulation of friends and brother warriors.

After the baby had fed, Talking Raven placed him in a bois d'arc cradle lined with velvety rabbit skins. The cradle's deep, rounded hood swallowed the tiny face, and when she hung it on the lodge pole, the bowed frame swung to and fro with a gentle rocking motion.

Watching from her pallet of buffalo robes, Mary was captivated by this blissful scene. For a moment her thoughts drifted back to the births of her own children, and she relived again the intense passion of squeezing a life from one's own body. How proud Two Moons must be, she mused, for every mother dreams of her first born being a son. Glancing at the girl, who was now sleeping peacefully, it occurred to her that all women, black or white, gentle or savage, were really no different beneath the skin. They lived solely for the love they could create, and whatever happiness they found was never far removed from the core of their own family.

Talking Raven's harsh voice shattered her dreamy ruminations. Tenderness had faded from the squaw's narrow features, and she was once more the demanding, sharp-tongued mistress of the lodge. There was dog meat waiting to be stewed, and a ready switch for those who lazed away the day with their head in the clouds. Mary felt herself jolted back to the reality of who she was and, more significantly, where she was. Hauling herself erect, she eased back the lodge flap and stepped outside.

Standing Bear was squatted before the fire, and he regarded her silently as she hung the kettle over the flames. As she stooped to stir the greasy mess, he leaned forward and patted her gently on the stomach. Startled, she found herself unable to move, and his probing fingers kneaded the flesh beneath her dress. Grinning wolfishly, he locked his arms together and rocked them like a cradle, then pointed suggestively back at her stomach. Suddenly his meaning dawned on her, and her mind reeled with visions of his chunky figure mounting her, ramming her legs apart, so that she too might become a good little Comanche mother. Straightening, she stepped back and met his smirking gaze with a level eye. While he couldn't understand her words, their substance was all too clear.

"You red nigger, you come around tryin' to stick that thing in me, and I'll make you wish you'd been born with a sweet potato between your legs."

Seven

The small column of riders seemed dwarfed by the vast openness of the rolling Plains. The grasslands had now become a gently swaying sea of chilled brown, and as autumn turned to winter, the slumbering landscape appeared more desolate than ever. Behind lay the granite towers of the mountains, and it had taken two days to reach a swirling dog leg of the lower Washita. Running Dog and Britt forded the stream first, then waited on the opposite bank while the women and older children gingerly eased their mounts across the shallow waters. The warriors then whipped their ponies across at a plunging run, spraying themselves and the squealing youngsters mounted behind them with geysers of icy water. Formed once more in a strung-out line, the party turned north and resumed their march. Ahead lay forty miles of barren, wind-swept prairie, and each of the riders had good reason to wish their journey concluded.

While the distance from Santana's camp to the Comanche village normally took only two days by horseback, Running Dog had purposely slowed the pace because of the tejano women and children. Under extreme conditions the Kiowas had many times crossed this stretch of empty wilderness without stopping. But the frail white-eyes were incapable of such a grueling march, and the Indians charitably held their ponies to a drowsy, ambling walk.

Altogether, Britt had ransomed four women and nine children, which accounted for all of the Kiowa captives. Though they were gaunt and crawling with lice, the captives were beside themselves with joy. Their ordeal was over, or almost over anyway, and within a fortnight they would once again be with their loved ones in Texas. Sarah Johnson had thrown her arms around Britt's neck and cried like a child when informed of the exchange. Afterward, he had talked with the four women for over an hour, reassuring them as best he could that they had nothing to fear from their captors.

Santana had been as good as his word, and as the tiny band thankfully departed the mountain stronghold, he pointedly reminded Britt that he was expecting twenty-one of the tejanos' finest horses. The cynical leader of the Kiowa also made good on his promise to see to it that Britt was properly escorted, and as the captives rode forth, they were accompanied by seven of the tribe's most formidable warriors. Their mission, Santana had declared, was to deliver the white-eyes unharmed to the Brazos and return with a herd of sleek, grain-fattened horses. And if they stumbled into a trap anywhere along the journey, they were to make sure that the first man to die was the tejano now called Black Fox.

Running Dog, foremost warrior of the Kiowa nation as well as a superlative horse thief, had been selected as leader of the escort party. Tall and lithely muscled for a red man, he made an imposing figure. Famed for his bloodthirsty ruthlessness in a fight, he was fiercely proud of his people and openly scornful of anything not Kiowa. Running Dog rarely smiled, and his infrequent bursts of humor were usually of a grim nature. This fearsome impact was not lessened by the cold intensity of his eyes, the jut of a heavy brow, and the wide, merciless slit of his thin-lipped mouth.

All things considered, he made the perfect choice for the leader of a band which might be called on to slaughter more than a dozen women and children. And the significance of his presence wasn't lost on Britt.

Still, Running Dog had gone out of his way to cultivate the black man, and before the march was a day old, it became obvious that the warrior found Britt to be a matchless, if somewhat puzzling, companion. The Plains Indians revered courage above all other personal attributes, and the black man's lone sortie into the Kiowa nation had made him something of an overnight legend.

Britt's obvious lack of fear, combined with an easy confidence and a natural friendliness, had greatly impressed Running Dog. But there were things about Black Fox that defied understanding, at least for an Indian. Like the jumbled parts of a riddle, these contradictions rattled irritatingly in Running Dog's head, and his normal taciturnity was slowly replaced by an almost childlike curiosity.

Britt, on the other hand, had experienced profound kinship with only one other man in his life, a white man, and as he felt himself being drawn irresistibly to this red savage, he became a confused and sorely perplexed man.

For all the confusion and lack of understanding, it remained a spontaneous admiration of one brave man for another. And from it sprang the genesis of a deep camaraderie that was to develop over the course of their journey together.

The weather was raw and blustery, and as the two men rode along, their words left frosty tentacles dangling in their wake. Running Dog had gradually become more inquisitive, peppering Britt with all manner of questions about the white-eyes' world. But until now he had skirted the thing that puzzled him most, the blacks themselves.

"There is this thing about the *Negritos* that has always eluded me, Black Fox. Maybe you could make it come clear." Running Dog glanced at Britt quizzically, who nodded, wondering exactly what the warrior had in mind. "The Kiowa comes into this life a free man, and until he crosses over to the other life, he is answerable to none save himself and the gods. Whether he chooses to sleep or steal horses or wander these Plains in search of his enemies, there are none to deny him. And a Kiowa would die fighting rather than bow before another man's will." Again he glanced at Britt, somewhat unsure as to how he should proceed.

Britt smiled soberly, now certain of the question about to follow. "What you wish to ask is why the *Negrito* has surrendered his freedom to the white-eyes."

"More than that, Black Fox. Freedom is but the first loss, and every warrior understands that this can happen in the defeat of battle. Even Kiowa women have been taken as slaves by the Ute and the Crow. But never a Kiowa man." For a moment he stared across the bleak prairie, attempting to phrase his next thought in a tactful manner. "And this is what eludes me. Rather than die, the *Negrito* has surrendered something beyond mere freedom. He has renounced his manhood."

Britt was stunned, and for a brief instant his eyes went cold with fury. Then he got a grip on himself, and reason slowly asserted itself once more. In his mind arose discarded memories of field hands cringing before a white overseer, and black women, like brood mares in heat, being mated to the stoutest buck in the slave quarters. The black man had indeed been emasculated, just as surely as a colt is gelded or a young bull is thrown to the ground and cut. The manhood of a people had been torn out, jerked from the sac as neatly as a rancher clips the balls from his frisky yearlings. And none knew it better than the black man himself. It wasn't possible. It was merely true.

"Running Dog sees much for a man who has never lived among the white-eyes."

"I watch with my mind, Black Fox, and I see that the white-eyes are not content to defeat a man in battle or even to kill him. They have this curious urge to strip a warrior of his manhood and bend him to their will, just as we would tame a dog or a fine horse." His eyes glazed over, and for several moments his mind seemed lost in a distant vision. "They leave a man nothing, neither freedom nor pride, and if they are not soon stopped, they will be the master of all. Even the Kiowa."

"If you hope to learn their secret from me, you have chosen a poor teacher." Britt fell silent and shivered from the icy claw deep in his gut. The moaning wind stung his face, stripping his thoughts of all pretense and artifice, and he wondered how long a race of men could hide from themselves. "Those who have been defeated are not always best suited to reveal the inner thoughts of their masters."

"That is true," Running Dog agreed. "But have I asked the question of the defeated ones? Would you have me believe that a *Negrito* who rides alone into the Kiowa nation has been stripped of his manhood?" He turned to look at Britt, and his piercing gaze seemed to search the black man's soul. "Among my people only a warrior would have dared such a thing."

"Perhaps even a man who lives in the white-eyes' shadow can remain a warrior. But that does not mean that he is proud of himself or would presume to advise those who still fight for their freedom."

"Your deeds contradict your words, Black Fox. While he might be a warrior, this person you speak of would only be half a man. Why would he not turn his back on what is past and join those who fight the oppression of the white-eyes?"

Why indeed? Britt silently demanded of himself. "There are some questions to which a man has no ready answers, Running Dog. But this is one I ask myself more and more as I walk among your people."

The Kiowa warrior nodded solemnly, as if the riddle had fallen together and he at last understood the black man who rode beside him. Dusk was approaching, and they would soon have to camp for the night. But they both knew that despite the warmth between them and the campfires they might share in the days to come, they would never broach the matter again.

In the distance Running Dog's keen eyes sighted a pack of wolves snapping and snarling over a lone buffalo carcass. Waiting patiently for the wolves to finish, two coyotes and a badger slowly circled the killing ground. Reining to a halt, the warrior touched Britt's shoulder and pointed to the unfolding tableau of survival on the Plains.

"There are few hunters, Black Fox, but many who want to eat the meat. The warrior must hold himself above the carrion eaters of this life, and when he has done so, then he will never again question his own manhood."

"And if those who wish to eat are his friends?"

"Then he must kill them swiftly and without remorse. For the scavengers of this earth have no friends other than their own greed."

Watching the wolves tearing at the carcass, Britt pondered the red man's words and felt himself growing more perplexed with each moment he spent in this strange wilderness. Choosing sides was easy, if that were all there was to it, for the Kiowas lived with a dignity that few black men even dared dream about. The trick was in killing the ghosts of those scavengers, especially the ones that haunted a man's past with kindness and love. And brotherhood.

Eight

Seated around the campfire that night, both men were at great pains to avoid any mention of *Negritos* or white-eyes. Running Dog was well aware that he had led the black man into a bramble patch of conflicting emotions, and he wisely limited the conversation to less troublesome matters. After a cold meal he spent most of the evening with the warriors, gambling and exchanging tales of battle. These stories were crusty with age, familiar to each man gathered around the fire.

But they were rarely dull. For the Kiowas were skilled in the art of exaggeration and enjoyed nothing quite so much as giving a tattered and worn tale a fancy new embroidery. Listening with one ear, Running Dog watched the man he now thought of as Black Fox out of the corner of his eye. Such men were welcome among the Kiowa, for they brought a fresh infusion of warrior's blood into the tribe, and Running Dog secretly schemed to make this black giant a brother of the True People.

Britt had spent the early part of the evening with the children, making the camp ring with laughter and squeals of terror as he acted out the scary ghost stories that had appealed so much to black youngsters. But his levity was an act and nothing more, for Running Dog's remarks of that afternoon lingered in his mind, suppurating as an open sore would fester and grow putrid with rot. Once the children settled down for the night, he talked with Sarah and the other women at great length, recounting the aftermath of the Brazos raid and what they could expect to find when they returned home. While sobered by the devastation, they had much to be grateful for, and their momentary gloom quickly disappeared beneath the merry chatter of those who have been given a second lease on life.

But the women were exhausted from three days of steady riding, and before long, their lightheartedness gave way to unsuppressed yawns. Finally they decided to call it a night and wearily crawled beneath the buffalo robes with the children. After they were settled, Britt stretched and approached the warriors, who were still trading yarns on the opposite side of the fire.

Glancing up, Running Dog greeted him in the broken

Spanish employed by the Kiowas. "*Hao*, brother. Be seated and join us. We were just speaking of the Comanches." Pausing, he flicked a wry smile at the other warriors. "You should listen well to this talk, Black Fox, for sometime tomorrow you will meet our fabled kinsmen."

"Running Dog's voice belies his words," Britt said in a joshing tone. "If I didn't know better, I might believe that the Kiowa mock their Comanche brothers."

"Huh!" snorted Running Dog. "You are well named, Black Fox. Among friends a truthful man might easily say that the Kiowa laughed behind their faces at the Comanche. Sit here by the fire and we will school you in ways to deceive our loutish kinsmen." The warriors crowded closer, vastly intrigued by the idea of conspiring against the detested northerners.

"Black Fox, the thing you must never forget in dealing with the Comanche is that they are thoughtless barbarians, completely untutored in the ways of enlightened people. They think with their gut and lack the vision to see beyond their next meal. They call themselves lords and sing praises to their own ferocity. But as wise men know, it is the dog that seldom barks who will tear your leg away at the roots. Is it not so, brothers?" The other warriors chuckled and murmured their assent, highly amused by this slanderous description of the haughty Comanches.

"I will illustrate for you, Black Fox, why enlightened men ridicule these barbarians." Grinning broadly, Running Dog resumed even though Britt seemed slightly taken aback by the sharp edge to his words. "The Kiowa will consider a matter at length, but when his mind is set, he will act quickly and firmly. The Comanche is like the butfalo, whose brain hangs between his legs. He decides a thing instantly, relying on instinct as does an animal, and then waits and waits some more, before he finally sucks up the courage to act. The Kiowa eats his food slowly and savors the taste fully. The Comanche wolfs his food like a starved beast and then accuses his neighbor of being the one who has broken wind. My words are crude, Black Fox, but from them you will see more clearly how to outwit the Comanche."

Puzzled by the Kiowa's cryptic remarks, Britt stared around the fire as the warriors waited for him to speak. "Running Dog's advice is like a knife that cuts with both edges. The Comanches act hastily, without considering a matter thoroughly, and thus can I hurry them into a stupid trade. But you also say that they are barbarians, who sit on a decision like a duck hatching eggs. This leads me to believe that they would later regret their haste and slit my throat to wipe away an unwise bargain."

The warriors all started talking at once, amazed that the black man could have made so much of such a simple thing. Finally a squatty, flat-nosed brave outshouted the others and spoke directly to Britt in a series of hoarse grunts. "You hear, but you do not see, Black Fox. The Comanches are barbarians, that is true. But there is a higher law that even the Comanches would not dare break. When a stranger comes to their lodges in peace, they are bound to accept him with a spirit of generosity and mercy." Shrugging his shoulders, the warrior made a chopping, dismissive gesture with his hand. "This is a thing that none among the True People would question. It is the law."

"My brother speaks straight," Running Dog interjected. "But there is a thing Black Fox would be wise to
remember in the days to come. Among the True People
it is known that one never stares at a Comanche. Not
even in a peace council. For as a wolf accepts a stare
as a sign of hostility, so it is with these barbarians. And
Black Fox must never forget that when he rubs shoulders with the Comanches he walks among the wild
beasts."

Britt felt the hair bristle on the back of his neck. The
men hunkered around this fire were savages, and yet
they were warning him against a people that they
themselves considered barbarian. Suddenly the chill
night wind sent a shiver down his spine, and he sensed
an ominous malevolence waiting just beyond the darkness.

Nine

The terrain had changed markedly just after midday.
Running Dog led them through a winding maze of deep
sandstone gorges, bounded on either side by sheer, red
cliffs. The floor of these formidable, uninviting canyons
was studded with trees and generally so narrow that a
man had the prickly feeling the earth was about to
close its jaws and devour him whole. High overhead,
springs gushed from crevices in the rocks, and water
gently cascaded down the crimson face of the menacing bluffs. But the abundance of vegetation and water
had little effect on the black man's edginess. While the
canyons teemed with life, they had about them the

stench of death, and Britt's backbone grew stiffer with each plodding mile.

Since breaking camp that morning, he had noticed a distinct change in the Kiowa warriors also. They were quieter, almost guarded, and as the column entered the sandstone canyons, their bantering conversation shriveled to grim grunts. Every now and then Britt would turn to look at the women and children, and it was obvious that they too felt the unseen evil that had stilled the Kiowas. Without knowing why, he began to wish they were back on the Plains. Whatever lurked in these canyons was hidden, a threat of the impending, and it preyed too much on a man's mind. While the prairie was desolate and windswept, at least a man could see his enemy and prepare for the worst. Britt chuckled to himself. What you don't see can't hurt you, people always said. Maybe not, he thought, but it can sure as hell make you touchier than a wet cat.

Later in the day, with the sun a cold ball of light in the overcast skies, they broke out of the canyons and halted on a barren plateau overlooking the Canadian. Along the tree-fringed riverbank they could see tendrils of smoke rising from the Comanche campfires and tiny, antlike figures of people moving about the village.

"There are your Comanche, Black Fox. Let us hope that the woman you seek is in this camp." Running Dog spoke with his eyes fastened on the village, and the other warriors stared glumly in the same direction.

Surprisingly Britt found that being free of the narrow gorges had done nothing to lessen his sense of dread. The unseen thing shadowing his thoughts waited in that village below, and as he had known all along, it had nothing to do with evil spirits. It was human, and it called itself Comanche.

Staring at the camp, he wondered if Mary and the children were down there right now. A hollow feeling gnawed at his gut, and he swallowed a huge lump lodged in his throat. Silently he called on the Lord God Jehovah to make him man enough and shrewd enough to bring off what must be done. On the spur of the moment he quickly added an entreaty to the gods of darkness—the juju gods that had ruled his grandmam's life to the final moment of her deathbed. When a man's in trouble, she used to say, he needs all the help he can get. And right now, Britt reflected, whatever's waiting down there is trouble enough for any man. Or his god.

"Waugh!" Running Dog's grunt broke the strained silence, and they all turned to look in the direction he was pointing. Far in the distance they sighted a herd of buffalo moving steadily across the plains to the west of the Comanche encampment. Each year, before the first snow, the buffalo migrated south for the winter, and the herd they were now watching numbered in the thousands.

The Kiowa leader gazed at the herd thoughtfully, and a sly glint slowly crept into his eyes. "Black Fox, we are about to make you a brother to the Comanche. Have I not told you they think with their gut? That they never look past their next meal? It follows then that the man who brings them the gift of food is a brother indeed." Observing Britt's quizzical expression, he grinned rakishly. "Have you ever killed a buffalo, brother? Well no matter. Today Black Fox becomes a hunter."

Gesturing toward the buffalo, Running Dog spoke to the warriors in a string of terse, guttural commands.

Clearly he had some scheme in mind and was instructing them in their parts. Britt was thoroughly bewildered, particularly when the warriors gigged their ponies and plunged down the incline that dropped off from the plateau. Running Dog watched until they reached the bottom and went thundering across the prairie toward the distant herd. Turning back to Britt, his eyes crackled with excitement, and the black man sensed that whatever he had planned was more than a mere hunt.

"Brother, what you do this day will be discussed in Comanche lodges for many snows to come. My warriors will cut out a plump cow from the herd and drive her toward the camp. You will then ride in and kill this cow in full view of the barbarians. You could offer them no greater honor than to drop a warm, tender cow right in front of Little Buffalo's lodge."

"Little Buffalo?" Britt echoed. "Is this the man who decides if the captives are to be ransomed?"

"No man decides that except the one who owns the white-eyes. But Little Buffalo is their *to-yop-ke*, and he can influence that decision." Glancing around, he noted that the warriors were rapidly approaching the herd. "Now pay attention, Black Fox, for you must learn the ways of the buffalo hunt with only one lesson."

Without wasting so much as a word, the warrior quickly explained the ancient method of dispatching a buffalo from horseback. While it sounded fairly simple, Britt realized that any skill in which the Indians took pride was never as easy as they made it sound. But there was no time to ask questions, for they could see that the braves had now cut a cow from the herd and were hazing her back over the prairie. Running Dog signaled for the women and children to follow, then kneed his pony down the slope. Still somewhat numbed by the rapid turn of events, Britt urged his horse forward, wondering if this wild man was going to get them all killed before they even had a chance to talk with the Comanche chief.

Moments later Britt found himself galloping full out amongst the howling warriors. A blinding cloud of dust enveloped him, coating his throat with a gritty layer of mud. But some ten lengths ahead he could make out the terrified cow lumbering toward the camp. Running Dog rode beside him, yipping like a madman in what Britt assumed to be shouts of encouragement. Spurring the chestnut, Britt pulled ahead of the Kiowas and began closing in on the buffalo. Slowly the gap narrowed, but the animal's ragged gait was deceptive, and it suddenly dawned on him that they were rapidly approaching the village. Raking with his spurs again, he urged the chestnut to a greater effort. But before he quite realized how it happened, he became aware that they were thundering down the main thoroughfare of the village with the cow still out in front.

Scattering dogs, lodges, and cooking pots in every direction, the cow roared through the camp like a shaggy, frothing tornado. Comanches ran from their teepees to gawk in disbelief as the great beast leveled a path through their village. But their stares turned to outright stupefaction when they awoke to the fact that the cow was being chased by a wild-eyed black man and a band of howling Kiowas.

Overtaking the cow at last, Britt kneed the chestnut alongside, matching her stride for stride. Caught up in the thrill of the hunt, he had no thought for anything

except the great, humped beast fleeing in terror not a
foot away from him. Jerking his Colt, he cocked it and
slammed two shots into her chest just behind the fore-
leg. Tumbling headlong in midstride, the buffalo rolled
end over end, cartwheeled high into the air, and
dropped with a shuddering crash not ten yards from
the medicine lodge.

Britt and the trailing Kiowas skidded to a halt in a
roiling upheaval of dust. Whirling their horses, they
trotted back to the fallen cow, as hundreds of Comanches began gathering around the medicine lodge. Covered with a mixture of grime and sweat, the black man
looked like some onyx centaur emerging from a
swirling duststorm. His face split in an enormous grin,
glistening with pearly-white teeth, and he seemed to
grow taller in the saddle as Running Dog proudly
gripped him by the shoulder.

As they reined to a halt before the gaping Comanches, Little Buffalo shoved through the crowd and
walked forward. His features were drawn in a tight
frown, and he had about him the lordly hauteur of a
war chief who can't quite believe that his defenses
have just been breached by the enemy. His eyes swept
contemptuously over the grinning Kiowas and came to
rest on Britt. The black man returned his scowl with a
lusty smile, unable to tear his eyes away even though
he remembered the warning that one should never
stare at a Comanche.

Running Dog nudged his pony forward and signed
greeting with an upraised hand. "*Hao*, Little Buffalo.
This man is Black Fox, brother of the Kiowa, and the
fat cow at your feet is his peace offering to the Comanche. Santana sends greetings and cautions you to treat

this man kindly, for his medicine is strong and he walks without hate among the True People. Black Fox has come to trade, and if the *to-yop-ke* is wise, he too may become a rich man." A murmur of excitement swept through the crowd, and out of the corner of his eye Running Dog saw Britt dismount.

Striding forward, the black man handed the still-warm pistol to Little Buffalo. The *to-yop-ke* accepted it solemnly and regarded Britt with a piercing gaze for a moment. Then his features relaxed, and his voice drifted across the council grounds. "Black Fox comes in peace, and he is welcome in the Comanche lodges."

Running Dog chuckled to himself, amazed by the audacity of his strange new brother. Black Fox had strong medicine all right. How else could one explain a man clever enough to disarm the barbarian by disarming himself? *Eeh-yah!* When the fox turns hunter, only his brothers can close their eyes!

♨ CHAPTER FIVE ♨

One

BRITT ACCEPTED THE LONG-STEMMED PIPE from Running Dog and puffed on it with grave dignity. It was an old pipe, worn and clogged with slime from years of use, and the pungent smoke left a dirty taste in his mouth. But he pulled on it steadily, ignoring the bitterness, for it was obvious that these Comanches regarded pipe smoking as serious business. Little Buffalo and Ten Bears watched closely, openly curious as to how a *Negrito* would handle a ceremonial pipe. Britt did his best to imitate the mannerisms and solemnity which they had displayed before passing the pipe around the fire. But it still seemed like a terribly clumsy way to get a smoke. With one final puff for good measure he let the smoke curl slowly from his mouth, then passed the pipe on to Little Buffalo.

The four men had been seated around the fire for more than two hours, and Britt began to wonder if these wearisome ceremonies would never end. Little Buffalo's wives had prepared choice hump cuts from the cow he had shot earlier, and throughout the entire meal not one reference had been made to either his mission or the captives. While shelter and food had been made available for the women and children accompanying the Kiowa party, the Comanche chiefs thus far had evidenced not the slightest interest in how they got there or to what purpose. Now the odorous pipe with its dangling feathers and sour taste was being passed around again, and there seemed no end in sight to this sterile formality.

Running Dog had warned him that the Comanches would test his patience by dragging the ceremonies beyond reason, but this was an exquisite form of torture that seemed a cut above mere barbarians. Suddenly it occurred to him that the Comanches might possess more cunning than the Kiowas gave them credit for, and he decided he had better watch his step. But before he could pursue that thought much further, Little Buffalo set the pipe to one side and nodded stonily to Running Dog.

"Brothers, this man comes offering many horses in exchange for the white-eyes taken in the Brazos raid." Running Dog spoke in Comanche, but Britt sensed that the words concerned him and knew the trading session had begun at last. "He is a good man, and unlike the tejanos, his heart bears no ill thoughts for the True People. The Kiowa have dealt with him as one warrior honors another, and we ask only that the Comanche consider his offer in a like manner."

Little Buffalo and Ten Bears stared inscrutably at the black man for a moment. Then the young *to-yop-ke* addressed Britt directly in coarse, broken Spanish. "The Kiowa call you Black Fox, and that warns me you are a sly man. The Comanche have no patience with devious men, but you are here, and we will listen to what you have to say."

"Little Buffalo is known as a just leader, and among such men there is no need for stealth." As he spoke, Britt mustered his thoughts quickly and decided that the man he faced was wholly unlike the vain and crafty Santana. "My mission among your people is stated simply and with nothing hidden in my words. I seek to ransom the captives you hold, and for their freedom I offer many horses."

"You speak plain, and that is good. But you talk to the wrong man. Among the Comanche only the warrior who owns a slave can agree to an exchange."

"This is what I have been told," Britt replied. "Yet I have also been told that among the Comanche there is no voice stronger than that of Little Buffalo. And my hope is that you will speak to the warriors in my behalf."

The *to-yop-ke* frowned, clearly reluctant to take the side of even a black tejano. But before he could speak, Ten Bears hurriedly joined the discussion. "This is a hard thing you do, Black Fox. The Comanche are a rich people and have many horses. They also find it belittling to trade women and children who have been adopted into the tribe." Then he paused, purposely lending weight to his next thought. "Unless, of course, the number of horses offered was so unusual that a man could overlook the grief of parting."

Britt's pulse quickened. This cagey old man was baiting him, and none too subtly either. Still, Santana had advised him that the Comanches were notoriously poor traders, and he might just be able to save the settlers a few horses. "Father, where the tejano's women and children are concerned, he can be generous indeed. I am empowered to offer one fat horse for each captive delivered unharmed to the Brazos."

"That is a madness that only a Kiowa could arrange," Little Buffalo said with biting sarcasm. "Still, a Comanche's courage is greater than a Kiowa's foolishness, and we have no fear of riding again to the Brazos."

"It is done then," Ten Bears pronounced. "Except for one thing, Black Fox. We must have two horses for each white-eye woman."

Britt frowned as the old chief eyed him shrewdly. This was better than he had hoped for, but he had to suffer a little to make it appear that they had ensnared the helpless *Negrito*. "Father, your stick is sharp, but it leaves me no choice. I accept, and though they will moan like squaws, the tejanos will honor my word."

Little Buffalo glanced at Ten Bears, who nodded with a gloating smile, and then back to Britt. "There is a thing you must consider, Black Fox. The white-eye captives are spread throughout our five bands, and it is you who must track each of them down."

"Give me a guide and I will do so gladly," the black man responded. "The only request I have is to be informed immediately of where I might find the *Negrito* woman and her children."

"That is simple enough," Little Buffalo said. "They are in this village. Not ten lodges from where you sit." The Comanche saw Britt's eyes come alive, and his face twisted in a stern warning. "Do not deceive yourself, Black Fox. You can see none of the captives before I counsel with the warriors who own them. Until then I caution you to walk lightly in this village, for the Comanche are not like the Kiowa. We may trade with the

tejanos, but my warriors would kill any man who over-
steps his welcome."

Little Buffalo's cold gaze swept across to Running
Dog, and the message was clear. Both the Kiowas and
their black brother could expect harsh reprisals if they
tampered with any of the captives before negotiations
were completed. They had come in peace, and tribal
law assured their safety. But only so long as they didn't
touch anything that belonged to a Comanche.

Two

The pitch black stillness of a starless sky had settled over
the camp when Britt and Running Dog made their way
back to the Kiowa lodge. Wood smoke hung beneath a
cloudy sky, and there was a hint of snow to come in the
crisp night air. Another week, maybe less, and icy winds
would blast down out of the north, bringing with them
the swirling snow-choked blizzards. Once started, the
storms would rage unabated throughout the winter, relentlessly sweeping the plains time and again with blinding ferocity.

Wandering across these snow-swept prairies in the
dead of winter was not a task to be taken lightly. As
Britt silently kept pace with Running Dog, he attempted to calculate the time needed to reach the far-
flung Comanche bands, but the variable of the weather
was too unpredictable. What might take days under
normal circumstances could turn into weeks if a blizzard refused to subside. And more than one man had
left his bones on the Plains because he miscalculated
the cussedness of prairie storms. Besides, there were

more immediate matters to be considered just at this moment.

Mary and the children were in this camp somewhere, and before anyone else got saved, he intended to see to it that his own family was well out of harm's way.

Near the western edge of the encampment, two lodges had been erected for the use of the Kiowas and their captives. The women and children had been quartered in the one closest to the river, and it occurred to Britt that he must talk with them sometime during the night. But that would have to wait. Right now he wanted to think and then talk with Running Dog where they would not be overheard by Comanches.

Entering the men's lodge, they found the warriors lounged around a small fire. Running Dog quickly briefed them on the meeting with Little Buffalo, and their sullen muttering made it clear that they resented having to wait while Black Fox trudged around the countryside collecting more white-eyes. Then one of the warriors made a comment, gesturing toward the black man, and Running Dog began questioning him intensely. While Britt couldn't understand the guttural flow of Kiowa, he knew from Running Dog's sober attitude that something ominous was being discussed. At last the two men fell silent, and Running Dog stared into the fire for a moment before looking around at Britt.

"Black Fox, I have bad news. My warriors went among the Comanche tonight, and they return with word of your woman. She is in the lodge of one called Standing Bear, and talk among the Comanche is that he will not consider trading her."

Britt's eyes widened with disbelief. Such a possibility

had never occurred to him, and for an instant he was gripped by sheer panic. "That's impossible! Or else they are lying. The Comanches want horses as much as the Kiowas. And besides, Little Buffalo agreed to the trade!"

"Calm yourself, brother," Running Dog said, "and think with your head instead of your heart. The *to-yop-ke* agreed only to counsel with his warriors. No man is obliged to act against his will. That is the law. And if Standing Bear refuses to trade, then it is out of Little Buffalo's hands."

"Well, it's not out of my hands!" Britt's voice dropped to a savage growl, and his eyes went cold. "I came here to get my woman, and by Christ, I will! Even if I have to steal her back and make a run for the Brazos."

"Your god cannot help you now, Black Fox. You are among the Comanche." There was a moment's stillness, broken only by the crackling fire and the warriors' grunted assent. "Should you steal the woman, the barbarians would run you to earth within a day. And then you would both roast over a slow fire. Besides, what would become of the white-eye women and children if Black Fox abandoned them?"

Britt's gaze remained flinty and remote, but the spark of reason once more entered his eyes. "You are right, of course. If I stole her, many would suffer for my selfishness. But I can't just get on my horse and leave her here. Would a Kiowa do that?"

"No warrior would do such a thing, brother." The Kiowa gave him a cool look of appraisal, almost as if he were sizing him up against some unspoken menace. "Still, there may be a way."

Britt stiffened, his features alert, and Running Dog continued in the same calm, dispassionate tone. "Standing Bear is a member of *ko-eet-senko*, the most highly honored warrior society, and as such, he could not refuse a fight. Since he stole your woman, you could challenge him to combat, and no one would question your right to do so. Should you win, then everything Standing Bear owns would become yours." The Kiowa regarded him silently for a moment, then stared impassively into the flames. "Of course, he might just as easily kill you. Even his own people say that he is more wild beast than Comanche."

Britt's eyes narrowed at the warning implicit in Running Dog's casual manner. Still, he had lived by hunches all his life, and instinct told him that fighting Standing Bear was the only way. But this was different somehow, for while he had killed, he had never before coldly planned another man's death. His eyes lost focus, and his gaze was absorbed in the flickering coals of the fire. Leering from the flames was the face of death, death's ugly, fleshless grin, and an icy hand squeezed down on his heart. He shivered imperceptibly, mesmerized by the specter he saw in the sparkling embers. Then he shook himself, like a dog rousing from a deep sleep, and wrenched his mind away from the grisly apparition. *Wake up. Get hold of yourself. You're one lone nigger in a Comanche village, and if you don't kill this man, your woman and kids ain't never again going to see Elm Creek.*

Tearing his eyes away from the fire, Britt became aware that the warriors were watching him curiously. His face creased in a tight smile, and he glanced at the Kiowa leader. "Running Dog must instruct me in how this thing is to be done."

"When a man has won the fight within himself," Running Dog commented, "all else comes easy. Tonight we will prepare you in the ways of the knife, for this is surely the weapon Standing Bear will choose."

The Kiowa drew a heavy, bone-handled fighting knife, and the other warriors moved back as he rose to demonstrate the surest way of gutting an arrogant Comanche.

Three

Talking Raven's rough, bony hands moved with nimble certainty as she wove porcupine quills into a diamond pattern on the buckskin shirt. Mary paused to watch, intrigued by the sight of those callused, thorny fingers performing a delicate task with such skill and grace. After a moment she returned to pounding the roots and berries which would be converted into bright dyes for staining more quills.

Work in a Comanche lodge was never ending, and there always seemed to be more chores at hand than the three women could possibly finish. Two Moons' new baby, along with George and Sue Ellen, made additional demands on their time, and from the crack of dawn till late at night the women rarely stopped to rest. Still, Mary normally welcomed the grueling workload, for it diverted her mind from her miseries, which in the past week had grown considerable.

But tonight her mind raced with newborn hope, and she was hardly aware of the tasks her nervous hands somehow managed.

Earlier in the day, near the center of the village, there

had been a commotion which ended in gunfire. Mary's foremost concern was for the children, for gunshots were almost unknown in the village itself, and she had hurried them inside the lodge. Though it was late in the year for a Crow raiding party, it was better to be cautious, and she stood guard in the entrance while Talking Raven watched from outside. Presently she heard Standing Bear's gruff voice, and she edged closer to the entrance flap. Though he and Talking Raven were speaking in hushed tones, she could still make out snatches of the conversation. Abruptly it dawned on her that they were talking about a tejano *Negrito* who had ridden into camp with a band of Kiowas. Then she heard Standing Bear order the squaw not to let their own *Negrito* out of the lodge until he returned. With that the conversation had ended, and Talking Raven entered the tepee, glancing at her with a curious, hidden look.

Concealing her excitement, Mary had busied herself around the lodge. Her mind flooded with a jumble of thoughts, each more tantalizing and seemingly far-fetched than the other. How could a black man have entered the village alive and in one piece? Was he really a Texan or just another renegade trader? And why was he riding with Kiowas? Oh God, could it be? Could Britt have somehow made friends with the Kiowas? Has he come to take us home? Merciful God, please let it be him.

But no matter how she talked to herself, it still didn't seem real or even possible. Texans just didn't ride into Indian lands and live to tell about it. Things like that just didn't happen. But why was Standing Bear holding her in the lodge? What was he afraid she would see? *Or was he afraid someone would see her?*

The day passed, and darkness fell without any resolution to her vexing questions. But as she pondered the situation at greater length, Mary came to the conclusion that if it was Britt, then there was a good chance Standing Bear would let her go. Especially since he had lost face so disastrously in their running battle of wits.

Since the day Two Moons' son was born, Standing Bear had nudged and pinched and leered at her so suggestively that everyone in the lodge became aware of his campaign to bed her. But it was only last week that he had finally managed to corner her alone. Late one morning Talking Raven and Two Moons had gone off on some errand, when the entrance flap suddenly flew open. Standing Bear stepped boldly into the lodge, and from the flushed expression on his face, Mary knew that her time had come. But she didn't intend to whelp any Comanche brats without a struggle.

Moving with the swiftness of a coiled snake, the warrior grabbed her shoulders and forced her toward a bed of buffalo robes. But the black woman was no novice at infighting, and she promptly sank her teeth into the meaty flesh of his forearm. Grunting with pain, Standing Bear cuffed her upside the head, and she dropped on the robes with a hollow ringing in her ears. Grinning like a wolf about to devour a hamstrung cow, the Comanche whipped his breech clout off, then straddled her, and began forcing her legs apart.

Dizzy and near passing out, Mary reared up with one last surge of strength, bucking the warrior's rump high into the air. Standing Bear laughed good-naturedly at this delaying tactic, but his humor quickly turned to a

roar of pain and animal rage. For when his rump came
down out of the air, Mary deftly planted her knee in his
crotch and again reared upward with all her might.

Only Talking Raven's timely appearance saved her
life. Between the spasms of retching and spewing sour
vomit around the lodge, Standing Bear grabbed a war
ax and was slowly crawling toward her. Just as Mary
found herself trapped against the wall, the lodge flap
opened and Talking Raven entered. There was a moment of embarrassed silence as the half-naked warrior
gasped for breath and darted guilty side glances at the
squaw. Then Talking Raven found her tongue and began to flay him, screaming that only a mindless *pawsa*
would kill a good slave just because she refused to
grease his pole. Finally unable to sand her screeching
harangue any longer, Standing Bear struck her in the
mouth, snatched up his breech clout, and fled from the
lodge.

Thinking back on the incident as she began dyeing
the porcupine quills, Mary was even more firmly convinced that Standing Bear would gladly see the last of
her. His pride had been gouged to the quick, and from
his sullen mood over the last week it was clear that he
had lost face among the other warriors. After all, if a
man couldn't bed a frail *Negrito* squaw, how could he
call himself a warrior? Absorbed in these pleasant
thoughts, Mary started as the entrance flap jerked back
and Standing Bear stepped into the lodge. For a moment it seemed like a terrifying repetition of their last
encounter, and she scuttled backward to where the
children were sleeping on their robes.

The warrior glowered around the lodge, then spoke
to the squaw even though his eyes remained fixed on

Mary. "The tejano *Negrito* comes to trade for this black bitch. She was his woman on the Brazos, and he thinks to take her from the Comanche."

Mary instinctively rose to her feet, aware only that Britt had actually come and that the words just spoken meant freedom. The children had awakened, sensing that something grave was taking place, and clung sleepily to her skirt. Standing Bear grinned evilly, his features twisted in a cruel smirk.

"Waugh! See how she comes alive with thoughts of rutting once more with her black dog." Snorting, he cast a sardonic glance at Talking Raven, then glared back at Mary. "Calm yourself, woman. This tejano *Negrito* must deal with me, and there will be no talk of trade. When he leaves, he will leave alone, for if you were both dead, you would be nearer to one another than you are at this moment."

Mary blanched and stared without moving, as if she had turned to stone. *This Comanche pig was going to refuse to trade and somehow force Britt to leave camp without us!* Suddenly all her pent-up anxiety exploded in a paroxysm of fury, and she launched herself at the warrior. Clawing and scratching, she screamed every vile name she could dredge up from memory, intent on nothing less than ripping his eyes clean from their sockets.

Standing Bear retreated cautiously before the force of her attack, but her rage was no match for his brute strength. Ducking beneath her blows, his arm swung in a rising arc, and the butt of his hand cracked solidly against her jawbone. Mary hurtled backward and dropped in a limp bundle on the robes. Her eyes blurred, fusing images in a shadowed fog, and a sharp,

brassy taste flooded her mouth. Dimly she sensed that
little George had leaped past her in a vain attempt to
halt the warrior. Then the boy fell beside her, his nose
bleeding from a vicious backhand. Blindly thrusting the
children behind her, Mary cowered before the Comanche, waiting for the death blow to fall.

But Standing Bear had other things in mind for his reluctant black squaw. Wiping the blood from a deep
gash on his cheek, his eyes hooded with sinister amusement. "Prepare yourself for mourning, woman. For before the sun sets again, I will show you how a warrior
spills blood."

Turning, he pushed through the entrance, and a chill
silence fell over the lodge. Mary shuddered, choking
back her tears, and the whimpering children clutched
her neck. Standing Bear's threat echoed in her head,
like a death knell for all she held dear. Filled with sickening dread, she implored her God to strike the heathen Comanche dead or else never let tomorrow come.

Four

Later that evening Britt left the warriors and walked toward the women's lodge. In a short time Running Dog
had taught him the rudimentary feints and slashes of
knife fighting as practiced by the Plains Indians. But
this brief lesson left him far short of the lethal skills developed and refined by warriors since childhood, and
once his anger had been replaced by reason, the odds
seemed to grow worse with each passing minute. From
what the Kiowas had said, Standing Bear was clearly a
formidable adversary, and the outcome of the duel he

intended to provoke tomorrow now seemed far less certain than it had an hour ago. Still, he dreaded talking with the settler women more than he disliked the idea of facing a foot of cold steel.

Most women, as he had learned from bitter experience, were highly unreliable where violence and blood spilling were involved. Their inborn aversion to such things tended to blind them to the harsh necessities sometimes demanded by life. And they failed to comprehend that a man must frequently take the ultimate gamble simply because he could do no less and continue to live with himself. Yet the lady called luck was the most capricious vixen of them all, and tonight even he felt a nagging irritant of doubt as to the aftermath of his scheme to free Mary. But that was a concern which at all costs must remain hidden from the Texas women and their brood.

Entering the lodge, he found the children blissfully asleep, and the four women hovered around a tiny fire. Their open, spontaneous smiles filled the tepee with warmth as they rose to crowd around him. This black man was their savior, and while he may have been an uppity nigger back on the Brazos, he was a lily-pure prince in a Comanche village. With the exception of Sarah Johnson, who had long ago accepted him as a member of the family, these women had not spoken a dozen words to him in the last ten years. But the specter of death has a way of leveling even the most rigid caste system, albeit the man bearing salvation is an untouchable and black as the ace of spades.

"Britt, we were getting worried about you," Sarah said, touching his arm lightly. "You've been gone so long, we were afraid those devils had done something to you."

"Now, Miz Sarah, you know there's nothin' that can touch old Britt." The black man chuckled with a levity that he hardly felt. "Matter of fact, I had supper with the head man of this bunch, and he's agreed to let us trade for their captives."

"Oh, Britt, that's marvelous," Sarah said excitedly. Then her face clouded with anxiety. "But what about Mary? Surely you must have learned something about her and the children."

"Bless me, Miz Sarah, I just plumb forgot to mention it! They're right here in the village, and we'll get them back sometime tomorrow."

The women clapped their hands and exclaimed happily. Then Maggie Williams pounded Britt on the shoulder. "Well, that's grand, just grand. If ever a man deserved to get his woman and little ones back, it's you." Looking around at the other women, she grinned with a sudden thought. "And that means we can start heading home tomorrow too."

"Well, no, not exactly," Britt said slowly. The women's eyes jerked around, and they peered apprehensively at him, like a flock of owls caught in an early sunrise. "Seems that the Comanches have split up into a number of bands, and the women and children have gone off with them. So it appears likely I'll have to hunt them down and bring 'em back here before we can leave."

"Why, that's . . . that's crazy!" Maggie Williams sputtered indignantly. "These red savages might take it in their head to murder us all while you're out galivanting around this god-forsaken wilderness." The other women

appeared stunned and for the moment, speechless.
"Now you just get it in your head that it's better to save
what you've got right now. A bird in the hand is worth
two in the bush, and you can always come back for
those others later." Then her face split in a sly, merce-
nary smile. "Besides, my man will pay you real good for
bringing us home."

Britt's eyes slitted, and the muscle in his jaw
clenched with repressed anger. A moment of strained
stillness ensued, and the women shrank before his cor-
rosive stare. "Miz Williams, I'll just pretend like you
didn't even say that. If I was after a reward, I'd have
made my deals before I left Fort Belknap. And if you
want something to think about, just remember it could
be you out there prayin' for somebody to come save
you from the Comanche."

"That's all well and good," Rachel Ledbetter snapped,
"but you'd better start thinkin' what you're gonna say to
our menfolks if these Indians decide to . . . well, to do
something bad to us women while you're gone."

"That's something I might not have to worry about."
Britt paused and glanced around at their fearful faces.
"Appears that the only way to save my own family is to
fight one of the Comanches tomorrow. And if things
don't go just exactly right, it won't much matter what
your menfolks think."

Sarah's mouth popped open, and she stared at Britt
with mounting terror. The other women appeared
equally appalled, and they watched him with unblinking disbelief. Then Maggie Williams found her tongue
and lashed out venomously. "You fool nigger! You
haven't got the sense God gave a piss ant. What do you

think will happen to us if you're killed? We'd be right back where we started!"

"Then I reckon you wouldn't be any worse off than before I got here," he said with chill dignity. "I came here to get the Johnson families, Miz Williams, and whether you know it or not, you're just ridin' on their coattails. If I can't save my own woman and kids, then I'm not going to bother my head too much about anyone else. Especially since I'd be dog meat anyway if I lose that fight."

"Britt's right!" Sarah's harsh tone cracked like a shot. "His first responsibility is to his own family, and if he gets us out along with them, then we can just count ourselves lucky. Instead of cursing him, you should get down on your knees and kiss his feet. And pray to God he wins that fight tomorrow."

Seething, she glared around at the other women. Their eyes dropped to the dirt floor, not in shame but with the manner of those who have been forced to look upon their own shabby corruption. Rather than self-loathing, they were gripped by bitter resentment and the abiding fear that their lives hung by a thread on the fighting skills of this fool nigger.

"Well, I'm sure as Christ not about to kiss his feet." Maggie Williams glanced around with a dour, unrepentant expression. "But you're right about one thing. We'd better ask the good Lord to make him strong as an ox, come daylight."

The black man regarded them stonily for a moment, then turned without a word, and walked from the lodge. Somehow life had become confusing, a frustrating riddle that threatened to penetrate his aloof shell with its barbed uncertainty. The Indians looked upon

him as a man, nothing more and nothing less. And they
accepted him for what he was, rather than what he had
been born. Yet tomorrow he would kill one of their
number and, in so doing, save the very people who
hated him for not being white. If there was a God, he
had a strange sense of humor. A white man's humor.

Five

The council ground was thronged with warriors, curious elders and a scattering of squaws. Little Buffalo and
Ten Bears stood before the medicine lodge, waiting patiently for the crowd to assemble so that the trading
session could begin. The *to-yop-ke* had called the council for midday, and the dull glow of the autumn sun was
now almost directly overhead. Presently Running Dog
and Britt shouldered their way through the swarm of Indians and came to a halt beside the Comanche chiefs.
After a brief exchange with the Kiowa and his black
brother, Little Buffalo stepped forward and the assembled warriors fell silent.

"Brothers, the tejano called Black Fox has come to
trade for those captured in the Brazos raid. He is a man
of honor and speaks straight. Both Ten Bears and I have
accepted him as a fair man, one who deals justly with
the True People. He offers two horses for each Tejano
woman and one horse for each child. We feel this to be
a worthy offer and have agreed to speak to you in Black
Fox's behalf. There is to be no haggling. This is the offer, and it is a good one. Now who will be the first to
trade with Black Fox?"

An undertone of muttering swept through the spectators' ranks, and Britt sensed something vaguely ominous in the sharp, disgruntled jabbering. There was unmistakable hostility in the warriors' glances, and he suddenly realized that something had inflamed them to the point of open belligerence. Then a stout, barrel-chested brave stepped forward, and when Running Dog nudged Britt with an elbow, he knew beyond question that this was Standing Bear. The black man eyed him closely, silently gauging his adversary. What he saw was a chunky man with a broad, spongy face, whose heavily muscled figure betrayed no sign of weakness. Standing Bear's glaring eyes slanted upward, hollow and cruel, and when he spoke, his words were riddled through with cold sarcasm.

"I, Standing Bear, will not trade with the *Negrito* dog! Like all tejanos, he thinks the Comanche are children who will fall before words of honey and shallow trickery. His words flow from both sides of his mouth, and as a *ko-eet-senko*, I am not bound to trade with a white-eyed liar."

Little Buffalo's eyes darted suspiciously at Britt as the warrior finished speaking. Something was afoot that surpassed understanding, and the *to-yop-ke* intended to have it out in the open. "You are within your rights, brother. As a Comanche you are bound by nothing but your own will. But you leave me wondering. Do you refuse because you wish to have Black Fox's family for your own? Or is there some greater thing that you back away from speaking?"

"The *to-yop-ke* forces words that I would have left unsaid," Standing Bear replied. "For they dishonor you and thereby make fools of all Comanches. The black dog laughs behind his face at us and would ridicule us

before our southern brothers. For he has offered us less
horses than those given to the Kiowa. I have this from
the mouths of the Kiowas themselves."

Little Buffalo's head snapped around, and his smoldering gaze came to rest on Britt and Running Dog.
The Kiowa leader cast a piercing glance at his warriors
who stood in a knot to one side, and from their crestfallen expressions he knew that they had bragged pre-
maturely and unwisely to their Comanche brothers.
Running Dog quickly translated for Britt what had occurred, and the black man's features stiffened under the
impact of this new crisis.

Britt instinctively sensed that all was lost unless he
moved quickly to regain the Comanches' confidence.
Mustering his most candid tone, he spoke in broken
Spanish to the *to-yop-ke*. "Great chief, hear my words.
Do not the Comanche seek the best terms when they
trade? Is it not so with all people? I sought not to cheat
the Comanche and certainly not to dishonor them, but
only to obtain the best bargain for my own people. This
is the accepted way of trade since our fathers and their
fathers before them. But if the Comanches doubt my
good will, then I will offer the same as given to the Kiowa. Three horses for each woman and one for each
child. Petty scheming to save a few horses is for children, not men. So let us trade as friends and have no
more talk of such things."

Little Buffalo stood motionless, unblinking, like some
great horned owl passing judgment on a nest full of fat
mice. He regarded Britt with disgust for a moment
longer, then turned back to the assembled warriors.
"The trade has been set, and the Comanches do not
step away from a promise. Those of you who would

trade will be given the same as the Kiowa. And as your *to-yop-ke*, I say give this *Negrito* your slaves and let us be done with the white-eye filth."

"No!" roared Standing Bear. "I refuse. You are the *to-yop-ke*, but you have no right to make us do this thing." Malevolence twisted his features, insidious and creeping like some cankerous growth, distilling the rage within him. Whirling on the black man, he shouted in bastard Spanish, *"Negrito*, your woman is mine to do with as I choose. From this day forward, she will labor like a horse, and her legs will spread for any Comanche who wishes to ram his pole in black meat!"

Britt's mind seethed and boiled with blind fury, searing out all thought. He started toward the warrior, determined to still that rancorous voice once and for all. But Running Dog grabbed his arm, restraining him, and after a moment his outrage gave way to calculated cold-bloodedness. Turning back to Little Buffalo, his words were spat out in a low, savage snarl. "I demand the right of combat with this coward who makes his fight on women. If he refuses, I will ride throughout the Comanche nation telling how he crawled before me like a whimpering dog."

"Show me your knife, *Negrito*!" Standing Bear shouted. "Step forward with steel in your hand instead of brave words and we will see who leaves his guts in the dirt."

"Hold your tongues," Little Buffalo growled. "Since you have both seen fit to involve me in this thing, it is I who will decide how this fight is to be made." His harsh glare shifted from one to the other as a startled murmur swept through the crowd, and the malice in his eyes was only partially obscured by a glaze of auto-

cratic hauteur. "When the sun drops below the earth, it
is then you will fight. And as you are each filled with
your own courage, I order it to be the Dance of Snakes.
Now a warning: should either of you attempt to back
away from this thing, I will gladly cut your throat with
my own hand."

The *to-yop-ke* spun on his heel and stalked off, followed closely by Ten Bears. Within moments the council grounds was deserted of Comanches, and the
Kiowas stood in a sober knot around their black
brother. Running Dog had difficulty meeting Britt's
eyes, and when he spoke, his words were halting,
shamed.

"Black Fox, the Kiowa are to blame for what has happened, and rightfully it is I who should fight Standing
Bear." He shifted uncomfortably under the black man's
quizzical look and rushed on. "Before we left the mountains, Santana ordered me to guide you in tricking the
barbarians into a poor trade. After you had gone, he
planned to taunt them with the thought that a *Negrito*
had made fools of the arrogant Comanches."

Britt shook his head with a wry, distant smile, finding
it difficult to be angry with the Kiowas and their childish games. Right now his thoughts centered on sundown and what he would face with the first shadows
of darkness. "Do not flay yourself needlessly, my friend.
What is done is done, and it is of no consequence. Instead, tell me of the manner in which I am to fight
Standing Bear. For the *to-yop-ke*'s words made clear
only that it would not be with knives."

"No, not with knives," Running Dog said with a
strange, hollow voice. "You are to face Standing Bear
over a pit filled with the evil ones, rattlesnakes. The fight

will end only when one of you has thrown the other amongst the crawling death." He faltered as the black man's face dissolved into an incredulous mask. "Little Buffalo chose the Dance of Snakes because he was displeased with you both. He felt you tricked him in the trade, and Standing Bear was fool enough to make this known in front of the other warriors. The *to-yop-ke* has lost face, and he means to regain it in the cruelest way known to the True People."

"I see," said Britt, somewhat shaken by the diabolic twist his simple scheme had taken. "But why must we wait until tonight? If this thing is to be done, why not do it now?"

"Black Fox, winter is near," Running Dog explained quietly. "The evil ones have already retreated to their dens. Little Buffalo made the fight for the hour of darkness because it will take many warriors the rest of the day to build fires and smoke them from their caves." The Kiowa glanced eastward and nodded toward the distant sandstone cliffs. "Bear in mind that with their winter sleep disturbed, the *to-yop-ke* knows the evil ones will be enraged beyond all belief."

Britt shuddered as the icy hand of death again clutched his heart. The fleshless specter he had seen in the fire last night took shape before his eyes, and for a brief moment he stared into a vision of writhing horror that seemed cleaved straight from the hell of a madman's demented ravings.

Six

Britt sat alone before the small fire. Running Dog and the Kiowa braves had fanned out through the village to arrange bets with the Comanches. Indians were inveterate gamblers, willing to risk everything they possessed on a toss of the bones or a fast horse, and the extraordinary fight to take place that evening had created a furor of betting within the camp. Moreover, the Kiowas had considerately absented themselves because they wanted Britt to have the lodge to himself. Black Fox had become one of them, and when a brother was to be reunited with his family, he deserved at the very least to be left alone.

Shortly after the discordant meeting that morning, Running Dog had approached Little Buffalo as an intermediary in Britt's behalf. There was every likelihood, he said, that Black Fox would never see another sunrise. And while bitterness now existed toward the *Negrito*, tribal law still dictated that the Comanche were his hosts. Therefore, it was not too much to ask that a man facing certain death be allowed to see his family one last time. After all, the Comanches were not heartless dogs like the Ute or the Crow, he had concluded, and even a condemned man had the right to make one final request of his accuser.

Little Buffalo wasn't for a moment deceived by Running Dog's deference, but he found the Kiowa's obsequious manner highly appealing and in some perverse way was immensely gratified by the life or death power he held over the black man. While he was not a vain man, he found himself curiously intrigued with the idea of manipulating the lives of lesser men, particularly those who had incurred his displeasure. But a great leader must be magnanimous as well as stern, and after deliberating for a few moments he had granted the request.

Standing Bear was summoned, and in no uncertain terms the *to-yop-ke* ordered that the tejano *Negrito* be allowed a brief visit with his family. The warrior's eyes crackled with resentment and indignation, but he had offended Little Buffalo enough for one day, and he reluctantly yielded to the demand. With a withering glance at Running Dog, he turned and stormed from the chief's lodge.

Now Britt waited tensely in the strangely silent Kiowa tepee. Needing some distraction to curb his impatience, he methodically cracked branches and fed them slowly into the fire one at a time. Almost a month had passed since he last saw Mary and the children, and the thought weighed heavily on his mind. What could happen to a woman in an Indian camp in a month's time wasn't pleasant to dwell on, and the treatment to which his family had been subjected might easily have affected them in some gruesome, unthinkable manner.

For that matter, he himself was hardly the same man who had ridden into the Wichita Mountains only a fortnight past. So much had happened to reshape his perspective of the world around him, and more significantly, the simple, unvarnished birthright that all men should reasonably expect from their short tenure on earth. The Kiowas had shown him a way of life where each man was his own master, beholden to none save his conscience and his god. Moreover, it was a federation of men based not on ancestry or race or the color of a man's skin, but rather upon the intrinsic qualities of one's manhood and the courage with which he faced life's uncompromising trials. It was a wild, exhilarating freedom unlike any he had ever known, and the thought coursed through his mind that he might never again be content to trod the nigger's path in the white man's shadow.

Suddenly the lodge flap whipped aside, and before he could move, Mary and the children swarmed over him with great wrenching sobs of joy. His eyes brimmed with tears, and a sodden, moist lump lodged in his throat. Wordlessly he swept them into his arms and hugged them fiercely, burying his face in the familiar scent of Mary's hair. Moments passed in silent physical communion, broken only by their sniffling cries and whispered words of endearment. Then as they gulped back their tears and dried their eyes, they began to see each other clearly for the first time, and it was a sobering experience.

"God a'mighty, it's good to see you, woman!" Britt hugged her again, trying to hide his shock at her greasy buckskin dress and worn features. "And would you just look at these two little Injuns!" Chuckling warmly, he scooped Sue Ellen and George up against his chest, and they clutched at his neck, smearing his face with wet, sticky kisses.

"Papa, have you come to take us home?" Sue Ellen said between hugs and kisses. "We been waitin' an awful long time."

Britt swallowed hard and felt his throat tightening. Thinner now, with her hair in braids, she had the cameo perfection of her mother's features, and her round, child's eyes stared trustingly into his face. The black man looked away, unable to stand her searching eyes, only to find his son watching him with the same unspoken question formed silently on his lips. Then the boy smiled bravely, choking back a fresh burst of tears. "It's not so bad, Pa. We can wait some more if you say so."

"Son, your waitin' is just about done with. This time tomorrow we'll all be back together again. That's a promise." Glancing at Mary, he saw fear kindle in her eyes, and he quickly looked back at the children. "Now you two just sit down here and be real quiet for a minute. Your mama and me has a lot to talk about, and we've only got a little time. Bet you never expected this old horned toad to come chasin' you down?" he said, forcing his voice to sound light and carefree.

Mary's eyes remained troubled, but she smiled and shook her head. "Lord, when I heard it was you, I just couldn't hardly believe it. How in the name of heaven did you keep 'em from killin' you? And how did you know where to find us? They said you was ridin' with the Kiowas, but I just don't—"

"Whoa! One question at a time, woman." Quickly Britt explained his curious alliance with the Kiowas and how he had come to the Comanche camp. Once or twice Mary interrupted with questions, expressing amazement at the sheer audacity of his scheme. When he came to the part about killing the buffalo cow, the black woman's jaw dropped open in utter astonishment.

"Gal, it wasn't nothin' but pure nigger luck. Just like a blind old boar hog stumblin' across an acorn." Then he smiled broadly and took her hand between his two meaty paws. "But that's all over and done with now.

Come tomorrow we'll be together, and there's nothin' ever again going to come between us."

Mary smiled shallowly, finding it difficult to meet his gaze. Then she glanced up and her eyes were rimmed with terror. "Don't try hidin' it from me, Britt. I know all about what's happening tonight. Standing Bear came back from the meetin' this morning and like to tore the lodge apart. He means to kill you, and you just haven't got any idea of what he's like when he's mad."

"Woman, don't you beat all!" he chortled. "When did you ever know ol' Britt to lose a fight? Why, if he's even twice as tough as some of those nigger studs I stomped back on the plantation, he still won't even get me breathin' hard. Or maybe you forgot how many I had to whip till they'd stay clear of you."

"No, I haven't forgot," she said grimly. "It was me that sewed you up and nursed you more times than I like to remember. But you was fightin' with knives and fists then."

"Ummm," he grunted with a wry smile. "Appears you've already heard how it's to be."

"Couldn't help but hear. It's all over the village. This is the first time they've had a fight like this in more'n six years."

"Little mama, don't get yourself all heated up." Britt lifted her chin gently in his hand. "I've been killin' snakes since I was old enough to spit. And I don't reckon it's botherin' me much to face some half-assed Comanche over a pit full of rattlers."

"Oh, Britt, how can you be funnin' at a time like this?" she cried. "That man's a devil, and he's gonna trick you somehow. I just know he is!"

"C'mon now! Have you forgot all that good juju my

grandmam taught me? You think I'm not going to peel
his red hide with some of that hoodoo double whammy
come nightfall?" Britt laughed deeply and gathered the
children in closely. "What do you say we quit borrow-
ing trouble before it even happens and start thinkin'
about what we're going to do with ourselves when all
this is over?"

The black man's light manner eased Mary's strained
face somewhat, but beneath his casual cockiness there
lingered the icy dread he had foreseen earlier. And
within the guileless crypts of his inner self there was
far less certainty of the night's outcome than he pretended. Shunting these grisly thoughts aside, he
laughed and joked, clowning with the children, and in
an engaging flow of anecdotes revealed to them the
warm, selfless humanism he had found among the men
he now called brothers.

All too soon the time would come to face Standing
Bear, and before that moment arrived, he wanted this
woman he loved so dearly to know of the burgeoning
dream that had taken form during his days with the
wild and fiercely proud Kiowas.

Seven

The entire Comanche camp was gathered near a large,
roaring fire as Britt, Running Dog, and the Kiowa
braves approached. The flames shot high in the air,
casting golden shadows across the hushed crowd, and
Britt noticed a deep pit off to one side of the fire. The
Comanche warriors and their squaws eyed the black
man speculatively, still somewhat awed by his enor-

mous size and yet curious as to how a *Negrito* would fare in the most deadly of all tests known to the True People. Rarely had warriors been subjected to the Dance of Snakes, and in the memory of the tribe no Comanche had ever refused this ultimate test of courage after being challenged. But the tejano *Negrito* was not a Comanche, much less a blooded warrior, and there was much concern that he might spoil this grand event by backing off at the last moment.

The fight was to be held on a flat stretch of ground near the riverbank, and the peaceful, rushing waters of the Canadian somehow seemed out of place with this eerie scene. A cavernous hole had been dug in the ground a few paces from the fire, and as Britt glanced quickly at the gaping pit, it appeared to be something more than six feet in length and breadth and quite deep. Strangely the darkened silence of its depths lent an added sense of evil and unseen menace to the pit, and Britt once again felt the cold, fleshless hand of death clutching at his spine.

Little Buffalo and Standing Bear stood alone before the fire, regarding the Kiowa party impassively as they drew nearer. As the Kiowa braves moved off to one side, Britt and Running Dog came to a halt before the two Comanches. Little Buffalo nodded solemnly and, without any attempt at ceremony, launched into the rules governing the fight.

"You men have sworn to kill one another, and that is a good thing, for a warrior is obligated to defend his manhood. But this thing tonight will be done with honor, so that the one who lives can justly lay claim to the possessions of the other." His stoic features betrayed no sign of compassion or mercy as he paused for a moment to gaze coldly into their faces. "Should either of you shame yourself before the fight is finished, my warriors have been instructed to kill you without hesitation.

"You will both be placed on opposite sides of the hole, and your purpose is to throw your opponent into the pit. How you do this is a matter of your own choosing. You can use no weapons, and you must never move past the outer edges of the pit. Should you break either of these rules or shame yourself with cowardice, you will be clubbed and thrown alive into the hole. If you do not understand what I say, then you must speak now."

"I have no questions, my *to-yop-ke*." Standing Bear's words were laced with sardonic brittleness, and he regarded the black man with a brash, amused impudence. "When a Comanche warrior lowers himself to fight a *Negrito* dog, then he asks only to have it done with."

Britt chuckled contemptuously, hoping to unsettle the warrior, and was rewarded with a brief flicker of uncertainty in the other man's eyes. Then he looked back to Little Buffalo. "What you have said is clear, but there is one thing that bothers me. We are not allowed to step past the outer edge of the hole, and this I understand. But is it also forbidden to cross over the pit itself? I would understand this thoroughly, for I have no desire to be killed by your warriors."

Standing Bear snorted as if confronted with the babblings of the village idiot, and Little Buffalo stared at the black man in some astonishment before speaking. "Black Fox, if a man is foolish enough to cross that pit, then his fate is such that he need not fear the Comanche." Turning, the *to-yop-ke* selected a stout branch from the pile of wood near the fire and tossed it into the hole. From within the pit the night was filled with a terrifying maelstrom of angry, buzzing whirs, and no man present doubted that a coiled, beady-eyed death waited just beneath the lip of that ominous trench.

Britt darted a glance at Running Dog, and the Kiowa's face was set in a grim frown. Clearly the floor of that deadly chamber was ankle deep in a writhing, twisting carpet of prairie vipers, and the man who tumbled into their midst would thrash out his life in an unimaginable hell.

Little Buffalo signaled a warrior at the edge of the crowd, and the man stepped forward with a lengthy rope of plaited rawhide. Quickly he secured one end of the rope to Britt's right wrist, and then bound Standing Bear in a similar manner with the other end. The *toyop-ke* then grabbed the middle of the rope and strode forward, forcing the antagonists to trail along like two yoked bulls. When he reached the center of the pit, Little Buffalo dropped the rope and returned to the sidelines. As he did so, a dozen or more warriors carrying heavy war clubs stepped from the crowd and formed a rough square around the two contestants.

This was to be a fight to the death, and Little Buffalo clearly intended that neither of the men would escape, should their bowels suddenly grow tight with fear.

Britt and Standing Bear faced one another across the yawning pit. The Comanche glared murderously at the black man and took a firm grip on the rope. Britt twisted the rawhide around his left hand, priming himself for the deadly tug-of-war that was about to ensue. The lives of his children and Mary hung in the balance as surely as his own, and the fate that awaited them, should he fail, seared his brain with the urgency to kill this man swiftly and without mercy. Both men leaned back into the rope, stretching it taut as they nervously awaited Little Buffalo's command.

"Impesa," the *to-yop-ke* shouted.

Without warning, Standing Bear leaped *forward*, throwing slack into the tight, quivering rope. Straining against the braided lariat, expecting the Comanche to pull in the opposite direction, Britt was taken totally unawares and tumbled backward to the ground. Raging at himself for having been maneuvered into such a childishly simple trap, the black frantically attempted to scramble to his feet.

The lousy, sneaking sonovabitch! Mary warned me! Warned me! Cursing himself, he suddenly realized that the rope had been jerked taut once more and he was being dragged like a bleating calf toward the open trench. Standing Bear had now thrown the rope over his shoulder, leaning into the dragging weight, digging furiously with the corded muscles of his legs to gain momentum. Skidding helplessly along the ground, Britt fought like a madman to regain his feet, but he was being dragged head first, and there seemed no way to halt the Comanche's relentless surge forward. Then, like some recurring nightmare come to life, the black man sensed that he was only a few yards from the gaping darkness of the pit.

For a moment he was paralyzed, unable to breathe or think, aware only that he was about to be buried in a seething, writhing hell. Then abruptly, his mind cleared, and his one hope dawned with the clarity that comes only to those who find themselves staring eyeball to eyeball with the specter of death.

Leaning into the rope with all the power of his massive shoulders, he jerked backward, twisting his legs forward and stiffening his body into a rigid slab in the same moment. Propelled forward by Standing Bear's violent heaving, he managed to gain a purchase on the ground with one foot and awkwardly launched himself into the air and over the pit.

Straining into the lariat with all his might, Standing Bear was caught completely by surprise as the slack now whipped in his direction, and he pitched to the ground like a felled ox. Dumbstruck but still game, the warrior rolled with the fall and came to his knees. But his recovery was short lived, for as he attempted to rise, the black man stepped forward and kneed him squarely in the face. There was a mushy sound, like a pumpkin being squashed on a sharp rock, and the mangled Comanche dropped in a gory, sodden heap.

Grasping the rope, Britt instantly hurtled back across the pit and charged forward, hauling Standing Bear closer to death with each quickening step. Instinctively he glanced back over his shoulder and saw the stunned warrior struggling to rise as his head cleared the edge of the trench. Standing Bear's face was etched with mortal terror as he clawed hopelessly at the crumbling earth, and for a moment in time the two men's eyes met in a frozen exchange of understanding. There was no question of asking or granting quarter, for one man must die, and neither would have expected any less from the other.

Setting himself, Britt jerked the rope, and the Comanche brave tumbled into the pit.

Suddenly the night was split with a shrill animal cry, and Standing Bear leaped erect, desperately trying to claw his way from the hole. His face and body were covered with a score of rattlesnakes, clutching and gouging, biting again and again as they sank their fangs into his defenseless flesh. Screaming with the fury of the damned, he tore at the snakes with both hands, his body oozing venom and blood as the flickering shadows of the fire played across the grotesque mask that had once been a face. Then as the venomed death sped through his system, constricting his heart, the warrior weakened, and his thrashing arms ceased to struggle. The silent gaze of the dead spread over his eyes, and without a sound he toppled backward into the pit. There was a brief flurry of angry rattles as the reptiles ravaged his lifeless form; then all was still.

The spectators were breathlessly silent, awed and more than a little frightened by the inhuman terror of a brave man's death. Running Dog strode forward and slashed the rawhide that bound the black man's wrist. Their eyes met, and the Kiowa clasped his shoulder compassionately. Black Fox had met the test, and while some killings would haunt a man even to his death bed, it was simply the price a warrior must pay if he chose to walk among the True People.

Britt suddenly felt very wary, as if the essential matter of his soul had shriveled into a hard, tight knot deep within his gut. Glancing about, he became aware of the curious, hollow stares of the hushed warriors. Then he looked at Little Buffalo and was momentarily startled by the Comanche's stern nod of approval. Silently he removed the rawhide loop from around his wrist and tossed it at the *to-yop-ke*'s feet. Turning, he walked slowly into the darkness, wanting only to be gone from this place and what lay at the bottom of that pit.

It had been a long night, and while the fleshless grin of death had passed him by for another, he felt small comfort in the fact.

Eight

The children were asleep, snuggled beneath the furry warmth of their buffalo robes. Britt and Mary sat close to the small fire, talking quietly. His arm encircled her waist protectively, and her head rested on his shoulder. For long moments they hardly spoke, cuddling close as they stared into the flames, grateful merely to be alive and together. Only that morning their chances of ever becoming a family again had appeared slim indeed, and now their lifetime stretched once more before them.

Shortly after the fight that evening, Britt had sent word to Little Buffalo that all he wanted from the lodge of Standing Bear was his own family. Moreover, he was awarding to the dead man's family the five horses that were rightfully theirs if the exchange had come off as originally planned. In effect, this made Talking Raven and Two Moons the richest squaws in the village. And while Standing Bear's body was barely cold, few doubted that any number of warriors would soon be extending offers of marriage to the two widows.

Struck by the black man's magnanimous gesture, Little Buffalo had ordered a lodge erected for Britt and his family. Further, he assigned a small party of warriors to lead the tejano *Negrito* to the outlying Comanche villages. The True People respected generosity second only to courage, and Black Fox had amply demonstrated that his character was that of a brother in heart, if not by birth. While this did not wholly erase the stigma of his bonds with the white-eyes, he was nonetheless elevated to a position of honor in the camp, and was to be accorded every courtesy.

Watching the flickering tongues of flame dance hungrily in the fire, Britt felt at peace for the first time in close to a month. His own family was now safe, and soon he would have arranged the trade of every captive taken in the Brazos raid. Looking back, he was more than a little amazed that he had been able to pull it off. Maybe it was like the white folks said after all, that God had a special way of watching over fools and dumb niggers. Whatever the variety of spirits that had protected him, he had done what he set out to do, and that was all that counted in the long haul. Nuzzling his head against Mary's cheek, he squeezed her tightly, reassuring himself that she was actually there and all his once more.

"Suppose I'll be ridin' out tomorrow." He felt her stiffen as she glanced up from his shoulder. "Snow's not going to hold off much longer, and if I'm going to get them women and kids out of the villages, I'd best be about it."

"I guess it's not like you have any real choice." She relaxed, snuggling closer again. "But God knows one night's not much to up and lose you again."

"You're not losin' me, woman," Britt chuckled. "Why, I'll be back here before you even know I'm gone. Way I got it figured, it won't take me more than three, maybe four weeks at the most."

"And if winter sets in?" she queried anxiously.

"Well, maybe a little longer," he admitted reluctantly. "But these Comanches guiding me know their way

around, and don't forget, they'll be wantin' to get back
here just as fast as I do. You know, it's not like they was
headin' out on this little jaunt just because they like
ridin' around in the snow."

"No, I guess that's right enough." She pressed closer to
his shoulder and watched the flames silently. Moments
passed as her mind drifted back over the day and everything that had happened. She shuddered slightly as she
recalled Talking Raven and Two Moons mutilating themselves as they wailed over Standing Bear's body, already
bloated and turning black from the massive injections of
venom it has absorbed. That foul, chewed-over horror
could just as easily have been Britt, and the sickening
thought made her stomach churn. Then something half-
forgotten flashed through her mind, and she looked up,
regarding the black man solemnly for a moment.

"You know what Talking Raven said to me when I
was leaving her lodge? She said, 'Make your man a coward so that he will not die fighting. Teach him to lower
his head and turn from trouble. Sap his manhood, let
him grow fat and afraid, for then at least your bed will
never be empty.' "

Mary paused, watching his face. "After today it makes
me wonder if she's not right. Maybe we ought to go
back where we come from. Even if they do treat you
like dirt on them plantations, at least you know you're
gonna live long enough to die peaceful."

Britt glanced at her and then stared back into the
flames. The silence grew, and she began to wonder if
he would speak or just ignore her comment. Then he
drew a long breath and exhaled it slowly. "Once a long
time ago that might have been enough for me too. But
I've seen something livin' with the Kiowas that I never

knew anybody could have 'cepting a white man. They're free, woman! Free as the wind or the tree, just like God meant for all natural things to be free." Then his voice lowered, impassioned with the vision that had slowly formed and taken root in his mind over the past month. "It's not just the South I'm talking about. I don't even know if I can ever go back to Texas again."

"Lord God, Britt, are you talkin' about livin' with these heathens?" Her eyes widened with fear, and she drew back from him. "They've already killed one of our boys. Or did you forget that? *Do you want Sue Ellen and Little George to grow up to be savages too?*"

"I haven't forgot nothin'." He sighed, rubbing his forehead with a gnarled hand. "I only know a black man's not free in a white man's world. Maybe never will be. The Kiowas accept you and me and these children for what we are. Not black or white, but just people. Human beings! And that's a hell of a lot more than we ever got in Texas, even with Allan's help."

"So you're just gonna throw all that over and be a red nigger instead of a black nigger?" Mary hesitated as tears welled up in her eyes, somewhat shaken by her own vehemence. "And what about Allan? All these years he's spent protectin' you from the white folks and helpin' us to make a decent life for ourselves. Don't you owe him anything?"

"Goddammit, don't crowd me, Mary!" He rose and jerked the lodge flap back, peering out into the night. The chill air swept gently over his flushed features, and after a moment his temper subsided. Finally he spoke, his voice weary and filled with uncertainty. "I don't know what to do. I'm not even sure I know what's right. I only know that with the Kiowas we'd be free and nobody would ever again be able to put his foot on our necks and grind us down into the dirt."

"And what happens when the whites kill all the Kiowas? Cause they will just as sure as there's a God in heaven."

Glumly he stared into the bleak darkness. What was it Running Dog had said about a man not being a man unless he held himself above the scavengers? Maybe it would be better to die fighting alongside the Kiowas. *At least you'd die free,* he thought, *like a man.* Not like some spineless, jelly-gutted thing always backing off from looking a white man straight in the eye. *But did he have the right to play God with the kids' lives?* Maybe if they lived to come of age, they'd rather be a live nigger than a dead free man. Sorely perplexed, he shook his head and turned back into the lodge.

"Let's go to bed, woman. I've got a long way to ride, and we've got plenty of time to decide what's best to do." Forcing a smile, he leered at her suggestively. "Besides, if you haven't forgot all them games we used to play, you might be able to whip me down just like that old squaw told you to do."

Her eyes hooded seductively, and a knowing smile played over her mouth. Stretching her hand to meet his, she followed him to their bed of buffalo robes. Curiously there was some strange new excitement which manifested itself at the thought of making love to the warrior that the True People now honored as the Black Fox.

❦ CHAPTER SIX ❦

One

CHRISTMAS HAD COME AND GONE, and a new year lay over the land. For the True People it was the time of the Snow Moon. But for Britt it was merely January, 1861, and a damned cold one at that.

Snow fell silently in the false dawn as they crested a hill east of Fort Belknap. Behind them the shivering band brought their mounts to a halt. Long moments passed as Britt and Running Dog sat gazing through the snow flurries at the fort below. The white stillness seemed deafening, broken only by the stamping hooves and frosty snorts of their horses. And somehow, for warriors and captives alike, there was a sense of the un-real about the dim outlines of the distant stockade.

Britt drew the buffalo cape tighter, burying himself deeper in its furry warmth, and stared at the fort with hollow, spent eyes. Three months had passed since he rode north from the Brazos, and in all that time he hadn't once slept the night through with any certainty of what the morrow would bring. The task of ran-soming only the Johnson families had somehow gotten out of hand. Once in the Indian camps he was unable to resist the pitiful stares of the Texan women and their children, and more by circumstance than design, he had found himself cast in the role of their savior. While this wholesale ransoming had been undertaken without any great reluctance on his part, the burdens it entailed had multiplied out of all proportion to anything he could have foreseen.

Somewhere along the line he became aware that each word he uttered, his every action, could affect the lives of more than twenty women and children. If it were the wrong word or some thoughtless gesture which offended the Comanche, then the effect could very well be permanent and deadly. The fight with Standing Bear had served to clarify this role even more in his own mind, and with it the responsibility he had assumed so lightly came crashing down on his shoulders. Whether the captives lived or died, remained slaves or returned to the Brazos, rested squarely on his head. And whatever the outcome, there was no one to blame but himself.

Upon leaving the Canadian in search of the far-flung Comanche bands, the dangers seemed very real, and the future never more uncertain. Then the howling blizzards broke across the Plains, and what began as a quick sortie into the other villages gradually evolved into a prolonged odyssey throughout a frigid, snow-bound wasteland. With the Comanche guides to lead the way and Little Buffalo's prestige backing him, the black man had eventually located each of the camps and was able to ransom the captives without any great difficulty. But it had required almost six weeks, and the

burden of that many lives, along with the grueling journey itself, had taken its toll.

Silently watching the fort through the predawn
gloom, Britt wondered what, if anything, he had actually accomplished. Certainly he had saved twenty-three
women and children from a miserable existence, and
that was something. But in the process he had the very
distinct feeling that he had lost his own soul. And he
wasn't at all sure that the settlers would evidence the
same gratitude as shared by those he had rescued. Especially when they heard how many horses it was going
to cost them.

Snow settled gently over his buffalo robe, spotting
his matted beard with flecks of white. Three months
without shaving had changed his appearance sharply,
and as droplets of frost formed on his moustache, it occurred to the black man that his insides were no longer
the same either. While a nigger had ridden forth
from the Brazos, a blooded warrior had returned. North
of the Red River he was known by another name, a respected name, and welcomed as a man of courage in
the camps of both Comanche and Kiowa. Below in that
fort he must once again resume the identity of Nigger
Britt, Allan Johnson's pet darkey. Assuming, of course,
that he wished to remain on the Brazos and live in
peace among the white man. And this was the gut-
wrenching decision he hadn't yet reconciled within
himself.

"Black Fox has the look of a man who sniffs rancid
meat." Running Dog's voice shattered the early morning
stillness, and the black man started as if an icy finger
had probed beneath his furry robe. The Kiowa's grave
look of concern rested only briefly on Britt before slid-

ing back to the fort. "Sometimes it is wiser for a man to go on instead of returning to what he has left behind."

"There is truth in that, brother. More than you know." Britt glanced wearily at the warrior, but his gaze was drawn once more to the distant walls. "My grandmother used to say that any man born of woman is few of days and full of trouble. It seems I have only begun to understand the wisdom of her words."

"Among the True People there are also women *puhakets*," Running Dog commented pointedly. "Perhaps we would all be better off if we heeded their counsel. But then even wise men have been known to ignore the counsel of those who offer it freely. Is it not so, Black Fox?"

Britt's head swiveled around, and he peered quizzically at the Kiowa's inscrutable features. With the dark, snow-flecked robe pulled up around his ears, the black man resembled a grizzled buffalo bull, but his hide wasn't nearly so thick. Running Dog's words stung, making him forget the bitter cold for a moment. They were the words of a friend, the counsel of one brother for another, and this significance was not lost on Britt. But still, they hurt.

"Your words have a bite to them, like the morning chill. Had I not heard Running Dog speak to his Kiowa brothers in the same manner, I would think he was addressing a white-eye."

"I do not talk to white-eyes, Black Fox. I kill them. The only reasonable discussion with a tejano is at the end of a gun."

"And if the tejano happens to be a brother in spirit? What then?"

"You speak of halfway things, my friend. And in this

life that is not to be found." The warrior looked at him steadily, searching his face. "Now that I think on it, your words have about them the sound of parting. It makes me wonder whether I speak with Black Fox or the tejano *Negrito*?"

"Can you not speak with both?" Britt asked, aware even before the words were out that he was still dealing in halfway measures.

But the question hung between them, for the Kiowa never had a chance to answer. From the fort came the sharp, rolling crack of a rifle. Their heads snapped around, and as they watched, they could see activity along the stockade walls. Their arrival had been timed to coincide with dawn, so that Britt could approach the fort without alarming its occupants. That possibility no longer existed, however, for it was clear that a sentry had spotted them, and the alarm had been sounded. Cautioning Running Dog to hold his position, the black man spurred his horse and rode through the swirling flurries toward Fort Belknap.

Two

Buck Barry came awake slowly. These mornings he never had to worry about the orderly awakening him. Along toward dawn his room in headquarters would become so cold that no amount of blankets could hold off the chill. Somehow it seemed that his toes always came awake first, growing frigid and brittle just as the biting darkness surrendered to the faint rays of dawn. Then the cold would slowly creep up his legs and across his body until he was full awake, shivering and cursing the lot of a civilian soldier.

Drawing his feet up below his rump, Barry snuggled deeper in the blankets, dreading that final moment when he must whip the covers back and jump from bed. Again he silently cursed the state militia and the deadwood that enlisted in order to avoid fighting Yankees. If this were the regular army, his orderly would already have a cheery fire blazing and a pot of coffee brewed long before he opened his eyes. But it wasn't the regular army or, for that matter, anything that even remotely resembled an army. It was a collection of misfits, sharpers, and outright cowards who had yet to fire a shot at an enemy, red or white. They had joined the militia to escape the hazards of a greater war, and so long as they had three squares and a warm bed, they couldn't have cared less about the fortunes of the South.

Such thoughts set his blood to boiling and warmed him for a moment. But the piercing cold quickly returned, and only with great concentration could he keep his teeth from chattering.

Lying there, shivering and still unwilling to forsake what warmth the blankets afforded, the nagging thought returned that some people might even consider him a coward. After all, if he was so brave, why wasn't he off fighting the Yankees with Lee and Beauregard? Damned good question, he answered himself. Thinking back, he cursed the day he had allowed the smooth-talking governor to convince him that he should head up a company of militia. The frontier needs defending just as badly from Indians, the gover-

nor had announced, as the Northern borders need to
be held against the Yankees!

Remembering the words, his temper flared briefly as
he reflected on the inequities of life. *Hell yes, the frontier needs defending! Except that we muffed our one
chance for a real fight. So now we sit on our ass and
wait for spring, until they're ready to raid again. And
while we freeze our butts off here, Stuart and Jackson
and Lee are makin' heroes out of themselves fighting
Yankees. What a way to fight a war! Waiting on a
bunch of bare-assed Comanches to come raidin' instead of moving up there in force and attacking their
winter camps.*

Thoroughly galled by the thought, he ripped the covers back and bounded from bed. Shivering violently
now, he threw a blanket around his shoulders and padded across the icy floor to the fireplace. Forcing his
numb fingers to remain steady, he quickly stacked a
handful of kindling and lighted it, then fed a load of
dried branches into the greedy flames. Soon he had a
roaring blaze going and the galvanized coffee pot perking merrily. Adding a log for good measure, he stood
with his back to the flames, luxuriating in the crackling
warmth, and slowly began dressing.

Thoughts of the distant war and the Indian raid last
October set Barry's mind off on a tangent all too familiar these days. While destiny passed him by, robbing
him of the glory that would surely have been his fighting with the Confederacy, he was saddled with playing
nursemaid to a pack of bellyaching settlers. After the
debacle in October they had moved into the fort lock,
stock, and barrel. Ever since, they had sat around swilling corn liquor and bemoaning the fact that the govern-

ment hadn't sent enough troops to protect them from the red savages. Of course, that didn't hold true for everybody.

There were some, like Johnson and Fitzpatrick, who rumbled out each morning in their wagons, come rain, sleet, or snow. Determined to rebuild what the Indians had burned to the ground, they hacked at frost-hardened trees with brittle axes and slowly snaked the logs back to their homesteads. Come spring they would be ready to start erecting cabins again, and unless the raids came earlier than expected, they would have crops planted and their cattle gathered before the Comanche struck. But there wasn't many like that. Most just sat around and slopped whiskey, declaring that when the winter storms finally broke, there would be plenty of time to start rebuilding. *Goddamned fools,* Barry fumed. *All they want to do is piss and moan and feed off the government till good weather forces them back to work.*

Thinking of the settlers brought the officer's mind around, as it invariably did, to Tom Fitzpatrick. While he admired the Irishman's gumption and his willingness to pitch in wherever help was needed, Fitzpatrick's constant presence in the fort was a grating irritant that chafed him raw. Generally they avoided each other, for it was clear that Tom would never forgive Barry for the way he had humiliated him the night Britt Johnson went away. But whenever they chanced to meet or found themselves in the same room, there was an astringent, smoldering expression to Fitzpatrick's face. And if he did speak it was through clenched teeth.

Clearly he harbored bitter resentment, if not outright hatred, toward the captain, and it was this unspoken animosity that continued to rankle Barry. Any man who carried a grudge couldn't be trusted, at least in Buck Barry's scheme of things. And lately he had grown increasingly suspicious of Fitzpatrick, convinced that the Irishman was only waiting to catch him off guard in order to exact some backhanded kind of revenge.

Buttoning his shirt, Barry next thought of Britt Johnson, for if anyone shared his dislike of Fitzpatrick, it was the black man. Idly he wondered what had happened to Britt. Probably skinned alive, he mused, and staked out for the Comanche squaws to torture till he begged for death! Still, you never knew. Some of those niggers had God's own luck, and he might just have pulled through after all. Of course, the settlers had their own theories about what had become of Allan's uppity nigger. Most believed that he was long dead, scalped and hacked to pieces not too many days after he had crossed the Red River. Otherwise, why hadn't he come back, they demanded, for as sure as a horse fart draws flies, no man in his right mind would willingly spend the winter in a Comanche camp. Not even a smart-ass nigger like Johnson's boy!

Others were of a different mind entirely. They knew niggers, by God, and this one wasn't no different than the rest of his breed. Sure as Christ was nailed to a cross, that black bastard lit out for parts unknown! Probably struck out for California to work in the gold fields or went north to join the Union Army. But you can bet your sweet ass on one thing, they chorused, that black sonovabitch never went anywhere near the Red!

While many a jug had been emptied in speculation as to Nigger Britt's fate, the settlers were unanimously undivided on the most chilling conclusion of all. Whether he had crossed the Red or simply kept on running, the women and children taken captive had long since been given up as dead. Perhaps some of them were still alive, they agreed, but by merciful Jesus, they'd be better off dead!

Barry rammed his foot in a boot and dismissed the subject from his mind. There were more important things to worry about than some fool nigger. Food was growing short with this many people drawing down on government provisions, and unless the settlers wanted real trouble before spring, they sure as Christ better start cinching their belts a little tighter. While there was plenty of meat available, what with so many cattle running loose, the supply of vegetables and tinned goods in the storehouse was running drastically low. And he sure as hell didn't intend to see the whole fort come down with scurvy or some other strange disease before the roads opened up that spring. Making a mental note to call a meeting that evening, he poured a cup of scalding coffee and gratefully let its warmth spread through his chilled innards.

Suddenly a rifle shot cracked from the direction of the front gate, and he froze with the cup half raised to his lips. *Goddamned fool probably shot his toe off. If those sonsabitches are shootin' at rabbits again, I'll peel their asses clear down to the backbone!* Slamming the coffee cup down on the mantel, he bolted through the orderly room and took off running across the parade ground.

Three

Buck Barry reached the catwalk along the stockade wall just as a horseman appeared on the forward slope of a hill to the east. Alerted by the sentry's rifle shot, settlers and the small contingent of militia poured from the barracks and went streaming across the parade ground toward the front gate. While the drifting snow partially obscured Barry's vision, there was something vaguely familiar about the way the approaching rider sat on his horse, and a wild thought suddenly raced through the officer's mind. Abruptly he grabbed the small telescope which sentries were required to carry and jammed it to his eye. As Barry peered into the distance, Allan Johnson scrambled up the ladder, half-dressed and squint-eyed from sleep, followed closely by Tom Fitzpatrick.

"Well, I'll be double goddamned!" Barry snorted.

"What is it, Captain?" Allan demanded. "Is it an Indian?"

The advancing rider certainly looked like an Indian, except for his wide-brimmed hat, but before answering, Barry elevated the telescope and scanned the distant hilltop. "Johnson, it appears that nigger of yours was as good as his word. That's him comin' across the flats, and unless my eyes are going bad, there's a bunch of Injuns holding our women and kids up on that far rise."

Leaping forward, Fitzpatrick snatched the telescope from Barry's hand and thrust it to his eye. His hand trembled with excitement but finally he steadied the glass on the group of riders crowding the hilltop. Suddenly his head jerked forward, and he studied the distant band even more intently for a moment. Then he slowly lowered the telescope, his face flushed with a stunned expression.

"Allan, it's them. All of 'em," he said in a hushed tone. "And my boy's with 'em!" Turning to the settlers jammed around the bottom of the ladder, his voice tremored with emotion. "Goddammit, men, he did it! That black devil has brought every one of them women and kids back with him."

There was a shocked, disbelieving murmur from the crowd, almost as if they were afraid to risk having their hopes dashed again. Then Captain Barry ordered the gates thrown open, and Britt Johnson trotted into the compound. Even before he could bring the chestnut to a halt, the settlers swarmed around him, laughing and shouting, each one trying to touch him in their mad unrestrained joy. Allan and Tom jumped from the catwalk and tore their way through the crowd. Barry chose the more dignified route down the ladder, but he was not far behind.

"Britt, you old war-horse!" Allan shouted. Physically dragging the black man from the saddle, he embraced him in a crushing bear hug. "Godalmighty, we gave you up for dead months ago! Where in the billy-blue hell have you been?"

"Allan, even if I told you, you wouldn't believe it. Sometimes I'm not real certain I believe it myself."

Suddenly Tom Fitzpatrick pushed forward, clasping the black man's hand and shaking it profusely. "I don't even have to ask you. I saw 'em up there. My boy and Allan's family too." For a moment the two men stared into each other's eyes, then the Irishman gave his hand another crunching squeeze. "Mister, I don't know how you did it but from now on you're ace high in my book.

Anything I said in the past, you just mark it off as a damned fool with his tongue unhinged."

Before Britt could answer, Buck Barry shouldered his way through the packed mob and gave the black man a jarring wallop across the back. "By Christ, it's good to see you, Britt. I don't mind admittin' I'd wrote you off a long time ago. Figured that topknot of yours was decorating some Comanche scalp stick."

"Cap'n, you don't know how close you are to bein' right." Britt smiled and glanced around the grinning crowd. "There was more'n once I thought they were gonna cash me in, but I guess I just got lucky somewhere along the line."

"Luck, my ass!" Barry boomed. "It takes more than luck to cross the Red and come back to tell about it." The settlers laughed in agreement and pushed closer, not wanting to miss a word. "Now level with us, Britt. How in Christ's name did you get them women and kids away from the Comanches?"

The black man looked around the anxious, curious faces and slowly shook his head. "Well, it wasn't just the Comanches, Cap'n. First I made friends with Santana. He's chief of the Kiowa. Then with his help I was able to get in good with Little Buffalo. He's the head-dog Comanche. The one that led the raid last fall." An angry muttering swept over the crowd at this last disclosure, and Britt glanced around in surprise. "I reckon you've all got reason enough to hate him, but I'm here to tell you that if it weren't for Little Buffalo, there wouldn't be any women and kids waitin' on that hill back yonder."

"By God, he's right, men," Allan announced forcefully. "Let's quit talking about Indians and start thinking of our families!"

"That's the ticket!" Fitzpatrick bellowed. "How many are there, Britt, and what'a we have to do to get 'em back?"

"Well, there's eight women and fifteen kids. I got 'em all back, but Miz Wilson. Way I heard the story from the Kiowas, she grabbed a knife and killed herself before they even got her across the Red."

The crowd grew silent, glancing at one another with undisguised skepticism. Then Buck Barry spoke up in a subdued voice. "Maybe it's just as well. We found Hank Wilson and their three kids butchered in some willows down by the creek. Looked like he went under tryin' to save the children."

The silence grew, and a few of the women wiped tears from their eyes. But the settlers were more interested in the living than the dead, and they quickly began peppering the black man with questions about their own families.

"Now if I was you, I wouldn't get my hopes up too high." Britt's sober tone stilled their anxious queries. "They're all alive, but they've been through a rough time. And you're liable to be a mite shocked when you see 'em."

"What about the women?" Lester Thomas asked quietly. "Did the Injuns . . . you know, did they . . . ?" His voice faltered, and he was unable to go on.

"Mr. Thomas, I reckon that's something you'll have to find out for yourself," Britt responded gently. "I didn't ask no questions. I just made the deal and got 'em out of there as fast as I could."

"That's good enough for me," Tom Fitzpatrick said.

"But you still haven't told us why the redsticks are holdin' them up on that hill."

The Irishman's question brought an alert look to the settlers' faces, and silence again fell over the crowd as they watched the black man curiously. Britt glanced around, aware that their stares demanded an answer. Determined that he wouldn't be intimidated by the throng of white faces, he drew a deep breath and let them have it squarely between the eyes.

"Now I know that none of you gave me leeway to make deals for you. But once I got up there and saw I was able to save 'em. I just sorta figured you wouldn't think the price was too high." The stillness thickened, like a murky fog settling to the earth, and he saw them stiffen with apprehension. "The deal I made was three horses for each woman and one horse for each child. And if I've calculated right, that means we've got to scare up thirty-nine horses to make the exchange."

The settlers stared at him incredulously, hardly able to believe their own ears. Then the storm broke. Their faces twisted with dismay and consternation, and all started shouting at once. Watching them, the black man somehow felt removed from the vortex of their anger, almost as if he had gone stone deaf and was aware of nothing but the movement of their lips. As their faces purpled and their abusive voices swelled in pitch, a tight smile played at the corners of Britt's mouth. No doubt about it, none at all. He was back in the land of the white-eyes. And things hadn't changed, not even by the width of a gnat's ass.

Four

"I don't give a goddamn what you say, this black scutter has sold us out to the Indians." Sam Ledbetter's eyes glistened with anger as he stared at Britt. Shifting his gaze, he glared at Buck Barry in baffled fury. "I say if you lie down with dogs, you get up with fleas. Only in his case he's probably crawlin' with Comanche lice."

"Ledbetter, offhand I'd say you weigh in at about twelve ounces of bullshit to the pound!" Barry's harsh growl momentarily stilled the rabid settlers. "Near as I recollect, your woman is waitin' up on that hill for you to come and get her, and all this yellin' about a few horses sorta leaves a man to ponder where your stick floats."

Still crowded around Britt, the settlers' eyes darted back to Ledbetter, tensely awaiting his reaction to the charge implicit in Barry's insult. Ledbetter's face went florid, and his eyes popped out of his head with rage. But only a fool tangled with Buck Barry, and when he spoke, his voice shook with restrained hostility.

"Cap'n, that's a low thing to say to any man. And you got no call to whipsaw me." Seeking support, he glanced around the watchful crowd, somewhat like a forlorn badger cornered by a sour-tempered grizzly. "I want my woman back as much as anyone here, but that don't change the fact that Johnson's nigger went out of his way to make the Indians rich at our expense."

"By God, he's right, Cap'n," Ike Claiborne snapped. "All them coons is tarred with the same brush, and whether he did it on purpose or just out of plain ignorance don't make no difference. The fact of the matter is that every man on the Brazos is gonna be left without a horse to his name."

"Well, I'm damned if I'd go along with that." Eli Thompson's grating voice jerked the settlers' heads around. Short and fat, with a mushy face, he quivered with rage like a lumpy bowl of oatmeal. "For my money, the nigger sonovabitch did it just out of pure spite. He was still carrying a grudge 'cause of what happened the night he left here, and he just flat went out of his way to break every man jack of us."

"Mister, I'm surely gettin' tired of all the horseshit you people are slinging around. *You especially!*" Tom Fitzpatrick jabbed the corpulent, heavily-jowled settler in the chest with a thorny finger. "And if you ain't real careful, I'm gonna strop up my skinnin' knife and make me two little fat men out of one big one."

Thompson's pudge features dissolved like a pail of lard in a hot sun, and he attempted to back away from the belligerent Irishman. But the settlers' packed ranks brought him up short, and for a moment it looked as if Fitzpatrick was actually going to jump him. Then Allan stepped forward, clasping Tom's arm firmly, and began speaking in calm, measured tones.

"Now hold on, Tom. There's no call to start fighting among ourselves." Looking around, he regarded the crowd with a benign expression for a moment, then resumed in a placating manner. "You men seem to have lost sight of what's at stake here. Whether Britt paid too high a price is no longer the issue. The fact is that the women and children are waiting up on that hill, and if we want them back, we're going to have to come up with enough horses to make the exchange. Personally I'm willing to throw in all the horses I own, and I'd think that every man with a family would feel the same way."

"Not by a damnsight!" Ike Claiborne snarled. "We got enough men and guns to go up there and make dog meat out of those red bastards. Why the hell should we give 'em good horses for women they stole from us in the first place?"

"Now you're talkin'," Sam Ledbetter whooped. "We could all mount up and be on 'em before they ever knew what hit 'em!"

A murmur of assent swept through the crowd, and they looked at one another as if this were the first sane idea they had heard all morning. Britt darted glances at Allan and Buck Barry, his face etched with a mixture of rage and disbelief. Clearly the situation was about to get out of hand, and if someone didn't act quickly, that distant hilltop would run red with blood before the sun was hardly over the horizon.

"Shut your goddamned mouths!" Britt commanded in a hoarse bellow. Backing a few paces away from the crowd, he let his hand come to rest on the Colt at his side. "Before you heroes get any fancy ideas, you'd better listen to what *I've* got to say. My family's waitin' on that hill too, and there's a Kiowa warrior up there with orders to cut the throat of every woman and kid if we even look like we're gonna pull a doublecross. So before you get through that gate, you'd better figure you gonna have to come over me."

Without warning, Tom Fitzpatrick suddenly leaped forward. Jerking a shotgun from the scabbard on Britt's horse, he backed up beside the black man. Slowly he cocked both hammers and glared at the settlers with a malevolent smile. "I stand with Britt. And the first sonovabitch that makes a move toward that gate is gonna get a quart of buckshot up his gizzard!"

The crowd wilted before the scatter gun. But a low rumble of sudden outrage spread virulently from man to man. While being backed down by Fitzpatrick was bad enough, the black man's contemptuous manner was almost more than they could swallow. But the sheer audacity of a nigger threatening white men with a gun was so shocking that for the moment they stood rooted in astonishment and confusion.

Then Tom's voice again split the compound, grating and wracked with emotion. "Just so there won't be any doubt as to where I stand, you boys better listen close. This man saved my little boy, the only family I got left. So far as I'm concerned, from now on, Britt Johnson's name might as well be Fitzpatrick, 'cause me and him are gonna be just about that thick. And any man ever again calls him *nigger* is gonna get the crap beat out of him by me personal."

Buck Barry regarded Fitzpatrick with an astounded expression, and the fleeting thought passed through his mind that he might just have misjudged this thick-headed Irishman. Glancing about the crowd, he saw that the settlers were equally bewildered and decided it was time to put a halt to this slack-jawed lunacy. Striding to a point directly between the two factions, he turned on the settlers with bristling anger.

"Gents, it's like the buzzard said when he dumped his load two miles up . . . a little of this shit goes a long way. And I've had about all I'm gonna take for one mornin'. Just between us *good neighbors*, I don't think the whole friggin' lot of you is worth the powder it'd take to blow you off a johnny pot. But that's neither

here nor there." Jerking a thumb in Britt's direction, he
glowered at the crowd with a shaggy, upraised brow.
"That man risked his life to save your women and kids!
But like a bunch of simple-minded turds, all you can do
is moan about how much it's gonna cost you. Well, by
Christ, I've had it! Either you rustle up them horses
pronto, or I'm gonna send Britt back up there and tell
them Injuns they can just keep your goddamned
women. Now make up your minds fast and not another
word from any of you!"

The settlers suddenly found themselves unable to
look at one another, shamed to the marrow by Barry's
stinging rebuff. With hang-dog expressions they slowly
separated and silently drifted one by one toward the
stables where their horses were quartered. Within minutes they rode through the front gate, led by Allan and
Tom. Hunched against the blinding snow flurries, they
thundered along the river trail toward their homesteads, intent now on collecting every loose horse in
the Brazos valley.

Five

Britt walked the chestnut across the parade ground and
dismounted before headquarters. Since it would take
the homesteaders at least two hours to gather a horse
herd and return, he had ridden back to the hilltop to
reassure Running Dog that plans for the exchange were
well underway. While the Kiowa was growing increasingly wary of remaining in such an exposed position,
he was willing to honor Black Fox's word, even though
the *Negrito*'s manner clearly indicated that something

sinister had taken place within the fort. Running Dog
had already sent warriors to fetch wood from a grove
along the river, and when Britt arrived, he found the
hostages huddled around a small fire. Though they had
eaten and were relatively warm, their faces were taut
with strain, and their eyes beseeched him to bring this
miserable waiting to an end.

When Britt had mounted after talking with the captives, Running Dog cautioned him that time was growing short. While he could control the Kiowa braves
easily enough, he had no real authority over the Comanches, and he sensed that they were growing more
edgy with each passing moment. Wondering how in
God's name he would ever pull this exchange off without bloodshed of some sort, the black man spurred his
horse and headed back across the flats.

Entering headquarters, Britt found Captain Barry
seated before the fireplace, sipping a mug of coffee
laced with whiskey. Noting the grave concern written
across Britt's face, the officer rose wordlessly and fixed
a similar concoction for the black man. Only when they
were seated before the fire, with Britt staring vacantly
into the flames, did the burly Texan speak.

"You look like a man that's carrying a heavy load.
And I reckon I don't have to ask what's botherin' you."
Barry took a long swig from the mug, letting the liquid
fire sear its way down his gullet. Thinking, he watched
the spitting logs for a moment. "You know, Britt, it's
not easy for these rockheads to live with the idea that
a colored man has suddenly become the community
hero. It sorta goes against the grain for a white man to
think that a nig— What I mean to say is that a black has
got more balls than they ever thought about havin'.

Something like that sorta knocks the pins out from
under their high and mighty attitudes, and it's a mite
hard to swallow gracefully."

"Why don't you just come right out and say it,
Cap'n?" Britt's flashing eyes reflected the white heat
from the fire. "If it had been anybody but a *nigger*,
they'd have pinned a medal on him and started shoutin'
hallelujah the minute he rode through the gate."

Barry hunched forward in his chair and sighed heavily. "That's about the size of it, for a fact. Instead of being grateful they resent what you've done. It's not the
horses they worried about, mind you. Hell, a man can
always get more horses. They're just downright jealous
'cause you showed 'em up where guts count, and
there's no gettin' around it."

"So I'm just supposed to bow my head like a good lit-
tle darkey and let 'em sit around cackling about how
Allan's fool nigger let himself get flimflammed by the
Comanche."

"Well, I reckon you could clean house, if it'd make
you feel any better. Looks like that thick-headed mick
has already come over to your side. And I suppose with
you and Allan and Fitzpatrick standin' back to back, you
could probably whip the whole goddamned bunch."
Barry leaned back in his chair, and a malicious gleam
flickered in his eyes. "Just between you and me, most
of these homesteaders are a pack of conniving little
mouse farts. There's not a man among 'em with
strength of character enough to pull his pecker out of
a pail of lard."

Britt chuckled in spite of himself. Glancing around,
he saw Barry's face twist in a cynical, wolfish grin. "And

where do you stand, Cap'n? With the big, bad nigger or agin' him?"

"Son, I gave up on the human race a long time ago, black or white. You could fit the brains of mankind in a thimble and still have room left over for a team of mules." Stretching, he took the jug from a nearby table and sloshed a healthy portion into his mug. "I figure every man is entitled to fight his own fights, and so long as he don't crowd me, I'm willin' to let him kick whosever ass seems most handy."

"But what if he don't want to fight, Cap'n? What if he just wants to be left in peace and allowed to live his life with the little bit of dignity every man has comin'?"

"Britt, assumin' there is a good Lord, he didn't put man on this earth to live in peace. Whatever anybody ever got out of life worth havin', they had to fight for. And more'n likely kill too. Leastways, that's been my experience." Sipping at the whiskey, he regarded the black man with a curious gaze for a moment. "Course, it might just be that you haven't got as big a fight on your hands as you think. Offhand, I'd say that sooner or later most of the folks hereabouts will come around to thinkin' you're a pretty good man to have as a neighbor. Might be they'll never invite you to break bread at their table or ask you to join their church. Maybe they'll never even work up the guts to thank you for savin' their women and kids. But I've got an idea they'll eventually get around to admitting among themselves that you've got more balls than a billygoat."

Britt shook his head with disgust and looked back into the fire. "What you're saying is to bite my tongue and act humble and maybe someday—*just maybe*—

they'll treat me and my family with the respect we're due."

"No, that's not what I'm sayin'," Barry growled. Leaning forward, he spit in the fire and studied his thoughts as the flames consumed the juicy wad in an angry hiss. "You're a colored man livin' in a white man's world, and no matter how hard you try to change it, you're gonna have to live according to his rules. You can kiss white ass and scrub your hide with lye soap the rest of your life, but when it comes time to plant you in a box, you'll still be as black as the day you were born. I'm not sayin' it's right, mind you. I'm only sayin' it's the nature of the beast, and there's not a goddamned thing you can do to change it."

"So what it comes down to is that the meek don't inherit the earth after all."

"Only six feet of it," Barry snorted cynically.

"The strong fight the strong for the right to harness the meek to the plow." Britt's eyes glazed over with the fiery glow of the flames centered in his gaze. There was a long pause, and his next thought was spoken absently, as if to himself alone. "And if one of the strong just happens to be black, then the best he can hope for is to get killed clean, without sufferin' too much."

The grizzly officer studied his face for a still moment in time, searching the black man's stoic mask for some deeper meaning behind the enigmatic words. Finally he drew a long breath and drained the mug.

"Britt, if I was a bettin' man, I'd say right about now you're entertaining some notion of joinin' up with the Comanches or maybe the Kiowas." The black man flinched imperceptibly, and Barry saw that his shrewd guess had struck home. "Thought so. Now let me tell you something, son. I don't care no more for you than I do the next man. Just happens that I've got a bigger distaste for these turdheads that call themselves settlers. But I'm gonna give you some advice, and you'd better think on it real careful."

Tilting back in his chair, he paused for a moment and gazed at the ceiling, as if some distant vision was unfolding on its beamed surface. "Long before the maker meant for you to die, this land is gonna be knee-deep in dead Injuns. 'Cause the whites mean to own this country, even if they have to kill everything that walks, crawls, or slithers on its belly. And even if some of the redsticks do come out of it alive, they're gonna be herded onto reservations just like so many cattle, 'cept theys won't be fed nearly so well. It happened back East, and in the South, and it's gonna happen out here. No two ways about it. And if I was a man with a family, I'd think real careful before I put 'em in that kind of fix." Again he hesitated, watching Britt steadily. "You know, sometimes dying is the easiest part of all. Mostly it's the livin' that forces a man to find out what kind of grit he's got in his craw."

"Cap'n, you're a real soothing kinda man." Britt smiled shallowly, regarding the officer with a shake of his head. "Fellow could listen to you for a little while and discover his problems were really only beginning."

"Son, you just haven't got enough faith, that's your problem." Barry's booming laugh shook the room, and his chair slammed to the floor as he leaned forward to shake Britt by the shoulder. "Listen, you're not some broken-down sodbuster with a couple of mangy cows and a boil on your ass. You and Johnson have got a good thing going for you, and if I *was* a bettin' man, I'd just be willing to wager you two will outlast that whole goddamned bunch of bellyachin' shitkickers."

"Hallelujah!" the black man chortled sardonically. "The great day is comin', and all the black folks has got to do is shuffle along and wait till it's our turn at the trough. Cap'n, you may not think much of mankind, but I'm damned if you wouldn't of made one hell of a preacher."

Buck Barry grinned like a shaggy dog trailing a butcher's gut wagon and refilled their mugs with his own special brand of liquid fire.

Six

Some two hours later Allan and Tom led the settlers back through the main gate, driving before them a herd of forty-one horses. With the exception of the mounts they themselves rode, this pathetically small *remuda* represented every remaining horse from Elk Creek in the north to the scattered homesteads on the South Brazos. While the men no longer appeared openly hostile, they continued to grumble sullenly among themselves. For it was apparent to everyone concerned that the settlement would be sadly lacking in mounts for many months to come. Leaving the other men to hold the horses bunched on the parade ground, Allan, Tom, and Grady Bragg rode on to headquarters and were dismounting just as Britt and Captain Barry stepped onto the porch.

"Well, I'm glad to see you boys didn't have any trouble," Barry said heartily. "For a while there I was begin-

ning to think I'd have to pony up some of the government mounts."

"I wouldn't exactly say we didn't have any trouble,
Captain." Allan's voice sounded cheerless and somewhat pensive, like a minister who had just discovered
that his congregation was composed primarily of agnos-
tics and fornicators. "Some of the men took a bit of per-
suading after we left the fort. They're still of a mind
that we could surprise the Indians or else ambush them
after the exchange has been made."

Barry shook his head derisively and stared across the
compound at the settlers. "Don't surprise me none.
Like I've said before, most of 'em don't have sense
enough to pour piss out of a boot."

"Cap'n, for once you and me agree about somethin',"
Fitzpatrick said. "If I had my way, we'd knock a few
heads together and let 'em worry about loose teeth instead of that sorry bunch of broomtails. But Allan's got
some fool notion we've gotta convince 'em polite like,
so that everyone can live peaceful when this thing's
over."

"Well, it's not all that cut and dried, you know."
Grady Bragg's tone was skeptical, edged with a faint
trace of ambivalence. "These men have lost everything
they owned, and it's only natural they'd think Britt sold
'em down the river."

Bragg glanced apologetically at Britt, and the others
watched silently, waiting for the black man's reaction.
But Britt merely regarded the pudgy settler with an indifferent look, as if he were weary of jousting with
dimwitted fools. After a moment of strained silence the
tension passed.

"*Horseshit!*" Buck Barry's explosive growl shattered

the stillness. "Grady, the only thing wrong with your friends is that they can't work up any courage except what they get suckin' on a bottle. Not one of those weak-kneed bastards had the guts to go anywhere near the Red. And if it weren't for Britt, their women would still be gettin' forked by the Injuns! For my money, they're the biggest goddamned bunch of ingrates I ever heard tell of."

"Cap'n, you might well be right. It's not for me to say." Bragg ducked his head, scuffing the powdery snow with the toe of his boot. "All I know is they're sayin' that horses are gonna be scarce as snake tits around here for a long time to come. And they figure any white man with a lick of sense could've made a better deal for the hostages."

"Jesus Christ! Any man that thinks like that is nothin' but a double-distilled sonovabitch. There's not one man in that bunch that could've crossed the Red without losing his hair. And knowin' the Comanch, they'd have cut his tallywhacker off and crammed it down his throat like a stuffed goose. Britt, am I right or not?"

"I can't rightly say, Cap'n. I know it was just pure luck that I was able to pull it off. And if the Indians didn't love horses so much, they might've fried me to a crisp anyway. What they would've done to a white man probably wouldn't be pretty to watch."

"You're goddamn right it wouldn't!" Barry gave the three white men a withering look, and his lip curled in a vicious snarl. "I guess you and those scissorbill heroes out there aren't aware that Britt had to fight a Comanche brave as part of the bargain. He told me all about it while you were out fetchin' them horses. Wasn't really much, you understand. Just had a friendly little tug-of-war over a pit full of rattlesnakes."

The men were thunderstruck, almost as if the officer's revelation defied comprehension. Their mouths popped open with astonishment, and they gaped at Britt as if some curious black deity had suddenly materialized before their eyes. Except for a muttered oath from Fitzpatrick, they stared wordlessly at the black man, their faces a stunned caricature of awe and supreme respect.

"C'mon! I thought we had this settled before you left to get them horses, but I see now it's time for a little ass-kickin'." Before they could recover their wits, the grizzly officer struck out across the parade ground, and the four men hurried along to keep pace. Never slackening his stride, Barry marched toward the milling horse herd and came to a halt before the mounted settlers. Where they had been grumbling among themselves only moments before, they now fell silent, sensing that the commander's surly disposition had somehow darkened during their brief absence from the fort.

"I understand some of you big-talkin' heroes still aren't satisfied with the way this exchange has worked out," Barry roared angrily. "Well, you'd better listen close to what I've got to say, 'cause I'm gonna say it once, and there ain't a sonovabitch among you that'll ever get to hear it a second time.

"Britt Johnson was seriously thinkin' of leaving the settlement because of the shitty way you people have acted since he got back. 'Course, if it had been up to you swizzleguts, your women and kids would still be north of the Red, and you could go right on feelin' sorry for yourselves. But instead of thanking him, you get up on your high horse and act like you been

robbed. Well, Bragg and Fitzpatrick and Johnson have
got the whole story of what he went through to save
your kinfolks. And if you've got any decency left at all,
you'll go to the trouble to find out how he damn near
got killed just to pull this deal off."

Barry turned and regarded the black man with a spec-
ulative gaze for a moment, then glared back at the settlers. "I think I've talked Britt into staying here. Leastways,
I hope so. It's a damn cinch this settlement needs a man
with a little starch in his backbone. But regardless of what
he decides, there's one thing I want to make clear. If any
of you *good citizens* try givin' him a hard way to go, I'm
gonna lay you out colder'n a well digger's ass. And the
way I feel right now, I'd purely welcome the chance to
give you a sample of what I've got in mind."

Tom Fitzpatrick stepped forward, shoulder to shoulder
with the burly captain. His eyes glinted fiercely, and his
ruddy face had gone almost ashen with wrath. "By Jesus,
I second that motion! And if there's anything left over
when the cap'n gets through, I'll give you boys a taste of
the best knuckle sandwich this side of St. Louis."

"All right, I think we understand one another," Barry
said, fixing the settlers with a malignant stare. "Now
you men just hold those horses right here till I tell you
different. It's not that I don't trust you, you understand.
But I think we'll just let Britt and his friends drive the
herd on up to those Injuns."

Dismissing the settlers with a contemptuous look, he
turned and motioned for Britt to follow. Silently they
walked toward headquarters, trailed closely by Allan
and Tom. After a moment the black man glanced at
Barry uncertainly.

"Cap'n, I want to thank you for what you done, but I'm not real sure—"

"Son, let me tell you something. Just one last piece of advice and then you decide what you want to do. There's generally three secrets in every man's life, whether he's black, white, or candystriped. *What you tell others. What you tell yourself. And the truth.* Most men play it so close to the vest they never even get a look at the truth. But if a man's able to handle it, he's pretty certain of finding out that what's true for him is the best road to travel. Course, most times it's a damn sight easier taking the right trail than it is ownin' up to the truth."

Britt stopped dead in his tracks. The white man's words had eviscerated his soul as neatly as a surgeon's scalpel, and he was appalled by the sudden truth he saw laid bare. Buck Barry's features twisted in a wolfish grin, and he walked on, leaving the black man to stare after him through the icy caress of the snowflakes.

Seven

Running Dog stood alone at the edge of the hill, watching the silent fort. Within him stirred a deep uneasiness. While there was no sun to measure the time, he knew that a reasonable hour for the exchange had long since come and gone. Already the Comanches suspected a trap and were talking among themselves of returning north, lest the white-eyes again trick them in some devious manner. Though the Kiowa braves trusted his judgment, they were still alarmed by the prolonged waiting and might easily be swayed by the Comanches' fears. Should the warriors become disgruntled or decide the tejanos were planning some underhanded scheme, he very likely would be unable to prevent the wholesale slaughter of the captives.

Something strange was going on inside that fort, and even he was growing skeptical that the white-eyes would honor their word. *Waugh!* But was that indeed so strange, for had not the tejanos fouled their honor with broken promises more times than a wise man could count.

Still, they had gathered the horses, for with his own eyes he had seen them driven through the gate. But if the white-eyes intended to complete the exchange, why were they taking so long? *Why indeed?* It was a good question, one which a leader worthy of his warriors' trust should be asking himself. And at the moment he had no reasonable answer.

The snow flurries had not slackened since dawn, and as he gazed across the white stillness, Running Dog's concern was as much for Britt as the worsening situation. *What fate had befallen Black Fox at the hands of the white-eyes?*

Certainly when he came with assurance of the exchange earlier that morning, there was much he had left unsaid. Even a *pawsa* could see that the black man was troubled beyond measure. It was in his eyes, his dispirited manner, and even more apparent in his open reluctance to return to the stockade. Clearly something was gnawing on Black Fox's vitals, and whatever the cause, it was to be found in that fort.

Perhaps the tejanos had berated him for trading so many of their horses. But how could men, even white-eyes, covet horses more than their own women and children? Still, one never knew. The white devils' greed and lust for possession was a thing that could not be disputed. Many snows had passed since the tejanos came to this land, and the True People had good reason to know of their hunger for what belonged to others. Had not this very land upon which he stood once been the home of their fathers before them? And their fathers' fathers? But still the white-eyes had driven them into the wilderness.

His anger flared briefly, remembering again the countless indignities his people had endured while being driven from their sacred lands. But there were more immediate matters to be considered, and his thoughts turned once more to Britt's curious manner.

Somehow, in ways which defied understanding, Running Dog sensed that the black man was struggling with a bitter inner conflict. He couldn't have explained how he knew, nor for that matter, did he fully comprehend it himself. It was a thing of the spirit, an instinct or sudden truth that revealed itself inside a man's being. Most often it occurred among men who stood as brothers. There was some spiritual communion that passed between them, and without speaking one man suddenly found himself possessed of the thoughts of his brother.

And as sure as he believed that *Tai-me* saw every frail imperfection in a man's being, the Kiowa knew that Black Fox was trapped in an obscure limbo between the True People and the white-eyes.

Abruptly his reverie was broken as the gates of the fort swung open. Nerves taut, squinting through the falling snow, Running Dog saw Black Fox and two tejanos drive the horses from the stockade. With the black man on point they hazed the herd across the flats and brought them to a milling halt at the base of the hill.

Alerted by the commotion, both the warriors and the hostages joined Running Dog on the edge of the forward slope. In the distance they could see that the settlers had now crowded through the gate and were staring anxiously toward the hill.

Britt motioned for Allan and Tom to remain with the herd, then sent his chestnut plunging through the snowdrifts covering the steep slope. Moments later he reined to a halt before Running Dog and dismounted.

"*Hao*, brother." Britt's smile seemed forced, his voice strained. "I bring you a herd of fine horses for the True People."

"Black Fox is a man of his word. But it must be said that there is doubt among us concerning the white-eyes." Nodding toward the men huddled outside the fort, the Kiowa's meaning was clear. "Must we guard against the tejanos after the exchange, or will we be allowed to depart in peace?"

Glancing back at the knot of settlers, Britt's eyes seemed hollow and worn. "Have no fear, brother. The white-eyes' courage has been spent in loud talk and empty threats."

Running Dog regarded the black man for a moment, somehow filled with regret that his suspicions had been confirmed. "It was no less than we expected. *Waugh!* Let us cease this talk of men without honor and have done with our business. How is this exchange to be conducted?"

Without a word Britt turned and signaled with a sweeping motion of his arm. Allan and Tom immediately began popping their lariats, hazing the horses up the snowy hillside. Once they had the herd halfway up the slope, the two men reined about and returned to the base of the hill.

Leaping to their mounts, the warriors plunged down the slope, circling the herd with shrill, yipping cries. The waiting had ended, and the white-eyes' horses were theirs at last! Now they could return to their warm lodges and their waiting women and spend the winter basking in the esteem of their brothers. *For were they not the chosen few among the True People, the ones selected to perform this ultimate humiliation on the tejanos!*

Britt and Running Dog watched silently as the braves drove the horses over the hilltop and milled them on the reverse slope. Then the black man glanced at the hushed, shivering captives and back at Running Dog. The Kiowa nodded solemnly.

"All right, ladies," Britt said. "You're free, and your menfolks are waitin'. There's nothin' holding you here anymore."

The women looked at one another as if they couldn't believe their ordeal had finally ended. Then their voices lifted in a spontaneous clamor of relief and joy as they realized they were free at last. Jerking their children along behind them, the women broke into an awkward, shambling run down the slope. Screaming the names of their men, they fell repeatedly in the deep snow, only to rise and begin lurching once more toward the fort they had never again expected to see.

A hoarse roar from the settlers split the air, and they began running across the flats. Waving, shouting jubilantly, they raced over the snow-covered ground toward their women and children. Within moments the two groups converged on one another, and the blustery day was filled with the cries and screams of families re-united. Tears streamed down the faces of both men and women as they wildly embraced one another. Scooping their children up between them, they danced and whirled through the snow in a mad, abandoned fit of pure joy. Even the militiamen were caught up in the spirit of the moment, and the crowd quickly became a frenzied mob, surging back toward the fort in a swirling crush of tumultuous shouting.

From the hilltop Britt watched impassively. Beside him Running Dog looked on with detached amusement, as if he were observing a pack of hungry dogs chasing after the same bone. Mary and the children stood off to one side, staring intently at Britt. Seemingly oblivious to the exuberant mob on the flats below, they waited uncertainly to see where the black man would lead them.

Looking around, Britt's eyes had a wary, defeated cast to them. After a moment he nodded to Mary, indicating the fort with a jerk of his head. Silently she gathered the children and descended the hill.

The two men stood alone, each gripped with the same thoughts, yet unwilling to hear them put into words. The raw wind made their faces tingle with the icy snowflakes, and they stared grimly as the last of the settlers disappeared into the fort.

"It comes to me that Black Fox has made his choice." The Kiowa's remark brought Britt's head around. "Yet I wonder if the path he chooses will be one a warrior can follow."

"A man must be many things it seems." Britt's eyes returned to Mary and the children, watching silently as they trudged through the gate. "And not always can he take the path that he alone would choose."

Running Dog nodded, observing the direction of the black man's gaze. "Brother, you are a man who pursues things that were not meant to be. Among the white-eyes you have suffered much in the past, and it will be so again. Today you have done them a great service, and for this they are thankful. But the tejanos' friendship is like the winter snow; it melts away when the sun once more appears."

"What you say is true. No man has better reason to believe that it will happen just so." Remembering the settlers' anger that morning, he now felt compromised and disgusted with himself. "But each man has an obligation to something greater than his own small cravings. Do not we all bear the responsibility of easing the way for those who follow?"

"Perhaps. But only the *puhaket*, the gifted ones, can say what the future holds. You and I, we are simply mere men and must do what seems best at the moment." Running Dog paused, turning to look at the warriors who waited for him on the backside of the hill.

"For the Kiowa there is only one road." He made the sign of death, one palm erasing life from the other. "Even if the tomorrows of our children are rubbed out, we must fight the white-eyes."

"Maybe what is to come will be better than we think." Britt's words had the ring of hope, but his voice lacked conviction. "Perhaps one day we will all walk this land as brothers, without hate or war."

"On that day will the sun rise from the west, and the mouse attack the bear." The Kiowa's face was grim, and for a long moment he stared sadly around the bleak hilltop. "What a strange place for Black Fox to die."

"Am I to die, brother?"

"No, not you. The man lives on, but the soul of Black Fox is no more. When I return to the mountains, I will carry with me the name and his spirit. And over the campfires we will often speak of that great warrior who chose to remain a tejano *Negrito.*"

"Running Dog's words sound bitter, and for that I am sad."

"No, it is I who am saddened. For even though you will remain as my brother, I must kill you, should we meet again."

Britt's throat tightened, and without shame he felt a mist form over his eyes. "What you said this morning about there being no halfway things in this life. Must that also include two men who have learned to walk as brothers?"

"Are we gods, that we can hold ourselves above our own people? I think not. So it is that any man who follows the path of the white-eyes is an enemy." His voice broke, and he was unable to look at the black man. "Even a brother."

Then the Kiowa's mouth curled in a tight smile, and he clasped Britt's shoulder. "*Walk boldly among the tejano dogs, Black Fox.* Do not let them break you. I carry your spirit in my heart. But I will make sacrifices to *Tai-me* in the hope that we shall never meet again."

Without another word Running Dog bounded onto his pony and rode to join the waiting warriors. Never looking back, he led the party north, toward the Red and the True People.

Britt watched until the small band was swallowed from sight by the gusting flurries. Then he turned and walked slowly toward the fort.

⚡ CHAPTER SEVEN ⚡

One

Spring came early to Fort Belknap. Warm March winds and a bright Plains sun had melted the winter snows, and the stockade once again became a beehive of activity. Each morning wagons loaded with settlers rumbled through the front gate, churning along a river trail that had been reduced to an axle-deep quagmire of mud and slush. The heavily laden wagons gouged deep ruts in the soft earth, and in the beginning the daily trips to and from the homesteads had been agonizingly slow. But as the month progressed and the sun grew hotter, the Brazos trail had hardened to the flinty surface of uncut granite. Shortly, even the sloughy Plains had baked out firm, and as one day faded into another, the wagons lumbered over the jolting trail with ever greater speed. But more than one man crawled into bed each night with an aching spine, dreaming fondly of a time when the bone-rattling trip had been made astride a light-stepping cow pony.

The settlement was still desperately short of mounts, and every saddle horse in the community had been

pressed into service pulling wagons. Even then the settlers had to share the teams, and only after a week of
argument and shouting did Buck Barry grudgingly agree
to loan them some of the government mounts. Slowly
trees were felled and snaked back to the homesteads,
awaiting the day when each family had accumulated
sufficient logs for a cabin raising. The settlers' idle winter spent in the fort was now to cost them dearly. For
if cabins were to be erected and fields plowed in time
to make a crop, it would require a herculean effort on
the part of every man, woman and child.

But there were some, like the Johnsons and Tom
Fitzpatrick, who had worked through the winter to be
ready for spring. And on a bright, cloudless morning in
late March, Britt whistled cheerily as he set out for another day on Elm Creek.

Perched atop a rattling wagon held together with spit
and rawhide, the black man reined his team away from
the stables and headed toward the front gate. Watching
the chestnut strain into the traces saddened him, for the
spirited gelding had served him well, and he hated to see
it reduced to a common work horse. Still, everyone was
in the same predicament and doubtless shared his feelings about their own prized mounts. Maybe even more
so, since he was the one responsible for trading nearly
every horse in the settlement to the Indians. But that had
all been settled, neatly and with a gratifying sense of finality, and it was a thought that rarely troubled him these
days.

Rounding the corner of the headquarters building,
he heard his name called and turned to see Buck Barry
leaning against the door jamb of the orderly room.
Reining the team to a halt, he returned the greeting and

waited as Barry ambled toward the wagon with the peculiar shuffling gait of broad-beamed men and large,
surly bears. Since returning to the fort, Britt had grown
quite attached to the militia commander, which gave
him charter membership among a singularly small
group of settlers. Strangely enough, Barry had also gone
out of his way to cultivate the black man's trust and
genuinely seemed to enjoy the friendship that had ensued over the past two months.

At first he had thought the officer's warm manner
stemmed from the fact that he alone was responsible
for Britt's decision to remain with the settlement. But
after pondering the matter at some length, he concluded it was just as likely that Barry sought his company simply as another means of antagonizing the
settlers. While hardly a cynic, Britt was aware that men
offered their hand in friendship for a variety of reasons,
not all of which were apparent on the surface. Yet
there was something guileless and earnest about the
burly soldier's nature, and Britt had long since resolved
to follow Barry's lead. Whatever his motives, the black
man liked him, and for the moment that was enough.

"Mornin', Britt. Where's your pardners?" Barry
hawked, cleared his throat, and spat a wad of early
morning phlegm on the crusted earth.

"Oh, they'll be along shortly," Britt said, glancing
back at the barracks. "Probably havin' a last cup of coffee."

"Figures," Barry snorted. "Lay up on their dusty butts
till the faithful ole darkey gets the team hitched."

"Now, Cap'n, what makes you say a thing like that?"
The black man smiled and shook his head humorously.
"You know as well as I do that we take turns with the

team every morning. Sometimes you put me in mind of a man back home that used to tie cats' tails together just to see 'em fight."

"Well, seein' as how cats are sorta in short supply around here, I just have to make do with what's at hand."

"Damned if I don't believe you, Cap'n. I never saw a man so all-fired on knockin' people's heads together."

"Christ, man, it gets boring around here!" Barry snapped with mock disgust. " 'Specially since you and your sidekicks trimmed Ledbetter's wick." A malicious gleam flickered in his eyes. "That was just naturally a stemwinder. Damned if it wasn't. You boys pulled it off slicker'n greased owlshit."

Britt grinned, still curiously amazed after all these months that a man of Barry's enormous physical power would remain so taken with such a minor incident. Thinking back, it all seemed so meaningless and insignificant now.

After the elation of being reunited with their families had passed, the settlers again started grumbling about their lost horses. Gathered outside the barracks one evening after supper, they pretended not to notice that Britt was standing on the fringe of the crowd along with Allan and Tom. The first flush of again having someone to warm their beds had worn off, and they were dismally bored with the inactivity of the fort. While they vaguely remembered Captain Barry's warning that the subject of their horses was a closed issue, they needed something to relieve the tedium. And at the moment Allan's pet coon seemed the most handy topic.

Then Sam Ledbetter made the untimely mistake of re-

ferring to Britt as "that ignorant nigger." Before anyone
had time to catch their breath, Tom Fitzpatrick jumped
Ledbetter, and both men went down in a thrashing tan-
gle of fists and hoarse grunts. When the dust settled,
Ledbetter was out cold, and his aroused cronies started
closing in on Fitzpatrick. Shouldering their way
through the crowd, Britt and Allan stood back to back
with Tom, fully prepared to take on the entire settlement if it came to that. But the homesteaders suddenly
found the odds not to their liking, and the moment had
passed with nothing more deadly than an exchange of
insults and hollow threats.

Still groggy from the beating, Ledbetter was hauled
away by his friends, and the crowd wandered off to lick
their wounded pride. Since then life in the fort had become a little more pleasant for Britt, and much as everyone expected, there was no further discussion of
the horses. Not within hearing of Tom Fitzpatrick, at
any rate.

Buck Barry had roared with laughter upon hearing of
the brazen stand-off and in the next instant began huff-
ing like a sore-tailed bear because he had missed out on
the action. Watching him now, Britt could see the glint
in Barry's eyes and knew that the militiaman was still
miffed over having lost the chance to crack a few
skulls.

"Cap'n, what you oughta do is get yourself a bulldog.
Then you could sic him on the settlers' hounds every
mornin' and have enough fights going to keep things
from gettin' dull."

Barry chuckled, but then the smile faded, and he
grew thoughtful for a moment. "By God, Britt, that's
not a bad idea, even if you were joshin'. If those bas-

tards in Austin keep me posted here much longer, I believe I might just do that." Puzzling over how in the hell he could get a bulldog transported halfway across Texas, the officer glanced up to find Britt observing him with a wry smile. "Well, goddammit, it is a good idea! Now quit your smirkin' and tell me what's happening out on Elm Creek."

"Just pluggin' along day by day, Cap'n. With three of us workin', things are moving steady. Cabins should be finished in a couple of weeks, and I'd say we've got about half the cattle corralled already. Few more days of warm weather, and the ground oughta be about ripe for plowin', so takin' things as they come, I'd say we're sittin' pretty good."

"Hell, it's better'n good. You boys are showin' the rest of these lardasses what it's all about. Maybe when they see what a little honest sweat can do, they'll get up off their haunches and start humpin' it too. Leastways, they'd better, if they want to eat next winter." Barry suddenly stopped, as if a forgotten thought had crossed his mind. When he resumed, his tone was more serious. "Say, that reminds me of something I been meanin' to ask you. Someone's gonna have to make a trip to Weatherford for supplies damn soon, and I was kinda hopin' you boys would volunteer for the job. Since you're way ahead of the others, it wouldn't set you back too much, and I'd sure feel easier knowin' it was in good hands."

"Well, it's all right by me, Cap'n. Course, I'll have to talk it over with Allan and Tom. But I got an idea they wouldn't mind turnin' the wolf loose. It's been a long time since they bellied up to a real bar."

"That's the ticket. Talk it over with them today and

lemme know tonight. Way I've got it figured, someone's got to leave here within the week." Abruptly his thick brow knotted in a frown, and his face clouded over. "Say, there's something else I meant to tell you about. Not that it's what you'd rightly call good news. Folks have been tryin' to keep it hush-hush, but I got wind of it last night. Seems like Miz Claiborne is in a family way. Rumor is she's about four months gone, which means Claiborne is gonna be jigglin' a half-breed on his knee come next fall. Course, knowin' Ike, he's not above stickin' the little bastard in a towsack and droppin' him in the river."

Britt's eyes narrowed, and he studied Barry intently for a long moment. "Cap'n, I'd purely appreciate it if you'd pass along word that Mary and me would be real proud to have that baby if the Claibornes don't want it." He turned, lifting the reins, and then paused. When his gaze swung around again, it had gone cold as ice. "Just so there won't be no misunderstandin', you might let the right parties know that if that baby ends up in a sack, he's gonna have a lot of company on the trip downstream."

Clucking to the team, Britt popped the reins across their rumps and drove off toward the gate. Thoroughly baffled, Barry stared after him in astonishment, wondering how in the name of God a white man could ever hope to understand what went on inside a nigger's head.

Two

Brooks and stream overflowed their banks in a wild rampage of rushing water as the snows melted in the craggy fastness of the Wichita Mountains. The Snow Thaws Moon had come and gone, and still the angry waters cascaded down from the foreboding granite palisades. Seated in his lodge, Santana could hear the roaring turbulence of a brook which bordered the village, and he idly wondered when the waters would once again return to their clear, sparkling beauty. It had been a hard winter, ravaging the mountains time and again with violent storms, and food was growing scarce in the camp.

The True People were meat eaters, and many moons had passed since they last tasted fresh venison or buffalo liver generously sprinkled with gall. Even thinking of it made his mouth water, and the husky chief resolved that within the week he would have the Dog Soldiers organize the first spring hunt. But for the moment there were more weighty matters to consider. Reluctantly he wrested his thoughts from savory visions of a hump roast growing crisp and succulent over a slow fire.

Little Buffalo would arrive sometime today, and the village was bustling with excitement and anticipation of this great event. For the first time in memory one of the haughty Comanche warlords was lowering himself to visit a Kiowa camp, and speculation was rife as to the purpose of this unprecedented honor. Only three days past, messengers had galloped in from the north to announce that Little Buffalo was even then departing the Canadian and would reach the mountain stronghold two suns hence. While the runners had no knowledge of what lay behind the Comanche chieftain's visit, they did know that a matter of great consequence was afoot. Surely it must be so, they had answered Santana's brusque questioning, because Little Buffalo had sat in counsel with Ten Bears and the tribal elders almost constantly for the past fortnight.

While curious and thoroughly puzzled as to this strange turn of events, the elation Santana felt at this moment stemmed from another source entirely. Unlike the Bud Moon of one snow past, there was no contemptuous summons for the Kiowas to appear on the Canadian at an appointed time. Instead, the Comanche dog was coming *here* to parley. And in that simple fact lay a kernel of truth ripe with possibilities.

The arrogant Comanches would never lower themselves in this manner unless they wanted something badly and were willing to pay a stiff price to get it. Something had happened throughout the winter to humble the Comanches, and whatever it was, Santa smelled a situation in which an ambitious man might further his own cause greatly. Though his scheme to humiliate Little Buffalo at the hands of the tejano *Negrito* had surpassed even his wildest expectations, he found it difficult to believe that this alone would prompt such civilized behavior from the barbarian. No, there was something unseen here, a thing yet to be revealed, and he was determined to make the Comanche dog squirm a little while the full truth was being extracted.

Suddenly there was a great clamor from the northern edge of the camp, and within moments the villagers' shouts became mingled with the thud of many hooves.

Rising slowly, Santana carefully straightened his robe
and adjusted the ceremonial headpiece he wore. Waiting until the horsemen and swarming Kiowas came to
a halt outside, he drew himself erect and stepped
through the lodge entrance with an air of regal hauteur.
Before him were some thirty mounted braves, the war-
lord's personal janissaries, and leading them, seated
astride the spotted *ehkasunaro*, was Little Buffalo.
Head erect, Santana smiled.

"*Hao*, brother." Little Buffalo broke the strained silence, aware even as he did so that the Kiowa had
deftly maneuvered him into a subordinate position.

"*Hao, to-yop-ke.*" Santana smiled crookedly, allowing
the merest trace of insolence to creep into his voice.
"My lodge is yours. Dismount and let us serve you.
While the Kiowa food is humble, I have no doubt that
the *to-yop-ke*'s words will add spice to the meal."

Little Buffalo's eyes flared briefly, but without a word
he slid from the pinto and entered the lodge. After seating themselves around the fire, they spoke obliquely of
the winter and the spring thaw, while munching on
pemmican and stewed jerky. Santana had not even
bothered to kill a dog for the occasion, and the significance of this social oversight was not lost on Little Buffalo. Finally, with the meal finished and the nonsense of
the ceremonial pipe out of the way, the two old antagonists got down to business.

Fixing Santana with a stony gaze, the *to-yop-ke*
launched into the reason for his presence in a Kiowa
lodge. "Brother, the war between the white-eyes grows
broader each day. From the east we receive word that
there are many battles, each more deadly than any the
True People have ever witnessed. With every new bat-

tle more of the accursed ones are rubbed out, and there is reason to hope that they might exterminate one another in this strange war they pursue. And while they fight among themselves, they have no time for concern with the lands stolen from our fathers. So it is that the True People are once again handed the opportunity of driving the tejanos from our sacred hunting ground for all time."

"These words you speak are somehow familiar to my ears. Perhaps it is because I heard them even more eloquently stated on the Canadian only a short time ago." The Kiowa's tone was sardonic, laced with derision, and his eyes held firm under Little Buffalo's murderous glare. "Tell me, great *to-yop-ke*, do you *also* receive word from the Brazos?"

The Comanche's copper features blanched, and he struggled to hold his temper in check. Only after a long moment of deathly silence was he able to resume in a composed manner. "You pose a question which has clearly been answered by your own scouts. The tejanos are even now rebuilding their log lodges, and before the snow flies again, all will be as it was before."

"But what of our raid on the Brazos? Ten Bears and the Comanche counsel led us to believe that this great raid would rid us of the white-eyes throughout the tomorrows of our children." Santana's words dripped with scorn, and his tight grin was that of a wolf with its adversary at bay.

"Do not push me too far, Kiowa," Little Buffalo grated. "What the counsel said then is even more true now, and only a *pawsa* would fail to see that we must mount a raid of even greater magnitude in the days to come."

Santana shook his head sadly, as if listening to the tantrums of a small child. "Save your threats for those who would wilt before a strong wind, brother. Even the Comanche *to-yop-ke* would be ill-advised to test Santana's medicine."

Returning Little Buffalo's glowering look, the Kiowa chief contemptuously spat into the fire. "Now let us speak reasonably, with the wisdom our warriors have a right to expect from their leaders. The Brazos raid was an act of foolishness, a salve for the vanity of the Co-manche. We burned the tejanos' lodges to the ground and stripped them of their horses, and by your own words all of this has accomplished nothing. Would you mount another great raid so that we might sit here at the next Bud Moon and repeat these same hollow words?"

The *to-yop-ke* stared blankly at Santana with the look of one who has discovered too late that great schemes do not make great men. "I wish only to see the white-eyes rubbed out, and for this reason alone have I come seeking the Kiowas' support."

"Brother, you are a great warrior, and for this I honor you. But do not mock me with deceit. You lower your-self to enter a Kiowa village because the Brazos raid was a failure. And for no other reason! You knew that if you again summoned the Kiowa to the Canadian, you would still be waiting when *Tai-me* called on us all to cross over to the other life."

Little Buffalo remained quiet, unable to refute the Ki-owa's devastating logic, and a tense stillness settled over the lodge. Watching him, Santana found that vic-tory had about it the taste of ashes, a bitter, unsavory taste. Rather than gloating, as he had long dreamt of doing, he was curiously filled with compassion for this proud warrior who had been humbled by the shifting winds of fate.

"Hear my words, Little Buffalo. For I too live only to see the tejanos destroyed. But great raids with hundreds of warriors riding under one shield are not the way to save the tomorrows of the True People. Instead, we must strike in small bands in a *hundred different places* on the same day. The tejanos must never know a moment's peace, always fearful of when or where we will strike next. What they build we will burn, and when they rebuild it, we will burn it again. Soon their terror will mount, for we will be as their shadow, waiting only until their backs are turned to strike where least expected. And only in this way, my brother, will you and I live to see the white-eyes rubbed out."

The *to-yop-ke* nodded, staring blankly into the fire, as if the answer somehow lay secreted in the flames. When he spoke, his voice was muted, and his eyes seemed focused on far-away things. "Ten Bears counsels that we no longer fight the white-eyes. His visions reveal that they are as leaves on the trees, and even the strongest medicine known to the True People could never rub out all of them."

"Ten Bears is old and feeble, like a woman," the Kiowa spat. "We must fight to survive, or else the accursed ones will take *all*. Even this wilderness where we now sit is not beneath their greed!"

"What you say is true, brother. And while it pains me to admit it, your words have about them more wisdom than any I have heard on the Canadian." Little Buffalo paused, reflecting for a moment. When he spoke, his voice was firm but resigned. "I will return to the Comanche and counsel them to adopt the cunning of the Kiowa leader."

"Now you begin to touch on the secret, brother. Once you grasp *that*, you will indeed be the *to-yop-ke*!" The Comanche's baffled frown brought the wolfish grin back to Santana's face. "Cunning, brother. Cunning! The kind of cunning the tejano *Negrito* used when he rode alone through the True People's nation. Why else do you suppose I named him Black Fox?"

"Yes, I see your point. The *Negrito* was all you say and more. He was a warrior, like few among us, and before this is over we may wish we had more like him riding at our side."

"Do not trouble yourself with what might be, brother. A power greater than you and I or all the peoples on this earth long ago laid out what would come to pass. Black Fox followed the road that was ordained for him, just as the True People must take the path that has been clear from the start. We were born to live free, as men should, and if a warrior must cross over defending that freedom, then it is a good day to die."

Past differences forgotten, their old animosities cleansed in the harsh glare of truth, the two warriors hunched closer to the fire and began planning for the Leaf Moon raids on the tejanos. Outside, the gentle spring winds whispered in from the south, and the rushing mountain waters glistened beneath the calm brilliance of a prairie sky.

Three

False dawn spread across the land as stars slowly faded
from view overhead. Two wagons stood silhouetted in
the dim light near the front gate, and the jangle of the
teams' harnesses seemed muffled by the damp morning
stillness. Seven men were gathered alongside the lead
wagon, and four hipshot saddle horses stood ground,
reined nearby.

Nearly a fortnight had passed since Buck Barry first
mentioned the trip to Weatherford, and supplies in the
fort commissary were running dangerously low. After a
tally of the remaining provisions and a few moments of
deliberation, Barry had sent for Britt the night before
and informed him that the trip could be delayed no
longer. Anxious to see the cabins completed before undertaking such an extended journey, Britt had put off
day by day as the work progressed on Elm Creek. But
the commander's gruff tone left no room for argument,
and after a hurried conference it was decided that Britt
and Tom would leave for Weatherford at sunrise. Since
Allan was more skilled at carpentry, he was to remain
behind and hopefully would have the cabin interiors
finished by the time they returned.

Now the first shafts of light were spilling over the
eastern horizon, and the supply party was about to depart. Britt and Tom were to drive the wagons, accompanied by four militiamen, and there was a stir of
excitement in the air. The two homesteaders hadn't
been in a real town in close to two years, and while
Weatherford was hardly a metropolis, the prospect of
visiting the bustling Plains community had left them
slightly dazzled. For the soldiers the trip was even more

heady. Bored with a year's isolation in the fort, they looked on the whole affair as something akin to a Roman holiday, and at the moment they were the envy of every militiaman in the compound.

With his great shaggy head framed against the distant sunrise, Buck Barry looked from face to face as he studied the six men intently. "Boys, I don't have to tell you how important this mission is to everyone in the fort. We've got to have enough supplies to carry us over till the first crop, and we're dependin' on you to get back here with them wagons loaded to the gunnels."

"Cap'n, you jest rest easy." Digging his buddy in the ribs with his elbow, one of the militiamen winked and grinned broadly. "With us along there ain't nothin' gonna go wrong, and we'll be back here quicker'n a cricket dancin' acrost a hot stove."

"Lemme tell you squirrelheads something," Barry rumbled. "I tapped you four to go along 'cause I felt you was the least likely to desert. And don't think you've got me fooled! You swizzleguts are gonna try and drink Weatherford dry in one night, and I knew it before I even picked you. But if you give these men any trouble, I'm givin' them permission to clean your plow right on the spot. Understood?"

The soldiers suddenly became very interested in their boot tops and sheepishly ducked their heads. Barry glared at them for a moment longer, then turned to the two settlers. "Tom, you make sure them storekeepers understand that my requisitions are the same as gold in Austin, and if they give you any argument, be sure and telegraph the governor just like I told you. But even if you have to load them wagons at the point of a gun, I want you back here pronto. Now how long do you think it's gonna take for you to get there and back?"

"Well, Cap'n, I can't rightly say." Fitzpatrick was still the cocky, fiery-tempered Irishman, but over the past year he sobered considerably. Frowning he concentrated on the problem for a moment. "Near as I recollect, it's about seventy miles as the crow flies. Course, we'd do best to follow the Brazos down and cut east at Mineral Wells, so that adds considerable. With any luck at all, though, I calculate we'd make it back in seven, maybe eight days."

"How about it, Britt?" Barry looked at the black man with a trace of skepticism in his eye. "That sound anywhere close to you?"

"Cap'n, since you asked, I'd have to say it don't." Britt glanced at the Irishman with a faint smile, trying to soften his discord. "Gettin' there shouldn't take more'n four days. But these cow ponies aren't built for pullin' heavy loads, and I figure we're gonna have to give 'em a breather every now and then comin' back. Way I see it, you shouldn't look for us back in less than ten days. Course, like Tom says, with luck we might just beat that."

"No, by God, you're right!" Tom nodded in agreement, slightly nettled that these same thoughts hadn't occurred to him. Grinning at the black man, he shook his head with disgust. "Jesus, as many wagons as I've hitched around, you'd think I'd know that saddle horses ain't got the grit of a work team."

"Well, boys, I've never set much store in luck," Barry said, "so I'm gonna top you both and figure twelve days. Besides, it appears to me you forgot to allow time to shop around for horses. You know, next to gettin' those supplies, horses is the thing this settlement is gonna need the most."

Britt and Tom exchanged a quick glance, then turned back as the officer resumed. "Now there's one other thing I want to caution you about." Casting a dark scowl over his shoulder, he froze the four militiamen in their tracks. "And you meatheads better pay particular attention to this. We all know the Injuns are on the loose again, so you're gonna have to be mighty careful. It's been near on a week since Fort Richardson sent word that they're raidin' heavy over that way, and if a man's smart, he's got to figure they've drifted south by now. Lookin' at it dead center, that means there might just be more'n one war party between you and Weatherford."

"Damned if there's any way to figure an Injun!" Fitzpatrick grunted. "Last year they rode through here with half the redsticks God ever created, and now they're back to raidin' with small bunches again. Just goes to show that there ain't nothin' dumber than a stinkin' Injun!"

"Irish, you're ridin' with a man that has good reason to disagree with you on that score." Barry regarded Britt's silent nod of confirmation. "And when it comes to fightin', I'd be the last man to ever underestimate a Comanche."

"Don't forget the Kiowa," Britt added. "Nobody ever saw them carryin' water for the Comanches."

"Damned right!" Barry snorted. "They're both dangerous as hell. And smart. Appears to me like they reared back and looked the situation over and saw real quick that the raid last year just didn't get the job done. Unless I'm way wide of the mark, I'd say we're in for a summer of more goddamn raids than you ever heard tell of. They're gonna hit quick and often, and before a man's got time to thumb the hammer back, they're gonna be off down the road, burnin' some other poor bastard to the ground."

"Well, goddammit, let 'em come!" Tom growled. "I got a few scores to settle with the sonsabitches. There ain't nothin' that'd please me more than to lay my sights down on some of that red hide."

"Trouble is, most of that red hide shoots back." Britt smiled, but his tone was far from amused. "Somehow, I just wish we could get all this fightin' done with so we could start in with the livin'."

"Amen to that!" Barry agreed forcefully. "But standin' around gabbin' like a bunch of hens at a church social isn't gonna solve it. Time's awastin', boys! Let's get this show on the road and see how fast you can make it back here with that grub."

Without another word the militiamen mounted hurriedly, glad to be out from under the critical eye of their churlish commander. Britt and Tom scrambled aboard their wagons, and Barry signaled for the gates to be opened. Walking forward to Britt's wagon, the officer extended a ham-sized fist and gave the black man's hand a crunching squeeze.

"Britt, bring 'em back safe. There's a lot of people dependin' on this food. And I don't have to tell you that it won't hurt none to have folks beholden to you for takin' on another risky job they should be doing themselves."

The black man nodded solemnly, filled with pride that Barry would entrust him with this vital undertaking. Then it dawned on him, and he felt like a fool for

not having seen it from the start. This great bear of a
man had purposely selected him so that the settlers
would be even more in his debt! Suddenly he saw the
burly officer in a whole new light, and with it came the
pleasant awareness that his life was slowly being embraced by the respect and dignity he had always
sought. *Yessir, for a nigger in a white man's world he
was doing very well indeed!* Grinning widely, he
gripped Barry's hand with renewed zest.

"Cap'n, you just set your mind to rest. We'll be back
before you even know it." Popping the reins, he sent
the horses lurching into the traces. The wagon creaked
and groaned as it gained motion, and his laughing voice
drifted back over the compound. "Hey, Cap'n! You remember that bulldog we was discussin'? Well, keep a
sharp lookout. 'Cause if Weatherford's got anything that
even looks like a bulldog, he's gonna be sittin' right
here on this seat when we get back!"

Barry's broad jaw twisted in a huge smile as he
watched the wagon disappear through the gate. *A bulldog!* Goddamn, if anybody could figure a way to get a
bulldog, it was that big black buck with his flashing
grin!

Over the distant horizon a flaming orange ball slowly
crept skyward as the sentry swung the gates shut. Startled by a shrill, discordant sound he stared open-mouthed
as Captain Buck Barry strode across the parade ground,
whistling at the top of his lungs.

Four

The wagons rumbled across the vast, rolling Plains, moving steadily in a southeasterly direction. For two days they had followed a trail roughly paralleling the Brazos, and gradually the contours of the land had become more defined, lending shape and substance to the earth even from a distance. Buffalo clover and bluebonnets were beginning to bud farther south, and already the prairie grasses were growing lush and green beneath the warm spring sun. They had made good time, pushing the horses at a ground-consuming pace from sunrise to dusk with only a short break for a cold meal at noon.

Thinking about it, Britt saw no reason to revise his original estimate. He still felt confident they would reach Weatherford sometime before sundown on the fourth day. While the horses remained sullen and balky at being hitched to the rattling wagons each morning, they quickly settled into the task and actually moved along at a faster clip than a work team could have sustained. Watching their corded flanks as they strained up a small knoll, Britt silently wished that the caravan's escort was as willing and eager as the horses.

The four militiamen rode bunched like a covey of quail far to the side of the wagons. Unsure of themselves on the open Plains, they preferred to let Britt set the course, even though a blind man could hardly have strayed from the rushing waters of the Brazos. While Britt and Tom were covered with grit from the shuffling hooves of the horses, the soldiers craftily remained upwind, free from the dust and grime of the trail. Glancing at them from the corner of his eye, the black man decided they looked like four schoolboys out on a summer lark. Clowning around with one another, laughing uproariously at an endless string of ribald jokes, they seemed concerned with nothing more than enjoying their respite from Fort Belknap. And getting to the fleshpots in Weatherford as fast as possible.

Though Britt had only a slight grasp of military tactics, he was painfully familiar with the ways of Indians, and with each passing mile his concern had grown. Instead of riding together, the four men should be scouting ahead and to the flanks, with one of their number always posted as rear guard. As it was, they could be ambushed without warning at any time, with never a chance to corral the wagons and use them as a barricade. Bunched together, the militiamen provided a highly tempting target, and in the event the caravan was bushwhacked, Britt had no doubt they would go under with the first volley of rifle fire.

Last night he had subtly broached the subject with Tom, keenly aware that the soldiers would only sullen up if the suggestion came from a black man. But when Fitzpatrick attempted to discuss it with them that morning, they jokingly assured him there was nothing to worry about. *They'd been fightin' Comanches all their lives, and there was nothin' an Injun respected more than seein' a bunch of white men formed and ready to fight as a unit!* Glancing at Britt, Tom had shrugged his shoulders in a gesture of futility. Short of knocking their heads together, there was nothing more the Irishman could do, and the situation remained unchanged.

But Britt was far from content to let it lay, and as the day progressed, he alternately studied and discarded various means of forcing the militiamen to take their escort duties a bit more seriously. Mulling the matter over shortly after their midday break, his concentration was abruptly shattered as a rider topped a distant hogback and galloped toward them. Jerking the team to a halt, he grabbed his rifle and shouted a warning to the four outriders.

Instantly they came alert, nervously milling their mounts as they attempted to form a line and bring their weapons to bear. Closing on them at a rapid pace, the horseman began waving his hat frantically, and within a matter of moments it became clear that he wore the makeshift garb of the state militia. Britt lowered his rifle and watched with growing apprehension as the soldier reached the bottomland near the river and pounded toward them. No man in his right mind pushed a horse that hard on the Plains. Not unless he carried bad news or was running from Comanches. Then the rider was upon them, wrenching his horse on its haunches as he came to a halt in a swirling cloud of dust.

"Howdydo, cousins," he greeted them, clapping the battered hat back on his head. "You boys wouldn't by any chance be from Fort Belknap, would ya?"

"Well now, ain't you the smart one!" cracked one of the militiamen. "Friend, we're not only from Fort Belknap, we're doin' our damnedest to get shed of it as fast as these nags'll travel."

"Do tell!" The rider's face twisted in a limpid smirk, and he stared at them for a moment. "I don't recollect hearin' Belknap was that bad. Matter of fact, when you hear what I got to say, you might just get to figurin' it's a regular little oasis."

"Mister, I don't mean to cut you short," Britt spoke up. "But we're a mite pushed for time, and we've got a long ways to go."

"Sambo, I don't remember sayin' nothing' to you. Or maybe you're the *boss* of this outfit." Turning back to the militiamen, he winked. "How about it, cousins? Is Sambo here ramroddin' your desperate little expedition?"

"Soldier, this outfit ain't got no boss." Dismounting from the wagon, Fitzpatrick walked forward, and his pugnacious manner wiped the smirk from the rider's mouth. "Now if you got something to say, spit it out. Otherwise, gig that runt you're ridin' in the ass and be on about your business."

"Mister, if I was you, I'd be more careful about who I started badmouthin'. It just so happens I'm on official business, carryin' dispatches from Fort Richardson to the commander at Fort Belknap."

"Well goody-two-shoes for you," Fitzpatrick replied caustically. "Now that you've impressed us, why don't you just pony up the good news, and we'll be on our way."

"Good news! Sodbuster, you're in for a real surprise." The courier patted the pouch strapped to his belt and snickered. "You know what's in here? Just a little scrap of paper sayin' some Yankee general name of Grant has whupped the shit out of the Confederates at a place called Shiloh. That's all!"

There was a moment of stunned silence from the supply party as they digested the courier's announcement. Then the militiamen began mumbling among themselves, uncertain as to how this defeat would affect their status at Fort Belknap. But the war was like some distant impersonal calamity, a tragedy from history that had befallen those unfortunate enough to be in the wrong place at the wrong time. Like an earthquake or a tornado. And besides, who the hell ever heard of a place called Shiloh? Still, the news was sobering, and for a terrible instant the war suddenly seemed much too close for comfort.

"Say, you boys wouldn't have any drinkin' whiskey, would ya?" The rider's nasal twang now seemed like the grating of an iron file. "Cousins, I'm here to tell ya I haven't swallowed anything 'cept spit since yesterday mornin'."

Still absorbed with their own thoughts, the others seemed disinclined to answer, and Britt finally spoke up. "No, we been drinkin' river water for two days. Captain Barry sent us to Weatherford to get supplies."

"Just my luck," the courier grumbled. Glancing around the solemn faces, he suddenly brightened. "Hell, boys, don't let it get you down. It's only a war. And it ain't over yet. Not by a damn sight!" Then his squinched, ferret eyes took on a superior look, and his tone was that of a gossipy old crone. "But I'll let you in on a little secret, cousins. Hard times is comin'. The tide's turned, and 'fore long there's gonna be lots of rebs swearin' they never heard tell of Dixie or the bonny blue flag."

"What about Indians?" Britt inquired quietly. "We heard they've been raidin' pretty heavy over around Fort Richardson."

"Goddamn, Sambo, don't you talk to me about Injuns. I seen enough of 'em to last me two lifetimes. They been burnin' and scalpin' over our way like there ain't no tomorrow. And everything I seen since I left

the fort says real plain they're movin' south and west
'bout as fast as them stump-legged ponies they ride will
carry 'em."

"Comanche or Kiowa?" Britt asked.

"Hell, who knows." The courier spit and sent a skittish glance around the skyline as if the subject had
somehow touched an exposed nerve. "Bastards all look
alike to me. Never could tell one from another."

"Seems like I've heard some folks say that about niggers." Britt's voice was sardonic, and there wasn't a hint
of a smile on his face.

"Yeah, well, I'll tell you how it is, Sambo." The courier's eyes flicked nervously around the group, and he
somehow had the feeling it was time to move on. "Between here and Weatherford you might see a shitpot
full of Injuns, and on the other hand, you might not see
nothin'. But if I was you, I'd sleep awful light." He
paused for a moment, then his thin, weasel face broke
out in a crooked grin. "Well, cousins, guess I better
shag it. All them folks at Belknap must be pinin' away
for a bit of *good news*, and we sure don't wanna keep
'em waitin'."

Lifting his hat in mock salute, he swatted his horse
across the flanks and galloped west along the river trail.
Silently they watched until he disappeared over a rise,
and the air suddenly seemed strained, fraught with
some unseen danger. The militiamen's levity had vanished as abruptly as the courier, and the four men
looked at one another with a tense wariness that had
not been present before. Britt clucked to the team and
headed the wagon once more in a southeasterly direction. Grinning to himself, he felt a twitch of perverse
amusement as he observed the militiamen separate and

take up scouting positions at the four points of the
compass.

Five

Dusk had fallen as the supply party prepared to make
camp for the night in a grove of cottonwoods along the
Brazos. The militiamen were still edgy, nervously peering over their shoulders and jumping at the slightest
sound from the deepening twilight. Their jocular ban-
ter of the last two days had dwindled to a strained
watchfulness, as if they had suddenly decided that this
escort detail wasn't just a simple lark after all. Britt suggested they make a cold camp, pointedly adding that a
fire might easily attract the attention of any hostiles in
the vicinity. The four soldiers merely grunted in agreement and continued scanning the darkening shadows
for any sign of the dreaded Comanches.

When the horses had been picketed, they consumed
a hasty supper of jerky and hardtack, forgoing even the
small comfort of an afterdinner pipe. The flare of a
sulphurhead might just be their undoing, and as they
were each well aware, the scent of smoke carried far
on the soft night breezes. Afterward, they spread their
bedrolls near the wagons and settled down for a sleepless night. Staring into the inky stillness, filled with a
sense of their own vulnerability, they wondered what,
if anything, lurked beyond the fringe of darkness.

Britt had volunteered to stand the first watch, and after tossing fretfully in his blankets for a short time, Tom
decided to keep him company. Seated on the ground,
with their backs propped against a cottonwood, they

listened to the unseen sounds of night and conversed in low tones.

"Did you notice how them soldier boys changed their tune?" Tom chuckled silently. "Damned if they ain't mopin' around like a bunch of shoat pigs that just paid a visit to the cuttin' pen."

"They got good reason," Britt observed quietly. "Indians don't like nothin' better than to leave a white man with a stump instead of a tallywhacker. Maybe if we can keep 'em scared, they'll guard these wagons like they should of from the start."

"What did you make of that courier? Reckon things are as bad as he painted 'em to be?"

"Wouldn't surprise me none if they was worse," Britt said with easy confidence. "Allan's daddy always said nobody but a fool would start a fight with them Northerners, and I got an idea we're gonna see that old man's words come true with a vengeance."

"Well, I ain't much for tellin' the future, but it sure enough looks like he was right." Tom grew silent for a moment, pursuing some elusive thought. The rustling of the leaves overhead was distracting, but after a time the right words finally came to him. "Course, if the Yankees were to win, that'd shore make life easier for the colored folks. What I'm tryin' to say is that there wouldn't be no more slaves then. See what I mean? *Everybody'd be free.*"

"Yeah, they'd be free all right," Britt rasped. "But bein' free is one thing, and havin' white folks treat you like a human being is somethin' else again."

There was a long silence as Tom pondered the black man's words, and Britt sensed that he was tussling with some hidden conflict within himself. After a while the

Irishman sighed heavily and stared off into the night. "You know, sometimes I get real stumped thinkin' about you and me. I was reared up in a neck of the woods where colored folks wasn't no more than a good mule, and a white man just naturally knew he was better'n the blacks. I mean, it was like the arithmetic you learned in school. Two and two made four, and there wasn't no way of disputin' a simple fact. That's the way things had always been, and there wasn't nothin' on God's green earth gonna change it."

He broke off and the silence deepened again as he struggled to find just the right words for the thoughts crowding his mind. "Now you come along and knock a hole in everything I was taught. I may be a thickheaded mick, like Captain Barry says, but I ain't no damn fool. Ever day I see ways you're smarter'n me. Like figurin' how long this trip would take. We both stood off and looked at the same thing, but you saw somethin' in it I didn't. It's like that two and two business. There just ain't no way of disputin' a simple fact. And to put the frostin' on the cake, I finally come around to seein' that you're the first *real* friend I ever had." He paused, mulling over the deeper implications of his words. "It sorta puts a man to thinkin'. Maybe lots of things we was taught ain't the way it really is. Leastways, it ain't the way it should be."

"*Should be* and *is* don't always turn out to be the same thing." Britt glanced at the Irishman and shook his head ruefully. "Maybe we're tryin' to do something that nature never meant to happen. Just for instance, have you ever noticed that animals only mix with their own kind? When did you ever see a buffalo chummin' around with deer or cows takin' up with horses?" Abruptly he snorted with disgust.

"Christ, that sounds like somethin' old Sam Ledbetter would say. It's a puzzle for a fact. When I stop and think about it, I'm not real sure I understand the way things should be either. But I do know that people are smarter'n animals, and damned if it don't seem like we oughta be able to figure out some way to live together."

They both pondered the problem for a moment, then the black man resumed on a brighter note. "You know, it's not like it's never been done before. Just look at us. I got you and Allan for friends and maybe even a few more. Stop and think what it'd be like if every nigger on this earth had two white men for friends. Why, in no time at all people'd forget about black and white and just get down to the business of livin' and let live."

"See, that's what I meant!" Tom's voice was filled with mild awe. "Jesus, a notion like that wouldn't of come into my head if I'd live to be a hundred."

"Maybe a man's gotta spend his life with his face squashed down in the muck before he gets thoughts like that."

"Could be. I can't rightly say. But I'll tell you one thing, Britt. You're wrong about people. I've seen my share and more, some of 'em are double wolf for guts and savvy. But most of 'em are just plain assholes."

Britt chuckled quietly. "You won't get no argument on that."

Tom smiled, suddenly filled with a sense of well-being, and glad that he had this soft-spoken black man as his friend. Then he thought back to the day Britt had returned his son to the fort, and with the thought came a nagging question that had bothered him ever since.

Reluctant to pry, he regarded the dim outline of his friend's face for a moment, then blurted it out.

"You know, there's somethin' that's had me in a quandary ever since you come back to the fort. Now I know it's none of my business, and if you feel like it, just tell me to shut my damn-fool mouth. But it'd purely settle my mind if I was to know the answer." Faltering, he felt the black man's eyes even in the dark and fumbled for the right words. "Well, goddammit, there just ain't no other way to say it. Captain Barry the same as told us you was meanin' to join up with the Injuns, and I'd just like to know why you didn't."

Britt stared at him for a long while, almost as if he were searching for a way to explain something that he himself had never fully understood. Finally, just when Tom had decided that the black man didn't intend to answer, Britt spoke up in a voice that was somehow eerie and illusive, like a risen ghost from a man's distant past.

"I guess that's what I really meant when I was talkin' about how animals stick with their own kind. Right or wrong, the whites are travelin' the road I want my kids to take. Maybe it's like the sparrow tryin' to join up with the hawks, I don't know. The way things are today, the white folks think the black man's the wrong color to fit in, and maybe there's nothin' that'll ever change their minds. But a man's got to have faith, otherwise he's no different than things that never learned to walk on their hind legs. And somewhere along the line he's got to have enough belief in his faith to make a start. I suppose that's what it all boils down to. Faith and belief that people really can change. Maybe not today or even next year but sometime. Sometime soon."

Tom stared at him, dumbstruck. He knew all about faith in the Good Book, and the kind of faith the fire and brimstone preachers ranted about. But this was something different. A faith in man's essential goodness. And that was a thing he had never even considered, much less credited to the shiftless, scheming blood-suckers he had known all his life. Watching Britt, he hoped that things could change, that men somehow could rise above the hateful ways they had been taught. But just in the event they couldn't, he silently resolved to beat the shit out of anyone who even looked like they were going to give the black man a hard time.

Six

Early in the afternoon, with the sun directly overhead, the supply detail halted at a tree-fringed clearing to water the animals and wolf down a quick meal. This was their third day on the trail, and without voicing it, each man felt the urgency of reaching Weatherford as rapidly as possible. Their chance meeting with the courier had occurred only yesterday, but his words lingered on. The warning was clear, and it had brought home the highly dangerous nature of a mission they had undertaken so lightly. Roving across the countryside were bands of hostiles who would like nothing better than to catch six men exposed and helpless on the open Plains. Captain Barry's terse warning had now become very real and threatening, and not a man among them doubted the menace they faced. While the likelihood of stumbling across a war party in this vast land was remote, many a man had sacrificed his life needlessly by scorning the capricious bitch called fate.

And right now their only thought was to reach the sanctuary of an organized settlement, just as fast as their horses could be pushed.

With any luck they should hit Mineral Wells tonight, and by the following evening sight Weatherford. But they still faced close to forty miles of exposed prairie, and since dawn there had been few smiles and even less conversation among the six men.

The day had been unseasonably warm, and the four militiamen appeared drowsy and somewhat fatigued. The tension curdled in their guts, along with a sleepless night, had drained their spirits and left them sapped of energy. Dismounting, they led their horses to the riverbank, then began splashing their own faces with the cool, invigorating waters of the Brazos.

Britt and Tom drove the wagons directly to the water's edge and let the horses begin swizzling greedily. They had no intention of unhitching the teams and allowing them to graze as they had done the last few days. This was to be a brief stop, limited to the essentials of watering and a few mouthfuls of food, and afterward they would again take to the trail with the utmost speed.

Britt jumped from the wagon and walked a few paces upstream. Kneeling, he dipped his hands in the rushing stream and brought them up to his parched lips. Sloshing the water around in his mouth, he felt the dust and grit loosen its hold on his throat and spat with an immense feeling of relief. Tom had hunkered down beside him and was noisily sloshing water over his entire head. Spewing and sputtering like a red-thatched whale, he then leaned forward and thrust his face into the cooling waters. Watching him, it occurred to Britt that the Irishman was really an overgrown boy, taking his pleasures from the simple things of life, as carefree as a yearling colt in a field of clover. Maybe they hadn't hit it off at first, but Tom had become a good friend, as good as any Britt had. And the black man somehow felt deeply grateful that this thickheaded mick had come over to his camp at last.

Suddenly Britt tensed, alert to some unseen danger. Instinctively wary and somewhat puzzled as to the cause, he glanced around the shaded glen. Something wasn't right, but as his eyes darted around the clearing, everything appeared calm and still. Maybe too still. Then the horses spooked, their eyes wide with fright. Rearing away from the water, they scrambled backward, jackknifing the wagons wheel to wheel in a splintering crash.

Springing toward the horses, the black man caught a glint of movement from the corner of his eye and halted in midstride. Looking downstream he saw one of the militiamen lurch forward with an arrow protruding from his chest. Grunting with pain, the soldier grasped the shaft with both hands, staring in horror as the blood gushed down over his arms. Then he pitched face down in the water and floated off with the current.

Stunned by the suddenness of the attack, the men seemed frozen in their tracks as they watched the soldier die. Before they could react, the trees on the opposite side of the stream exploded with gunfire and a shower of arrows. The horses screamed and reared, digging furiously with their hooves as they whirled up the slight incline leading to the bank. Desperately the militiamen fought to control their mounts, clutching the reins tightly in a vain effort to stop the horses from stampeding. Clawing pistols from their holsters, the soldiers jerked at the reins while firing blindly at the trees across the river. But the plunging horses spoiled their aim, and the slugs harmlessly kicked up geysers of water in midstream.

While the militiamen cursed their horses and thumbed off shots at an unseen enemy, Britt and Tom sprinted forward in a running crouch and dove headlong under the nearest wagon. Though terrified and still fighting at the traces, the two teams were unable to move as the rear wheels of both wagons were now locked in a grinding embrace. Slithering on their bellies, the men crawled to a position between the wagons and jerked their six-guns. Peering through the spokes of the wheels, their gaze swept back to the riverbank just in time to see the soldiers play out the final act in futile courage.

Realizing too late that they couldn't save both themselves and their mounts, the three militiamen released the horses and began backing toward the wagons. Britt and Tom watched helplessly as the men advanced step by step, firing bravely as they moved in a huddled bunch across the open ground. Then the opposite treeline erupted in a fusillade of rifle fire and gleaming feathered shafts, raking the clearing with an invisible hail of death. The three men spun backward, their clothes pocked by the dusty spurts of lead, arrows jutting cruelly from their torn bodies. As if a giant scythe had swept over a field of wheat, the men fell before the bloody storm and pitched to the ground.

Britt stared at the shattered bodies in an agonized

trance, unable to believe that four men had been
brought to death in only a matter of moments. Somehow it didn't seem real, as if he were merely a spectator at some grim ritual that would abruptly end with a
burst of applause. Every muscle in his body strained as
he waited for the men to rise, willed them to stand
again. But their lifeless forms lay unmoving, crumpled
in the impersonal savagery of death, and he knew then
that it was absolute. Blinking, his senses slowly returned and he became aware of Tom's hoarse muttering
beside him.

The Irishman's eyes were wild with rage, bulging
from their sockets, shot through with red, swollen
veins. From his throat came a dry, deathlike rattle as his
lips moved soundlessly, and his face was contorted
with the horror of a man who has looked into the pits
of hell and come away demented. Leaping to his feet,
he scrambled from the ground, clawing his way up the
side of the wagon, screaming with crazed, maddened
fury.

*"You murderin' sonsabitches! Come on out and
fight like men! Where are you? Stand up and fight,
you yellow bastards!"*

Startled by the Irishman's frenzied actions, Britt
moved too late to drag him from atop the wagon. The
crack of a single rifle shot split the air, and Tom staggered, mortally wounded. Slowly he fell away from the
wheel and dropped between the wagons in a sodden
lump.

Britt grabbed his shirt and dragged him underneath
the wagon, searching frantically for some sign of life.
The Irishman's breathing was labored and shallow, and
a dark, crimson blotch covered his chest. Working fe-

verishly, the black man ripped his shirt open and stared
sickenly as a small, neat hole beneath the breastbone
pumped a bright fountain of blood. Tearing a strip from
the shirt, he jammed it against the wound, trying desperately to staunch the bubbling hole. But even as he
did so, he knew that Tom was dying. Numb with grief,
he stared on helplessly as the Irishman's life spurted
out beneath his hand.

Then Tom's eyes slowly opened and focused on the
black man with glazed brightness. His arm raised ever
so gradually, as if he had all the time in the world, and
his rough, thorny hand clasped Britt gently around the
neck. "I wish I'd been born a nigger. Couldn't we've
had fun?"

He chuckled, as though the thought pleased him
greatly, and a thin trickle of blood seeped from his lips.
Then he closed his eyes and died.

Britt stared vacantly at his dead friend, overcome
with a shuddering sense of loss. Tears streamed down
his face, and his breath came in great, sobbing gasps, as
if a steel band was constricting ever tighter around his
chest. The pallor of death had settled over the Irishman's features, but his mouth was frozen in a gentle
smile, and Britt unconsciously found himself returning
the smile. Tom had greeted death with the same cocky
devilishness with which he had faced life, and the black
man somehow felt proud that he had passed over with
his swaggering spirit intact. Still, his own life was diminished beyond measure by his comrade's abrupt end,
and a sour bile swelled in his throat as he once again
heard the Irishman's jaunty words. *Couldn't we've had
fun?*

Bit by bit, Britt's mind emerged from the brutal funk

of his despair, and he slowly became aware that a deep, unnatural stillness had settled over the clearing. There was something abnormal and strangely eerie about the silence, as though the ghosts of the dead had taken with them every creature and sound from the grove of cottonwoods. Crawling forward to the front of the wagon, he cautiously scanned the riverbank. Then his eyes were drawn to the opposite shore, and he sucked in his breath with the wheezing gasp of a man who had been kicked in the pit of the stomach.

Crowding the far bank, eleven Kiowas sat mounted on ponies, their war paint and garishly decorated shields glistening in the bright spring sun. Motionless, they waited in the deepening silence, staring with grim, patient eyes at the wagons. Britt's startled gaze darted from face to face, recognizing each in turn as warriors from Santana's village. Then he grunted with shock as his eyes locked incredulously on the stern, tight-lipped visage he remembered so well. *Running Dog!*

Cursing beneath his breath, he damned the gods, *Tai-me* and Jehovah alike, for amusing themselves with a deadly little game between mere mortals. Wherever they sat in judgment, it must be a festive day indeed, for what better sport than to pit brother against brother in the ultimate test? How very fickle they were with men's lives, looking on with detached smiles as they snuffed out a man like a mindless child squashing a beetle. *What a joke! A filthy, rotten, bastardly joke that could have only one end.*

Crawling from beneath the wagon, Britt stepped a few paces into the clearing, vaguely aware that he still clutched the Colt in his right hand. Holstering the pis-

tol, he faced the Kiowas and waited for some sign of
how this thing was to be done. Their features were
cold, remote, as if they were observing a white-eye
who by some quirk of fate happened to be black. Their
manner made it clear that no quarter would be granted,
and Britt smiled thinly in admiration. They were the Kiowa, the True People, and he really hadn't expected
any less.

Then the black man raised his arm in salute. "*Hao*,
Running Dog! It appears that *Tai-me* sees fit to bring us
together one last time."

The Kiowa regarded him stoically, but beneath the
dull sheen of his eyes there was an infinite sadness.
Within him coursed the bittersweet sense of pride and
dismal sorrow. How fine and brave Black Fox looked
standing there! Straight and tall, alone but unafraid,
flaunting his courage as a warrior should when he
crossed over. Somewhere on the other side they would
meet again, and *Tai-me* in his wisdom would at last allow all men to walk side by side in peace.

"Make your fight, brother," Running Dog ordered. "It
is a good day to die!"

Understandingly, Britt nodded, certain now that Running Dog had instructed the other warriors on how it
was to be. The Kiowa meant for Britt to kill him so that
they might cross over together. And only after the black
man's shot had struck home were the remaining warriors to open fire.

Drawing his Colt, Britt raised the pistol and sighted
on Running Dog. Then with an imperceptible movement of his wrist he lowered the sights and fired. The
slug kicked up a spurt of sand at the hooves of Running

Dog's pony, and in that same instant came the whispered twang of a bow string.

The black man lurched backward, his chest pierced by the feathered shaft, and slowly sank to his knees. Running Dog looked on without expression, more proud than ever that Black Fox had ridden with him as a brother. Yet while he was unwilling to be the instrument of the black man's death, he was equally unable to halt the inevitable.

Gritting his teeth, Britt fought against the swirling darkness of pain and willed himself to stand erect. Thrusting the Colt to arm's length, he steadied himself and fired blindly into space. With the report of the pistol a rifle exploded on the opposite bank, and a puff of dust leaped from his shirt front. He staggered, releasing his grip on the gun, and like a giant tree torn from its roots, toppled to the earth.

Silence once more settled over the clearing, and the Kiowa braves watched impassively to see if Black Fox would rise again. But it was over, and there was no need for further waiting. Running Dog gave the signal, and the warriors kneed their ponies into the water, whooping shrill war cries of victory as they splashed across the river. Leaping from the ponies, they swarmed around Tom and the fallen soldiers, their scalping knives glinting in the shining rays of the sun.

Running Dog slid to the ground and stood for a moment looking down on Britt. Kneeling, he jerked the arrow free and gathered the black man in his arms. Struggling under the weight, he carried the body to the riverbank, near a clump of trees. Lowering the great frame gently, he propped the black man against a towering cottonwood. Working swiftly, he tugged and

pulled until he had the body sitting in an upright position, carefully arranging it so that it wouldn't fall over.
Walking back to the wagon, he collected Britt's rifle
and returned to the tree. Checking to make sure the
gun was loaded, he placed it across the black man's lap,
then stood back to observe his handiwork.

Approaching, one of the braves grinned broadly, dis-
playing a curly, burnished gold scalp. Running Dog ignored the gory trophy, and sensing his mood, the
warrior's grin vanished. Looking at the body, he studied
it solemnly for a moment, then glanced back at Running Dog. Nodding his approval, he grunted with deep
respect. "Only the earth endures forever, brother. Black
Fox died a good death."

"*Waugh!* He was a warrior!" Running Dog grated.
"And there are not many of us left."

Having bestowed the final epitaph on his friend, Running Dog abruptly strode to his pony and mounted.
This was the signal for the braves to have done with
scalping and plunder, and within moments he led the
war party back across the stream. Halting on the opposite bank, he wheeled his pony and stared back at the
body for a moment. Then his arm raised in salute, and
his voice boomed proudly across the glen. *"Hao, Black
Fox!"*

The sun rippled fleetingly on the shining water, and
the man called Britt Johnson gazed peacefully upon the
tranquil solitude of the cottonwood grove.

Black Fox had crossed over at last.

Outlaw Kingdom

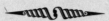

Praise for Matt Braun and
OUTLAW KINGDOM:

"Matt Braun brings back the flavor of early Oklahoma and the grit of the men who brought law to an outlaw territory. He is a master storyteller of frontier history."   —Elmer Kelton

"In OUTLAW KINGDOM I once again see the unique talent that placed Matt Braun head-and-shoulders above all the rest who would attempt to bring the gunmen of the Old West to life. In place of the laconic, two-dimensional gunslinger of Hollywood and so much pulp fiction today, Braun has given us his Bill Tilghman— a man of flesh and bone, blood and sinew, a man we can see ourselves joining as he walks down those dusty streets of Oklahoma Territory."

—Terry Johnston, author of the Plainsmen series

"Matt Braun is just as fearless as the man of the West he brings to life in his novel, OUTLAW KINGDOM. Braun tackles the big men, the complex personalities of those brave few who were pivotal in the settling of an untamed frontier. OUTLAW KINGDOM is an indelible portrait of a hard man living in dangerous times who was also a compassionate human being. I think old Bill would have said what I feel after reading this novel: 'He told it straight—and he told it well.' "   —Jory Sherman, author of *Grass Kingdom*

"In OUTLAW KINGDOM, a mighty novel of Oklahoma in the Land Rush days, Matt Braun has brought back to life that sadly and inexplicably forgotten lawman Bill Tilghman. Braun is an Oklahoman and he has a deep knowledge and appreciation of the territorial history of his state. He has depicted splendidly the era when the Doolin gang made Oklahoma a killing ground and when Bill Tilghman stood for law in a lawless land."   —Dale Walker

"Braun blends historical fact and ingenious fiction . . . A top-drawer Western novelist!"—Robert L. Gale, Western Biographer

"Braun gives human depth and a poignant love to mythic Bill Tilghman, the West's most admirable lawman."
—Jeanne Williams, author of *A Lady Bought with Rifles*

"Matt Braun has a genius for taking real characters out of the Old West and giving them flesh-and-blood immediacy."
—Dee Brown, author of *Bury My Heart at Wounded Knee*

To
Kim and Tracey
Jesseca and Eric
Who give the world special meaning
and, as always,
to Bettiane

AUTHOR'S NOTE

Outlaw Kingdom is based on a true story. Bill Tilghman was the prototype for the mythical gunfighter-marshal of Old West legend. Yet there was nothing mythical about Tilghman, or his exploits as a lawman on the frontier. He was the real thing.

Bill Tilghman's life on the plains spanned a time from the buffalo hunters to the oil boomtowns. His career as a lawman encompassed fifty years, ending in 1924 when he was the age of seventy. During successive eras, he served as deputy sheriff, town marshal, deputy U.S. marshal, sheriff, and chief of police. None of the lawmen fabled in Western myth—including Wild Bill Hickok, Bat Masterson, and Wyatt Earp—came close to matching his record. He was without equal among men who wore a badge.

Outlaw Kingdom deals with one era in the lifetime of Bill Tilghman. The great Land Rush of 1889 opened parts of Indian Territory to settlement, and resulted in the creation of Oklahoma Territory. Those early days of settlement gave rise to outlaw gangs who robbed and pillaged on a scale unmatched in the annals of crime. Oklahoma Territory became a battleground where deputy U.S. marshals fought a bloody and vicious war against marauding gangs. In a literal sense, the land became a killing ground.

During the era of the outlaw gangs, Bill Tilghman performed valiant service as a deputy U.S. marshal. In telling his story, fact is presented in the form of fiction, and certain license is taken with time, dates, and events. Yet there is underlying truth to the daring and courage of a man whose exploits were the stuff of legend. His record as a lawman needs no exaggeration, and his dedication to taming a raw frontier stands in a class all its own. His days on the killing ground of Oklahoma Territory were, in a very real sense, larger than life.

William Matthew Tilghman was the last of a breed. To friend and foe alike, he was known simply as Bill Tilghman, and the name alone struck fear in those who lived by the gun. Determined and deadly, sworn to uphold the law, he was a man of valor.

PART ONE

CHAPTER 1

A sea of campfires spread endlessly across the plains. Forty thousand people camping under a star-studded sky waited for the Oklahoma Land Rush.

Tilghman stood with his hands jammed in the pockets of his mackinaw. Though a brisk wind drifted down from the north, his coat was unbuttoned, and his gaze swept an inky darkness dotted with tongues of flame. His camp was located near the train tracks, and as far as the eye could see, the shadows of men were cast against the glow from thousands of campfires. Like him, they stared southward, awaiting the break of dawn.

"What're you thinking about, Bill?"

Tilghman turned to face Fred Sutton. Old friends, they were partners in certain ventures revolving around the land rush. Sutton had operated a saloon and gambling establishment in Dodge City, where Tilghman had served as town marshal.

"Way it appears," Tilghman said, "lots of folks are gonna get the short end. I calculate more people"—he motioned toward the blinking campfires—"than there are homesteads."

Sutton nodded, looking out over the mass of humanity. He was a man of medium height, square-faced and clean-shaven, a greatcoat thrown over his shoulders. He held his hands out to the warmth of the fire.

"Same old story," he said with a wry smile. "Offer something for nothing and the world beats a path to your door. Simple human nature."

"No argument there," Tilghman agreed. "Everybody and his dog turned out for this one."

Their camp was on the line separating the Cherokee Outlet from the Unassigned Lands. Tomorrow, for the first time, land would be opened to settlement in Indian Territory. By government decree, a man could claim one hundred sixty acres for a nominal filing fee. The lodestone of free land had drawn eager homesteaders from coast to coast.

Tilghman wagged his head. "Figures to be devil take the hindmost. Ought to be a helluva race."

At root was the scarcity of good farmland. The flood of settlers pouring west had already claimed the choice homestead lands; the clamor to open Indian Territory to settlement had swelled to a public outcry as western migration intensified. The primary goal of this land-hungry horde was known as the Unassigned Lands.

Embracing some two million acres of well-watered, fertile plains, it was land that had been ceded by the Creeks and Seminoles, as a home for tribes yet to be resettled. But the government eventually announced that it had no intention of locating Indians on these lands. The howls of white settlers then rose to a fever pitch, and their demands now included the Cherokee Outlet, which abutted the northern border of the Unassigned Lands.

The settlers were backed by several influential factions, all of whom had a vested interest in the western expansion. Already the Santa Fe and other railroads had crossed through Indian Territory, and competing lines had no intention of being left behind. Pressure mounted in Washington for a solution, equitable or otherwise, to the problem.

Opposed to settlement were the Five Civilized Tribes, who occupied the eastern half of Indian Territory, and a diverse group of religious organizations. The churches and missionary societies asserted that government dealings with Indians formed a chain of broken pledges and unfulfilled treaties. In that, the Five Civilized Tribes agreed vehemently. They had ceded the western part of their domain to provide other tribes with a home—not for the enrichment of white farmers and greedy politicians.

Tilghman took the pragmatic view. While serving as marshal of Dodge City, he had watched the Indians fight what was clearly a losing battle. At the forefront of the struggle was Captain David Payne. A drifter and ne'er-do-well, Payne had served briefly in the Kansas militia and the territorial legislature. Yet he was a zealot of sorts, and in the settlement of Indian lands he had at last found his cause.

Advertising widely, Payne made fiery speeches exhorting the people to action, and gradually organized a colony of settlers. Every six months or so he'd led his scruffy band of fanatics into the Unassigned Lands, and just as regularly, the army ejected them. After several such invasions, each of which was a spectacular failure, Payne's followers had become known as the Boomers. They were said to be *booming* the settlement of Indian Territory.

Though saner men deplored his tactics, Payne wasn't alone in the fight. Railroads and politicians and merchant princes, all with their own axes to grind, had rallied to the cause. That they were using the Boomers to their own ends was patently obvious. But Payne and his rabble scarcely seemed to care. Frustrated martyrs in a holy quest, they would have joined hands with the devil himself to break the deadlock.

Tilghman's woolgathering was broken by the sound of curses and shouts. Several camps down, where a fire blazed beside an overloaded wagon, two men squared off with knives. A crowd had formed a circle around them, goading the men on with guttural murmurs. Fights were common, fueled by liquor and building tension as the day for the land rush approached. But thus far no one had resorted to weapons.

No longer a lawman, Tilghman nonetheless reacted out of ingrained instinct. He hurried forward, Sutton only a step behind, as the two men slashed at one another, the steel of their knives glinting in the firelight. Shoving through the crowd, he swept his coat aside, drew a Colt Peacemaker from the holster on his hip, and thunked the nearest man over the head. The man went down as though struck by a sledgehammer.

The crowd was stunned into silence. But the other man instantly turned on Tilghman with his knife. His eyes were bloodshot from too much whiskey, his face contorted in an expression of rage. He advanced, flicking the blade with a drunken leer.

"C'mon ahead," he said in a surly voice. "Just as soon cut you as him."

Tilghman was tall, broad through the shoulders, hard as spring-steel. The firelight reflected off his cold blue eyes, showering his chestnut hair and brushy mustache with a touch of orange. He thumbed the hammer on his Colt, the metallic sound somehow deadlier in the stillness.

"Drop the knife," he said quietly. "Otherwise you won't be making the run tomorrow."

"Kiss my rusty ass!" the drunk snarled. "You got no call buttin' in on a private fight."

Tilghman stared at him. "Let's just say I made it my business. Do yourself a favor—don't push it."

"Gawddammit to hell anyway!"

The man tossed his knife on the ground. He whirled

around, bulling his way through the crowd, and stormed off into the night. Tilghman slowly lowered the hammer and holstered his pistol. He turned, nodding to Sutton, and walked back toward their camp. Sutton whistled softly under his breath.

"Jumpin' Jesus, Bill! You could've got yourself killed."

"Not much chance of that, Fred. Those boys were blind drunk."

"Yeah, but you're not wearin' a badge anymore—remember?"

"I reckon old habits die hard. No sense letting them carve on one another."

Tilghman's tone ended the discussion. At the campsite, he poured coffee into a galvanized cup and resumed staring into the night. Sutton, who understood the solitary nature of his friend, squatted down by the fire. He idly wondered if Tilghman had done the right thing by resigning as a lawman.

For his part, Tilghman dismissed from mind the knife fight. During his years in Dodge City, he had buffaloed countless drunken cowhands, whacking them upside the head with a pistol barrel. In the overall scheme of things, one more troublemaker hardly seemed to matter. His thoughts returned to tomorrow, the land rush, a new life. Oklahoma Territory.

Never had there been anything like it. President Benjamin Harrison's proclamation opening the Unassigned Lands to settlement had created a sensation. Newspapers across the nation carried stories of the "great run" and what was described as the "Garden Spot of the World." America turned its eye to Oklahoma Territory, drawn by the prospect of free land. The scintillating prose of journalists brought them hurrying westward by the tens of thousands.

Unstated in these news stories was the tale of intrigue and political skulduggery which lay behind the opening of Indian Lands. The Boomers' squalling demands, though loud and impressive, were merely window dressing. Instead, it was the railroads—and their free-spending lobbyists—who brought unremitting pressure to bear on Congress. The first step had been to declare the right of eminent domain in Indian Territory.

By 1888 four railroads had laid track through the Nations, the lands of the Five Civilized Tribes. This cleared the way for settlement, and shortly after his inauguration, President Harrison decreed that the Unassigned Lands would be opened to homesteading at high noon on April 22, 1889. But it would be on a first-come-first-served basis, a race of sorts with millions of acres of virgin prairie as the prize.

The land-hungry multitudes cared little for whose ultimate benefit it had been organized. Hundreds of thousands of immigrants were pouring into America each year, and they were concerned not so much with the land of the free as with free land. Here was something for nothing, and they flooded westward to share in the spoils.

Nearly one hundred thousand strong, they gathered north and south along the borders of the Unassigned Lands. They came in covered wagons and buckboards, on horseback and aboard trains, straining for a glimpse of what would soon become Oklahoma Territory. And of a single mind, they came to stay.

Among them was Bill Tilghman. Like thousands of others, he had come seeking opportunity, and in no small sense, a place to start over. The old life was gone, withered to nothing, and his gaze had turned toward the last frontier. A land where men of purpose might scatter the ashes of the past and look instead to the future.

A westering man, Tilghman had moved with his family in 1856 to a farm near Atchison, Kansas. At sixteen, he became a buffalo hunter, and later, operating out of Fort Dodge, he'd scouted for the army. In 1877, serving under Bat Masterson, he had been appointed a deputy sheriff of Ford County. Over the next several years he had worked closely with fellow peace officers such as Jim and Ed Masterson, brothers of Bat Masterson. During the same period, he'd developed a friendship with Wyatt Earp, assistant town marshal of Dodge City.

In 1884, Tilghman himself had been appointed town marshal, where he served for four years. Though Wyatt Earp later captured national headlines after the Gunfight at the O.K. Corral, Tilghman's fame was far greater among outlaws and in western boomtowns. He was considered the deadliest lawman of all the frontier marshals, having killed four men in gunfights. Earp and Masterson and Wild Bill Hickok got the headlines. Tilghman got the reputation as a man to avoid at all costs.

Yet, unlike many peace officers, he was a family man. He'd married a Kansas girl, and together with another old friend, Neal Brown, they had built a ranch outside Dodge City. Their principal business was raising horses, providing saddlestock for the Army as well as other ranches. Then, not quite six months past, Tilghman's wife had suddenly taken ill with influenza and died.

To Tilghman, her death somehow represented an end to that part of his life. Shortly afterward he'd sold the ranch except for the finest breeding stock, and resigned as marshal of Dodge City. The Oklahoma Land Rush was forthcoming, and he had seen that as a new beginning, a place without raw memories. Once he was settled, he planned to send for Neal Brown and the horses. His attention was now fixed on Oklahoma Territory. *A new life.*

Tilghman and Sutton had arrived early that afternoon aboard the lead train in a caravan of eleven trains organized by the Santa Fe. Their immediate goal was the townsite of Guthrie, some twenty miles south, situated along the railroad tracks just below the Cimarron River.

Tilghman had chosen Guthrie over the other major townsite, Oklahoma City, based on his assessment of the economic future of the territory. Before nightfall tomorrow he meant to have a sizable stake in that future.

Behind him in Kansas, Tilghman had left fame. Somehow, once he'd buried his wife, his reputation as a lawman had ceased to matter. The new life he envisioned was that of a businessman, a man of property and substance. Others would come along to take up the badge, enforce the law, and put the lawless behind bars. He was content to leave the past in the past.

Fred Sutton moved to stand beside him. For a moment, they stared out over the campfires, into the darkness beyond. Then, with a bemused smile, Sutton motioned southward.

"What do you see out there, Bill?"

"Nothing," Tilghman said slowly. "And everything."

What he saw was a land where a man of thirty-five could start fresh. A world newborn.

CHAPTER 2

The noonday sun was almost directly overhead. A cavalry officer, followed by a trooper with a bugle, rode slowly to a high point of ground. Below, a thin line of mounted troopers, extending east and west out of sight, held their carbines pointed skyward.

Silence enveloped the land. The quiet was eerie, an unnatural stillness, broken only by the stamping hooves of horses and the chuffing hiss of locomotives. On the small knoll the army officer stared at his pocket watch, and in the distance, hushed and waiting, over fifty thousand homesteaders stared at the knoll. The Oklahoma Land Rush was about to begin.

Tilghman and Sutton were seated in the first passenger coach on the lead train. They watched through the windows as men on swift ponies and those aboard wagons struggled to hold their horses in check. Tilghman knew that the horseback riders, at the beginning of the race, would outdistance the train. But the Guthrie townsite was twenty miles south, and no horse could outrun a train over that distance. He was confident of winning the race.

Overnight the news circulated that added trains had been laid on at the southern boundary of the Unassigned Lands. Yet Tilghman was unconcerned, for the

jump-off point was the South Canadian River, closer to
the Oklahoma City townsite than to Guthrie. That news,
along with thousands more arriving at the northern
boundary during the night, widely increased the air of
tension and excitement. There were now over one hundred thousand poised for the land rush.

The troublesome thing to Tilghman was not the number of people. Instead, he was bothered by those who
refused to play by the rules. These men were being
called Sooners, since they crossed the line too soon. Despite the soldiers' vigilance, they had sneaked over the
border under cover of darkness, planning to hide until
the run started and then lay claim to the choice lands.
Cavalry patrols had flushed hundreds of them out of
hiding, but word spread that there were several times
that number who had escaped detection. This left the
law-abiding homesteaders in an ugly mood.

All along the line people were gripped by the fear
that there wouldn't be enough good land to go around.
As noon approached, and the tension became pervasive,
their mood turned to one of near hysteria. Since early
morning the Santa Fe had moved four additional trains
into position, fifteen now one behind the other, loaded
with still more land-hungry settlers.

The men on horseback were reasonably certain they
could outdistance the trains in the short run. But those
in wagons and buckboards (by far the greater number)
knew they would arrive too late for a chance at the most
desirable claims. Tempers flared, fistfights broke out,
and as the minutes ticked away fully fifty thousand people jostled and shoved for a better spot along the starting line.

On the knoll, the cavalry officer stared intently at his
pocket watch. As the hands of the watch merged, precisely at high noon, he dropped an upraised arm. The
trooper beside him put the bugle to his mouth and blew
a single piercing blast. On signal, the cavalrymen below

discharged their carbines into the air, but the gunfire was smothered beneath a thunderous human roar. The troopers scattered to avoid the onrushing stampede.

Horses reared and whips cracked, men dug savagely with their spurs, and in a sudden dust-choked wedge, a wave of humanity surged across the starting line. At first it seemed a mad scramble, as the earth trembled and trains gained headway. But within moments the race was decided for choice claims to the immediate south of the border.

Out of the blinding dust cloud emerged the swiftest horses, spurred into a wild-eyed gallop. Behind them, strung out and gaining speed, came the trains. Scattered across the countryside, quickly losing ground, wagons and buckboards, and even one solitary soul on a high-wheeled bicycle, brought up the rear. America's first great land rush was under way at last.

From the lead train, Tilghman watched as the horsemen broke clear and sped off into the distance. Not far away he saw two wagons collide and upend, spilling people and household goods across the prairie. He and Sutton exchanged an amused look as the adventurous soul on the bicycle quickly fell behind, obscured in a whirling cloud of dust. Then, as the train gathered speed, smoke and soot from the engine drifted through the open window. They sat back in their seats.

"Judas Priest!" Sutton hooted. "Never saw anything that could hold a candle to that. We could've sold tickets!"

Tilghman smiled. "Hell, that's just the start. The real fun's yet to come"—he nodded out the window—"when they butt heads with the Sooners."

"Yeah, I suppose you're right. There's liable to be some knock-down-drag-out brawls before this day's over."

"Fisticuffs would be the least of it, Fred. There's people out there willing to kill for a choice piece of land."

Sutton looked somber. "You think we'll run into trouble at Guthrie?"

"All depends," Tilghman allowed. "We'll see if anybody's on the ground when we get there. Or leastways, the piece of ground we want."

Every townsite claimant was entitled to stake out two lots. Between them, Tilghman and Sutton planned to stake claim to four lots. One of those, the choice lot, would be devoted to their joint enterprise. They intended to open the first sports-betting emporium in Oklahoma Territory.

In recent years, a cottage industry had sprung up around sports betting. Horse races, such as the Kentucky Derby, and championship prize fights had become national in scope with the advent of the telegraph. The results, transmitted from coast to coast by wire, enabled bettors to wager on a multitude of sports events. Sutton, along with other saloonkeepers in Dodge City, had provided an informal service for his customers. In Guthrie, he and Tilghman meant to corner the market with an across-the-board sports book. They envisioned it as becoming a veritable money tree.

"Mr. Tilghman?"

A man of distinguished bearing stood in the aisle beside their seats. He was perhaps fifty, with a mane of silver hair, and dressed in finely tailored clothes. He smiled pleasantly.

"William Tilghman?" he inquired. "Formerly the marshal of Dodge City?"

"Guilty on all counts," Tilghman said, climbing to his feet. "What can I do for you?"

"Allow me to introduce myself. Colonel Daniel F. Dyer, formerly adjutant to General Sherman and late of Kansas City. I dabble in real estate and other ventures."

Tilghman accepted his handshake. "You aim to settle in Guthrie, Colonel?"

"Indeed," Dyer affirmed. "A burgeoning new land

with unlimited opportunity for investment. Of course, the magnitude of such opportunity attracts the undesirable element as well."

"Likely draw them like flies to honey."

"Mr. Tilghman, I am a man of some wealth and political influence. I intend to play an instrumental role in making Guthrie the capital of Oklahoma Territory. I would like to enlist your aid in furthering that goal."

Tilghman appeared puzzled. "Politics aren't my game, Colonel."

"Quite so," Dyer agreed. "Yet you are a law officer of the first order, Mr. Tilghman. And Guthrie, as the territorial capital, must set an example for law and order."

"Sounds like you're offering me a job."

"All in good time, when we have established a city government. But, yes, Mr. Tilghman, I would be honored to propose your name for chief of police."

"Sorry," Tilghman said amiably. "I quit law work when I left Dodge. Business is my game now."

"Is it?" Dyer said with a dubious expression. "Last night, I observed your rout of those two unsavory characters. From all appearances, you've hardly lost your taste for law enforcement."

"Chalk it up to old habits, Colonel. I'll have to wean myself off that one."

"No need for a hasty decision, Mr. Tilghman. Think it over at your leisure. We'll talk again."

Tilghman grinned. "Talk won't change things, Colonel. I've got other irons in the fire."

"Nonetheless, you are admirably suited to the law, Mr. Tilghman. Give it some thought and we'll talk in Guthrie."

Dyer strolled off down the aisle. Tilghman resumed his seat and traded a look with Sutton. After a quick glance over his shoulder, Sutton shook his head.

"There's a gent not accustomed to taking 'no' for an answer."

"Guess he'll just have to learn. Like I told him, I'm done with law work."

Sutton silently wondered if that were the case. Some habits were harder to break than others.

Shortly before two that afternoon, Tilghman and Sutton stepped off the train at the Guthrie townsite. Neither of them had ever traveled this far into Indian lands, and they took a moment to get their bearings. What they saw hardly had the look of the future capital of Oklahoma Territory.

Before them stretched a rolling plain, bordered in the distance by stunted knolls. The Santa Fe tracks curved off to the southwest, roughly paralleled on the west by Cottonwood Creek. East of the tracks, directly across from a meandering bend in the stream, was a small depot flanked by a section house and a water tank. Several hundred yards east of the depot was an even smaller structure, the federal land office. The rest was empty land.

Three buildings and a water tank constituted the town of Guthrie.

Tilghman and Sutton skirted the depot, headed on beeline for the land office. There were now only minutes to spare, for hundreds of men were pouring off the train and running in the same direction. Reason dictated that the center of town would be located near the land office, and it was here that Tilghman meant to stake their lots. But as he hurried forward several men were already erecting a tent catty-cornered from the land office.

Tilghman immediately tagged them as Sooners. Yet there were other lots and he was satisfied to let latecomers argue the matter. He paced off twenty steps due north of the land office and an equal distance east of the tent. There he drove his stake, with his initials carved in bold letters at the top. Then, moving quickly, he repeated the process, hammering a second stake into an adjacent lot.

Sutton, meanwhile, was scurrying around what would logically represent an opposite corner. He jabbed two stakes in the ground on lots side by side, and not a minute too soon. The landscape all of a sudden sprouted horsemen and a bedlam of humanity emptying off of trains. Where moments before there had been a tranquil prairie the earth was now covered with a frenzied swarm of men, racing mindlessly to plant their stakes in what seemed the choicest spot.

Disputes erupted immediately as men attempted to claim the same lots, and within minutes a dozen slugfests were in progress. But no one came anywhere near the corner north of the land office, or the corner directly opposite. Tilghman stood between his stakes, hand on his pistol, and Sutton adopted a similar posture across the way. The message was clear, and however desperate for land, other men heeded it.

By nightfall Guthrie was a city of tents. Still, rather than sanity restored, pandemonium continued to reign. The Santa Fe station agent quit his post to stake a claim, and a southbound train collided head-on with a northbound from Oklahoma City. Cavalry troopers battled mobs of claim jumpers, who found their dirty work easier done in the dark. Saloons conducted a thriving business from planks resting across barrels, and bordello tents began servicing customers who apparently had a highly attuned sense of direction. Torches lit the night on what gave every appearance of a demented anthill.

Tilghman and Sutton maintained their vigil on opposite corners. They watched as land speculation flourished, rising to a fever pitch in the glow of blazing torches. Hundreds of men had staked claims for no other purpose than to sell them to the highest bidder, and many lots were resold on the hour. Speculators moved swiftly from location to location, dickering and swapping as the future shape of the city took form.

There were no sanitation facilities and no law enforcement. Unfouled drinking water was in short supply, and the stench of a garbage dump slowly settled over the land. By late that night scores of drunken men lay where they had fallen, brought down by the effects of cheap pop-skull whiskey. Yet there were better than ten thousand delirious souls squatted on their claims, and drunk or sober, they were in an exultant mood. They had themselves a town.

Tilghman thought it the greatest circus ever to hit the plains.

CHAPTER 3

There were never enough hours in the day. Tilghman had four projects in various states of completion, and his workday generally stretched from sunrise to well after dark. He often felt like a juggler with one too many balls in the air.

The intersection of Oklahoma Avenue and Second Street, just as he'd surmised that first day, had become the hub of downtown Guthrie. City Hall was taking shape on the southeast corner, and opposite that the post office was under construction. He and Sutton, their claims duly filed, owned the other two corners.

A sawmill as well as a brick kiln were now in operation on the outskirts of town. To meet building demand, the Santa Fe continued to haul in carloads of finished lumber and fixtures from Kansas. Along with the supplies a regiment of carpenters, bricklayers, and stonemasons had arrived in Guthrie. Their services, in the boomtown growth, went to the highest bidder. Others joined a long waiting list.

Tilghman's bankroll, though not inexhaustible, was larger than most. The funds from the sale of his Kansas ranch allowed him to purchase a carload of lumber and secure the services of a half dozen carpenters. On his lots, the sports book (dubbed the Turf Exchange) and a mercantile store, already rented, were nearing completion. Across the way, Sutton was building the Alpha Saloon and a storefront leased to a hardware dealer.

Some blocks north of downtown Tilghman had bought a lot from the original claimant. There, with yet another crew of carpenters, he was building a frame house. A modest affair, the house would have five rooms with a roofed porch. Tired of bunking in a tent, he had already ordered furniture, including a cushy bed, for delivery from Kansas. Sutton, who preferred to be closer to his work, was building living quarters over the saloon.

Hustling back and forth between projects, Tilghman rarely had a moment to spare. Yet his dawn-to-dark workday seemed somehow normal amidst the hectic sawing and hammering along every street. By the close of the second week a small miracle of sorts had taken place on the once-barren prairie. The tent city had virtually disappeared, and from this humble beginning, a town had emerged. Guthrie took on a solid look of permanence and bustling industry.

Saloons and gambling dens were everywhere in evidence, as well as several sporting houses. The most spectacular of the lot was the Reaves Brothers Casino, where it was advertised men could find honest games and fine whiskey. The sporting life, particularly at the start, was the economic mainstay of any boomtown. But Guthrie was gearing itself to become the center of commerce for the entire territory.

Under the sure hands of carpenters and stonemasons, some fifty buildings were in various stages of construction. Among them were three banks, two newspapers, three hotels, and several office buildings. While the activity was noteworthy in itself, what distinguished Guthrie from other towns was its leaders and their vision of the future. The structures they erected were being built to last, at least a third constructed of brick and stone.

Their common goal was to make Guthrie the frontrunner in the fledgling territory.

Tilghman was no less enterprising. His latest project had to do with the field south of town where the local elections had been held. The land was owned by a homesteader, who was an enterprising man himself. Originally, like other homesteaders, his plan had been to farm the land. But with the explosive growth of the town, he saw greater opportunity on the horizon. One day soon, Guthrie would spread beyond the townsite, and his land bordered the town limits. He figured he was sitting on a fortune in future town lots.

Though of a similar opinion, Tilghman's experience as a horse trader gave him an edge. The first step had been to convince the homesteader that his bonanza in town lots was at least a year down the road. With that accomplished, he'd persuaded the man that leasing the field near town would be more profitable than planting it in crops. After that, they got down to serious dickering over the price. The homesteader was wily, but no match for a seasoned horse trader. In the end, Tilghman got a one-year lease for three hundred dollars.

The lease enabled Tilghman to move ahead with a certain moneymaker. Horse racing in the west was, if anything, more wildly followed than in the east. Western races were smaller, usually of a regional nature, but widely attended, something of a festive event. Entry fees from horse owners made for large purses, and the betting was always heavy. So Tilghman, playing the game at both ends, intended to collect on a double hit. He would operate a racetrack and book the bets at the Turf Exchange.

Today, standing at the edge of town, he watched as workmen put the finishing touches on the racetrack. A crew of graders had leveled the field and then laid out an oval track a half mile around. At the southern side of the field a stable had been built large enough to house

ten horses. The stable and the railing around the track
were now in the process of being whitewashed. The
overall visual effect was one of a professional operation.

Tilghman thought of it as a license to print money.
The first race, advertised with posters around town,
would be held Saturday, only three days away. His cut
from the entry fees would be substantial, and weekly
races would ensure a tidy profit. The Turf Exchange,
though in the final stages of construction, was the only
full-fledged sports book in Guthrie. There, eager for entertainment and generally enthused about horse racing,
the townspeople would wager large sums. Westerners,
who were inveterate gamblers, would bet on anything,
especially a favorite horse. The races would do a landslide business.

Eleven horses had already been entered in the Saturday race. Some of them he'd seen working out on the
track, and he wasn't overly impressed. His own string of
four horses arrived today on the noon train from Kansas, still under the care of Neal Brown. He planned to
run a leggy chestnut gelding in the race, and he thought
the prospects of winning were far better than average.
All that remained was for he and Sutton to calculate
odds on the horses entered. He planned to post the
board late that afternoon.

On his way to the train station, Tilghman passed
through the heart of the business district. Citizen's National, the first bank to open its doors, would ultimately
dominate the downtown area. Three stories high with a
massive cupola, it was being constructed of native stone.
Already the ground floor was completed, and as offices
on the second and third floors were finished they would
be leased to professional men and business concerns.
Lawyers and physicians, arriving daily, were competing
for office space.

Around the corner, the Palace Hotel presented an
equally imposing sight. Four stories high, with polished

granite columns at the entrance, it was intended to be a plush affair. The rooms were spacious, with all the latest conveniences, suitable to attract a select clientele. Other hotels were being built, but everyone agreed that the Palace was indeed palatial. Big and elegant, and with just the right touch of class.

Tilghman, as he passed by, was reminded that Guthrie's leading citizen occupied one of the ground-floor rooms. George W. Steele, formerly of Indiana, had been selected as the first governor of Oklahoma Territory. In the Organic Act, passed by Congress, the new territory comprised all Indian lands west of the Five Civilized Tribes, once those lands were opened to settlement. The territory was divided into seven counties, with lawmaking powers vested in a legislature to be elected by the people. The office of governor had been filled by presidential appointment.

Some thought Governor Steele was a tool of the railroads, a friend to robber barons. Others were equally firm in their belief that the new governor was a man of integrity. Tilghman, who preferred to judge a man on performance, thought Steele was handling the job pretty well. Elections were to be held shortly, and a sitting legislature would soon address the business of territorial government. Everyone, regardless of political persuasion, was jubilant that Guthrie had been designated the territorial capital. Confident of greater days ahead, the city council set aside four square blocks at the end of Oklahoma Avenue for the future capitol grounds.

At the Santa Fe depot, Tilghman got a pleasant surprise. The noon train was on time, and Neal Brown hopped off the steps of the caboose. Brown was short and wiry, with a quick smile and an uncanny way with horses. He waved, motioning toward the last boxcar on the freight train. His mouth split in a grin.

"By God!" he said, pumping Tilghman's arm. "Thought you never was gonna send for me."

The telegraph lines were now operating out of Guthrie. Two days before Tilghman had wired instructions for shipping the horses. "Good to see you," he said as they shook hands. "How was the trip?"

"Smooth as butter," Brown assured him. "Think the horses slept all the way."

"Glad to hear they're rested and full of vinegar. Big Red's scheduled for a race on Saturday."

The reference to the long-legged chestnut caught Brown short. "Gawdalmighty, Bill," he said, somewhat amazed. "That's pretty quick, ain't it?"

"Quick enough," Tilghman informed him. "The racetrack's all but done, and no need to dally around. You can start working Big Red this afternoon."

"You just move right along, don't you?"

"Timing worked out perfect, Neal. There's a prize fight set for Saturday, heavyweight championship. The bout's scheduled to start right after the race. We're bound to draw a big crowd."

"Goddamn," Brown said in mild awe. "Told me you aimed to make your fortune down here. Guess you wasn't kiddin'."

Tilghman smiled. "Never kid about money, Neal. Let's get those horses unloaded."

Brown began barking orders at the train crew. A ramp was rolled into place and the boxcar door thrown open. Big Red was the first in the string to set hoof on Oklahoma Territory.

The Turf Exchange was mobbed Saturday morning. The doors opened at eight o'clock and Tilghman and Sutton worked the betting cages straight through until noon. Guthrie had again led the way, staging the first sporting events in the territory, and people treated it like a civic celebration. Hardly a man in town failed to wager a bet.

Saloons and gambling dives also took bets. But just as Tilghman had foreseen, the public flocked to what was considered a legitimate sports book operation. To such a degree, in fact, that Tilghman and Sutton had deposited over thirty thousand dollars in wagers at the Citizen's National Bank. A nightly tally of the betting slips indicated that the wagers were roughly split between the prize fight and the horse race. At noon, with bettors still waiting in line, they were forced to close the doors. Their bankroll, taken with the odds, would cover no more wagers.

Post time at the track was scheduled for two that afternoon. An hour before some fifteen thousand spectators were mobbed around the track railing. On trains, by buggy and horseback, people had traveled from across the Territory to witness a double-barrelled sports extravaganza. Cafes and saloons also had struck pay dirt, and half the crowd was ossified on spirits by post time. The police force, led by the newly appointed town marshal, finally called it quits. There was no way to control such a large crowd.

The race went off shortly after two o'clock. Big Red, with Neal Brown aboard, surged across the starting line and took an early lead. Half a length behind was a roan stallion, imported for the event by a rancher outside of Oklahoma City. The rest of the pack, never really in the race, were strung out some distance behind. Big Red set the pace, but by the far turn the roan was edging closer. In the homestretch, the roan's rider applied the quirt and the stallion made it a neck-and-neck race. Valiant to the end, with Brown urging him on, Big Red matched the roan stride for stride. At the finish line, the roan at last gained half a step and won it by a nose. The crowd, hoarse from shouting, roared approval for both horses. Talk of a future rematch instantly swept the track.

An hour later, in a field west of the track, the prize fight got under way. Paddy O'Shea, the heavyweight champion of Kansas, was matched against Davy Dolan, a pugilist from St. Louis. The match was bare-knuckle, conducted under Marquis of Queensberry Rules: no hitting when a man was down. The crowd, raucous with excitement by now, surrounded an earthen ring of posts and ropes in the center of the field. At the opening bell, O'Shea proceeded to give the contender a lesson in the gentlemanly art of boxing. By the twenty-third round, Dolan looked like a man who had been savaged by wildcats. O'Shea charitably put him down and out with a clubbing right to the jaw.

The crowd went wild as O'Shea strutted around the ring. Tilghman and Sutton, who were standing near one of the corner posts, were only slightly less restrained. Laughing, pounding one another on the back, they exchanged mutual congratulations. Neal Brown, who had only just finished tending Big Red, found them moments after the fight ended. Consternation swept his face when they grabbed him, still laughing, and heartily shook his hand.

"What the hell you two lookin' so happy about? Our horse lost!"

"Who cares?" Sutton crowed. "Won or lost, it's all the same!"

"You gone nuts?" Brown demanded. "Won or lost ain't the same a'tall."

"Yeah, it is," Tilghman said. "Leastway if you're running the right kind of business."

"You're gonna have to spell that out for me, Bill."

Tilghman pulled him aside and told him. No matter who won or who lost—horses, baseball, or pugs—the oddsmaker had it covered both ways. The Turf Exchange, Tilghman revealed with a low chuckle, was the biggest winner of all.

"We cleared better than ten thousand dollars for the day!"

CHAPTER 4

Late Monday morning Tilghman and Sutton finished the accounting. Sutton was the bookkeeper of the partnership, and by his calculation they had netted closer to twelve thousand dollars. Their jubilance had abated none at all, and even more, they were of one mind. The Turf Exchange was indeed a license to print money.

Tilghman began laying out plans for the next race. He wanted to build bleachers on the south side of the track, in front of the finish line. People would pay top dollar for seats with a view, and the admission charge would further increase profits. As well, he wanted to install vendors' booths around the track, where spectators could purchase drafts of keg beer to quell their thirst. The money to be made, in his view, was there for the taking. Several thousand people could drink a lot of beer.

"Mr. Tilghman?"

A young boy stood in the doorway. Tilghman moved to the betting window at the counter. "I'm Tilghman," he said. "What can I do for you, sonny?"

The boy stepped into the room. "Marshal Grimes wants to see you over at his office. He told me to fetch you."

"I don't suppose he told you what it's about?"

"No sir, he didn't. Just said to bring you along."

Sutton turned from the ledger on his desk. "We haven't got any business with a federal marshal. Last I heard, it's no crime to take bets."

"We'll find out quick enough." Tilghman nodded to the youngster. "What's your name, sprout?"

"Tommy Brewster," the boy replied with a gap-toothed grin. "I run messages for folks over at the territory capitol."

"Well, lead the way, Mr. Brewster. I'm right behind you."

Tilghman followed the boy out the door. On the way across town, he reviewed what he'd heard of the newly appointed U.S. Marshal. Formerly from Nebraska, Grimes had made the land rush and claimed a homestead near the townsite of Kingfisher. Word had it that he had served two terms as a sheriff in Nebraska and had an enviable record for his hardline attitude toward outlaws. The way the grapevine told it, he'd sent a good many bad men to the gallows. President Harrison, at Governor Steele's urging, had appointed him United States Marshal only last week.

Until a capitol building was constructed, all territorial and federal offices were housed in the Herriott Building, located at the corner of Division and Harrison. Tilghman followed the boy to the second floor, still new with the smell of fresh lumber. There the boy left him at a door with a newly painted placard denoting UNITED STATES MARSHAL, OKLAHOMA TERRITORY. He rapped on the door.

"Door's open," a voice called out. "C'mon in."

Tilghman entered a room that had the look of a monk's cell. There was one desk, a battered veteran of better days, and three wooden chairs. A file cabinet flanked the desk, and a Winchester rifle was propped in one corner. A man he took to be Grimes was seated behind the desk, and a man unknown to him occupied

one of the chairs. Chris Madsen, a deputy marshal he'd
met around town, moved forward to greet him.

Short and barrel-chested, Madsen's name was known
across the frontier. A soldier of fortune, Danish by
birth, he had fought under Emperor Louis Napoleon in
the Franco-Prussian War and later served in the French
Foreign Legion. Emigrating to America in 1876, he had
joined the army and distinguished himself in the wars
with the Plains Tribes. Last year, he'd resigned from the
army and accepted appointment as a deputy marshal
working Indian Territory. His reputation was hard but
fair, and deadly with a gun.

"Bill," Madsen said amiably, "good to see you. I'd
like you to meet our federal marshal, Walt Grimes."

"Mr. Tilghman." Grimes rose, offering his hand
across the desk. "Pleasure to make your acquaintance."

"Mutual," Tilghman said. "Congratulations on your
appointment."

"Consolation might be more in order. Seems I've
walked into a hornet's nest."

"How's that?"

"The Dalton boys," Grimes said tersely. "They're
shooting up the territory."

"Who are the Dalton boys?"

"Hell, I jumped the gun. Before we get to that, I want
you to meet one of our deputies. This here's Heck
Thomas."

The man in the chair stood and shook Tilghman's
hand. He was a lean six-footer, with steel-gray eyes and
hard features. A slight smile touched one corner of his
mouth.

"Bill Tilghman," he said. "Late of Dodge City and
thereabouts. Your reputation travels."

"Not near as far as yours," Tilghman replied.
"Pleased to meet you."

Tilghman's remark was hardly an overstatement.
Heck Thomas was a renowned mankiller, one of the

foremost lawmen in the West. A Georgian, he had served as a policeman in Atlanta before migrating to Texas. There, he had operated as a private detective prior to appointment as a deputy U.S. marshal. Later, he'd served under Judge Isaac Parker, the hanging judge, headquartered at Fort Smith but trailing outlaws who sought refuge in Indian Territory. He was reputed to have killed six men.

"Have a seat," Grimes said. "Let me tell you about the Daltons."

Tilghman reluctantly took a chair. He sensed that this was something more than a social visit. Thomas resumed his seat and Madsen moved to a window, staring outside. Grimes waved his hand as though batting at flies.

"There's four Daltons, all brothers. Crazy bastards decided to turn desperado, the whole bunch."

Grimes went on with a thumbnail sketch of an entire family turned outlaw. Former cowhands, three of the brothers had at one time served as deputy U.S. marshals. But Bob Dalton was fired for taking bribes, and the other two, Emmett and Grat, resigned amidst rumors that they were rustling cattle on the side. Afterward, fancying himself another Jesse James, Bob formed a gang that included Emmett, Grat, and the fourth brother, Will, along with a pack of some eight cutthroats. The outlaw band, like other predatory gangs, operated out of Indian Territory.

"Helluva note," Grimes concluded. "I'm one week on the job and they've robbed two trains. Hit the Santa Fe up in the Cherokee Outlet and the Katy express down in the Creek Nation. Then they're off and gone, like a goddamn puff of smoke."

"Where to?"

"Where else?" Grimes said hotly. "The Nations."

Any peace officer, even those who served in Dodge City, had heard tales about the Nations. But Tilghman

had always thought them overblown, half hot air and
half truth. He listened attentively as Grimes described
the strangest circumstances ever faced by men sworn to
uphold the law.

With wider settlement of the frontier, a new pattern
of lawlessness began to emerge on the plains. The era of
the lone bandit faded in obscurity; outlaws began to run
in packs. Bank holdups and train robberies were boldly
planned and executed, somewhat like military cam-
paigns. The scene of the raids often resembled a battleground, strewn with the dead and dying.

Local peace officers found themselves unable to con-
tend with the lightning strikes. Instead, the war evolved
more and more into a grisly contest between the gangs
and the federal marshals. But it was a game of hide-and-
seek in which the outlaws enjoyed a sometimes insurmountable advantage. A deadly game that was unique
in the annals of law enforcement.

Gangs made wild forays into Kansas and Missouri
and Oklahoma Territory, terrorized the settlements, and
then retreated into the Nations. There they found virtual immunity from the law, and perhaps the oddest
sanctuary in the history of crime. Though each of the
Five Civilized Tribes had its own sovereign government,
their authority extended only to Indian citizens. White
men were untouchable, exempt from all prosecution except that of a federal court.

Yet there were no extradition laws governing the Nations. Federal marshals had to pursue and capture the
wanted men, and return them to white jurisdiction. In
time the country became infested with hundreds of fugitives, and the problem was compounded by the Indians
themselves. They had little use for white man's law; the
marshals were looked upon as intruders in the Nations.
All too often the red men connived with the outlaws,
offering them asylum.

For the marshals, the chore of ferreting out lawbreakers became a herculean task. Adding yet another obstacle, even the terrain itself favored the outlaws. A man could lose himself in the mountains or along wooded river bottoms, and in some areas there were vast caves where an entire gang could hole up in relative comfort. The tribal Light Horse Police refused all assistance, and the gangs usually chose to fight rather than face a hangman's rope. It was no job for the faint of heart.

"There you have it," Grimes concluded. "The Daltons are running wild and their example just breeds more gangs. We need the help of experienced lawmen. Men like yourself."

Tilghman arched one eyebrow. "Are you offering me a job?"

"Hear him out," Madsen interjected. "I told the marshal how you'd made your mark in Kansas. We think you're the right man for the job."

"Chris makes a good point," Grimes added. "You proved yourself in Dodge City, and that's high recommendation. You're the kind of man we want."

"I appreciate the—"

"Let me finish," Grimes cut him off. "I've been authorized to recruit sixteen deputy marshals to police the territory. Chris and Heck are the first to sign on, and you'd be the third. That's pretty select company, Mr. Tilghman."

"Another day, another time," Tilghman said, "I'd be honored to serve with these men. But I've put law work behind me, marshal. I'm a businessman, now."

"So I hear," Grimes said shortly. "To be frank about it, that has me stumped. You're one of the best peace officers ever to pin on a badge. Why quit now?"

"Let's write it off to personal business and leave it there."

"Goddammit, Tilghman, this *is* personal business. You settled here, and men like you have a responsibility to make the territory safe for everyone. Where's your public spirit?"

Tilghman stood. "I generally don't overlook insults. In your case, I'll make an exception." He nodded to Madsen and Thomas. "See you gents around."

"Hold on!" Grimes said crossly. "I'm just trying to—"

Tilghman turned, ignoring him, and walked to the door. Heck Thomas rose from his chair and hurried into the hallway. He caught Tilghman at the landing to the stairs.

"Don't take it personal," he said amiably. "What with the Daltons and all, Grimes has a load on his shoulders. He's under a lot of pressure."

Tilghman shrugged. "A badge doesn't excuse bad manners. He ought not to push so hard."

"I tend to get riled on things like that myself. 'Course, he's right when he says that some men have more responsibility than others."

"Way I see it," Tilghman said, "I've done my duty more than most. I won't lose any sleep over it."

Thomas searched for a convincing argument. Over his years as a lawman he had learned a little about life and a great deal about death. He had few illusions left intact, and instead of thirty-nine, he felt fifty going on a hundred. These days, he saw people not as he wished them to be but simply as they were. He understood Tilghman.

In the Nations, even among other peace officers, Thomas had seen his share of hardcases. Yet there was nothing loud or swaggering about Tilghman, nothing of the toughnut. Instead, he seemed possessed of a strange inner calm, the quiet certainty more menacing than a bald-faced threat. Thomas respected a man of cool judgment and nervy quickness in tight situations. Those were the traits he wanted in men who rode beside him. The traits he saw in Tilghman.

"Funny thing," he said now. "Seems like I've been

wearin' a badge all my natural born life. Hard to remember a time when I wasn't."

"Same here," Tilghman admitted. "What with scouting for the army, and law work, it seemed like every day led to another fight. I never had time for anything else."

"Maybe there's a reason," Thomas said. "Some men are good at it and some men aren't. I suspect you and me are two of a kind."

Tilghman wondered about that. For the past several years, Thomas had served as a marshal under Judge Parker. Until the Oklahoma Land Rush, Parker's court in Fort Smith had had sole jurisdiction over the Nations. Parker's administration of justice had been punctuated repeatedly by the dull thud of a gallows trap. Almost seventy men had been hanged, but in the process sixty-five marshals had lost their lives tracking outlaws across the Nations. The job was dirty and dangerous, and Heck Thomas had survived because he was a highly skilled killer of men. Though he was equally skilled, Tilghman wanted something more from life. He thought he'd found it in Guthrie.

"Yeah, I reckon we're alike," he agreed now. "But some men burn out faster than others. Figure I've run the course."

Thomas eyed him with a shrewd smile. "You know, it's curious how being a lawdog gets in a man's blood. I'd wager you're not shed of it yet."

"Would you?" Tilghman liked his easy humor, his open nature. "Well, Heck, that's one bet you're bound to lose. I've hung up my badge—for good."

"You wouldn't take offense if I brought it up now and again, would you? Just by way of testin' the water."

"You've got a streak of stubborn, don't you?"

"Damnedest thing." Thomas laughed. "I got the same notion about you."

They parted with a warm handshake. Tilghman went down the stairs and disappeared into the street. Thomas stood there for a long moment, turning the conversation over in his head. Then he chuckled softly, nodding to himself.

Bill Tilghman was going to make a hell of a marshal.

CHAPTER 5

The day was bright as brass, without a cloud in the sky. A gentle breeze drifted in from the south, and huge white butterflies floated lazily on warm updrafts of air. High overhead a hawk hung suspended in the sky, a speck of feathers caught against the blaze of a noonday sun.

Tilghman shaded his eyes against the glare, watching the hawk. He was mounted on a dun mare, one of his string quartered in Guthrie. The mare cropped grass where they had paused on a knoll overlooking a wooded stream. The hawk floated away and his gaze swept out across the land. There was something familiar about it, a distant memory.

The valley was located in the Sac and Fox tribal reservation, some forty miles southeast of Guthrie. He'd departed town yesterday afternoon, camping overnight on the trail, and pushed on steadily through the morning. The purpose of his trip was to inspect the horse herds of the Sac and Fox, famed throughout Indian Territory for their high-bred stock. Swift ponies with the endurance of plains horses would add to the bloodline of his racing stable.

The land before him stretched onward in gently rolling prairies and wide valleys. Like a latticework of water, the Deep Fork of the North Canadian fed the tributaries of Dry Creek, Bell Cow, Quapaw, and the Kickapoo. The streams were bordered on either side by trees, and an occasional timbered woodland stood stark against the sunlit plains. The earth seemed to sway with wave upon wave of lush tall grass.

The morning's ride had convinced Tilghman that the reservation was a wildlife paradise. While the buffalo herds were now gone, there was still an abundance of game. Great flocks of turkey swarmed over the woodlands; at dusk the timber along the creeks was loaded with roosting birds. Deer were plentiful, and grouse and plover were everywhere in the tall grass. Fat, lazy fish crowded the streams and river shallows, eager to take a hook baited with grasshopper. It was a land where no man need go hungry.

Summoned from long ago, Tilghman suddenly realized why the land appeared so familiar. From his boyhood on the farm in Kansas, he remembered these same rolling prairies and waves of grass. In his youth, he had hunted the woodlands and fields, and fished the creeks. He recalled returning home at sundown with his game bag stuffed full, and the savory smells in the kitchen as his mother cooked what he'd harvested from the wild. Those were good memories, fond memories, long ago of another life. Oddly, looking out from atop the knoll, he felt as though he'd somehow come home.

Tilghman shook it off, gently nudged the mare with his boot heels. His immediate destination was the reservation agency, where he intended to talk with the Indian agent. But as he rode across the prairie, unbidden thoughts intruded on the business at hand. Perhaps it was stumbling over old memories, made vivid in his mind's eye by the haunting familiarity of the land. Whatever the source, unbidden or not, he was forced to admit something he'd avoided until now. There was a restlessness within him, some inner spark of discontent with the way things were. He felt as though he'd taken a wrong turn in the road.

All of which left him thoroughly confused. A month ago, after that first horse race, he had thought of himself as a man with the world on a downhill slide. Everything had fallen into place just as he'd planned, one piece dovetailing with the other in rapid order. Even now, the Turf Exchange and the racetrack were coining money faster than he and Sutton could count. He owned several properties, his business concerns were a resounding success, and he was on a first-name basis with the civic leaders of Guthrie, including the governor. So he had to wonder about this nagging sense of discontent. No ready answer presented itself, and that bothered him even more. He was a man who'd always known himself.

A short while later he rode into the agency compound. Headquarters was a whitewashed frame house with a shaded porch out front. The agent, Joseph Monroe, was a spare man with spectacles and a talkative nature. He invited Tilghman inside, where one part of the parlor served as an office. There, once they were seated, he waved off into the countryside.

"What brings you to the reservation, Mr. Tilghman?"

"Horses," Tilghman remarked. "I hear the Sac and Fox breed good stock. I'm interested in buying."

"Well then," Monroe said jovially, "you've come to the right place. No tribe raises finer horses than the Sac and Fox."

"How would you suggest I go about it?"

"Oh, there's a certain protocol to these things. You'll have to deal with the chief, at least at first. His name is Moses Keokuk."

"Moses?" Tilghman said quizzically. "Where'd he get a name like that?"

"Fairly common," Monroe noted. "The original agent here was a missionary. He liked Biblical names!"

"So did Moses lead the Sac and Fox to the Promised Land?"

"Well put, indeed, Mr. Tilghman. And not far from the fact, I might add. The Sac and Fox are the most influential tribe on the reservation."

"How many are there?" Tilghman said. "I only heard about the Sac and Fox because of their horses."

Monroe warmed to his favorite subject, the diverse nature of his wards. He explained that the reservation was home to several tribes, each relocated from distant parts of the country. The Sac and Fox, still nomadic in their ways, roamed the reservation with their horse herds. The Iowas, who followed the white man's road, were now farmers with thousands of acres under cultivation. The Shawnee-Potawatomi were middle of the road, still in transition to becoming white Indians. Other than sharing a reservation, the tribes had little in common.

A good listener, Tilghman discerned that Monroe had little in common with those who ran the Bureau of Indian Affairs. The agent went on to relate that Washington was devouring Indian lands piecemeal. In their latest move, the bureaucrats had secured agreements by which members of the three tribes were each allotted one hundred sixty acres in severalty. The remainder of their lands, something over a million acres, had been ceded to the government. Thus another land rush, opening the land to settlers in early September, had been put in place. The reservation, for all practical purposes, was even now part of Oklahoma Territory.

To underscore the point, Monroe wryly observed that the Secretary of the Interior had already divided the reservation into two counties. One was named Lincoln, and in a twist of bureaucratic humor, the other was to be called Potawatomi. Federal surveyors had recently designated their boundaries and selected the county seat townsites. Washington, in a fit of noblesse oblige,

had left it to the territorial legislature to provide for
local government of the new counties. Which, in
Monroe's opinion, would allow Governor Steele to
award plum positions through patronage.

"All neat and tidy," he said with mild sarcasm. "Another instance of politics as usual."

"Way it sounds," Tilghman commented, "you'll soon
be out of a job."

"Well, perhaps it's a blessing in disguise. Working for
the Great White Father sorely tests a man's conscience.
I intend to join the land rush and stake a claim."

"A homestead?"

"Hardly," Monroe said with a gruff chortle. "I'm no
farmer, Mr. Tilghman. The townsite for the seat of Lincoln County will be called Chandler. I plan to stake out
a town lot."

"Good idea," Tilghman said. "What business have
you got in mind?"

Monroe laughed. "I think I'll open a saloon. Hard
times or not, people always have money for liquor. I'll
probably wind up a rich man."

"Never saw a saloonkeeper yet who went to the poor-
house."

Monroe appreciated a man with a sense of humor.
He decided to personally escort Tilghman and introduce him to the Sac and Fox chief. Otherwise, given the
tribe's nomadic wanderings, Tilghman might never find
them. They went out to the corral to saddle Monroe's
horse.

Toward midafternoon, they found the tribe camped
on Bell Cow Creek. Tilghman was again struck with a
sense of familiarity about the spot. A grove of trees
bordered a bend in the creek and the surrounding prairie was a natural grazeland. There was an eerie similarity to the family farm site of his boyhood.

Moses Keokuk, chief of the Sac and Fox, was something of a surprise. A commanding figure, grown heavy

with age, he spoke his own brand of broken English. His angular features and hawklike nose were offset by the humorous cast of his eyes. He looked like a red-skinned pirate who enjoyed his work.

Monroe performed the introductions. He explained that Tilghman was interested in horses and had ridden a long way to look at the Sac and Fox herds. Tilghman seemed uncertain as to how he should address the tribal leader, and there was an awkward moment. Then Moses Keokuk gave him a sly smile.

"We talk trade. Mebbe you call me Moses. Mebbe you call me Chief. We see."

"Sounds fair," Tilghman said, warning himself that the man was shrewder than he pretended. "I've heard the Sac and Fox raise fast horses."

"Plenty fast," the chief said proudly. "Wanna eat dust, try to outrun our ponies."

"Well, that's good to know. What I'm looking for is a couple of stallions."

Moses Keokuk grunted. "Gonna breed 'em to that mare you ridin'?"

"I might," Tilghman said. "Then again, I might just race them. Either way, they've got to be fast."

"Told you, we ain't got no horses ain't fast. Stallions, mares, all the same."

"You suppose I could have a look at some?"

"Do lots better," the chief said. "Let you see 'em run."

Moses Keokuk was as good as his word. Several stallions were selected from scattered herds grazing at different points on the prairie. Lean, young horse herders bounded aboard the stallions and rode them at top speed. Any questions about stamina were resolved, and the rumors were indeed true. Sac and Fox horses were fast.

Tilghman settled on only one stallion, a sorrel stud that seemed like the wind in motion. Moses Keokuk, adopting the stony-faced manner of a poker player, proved to be a haggler of the first order. In the end, certain that they would do business again, Tilghman decided not to dicker too hard. He allowed the chief to extract a price that was high, but still short of robbery. They solemnly shook hands on the deal.

By then it was nearing sundown, and Monroe invited Tilghman to stay the night. The agent's wife, a pleasant woman and a passable cook, laid out all the fixings for supper. Afterward, seated in rockers on the porch, Tilghman listened while Monroe stoked a pipe and told blistering tales about the Bureau of Indian Affairs. The stories dealt with a bureaucracy that operated on the principle of incompetence mixed with corruption. If nothing else, the evening convinced Tilghman that Monroe would make a good saloonkeeper. The man was too honest for government work.

Early next morning Tilghman rode out leading the sorrel stallion. The impressions of yesterday came over him again as he retraced his route across the reservation. The rolling prairies rekindled old memories, some better than others. He was realist enough to admit that part of his discontent was deeply personal. Though he'd never discussed it with anyone, he still mourned the loss of his wife. His fresh start, the excitement of Oklahoma Territory, was a poor substitute for the woman who had graced his life. His grief was hidden, but not gone.

Yet, however great his personal loss, there was more to the overriding sense of restlessness. The Turf Exchange and the racetrack, all the money in the bank, had failed to slake some inner need. Seemingly, he had the world by the tail, but in the midst of all he'd accomplished, something was missing. He felt as though he had wandered astray, somehow lost his way, and try as he might, he couldn't regain his sense of direction. He was searching for something and it was elusive. Hard to identify, or put into words.

Late that morning, as he approached the Deep Fork of the North Canadian, he was reminded of Bell Cow Creek. The lay of the land, the rushing stream and the grove of trees, all triggered a feeling that had come over him just yesterday. A spooky feeling, one that defied logic, but nonetheless real. A sense that he'd come home.

So maybe he wasn't lost. Instead, he told himself as he forded the river, maybe he had found the path after all. A path that could end his search. One thought triggered another and then another as he rode toward Guthrie.

CHAPTER 6

By midsummer the frontier boomtown was gone.

In its place was a city unlike any imagined by the original settlers. Guthrie was now a thriving metropolis, the population swelled to more than twelve thousand. A waterworks and pumping station were under construction, and along with it, a rudimentary sewerage system. Tracks were laid on Oklahoma Avenue and a horse-drawn streetcar began servicing one of the town's main thoroughfares.

A group of private investors had obtained the license for a generating plant. By early next fall they would provide streetlights at major intersections, and the wonder of electric illumination in offices and business concerns in the downtown area. Their plans, though considered overly ambitious by some, were to extend this remarkably efficient service to every home in town. The coal-oil lamp, astounding as it seemed, would soon become a thing of the past.

Near the Santa Fe railyards at the west end of Cleveland Avenue, another investor had built a warehouse and organized Guthrie's first wholesale grocery company. Directly across the street still another go-getter had established the town's largest lumberyard, buying in trainload lots, and outselling all other competitors combined. Mayor Dyer, by now a pillar of the community, had been instrumental in bringing all these improvements to the city.

But the mayor, for all his civic virtue, was a strong advocate of the free enterprise system. After sampling the water at a mineral well southwest of town, he bought the land, organized a bottling plant, and began selling Mineral Wells Elixir Water throughout the territory. Then, exploiting his scheme to the fullest, he built a bathhouse near downtown, piped the water in from the well, and charged outrageous prices for people to luxuriate in the warmth of a mineral bath. Nothing with the smell of profit escaped attention.

An accelerated rate of growth, stimulated by supply and demand, attracted investment at a dizzying pace. City Hall had approved the blueprints for a flour mill, two creameries, a distillery, and a bookbinding factory. The newspaper reported as well that approval was forthcoming for a wholesale meat company, a gristmill, and a cotton gin. By next summer, when the first full year of crops were harvested, the homesteaders would lack for nothing. To quench their thirst, Pabst was designing a brewing plant large enough to service the entire territory.

Growth was evident as well in the professions and retail establishments. A city directory listed fourteen doctors and thirty-six lawyers, half a dozen mercantiles, twenty-three cafes, and four drugstores. The public servants who prepared the directory were nothing if not discreet, and unlisted were eighteen saloons, five gambling dives, and several flourishing whorehouses. Still, in its own unobtrusive way, the sporting crowd did quite well in Guthrie.

For all that, Tilghman watched the surge of growth with mixed emotions. The Turf Exchange, with results relayed directly from the telegraph office, was now booking bets on horse races, prize fights, and baseball games from all across the country. The racetrack was mobbed every Saturday afternoon, and now drew horse owners from as far as Missouri and Texas. To run the whole operation required a payroll of twelve employees.

By some accounts, Tilghman and Sutton were two of the wealthiest men in town. But Tilghman rarely looked at his bank balance, and he'd turned down countless investment opportunities, including Mayor Dyer's mineral-water bonanza. For the most part, his days were spent at the track with Neal Brown, training horses, talking bloodlines, and planning the breeding program for their stock. He took greater pleasure in speculating on the foals sired by the Sac and Fox stallion than he did in the daily receipts from the Turf Exchange. His spark for business grew dimmer by the day.

The final blow occurred toward the end of June. The Guthrie *Statesman* reported that the wondrous invention of Alexander Graham Bell was coming to the territorial capital. The telephone, grown quite sophisticated since its invention in 1876, had spread rapidly to cities throughout America. According to the *Statesman*, plans were under way to provide Guthrie with telephone service by the fall of 1890. The age of science had overtaken the frontier.

Tilghman saw it in another light entirely. The frontier he'd known, from buffalo hunting to the cowtowns to the land rush, was swiftly vanishing. The telephone, rather than a modern convenience, represented the death knell of a way of life. To him, the jangle of a telephone bell was a sound he was never meant to hear. He didn't want to be there when it arrived in Guthrie.

On the Fourth of July, he made his decision. By a small quirk of nature, the fourth was also his birthday, and he thought it an auspicious time to put his life in order. The town celebrated the holiday with a parade and fireworks, and the Turf Exchange pulled down the largest single daily gross since the doors opened. A spectator of sorts, Tilghman celebrated his thirty-sixth birthday by stepping across a line he'd skirted for the last month. He decided to sell out.

The next morning he discussed his plans with Neal Brown. The reaction he got was much as he'd expected. Brown was more comfortable with horses than he was with people. Apart from a Saturday night on the town, he much preferred wide open spaces and working with horses. His years on the plains had left him with a general distaste for towns and an ingrained distrust of townspeople. Guthrie, with its mushrooming growth and hurly-burly of people, was for him the worst of all worlds. He'd stayed on only out of loyalty to Tilghman.

Early that afternoon Tilghman entered the Alpha Saloon. The interior was pleasantly cool, despite sunlight streaming through the front windows. A long mahogany bar occupied one wall, behind it a large mirror flanked by the ubiquitous nude paintings popular in Western saloons. Opposite the bar were faro and twenty-one layouts, with poker tables toward the rear. A four-man poker game was under way at one of the tables, and Fred Sutton, finishing a breakfast of ham and eggs, was seated at a nearby table. Tilghman took a chair across from him.

"Afternoon," he said. "Or by the looks of your plate, it's still morning."

"Late night." Sutton waved his fork around the room. "We had a crowd in here till the wee hours. Wish the Fourth of July came more often."

"Older I get, the less I like it. Just adds another year to my calendar."

"Damn!" Sutton dropped his fork and extended his hand. "What with the crowds and everything, I forgot to wish you happy birthday. All the best, Bill."

"Thanks." Tilghman shook hands, then nodded toward the nearby poker table. "Those boys been at it all night?"

The four men were hunched over their cards. One of them, attired in a checked suit and derby hat, had at his elbow stacks of gold coins and a large stack of greenbacks. The other three, scowling at their cards, were clearly losers.

"Some fools are born losers," Sutton scoffed. "The big winner's a tinhorn who passed himself off as a notions drummer. He's plucking the other three."

"Honest game, or is he a cardsharp?"

"Way it appears, he's just got 'em outclassed. 'Course, I've been fooled before. Some are slicker than others with a deck of cards."

Tilghman lost interest. "Want to talk to you," he said. "Are you satisfied with our take from the Turf Exchange?"

"Satisfied!" Sutton said, a bite of ham speared on his fork. "Christ, it's like a license to steal. We own the mint."

"How'd you like to own it all?"

"I don't follow you."

"Simple," Tilghman said. "I'm thinking of selling out my half. Thought I'd offer it to you first."

"Sell out?" Sutton said, astounded. "Why would you do a damnfool thing like that?"

"Fred, I'm wore out on the city life. Guthrie got too big, too fast for my tastes. I'm thinking of moving on."

"Where would you go? What would you do?"

"Figured to raise horses," Tilghman said. "There's another Land Rush toward the end of September. I've got a spot picked out on the Sac and Fox reservation."

"I'll be dipped." Sutton shook his head. "You're just a sackful of surprises."

"Hell, Fred, I wasn't cut out to be a businessman. All a pipe dream, and no sense kiddin' myself any longer. I see that now."

"Sort of sudden, isn't it? You never gave a clue."

Tilghman thought of it another way. He kept his own

counsel, rarely seeking the advice of others. Still, in looking back, there had been nothing sudden about his decision. A great deal of weighing and deliberation had taken place over the past month. The idea of telephones in Guthrie had merely been the last straw.

"Sudden or not," he said, "I aim to sell out. You interested?"

Sutton took a swig of coffee. He set the mug back on the table, his features unreadable. "What've you got in mind?"

Tilghman sensed that the mood between them had changed. Friendship was one thing, business was another. Sutton would attempt to drive a hard bargain.

"Fred, I'm not one to haggle. So I'll make you a fair deal."

"Go ahead."

"Twenty thousand cash," Tilghman said, "plus thirty percent of profits for six months. After that, I retain ten percent interest."

Sutton frowned. "Sounds pretty steep to me, Bill."

"I've thought on it, and that's my only deal."

"Are you saying, take it or leave it?"

"Yeah, I reckon so," Tilghman told him. "Lots of people would jump at the deal. I'd rather sell to you."

Sutton was silent a moment. "What about the racetrack? You plan to unload that, too?"

"Ten thousand cash buys the lease, the stables, the whole works."

"Throw in your house and we'll shake on it."

"Nope," Tilghman said slowly. "The house will fetch a good price on its own. We're talking the track and the sports book."

"Goddamn," Sutton grumbled. "Anybody says you're not a businessman, he's loco. You squeeze the turnip."

"One horse trade's like another, Fred. We got a deal?"

"Hell, why not! I'm partial to owning the whole she-bang anyhow. I'll have a lawyer draw up the papers."

"Sooner the better, so far as I'm concerned."

A snarled curse from the poker game filled the room. "You tinhorn sonovabitch! You're cheatin'."

"Am I?" the man in the derby hat replied. "How do you propose to prove it?"

"Don't have to prove it!" The accuser kicked back his chair and started around the table. "I'm just gonna beat the livin' shit out of you."

The gambler rose, pulling a bulldog pistol from his waistband. "Stop right there."

The other man shoved the table aside and lunged forward. At point-blank range, the pistol roared and the powder flash set his shirt afire below his breastbone. He staggered sideways, his eyes wide with shock. Then he dropped dead on the floor.

Tilghman stood, his reaction one of visceral instinct. He pulled his Colt and thumbed the hammer. "Drop that gun."

The gambler crouched, wheeling around, and brought the bulldog pistol to bear. Tilghman shot him in the chest, nicking the edge off the lapel on his coat. The impact drove him backwards, his feet tangled, and he collapsed onto the wreckage of the poker table. A trickle of blood leaked out of his mouth and his eyes rolled back in his head. He lay still.

"Jesus," Sutton mumbled hollowly. "Why'd you take a hand? Wasn't your fight."

The question, though phrased differently, was put to Tilghman several times over the course of the afternoon. Ed Kelly, the first lawman on the scene, was dumbfounded. He clearly thought it a mild form of insanity to take part in someone else's fight. There would be a coroner's inquest, with those who witnessed the double shooting required to testify. No one doubted that Tilghman would be cleared.

Heck Thomas arrived as the bodies were being carried out. When he posed the question, there was not a trace of surprise on his face as Tilghman explained that murder required a response. He felt confident that, with or without a badge, Tilghman would respond to any killing in exactly the same way. The traits that had made him an outstanding lawman were the traits that would permit him to do no less. To Thomas, it was a fundamental part of certain men's character.

Outside, they stood talking for awhile on the street. Thomas related that the Dalton gang had robbed yet another train, and vanished into the Nations. Tilghman, though he'd just killed a man, listened closely and asked questions that would have occurred only to a lawman. Still, despite his interest, he evidenced no sudden urge to pin on a badge. He meant to raise horses, not chase outlaws.

Upon parting, Thomas told himself that it was only a matter of time. Tilghman was one of that rare breed with no tolerance for those who stepped outside the law. He'd been born to wear a badge.

CHAPTER 7

The sun dipped lower, splashing great ripples of gold across the water. Overhead a hawk veered slowly into the wind and settled high on a cottonwood beside the stream. The bird sat perfectly still, a feathered sculpture, flecked through with a bronzed ebony in the deepening sunlight. Then it cocked its head in a fierce glare and looked down upon the men.

There were five of them, all lean and hard, weathered by wind and sun. Four were Sac and Fox tribesmen, their features like the burnt mahogany of ancient saddle leather. Tilghman watched as they wrestled a stout log onto their shoulders and jammed the butt end into a freshly dug hole. Small rocks and dirt were then tamped down solidly around the log until it stood anchored in the earth. This was the last in a rough circle of wooden pillars embedded in the flinty soil.

Tilghman had hired the men through Moses Keokuk, chief of the Sac and Fox. While they continued work on the corral, he slowly inspected the ranch compound. His homestead centered on a wide expanse of woodland, with cottonwoods along Bell Cow Creek and a grove of live oaks stretching westward for a quarter mile. Bordering the shoreline was a natural clearing, with a rocky ford and a stunted hill to the north, which would protect it from the winter blast of a plains blizzard. The terrain rolled away from the creek in virgin grassland.

Not quite three weeks past, in early September, Tilghman and Neal Brown had joined twenty thousand homesteaders in the land rush. Tilghman had claimed one hundred sixty acres along Bell Cow Creek, three miles northwest of the Chandler townsite. Farther west along the creek, Brown had staked a homestead abutting Tilghman's land. Their combined holdings provided over three hundred acres of natural pasture for raising horses.

The ensuing weeks had been a time of sweat and labor. Tilghman drove himself and the tribesmen at a furious pace, working from dawn to dusk, seven days a week. At the outset, he had informed them that two buildings must be erected, a main house and a stable for twenty horses. They felled trees, snaked logs to the clearing, and worked without respite under his relentless urging. The buildings were completed, including planked floors and a stone fireplace in the house, in less than three weeks.

Now, as dusk settled over the clearing, they stood back and marveled at the fruit of their labors. Set off away from the creek, shaded by tall cottonwoods, was a sturdy, shake-roofed log house. It had five rooms with windows overlooking the stream and an oak door with iron fittings. Across the clearing, set flush with the terrain, was the stable, also constructed of logs. Half the stalls were filled with brood mares, most of them topped by the Sac and Fox stallion and ready to foal in late spring. The stallion, by now named Steeldust, stood at his stall door watching the men.

The corral sat squarely in the middle of the clearing, a short distance from the stream. The cross posts were springy young logs, designed to absorb punishment from milling horses without snapping. There, in time to come, young horses would be gently educated in the ways of man and saddle. For the moment, the corral would serve as exercise ground and breeding pen for the stock. The tribesmen, all experienced horse herders, daily took the stock to graze on the prairie bordering the creek.

Moses Keokuk rode into the compound as the men stood admiring their handiwork. He was astride a prancing black stallion with fiery eyes and a flowing mane. As he reined to a halt, one of the tribesmen came forward to hold his horse. He stepped down from the saddle, grinning at Tilghman.

"Heap lotta work," he said, waving around the compound. "When you gonna stop?"

Tilghman smiled. "We ought to finish by tomorrow. Just odds and ends left to be done."

"You white men all the time work. Got no time for play."

"Well hell, Moses, only chiefs have time to loaf. The rest of us have to bust our humps."

Over the past several weeks Tilghman and Keokuk had become great friends. They were honorable men, steadfast in manner, with similar views on life. Of equal significance, they shared a fondness for sweeping plains and fast horses. By now, they enjoyed the bantering relationship of men who respected one another.

"Brown the same," Keokuk said, shaking his head. "Just come from his place. Work my men mighty hard."

"Good wages, though," Tilghman remarked. "Gives your boys hard money in their pockets. They like that when they go to town."

"Old days was lots better. Never needed money."

Tilghman understood the sentiment. With the land rush, the nomadic life of the Sac and Fox had ended. Tribal members were each awarded one hundred sixty acres, the same as their new white neighbors. But farming was foreign to their nature, and they hadn't yet taken to the white man's road. They still counted their wealth in horses.

For all that, Moses Keokuk had urged his followers to take work where it could be found. The reservation was gone, and with it the monthly food allotments. Tilghman had put four men on the payroll, and Neal Brown, who was building a small cabin on his claim, had hired two Sac and Fox. The old days were no more, but cash money gave them an independence of sorts. Their trade was welcome at the stores in Chandler.

"How 'bout tonight?" Keokuk asked. "You gonna go to town?"

"Wouldn't miss it," Tilghman said. "Figures to be quite a shindig. What about you?"

"Sure, I go." Keokuk gave him a sly grin. "Mabbe see white man not all work."

"Moses, I just suspect you will."

Three days ago elections had been held for town and county offices. To honor the occasion, the leaders of Lincoln County had organized a celebration. Everyone from miles around would attend, and there were certain to be large crowds. Chandler, as the county seat, was now a hub of activity. And a great curiosity to the Sac and Fox.

Keokuk grunted, looking thoughtful. "So you still not be a law chief. How come you turn 'em down?"

Tilghman had been asked to run for county sheriff. Though the arguments were persuasive, presented by several influential townspeople, he had declined. "Told you before, Moses," he said now. "Horses are my business, not the law. I've got all I can handle here."

"You're funny man, Bill Tilghman. Big honor to be chief."

"I'll stick to raising horses. Let me get washed up and we'll ride into town together."

Tilghman walked toward the house. Moses Keokuk stared after him, considering. In his mind, the position of law chief was on a magnitude of the red man's war chief. An honor not to be dismissed lightly.

White men, even those he knew well, were still a mystery. Tilghman more so than most.

The town square was a tableau of thriving commerce. In only three weeks, shops and business establishments had been hammered together with wagonloads of lumber imported from Guthrie. People already referred to it as Courthouse Square, though a courthouse, planned as a stone edifice, was yet to be built. The town leaders meant for Chandler to make its mark on the map.

The boardwalks were crowded with people, and farm wagons lined the street. By nightfall, over a thousand homesteaders and townspeople were gathered for the celebration. One part of the square was devoted to a feast, where quartered beeves roasted over low fires. On the opposite side, where a band blasted out merry tunes, a large section of level ground served as a dance floor. The climax of the evening would be an elaborate display of fireworks.

Tilghman and Keokuk drew stares as they walked through the milling throngs. A white man in company with an Indian aroused curiosity in itself. But a former lawman, known to have declined the post of sheriff, and the chief of the Sac and Fox attracted attention wherever they went. Tilghman, all too aware of the attention, thought Neal Brown had made a wise decision. Never one for large crowds, Brown had elected to forego the celebration. He was content to spend the evening in his cabin on Bell Cow Creek.

Keokuk abruptly grunted a low chuckle. He took Tilghman's elbow, tugging him along. "See a man you oughta know. Pretty honest, for a white man."

"Who's that?"

"Amos Stratton," Keokuk said. "There, with the girl."

Up ahead, Tilghman saw a man in his late forties attired in a dark suit and hat. But his attention was drawn to the girl and stayed there. He couldn't take his eyes off her.

Keokuk performed the introductions. Stratton and his daughter, Zoe, had made the land run and staked a claim on Quapaw Creek. Like Tilghman, Stratton fancied horses and had bought several head of breeding stock from the Sac and Fox. Tilghman listened, nodding in all the right places, occasionally offering a comment. His attention was fixed on the girl.

Zoe Stratton appeared to be in her early twenties, perhaps younger. She was tall and statuesque, with a rounded figure and a tiny waist. She had extraordinary green eyes, exquisite features, and a cloud of auburn hair worn in the upswept fashion. She carried herself erect and proud, and when she smiled Tilghman was mesmerized. He thought her the loveliest woman he'd ever seen.

After some moments of conversation, Stratton excused himself and strolled off into the crowd with his daughter. Tilghman considered the brief interlude all too short, and reluctantly turned away. As he fell in beside Keokuk, he found Heck Thomas approaching them. He introduced Keokuk, who seemed drawn now by the savory aroma of the roasting beef. Announcing that he was hungry, the chief walked off toward the fire spits.

Thomas smiled. "Looks like you made yourself a friend, there."

"Good one, too," Tilghman acknowledged. "Him and his men have been a big help in getting the ranch started."

"Sounds like you've got things well in hand."

"No complaints so far. What brings you to Chandler, Heck?"

"Same old thing," Thomas said. "Trailin' the Dalton boys."

"Thought you would've caught them by now."

"Yeah, me too."

Thomas appeared somber. He went on to relate that the Dalton Gang had robbed two trains within the last month. One was on the Santa Fe line, and the other was an express car on the Katy line. In the latter holdup, the express car guard resisted and had been killed. After each robbery, the gang had vanished into the Nations.

"Got a tip," Thomas concluded. "Word's around that some of the gang was sighted north of here."

"In Oklahoma Territory?" Tilghman said quizzically. "Why wouldn't they stay holed up in the Nations?"

"Damn good question." Thomas frowned, clearly troubled. "These boys are runnin' us ragged, Bill. We're always a day late and a dollar short."

"I remember the feeling, Heck."

"Last week Jim Masterson signed on as a marshal. But hell, he's only one man, and we're still spread thin. We need somebody that knows the ropes."

Tilghman stared at him. "Why do I get the notion you're here to see me?"

"Saw through it, huh?" Thomas shrugged, lifting his hands. "You're too good a lawman to sit this one out, Bill. Forget duty and obligation and all that. I came here personal to ask your help."

Tilghman was silent for a long moment. He still felt a strong reluctance to again become involved in law work. Yet he found it difficult to refuse a personal appeal from a man he respected. One who had now become his friend.

"Let's say I signed on," he said. "You understand it wouldn't be permanent?"

"Any way you want it," Thomas quickly agreed. "Just stick with me till we clean out this bunch."

"I'll need a week to get things squared away at the ranch. Then we'll call it official."

"Goddamn, I knew you wouldn't turn me down! We're gonna nail those bastards, Bill. Mark my word!"

"So far as I'm concerned, the sooner the better."

Tilghman's attention was distracted. Through the crowd, he saw Amos Stratton and his daughter watching couples swirl around the earthen dance floor. He nodded to Thomas, leading the way, and cleared a path through the spectators. Halting beside the Strattons, he tipped his hat to the girl.

"Miss Stratton," he said, smiling. "I'd count it an honor if you'd like to dance."

Amos Stratton gave him a sour look. But the girl graced him with a radiant smile and accepted his hand. He led her onto the dance floor, holding her at a respectful distance, and caught the beat of the music. They glided off into the throng of dancers.

Heck Thomas watched them with a broad smile. His toe tapped in time to the music and he mentally patted himself on the back. By his reckoning, the ride to Chandler had been worth every mile.

He'd landed his man.

CHAPTER 8

Trees along Red Rock Creek clattered in a bright and nimble wind. The tawny grasslands bordering the stream were littered with drifts of scarlet and gold. There was a frosty nip in the air, and at night, streamers of ice had begun to form along the banks. To those who could read the sign, it was a portent of a long winter.

Early in November Tilghman and Thomas forded Red Rock Creek. They were south of Nowata, a backcountry crossroads located deep in the Cherokee Nation. Their trail had led from Oklahoma Territory to the Kansas border, and then into the hinterlands of Indian Territory. They were tracking Tom Yantis, a member of the Wild Bunch.

In late September, Tilghman had taken the oath in Guthrie and pinned on the badge of a deputy U.S. marshal. He'd done so with lingering reservations, partly due to his reluctance to be away from the ranch. A new aspect, and perhaps a larger part, was his reluctance to be away from Zoe Stratton. After the election day celebration in Chandler, they had begun keeping company on an informal basis. Nothing serious but nonetheless a budding relationship, one he intended to pursue.

Then, hardly a week after he'd been sworn in, the Dalton Gang had staged a daring raid. Bob Dalton and his band of renegades had attempted to rob two banks simultaneously in Coffeyville, Kansas. Their plan went awry from the beginning, and armed townspeople blocked any hope of escape. When the gunfire ended eight men—four citizens and four bandits—lay dead in the street. Three of the Dalton brothers, Bob, Emmett, and Grat, were among the dead.

The Dalton Gang had been wiped out on the streets of Coffeyville. Only two of the outlaws had escaped, a blooded killer named Bill Doolin and the last of the brothers, Will Dalton. For a week or so, federal marshals thought their major problem had been eliminated. Tilghman had signed on to help rid the territory of the Daltons, and for all practical purposes, the Dalton Gang had ceased to exist. His thoughts turned to the ranch, and Zoe, and he began planning a tactful way to resign his commission. Once again, thanks to the citizens of Coffeyville, he could put aside the badge.

But then, as though risen from the ashes, Bill Doolin took up the mantle. Within a week of the Coffeyville massacre he had formed a gang of his own, and apparently devoted considerable time and thought to making fools of the lawmen who chased him. From the little known of Doolin, he had worked as a cowhand in the Cherokee Outlet until a drunken spree resulted in a shootout with lawmen. When the smoke cleared, Doolin was still standing, miraculously unscathed, and two peace officers were dead. A killer with a price on his head, he'd taken what seemed the logical step. He joined the Dalton Gang.

From all appearances, he had learned well riding with the Daltons. His first move in forming a gang was to appoint Will Dalton as his second in command. Then, according to the grapevine, he had recruited a band of misfits and killers far worse than the Dalton Brothers. Among those he'd enlisted were Red Buck Waightman, Tulsa Jack Blake, Dynamite Dick Clifton, and Cimarron

Tom Yantis. Their nicknames, like badges of dishonor, tagged them one and all as renegades. Under Doolin's leadership, they began terrorizing the territory.

Tilghman, as well as Thomas and the other marshals, was taken by surprise. Doolin moved quickly, forging a gang while on the run, and proved to be far craftier than any of the Daltons. Less than a fortnight after the Coffeyville massacre, he and his gang robbed the Missouri-Pacific express on its passage through Indian Territory. After the holdup, Doolin adopted a new tactic, scattering his band to the winds throughout the Nations. The federal marshals were left with too many trails and too few clues. The chase ended hardly before it had begun.

U.S. Marshal Grimes then adopted a new tactic of his own. He summoned Tilghman and Thomas to Guthrie, and assigned them full-time to the Doolin Gang. By then the newspapers, always alert to a catchy headline, had dubbed this latest band of outlaws the "Wild Bunch." No sooner were the Daltons wiped out than the Wild Bunch appeared, and Grimes was under immense pressure from the governor to bring them down. Given the circumstances, Tilghman saw no diplomatic way to turn in his badge. The ranch, and Zoe, would have to wait.

With Heck Thomas, he began scouring every known outlaw haunt in the Nations. Then, during the last week in October, the gang struck again. Crossing the border into southwestern Kansas, Doolin and his men robbed the bank in Spearville. The Ford County sheriff pursued the band as they fled southeast and crossed the line into Oklahoma Territory. There his jurisdiction ended and pursuit became a matter for the federal marshals. But the robbers scattered once more, taking refuge in the Nations. Organized pursuit ended at that point.

Tilghman and Thomas, still operating on their own, began searching for leads. Over the years, working as a marshal out of Fort Smith, Thomas had developed informants throughout the Nations. For the most part, they were Indian farmers who believed that lawlessness, whether red or white, ill-served the Five Civilized Tribes. Their information came from a backwoods grapevine that was part fact and part rumor, and often unreliable. Fearing for their lives, few red men told the whole truth where white outlaws were concerned. Even fewer risked being identified as the source.

Late that afternoon a farmer outside Nowata had taken the risk. Unlike most Cherokees, his resentment of white men was not wholesale. Some he trusted and some he didn't, and Heck Thomas had long ago earned his confidence. The rumor he'd heard placed Tom Yantis at the home of a farmer on Red Rock Creek. Word had it that Yantis paid a steep price for refuge and the farmer's silence. But only yesterday, at the general store in Nowata, the farmer had displayed newfound wealth. When asked about his sudden prosperity, he'd been unable to resist a brag. He had a generous friend, one of the notorious Wild Bunch. Cimarron Tom Yantis.

Shortly before sundown, Tilghman and Thomas made camp along the creek. Though they both wore mackinaws, the night promised to be cold, and they selected a sheltered spot in a grove of trees. After tethering their horses, Tilghman began dressing a rabbit he'd shot along the trail. Thomas gathered wood, built a fire, and soon had a coffeepot perking. They traveled light, but there was always room for a small pot and a bag of coffee beans in their saddlebags. That was one luxury neither of them were willing to forego on a manhunt.

By dusk, they were seated around the fire with steaming cups of coffee. Their saddles served as comfortable backrests, and they watched as the rabbit roasted on a spit made of green tree limbs. There was now an easy familiarity between them, borne of long days and nights on trail. Neither of them was given to small talk, nor were they bothered by silence. Any conversation generally centered on their work.

"Funny," Thomas said in a musing tone. "You bust your ass chasing all over creation and getting nowhere. Then you ask a simple question and presto! You're on the right track."

Tilghman sipped coffee, warming his hands on the metal cup. "Guess it all depends on who's being asked the question. Not many Cherokees would give a straight answer."

"Cherokees, Choctaws, they're all the same. I must've spent a year in the Nations before anybody would talk to me. They just don't cotton to white men—lawmen especially."

"How'd you finally get on their good side? The ones that give you leads?"

"Wasn't easy," Thomas allowed. "Took time to get 'em to trust me. 'Course, there's damn few that give a hoot in hell about lawbreakers. Most figure it's just white man's business."

"Understandable," Tilghman said. "Leastways if you look at it from their standpoint. Whites aren't known for giving Indians a square deal."

"Christ, tell me about it! After all these years, there's still not more than a handful that'll part with information."

"Well, we got it today, Heck. I reckon that's what counts."

According to their source, the farm they sought was another three or four miles upstream. They planned to camp overnight and be on the trail before first light. Years of experience had taught them that dark nights were a dangerous time to confront men with guns. Dawn was the better time, when men's heads were fuzzed with sleep. That was their plan for tomorrow.

"Liable to be fireworks," Thomas said grimly. "Yantis

has a reputation as a hardcase. I doubt he'll go peaceable."

"Let's hope otherwise," Tilghman replied. "Dead men don't tell tales."

"You talkin' about Doolin?"

Tilghman nodded. "We need to take Yantis alive. He likely knows where Doolin's holed up."

Thomas snorted. "But will the scutter talk, or even surrender? I'd say he's more likely to fight."

There was no arguing the point. Despite the efforts of federal marshals, Oklahoma Territory remained a spawning ground for outlaws. The men who rode the owlhoot refused to acknowledge either the rights of the people or the might of the law. Over the line, in Indian Territory, the deadly game of hide-and-seek raged on unabated. The marshals held their own, generally killing more than they captured since the wanted men seldom surrendered without a fight. Yet there were scores of fledgling badmen waiting to fill the boots of every outlaw killed. Across the blackjack-studded hills of the Nations there was no end in sight.

"All the same," Tilghman said now, "Doolin's the prize catch. Let's try to take Yantis alive."

"No harm in tryin'," Thomas conceded. "Just don't get yourself killed in the bargain. Or me either."

On that note they fell silent. The rabbit, already split down the backbone, was removed from the spit. Fairly tender, dripping with succulent juices, the meat satisfied their hunger. After a final cup of coffee, the fire was built up against the chill night's wind. Then, their thoughts on tomorrow, they crawled into their bedrolls.

No more was said about Tom Yantis.

A faint streak of silver touched the eastern sky. The cabin stood in a clearing with a ramshackle shed and a corral off to one side. Beyond, in a large field, withered corn stalks bent beneath the morning frost. A tendril of smoke drifted skyward from the cabin chimney.

The lawmen waited in a stand of trees along the creek. Their horses were securely tied in a similar grove some hundred yards downstream. On foot, they had made their way along the north bank and taken a position opposite the front door of the cabin. They waited now for full dawn.

Tilghman carried a Winchester .44–.40 saddle carbine with a shell in the chamber. Thomas was armed with a 10-gauge double-barrel shotgun loaded with buckshot. Though both men packed pistols, experience dictated that a long-gun served better in the event of trouble. Given a choice, no man resorted to a pistol in a gunfight.

The sky slowly paled into full light. Neither of them spoke, for their plan was already in place. Thomas stepped clear of the trees, his shotgun extended, and advanced toward the cabin. Tilghman skirted the clearing, moving toward the shed, to cover the rear of the cabin. Three horses stood hip-shot in the corral, eyeing him warily as he approached. One of them suddenly snorted, and the other two took alarm. Hooves clattering on the frozen ground, they bolted to the opposite side of the corral.

The noise was like a drumbeat in the still air. From inside the cabin someone yelled, and the sound of feet on plank floors was plainly heard. Tilghman ducked behind the shed, thumbed the hammer on his carbine. Out front, Thomas threw the shotgun to his shoulder.

"Tom Yantis!" he shouted. "Federal marshals. Give yourself up!"

The back door burst open. A man in long johns and mule-eared boots rushed outside. He was carrying a cocked pistol in one hand and his pants in the other. As he turned toward the corral, he spotted Tilghman and abruptly stopped. His eyes were wide with fear.

"Hold it!" Tilghman ordered. "Drop the gun!"

Yantis reacted as though galvanized by the command. He snapped off a shot which thunked into boards of the shed. Thomas stepped around the corner of the house as Tilghman brought his Winchester to bear. The crack of the carbine mingled with the roar of the shotgun.

Struck from the front and the side, Yantis stumbled away in a nerveless dance. His long johns went red with blood and the pistol dropped from his hand. Then, arms flailing, he pitched to the ground.

Thomas advanced slowly, covering the rear door with his shotgun. He saw the Cherokee farmer dart a look through the open door, then slam it shut. Tilghman walked forward and knelt beside the fallen outlaw. He was amazed to find Yantis conscious, still alive.

"Tom," he said urgently. "Can you hear me?"

"Sonovabitch, you done killed me."

"Where's Doolin, Tom? Go out with a clear conscience. Tell me where to find Doolin."

Yantis smiled. "Go to hell."

Wet bubbles frothed his mouth with blood. The smile slipped, then vanished, and his eyes went blank. One boot wiggled in a spasm of death.

Thomas came closer. "What'd he say, Bill?"

"Told me to go to hell."

"Stupid bastard! Dumb as a goddamn rock. They all are!"

"Yeah, but he went out like a man, Heck. Leastways according to his lights."

"What d'you mean?"

"He died with his boots on."

Tilghman climbed to his feet. He stared down at the body, thoughtful a moment. Then he turned, headed back toward the creek. His features were solemn.

So much for taking Tom Yantis alive.

CHAPTER 9

The sky was dull as pewter. Tilghman studied the western horizon, where roiling clouds screened a late afternoon sun. There was a crisp smell in the air, and with Christmas only two days away, he wondered when it would snow. He hoped it would hold off until after tonight.

The Methodist Church in Chandler was holding a tree-decorating party. There would be food and fruit punch and carols to launch the Christmas season in proper style. Zoe had invited him to escort her to the party, even though he was a backslider where church was concerned. She jokingly threatened to bring him back into the fold.

Tilghman was still somewhat astounded by his own behavior. As he drove a buckboard toward the Stratton ranch, he calculated that he'd known Zoe not quite three months. In that time, he'd turned from a mature, sober-minded man to a moonstruck schoolboy. Or at least, in private moments, that's how he sometimes thought of himself. A man addled by a bewitching young woman.

Up ahead, in the deepening twilight, he saw the glow of lamps from the Stratton house. The ranch was situated along the banks of Quapaw Creek, with a sprawling log house overlooking the stream. To the rear of the house, there was a log barn with a corral attached to one side. The barn had stalls for ten horses and a milch cow, with cleared ground to the north for further expansion. There was a solid look of permanence about the place.

Outside the house, Tilghman reined his team to a halt. He stepped down, snapping a lead rope onto one horse's bridle, and left the team tied to a hitch rack. The air was sharp and brittle, and as he walked toward the house, it occurred to him that there was little question of a white Christmas. He crossed the porch and rapped lightly on the door. From inside, he heard the sound of footsteps.

Amos Stratton opened the door. "Good evening, Bill." He motioned inside. "Come in out of the cold."

"Evening, Amos." Tilghman stepped through the door, removing his hat. "Looks like we'll get snow before long."

"I would judge tomorrow at the latest."

Stratton led him into the parlor. By now they were on a first-name basis, though Tilghman was never comfortable in the man's presence. There was a forced cordiality between them, and he sensed that Stratton somehow disapproved of him. Nothing spoken, but nonetheless there.

A stack of logs blazed in the fireplace. Tilghman shrugged out of his greatcoat and hooked it on a coatrack beside the door. As he entered the parlor, Stratton waved to a sofa.

"Have a seat," he said. "Zoe will be along directly. She's still getting ready."

"Fire feels good tonight."

"Yes, you'll have a cold ride into town."

Tilghman took a seat on the sofa. Stratton dropped into an easy chair and began loading a pipe. Watching him, Tilghman thought he had the look of a lonely man.

Zoe's mother had died several years ago, and Stratton, who owned a farm in Missouri at the time, had taken it hard. Later, after selling the farm, he'd decided to join the Land Rush and homestead land in Oklahoma Territory. From his manner, he had yet to escape the ghosts of his past.

Stratton struck a match, lighting his pipe. He puffed a wad of smoke and tossed the match into the fireplace. "How're things?" he said distantly. "Your horses making out all right?"

"Ask me come spring," Tilghman said. "I'm hoping Steeldust sired some fast-steppers."

"Never understood what interests you about race-horses."

"Lots of money to be made with racing. Not bragging, but I did pretty good with that operation over in Guthrie."

"Saddle stock," Stratton announced. "There's always a market for saddle horses. Good business, solid and dependable."

"That why you got into it?"

"Farmed most of my life and little to show for it. Horses look to me to have a brighter future. Saddle horses, anyhow."

"Yeah, you're right," Tilghman agreed. "I see racing as a sideline with big potential. The other part of my breeding is for ranch stock, good cow ponies. That's steady business."

A silence fell between them. Stratton stared off into the fire, puffing his pipe. Tilghman got the impression that the other man was trying to pick an argument. But to what purpose, or for what reason, was unclear. At length, Stratton looked around.

"What's new with the Wild Bunch?"

"Not a whole lot," Tilghman admitted. "Seems like they've gone to ground."

"You think they've quit the territory?"

"Doolin's not the type to quit and run. Not from what I've heard, anyway. I tend to doubt we've seen the last of him."

Stratton grunted. "So why's he laying low?"

"One guess is as good as another. I reckon only Doolin knows the answer."

For all their determination, the federal marshals had been singularly unsuccessful in running Doolin to earth. The gangleader and his Wild Bunch seemingly had vanished into thin air. Nearly two months had passed with no robberies, and no reported sightings of Doolin or his men. Nor were the informants of Heck Thomas able to turn up a lead in the Nations. Despite rewards now totaling ten thousand dollars, there was nothing but silence. No one knew anything.

Tilghman suspected that it was somehow tied to the death of Tom Yantis. The killing might well have convinced Doolin and his gang to take a breather. Or for that matter, what with the cold and snow, the Wild Bunch might simply have taken the winter off. They had money in their pockets from the last bank holdup, and they could easily have decided on a holiday. For all anyone knew, they were in New Orleans or St. Louis having the time of their lives. After their money ran out and the manhunt subsided, they could return to work. There was always another train to rob.

In the meantime, Tilghman had kept himself occupied with the ranch and the routine tedium of a lawman. While liquor was legal in the territory, its sale was restricted to white men. Federal law made it a felony to sell alcoholic spirits of any variety to an Indian. The prohibition made for a brisk business in Oklahoma Territory, particularly along the borders of the Creek and Seminole nations. Over the past month Tilghman had arrested eight whiskey peddlers and confiscated their wares. All of them had been treated to a swift trial, and convicted.

Still, Tilghman had little interest in apprehending
backwoods whiskey smugglers. He was convinced
Doolin would resurface, and he stayed on because he'd
given his word to Heck Thomas. Beyond that, he saw a
pattern of lawlessness developing in Oklahoma Territory. Before the land runs, Texas ranchers had leased
great tracts of grazeland from various tribes. But with
settlement, farms had displaced the cattle spreads, and
hundreds of cowhands were thrown out of work. Left to
idle in saloons and contemplate the menace of railroads
and sodbusters, many felt they had been dealt a low
blow. They righted this seeming injustice by turning to
an occupation with short working hours and incompara-
ble wages. They became outlaws.

Just in the past week, working with the county sheriff,
Tilghman had caught three former cowhands turned
horse thieves. Given different circumstances, or bolder
spirits, they could have easily robbed a bank. One crime
led to another, and in the end, any man who rode the
owlhoot was capable of killing to avoid a stretch in
prison. The more he thought about it, the more Tilghman realized that it wasn't altogether his word to Heck
Thomas that kept him on the job. Though he wouldn't
admit it to anyone, he'd grudgingly come to accept what
Neal Brown and other friends had told him for many
years. He had the calling to be a lawman.

Stratton's voice intruded on his woolgathering. "Zoe
tells me you've been married before."

"Yeah, I was," Tilghman said without inflection. "My
wife died last year. Influenza."

"Sorry to hear it." Stratton stared at him, puffing on
his pipe. "You looking to get married again?"

Tilghman shrugged it off. "I haven't given it much
thought."

"High time, then," Stratton said in a hard voice. "A
man your age ought not to toy with the affections of a
young girl."

"A man my age?"

"Zoe tells me you're thirty-six. She's barely twenty, and the way I figure, that's a sight of difference. Aren't you a little old for her?"

Tilghman saw where the argument lay now. By all appearances, he and Stratton were separated in age by not more than ten years. Stratton clearly thought of him as an older man, someone in his own generation. Far too old for his daughter.

"I'm younger than I look," Tilghman said in an off-hand manner. "And I don't have any wrong intentions toward Zoe. You can rest easy on that score."

"Never said otherwise," Stratton muttered. "What I'm saying is, she hasn't so much as looked at another man since you came on the scene. Don't you think she deserves a man her own age?"

"I think that's for Zoe to decide. She's free to see whoever she wants."

"Not as long as you're around," Stratton said harshly. "She's got stardust in her eyes. Any fool can see that."

"Look, I'm not trying—"

"Good evening." Zoe suddenly swept through the entrance to the parlor. "Did I interrupt something?"

"No, no," Stratton said hurriedly. He rose, moving to the fireplace, and knocked the dottle from his pipe. "We were just debating the merits of racehorses versus saddle stock."

She looked at Tilghman. "Believe it or not," she said brightly, "I'm finally ready. Shall we go?"

"You bet." Tilghman walked to the door, gathering his hat and greatcoat. "Nice talking with you, Amos."

"You too, Bill," Stratton said amiably. "We'll have to do it again."

Zoe kissed her father good night while Tilghman shrugged into his coat. He helped her into a long cape with a fur-trimmed hood and they went through the door. Outside, he got her settled in the backboard and draped a woolen blanket over her lap for added warmth. Then he unhitched the horses and climbed into the driver's seat. He popped the reins.

"Well now," he said, glancing at her. "You're looking mighty pretty tonight."

She sniffed. "Don't try to pretty-please me, Bill Tilghman. What were you and father talking about?"

"Like he told you—"

"Honestly! You must think I'm a little scatterbrain. I want to know what you were arguing about—right now!"

Tilghman was tempted to kiss her. She was full of spirit and spunk, and he could imagine her eyes flashing green in the dark night. There was a vibrancy about her so compelling that he felt captivated all over again. He chuckled softly.

"You want the truth?"

"Yes, I do! And with no soft-soap, Mr. Tilghman."

"You won't tell him I told, will you?"

"Cross my heart," she said pertly. "So what did he say?"

"Well, in a nutshell—" Tilghman watched her out of the corner of his eye. "Your pa thinks I'm too old for you."

"Does he indeed?" she said in a exasperated tone. "And what did you say?"

"I told him I'm younger than I look."

"Of course you are!"

Tilghman suppressed a smile. "And that I have no improper intentions toward you."

"You didn't!" Her eyes danced with merriment. "You actually said that to him?"

"Seemed like the right thing at the time. What with you being so young and innocent, and all."

"Oh, fudge!" She dug him in the ribs with her elbow. "You're teasing me, aren't you?"

"Who, me?" Tilghman said with mock concern. "You think I'm one to step out of line?"

"Nooo," she said slowly. "But sometimes I wish you'd try—just a little."

"I'll be switched. I think you mean that."

"I never say anything I don't mean. You should know that by now."

"In that case," Tilghman prompted her, "what are you going to tell your pa?"

"I'm going to tell him to mind his own business. I'll decide who's too old and who isn't."

"So where does that leave me?"

"Just exactly where you belong."

She scooted closer, throwing the blanket over his lap as well. She put her arm through his, hugging him, and nestled her head against his shoulder. Then, closer still, she uttered a low, throaty laugh.

"Doesn't that feel about right?"

Tilghman smiled. "I think it's Christmas already."

The cold forgotten, they drove toward town.

CHAPTER 10

The corner of Harrison and Second was the liveliest spot in Guthrie. Chambers for the territorial legislature occupied the upper story of the International Building, which was located on the southeast corner. Across the street was the Palace Hotel, where the politicians made their home away from home when the legislature was in session.

The Reaves Brothers Casino, fanciest sporting emporium in the territory, stood three stories high on the northwest corner. Directly opposite was the Blue Bell Saloon, a most democratic bucket of gore catering to anyone with the price of a drink. A hangout for the town's rougher element, it was known by such aphorisms as the Slaughterhouse and the Butcher Shop.

On any given night the intersection was a beehive of activity. The hotel was elegantly posh, the casino was an orderly temple of vice, and the saloon was a riotous circus of mayhem. Businessmen and gamblers, hardcases and politicians, whores and barflies came there in a sweaty pursuit of the fast life.

Tilghman dismounted outside the hotel early that evening. A groom took his horse to a stable around the corner and he entered the hotel with his warbag. After registering, he went to his room and sponged off trail-dust in the washbasin. Then, downstairs again, he treated himself to a steak dinner in the dining room. By eight o'clock he was headed uptown.

A few minutes later he knocked on the door of Heck Thomas's home. When Thomas opened the door, his face creased with surprise. "Bill!" he said, grinning. "Where'd you come from?"

"Just rode in," Tilghman said. "Took a room down at the Palace."

"Well, don't stand there." Thomas turned, shouting to his wife, "Hey, Dottie, look who's here."

Dorothy Thomas was a plain woman with an engaging manner. She greeted Tilghman warmly and served coffee after the men were seated in the parlor. Then, aware that Tilghman's visit was business rather than social, she excused herself. Thomas drained his coffee cup.

"I take it you're here for the big powwow tomorrow?"

Tilghman nodded. "Got my invite yesterday."

"Helluva note," Thomas observed. "Just tied a can to Grimes's tail. He deserved better."

"That's politics, Heck. One day here, the next day gone."

Tilghman's remark went to the heart of the matter. The new year had gotten off to an unsettling start when President Benjamin Harrison reaffirmed the old adage that politics does indeed make for strange bedfellows. He opened 1890 with sweeping changes in the political hierarchy of Oklahoma Territory. The changes were the result of widespread criticism about what the newspapers termed the "anarchy of outlawism." Factions in Congress declared it a national disgrace.

Until statehood was granted, a territory was at the mercy of the federal government. The president, by the stroke of a pen, could alter virtually any aspect of territorial affairs. Which was precisely what President Harrison had done shortly after the first of the year. In one surgical stroke, after weighing the counsel of his advisors, he removed the Republicans and replaced them with Democrats.

Heading the list was Governor George Steele. He was unceremoniously dumped, and overnight, William Renfrow, a banker from the town of Norman, was sworn in as the new governor. Political wags were quick to note that he had been responsible for naming a street in the territorial capital after President Harrison. Apart from the governor, the shakeup extended to the territorial supreme court as well as district courts throughout Oklahoma. Over twenty political appointees fell before the axe.

For Tilghman, the general upheaval had only passing interest. He studiously avoided the political arena, and he held most politicians in low regard. Yet the U.S. marshal, who had served with distinction, had ultimately won his respect. Unlike most appointees, who saw themselves as administrators, Walt Grimes had often accompanied his deputies into the field, and traded shots with outlaws. Still, despite his efforts to establish law and order, he belonged to the wrong political party. He'd been swept out with the other Republicans.

The man who replaced him was Evett Nix, a staunch Democrat. Though he had no law enforcement experience, Nix was a prominent figure in Guthrie political circles. A former Kentuckian, he had joined the first land rush, and was a partner in the town's leading wholesale grocery concern. Quoted widely in the newspapers, he had vowed to rid Oklahoma Territory of its outlaw element. Upon appointment as U.S. marshal, he had requested authorization for a hundred deputies, five times the number currently serving. If nothing else, his brash demands kept his name in the headlines.

On January 8, the day after Nix's appointment, Tilghman received a tersely worded summons. He was to report to the marshal's office in Guthrie on the morning of January 10. The message gave no reason as to the

purpose of the summons, or Nix's intentions. But Tilghman, figuring it was politics as usual, had a hunch his
commission would be revoked. What surprised him
most was that he found the thought curiously unsettling,
not at all to his liking. He'd somehow experienced a
turnaround during his months on the trail with Heck
Thomas. He wanted to stay on as a deputy.

Tilghman departed the afternoon before the meeting.
There was no train service between Chandler and Guthrie, though the stagecoach line made twice-daily stops.
Still, he had no fondness for crowded coaches, and the
inevitable conversations that developed with other passengers. He decided to travel on horseback, which gave
him time to further ponder the situation. The ranch, as
was customary during his absences on law business, was
left under the care of Neal Brown. As he rode out, it
occurred to him that his old friend was more essential
than ever to the operation. Except for Brown, he could
never have signed on as a marshal.

Outside Chandler, on the road to Guthrie, he'd been
struck by a thought that kindled mixed emotions.
Should he be dismissed as a deputy, that would allow
him far more time to spend with Zoe. Since Christmas,
he had seen her at every opportunity, and she clearly
welcomed his company. Whatever she'd said to her father, Amos Stratton had never again raised the subject
of their age difference. Yet, however much he wanted to
be with her, he was uneasy with the idea of no more law
work. The months spent tracking Doolin and the Wild
Bunch had reawakened his taste for challenge. His life
was somehow fuller as a lawman.

All in all, it required a fine balancing act. The ranch,
and Zoe, and working as a lawman, kept him hopping
like a one-legged man in a footrace. But he'd somehow
come to the point that he wanted it all, the ranch and
Zoe and the badge. Of course, as he pondered it now,
the thought occurred that he might no longer have a

problem. Evett Nix, the new U.S. marshal, might solve it for him. He could lose his badge tomorrow.

"For all we know," Thomas said, as though reading his mind, "we could be out of a job ourselves."

"Have you talked to Nix?"

"Not to speak of," Thomas replied. "Went by the office the day he took over. We shook hands and danced around the mulberry bush. He told me to sit tight until the meeting tomorrow."

"That's it?" Tilghman said. "No clue about what he intends?"

"Whatever it is, he wasn't talkin'."

"How'd you size him up?"

Thomas frowned. "Way I figure it, he's a crossbreed. Half go-get-'em businessman and half politician. Likeable enough, but a quick, no-nonsense way about him."

"What's the word around town?" Tilghman asked. "Does he aim to use the marshal's office as a stepping-stone to something bigger?"

"Haven't heard anything, but it wouldn't come as no shock. He's like fleas on a dog with the bigwig Democrats."

Tilghman knuckled his mustache. "So we're betwixt and between until tomorrow. Nothing to go on."

"Looks that way," Thomas grumped. "Just a cog in the wheel."

"What about Chris Madsen? Hear anything about him?"

"Yeah, he rode in late this afternoon. Sat where you're sittin' and asked the same questions. I had no more answers then than I do now."

Tilghman caught the concern in his voice. "What will you do if Nix turns us out to pasture?"

Thomas suddenly laughed. "Bill, I've been a lawdog most of my life. Never yet had a problem finding another badge."

"All the same, we started out to catch Doolin. I hate to leave a job undone."

"You've shore swung around, haven't you?"

"How's that?"

Thomas grinned. "Hell's bells, I had to twist your arm to sign you on. Now, you're worried it won't last. Go ahead and tell me I'm wrong."

"You're a bad influence," Tilghman said with a slow smile. "Knew it the day I met you."

"Howsomever, we're alike in one way, my friend."

"What way is that?"

"We feel naked without a badge—don't we?"

Their eyes locked in a moment of silent communion. Then, slowly, Tilghman nodded.

The following morning, at eight o'clock sharp, Thomas, Madsen, and Tilghman trooped into the U.S. marshal's office. To their amazement, they were the only ones there. None of the other deputies had been summoned.

Evett Nix was a stocky man, on the sundown side of forty. His manner was brusque and businesslike, his eyes penetrating and shrewd. He greeted them with a perfunctory handshake and asked them to be seated. Then, wasting no time, he went straight to the point.

"First things first," he said. "All the deputies on the roster still have a job. That includes you three."

A sense of tension seemed to melt from the room. He waited a moment, allowing them to absorb the news, then went on. "Walt Grimes lost his job for two reasons, gentlemen. One, which amounts to bad luck, he was a Republican. And second, which was a matter of poor timing, he failed to bring Bill Doolin to justice."

Again, he paused, awaiting a reaction. When none of the men spoke, he continued. "One day, I may lose this job because I'm a Democrat. But, gentlemen—" He stopped, looked each of them directly in the eye. "I assure you I will not be turned out because of some half-assed desperado. *Bill Doolin will be caught.*"

Nix let the words hang in the air. He had been standing during the entire speech, and now he took a seat behind his desk. He steepled his fingers into a church, staring at them.

"Mr. Thomas. Mr. Tilghman. In your opinion, why is Doolin still on the loose?"

Thomas and Tilghman exchanged a look. After a moment, Tilghman took the lead. "You'll recollect that Jesse James was betrayed and killed, but never caught. That's because he adopted the tactics of Quantrill, the Civil War guerrilla. Doolin operates the same way."

"Hit and run," Thomas added. "Then scatter and go to ground. Like Bill says, he's real slippery."

"I agree," Nix said, surprising them. "So we're going to increase the heat on Doolin. As of today"—he nodded pointedly to Chris Madsen—"you three are assigned to the Wild Bunch."

Tilghman looked uncomfortable. "Are we being transferred?"

"No," Nix said. "You'll stay in Chandler. Mr. Madsen remains in El Reno. And Mr. Thomas here in Guthrie. But starting now, you forget whiskey smugglers and other small-timers. Your efforts will be solely directed to Bill Doolin."

"Amen to that," Thomas said approvingly. "Do we work separately or as a team?"

"Do whatever the situation demands. Just get the job done quickly. Understood?"

Without waiting for a response, he looked at Tilghman. "An unsigned letter arrived the day I took office. Are you familiar with the town of Ingalls?"

"Never been there," Tilghman said. "It's about a half day's ride north of Chandler."

"According to the letter, Doolin has a hideout somewhere around Ingalls. I want you to scout it out on the quiet. Any questions?"

There were no questions. Nix shook their hands and the three lawmen walked to the door. In the hallway, Tilghman looked first at Madsen and then at Thomas. His expression was quizzical.

"What do you think, Heck?"

"Boys, I think we've got ourselves a marshal. Hooray and hallelujah."

CHAPTER 11

Three days later Tilghman rode into Ingalls. He wore rough range clothing and he was posing as a horse trader. The name he'd adopted was Jack Curry.

Tilghman had given considerable thought to the assignment. He was working on the premise that the information received in the anonymous letter was correct. If so, then Doolin was hiding out in the vicinity of Ingalls, betrayed by someone for reasons as yet unknown. Outlaws were oftentimes brought down by betrayal rather than good detective work.

Still, the letter itself was just a starting point. To pinpoint the location of Doolin's hideout would require detective work. So Tilghman had decided to operate undercover, adopting a disguise. In small towns, particularly one harboring a fugitive, any stranger was suspect. But horse traders, who commonly traveled the backcountry, were less suspect than most. Jack Curry might get someone to talk.

Ingalls was about what Tilghman had expected. The main street was less than a quarter mile long, with frame structures wedged together in a small business district. There were the usual shops and stores, with a saloon situated across from a two-story hotel. At the far end of the street, a livery stable was separated from the other buildings. Houses were randomly scattered across the land surrounding the business district. From all appearances, the population was less than four hundred people.

Tilghman tried to think like the man he hunted. From Doolin's standpoint, there was a certain warped logic in choosing Ingalls as a hideout. The town was located close to the Kansas border, and Doolin could easily stop off there after raids across the state line. Moreover, Guthrie was only a half day's ride to the west; no one would expect the Wild Bunch leader to hole up so near the territorial capital. With the rest of the gang scattered throughout the Nations, Ingalls was the last place anyone would look for Doolin. In many ways, it was a perfect hideout.

Tilghman reined to a halt outside the saloon. A recent snowfall had melted off, and the street was thick with mud. As he stepped down from the saddle, he was aware of the scrutiny of people along the boardwalks. Word spread quickly in a small town, and he warned himself not to overplay his hand. One misstep, particularly among people friendly to Doolin, and he would be pegged as a lawman. He took his time, acting the casual traveler, and loosened the cinch to give his horse a breather. Then, stamping mud from his boots, he entered the saloon.

The interior was bathed in sunlight from the front windows. Along one wall was the bar, and tables and chairs were arranged along the opposite wall. Halfway down the bar, in the middle of the room, a large pot-bellied stove glowed with heat. A lone customer stood with one foot hooked over the brass rail, staring into a whiskey glass. The barkeep, sporting a handlebar mustache, was wiping down the counter. His expression was neutral.

"Help you?"

"Gimme a beer," Tilghman said. "Little early for the hard stuff."

"Says you," the customer retorted in a slurred voice. "Ain't never no bad time for a drink."

"No offense, mister. Just makin' conversation."

Tilghman removed his mackinaw and draped it over the counter. The bartender filled a schooner from the tap, then walked back and placed it in front of Tilghman. Leaning closer, he cut his eyes at the other customer. He spoke in a muffled voice.

"Don't pay him no mind. He's got a snootful."

"Likes his liquor, does he?"

"Every town's got a barfly. He's ours."

"Know what you mean," Tilghman said. "In my business, I see lots of towns. They're all the same."

"What line you in?"

"Horse trader." Tilghman stuck out his hand. "Name's Jack Curry."

"Joe Harmon." The barkeep accepted his handshake. "You from hereabouts?"

"Here, there, and everywhere. I buy stock for the army."

"Army payin' good these days?"

"Top dollar." Tilghman sipped beer, wiped foam off his mustache. "Government buys the best for its soldier boys."

Harmon nodded. "That what brings you to Ingalls?"

"Heard there were some good size ranches around these parts. Thought I'd have a looksee."

"Yeah, there's some with horses."

"Anybody special?" Tilghman inquired. "I'm lookin' for top-notch stock."

Harmon considered a moment. "You might try the Dunn brothers. Got a spread out on Council Creek."

"Yeah, you do that," the barfly crowed, chortling a drunken laugh. "Careful of their visitor, though. He don't cotton to strangers."

"What visitor's that?"

"Why, the big man hisself—"

"Close your trap!" Harmon thundered. "Or some-body'll close it for you."

"Hell, Joe, I ain't tellin' tales outta school. Everybody in town knows."

"You heard me, you stupid son-of-a-bitch. Button your lip!"

"Aww, for chrissakes."

The man wobbled away with his whiskey glass, drop-ping into a chair at one of the tables. Harmon stared at him angrily, then let out a long sigh. He shook his head, glancing at Tilghman.

"Pay him no mind. Just a drunk runnin' off at the mouth."

"None of my business," Tilghman said pleasantly. "Sounded like hot air to me."

"Bastard's full of it, all right."

"Let's get back to horses. You were tellin' me about—what'd you say—the Dunn brothers?"

Harmon appeared troubled. He wrestled with it a moment, then shrugged. "Bee and George, they're brothers. Always got horses for sale. Ask for either one."

Tilghman got directions while he finished his beer. After paying for the drink, he gathered his mackinaw and headed for the door. The barkeep's display of tem-per convinced him that he'd struck a nerve. Even more so from the barfly's slip of the tongue. The Dunn broth-ers were hiding someone.

Outside, Tilghman surveyed the street. Across the way he saw a barber shop, and decided to probe a bit further. A few minutes later he was seated in the bar-ber's chair, once again relating his business as a horse trader. The barber was a loquacious man who admired the sound of his own voice. His shop, just as Tilghman had suspected, was a clearing house for the town's gossip.

"Yessir," the barber said, snipping away with his scissors. "The Dunn boys pride themselves on their horses. You ought to do right well."

"Guess they made the run like everybody else?"

"Ummm." The scissors stopped, and the barber's voice dropped to a confidential tone. "Don't tell 'em I told you, but they were Sooners. Got themselves the best piece of land on Council Creek."

"Mum's the word with me," Tilghman promised. "Curious you mention it, though. I heard something over in the saloon that's hard to believe."

"Oh, what's that?"

"Well, there was this drunk—"

"Lon Anderson, a first-rate boozehound!"

"Never caught his name," Tilghman went on. "Anyway, he says the Dunns are hidin' that outlaw, Bill Doolin. Damn hard to believe."

The barber glanced around the empty shop, as though he might be overheard. "Not exactly a secret," he said softly. "Everyone in town has known about it for months."

"You're joshin' me!"

"No, it's the truth. Way I hear it, Doolin's sweet on Edith Ellsworth. The postmaster's daughter."

Tilghman looked worried. "Maybe I ought not to pay a call on the Dunns. I'd sure hate to run across Bill Doolin in the flesh."

"Well—" the barber started snipping again. "So I'm told, he's not there now. Took off a couple of days ago."

"By golly, for an outlaw, he's got damn few secrets. Seems a mite strange."

"The Ellsworth girl tells her friends, and they tell their friends, and word gets around. Not many secrets in a small town."

"And nobody's turned him into the law?"

The scissors stopped. "I wouldn't risk my life against him and his Wild Bunch. Would you?"

"Nosiree," Tilghman said, wagging his head. "Let him rob all the banks and trains he wants. Live and let live, that's my motto."

"Exactly right, Mr. Curry. Why borrow trouble?"

Early that afternoon Tilghman reined to a halt on Council Creek. He was two miles southeast of Ingalls, and ahead, beyond a bend in the stream, lay the Dunn brothers' ranch. Dismounting, he took a folding telescope from his saddlebags and left his horse tied in a grove of trees. He walked forward, taking cover in the treeline.

Extending the spyglass, he slowly studied the ranch compound. The main house was a log and frame structure, situated at the bottom of a low knoll. A short distance away was a large corral with some thirty head of horses standing hip-shot in the corral. East of the house a storm cellar had been dug in the hillside and roofed with heavy timber. Smoke funneled from the house chimney, indicating it was occupied. But no one was in sight.

After a thorough inspection, he collapsed the spyglass. Based on the barber's information, he hadn't expected to spot Bill Doolin. Still, he'd wanted to scout the lay of the land, perhaps have a word with the Dunns about horses. But now, having seen it, he decided there was no point in pushing his luck. Better to return another day, when he was certain that the gangleader was there. The idea was to capture Doolin, not put him on guard.

On the way back to town, Tilghman sorted through the pieces. There was no reason to disbelieve a talkative drunk or a gossipy barber. In fact, from their reactions as well as their words, there was good reason to believe they were telling the truth. All of which would explain where Doolin had spent the winter months, and why. Even outlaws had a personal life, and everything indicated that Doolin was serious about the Ellsworth girl. The masterstroke was that no one would have looked for Doolin so close to Guthrie. He'd fooled them all.

Yet one piece of the puzzle was still to be found. The letter to the U.S. marshal left no doubt that someone had a score to settle with Doolin. A grudge so strong, in fact, that someone had betrayed him to the authorities. Whoever it was preferred to remain anonymous rather than risk death. But the letter had been postmarked from Ingalls. . . .

Tilghman played a hunch. Earlier that day, he'd noticed a post office sign hanging over the door outside the general store. A bitter wind blew in from the north as he dismounted before the store and looped the reins around a hitch rack. Inside, a woman waited while a man behind the counter made change for her purchases. She was the only customer in the store.

A cage at the rear fronted a space that served as the post office. Tilghman walked to the cage window and halted, leaning on the counter. The storekeeper was in his early forties, a heavyset man with thinning hair and wire spectacles hooked over the bridge of his nose. When the woman departed with her parcels, he turned and moved toward the rear. He nodded to Tilghman.

"Afternoon."

"Howdy," Tilghman said. "Got anything general delivery for Jack Curry?"

The storekeeper glanced at a rack of mailboxes on the wall. "Sorry," he said. "Nothing for general delivery at all."

"Too bad." Tilghman looked at him through the cage. "You the postmaster?"

"John Ellsworth," the man said, nodding. "I take it you're Mr. Curry."

"That's me," Tilghman said. "Just got to town today, and you know—I heard the darnedest thing."

"What might that be?"

"Heard your daughter's keeping steady company with Bill Doolin."

Ellsworth's face blanched. His jowls rippled as he shook his head. "You heard wrong, Mr. Curry."

"Think not," Tilghman corrected him. "Not after that letter you sent to the U.S. marshal."

Ellsworth blinked, his features suddenly gone pasty. "I don't know what you're talking about."

The startled reaction was all Tilghman needed. He now had the answer as to who had written the letter. A respectable storekeeper, trying to protect his daughter, had silently betrayed an outlaw. He nodded to Ellsworth, then walked toward the door.

"Give my regards to Doolin next time he calls on your daughter."

CHAPTER 12

The plains of western Kansas were blanketed with light snow. Overnight the skies had cleared and a warm morning sun was slowly melting the snowfall. Wet and glistening, a ribbon of steel, the Santa Fe tracks stretched onward to the horizon.

The California Express hurtled through the town of Cimarron. Coupled to the rear of the engine and the tender were an express car and five passenger coaches. As the locomotive sped past the small depot, the engineer tooted his whistle. The train's final destination was Los Angeles.

A mile west of town, on a dogleg curve, a tree had been felled across the tracks. The engineer set the brakes, wheels grinding on steel rails, and the train jarred to a screeching halt. The sudden jolt caught the passengers unawares, and there was a moment of pandemonium in the coaches. Luggage went flying from the overhead racks as women screamed and men cursed.

Then, suddenly, a collective hush fell over the coaches. From under the bridge where trees bordered the river, a gang of riders burst out of the woods. Four men rode directly to the express car, pouring a volley of shots through the door. Another man, his pistol drawn, jumped from his horse to the steps of the locomotive.

The engineer and his fireman dutifully raised their hands.

The three remaining gang members, spurring their horses hard, charged up and down the track bed. Their pistols were cocked and pointed at the passengers, who stared open-mouthed through the coach windows. No shots were fired, but their menacing attitude and tough appearance made the message all too clear. Anyone who resisted or attempted to flee the train would be killed.

The threat made eminent good sense to the passengers. Like most railroads, the Santa Fe was not revered by the public. For thirty years, Eastern Robber Barons had plundered the West on land grants and freight rates. A holdup, according to common wisdom, was a matter between the railroad and the bandits. Only a fool would risk his life to thwart a robbery. And there were no fools aboard today.

From the coaches, the passengers had a ringside seat. They watched as the four men outside the express car demonstrated their no-nonsense approach to train robbery. One of the riders produced a stick of dynamite and held the fuse only inches away from the tip of a lighted cigar. Another rider, whose commanding presence pegged him as the gangleader, gigged his horse onto the road bed. His voice raised in a shout, he informed the express guards that they had a choice.

"Open the door or get blown to kingdom come!"

The guards, much like the passengers, were unwilling to die for the Santa Fe. The door quickly slid open and they tossed their pistols onto the ground. Three of the robbers dismounted and clambered inside the express car. The leader, positioned outside the car, directed the operation from aboard his horse. His tone had the ring of authority, brusque and demanding. His attitude was that of a man accustomed to being obeyed.

From start to finish, the holdup took less than five

minutes. The robbers inside the express car emerged
with mail sacks stuffed full of cash and mounted their
horses. On signal from their leader, the gang raked the
length of the train with a barrage of gunfire. The shots
were purposely placed high, but windows shattered and
wall panels splintered. As bullets ripped through the
coaches, everyone dove for the floor and prudently
stayed there. A moment later the thud of hoofbeats
drummed the earth.

Bill Doolin led his gang down the embankment at the
edge of the bridge. They disappeared into the trees and
rode single file along the river. To their rear, they heard
the train get under way and commence backing toward
the town of Cimarron. Within the hour word of the
holdup would spread across Kansas by telegraph. But
for now, there was no pursuit and they'd looted the train
without taking casualty. Their excitement erupted as
they turned south toward the state line.

"Gawddamn!" Dynamite Dick Clifton whooped. "We
pulled it off slicker 'n greased owlshit!"

"Bet your sweet ass!" Tulsa Jack Blake howled. "How
much you think we got, Bill?"

"Enough," Doolin said shortly. "Quit yellin' and keep
your mind on business. We're not out of the woods yet."

"Aw hell, Bill," Blake protested. "Don't be a spoil-
sport. We done good."

"There's time to celebrate when we cross the line.
You boys keep a sharp lookout."

Doolin set a faster pace. He understood their need to
let off steam, but his mind was fixed on eluding pursuit.
He found it impossible to unwind until they crossed the
border, split the loot, and scattered. His tireless vigilance, mixed with a healthy respect for lawmen, was the
reason he'd never been caught. Unlike most outlaws,
who viewed their profession with a degree of fatalism,
he had no intention of dying with his boots on. That was
for suckers and superstitious dimdots.

Apart from brutish courage, the men he rode with had contributed little to the gang's unblemished record. They were vengeful and reckless, superb haters, but not a mental wizard in the bunch. To a man, they gloried in their nicknames—Bitter Creek, Tulsa Jack, Dynamite Dick—devoting considerable thought to the selection of a *nom de guerre.* That was their mark in life, the prize sought by emotionally stunted men. A badge of distinction in a world that had branded them outcasts.

It took a strong man, someone with brains and nerve, to hold them in line. Doolin imposed his will by force when necessary, but more often through cunning and a steel-trap mind. There was nothing striking about his appearance, for he was lean and of average height, his skin seared by years of wind and sun. Yet he was hard and ruthless, deadly when provoked, with a certain genius for channeling the hate of others to his own ends. His manner was like that of a crafty savage.

When he'd organized the Wild Bunch, he had started with a band of congenital misfits. With leadership and discipline, he had converted them into a fierce, tightly-knit gang, and never for a moment had he let them forget that it was his savvy which kept them alive. Every job was planned in detail, and the holdups were staged with a military sense of precision. Anyone who got in the way was dispatched with businesslike efficiency, and the raids were characterized by the gang seemingly vanishing in a cloud of dust. His men looked upon him with the awe of stupefied boys watching a magician.

Today, as on other raids, Doolin's attention centered on the next step in the plan. Telegraph wires were singing and pursuit by Kansas lawmen was certain. The immediate goal was to cross the line into Oklahoma Territory, where Kansas jurisdiction ended. Even then, sheriffs and federal marshals throughout the territory would have been alerted by telegraph. But once the loot was split, and the gang scattered, the odds improved greatly. There would be eight trails to follow instead of one, and the law hadn't yet proved equal to the task. Still, he relied on caution as much as guile, for there were no old, bold outlaws. A man survived on the owlhoot by taking nothing for granted.

He led his men toward the border.

Late the next day Doolin rode into Ingalls. He was accompanied by Jack Blake and Dick Clifton, who stared suspiciously at passersby on the street. Outside the hotel the men assisted him off his horse and he hobbled inside on one foot. The desk clerk nodded to them with a sallow smile.

"Afternoon, gentlemen."

"I want a room," Doolin ordered. "Give me one on the ground floor."

"Yessir," the clerk said. "How long will you be staying with us?"

"Till I'm ready to leave. Let's have a key."

Doolin signed the register as John Smith and took the key from the clerk. Then he turned to his men. "Jack, go find the local sawbones and send him over here. After that, get the girl I told you about and bring her along. Got it straight?"

"Sure thing, Bill."

Blake hurried out the door. Doolin, one arm around Clifton's shoulders, limped off down the hallway. Once inside the room he tossed his hat aside and flopped down on the bed. A dark stain, crusted with blood, covered the arch of his left boot. He pulled a jackknife from his pocket and flicked open the blade. He handed it to Clifton.

"Let's get that boot cut off, Dick. Hurts like a bastard, so take it easy."

While he watched Clifton work on the boot, Doolin silently cursed poor timing and bad luck. Yesterday, as the gang crossed into Oklahoma Territory, they'd been intercepted by the Beaver County sheriff and a posse. A running gunfight ensued, and a stray bullet had hit Doolin in the foot. None of the other men were wounded, though over a hundred shots had been exchanged. Finally, under cover of darkness, they had escaped the posse.

Doolin had made an on-the-spot decision. With the alarm sounded, every lawman in the territory would be on the scout. There was safety in numbers, and he'd chosen to keep the gang together. The nearest hideout was the Dunn brothers' ranch, and he had led his men eastward through the night. Some of the men already knew about the Dunn brothers, and he saw nothing to lose by taking them there. He had to get them out of sight as fast as possible.

Bee and George Dunn were of another mind. Hiding Doolin was one thing, but harboring the entire gang was a far riskier matter. Harsh words were exchanged, and the Dunns had finally agreed after being given a full share in the loot from the holdup. Doolin had left Will Dalton in charge, and departed for town with Blake and Clifton. The law knew nothing of the Dunns or his visits to Ingalls, so there was little chance of being caught out. All the more so since the townspeople could have long ago betrayed him. His affair with the Ellsworth girl was hardly a secret.

The doctor arrived first. After examining Doolin's foot, he found that the bullet was embedded on the inside of the arch. He gave Doolin a dose of laudanum to kill the pain, and then began laying out instruments. While Clifton held Doolin's foot steady, the doctor went to work with a scalpel. Doolin gritted his teeth, clutching the bedposts, his forehead beaded with sweat. At last, with the incision completed, the doctor extracted the slug with a pair of forceps. He dropped it into a johnnypot at the side of the bed.

Edith Ellsworth arrived just as the doctor finished

stitching the wound. The laudanum had taken effect, and Doolin seemed to have recovered his composure. He ordered Clifton to pay the doctor and wait in the lobby with Blake until he sent for them. The doctor promised to return in the morning and change the dressings he'd applied on Doolin's foot. Then, nodding to the girl, he followed Clifton out of the room.

The girl was nothing if not brave. She had long ago accepted the fact that the man she loved was an outlaw. He explained the events of the last twenty-four hours, and she listened without tears. She was short, somewhat plump, by no means the prettiest girl in town. But he'd treated her like a lady and often declared his intention to make an honest woman of her. There was never any question in her mind that she would stand beside him. Wounded, he needed her more than ever.

"Don't worry," Doolin said, holding her close. "I'll be as good as new before you know it."

She was silent a moment. The outlaw life frightened her, though she'd never voiced her fears before. Still, given the situation, she thought it was worth a try. She wanted a live husband.

"Bill," she said softly. "Did you mean it, all those times you told me we'd get married?"

"Why sure, I meant it." Doolin was somewhat taken aback by the question. "Why'd you bring that up now?"

"Would you quit?" she asked, beseeching him. "Would you marry me and leave this life? Start over somewhere?"

"Honey, I always intended to quit. Just as soon as I build us a stake."

"What good's a stake if you're dead? You always said the law wouldn't get you. Now, here you are shot and hurt and the law—"

"Won't happen," Doolin interrupted. "The law's not gonna get me. Don't fret yourself about it."

Tears welled up in her eyes. "I waited to tell you till I

was sure. . . ." She wiped away tears, took a deep breath. "Bill, I'm in a family way. I want a father for our baby. And I want a husband—a live husband!—not a memory."

"Godalmighty." Doolin stared at her with a foolish grin. "I'm gonna be a daddy?"

"Yes, I'm almost two months along."

"Then it's high time we got married. You go round up a preacher. Bring your ma and pa along, too."

She looked stunned. "You mean now—here?"

"Nothing else," Doolin said, laughing. "Today's our weddin' day!"

"And you'll quit?" she pressed him. "We'll go away?"

"Honey, I've got a plan, had one all along. I've been buildin' us a nest egg, a real stake."

"Bill—"

Doolin stopped her, cupped her face in his hand. "Just gimme a little time. That's all I'm askin'. Then we're headed for California."

"California?"

"Told you I had a plan. We'll leave all this behind. Build ourselves a good life out there."

She searched his eyes. "You really mean it?"

"Honest to God," Doolin promised. "You got my word on it."

"Oh, God, Bill, don't let me down."

"Honey, we're as good as on our way."

A preacher married them in a private ceremony that evening. By nightfall everyone in town knew that the Ellsworth girl and Bill Doolin were man and wife. Their wedding night was for her one of joy and lingering anguish.

She prayed he would keep his word.

CHAPTER 13

Tilghman rode into Guthrie the following afternoon. Yesterday, upon his return from Ingalls, he'd stopped off at the ranch and then spent the evening with Zoe. Had he located Doolin, he would have ridden straight through to the capital. But with Doolin gone, there was no rush to deliver his report. Today seemed soon enough.

On Division Street, he left his horse at a stable, then walked over to the Herriott Building. Upstairs, the hallway was crowded with people rushing in and out of the governor's suite. So much activity was unusual, but he didn't pause to inquire the reason. He made his way to the marshal's office and pushed through the door. Heck Thomas turned from the window with a startled look.

"Bill!" he said loudly. "Goddamn, am I glad to see you."

"What's all the excitement at the governor's office?"

"Oh, that," Thomas said dismissively. "The president's just authorized opening the Cherokee Strip. There's gonna be another land rush."

Tilghman was impressed. The Strip included the former Cherokee Outlet as well as parts of the Pawnee and Tonkawa reservations. In total, the president's proclamation opened some eight million acres to settlement.

By far the largest land rush to date, it would add more than nine thousand square miles to Oklahoma Territory.

"That's some news," Tilghman said. "Ought to draw lots of people."

"Liable to be a stampede," Thomas told him. "There's talk it'll pull a couple of hundred thousand settlers into the territory."

"Have they set a date for the opening?"

"Looks to be May fifteenth. The governor called Nix down to his office to start planning. They want federal marshals to police the townsites."

"Any idea when Nix will be back? I've got word on Doolin."

Thomas gave him a strange look. "What kind of word?"

"I scouted things out," Tilghman said. "That letter was right on the money. Doolin holes up there at a horse ranch on a regular basis. Got himself a girl in Ingalls, too."

"When were you in Ingalls?"

"Day before yesterday. Stopped by Chandler and rode on here."

"I'll be damned," Thomas mumbled. "You haven't heard about the holdup, have you?"

"Holdup?" Tilghman said, amazed. "Doolin pulled another job?"

Thomas quickly recounted details of the Santa Fe robbery in Kansas. He went on to relate the gun battle between the Wild Bunch and the Beaver County posse. He ended with Doolin's escape.

"But that's old news," he hurried on. "This morning we got the latest, and you're not gonna believe it. Doolin's holed up in a hotel in Ingalls."

"Hotel?" Tilghman said skeptically. "Why would he come out in the open like that? Where'd you get this story?"

"From a preacher." Thomas grinned, shaking his

head. "Old bird was hot under the collar, too. Rode all night to get here."

"What's a preacher got to do with Bill Doolin?"

The preacher, according to Thomas, had been struck by a sudden fit of conscience. After the wedding ceremony, he'd become incensed that a decent girl would marry an outlaw. All the worse, he speculated that it was a shotgun wedding, the girl in a family way. He also reported that Doolin had been wounded in the foot.

"To cork it," Thomas concluded, "Doolin brought the whole gang into town to celebrate his weddin'. I tell you that preacher was plenty pissed."

Tilghman took a moment to digest what he'd heard. His forehead wrinkled in thought. "Doolin's no dummy. He won't stick around Ingalls too long. He knows the word will leak out."

"Exact same thing I told Nix. We've got to hit Doolin tomorrow. Next day might be too late."

"Does he agree?"

"We got in an argument," Thomas said flatly. "He wants to send an army up there, and I'm against it. Too many men just get in one another's way. A couple of good ones, maybe three, that's all we need."

"We'd never get Madsen here from El Reno in time."

"There's always you and me, Bill. I'm not one for big posses and lead flyin' every whichaway. Just the two of us, we'd figure a way to nail Doolin."

"How'd you leave it with Nix?"

"We were still at it hot and heavy when the governor sent for him."

The office door opened. Evett Nix entered, his expression harried as he walked to his desk. He took a seat, nodding at Tilghman. "Has Heck filled you in?"

"We both did the honors," Tilghman said. "I just got back from Ingalls, so it wasn't a surprise. Doolin's been hiding out there off and on for months."

"Which means our outraged parson was on the mark.

We have an opportunity to rid the territory of Doolin once and for all."

"Looks that way."

Nix's gaze shifted to Thomas. "Have you changed your mind?"

"Nope," Thomas said, his eyes narrowed. "You send a crowd and there'll be hell to pay. Seen it happen time and again."

"Heck, I know your opinion of me as a lawman. But good judgment dictates that two or three men have no chance against a gang that large. I won't risk it."

"Heck's right," Tilghman interceded. "The larger the posse, the greater the risk of failure. Let the two of us handle it and the odds improve on getting Doolin. He's the main target, more so than his gang."

"I disagree," Nix said. "I want Doolin *and* his gang. Now, I stepped out of the meeting with the governor to settle this matter, and it's settled. Let's leave it at that."

Thomas scowled. "You're fixin' to get some men killed to no good end."

"Enough!" Nix said sharply. "We have local officers who carry standby federal commissions. Get them together and do your job."

Nix rose, rapidly crossing the room. He paused at the door, looking back. "Heck, despite any differences, you're our most experienced marshal. You'll be in charge."

"Christ!" Thomas snorted when the door closed. "What d'you think of them apples?"

"Well, Heck," Tilghman said, "I think he just put the bee on you."

"Guess he did, 'cause I sure as hell feel stung."

The sky was heavy with clouds, and beneath it the earth was cold and still. Trees along the creek swayed in the wind, bare branches crackling like the bones of old skeletons. A flock of crows fluttered against the sky, then wheeled and vanished beyond the treeline.

There were nine men in the posse, bent low as they crept forward in single file. The creek bank covered their movements, and the rush of water deadened the sound of their footsteps. A mile or so downstream where the creek angled southeast, they had left their horses hidden in a stand of trees. Stealthily, as though stalking game, they had spent the last hour working their way up the rocky stream.

Ahead, the bank sloped off sharply, and Council Creek swung westward in a lazy curve. Beyond the bend, hardly more than a stone's throw away, stood a squalid collection of buildings. Heck Thomas held up his hand and the men halted, flattening themselves against the creek bank. Except for Thomas, who carried a double-barrel shotgun, every man in the party was armed with a Winchester. A sense of suppressed violence, something unseen but menacing, hung over the ramshackle town.

Tilghman scrambled forward on his hands and knees. He stopped beside Thomas, who nodded and jerked his thumb toward the town. They removed their hats, still hunched low, and slowly eased themselves to eye level at the top of the bank. Their weapons held at the ready, they subjected the huddled buildings to an intense, door-to-door scrutiny. For a time, with the squinted gaze of veteran scouts, they absorbed every detail.

Ingalls under an overcast sky was little more than a backwoods eyesore. The single street, rutted and dusted with snow, petered out into a faint wagon road on either side of town. Nearest to the creek was a blacksmith shop, beside that a mercantile emporium, and farther along the dulled windows of the two-story hotel. Across the street was a seedy-looking saloon, flanked on one side by a cafe and on the other by a general store. Beyond, a short distance upstreet, was the livery stable.

Heck Thomas whistled softly between his teeth, mo-

tioned toward the town. Everyone already had their instructions, and as they scrambled over the creek bank,
the lawmen split into two groups. Tilghman headed for
the cafe, trailed by three men, and Thomas led the others on a direct line to the smithy. Taking one building at
a time, they were to work both sides of the street, one
party covering the other, until they flushed the gang. A
metallic snick broke the stillness as one man after another eased back the hammer on his Winchester.

Then, too quick to fathom, their plan came unrav-
eled. The door of the cafe opened, and a man accompanied by a young boy emerged onto the street. A moment
later Bitter Creek Newcomb stepped through the door
of the saloon, a bottle in hand, and started across to the
hotel. On the instant he spotted Thomas, then his eyes
flicked past the man and boy to Tilghman. His reaction
was one of sheer reflex, without regard for the conse-
quences. He jerked his pistol and fired.

Tilghman's shouted warning to the man and boy
melded with the gunshot. The marshals behind him and
those across the street shouldered their rifles in unison.
The first sharp crack blended into a rolling tattoo, and
Newcomb was struck in the left arm, dropping his bottle. Caught in the crossfire, the man outside the cafe
went down like a puppet with his strings gone haywire.
Beside him, jolted back by the impact of a slug, the boy
dropped onto the boardwalk. Newcomb took off running for the stable.

Suddenly the street came alive with sizzling lead.
Someone fired from an upstairs room in the hotel, and
the front of the saloon appeared wreathed in a wall of
flame as men opened fire through the door and windows. The marshal behind Tilghman grunted, clutching
at his stomach, and dropped to the ground. Tilghman
hefted his rifle and levered four shots into the upper
floor window of the hotel. Glass shattered and a mo-

ment later Arkansas Tom Daugherty toppled over the windowsill. His rifle clattered to the boardwalk below.

From across the street, Thomas let go with his shotgun. Tilghman was aware that the other officers had concentrated their fire on the saloon, and he swung his rifle in that direction. Another lawman went down, a dark splotch blossoming on his coat, but the remaining Winchesters hammered out a withering barrage. The saloon windows disintegrated in a maelstrom of glass, and the building jounced as heavy slugs shredded the front wall. A third marshal swayed and crumpled to the earth.

Doolin suddenly leaped through the saloon door, followed by Clifton and Raidler. They sprinted toward the stable, where Newcomb was popping off shots at the lawmen. Tilghman fired simultaneously with the roar of Thomas's shotgun, and the four remaining officers loosed another volley. Clifton staggered, then righted himself, as slugs pocked the walls of the general store. He darted into the stable on the heels of Doolin and Raidler.

There was a momentary lull in the gunfire. Then, as though prearranged, Will Dalton, Jack Blake, and Red Buck Waightman rushed out of the saloon. Doolin and the men in the stable covered their retreat, emptying their pistols rapid fire at the marshals. The officers returned fire, Thomas fumbling to reload his shotgun, and Tilghman winging Blake in the arm. The three outlaws, dodging and twisting through a hornets' nest of lead, raced past the store and ducked into the stable.

An eerie stillness settled over the street. The marshals waited, staring over their sights at the stable. But the outlaws, unaccountably and all too abruptly, had ceased fire. Then, as Thomas cautiously motioned the officers forward, the screech of rusty door hinges broke the stillness. Doolin and his men, mounted on their horses, suddenly burst through a rear door of the stable and pounded across the countryside. They disappeared into a stark timberline at the north edge of town.

"Goddammit!" Thomas roared, hurling his shotgun to the ground. "The bastards already had their horses saddled. We let 'em get away."

Tilghman crossed the street. "Why should that surprise you, Heck? Doolin's smart and he always thinks ahead. He was fixed to run if anything happened."

"Would you look at this?" Thomas stormed, gesturing wildly around the street. "Holy Jesus Christ!"

The man and the small boy lay dead outside the cafe. Nearby, one of the marshals in Tilghman's group stared sightlessly at the overcast sky. Opposite them, in front of the blacksmith's shop, two other lawmen were sprawled on the ground. The smell of blood was ripe in the cool, still air.

Along the street, townspeople slowly emerged from the shops and stores. The blacksmith walked forward, knelt beside the fallen marshals, and shook his head. A woman outside the cafe gently cradled the dead boy in her arms.

"A goddamn bloodbath!" Thomas raged, shaking his fist at the hotel. "All for that."

Arkansas Tom Daugherty, arms dangling, hung from the hotel window.

PART TWO

CHAPTER 14

"Never saw a horse so proud of himself."

Neal Brown laughed. "Figures he's cock-o'-the-walk around here."

"Guess that's not far from the truth."

Tilghman led the sorrel stallion from the stable to the corral. The weather was brisk even though a bright noonday sun stood at its zenith in a cloudless sky. The stud was frisky, impatient to be turned loose. He snorted, frosty puffs of air steaming from his nostrils.

Brown swung open the corral gate. Tilghman led Steeldust into the enclosure and unsnapped the lead rope. The stallion raced away, crossing the corral in a few strides, then swerved away an instant before colliding with the fence. Snorting frost, heels kicked high in the air, he circled the corral. His eyes were fierce with freedom.

Tilghman stepped outside as Brown latched the gate. They stood, shaking their heads with amusement, watching the sorrel stud cavort around the corral. Brown took out the makings, spilling tobacco into a paper, and rolled himself a cigarette. He struck a match on his thumbnail.

"Tell you what's a fact," he said, puffing smoke. "That critter almost makes me wish I was a horse."

Tilghman smiled. "Yeah, he leads a pretty cushy life."

"Cushy!" Brown hooted. "All he can eat, not a lick of work, and all the mares he can service. I'd trade places with him any day of the week."

"I suspect lots of folks would, Neal."

Tilghman was in a rare good mood. A month had passed since the murderous shootout at Ingalls. At first, the press had lambasted U.S. Marshal Evett Nix and the deputies involved for the debacle. Innocent citizens gunned down, one of them a nine-year-old boy, and three lawmen killed. On the other side of the ledger, only one outlaw had been slain and the Wild Bunch had escaped. Headlines denounced it as a tragic disaster.

Republicans, widely quoted in the newspapers, demanded Nix's resignation. Neither Heck Thomas nor Tilghman offered any comment. In private, they reminded Nix that they had been opposed to such a large raid from the outset. In public, they quietly accepted the brunt of the blame, refusing to make Nix the scapegoat. Thomas, as leader of the raid, was vilified in the press.

Tilghman, the memory raw in his mind, had relived the bloody fight again and again. Fragmented in time, those moments were so brutalizing that the smallest detail would remain vivid all the rest of his days. Awake and in his dreams, he saw again the man and the boy step from the cafe only to be chopped down in a hail of gunfire. He wondered what would have happened if they had taken longer with their meal, remained in the cafe. At the very least, he ruminated, they would still be alive.

For the other part, though, nothing would have changed. He often reflected that fate, or perhaps simple bad luck, had brought Bitter Creek Newcomb through the door of the saloon at that particular moment in time. Given another minute, the marshals would have gained the element of surprise, trapping the gang in the saloon. But they'd lost the edge, and with it their composure, their ability to shoot straight in a moment of stress. Over and over in his mind he saw the outlaws retreating along the boardwalk toward the stable. He was still astounded that the other marshals, their guns blazing, had hit nothing.

In times past, from talking with Civil War veterans, he'd heard that most of the shots fired in battle never hit the mark. Still, looking back on Ingalls, there was no accounting for the marshals' inaccuracy at such short range. After all, the Wild Bunch had killed three lawmen, and probably fired fewer shots. The whole affair reminded him of the cardinal rule for survival in a gunfight: Speed's fine but accuracy is final. He took small consolation in the fact that he had killed Arkansas Tom Daugherty. The score was still three to one.

To make matters worse, Doolin and the Wild Bunch had again pulled their vanishing act. Following Ingalls, every lawman in Oklahoma Territory and the surrounding states had been put on alert. The rewards had been increased to five thousand dollars on Doolin and two thousand on every member of the gang. But there had been no sightings, no reports, absolutely nothing on where the gang had gone to ground. There was a rumor that they had crossed the Red River, taking refuge in Texas. Yet federal marshals and local lawmen in Texas had been unable to verify the story one way or another. The Wild Bunch, as a practical matter, had again disappeared.

Only one thing was known for certain. The doctor in Ingalls had confirmed that he'd treated Doolin for a gunshot wound to the foot. The wound, as near as Tilghman could piece it together, had been suffered in the running gunfight with the Beaver County posse, two days before the raid on Ingalls. Edith Doolin, the outlaw's new bride, refused to confirm or deny any part of the story. Yet the wound, to some small degree, explained the month-long absence of the Wild Bunch. Doolin would stick to cover until his foot was healed.

"Consarn it," Brown grumbled. "You got to where you just drift off, don't you?"

Tilghman realized he'd been staring into space. "Only now and then," he said lightly. "What'd I miss?"

"I asked you when we was gonna buy some more mares. We got land enough for a herd four or five times this size."

"Well, I thought we might hold off till spring. I'd like to take a look at brood stock up in Missouri, or down south. Maybe improve our bloodlines."

"Time's a-wastin'," Brown said. "Why wait till spring?"

"Unfinished business," Tilghman replied. "You know I can't leave."

"You're talkin' about Doolin and his bunch, aren't you?"

"Who else?"

Brown took a final drag on his cigarette. He dropped the butt and ground it underfoot. "So you're stuck here," he said. "I'm a pretty fair judge of horseflesh. Why don't I go?"

"You're stuck, too," Tilghman said. "I wouldn't trust anybody else to run the place."

The Sac and Fox tribesmen were reliable workhands. Under Brown's supervision, they cleaned out the stables, fed and watered the stock, and saw to it that the horses were exercised regularly. But Tilghman was wary of entrusting the brood mares, or Steeldust, to outsiders. He relied solely on Neal Brown.

"Helluva note," Brown said, kicking at a clod of dirt. "We're markin' time till Doolin pops up again. Somebody oughta shoot the bastard."

"Somebody will," Tilghman observed. "His kind always gets it, sooner or later."

"Trouble is, sooner's already past. We're workin' now on later."

Tilghman caught the disgruntled tone in his voice. Off and on, they'd had similar conversations several times over the last few months. Brown never stated it openly, but his opinion on the matter was hardly in question. All the more so since the vitriolic newspaper articles and editorials following the Ingalls shootout. He thought the job of federal marshal was a thankless task, often drawing criticism but seldom praise. Horses, in his view, were of far greater consequence than outlaws.

Before Tilghman could reply, a buggy rolled into the compound. Zoe waved gaily, gently hauling back on the reins, and brought her team to a halt. Tilghman walked forward as she scooted across the seat. He assisted her down from the buggy.

"Welcome surprise," he said, grinning. "What brings you over this way?"

"Oh, just passing by," she said, smiling past him at Brown. "Hello, Neal."

"Howdy, ma'am." Brown touched the brim of his hat, shy and curiously tongue-tied in the presence of a pretty woman. "Bill, I'd better check on things down at the stables. Nice seein' you, Miss Zoe."

"Nice seeing you too, Neal."

Brown bobbed his head and walked off. Zoe stared after him a moment. "After all this time, he still runs whenever he sees me. Am I that forbidding?"

"You're a woman," Tilghman said simply. "And Neal's not exactly a ladies' man. He's lots more comfortable with horses."

"And you?" She looked at him, amused. "Are you a ladies' man?"

"Common knowledge that I hold the title in Lincoln County. 'Course, I limit my attentions to one lady."

"How gallant of you, Mr. Tilghman."

"Believe me, it's my pleasure."

She laughed, touching his arm. Then, a startled look in her eyes, her gaze went past him. On the opposite side of the fence, Steeldust charged toward them, suddenly pulled up short, and whinnied a shrill blast of greeting. He was barrel-chested, standing fifteen hands high, his hide glistening in the sun. He watched them, pawing the earth as though he spurned it and longed to fly.

Tilghman smiled. "I think Steeldust likes you, too."

Zoe nodded, her gaze abstracted. The stallion came on at a prancing walk, moving with the pride of power and lordship. Always protective of his mares, who returned his whinny from the stables, he halted a few paces short of the fence. Then he stood, nostrils flared, like a statue bronzed by the sun. He tested the wind, staring directly at Zoe.

The stallion fascinated her. Whenever he came this close, she always felt a curious sensation in her loins. Oddly enough, Tilghman and Steeldust were somehow intertwined in her thoughts. On occasion, when she looked at Tilghman, a fleeting image of the stallion flashed through her mind. The feeling she experienced made her skin tingle and left a sweet aftertaste in her mouth. Almost as though she'd bitten into a moist peach.

"Goodness," she said softly. "He's a handsome brute, isn't he?"

"King of the mountain." Tilghman chuckled. "Thinks he owns everything between here and St. Louis."

"You certainly made a good choice. Father says you bought the best the Sac and Fox had to offer."

"I reckon we'll find out come spring. His foals will tell the tale."

Tilghman's breeding program centered on Steeldust. The stud had the spirit of his noble ancestors, the Barbs, the forerunners of all Indian horses. From generation upon generation of battling to survive on the plains, an almost supernatural endurance had been passed along to Steeldust. From this fusion with his Kansas mares, Tilghman hoped to breed colts and fillies with the speed for racetracks.

The brood mares he'd bought from the Sac and Fox were another matter entirely. By culling them, continually breeding up, he planned to breed the ultimate range horse. With Steeldust as the original sire, the offspring would have the stamina and catlike agility necessary for working cattle. Some would fall short of the mark, but with the sorrel stallion's blood, he nonetheless thought they would have great value. He planned to sell them to the army, or horse dealers, for saddle mounts.

"So?" Tilghman said as Steeldust turned and loped across the corral. "What brings you over our way?"

Zoe rolled her eyes. "Don't tell me you've forgotten!"

"Forgotten what?"

"The dance in town tonight. Have I lost a day somewhere? This is Saturday, isn't it?"

"Let me think." Tilghman feigned confusion. "No, by golly, you're right. Today's definitely Saturday."

"See!" she teased. "You needed reminding after all."

"Then it's good you dropped by. I'll make it a point to be at your place on time."

"Actually," she paused, gave him a minxish look, "I came by to invite you to Sunday dinner."

Tilghman cocked one eyebrow. "You could've done that tonight."

"Yes, but this gave me an excuse to see you."

"I get the feeling there's something missing here. What's the rest of the story?"

"Well," she said coyly, "as long as you're coming for Sunday dinner—"

"Now I get it," Tilghman broke in, wagging his head. "Why not make a day of it and escort you to church, too. That the idea?"

"How gracious of you to ask. I accept."

"Accept, my foot! You tricked me into it."

"A little religion never hurt anyone, especially you. God loves a heathen."

"Heathen!" Tilghman appeared wounded. "I'm as good a Christian as the next man."

She patted him on the cheek. "Then I'm sure you'll enjoy tomorrow's sermon. See you tonight."

When she drove off, Tilghman turned back to the corral. He stood watching Steeldust, wondering at the ways of women. A few moments later Brown walked up from the stables.

"You're a goner," he said ruefully. "That little lady's got the look in her eye."

"You think so, Neal?"

"I'd bet on it and give you good odds."

Tilghman smiled. "No bet."

Steeldust pawed the ground, fierce eyes fixed on the stables. His nose to the wind, he scented his mares.

CHAPTER 15

The men rode into town in three groups. Doolin and Dick Clifton entered by the farm road from the south. Charley Pierce, Jack Blake, and Red Buck Waightman appeared on the road north of town. Bill Raidler and Little Dick West rode along a sidestreet from a westerly direction.

Located in the southwest corner of Missouri, the town was aptly named Southwest City. A farm community with a population of less than a thousand, it lay some five miles east of the border with the Cherokee Nation. Hardly a center of commerce, it was nonetheless a thriving hamlet built on the trade of the area's farmers.

Southwest City, like most farm towns, was bisected by a main thoroughfare. The business district, small but prosperous, consisted of four stores, a saloon and a blacksmith shop, and one bank. There were few people about and little activity on a Monday afternoon. Typically the slowest time of the week, it accounted in part for the seven strangers. Their business was better conducted without crowds.

A week past, Doolin had assigned Jack Blake to scout the town. Blake had returned with a crudely sketched map after stopping for a drink in the saloon. He reported that the bank was manned by only the president and two tellers. Law enforcement consisted of the town marshal, who operated without regular deputies and rarely patrolled the streets. The townspeople, apart from shopping and the usual errands, were seldom about on weekdays. All in all, Southwest City looked like easy pickings.

Doolin had selected the farm town for just that reason. He needed a simple job, and one that would give his men a decent payday. After the Ingalls shootout, he'd been roundly criticized by Will Dalton for poor leadership. Dalton blamed him for keeping the gang in Ingalls too long, creating a situation that fairly begged for a raid by the law. The argument became heated, with Doolin prepared to kill in order to hold the Wild Bunch together. Dalton wisely avoided a showdown, for he was no match for Doolin with a gun. Instead, he'd quit the gang and taken off on his own.

The others had elected to stick with Doolin. He had persuaded them to scatter throughout the Nations and stay in deep cover until he felt it was safe to resume operations. When the heat died down, he'd promised them, there would be more and bigger paydays. With money in their pockets from the last robbery, the men had kept out of sight for the past four months, all of them still somewhat spooked by the close call at Ingalls. But finally, short on money and tired of hiding out, they seemed on the verge of splitting apart. Doolin had no choice but to plan another raid.

From a personal standpoint, Doolin was no better off than his men. He was nearly broke, and his foot wound had healed poorly, leaving him with a pronounced limp. Even worse, his wife was with child, and given the circumstances, there was no way for them to be together. Every few weeks he'd managed to sneak into Ingalls, always under cover of darkness, and visit her for a night. But she was afraid and dispirited, and constantly bad-

gering him to quit the outlaw life. For that he needed a
stake, and he'd decided to resume operations with a job
that offered quick escape into the Nations. Southwest
City appeared to fit the bill.

The men held their horses to a walk. Travelers con-
verging from different directions, they proceeded
toward the center of town. Outside the bank Doolin and
Clifton wheeled to the right and halted before the hitch
rack. Upstreet, the three men approaching from the
north stopped in front of a mercantile store. Down from
the bank, Raidler and West reined in on the same side
of the street.

There was a military precision to their movements,
smooth and coordinated, somehow practiced. The riders on either side of the bank dismounted and took positions to cover the street in both directions. Some
checked their saddle rigging, others dusted themselves
off, and to a man their eyes checked nearby buildings.
Doolin paused a moment and subjected the whole of
the business district to a slow, careful scrutiny. Then,
followed by Clifton, he turned and entered the bank.

Inside the door, Doolin quickly scanned the room.
The cashier's window was to the rear, and beyond that
the vault door, which was open. To his immediate left,
seated behind a desk, the bank president was engaged in
conversation with a man dressed as a farmer. One teller
stood at the cashier's window while the other worked on
a set of books.

"This is a holdup!" Doolin announced. "Keep quiet
and you won't get hurt."

There was an instant of leaden silence. At the desk,
the president stared at him with disbelief, and the
farmer swiveled around in his chair. The cashier froze,
watching him intently, and the other teller paused with
his pen dipped in an inkwell. Clifton positioned himself
to cover everyone in the room.

"Don't nobody get stupid," he said jovially. "Hell, gents, it's only money."

Doolin walked to the cashier's window. He casually wagged the snout of his pistol, nodding to the teller. "Forget your cash drawer. Empty the vault and be quick about it."

"What'll I put it in?"

From inside his coat, Doolin pulled out two neatly folded gunnysacks with draw strings. He pushed them across the counter, motioning with his gun, and the teller turned toward the vault. The other teller suddenly dropped his pen and jerked open the drawer of his desk. He stood, panic written across his face, a pistol in his hand.

"No!" Doolin thundered. "Drop it!"

From the door, Clifton sighted and fired. The slug punched through the teller's head and tore out the back of his skull. A halo of bone and brain matter misted the air, and he stood there a moment, dead on his feet. Then he pitched headlong onto the floor.

"Goddammit!" Doolin shouted. "I had him covered. Why'd you shoot?"

Clifton shrugged. "Bastard shouldn't've pulled a gun."

"Well, you damn sure put the town on notice." Doolin turned to the teller at the vault. "Get them sacks loaded. Muy goddamn pronto!"

A roar of gunfire, several shots in rapid succession, suddenly sounded from outside. Clifton glanced through the front window and saw gang members popping shots at merchants who had appeared in doorways along the street. Across the way the town marshal emerged from his office, pistol in hand, and started along the boardwalk. Another volley erupted and his right leg buckled under the impact of a slug. He went down on his rump.

"Hop to it!" Clifton yelled. "We got trouble."

The teller shoved the loaded sacks across the counter. Doolin grabbed them, backing to the door, and tossed one to Clifton. The gunfire swelled in intensity as they rushed outside and moved toward the hitch rack. On either side of them, the men posted as guards were trading shots with merchants up and down the street. Their horses were wall-eyed with fright as they bounded into the saddle.

A rifle ball opened a bloody gash on Clifton's forehead. He whirled his horse and fired, dropping the owner of the mercantile store. Across the street, the town marshal rose unsteadily to his feet and triggered three quick shots. One of the slugs sizzled past Doolin's ear and he wheeled about, fighting to control his horse, and ripped off two shots in return. The lawman staggered backward, crashing into the wall of a building. He slumped to the boardwalk.

All along the street storekeepers were firing from windows and doorways. The other gang members hastily mounted, their pistols barking flame in a steady roar. Upstreet a merchant pitched forward in his doorway, and in the opposite direction, the blacksmith tumbled to the ground. Then, with Doolin in the lead, the gang reined their horses around and spurred for the south edge of town. Behind them, the townspeople peppered their retreat with a barrage of lead.

The Wild Bunch thundered west toward Indian Territory.

Will Dalton and Jim Wallace dismounted in the alley beside the bank. A few moments later Asa and Tim Knight entered the alley from the opposite direction. After they dismounted, Tim Knight took the reins of the other two men's horses. Dalton and Wallace walked toward the street.

The town of Longview was the center of trade for farmers and several large logging operations. Located in northeastern Texas, it was some eighty miles south of the Red River, the boundary between the Lone Star State and the Choctaw Nation. A prosperous community, Longview was the county seat, with a stone courthouse dominating the town square.

The First National, the largest bank in town, was located on the north side of the square. Dalton had selected the bank as the first full-fledged job for his newly formed gang. After splitting with Doolin, he had joined forces with Wallace, a small-time bandit who operated out of the Chickasaw Nation. Wallace had in turn introduced him to the Knight brothers, former loggers turned outlaw who were originally from Longview. Their tales of a vault stuffed with mountains of cash had sold Dalton on the First National. He meant to eclipse the record of the Wild Bunch with a single holdup.

Dalton led the way into the bank. He covered the door, his pistol drawn, and commanded everyone to lie on the floor. Wallace collared the bank president, put a gun to his head, and forced him to unlock the vault. The shelves lining the walls, just as the Knight brothers had promised, were stacked with piles of cash. At first overawed, Wallace quickly located the shelves with bills of larger denominations. He produced cloth sacks from inside his coat and ordered the president to get busy.

"Whooee!" he yelled out to Dalton. "We're gonna be rich. Filthy rich!"

"Tell me about it later," Dalton said sternly. "Get them sacks filled and let's get out of here."

Only a few minutes were required to complete the job. Wallace came out of the vault, struggling with two heavy sacks thrown over his shoulder, and moved to the front of the room. Dalton glanced through the door window, watchful a moment as townspeople went about their business on the courthouse square. Then, turning back, he fixed those in the bank with a menacing scowl.

"Stay put and don't get brave! Anybody comes out this door will get his head blowed off."

Dalton stepped through the door, followed by Wallace. On the street, passersby spotted their drawn guns and immediately ran for cover. By a fluke of timing, in that same moment, Town Marshal George Muckley and his deputy, Wally Stevens, emerged from the courthouse. Their attention drawn by the commotion, they saw the two men hurrying from the bank and the Knight brothers holding four horses in the alley. The Knight brothers, who had fled Longview after a string of petty robberies, were known to them on sight. On the instant, they realized the bank was being robbed.

The lawmen pulled their guns and opened fire. Muckley, hoping to spook the horses and prevent escape, let off three quick shots at the Knight brothers. One of the slugs caught Asa Knight in the chest and he fell spread-eagled in the alley. Deputy Stevens trained his fire on the two men scurrying along the boardwalk outside the bank. A bullet shattered the bank's plate-glass window in an explosion of jagged shards.

Dalton and Wallace, firing as they ran, reached the entrance to the alley. Their shots were wild and for the most part pocked harmlessly into the front of the stone courthouse. But a wayward ball drilled the marshal through the bowels and he folded at the waist, then keeled over. Stevens dropped to one knee, stone chips flying all around him, and emptied his gun. A townsman passing the courthouse was caught in the crossfire and took a slug through the lungs. He toppled to the ground.

In the alley, Tim Knight fought to control the horses as he knelt to check on his brother. His face blanched with rage as he saw the sightless eyes and realized Asa was dead. He climbed to his feet, the horses' reins clutched tightly in one fist, and winged a shot at Stevens on the courthouse steps. The deputy shucked spent car-

tridges and reloaded as a merchant opened fire with a
rifle from the corner. Upstreet, in the opposite direction, a saloonkeeper armed with a sawed-off shotgun
joined the fight.

Buckshot and lead whistling about their ears, Dalton
and Wallace returned the fire. Wallace's snap-shot
singed the merchant's coatsleeve and drove him back
into his store. Dalton halted, took deliberate aim, and
loosed a round to silence the shotgun. The saloonkeeper staggered backwards, arms windmilling, then
dropped the scattergun and crashed to the boardwalk.
Still leading the way, Dalton darted into the alley.

Tim Knight was already mounted. Holding the reins,
he waited while Dalton and Wallace scrambled aboard
their horses. Encumbered with the money sacks, the two
men were forced to holster their pistols as they reined
away. Knight covered their retreat, emptying his gun
across the courthouse square. The three men spurred
toward the end of the alley.

Deputy Stevens, his gun reloaded, got off one last
shot. Then, as the outlaws disappeared, he stared
around at the carnage with a stunned expression. The
marshal lay dead at his feet, and the townsman caught
in the crossfire was knotted in a grotesque heap. Across
the street on the boardwalk, the saloonkeeper lay pud-
dled in blood.

The courthouse square looked like a slaughterhouse.

CHAPTER 16

OUTLAW GANGS ROB TWO BANKS IN THREE DAYS
THE WILD BUNCH STRIKES MISSOURI AND TEXAS

The headline in the Guthrie *Statesman* covered the width of the front page. The dateline was May 22, 1890, and fully half the page was devoted to coverage of the robberies. In separate articles, the newspaper reported on the May 19 holdup in Missouri and the May 21 raid in Texas. An editorial by the publisher, enclosed in a black border, rendered a blistering attack on the U.S. marshal.

Evett Nix slammed the paper onto his desk. Lined up before him were Tilghman, Heck Thomas, and Chris Madsen. Upon news of the first robbery, he had recalled the three deputy marshals from their assignments in the Cherokee Strip. The telegraph report on the second holdup had arrived even as they rode into Guthrie late last night. Today, facing him across the desk, they waited for Nix's tirade to subside.

None of the deputies responded as he paused to take a breath. Nor were they expected to respond, for Nix was clearly not finished with his harangue. He scooped the newspaper off the desk, balled it into a wad, and hurled it across the room. His features were mottled with anger.

"What happened?" he demanded. "Why were we caught flat-footed? Why weren't you men on the case?"

"Maybe you forgot," Thomas said with intended irony. "You sent us to play po-licemen in the Cherokee Strip. We were just a tad out of touch."

Tilghman thought it a telling remark. In the four months since the Ingalls shootout, federal lawmen had been assigned to police the Cherokee Strip land rush, which brought over two hundred thousand settlers pouring into the Territory. During all that time, not a single lead had been uncovered as to the whereabouts of the gang. There was widespread speculation, particularly in the newspapers, that the Wild Bunch had quit Oklahoma Territory altogether. The federal marshals, Tilghman more so than most, were not wholly persuaded by the argument. Doolin's wife, rumored to be with child, still lived in Ingalls, and showed no signs of leaving. That alone indicated Doolin had not gone far.

Over the last four months Tilghman had occasionally slipped out of the Cherokee Strip to scout Ingalls and the Dunn brothers' ranch. His attempts to interrogate Doolin's wife and her storekeeper father had proved to be an exercise in futility. Their attitude was polite but distant, and both of them denied any knowledge of Doolin's whereabouts. The townspeople, fearing reprisals from men quick to kill, were even less willing to discuss the Wild Bunch. As a practical matter, Doolin and his gang seemed to have disappeared off the face of the earth. The federal marshals were stymied, their search seemingly at a dead end. Until today.

"Excuses, nothing but excuses!" Nix thundered now. "You're supposed to keep your ear to the ground. How could you not get wind of something this big?"

"Why would we?" Tilghman said, tired of being bullied. "You want a fortune teller, get yourself another crew. None of us have a crystal ball."

"Bill's right," Madsen chimed in. "We had our hands full with the land rush and claim jumpers. You're the one that pulled us off the Wild Bunch."

"That's not true!" Nix said hotly. "The governor wanted federal marshals assigned to the Strip."

"Then blame him," Thomas said with an edge to his voice. "We're not gonna be your whipping-boys, Mr. Nix. That's the end of that story."

Nix stared at them in baffled fury. They were united, obviously unfazed by his harsh manner, and on the verge of telling him to go to hell. What with the newspaper articles and censure from Washington, he could hardly afford to risk losing his top three deputies. He decided to switch tactics.

"Let's all cool down," he said, dropping into his chair. "Nothing to be gained in arguing amongst ourselves. You gentlemen have a seat."

The deputies took chairs ranged before his desk. He massaged his forehead, got a grip on himself. "Tell me this," he said in a calmer tone. "Where have Doolin and his gang been all this time? Why have they suddenly reappeared . . . after four months?"

"Wrong question," Tilghman corrected him. "How could they pull two holdups in three days—over three hundred miles apart?"

"They couldn't," Thomas said simply. "Horses don't have wings."

Madsen nodded sagely. "Doolin was identified in the Missouri job. So the one in Texas had to be somebody else."

"Yes and no," Nix said quickly. "I received a wire this morning from the U.S. marshal in Texas."

From the clutter on his desk, Nix showed them a two-page telegraph message. The gist of it, he related, was that a posse comprised of Longview citizens and federal

marshals had tracked the outlaws to the border of Indian Territory and west along the Red River. There the
trail had petered out, lost in the Chickasaw Nation.

"Here's the corker," he concluded. "The town deputy
in Longview positively identified Will Dalton. Recognized him from those wanted posters we circulated
months ago."

"Holy Christ," Thomas said softly. "You mean to say
Doolin's operatin' two gangs now?"

"Sounds odd," Tilghman observed, shaking his head.
"Will Dalton was the runt of the litter, and no wizard.
Doolin wouldn't trust him to pull a job on his own."

"You betcha not," Madsen agreed. "Doolin's the
brains of that outfit. He'd never let Dalton branch off."

Thomas clucked to himself. "Whole thing's fishy as
hell. There were seven men in the Missouri raid and
four in Texas. Where'd all these gawddamn desperadoes
come from?"

"Oh, I forgot," Nix broke in, waving the telegram.
"The other men in the Longview robbery were identified as well. Asa Knight was killed, and his brother, Tim,
got away. The last one is a known friend of theirs, Jim
Wallace."

"Kiss my rusty butt!" Thomas said, astounded. "The
Knights and Wallace are wanted men, known throughout the Chickasaw Nation. Wallace has a brother
down there—lemme think—Houston Wallace, that's his
name."

"Down there?" Tilghman repeated with a questioning
look. "You mean the Chickasaw Nation?"

"Yeah," Thomas said. "Near as I recollect, it's somewheres around Ardmore. Heard he married a Chickasaw woman, turned farmer."

Nix appeared surprised. "Are you saying he owns
land in the Nations?"

"Long as he stays married."

Thomas briefly expounded on his remark. The Chickasaw Nation, like all the Five Civilized Tribes, was virtually an independent republic. Unlike the western Plains Tribes, the Nations had never accepted annuities or financial assistance from Washington. Thus they had maintained their independence as well as their own courts and legal system. By law, white men were not allowed to own land or property in the Nations except through intermarriage. Their Indian wives, in effect, controlled the purse strings. Divorce could reduce a man to a pauper.

"That raises a legal question," Nix said when he concluded. "Let's presume Wallace provides a hideout for his brother and Dalton. That makes him an accomplice to robbery and murder."

"So?" Thomas replied. "What's the question?"

"Well, as you've said, he's married to an Indian woman. Does that make him a Chickasaw citizen and immune to federal law? Or do we still have jurisdiction?"

"The courts ruled on that a long time ago. He's white, and married or not, we've got first dibs."

"Do you know Wallace?" Tilghman asked. "Was he ever on the owlhoot?"

"Not that I heard," Thomas said. " 'Course, it makes sense he'd let his brother hide out there. For all we know, that's where Dalton's been holed up the past four months."

Madsen grunted sourly. "That would explain how he got tied in with the Knight brothers and Jim Wallace."

"Maybe," Tilghman said. "But it still doesn't explain why he pulled a job without Doolin."

"Neither here nor there," Nix informed them. "The attorney general wants results, and an end to these damnedable newspaper articles. Right now, Dalton is the only lead we have."

Thomas raised an eyebrow. "Dalton's a small-fry

compared to Doolin. Are we gonna let Washington politicians tell us how to do our job?"

"Indeed we are," Nix said sharply. "Not to mention the fact that three men were killed in the Longview robbery. That makes Dalton a prime target."

"Makes good headlines, too," Thomas said with a caustic smile. "Assuming we catch him."

Nix tossed another telegram across the desk. "Forget catching him, gentlemen. Those are your marching orders."

The deputies scanned the telegram. The message was terse and pointed, an official directive without equivocation. It was, in effect, a death sentence from the United States Attorney General.

I have reached the conclusion that the only good outlaw is a dead one and I order you to employ extraordinary measures in resolving this problem. You are directed to instruct your deputies to bring the Wild Bunch in dead.

"Judas Priest!" Thomas muttered. "It's open season on outlaws."

"I don't like it," Tilghman said quietly. "That makes us judge, jury, and executioner—hired guns."

"Think about it, Bill." Thomas looked dour. "None of the bastards ever surrender peaceable. They always put up a fight."

"Heck's right there," Madsen added. "They're like a pack of rabid dogs. I say better them than us."

Tilghman still appeared doubtful. Before it could go any further, Nix took the lead. "Orders are orders, and we have ours. I want you gentlemen to locate Will Dalton."

The three lawmen stared at him without expression.

Though couched in subtle terms, there was no ambiguity in his directive. Nor was he allowing them a choice.

Will Dalton was to be found and killed.

Four days were required to locate the farm of Houston Wallace. By horseback, it took three days for the lawmen to reach the heart of Chickasaw country. Another day was spent in clandestine meetings between Heck Thomas and informants he had developed over the years. Finally, by early afternoon on the fourth day, they had a solid lead. The farm was situated south of Ardmore, on Elk Creek.

The need to move quickly was all too apparent. The Chickasaws, like tribesmen throughout the Nations, were openly defiant of federal marshals. Word would spread rapidly that they were in the area, clearly there in search of white outlaws. Will Dalton and his men, if they were hiding on the Wallace farm, would be warned no later than tomorrow. There could be no delay in staging the raid.

Tilghman was elected to scout the farm. Based on their information, the Wallace place was a mile or so west off the wagon road leading south from Ardmore. He left Madsen and Thomas with their horses in a grove of trees not far from the road. A rutted trail bordered the creek, and he cautiously made his way upstream. Late that afternoon, rounding a gentle curve in the stream, he suddenly stopped and ghosted into the woods. He had found their quarry.

The farmhouse was a crude log affair, on the north bank of the creek. A buck deer hung from the limb of a tree, and an Indian woman was busy skinning the carcass. Four men were seated outside the house, basking in the late afternoon sunshine. A jug of whiskey passed from man to man, and their laughter carried across the clearing. From wanted dodgers, Tilghman recognized one of the men as Will Dalton. There was a family resemblance between two of the men, probably Houston and Jim Wallace. The fourth man he took to be Tim Knight.

An hour later, downstream again, he briefed Madsen and Thomas. Sundown was close at hand, and from Tilghman's description, the gang was lazing around, swigging whiskey, waiting on a supper of venison steaks. Tilghman sketched a map in the dirt, and from the layout, there was no way to circle the house without being spotted. After weighing tactics, they decided to advance on line through the woods and take positions east of the house. That would allow them to cover the corral, which was off to the rear of the house, in case any of the outlaws made a break for their horses. Thomas was elected to issue a single warning, demanding surrender. Anyone who resisted was fair game.

By dusk, they were positioned in the treeline beside the clearing. There was still adequate light to see and sight, and each of them carried a Winchester carbine. Tilghman was nearest the creek with Thomas off to his right, and Madsen several paces farther north. To their front, the three outlaws and Houston Wallace were still seated outside the house. A lamp glowed inside, and through a window, they could see the woman working over a wood cookstove. Thomas raised his voice in sharp command.

"Federal marshals! Surrender or be killed!"

Dalton scrambled off the ground, clawing at his holster. Knight and Jim Wallace were only a beat behind, their pistols clearing leather. The lawmen's carbines, like rolling thunder, cracked in swift unison. Knight and Wallace went down as though struck by the fist of God. Dalton stumbled sideways, still trying to raise his pistol, and Tilghman shot him again. Driven backward, he sagged to the ground.

Houston Wallace, a farmer with no wish to die, stood with his hands overhead. He stared down at the body of his brother as if unable to comprehend the terrible suddenness of death. The lawmen moved out of the treeline, their carbines held at the ready, and crossed the clearing. Wallace's wife, hovering inside the doorway, watched them with a hand pressed to her mouth. She fully expected them to kill her husband.

Tilghman kept Wallace covered while Madsen and Thomas checked the bodies. A quick search of the house turned up two burlap bags, stuffed with the loot from the Longview bank robbery. Then, in an unusually kind voice, Thomas subjected the farmer to a skilled interrogation. Wallace told him everything.

Will Dalton, as they'd suspected, had used the farm as a hideout. The story of his split with Doolin, brought out under close questioning, revealed that he had quit the Wild Bunch several months ago. Afterward, he'd returned to the farm and eventually formed his own gang with Jim Wallace and the Knight brothers, who frequented the Chickasaw Nation. The time since had been spent in planning the Longview holdup.

The woman, still convinced they would kill him, watched fearfully as Madsen stood guard over her husband. Tilghman and Thomas walked off a short distance, to confer in private. Thomas glanced back at the farmer, who now seemed unable to look at the bodies. He wagged his head.

"Hard thing," he murmured. "Seeing your brother shot down like that."

"Always knew it," Tilghman said with a slow grin. "You're just an ole softy at heart."

Thomas was embarrassed. "Hell, Bill, you know what'll happen if we take him back. Gawddamn Nix will have him hung for accomplice to murder."

"You know what I think?"

"What?"

"Three dead men will get Nix all the headlines he wants. Let's leave it at that."

"And if Nix don't like it, to hell with him!"

Thomas issued a stern warning to the farmer about the wages of crime. Then, pressing the advantage, he converted him into an informant. The woman, still watchful, uttered a silent prayer of thanks to the white man's god. Ten minutes later, as darkness fell, the marshals walked off to gather their horses.

They left Houston Wallace to bury the fallen outlaws.

CHAPTER 17

Word preceded them by telegraph on the shootout. Three days later, when they rode into Guthrie, their names were the talk of the territory. People stopped to cheer them on the street outside the Herriott Building.

Upstairs, they found Evett Nix in a wildly euphoric mood. Newspapers throughout the territory lauded the marshal and his deputies, where only a week before they had been vilified. There was particular praise on the death of Will Dalton, generally accepted as second-in-command of the Wild Bunch. The Guthrie *Statesman* recommended the same fate for every member of the gang.

Nix hurriedly arranged a press conference. His stated purpose was to provide the newspaper with a first-hand account from the men who had brought down a notorious outlaw. Unstated, though clearly understood, was an attempt to gain political mileage for himself from the exploits of Thomas, Tilghman, and Madsen. The reporter from the *Statesman*, usually one of their harshest critics, was today their enthusiastic supporter. All the more so since the interview represented a scoop on other newspapers.

"Tell me this," he said, pencil poised over his notepad. "Which one of you actually killed Will Dalton?"

Thomas and Madsen looked at Tilghman. After a moment, he offered a casual shrug. "What with all the shooting, things were pretty confused. Just say we all had a hand in it."

The reporter scribbled furiously. "The last of the Dalton brothers. The outlaw family that spawned Bill Doolin and the Wild Bunch. Killed by—" He paused, momentarily stumped. "I need a name for you three. Something with a ring to it."

"Excellent idea," Nix prompted him. "They're our top three deputies, guardians of law and order."

"That's it!" the reporter said, wide-eyed with a sudden fit of inspiration. "The Three Guardsmen! France had the Three Musketeers. We have the Three Guardsmen."

Nix beamed. "A fitting analogy. For a fact, they do guard Oklahoma Territory."

"The public will love it." The reporter appeared overjoyed with himself. "Now, let me ask you gentlemen—" he stopped, looking from man to man. "Having rid the territory of Dalton, what are your plans for Doolin and the rest of the Wild Bunch?"

"You can quote me directly," Nix said, desperate to insert his own name into the interview. "We are hot on the trail of Bill Doolin and his gang. Results will be forthcoming shortly."

"That's the headline! Three Guardsmen Hot On The Trail! What a story!"

On that high note, Nix tactfully ended the interview. Grinning broadly, he ushered the reporter to the door and saw him off with a warm handshake. Then, turning back into the room, his grin melted away. He took a seat behind his desk.

"Reporters," he said with mild disgust. "One day your friend, the next your nemesis."

Thomas snorted. "We'll play hell livin' down that tag he hung on us. The Three Guardsmen! Jesus Christ."

"Don't worry about it," Madsen said jokingly. "Tomorrow it will be old news."

"Speaking of which," Nix interjected, "I still wish you'd arrested that farmer. I just can't believe he knew nothing of Doolin's whereabouts."

"Done told you," Thomas said crossly. "I grilled him six ways to Sunday. He would've spilled it if he knew."

"Nonetheless, what Chris said is true. We need a new headline for tomorrow. One with Doolin's name in it."

"Fat chance," Tilghman remarked. "We're not even close to being hot on the trail. Maybe you should've told that reporter the truth. There is no trail."

"I've been thinking about that," Nix said. "What about that ranch outside Ingalls? Where Doolin holed up before?"

"The Dunn brothers," Tilghman noted. "What about them?"

"I think we should raid the place. Who knows, Doolin could be there right now. At the very least, we might uncover a lead through the Dunns."

"Bad move," Tilghman said. "Doolin's nowhere near Ingalls or that ranch."

"Oh?" Nix sounded dubious. "What makes you so certain?"

"By now, Doolin knows we know he married that girl. He'll steer clear of her—and the Dunn ranch—until he's ready to move her somewhere else."

"You believe Doolin will move his wife?"

"Has to," Tilghman affirmed. "Otherwise they'll never be together."

Nix considered a moment. "Then perhaps we should put surveillance on his wife."

"Town that small, Doolin would get wind of it. His wife and the Dunn ranch are our only solid leads. Touch either one and we tip our hand to Doolin."

"So what are you suggesting?"

"Wait and see," Tilghman said. "Somebody in Ingalls

—the preacher, the doctor, maybe the girl's dad—will let us know when Doolin shows up again. Until then, we sit tight."

"Sit tight?" Nix repeated testily. "Are you saying we do nothing?"

"We wait for Doolin to make a mistake. Often as not, that's what ends a manhunt—the other fellow gets careless."

"Bill's got a point," Madsen broke in. "Any move on the girl, or the Dunns, would cause Doolin to back off. We just have to wait it out."

"All right," Nix said reluctantly. "But let's have it understood, I won't wait too long. I want results."

"So do we," Thomas told him. "Don't you worry, we'll keep our ears open."

Their meeting ended on that note. Nix wasn't pleased, but he saw little choice in the matter. A good leader, he reminded himself, listened to the advice of his men. Yet he was uncomfortable with the outcome.

He needed Bill Doolin. Dead.

Tilghman rode straight through to Chandler. He arrived late that night, weary from ten hard days in the saddle. Too tired to eat, he had a cup of coffee with Neal Brown, relating only the bare details of the manhunt. Then, unable to resist sleep any longer, he went to bed.

The next morning, feeling rested, he was up early. He ate a large breakfast of bacon and eggs, sourdough biscuits, and strong black coffee. Afterward, he and Brown spent the morning going over the books and discussing ranch matters. Following the noon meal, he retired to a tub of hot water and soaked away the layers of grime accumulated on the trail. He then stropped his straight razor, gave himself a close shave, and splashed on a touch of bay rum lotion. He felt like a new man.

Late that afternoon he emerged from the house. He was attired in a blue serge suit, a starchy white shirt cinched at the collar with a tie, and his Sunday hat. As he stepped off the porch, Neal Brown walked up from the corral. Brown gave him a slow once-over.

"You headed for church on a weekday?"

"Nope," Tilghman said. "Tonight's Zoe's birthday party. Promised her I wouldn't miss it."

Brown sniffed the air. "You shore smell sweet. Sorta like a petunia."

"You ought to try it yourself sometime."

"Take a bath ever' time it rains. Reckon that's enough."

"Anybody downwind wouldn't doubt it."

"Sorry state of affairs," Brown grumped. "That little lady's got you turned inside out."

"Neal, you've got no idea."

A short while later Tilghman drove off in the buckboard. He often thought that Brown was right, that he was addled by a younger woman. Though their birthdays were only a month apart, he and Zoe were separated by a span of years. She was now twenty-one, and come July 4 he would be thirty-seven. Still, for him, the years seemed to have fallen away. He felt like a kid again.

Not long after dark he arrived at the Stratton place. The buggies and buckboards of neighbors were parked outside, and the house was ablaze with lights. Gaily colored Chinese lanterns had been strung between the roof and nearby trees, and the crowd had spilled out onto the yard. Zoe saw him step down from the buckboard, and she excused herself from her guests. She hurried toward him.

"You're here!" she said, her eyes radiant. "Somehow I knew you would make it."

"Told you I would," Tilghman said, taking her hands. "How could I miss your birthday?"

"When did you return?"

"Late last night."

"Everyone's heard," she paused, searching his eyes. "About Dalton, I mean. Was it bad?"

"Time for that later," Tilghman said, smiling at her. "I thought you invited me to a party."

"Yes, of course, you're right. Come and say hello to everyone."

She led him to the guests congregated under the Chinese lanterns. The women smiled, watching him with curious expressions, and the men shook his hand, greeting him warmly. Several offered their congratulations, alluding to Dalton, and waited expectantly for details. But Zoe warded them off, pulling him through the crowd toward the house. Her father came through the front door.

"Look who's here," she said, leading Tilghman onto the porch. "He got in just last night."

"Bill." Amos Stratton extended his hand. "Glad you could make the party."

"Glad to be here, Amos. Looks like everyone in the county turned out."

"That reminds me," Stratton said. "Zoe, you'd better check the punch bowl. It's just about empty."

"Oh, fudge!" She squeezed Tilghman's hand. "Don't run off. I'll be right back."

She hurried into the house. Stratton was silent a moment, then cleared his throat. "Your name's been in the papers the last couple of days. Way it sounds, Dalton put up a stiff fight."

"Nothing out of the ordinary," Tilghman said. "Like most, he didn't know when to quit."

"Zoe worries about you something terrible. She'd never say so, but it's a fact."

"Not all that much to worry about. I look after myself pretty close."

"You must," Stratton said amiably. "Or maybe you carry a lucky charm?"

"Never tried that," Tilghman said with a good-humored smile. "I always figured a man makes his own luck."

"I suspect that's so in your line of work."

"Daddy!" Zoe came out the doorway. "No talk of work tonight. This is a party!"

"Whatever you say, honey. It's your night."

She kissed her father on the cheek. Then, hooking her arm through Tilghman's, she turned back into the yard. Smiling, nodding to her guests, she led him under the Chinese lanterns, leaving the crowd behind. They paused beneath a tree.

"I know it's shameless," she said gaily. "But I don't want to share you with anyone tonight."

"Same here," Tilghman said. "Fact is, I was wondering how I could get you alone."

"Were you really?"

"Well, you see, I've been thinking about your birthday present. So I went by a shop over in Guthrie yesterday."

"You got me a present?"

Tilghman took a small box from his coat pocket. He snapped open the lid and the light from the lanterns sparkled off a diamond set in a slim gold band. Her mouth ovaled in a silent gasp and she stared at it as though bewitched. She finally looked up.

"Bill—"

"No, let me talk. You're everything a man could want in a wife and . . . well, if you'll have me, I'm, proposing marriage."

"Yes."

"What?"

"I said 'yes.' I'll marry you."

"You will?"

"Of course I will. Just tell me one thing . . . do you love me?"

"So much it hurts like a toothache."

Though hardly poetic, the sentiment was there. By now, she knew he was a man rarely given to a display of emotion. Still, once they were married, she could change that easily enough. She held out her hand.

"Put the ring on, Bill."

Tilghman slipped the ring on her finger. The sparkle in her eyes was no less than that of the lantern light off the diamond. She kissed him soundly on the lips.

"I do love you, Bill," she murmured. "So very much."

Tilghman enfolded her in a great hug. Across the yard there was a buzz of conversation. Then the crowd went silent, staring at them. She stepped out of his embrace, took his arm. She nodded to the watchful crowd.

"Shall we?"

"Shall we what?"

"Announce our engagement."

Tilghman grinned and led her toward the house.

CHAPTER 18

Tilghman still felt slightly dazed. The party had ended with another round of handshakes and warm congratulations from all their neighbors. Even Amos Stratton had pumped his arm, welcoming him into the family. Then Zoe had seen him off with a long, lingering kiss.

A full moon bathed the landscape in a spectral glow. He was humming to himself, filled with a sense of well-being for the moment and the future. Though he'd hoped to be married sooner, Zoe had insisted on an engagement period of six months. She wanted everything done in the proper manner, and she needed time to plan the wedding. The way he'd felt tonight he could refuse her nothing. He told himself six months wasn't long to wait.

The buoyant mood suddenly evaporated. As the buckboard rolled into the compound, he spotted two horses hitched outside the corral. A moment later two men rose from where they were seated in shadows at the front of the house. When they stepped into the moonlight, he saw that it was Heck Thomas and Chris Madsen. He brought the buckboard to a halt, swearing softly under his breath. He knew without asking that it was bad news.

"Look who's here," he said, stepping down from the buckboard. "Where'd you come from?"

"Guthrie," Thomas replied. "We've got trouble, Bill."

"Figured that when I saw you. What's the problem?"

"A warrant's out on the Dunn brothers."

"On what charge?"

"Horse stealing."

Thomas quickly related the details. The sheriff of Payne County had obtained a warrant against the Dunns on charges of horse stealing. There was evidence that the brothers bought rustled stock from horse thieves and later resold it after altering the brands. Evett Nix had learned of the charges only that afternoon, and he'd moved quickly to forestall the Dunns' arrest. In effect, he had made a deal with the Payne County sheriff.

"We bought some time," Thomas concluded. "The sheriff will hold off till we finish our investigation. But if we don't move on the Dunns, he will."

"What's his hurry?" Tilghman asked.

"Longer he waits, the more horses get stole. He wants the Dunns behind bars."

Tilghman was thoughtful a moment. Some months ago, when he'd posed as horse trader in Ingalls, he recalled the saloonkeeper mentioning that the Dunns had horses for sale. He saw now that their ranch was actually a way station for rustled stock. As well, it explained their connection to Doolin and the Wild Bunch. Thieves were drawn to thieves.

"Birds of a feather," he said at length. "The Dunns probably met Doolin through the horse thieves. All that crowd knows one another."

"Likely so," Thomas agreed. "We're gonna find out pretty damn quick. Nix wants us to raid the Dunns."

Madsen chuckled. "Told us to tell you it's a direct order. He figured you'd object."

"Nothing's changed," Tilghman said. "All we'll do is tip our hand to Doolin."

"Orders are orders," Madsen said. "Besides, if we don't, the sheriff will. Might as well be our play."

"You've got a point there, Chris."

Thomas held his pocket watch to the moonlight. "Quarter till eleven," he said, glancing at Tilghman. "You reckon we could hit the Dunns by sunrise?"

"Yeah, I suppose so." Tilghman's gaze went past him to the house. "You boys seen Neal Brown?"

"Gave us short shrift," Madsen said in a bemused tone. "Wouldn't say where you were, and told us to wait for you outside. Not the friendly sort, is he?"

"Neal figures I'm in the wrong line of work."

Thomas eyed him closer. "Where you been, anyway? Never saw you in duds like that."

"Well, Heck, you might say I dressed for the occasion. I popped the question tonight, and she said yes."

"You're gonna get married?"

"C'mon, I'll tell you about it while I change clothes."

Tilghman led them into the house. They pumped him with questions and laughingly joshed about the bliss of wedded life. The commotion awakened Brown, who grumpily went to make a pot of coffee. Then, figuring it might be a long time between meals, they all trooped into the kitchen. A short while later everyone sat down to a hurriedly prepared breakfast.

They toasted his engagement with flapjacks drowned in sorghum.

The moon heeled over to the west. The lawmen were some twenty miles north of Chandler, their horses held to a steady trot. All around them, the plains were awash in moonglow, the terrain clearly visible. Their thoughts were on the job ahead.

On the ride north, Tilghman had described the layout of the Dunn ranch. The main compound, he told Mad-

sen and Thomas, was situated on Council Creek southeast of Ingalls. The house was set back off the creek,
with a low knoll to the rear. To the west was a large
corral, and east of the house was a roofed storm cellar.
He recalled a stovepipe protruding from the storm cellar, and they all agreed that visiting outlaws were probably quartered there. After some discussion on tactics,
they had agreed on a plan. Their raid would be staged
from three directions.

Some miles south of Council Creek, the lawmen suddenly reined to a halt. Ahead, like an illusory phantom,
a rider materialized out of the moonlit night. Without a
word being spoken, they spread out, hands resting on
the butts of their pistols. The rider slowed to a walk,
then halted a few yards away. There was a moment of
tense silence.

"Howdy," Tilghman finally said. "You gave us a
start."

"You like to scared the pee outta me, too."

The voice startled them even more. They peered
closer, squinting in the moonlight, and saw that the
rider was a girl. She was dressed in men's clothing, pants
stuffed in her boot tops, a vest over her shirt, and a
weather-beaten hat. She looked to be no more than sixteen or seventeen.

"I'll be switched!" Thomas said, amazed. "Your folks
know you're out so late, missy?"

The girl stiffened. "Don't see as how that's any of
your business."

Her voice was tough, high-pitched but oddly hard.
Staring at her, Tilghman suddenly realized that she was
armed. The stock of a Winchester protruded from her
saddle scabbard and a holstered pistol was strapped
around her waist. He casually motioned off into the
night.

"You live around here?"

"What's your name, Nosey Ike? You gents ask a lotta questions."

Tilghman shifted in the saddle, and a flash of moonlight glinted off his badge. "We're just surprised to see a girl out here by herself. Where you headed?"

The girl hesitated, staring at their badges. Then, hauling the reins about, she gigged her horse. "Don't nobody follow me!" she yelled. "You'll git yourself shot."

She pounded off toward the east. Somewhat stunned, the lawmen were speechless, watching her disappear at a gallop across the plains. Finally, the first to recover, Thomas found his voice.

"What the hell do you make of that?"

"You got me," Tilghman said. "Did you see the hardware she was packin'?"

"A real spitfire," Madsen said in wonderment. "Maybe she's the daughter of some rancher around here."

"Well, boys," Thomas allowed, "whoever she was, she's gone now. Guess we'll never know."

Tilghman studied the sky. "Couple of hours till first light. Let's move out."

They rode toward Council Creek.

A shaft of golden sunlight touched the horizon. The lawmen, their horses hidden, were secreted in stands of trees around the Dunn ranch. Sunrise was their prearranged signal, and they started forward.

Tilghman approached from the creek, Winchester in hand, and headed toward the house. Thomas, carrying a shotgun, moved on a direct line to the storm cellar, the sun at his back. To the north, Madsen came down the knoll, with a line of fire to the rear of the house as well as the storm cellar. They moved quickly, every sense alert.

A hand signal between Tilghman and Thomas kicked off the raid. One pounded on the front door of the house and the other rattled the stovepipe on the roof of the storm cellar. In loud voices, they identified themselves as federal marshals and ordered everyone outside. Tilghman waited at the side of the house, his carbine trained on the door. Thomas, standing on top of the storm cellar, covered the entrance with his shotgun.

"Hold your fire!" someone yelled from inside the house. "We're comin' out."

From the storm cellar, as though echoing in a cave, a voice cried out. "For chrissakes, don't shoot! We're not gonna fight!"

The door of the house creaked open. Hands raised, two men in filthy long johns and their women in nightdresses stepped outside. At the storm cellar, three men in hastily buttoned pants, their boots forgotten, moved into the daylight. While Tilghman and Thomas kept them covered, Madsen quickly searched the house. Then, crossing the yard, he cautiously inspected the storm cellar. He waved an all clear signal.

The men at the house identified themselves as the Dunn brothers, Bee and George. From the storm cellar, his features wreathed in disgust, Thomas called out, "These boys are a sorry lot of two-bit horse thieves. I arrested one of them before. Know the other two on sight."

Tilghman interrogated the Dunn brothers. Thomas poked the man he'd arrested in the belly with his shotgun. The man blanched, his knees wobbly, and began answering questions. Some while later, they herded everyone together in the yard of the house. The lawmen walked off a short distance.

"You first," Thomas said, nodding to Tilghman. "What'd you find out?"

"Nothing much," Tilghman admitted. "The Dunns say they never saw your horse thieves until last night. Claim they just gave them a place to sleep."

"One part jibes," Madsen said. "I took a good look

around that storm cellar. There's eight bunks and a
wood stove. Stinks like a wolf den."

Thomas gave them a dour look. "That knothead I
questioned spilled his guts. You remember the girl we
ran across last night?"

"Yeah?" Tilghman said. "What about her?"

"She goes by the handle of Cattle Annie. Her and
another girl—calls herself Little Breeches—run together. Sounds so dumb it's got to be true."

"So?"

"Turns out they're friends of the Wild Bunch. Cattle
Annie damn near killed her horse to beat us here.
Guess who she brought a warnin' to?"

"You serious?" Tilghman said. "Doolin was here?"

Thomas nodded. "Bastard rode out before dawn."

CHAPTER 19

The lawmen were in a quandary. Doolin's trail was still fresh, less than two hours old, and they needed to start tracking. Yet they weren't sure they'd heard the full story. Or the entire truth.

After a hurried conference, they decided to have another talk with the horse thieves. Then, depending on what was learned, they might question the Dunns further. Their thought was that the Dunns, hoping to avoid prison and thereby save their ranch, would admit nothing. The horse thieves, with less to lose, would be more cooperative. They simply wanted to stay out of jail.

The Dunn women were ordered to brew coffee. While they were inside, Madsen kept their husbands under guard in front of the house. Tilghman and Thomas marched the three horse thieves back to the dugout storm cellar. Thomas adopted the role of the tough but sympathetic lawman, explaining that he was merely following orders. The man in charge, he told them, wasn't satisfied with their story. He then gave the stage to Tilghman.

Tilghman was no slouch as an actor himself. Over the years he had played out the same routine with such consummate performers as Bat Masterson and Wyatt Earp. He stuck his thumbs in his gun belt, the Winchester in the crook of his arm, and squinted at the thieves with a fierce glare. His voice was lowered to a harsh rasp.

"Horse stealing," he said bluntly, "carries a sentence of five to ten years. I figure you boys deserve the maximum."

The three men looked stricken. Tilghman allowed a moment of silence to underscore the message. Then, his voice cold and threatening, he went on. "This is your last chance," he said. "Tell me the truth and we might cut a deal. Lie to me and I'll put you away for ten years. I guaran-goddamn-tee it."

The thieves tripped over one another to save themselves. As the story unfolded, one then the other rushed to provide missing details. Doolin had ridden in late last night, after visiting his wife in Ingalls. An hour or so later Cattle Annie had rapped on the door of the storm cellar and called Doolin outside. Within minutes, Doolin had collected his gear, saddled his horse, and galloped off with the girl. One of the men, who had stepped outside to relieve himself, saw them ride southeast along the creek.

Probing further, Tilghman discovered that the thieves felt they'd been betrayed. Doolin or the girl could have warned them that lawmen were headed for the Dunn ranch. Yet they were left in the lurch, probably in the hope that they would engage the marshals in a long, time-consuming gun battle. To their way of thinking, Doolin had been willing to sacrifice them in order to cover his own escape. Had they put up a fight, the plan would have worked without a hitch.

Tilghman intended to wait until full sunrise before he started tracking. He checked the horizon, saw that he still had a few minutes, and prodded the men to talk about Cattle Annie. The girl's real name, they told him, was Annie McDougal. Her partner, known as Little Breeches, was Jennie Midkiff. Word had it that they were runaways, formerly from somewhere in Ohio. They

rustled a few cattle, whored for members of the Wild
Bunch, and looked upon Doolin as their idol. Their
hideout was a mile or so north of where Council Creek
fed into the Cimarron.

The Dunn brothers, the thieves hastened to add, were
known to everyone on the owlhoot. For a price, they
provided Doolin with a refuge from the law. Their regular business was operating in stolen horses and occasionally rustled cattle. The Dunns never tried to gouge,
always paying a fair price for good stock. George, who
was an artist with a running iron, skillfully altered the
brands. Bee was the thinker of the family and attended
to business matters. The stolen horses were sold to a
network of crooked livestock dealers.

"Here's the deal," Tilghman told the thieves when
they finished talking. "We'll tell the judge you boys were
a big help with information on the Wild Bunch. I think
he'll agree to probation."

"Probation?" one of them parrotted with disbelief.
"You mean he'll turn us loose?"

"Yeah, probably, on the condition that you go
straight. Steal another horse and you're on your way to
prison."

Tilghman turned, exchanging an amused look with
Thomas, and walked back to the house. He took Madsen aside, quickly explained the situation, and secured
agreement to go along with a plan he'd hatched over the
past few minutes. Then, while Madsen went to retrieve
their horses, he moved back to the Dunns. He addressed his remarks to Bee.

"Those boys," he said, nodding toward the storm cellar, "are headed for jail in Guthrie. You and your
brother are working on borrowed time."

Dunn was a short man with a potbelly and beady eyes.
His brow furrowed with skepticism. "Why aren't you
arrestin' us too?"

"Simple," Tilghman informed him. "You gents will

keep your mouths buttoned about today. When Doolin asks, you'll tell him nobody spilled the beans about him being here. Just say we were after horse thieves."

"And if we don't?"

"Then I'll personally escort you to federal prison."

Dunn frowned. "What makes you think Doolin will buy that story?"

"You'll convince him," Tilghman said with a hard grin. "That's what I meant about borrowed time. Either way, if you don't convince him, you lose. He'll kill you or I'll put you in prison."

"Cold one, aren't you?" Dunn said. "I'll bet you piss ice water."

"Let me down and you'll find out."

Some ten minutes later Madsen rode south with the horse thieves. The men were mounted, hands manacled behind their backs, their horses hitched to a rope attached to Madsen's saddlehorn. The Dunn brothers watched silently from the house.

Tilghman and Thomas rode southeast along Council Creek. The tracks, churned earth of horses at a gallop, were simple to follow. Downstream a ways, Thomas finally broke the silence. His expression was somber.

"Why'd you let the Dunns off the hook?"

"Hedged our bet," Tilghman said. "We've lost nothing in the bargain if we catch Doolin. But if we don't catch him, then maybe he'll still believe the Dunns' place is a safe hideout. Down the road, that might be our ace in the hole."

"Jesus," Thomas said in an admiring tone. "You're a lot more devious than I gave you credit for."

"Learned it all watching you, Heck."

"Hell, don't lay it off on me. Nix is gonna have kittens when he hears about this."

"Let him," Tilghman said easily. "Last few months, we've got a better handle on Mr. Nix. When the three of us stick together, he folds like a house of cards."

"By God!" Thomas said with a sudden grin. "Never thought of it that way, but you're right. We do have his number."

"Well, look here." Tilghman reined to a halt, studying the tracks. "Doolin and the girl parted company. She went on downstream, probably headed for her place. He took off on a beeline for the Nations."

"How do you know him from her?"

"I got their tracks separated out back at Dunn's corral."

Thomas decided to keep quiet, and let him sort it out. Tilghman's experience as an army scout made him the most skilled tracker of all the marshals. His experience as a peace officer had taught him an equally important lesson, perhaps a cardinal rule. He'd learned long ago that a wilderness manhunt requires patience.

For that reason, like any seasoned tracker, he had awaited full sunrise before trying to cut sign. On hard ground the correct sun angle made the difference between seeing a print or missing it entirely. The tracker stationed himself so that the trail would appear directly between his position and the sun. In early morning, with the sun at a low angle, he worked westward of the trail. The easterly sunlight then cast shadows across the hoofprints of a horse.

A tracker seldom saw an entire hoofprint unless the ground was quite soft. On hardened terrain the tracker looked for flat spots, scuff marks, and disturbed vegetation. Of all sign, flat spots were the most revealing. Only hooves or footprints, something usually related to man, would leave flat spots. Small creatures might leave faint scuff marks or disturb pebbles. But a flat spot, unnatural to nature, was always made by a hooved animal or a man. A shod horse made the sign even simpler to read.

Tilghman kept the sun between himself and the hoofprints. The trail angled across the plains, the direction east by southeast. He looked for the change of color caused when the dry surface of the earth is disturbed to expose a moister, lower surface. Heat increased the rate at which tracks age, and the sun had been out now for more than a hour. The under-surface of the prints, he noted, was almost restored to the normal color of the ground. All the sign indicated that Doolin was slightly more than two hours ahead.

The tracks took on an irregular zigzag pattern through streams and timbered woods. Whenever possible, Doolin chose rocky terrain or ground baked hard by the summer sun. He clearly suspected he was being pursued, and he'd resorted to evasive tactics. Yet his general direction never deviated, even though he had elected to take a winding route. He was headed for a sanctuary somewhere in the Nations.

By midday, the lawmen had covered better than ten miles. A good part of the time Tilghman was forced to dismount and conduct the search on foot. At several points, particularly on hard ground, the hoofprints simply disappeared. He then had to rely on pebbles and twigs dislodged as horse and rider had passed that way. The direction in which the ground was disturbed, invisible except to a veteran tracker, indicated the line of travel. Slowly, sometimes step by step, he clung to the trail.

Shortly after noonday Tilghman located a troubling sign. Upon crossing the Cimarron, he discovered that Doolin had stopped to watch his backtrail. The spot was located at a bend in the river where a stand of trees bordered the shoreline. Hidden behind the trees, Doolin had dismounted and waited, with an open field of fire across the width of the Cimarron. From there, with a lever-action rifle, he could have ended the chase. Or at the very least, discouraged further pursuit.

On foot, Tilghman inspected the spot. Farther into the trees he found where Doolin had tied his horse sometime before midday. The prints were deep and clear, the ground thoroughly scuffled, indicating a wait of close to an hour. Nearer the river bank, screened by the treeline, he saw where Doolin had selected a vantage point with a field of fire covering the stream and the opposite shoreline. Imprints of his boots were recorded in the soft earth beneath the trees.

"Doolin's tricky," Tilghman said. "Glad we didn't ford the river an hour ago."

Thomas was still mounted. He'd halted on the river bank and watched the search from a distance. "Hope you're jokin'," he replied. "The bastard was gonna bushwhack us?"

"Way I figure it, he would've waited till we were in the middle of the river. Then he'd have cut loose."

"And us stuck out there like sitting ducks. No place to run, no place to take cover."

"Heck, I just suspect we would've been dead ducks. Wouldn't have taken more than two shots."

"Goddammit!" Thomas exploded. "If he tried it here, he's liable to try it somewheres up ahead. We're gonna have to keep a sharp lookout."

"No argument there." Tilghman walked back to his horse, stepped into the saddle. "Maybe he didn't get us, but he sure as hell slowed us down. Told you he was tricky."

"What I wouldn't give to get that sonovabitch in my sights."

"Count your lucky stars, Heck. An hour ago he would've had us in his sights."

Tilghman led the way. He started at the tree where Doolin had tied his horse and began tracking from there. Yet another element, the prospect of an ambush, had entered into the chase. They both kept a wary eye on the terrain ahead as they moved off through the woods. The hunters, in no small sense, had now become the hunted.

Late that afternoon, Tilghman reined to an abrupt

halt. Before him lay a wide stretch of rocky terrain bordering the Cimarron. Not far ahead he spotted sign where Doolin had crossed the river onto soft ground along the opposite bank. A short distance beyond that point the sun had baked the upper shoreline as hard as brick. There, as though Doolin's horse had taken wings, the tracks disappeared.

By sundown, Tilghman had walked the ground a mile in each direction on both sides of the river. There were no tracks, no upturned pebbles, no disturbed vegetation. Finally, with a grudging sense of admiration, he ended the search. Doolin had once again outfoxed them.

CHAPTER 20

The moon stood like a mallow globe in a starlit sky. Where they'd lost the trail, they made camp along the banks of the Cimarron. Their horses were hobbled, grazing on a nearby patch of grass. The swift rush of water was the only sound in the night.

Their supper consisted of hardtack, jerky, and thick black coffee. Seated around the fire, they stared into the flames, their mood at a low ebb. The chase, ending in yet another stalemate, had left them withdrawn and thoughtful. Neither of them had spoken in a long while.

Thomas cracked a twig, tossed it into the fire. He rubbed his whiskery jaw, suddenly restless with the silence, and finally broached the subject that had them both disturbed. "How you reckon he ditched us?"

"Wish I knew," Tilghman said dully. "Just a guess, but he might've doubled back on that hard ground and taken to the river. He could stick to the shallows a long ways downstream."

"We could ride both banks in the mornin'. Might just turn up some sign."

"I'd seriously doubt it. Doolin's slicker than I thought."

"You mean the way he gave us the slip?"

Tilghman knuckled his mustache. "Wherever he

learned it, he knows every trick in the bag. Probably took lessons from his Indian friends."

"I hear you right," Thomas observed, "you're sayin' we lost him."

"Heck, he's long gone into the Nations by now. We're playing a busted flush."

"Sorry bastard's got more lives than a cat."

"I've been sittin' here studying on that. Appears to me there's only two ways we'll catch him. One's by pure accident, the right place at the right time. The other's through his wife."

"You got a point," Thomas agreed. "He's sure enough been bit by the love bug."

"No doubt about it," Tilghman said. "For a smart man, he takes lots of risks to be with that girl. Ingalls ought to be the one spot he avoids at any cost."

"Which is just where he was last night. Before he rode out to the Dunns' place."

"Well, I imagine the girl being in a family way has a lot to do with it. Doolin strikes me as a man who takes his obligations pretty serious."

"Life's funny," Thomas said without mirth. "Here's a goddamn robber and killer with all the conscience of a scorpion. But he's true blue to his woman. What a joke."

Tilghman chuckled. "You're startin' to sound like a philosopher."

"A plumb pissed-off philosopher. I thought for sure we had him this time."

"The accident went against us this time, Heck. Bad luck in spades when we stumbled across that girl."

"Cattle Annie?"

"Miss Annie McDougal, every outlaw's sweetheart. Except for her, we would've caught Doolin sound asleep."

Thomas grunted. "Somebody ought to pull her drawers down and spank her butt."

"That's a dandy idea." Tilghman suddenly grinned, nodding to himself. "Why go back to Guthrie empty-handed?"

"You talkin' about arresting the girl?"

"Don't see any reason why not. We've got her on obstruction of justice and aiding a fugitive. All federal charges, too."

"By God!" Thomas's mood brightened. "I like it."

"Another thing," Tilghman added. "Lock her up and she won't be giving Doolin the tip-off anymore. Starts to sound better all the time."

"What about her pardner, Little Breeches? Wonder how the hell she got that name?"

"However she got it, she's in thick with Doolin too. We'll arrest her on the same charges."

Thomas took the small, galvanized coffeepot from the edge of the fire. He poured himself a cup, his expression abruptly solemn. "You know we're gonna get razzed for bringin' in girls instead of Doolin. Christ, I can hear it now."

"You forget," Tilghman advised him. "Annie was carrying a pistol and a rifle. Threatened to blow our heads off, as I remember."

"You really think they'd fight?"

"I think we'd be smart to approach it that way. A gun doesn't care who pulls the trigger."

"Yeah, you're right," Thomas said thoughtfully. "That could be downright embarrassin'!"

"What?"

"Gettin' yourself shot by a girl."

Tilghman started laughing, and a moment later Thomas joined in, struck by such a preposterous notion. But later, as they lay in their bedrolls, Thomas stared soberly at the star-studded sky. He hoped Tilghman was wrong, that they wouldn't fight. He'd never before killed a woman. Or even worse, a girl.

Tomorrow, he told himself, wasn't the time to start.

* * *

Late the next afternoon, west along the Cimarron, they sighted Council Creek. They turned northwest where the tributary emptied into the river, sticking to the shoreline. Their information, squeezed from the horse thieves at the Dunns' ranch, was that the girls had a hideout a mile or so upstream. Half a mile farther on they dismounted, leading their horses.

A short while later the wind shifted and they caught the scent of woodsmoke. Up ahead, through trees crowding the creek bank, they saw the outlines of a small cabin. As they approached nearer, it became apparent that the cabin was a crude one-room affair thrown together with logs, a stovepipe sticking out of the roof. On the wind, they heard the sound of girlish laughter.

Tilghman motioned a halt at the edge of the treeline. Beyond was a clearing, the cabin set back a short distance from the creek. At the far corner of the cabin, hitched to a metal ring in the wall, two horses stood hipshot and saddled in the heat. The door was open, and through it, they saw shadowed movement as one of the girls moved across the cabin. The sound of voices was followed by another burst of laughter.

The lawmen left their horses in the trees. Then, circling through the woods, they approached the cabin from the rear. Their pistols drawn, they flattened themselves against the wall and moved to the front of the cabin. As they stepped around the corner, one of the horses at the opposite end awoke with a start and snorted in alarm. Swiftly now, afraid the girls had been alerted, they hurried along the front wall of the cabin. But even as the horses reared back in fright, there was still another round of laughter from inside. They jumped through the open door.

"Hold it!" Tilghman ordered. "Federal marshals."

The girls froze, their laughter stilled. Little Breeches,

a tiny waif of no more than fifteen, was stretched out on a bunk bed. On the opposite side of the room, Cattle Annie stood silhouetted before an open window. They were both dressed in men's clothing, holstered pistols strapped around their slim hips. For an instant, thunderstruck, they stared with their mouths ajar.

"Easy now," Thomas said in a loud voice. "Don't try anything foolish."

Cattle Annie dived through the open window like a dog through a hoop. Tilghman turned back toward the door as Little Breeches leaped off the bed. Thomas crossed the cabin in three swift strides and caught her wrists as she pulled her pistol. He bore down, squeezing hard, and the gun dropped from her hand. Holstering his pistol, he smiled down on her.

"Now I know why they call you Little Breeches."

She slugged him in the balls. His mouth ovaled in a whoosh of air and he bent double, clutching at his groin. The girl loosed a shrill screech and attacked him with the ferocity of a wildcat, clawing and scratching as he hopped around with fire in his crotch. Her nails raked his face from forehead to chin.

After several moments, battered and savaged by her assault, Thomas was finally able to draw a full breath. He warded her off with one arm, still clutching his groin with the other hand, and she kicked him in the shins. Howling with pain, he grabbed her by the hair and lifted her off the floor. The girl screamed like a banshee, flailing and thrashing while he held her at arm's length. His face was ribboned with purple welts and bloody slashes.

Outside the cabin, Cattle Annie bounded onto her horse like a circus acrobat. She wheeled away at a lope as Tilghman came through the door. He jerked the reins loose on the other horse, vaulting into the saddle, and took off after her. A beaten path behind the cabin tunneled through the woods and emerged onto an open prairie. The girl whipped her horse into a headlong gallop.

Tilghman was perhaps ten yards behind when he cleared the treeline. The girl looked over her shoulder, her features contorted, screaming obscenities that were lost on the rush of wind. Then, as he booted his horse and closed the distance, her eyes went round with panic. She pulled her pistol, turning in the saddle, and fired three quick shots at Tilghman. The slugs whizzed past him with an angry snarl.

Hauling back on the reins, Tilghman brought his horse to a skidding halt. He grabbed the stock of a Winchester carbine, jerking it from the scabbard as he stepped out of the saddle. A quick glance confirmed that it was much like his own carbine and he levered a shell into the chamber. The butt snugged into his shoulder, he caught the sights and drew a bead on the girl's horse. When he fired, the horse went down forelegs first, dead even as it struck the ground. The girl was hurled out of the saddle like a cannonball.

Tilghman led his mount to where Cattle Annie lay sprawled on the prairie. The jolt had rattled her senses and sapped her will to fight. He took her pistol, then unbuckled her pants belt and pulled it loose. She moaned, her eyes fluttering, as he cinched her wrists together with the belt. Before she could resist, he hefted her off the ground and dumped her over the saddle. She began cursing as he mounted behind her and rode back toward the creek.

Thomas was waiting outside the cabin. Little Breeches was seated on the ground, her wrists bound with rope and a bandanna stuffed in her mouth. Her eyes welled up with tears as Tilghman reined to a halt and dropped Cattle Annie at her feet. He stepped out of the saddle, eyeing the latticework of scratches across Thomas's face. Tilghman's mouth lifted in a crooked grin.

"Looks like you got the worst of it, Heck."

"No laughin' matter," Thomas said sourly. "She's mean as tiger spit and twice as deadly. I've fought men no tougher'n her."

"You lousy bastards!" Cattle Annie shrieked. "Take that gag outta Jennie's mouth. She's just a kid!"

"Some kid," Tilghman commented dryly. "Quit yellin' or I'll gag you. We've had enough nonsense for one day."

She fell to her knees beside Little Breeches. Thomas studied them a moment, then looked at Tilghman. "What was all that shootin'?"

"Annie tried to stop my clock. I brought her horse down with a saddle gun."

"Jesus Crucified Christ! We're never gonna live this down."

"Think not?"

"Know not," Thomas grumped. "You tradin' lead with a slip of a girl. And me cut up like I'd tangled with a grizzle bear." He gingerly touched a bloody gash on his jaw. "Wish't I'd never let you talk me into it."

"Whoa now," Tilghman said with a wry smile. "I seem to recollect it was your idea."

"Whoever thought it up," Thomas retorted indignantly, "it was a pea-brain notion. Here on out, I'm not chasin' any more girls."

"Way you look, I don't blame you, Heck."

"Don't you start on me! I'm warnin' you."

A short time later they rode out of the clearing. The girls were mounted double on Little Breeches's horse, hands now secured behind their backs. Tilghman took the lead and Thomas brought up the rear, nursing his wounds with a kerchief dipped in creek water. Little Breeches, whose gag had been removed, taunted him in a shrill voice.

"Hey, you big sissy! Hurt bad, are you?"

"Close your trap or I'll close it for you."

"Yeah!" Cattle Annie chimed in. "Way you jumped us, you're nothin' but cowards. Let's try it fair and square."

"Awww, for chrissakes," Thomas moaned. "It's never gonna end."

The Guthrie *Statesman* ran a front-page story two days later. A banner headline confirmed Heck Thomas's worst fears.

STALWART MARSHALS APPREHEND DESPERADOES
CATTLE ANNIE AND LITTLE BREECHES NABBED

CHAPTER 21

A fortnight later the girls were still in the news. After being lodged in the Guthrie jail, Cattle Annie and Little Breeches had escaped. There was lax security for women prisoners, and they had managed to outwit the night guard. The newspaper, with caustic humor, played it as farce.

Sheriff's deputies recaptured the girls the following day. From that point, justice moved swiftly for the young runaways. They were brought to trial and rapidly convicted on testimony by the three horse thieves captured at Dunns' ranch. The judge, though lenient, passed sentences the same day.

Annie McDougal and Jennie Midkiff, being underage, were not sentenced to prison. Instead, they were committed to a reform school in Massachusetts for two years. The girls, who considered themselves full-fledged outlaws, took it as a personal insult. A day later, on Tilghman's recommendation, the horse thieves were sentenced to five years' probation. They were admonished to follow the straight and narrow.

To Evett Nix's dismay, he was again lambasted in the press. As U.S. marshal, according to the newspapers, he was hell on underage girls but no significant threat to the Wild Bunch. Doolin and his gang had vanished in yet another puff of smoke, leaving no trace as to their whereabouts. They were generally thought to be hiding out in the Nations, but no one had a clue. Once again, they'd gone to ground.

Tilghman returned home following the court proceeding. Nix had ordered him, as well as Madsen and Thomas, to redouble their efforts. Still, without a tip from an informant, or another holdup by the Wild Bunch, the trail was cold. On the ride to Chandler, Tilghman had pondered the matter at some length. Thomas and Madsen would work their informants, and hope for a break. He decided to take more direct action.

On his first morning at home, Neal Brown brought him up to date on ranch operations. The mares had foaled a week past, dropping four colts and six fillies. An inspection of the stables confirmed that all were doing well under the care of the Sac and Fox hands. The offspring were frisky, their legs sturdy, and all clearly had the conformation of their sire, Steeldust. The breeding program was off to a rousing start.

Tilghman was immensely gratified with the results. For the first stage, he thought the crop of colts and fillies held great promise for the future. When time permitted, he still intended to expand the bloodlines with another stallion and other thoroughbred mares. But for the moment, with his duties as a lawman, he was content with the progress thus far. Steeldust had performed admirably as a stud, and there was reason to be pleased.

At the noon meal, Brown finally ran out of talk about horses. He looked up from his plate with mock solemnity. "Those girls you arrested?" he said, waving a fork. "From the newspapers, sounded like you had your hands full."

"Yeah, couple of real hardcases." Tilghman played along, aware that he was being ribbed. "First time I ever traded shots with a female."

"So what happens to them now?"

"Tried, convicted, and sentenced. They're on their way to reform school."

"No joke?" Brown asked idly. "Well, I guess reform school's the right place for pint-sized desperadoes. Evett Nix must've been tickled you brought 'em in."

"After a fashion," Tilghman said, laughing. " 'Course, I think he would've preferred Doolin."

"What the hell," Brown said in a bantering tone. "You got your man—uh, girl. That's what counts."

"Too bad you weren't with me, Neal. Things might have gone better."

"Think so, do you?"

"Yeah, I do," Tilghman said, nodding. "Fact is, I wanted to ask your help on another matter."

Brown squinted at him. "You talkin' about law work?"

"Not anything all that risky. I just need someone to cover my back."

"Cover your back where?"

Tilghman sipped his coffee. "Thought I'd scout the Dunn ranch again. It's been two weeks since that last raid, and who knows? Doolin might figure we wouldn't look there so soon."

"Why me?" Brown said crossly. "I ain't no lawdog."

"Well, you might say it's a secret mission. I halfway forgot to clear it with Nix. Thought I'd have a looksee on my own."

"Just a looksee?" Brown scoffed. "What if we stumble acrost Doolin and his bunch?"

"Doubtful," Tilghman replied. "I had in mind a quick scout, in and out. Figured you wouldn't object to lending a hand."

"You get my ass shot and I won't never forgive you."

"Appreciate the assist, Neal. Knew I could count on you."

"Yeah, sure," Brown said gruffly. "Just a prize sucker, that's me."

"You're an upstanding citizen, always were."

"Tell me that when the shootin' starts."

Early that evening Tilghman called on Zoe. She hadn't expected him, unaware that he had returned to Chandler. But she pulled him into the house, insisting that he stay for supper. He gladly accepted.

"Just potluck," she said, walking him into the parlor. "Nothing special, I'm afraid."

"Beggars can't be choosers," Tilghman said. "Don't put yourself to any trouble."

"I'm so happy to see you I could skip supper. Who needs food?"

She squeezed his arm as they entered the parlor. Amos Stratton smiled and rose from his easy chair, extending his hand. After a moment, Zoe excused herself and hurried off to the kitchen. Stratton motioned him to a chair.

"When'd you get back, Bill?"

"Late last night. Rode in from Guthrie."

Stratton struck a match, lit his pipe. "We read about you in the newspaper. Those two little girls must've been a sorry pair."

"Sad thing," Tilghman observed. "They got mixed in with a bad lot."

Stratton now took an interest in his work. Their conversation, rather than stiff and formal, had become a casual exchange between friends. Tilghman was treated more as a family member, his calls a welcome occasion. Their talks often ranged over a wide variety of subjects.

"Speakin' of news," Stratton said, nudging a crumpled newspaper at the foot of his chair. "You heard the latest on the statehood movement?"

"Heard it yesterday," Tilghman acknowledged. "There's talk of little else in Guthrie."

"Yeah, I'd bet they're beatin' the drum over there. Big things are in the works."

"Guess it depends on whose ox gets gored."

"Same as always," Stratton said easily. "The Indian's got to make way for progress."

"There's a difference here, Amos. We're talking about the Five Civilized Tribes."

Tilghman's remark went to the heart of a wide-ranging debate. The battle for statehood had been joined, and at stake was twenty million acres of land in the Nations. The debate, by now a matter of national interest, raged in the halls of Congress as well as the White House itself. No one doubted that the future of both Oklahoma Territory and Indian Territory would be played out along the banks of the Potomac. There, in the political arena, the issue of statehood would be decided.

The key to the debate was that the Nations possessed almost all of the mineral wealth to be found in both territories. Coal mines had begun operating on tribal lands as early as 1871, when the Katy railroad first laid tracks through the Nations. The largest of these mines was located in the Choctaw Nation, and for the most part had remained under strict tribal control. But with the rapid growth of Oklahoma Territory, and a steadily increasing demand for coal as fuel, the situation had changed. White entrepreneurs, as well as government, now coveted the red man's natural wealth.

"Indians are Indians," Stratton said. "I never bought that stuff about the Five Civilized Tribes. Don't appear all that civilized to me."

"You've never been there," Tilghman observed. "They have towns and schools, and laws and courts. Their system of government's even patterned on ours."

"Maybe so, but they've had that land for fifty years. What've they done with it?"

Zoe called them to supper. At the table, the conversation resumed with the give and take of a friendly debate. Tilghman's view of the Nations, a subject they'd never discussed, was a pleasant surprise for Zoe. She found herself nodding with his defense of the Five Civilized Tribes.

The power brokers, Tilghman commented, had decided that Oklahoma Territory and Indian Territory should be joined as one state. Indian leaders, on the other hand, had lodged fiery protests against single statehood. They feared, and rightly so, that Oklahomans would monopolize government and politics, and the rule of law. As the Plains Tribes had been dispossessed of their lands, it now appeared that similar tactics were to be used against the Five Civilized Tribes. There was an odor of conspiracy involving white money barons and the federal government.

The Indians, Tilghman went on, were right in their suspicions. Joint statehood would be impossible until all Indian lands had been allotted in severalty and the tribal governments abolished. Quick to respond to pressure from Congress, the president had appointed a commission and ordered that negotiations commence with the Five Civilized Tribes. The purpose was to extinguish tribal title to their lands, and Indian leaders were aligned in their determination to resist. The last battle was about to be joined.

"I don't get it," Stratton said, puzzled. "Everybody in the Nations sides with outlaws and works against federal marshals. Why would you take up for them?"

Tilghman helped himself to a second serving of beef stew. "Question of what's right," he said. "Fifty years ago we took their homelands in the South and forced them to move out here. Not right to rob them again."

"The same could be said of the Plains Tribes. We took their land."

"Yeah, but there's a difference. The Plains Tribes were nomads, lived off the buffalo. The people in the Nations operate businesses and run farms. They adopted our way of life."

Stratton sopped stew gravy with a hunk of bread. He chewed thoughtfully a moment. "No offense, Bill," he said finally. "But you and me wouldn't have land except for broken treaties. What changed your mind about the Nations?"

"Hard to say," Tilghman admitted. "What seemed fair yesterday doesn't seem so fair today. Maybe we ought to stop breaking treaties."

"Sounds like wishful thinkin' to me. Would you return your land to the Sac and Fox?"

"Too late now to turn back the clock. But we've got a chance to do the right thing in the Nations. We owe those people more than a hundred sixty acres."

Congress had directed that a roll be taken of every man, woman, and child in Indian Territory. Clearly, this was a preparatory step to allotment of lands in severalty, one hundred sixty acres to a family. Yet the rolls being taken were also a death knell for a way of life. It was the first step in the dissolution of the Five Civilized Tribes.

Amos Stratton saw it as progress. To his way of thinking, at least ten million acres would be opened to white settlement in Indian Territory. But for Tilghman it had slowly become a symbol of all that was wrong between the white man and the red man. He had pioneered the opening of Oklahoma Territory, and he was proud of what had been achieved. Still, in retrospect, he saw that it could have been handled in a more equitable manner. He thought the Five Civilized Tribes deserved better.

After supper, Zoe shooed her father back into the parlor. Then, once the table was cleared, she and Tilghman walked down to the creek. The summer sky was ablaze with stars, and they paused beneath the dappled shadows of a tree. She took his face in her hands, kissed him softly on the mouth. Her eyes shone in the starlight.

"You're a good man," she said in a dreamy voice. "I'm so proud of you."

Tilghman was taken aback. "What makes you say that?"

"Because I saw a different side of you tonight. You believe right is right—even for Indians."

"Took a while," Tilghman confessed. "Working over in the Nations opened my eyes. They've got reason not to trust whites. We don't keep our word."

"That's why it bothers you," she said, staring at him. "You do keep your word."

"Watch out," Tilghman said with a roguish smile. "You're liable to give me a swelled head."

"No fear of that."

"You think not, huh?"

Her voice was husky. "Hold me, Bill. Hold me tight."

Tilghman enfolded her in his arms. She stood quietly in his embrace a moment, and then looked up, her mouth moist and inviting. He kissed her beneath the dappled starlight.

The katydids along the creek went silent.

CHAPTER 22

Tilghman and Neal Brown rode north the following night. The plains glimmered beneath bright starlight and a cloudless sky. A soft breeze whispered through the rolling sea of grass.

By now, the trail was a familiar one to Tilghman. His previous scouts to Ingalls and the Dunn ranch had left a map of the landscape imprinted in his mind. He timed their departure to put them on Council Creek shortly before dawn. He planned to be in position by sunrise.

Brown was in a grumpy mood. He'd arranged for the Sac and Fox workhands to look after the stock while they were gone. One day would suffice for the trip, and he had told them he would return by the next evening. But that was based on the assumption that he and Tilghman would encounter no problems. His sour mood indicated that he wasn't sold on the argument. To him, outlaws were always a problem.

"No end to it," he muttered as they rode along. "Doolin or somebody else, there's gonna be robbers and such till hell freezes over. You'll never catch 'em all."

Tilghman nodded agreeably. "Never said I would, Neal. Doolin's the one I'm after."

"Who you kiddin'?" Brown said with a short laugh.

"Once't you catch Doolin there'll be another one, and then another one. You've got the tin badge disease."

"Well, lucky for you, it's not contagious."

"Bet your life it ain't! I'll stick to horses any ole day. You oughta do the same."

Tilghman couldn't argue the point. As a practical matter, there was a greater future in horses than in outlaws. But the challenge of capturing Doolin was one he'd been unable to resist. Even with Doolin caught, he wasn't entirely sure that he would ever quit as a lawman. So he had to consider that Brown was right, after all. Perhaps he had contracted the tin badge disease.

"Hard to quit," he said now. "Thought I'd put it behind me when we left Kansas. Guess that's not the case."

"No guesswork about it," Brown said gloomily. "You'd lots rather be off chasin' desperadoes. Don't see nobody twistin' your arm."

"You got me there, Neal."

"What's Miss Zoe say about all this? She don't worry about you gettin' yourself killed?"

"She never says one way or another. I reckon she figures she got the badge in the bargain."

"Damn poor bargain." Brown rubbed the bridge of his nose. "You must've sold her a bill of goods."

"Maybe she's just not a worrywart . . . like some people I could name."

"Think that's what I am, do you?"

"Never thought otherwise."

Brown mumbled something under his breath. He let the matter drop, reminded all over again that it was probably a lost cause. They rode in silence toward Council Creek.

Sunrise found them positioned in the treeline east of the Dunn ranch. Below, apart from some thirty horses in the corral, there was no sign of movement across the compound. Armed with Winchesters, they settled down to wait.

Tilghman had no immediate plan of action. He intended to watch and react as developments unfolded. Should Doolin appear, then he would play the situation as the moment dictated. If Doolin failed to appear, then he would pull back and await another day. Like most manhunts, it was all a roll of the dice.

A short while after sunrise smoke began billowing from the chimney on the house. Some moments later Bee Dunn stepped through the doorway, followed by his brother, George. They paused in the yard, talking briefly, then Bee ambled off toward the dugout storm cellar. George yawned, stretching his arms to loosen his shoulders, and walked to a haystack near the corral. He began forking hay to the horses.

Bee gave three sharp knocks on the door of the storm cellar. Then he pulled the door open, moved inside, and closed it behind him. The walls of the dugout deadened any sound, and there was no way to tell if anyone else was inside. After a few moments, tendrils of smoke drifted from the stovepipe on top of the roof. Someone had clearly stoked the fire in the stove.

Tilghman waited, his gaze fixed on the door. Several minutes passed, and Bee Dunn still hadn't emerged from the dugout. Across the way, George Dunn finished forking hay to the horses and walked back to the house. A stillness settled over the compound.

Brown jerked his chin at the dugout. "What d'you make of that?"

"Somebody's in there," Tilghman said. "Otherwise he wouldn't have knocked, or started a fire."

"Why would anybody build a fire in the summertime?"

"Way it appears, he just woke somebody up. They're fixing morning coffee."

Brown grunted. "You think it's Doolin?"

"Maybe," Tilghman said. "Then again, maybe it's another crew of horse thieves. Hard to tell."

"So what's our next move?"

Tilghman considered a moment. Dunn had been inside for some time, and showed no signs of coming out. By now, it was clear that he was talking with someone in the dugout. Whether to wait and see what happened, or force the issue seemed to Tilghman a tossup. He decided to act rather than react.

"Here's how we work it," he said. "I want you to stay here and give me cover. I'll see who's in that dugout."

Brown gave him a bewildered look. "You're gonna go down there?"

"That's the general idea."

"Gawddamn, Bill, you're liable to get yourself shot. Wouldn't it be safer to wait and see who comes out?"

"Not much," Tilghman said. "I think I'd rather flush them out."

"Crucified Christ." Brown's voice sounded parched. "What'll I do if something goes wrong?"

"Keep one eye peeled on the house. Anybody comes out with a gun, let loose in a hurry."

"You want me to kill him?"

"Whatever it takes to stop him. I'm liable to be too busy to handle it myself."

"Gawdalmighty," Brown said with a bleak expression. "Knew I wasn't cut out to be a lawdog."

Tilghman handed over his Winchester. "That'll save you from having to reload. Shoots a hair to the right."

"Sounds like you're plannin' on fighting a war."

"Just figure to have a looksee, Neal."

"Do me a favor next time."

"What's that?"

"Don't ask me along."

Tilghman moved clear of the treeline. He crossed the open ground on a direct line to the dugout. He pulled his pistol as he halted before the door. For a moment, he waited, listening, but there was no sound from inside. He rapped on the door three times.

A beat of silence slipped past. Then, deadened by the sod wall, a voice called out. "Who's there?"

"Federal marshal," Tilghman said. "Come on out, Bee."

There was no reply for several moments. "Door's unlatched," Dunn finally yelled back. "C'mon in."

Tilghman debated briefly with himself. Then, standing to one side of the door, he flung it open. Sunlight flooded the inside of the dugout, which resembled a barracks. Four double bunks lined either side of the room, with blankets draped over the front for privacy. There was no way to tell if the bunks were occupied, someone hidden behind the draped blankets.

Dunn stood at the far end of the room. Beside him, on a small wood stove, a coffeepot began to belch steam. The dugout was a rainbow of odors, stale sweat mixed with dried earth and the aroma of coffee. Tilghman took one step inside the door, halting at the edge of the first bunk. He kept his pistol trained on the rancher.

"Expecting company, Bee?"

"No, I'm not," Dunn said hastily. "Always come down here for coffee in the mornin'. Old lady raises hell if I get her up too early."

Tilghman motioned with the pistol. "Eight bunks and a stove, all the comforts of home. You running a hotel?"

"Well, you know, people stop over and want a bed. I try to oblige."

"Yeah, I recollect you're the obliging sort. Last time I was here, you had three horse thieves holed up."

Dunn shifted from foot to foot. "Told you I never saw those boys before. Just let 'em stay the night."

Tilghman noted that he appeared agitated. His voice was an octave too high and a muscle ticced along his jawline. He seemed unable to stand still.

"How about today?" Tilghman waggled the snout of his pistol. "Anybody in those bunks?"

A slight rustling noise sounded as someone shifted in the farthest bunk. On two of the bunks closer to the door, the draped blankets moved as though touched from behind. Dunn's eyes went wide with fright.

"Nobody's here," he said in a shaky voice. "Told you, I'm just makin' coffee."

Tilghman sensed that he'd stepped into a vipers' den. There were at least three men, probably more, hidden behind the draped blankets. He was outnumbered and outgunned, and the wrong word now would be his last. He was reminded that discretion often proved the better part of valor.

"I'm after three bank robbers," he lied casually. "Got a posse of ten men waitin' in the woods. Any strangers come through here last night?"

Dunn's mouth twitched. "Nobody come through here."

"You're real sure about that, Bee?"

"Plumb certain."

Dunn stole a furtive glance at the bunks. For a moment, the silence in the dugout was like breathing suspended. Tilghman knew then his bluff had worked; the men in the bunks believed he had a posse outside. They were convinced for now that their only chance was if he left the dugout alive. He decided not to press his luck.

"We're headed north," he said, underscoring his bluff. "Do yourself a favor and keep your nose clean. Get my drift?"

"Don't worry, marshal." Dunn bobbed his head. "I'm not lookin' for trouble."

"Then I guess we understand one another. See you around, Bee."

Tilghman took a step backwards through the entrance. He purposely slammed the door shut, a signal to everyone inside that he was gone. Holstering his pistol, he turned from the dugout and walked toward the trees. All the way across the open ground he felt as though he was lugging an anvil on his shoulders. Yet he forced himself to maintain a brisk, unconcerned pace.

Brown waited behind a large live oak. He kept his carbine trained on the compound until Tilghman was well within the treeline. Then, a Winchester in either hand, he retreated deeper into the woods. He let out a huge sigh of relief.

"What happened?" he said nervously. "I started to think you was a goner."

"So did I," Tilghman replied. "I think Doolin and some of his men are in that dugout."

"How'd you get out alive?"

"They thought I had an ace in the hole."

"Ace in the hole?" Brown looked rattled. "What the hell you talkin' about?"

"I'll tell you about it later. Let's see what they do now."

Tilghman retrieved his carbine and motioned Brown to follow. Crouched low, they moved forward to a patch of shadows just inside the treeline. There they went belly down on the ground, hidden from sight. Quiet and still, careful not to betray their position, they waited.

A long half hour passed in silence. Then with a screech of hinges, the door of the dugout swung open. Bee Dunn moved into the sunlight, blinking against the glare. He shaded his eyes with one hand and slowly examined the woods on all sides. Finally, satisfied that no one waited in ambush, he turned back toward the door. His voice was muffled.

Red Buck Waightman emerged from the dugout. He was followed by Doolin, and then, one at a time, the rest of the Wild Bunch. They stood ganged together, eyes shaded against the sunlight, searching the woods. Dunn's woman appeared in the doorway of the house and her call to breakfast sounded across the compound.

On signal from Doolin, the men trooped toward the house.

Tilghman shouldered his Winchester. He caught the sights and drew a bead on Doolin's back. A touch on the trigger, one shot, and the leader of the Wild Bunch would be dead. The urge to fire and end it here was almost overwhelming. But he found himself unable to squeeze off the shot. He was no assassin.

Doolin and his men entered the house. Tilghman lowered the hammer on his carbine and rose to his feet. Brown gave him a strange look. "Where you headed?"

"Guthrie," Tilghman said. "We're coming back with more men."

He walked off toward their horses.

CHAPTER 23

"Are you serious? You had him in your sights?"

"That's about the size of it."

Evett Nix stared at him with a flabbergasted expression. Tilghman was seated before the desk and Heck Thomas stood at the window. There was a moment of strained silence.

"For God's sake!" Nix snapped. "Why didn't you shoot him?"

Tilghman's gaze was steady. "I'm no bushwhacker."

"We're not discussing some gentlemanly code of honor. We're talking about a cold-blooded killer!"

"Speak for yourself. I don't shoot men in the back."

"Those were your orders," Nix said indignantly. "Bring them back dead, which is to say, kill them. Who are you to decide the right or wrong of it?"

"I've already told you," Tilghman said levelly. "I won't kill a man without fair warning."

Tilghman had briefed them on his scout of the Dunn ranch. He'd spared no details, nor had he spared himself. The tense moments in the dugout, as well as the chance to kill Doolin, had been recounted at length. He had offered no excuses.

"Now that I think of it," Nix said, "who authorized

you to go off on your own? You didn't clear that with me."

"The man on the spot has to make his own decisions. I played a hunch."

"Let's get this straight," Nix ticked off points on his fingers. "You went to the Dunn ranch without authorization. You placed yourself in jeopardy by acting on your own. You disobeyed a direct order to shoot Doolin on sight. Does that about cover it?"

Tilghman waggled one hand. "I reckon you hit the high points."

"Careful with your tone of voice, Mr. Tilghman. I will not tolerate insubordination."

"Try a civil tone of voice yourself. You want respect, then give it."

Nix swelled up like a toad. "Don't push me too hard. I hired you and I can fire you."

"Tell you what," Tilghman said bluntly. "Anytime you want my badge, all you have to do is ask."

"Hold on!" Thomas broke in, turning from the window. "Just back off before things get out of hand. That goes for both of you."

"Indeed?" Nix said stiffly. "Are you issuing the orders around here now?"

"Not orders," Thomas said with restraint. "I'm talkin' common, ordinary horse sense. We'll get nowhere fightin' amongst ourselves." He paused, looking from one to the other. "Let's stick to fixin' Doolin's little red wagon."

Nix took a deep breath, collected himself. "All right," he said. "What's to be done now that Doolin has escaped?"

"Who said he'd escaped?" Tilghman asked. "Odds are he's still at the Dunn place."

"Really?" Nix said with skepticism. "After your surprise visit, I hardly think he'd hang around."

"Well, first off, he doesn't know we know he uses the

Dunn place as a hideout. So there's no reason for him to run."

"Prudence would dictate otherwise. But go on with what you were saying."

Tilghman ignored the interruption. "Doolin probably brought the gang together to pull another job. Depending on his timetable, they might still be there. Or they might come back there after pulling the job."

"You got a point," Thomas said thoughtfully. "Leastways where Doolin's concerned. He'd likely want to see his wife again."

"So?" Nix prompted. "What are you suggesting?"

"Another raid," Thomas said. "Bill and me could make it up there by late tonight. I vote we hit them first thing tomorrow mornin'."

Nix regarded him a moment. "We don't have time to get Madsen here from El Reno. But on the other hand, two against eight make for poor odds. I think we should deputize some of the local officers."

"Count me out," Thomas said bitterly. "We'd more 'n likely wind up with another bloodbath like Ingalls. I want no part of it."

"Heck's right," Tilghman cut in. "You'll recollect we told you the same thing before the raid on Ingalls. Let the two of us handle it."

"Suppose I do?" Nix said pointedly. "And suppose you have another crack at Doolin? Will you kill him?"

Tilghman held his gaze. "Any man deserves a warning, and that includes Doolin. But if he resists, I'll get the first shot."

Nix sounded weary. "You have a way of making your own rules. I'd think orders would mean more to a lawman."

"Guess that all depends on the orders. Even a lawman's got to live with himself."

"So it appears." Nix summoned a tight smile. "Gentlemen, I wish you good hunting. Bring me Bill Doolin —dead."

Outside the office, Tilghman and Thomas made their way down the stairs. On the street they paused to watch a horse-drawn trolleycar clang past. The sight seemed curiously at odds with their backcountry pursuit of outlaws.

"You're a hard one," Thomas said with amusement. "Thought you were gonna give Nix a heart attack."

"Him and his orders," Tilghman said heavily. "I'd wager he's yet to kill his first man. Doubt he's got the stomach for it."

"Most don't," Thomas allowed. "Sounds easy till you're set to pull the trigger. Guess that's why there's fellers like us."

Tilghman considered a moment. "Tell me the truth, Heck," he said finally. "Would you have back-shot Doolin?"

"I'd have been sorely tempted."

"Yeah, but would you have done it?"

"Probably not," Thomas admitted. "Like you said, a man's got to live with himself. I wouldn't be partial to that kind of dream."

Tilghman looked surprised. "You dream about the men you've killed?"

"Only on bad nights. How about you?"

"Once a month or so. Nothing regular."

Thomas laughed. "We ought not let Nix hear us talkin' this way. He'd figure we'd lost our nerve."

"Guess he would," Tilghman said, grinning. " 'Course, for a brave soul like him, what's another dead man?"

"Ink on paper, my friend. A nice, big headline."

An hour later they rode out of Guthrie. The trail, once again, led toward Council Creek.

* * *

Before dawn they moved into position. Thomas was hidden in the treeline by the creek and Tilghman was directly opposite the dugout. They settled down to await sunrise.

Their plan was simple. From their positions, they were afforded an interlocking field of fire on the storm cellar. When the gang emerged for breakfast, Tilghman would order them to surrender. At the first sign of a fight, both lawmen would open fire on Doolin. The gang, with their leader dead, would almost certainly scatter and run.

Tilghman briefly had considered the same plan yesterday morning. Yet he had discarded it just as quickly because of Neal Brown. His friend could have provided covering fire, but Brown lacked the experience for a pitched gun battle. Today, should the gang fight rather than run, Tilghman was confident that Thomas would hold his own. Hidden in the treeline, firing on men in the open, there was no question of the outcome.

Shortly after sunrise George Dunn stepped through the door of the house. He walked directly to the corral and forked hay to the milling horses. Then, his morning chore completed, he returned to the house and disappeared inside. There was no sign of Bee Dunn, even though smoke funneled from the chimney. Nor was there anything to indicate that the bunkhouse in the dugout was occupied. The stovepipe on the roof stood as further proof. No smoke appeared.

Tilghman waited until full sunrise. Finally, troubled that their plan had gone awry, he circled back through the trees to the creek. He found Thomas leaning against a tree, watching the house. They exchanged an unsettled look.

"What d'you think?" Thomas said. "Anybody in that dugout?"

"Doesn't look that way," Tilghman said. "By now,

they'd be up and making coffee. Not a trace of smoke from the stovepipe."

"Maybe they rode out to pull a job. Could've left yesterday after you were here."

"I've got an inkling that's the case."

"We could wait," Thomas suggested. "Like you said, they might come back this way."

"Yeah, they might." Tilghman stared at the house a moment. "What say we have a talk with the Dunns?"

"Any particular reason?"

"They'll likely know Doolin's plans. Leastways they'll know more than we do."

"That'll tip our hand," Thomas said. "Dunn will figure we're keepin' a watch on his place."

"Things have changed," Tilghman observed. "After yesterday, we've got solid proof he was harboring fugitives. I'd say it's time to convert him."

"Turn him into an informant?"

"You're reading my mind, Heck."

Ten minutes later they rode into the compound. Outside the corral, they dismounted and hitched their horses. Bee Dunn appeared in the doorway of the house, his expression unreadable. He spoke to someone over his shoulder, then walked toward the corral. His brother took a position at the door, stationed to act as a watchdog.

Dunn halted before the lawmen. "You gents are gettin' to be regulars."

"Listen close, Bee." Tilghman nodded toward the house. "George looks like he might have a rifle hidden behind that door. If he tries anything, you're a dead man."

Dunn motioned his brother into the house. When the door closed, he turned back to Tilghman. "Satisfied?"

"For now," Tilghman said. "That dugout appears to be empty. Where's Doolin?"

"How would I know?"

"Don't dance me around, Bee. I stayed behind yesterday and waited to see what happened. You treated Doolin and his boys to breakfast."

Dunn gave him a sharp, sudden look. "I'll be gawddamned! You didn't have no posse up in the woods. You were by yourself, weren't you?"

"Maybe, maybe not," Tilghman said. "Either way, I'm eyewitness to the fact that you're harboring fugitives. You've been caught out, Bee."

"So what d'you want from me?"

"Let's take first things first. Where's Doolin?"

"Gone," Dunn answered in a monotone. "You spooked him with all that talk of a posse. Him and his boys went back to the Nations."

Tilghman appraised him. "Were they planning a holdup?"

"I'm not privy to Doolin's plans. He keeps such to himself."

"Where does he hide out in the Nations?"

"Dunno," Dunn said stonily. "Never asked him."

"You think we're stupid?" Thomas demanded, poking him in the chest with a thorny finger. "You'd better come up with some answers, pronto! Otherwise you're up shit creek."

"What's that supposed to mean?"

Tilghman riveted him with a look. "By law, you're an accomplice after the fact to murder, robbery, and conspiracy to commit criminal acts. How'd you like to take a short drop on a hangman's rope?"

"Jesus Christ, I never killed nobody!"

"You're still guilty under the law. A judge and jury would convict you in a minute."

"What if they would?" Dunn sounded unnerved. "Why haven't you arrested me?"

"Here's the deal." Tilghman's eyes were like nail heads. "We'll drop all charges against you, even for horse stealing. In exchange, you feed us information on

Doolin and his gang. Their whereabouts, their plans—anything you know."

"You expect me to inform on Bill Doolin?"

"Get the wax outta your ears," Thomas warned. "You waltz us around and we'll put your ass smack-dab on the gallows. You hear me?"

"Yeah," Dunn said dully. "I hear you."

"So let's try again," Tilghman said. "Where's Doolin hole up in the Nations?"

"Swear to God I don't know. I'm tellin' you the truth."

"You ever lie to me and I'll personally put the rope around your neck."

Dunn's expression became one of bitter resignation. "You done convinced me, awright? I got the message."

Tilghman quickly laid out the ground rules. He explained the location of his ranch outside Chandler as well as the marshal's office in Guthrie. Dunn was to get word to him whenever there was information on Doolin. He underscored the urgency should Doolin return to the Dunns' ranch.

"One last thing," he concluded. "Your brother's as guilty as you are. Any slipups and you'll both swing."

"Don't worry about George," Dunn said weakly. "He does whatever I tell him."

"We'll expect to hear from you, Bee—real soon."

The lawmen mounted and rode toward the creek. Dunn stared after them a moment, his pudgy face wreathed with disgust. His mind whirled at what he'd done.

He was now the Judas goat for the certain execution of Bill Doolin.

CHAPTER 24

Late that afternoon Tilghman and Thomas rode into Guthrie. On the street, they hitched their horses and then trudged into the Herriott Building. Neither of them relished the thought of delivering their report.

Evett Nix greeted them with an expectant look. But as Tilghman related the details of the raid, his expression changed. His eyes hooded and his mouth set in a razored line. Finally, unable to suppress his anger, he slapped the top of his desk with the flat of his hand. His voice was tense.

"You say Doolin and his gang were gone. Gone *where*?"

"The Nations," Tilghman told him. "They pulled out yesterday morning."

Nix glared at him. "After you failed to shoot Doolin —despite your orders."

"We've already covered that ground."

"And you assured me Doolin would be caught. But now, he's escaped again. For the umpteenth time!"

Tilghman hadn't slept for almost two days. His features were drawn, and he was in no mood to be bullyragged. He shifted in his chair, his temper frayed, on the verge of replying in kind. Thomas swiftly interrupted.

"You're overlooking something," he said to Nix. "Doolin and his boys were plannin' on pulling a holdup somewheres. Bill's visit there yesterday gave them cold feet. Except for that, the newspapers would be hawkin' another robbery."

"Thank God for small favors," Nix scoffed. "The fact remains that the Wild Bunch has once again slipped through the net. Why are you sitting here telling me this? Why aren't you on their trail?"

"Waste of time," Thomas said. "They're scattered all over the Nations by now."

"So you intend to twiddle your thumbs and wait for them to commit yet another robbery. Is that it?"

"Well, no, not just exactly. We've got ourselves a new informant."

Nix looked at them speculatively. "Do you indeed? And who might that be?"

"Bee Dunn," Tilghman replied. "We made a deal with him. All charges will be dropped against him and his brother. Horse stealing. Harboring a fugitive—"

"*What?*"

"—accomplice to murder. The whole works."

"Are you addled?" Nix said, flaring. "You can't just willy-nilly drop such charges."

"In exchange," Tilghman went on, ignoring the outburst, "Dunn will tip us the next time Doolin shows at his place. Or let us know anything he learns about Doolin's plans."

"You had no authority to make that kind of deal. Good God, you've given the man virtual immunity!"

"Arresting Dunn wouldn't have gained us anything."

"On the contrary," Nix said irritably. "His arrest would have shown that we're capable of putting away Doolin's cohorts. The newspapers would have loved it."

"I'm not interested in headlines," Tilghman said. "With Dunn, we've got a real chance at Doolin. I'll settle for that."

"What makes you think Dunn will keep his word?"

"No fear of that," Thomas said with a sardonic half-smile. "Unless he squeals on Doolin, the charges don't get dropped. He'll hold up his end."

Nix scowled. "You place a good deal of faith in a horse thief."

"I put my faith in him being a coward. He's more afraid of a hangman's noose than he is of Doolin."

"Even so—" Nix paused, his gaze shifting to Tilghman. "I have no authority to authorize this deal. You may have misled Dunn."

Tilghman stared at him. "U.S. marshals make deals all the time."

"Perhaps," Nix said curtly. "But this one requires the approval of the governor and the U.S. attorney general. Otherwise there could be serious repercussions."

"How so?"

"Because it involves Bill Doolin and the Wild Bunch. I won't take that responsibility on myself."

"Even if it means catching Doolin?"

"And if you don't?" Nix let the question hang a moment. "Then it would put me out on a limb, wouldn't it? Had you thought of that?"

"What the hell," Tilghman said, motioning to include Thomas. "We put our necks on the line every time we ride out. Thought you knew, that's part of being a lawman."

"Don't presume to lecture me," Nix said furiously. "You'll overstep yourself once too often."

"Look here," Thomas broke in before it could go any further. "What we're talking about is the fastest way to catch Doolin. Am I right?"

When they both nodded, he looked at Nix. "You say you need approval," he noted. "But all that takes is for you to endorse the deal we made with Dunn. Do that and we're in business."

"You expect me to sell the idea, is that it?"

"Yeah, I do," Thomas said breezily. "Leastways if you expect us to catch Doolin."

A vein stood out on Nix's forehead. "You're quite a pair," he said in a tight voice. "What I'm hearing sounds vaguely like extortion."

Thomas waved it off. "We're just trying to do our job. Why take it personal?"

Nix glowered at them a moment. "All right," he said, rising from his chair. "For what it's worth, I'll have a word with the governor. Wait here."

Neither of them spoke as he crossed the room. When the door closed, Tilghman shook his head. "Turned out to be just another gutless wonder. He should've stuck to the grocery business."

"Hell, Bill," Thomas said without rancor, "all politicians are the same. Let somebody else make the decision in case it goes sour. That way your butt's covered."

"Guess that's my problem," Tilghman observed. "I was never much good at politics. Too slick a game for me."

"Trouble is, you expect everybody to be on the up and up. Politics is like cardsharps being elected to office. You gotta allow for dealing from the bottom."

"Tell you the truth, I'm startin' to wonder if it's worth it. There's better ways to spend your life."

"Name one," Thomas said, grinning. "You and me, we're two of a kind, Bill. We'll be old and feeble when we lay down the badge."

"Don't bet on it," Tilghman said. "One more go-round with Nix might be the last. All he wants are the headlines."

"I've heard of worse bargains. For him to get what he wants, we get what we want."

"You talking about Doolin?"

"Only in passing," Thomas said. "Nix and his crowd, they're after higher office, runnin' things. We're simpler, the way we look at it. All we want is law and order."

"Maybe we're not simpler," Tilghman said, unable to resist smiling. "Maybe we're outright simpletons. We do the work and they get the glory."

"When the history books get written, things don't always work out that way. Lemme ask you a question."

"Shoot."

"Who killed Billy the Kid?"

"Pat Garrett," Tilghman said. "So what?"

"When Garrett shot the Kid"—Thomas gave him a sly, sideways glance—"who was governor of New Mexico Territory?"

"I haven't got the least notion."

Thomas grinned. "I rest my case."

"Pretty funny," Tilghman said, his smile wider. "Guess that means one of us will have to kill Doolin."

"Don't worry about it, Bill. One of us will."

A short while later Nix came through the door. He walked to his desk and sat down in the swivel chair. His expression was curiously benign.

"The governor bought it," he said in a cheery voice. "In fact, he thought it was a top-notch idea. We have his full endorsement."

Neither Tilghman nor Thomas missed the use of "we" in his statement. Clearly, with the governor's endorsement, Nix was now a staunch advocate of the plan. Thomas managed to keep a straight face.

"So what d'you think?" he asked. "Will the attorney general approve the deal with Dunn?"

"No question of it," Nix said genially. "I'll draft a telegraph message that includes the governor's endorsement. We should have approval from Washington by tomorrow."

Nix was still beaming when they went out the door. On the street, they paused as passersby hurried along the sidewalk. Then, unable to restrain himself, Thomas burst out laughing.

"Whatta world!" he said. "Before long, Nix will think we hung the moon."

"All the same," Tilghman said with some amusement, "he's still a gutless wonder."

"You clean forgot what I told you."

"What's that?"

"You know—" Thomas hesitated, grinning. "Who shot Billy the Kid?"

"One thing's for certain, Heck."

"Yeah?"

"It damn sure wasn't Evett Nix."

Tilghman called on Zoe the following evening. After riding in from Guthrie, he'd managed a full night's sleep, and he once again felt rested. Yet, for all that, his good humor seemed somehow forced. He was still thinking of the encounter with Nix.

Following supper, Zoe banished her father to the parlor and his newspaper. She led Tilghman outside, and they seated themselves in the porch swing. A breeze off the prairie had displaced the day's heat shortly after nightfall. Off toward the creek, fireflies blinked dots of light in the dark.

For a while, lulled by the motion of the swing, they talked of his upcoming birthday and her plans to hold a party. Yet, beneath the surface, she sensed that he was not himself tonight. By now, she could detect the slightest shift in his mood, particularly when he was troubled by something he was trying to hide. She knew, despite his pleasant manner, that his mind was worlds away. He was brooding on something.

"All right," she said, squeezing his arm, "tell me all about it."

"All about what?"

"You're not fooling me for an instant. I can almost hear the wheels grinding. What's bothering you?"

"Nothing much," Tilghman said, avoiding a direct answer. "Besides, I'd rather spend our time together talking about us. Why spoil it talking about business?"

"Because we should share things," she persisted. "The good as well as the bad. Are you talking about ranch business or law business?"

"Won't give up, huh?"

"Oh, for goodness sakes! Anything that involves you involves me. You should know that by now."

Tilghman was silent a moment. Then, aware that she wouldn't be put off, he finally told her. His voice quiet with anger, he related the encounters over the past few days with Evett Nix. His words were filled with loathing.

"Hate to admit it," he concluded, "but I'm about at the end of my rope. Nix looks at Doolin as just another feather in his cap. He's a politician, pure and simple."

"He sounds perfectly terrible," she said. "But on the other hand, he is the U.S. marshal. How do you get around that?"

"Short of quitting, there's no way around it. I'm stuck with him."

She often experienced a whipsaw of emotions about his job as a lawman. She was constantly frightened for his safety, terrified that he would ride out one day and never return. Yet his devotion to the law, his inner conviction that right should prevail, was all too apparent. She had long since reconciled herself to the fact that he would not be the same man without a badge. Nor would she attempt to change him.

"You know what I think?" she said with a disarming smile. "You hate taking orders from a man you don't respect. You feel like you've compromised yourself."

"How'd you know that?" Tilghman said, slightly astounded. "You a mind reader, or something?"

"No," she said softly. "But I know you."

"Well, you hit the nail on the head. Half the time, I feel like kicking myself for not turning in my badge."

"And yet, turning in your badge isn't the answer, is it? You take great pride in being a lawman."

Tilghman nodded. "Not bragging, but I'm good at it. Sort of comes natural."

"Then you shouldn't quit," she said confidently. "People always say you have to take the bitter with the sweet. Nothing's ever perfect."

"Evett Nix is a bitter pill, all right. One that I find damn hard to swallow."

"Perhaps that isn't the answer, either."

"How do you mean?"

"Well—" She hesitated, searching for the right words. "Where you're concerned, I'm hardly impartial. But you're a resourceful man, the most determined man I've ever met. I just suspect you'll find a way to deal with Mr. Nix."

Tilghman put his arm around her. He held her close and she snuggled into the hollow of his shoulder. He stared off into the dark for a time, thinking about what she'd said. Then, finally, he chuckled and hugged her tighter.

"You know, I just suspect you're right. One way or another, I'll deal with Nix."

CHAPTER 25

A fortnight slipped past with no word on the Wild Bunch. Then, as though contemptuous of the law, they struck in the heart of Oklahoma Territory. On a dark night, late in July, the gang robbed a train outside the town of Dover. They got away with over twenty thousand dollars from the express-car safe.

News of the holdup went out on the telegraph before midnight. Tilghman, who was in Guthrie at the time, was awakened shortly afterward in his hotel room. Less than an hour later, he and Thomas met with Evett Nix to map out a strategy. There was no train between Guthrie and Dover, and they had no choice but to travel by horseback. By two o'clock, they rode west into the night.

Dover was a small town north of the Cimarron River, located some thirty miles northwest of Guthrie. El Reno, where Chris Madsen was posted, was some sixty miles south of where the robbery had occurred. The Rock Island railroad had service from there northward, and Nix ordered him by telegraph to commandeer a train. He was to meet Tilghman and Thomas in Dover.

An hour or so after sunrise Madsen's train pulled into the station. Tilghman and Thomas, sipping coffee provided by the stationmaster, were standing on the depot platform. They waited while Madsen unloaded his horse from a boxcar behind the locomotive. The three men had about them a sense of grim determination, as well as quickened excitement. The Wild Bunch, missing since the raid on Dunn's ranch, had at last surfaced. This time, they meant to run the gang to earth.

Once they were mounted, they rode south along the railroad tracks. Some three miles outside town a trestled bridge spanned the Cimarron. At the northern end of the bridge, the bandits had felled a tree to halt the train. Following the robbery, a posse had been hastily organized by the Dover town marshal. Working by torchlight, they had attempted to uncover the gang's trail, and finally abandoned the search. Their horses had churned the earth on both sides of the tracks.

"Helluva note," Thomas muttered, staring down at the jumbled hoofprints. "Had good intentions, but they sure left a pretty mess. How're we gonna find the trail?"

Tilghman studied the terrain a moment. On the opposite side of the bridge were rolling hills, studded with trees. To their immediate east, bordering the river, the land was flatter, less wooded. He shaded his eyes against the sun.

"You and Chris stay here," he said. "I want to have a look at that flat ground."

"Figure they're headed for the Nations?"

"So far they've run true to form. I'll just have a look-see."

Ten minutes later Tilghman cut sign a hundred yards downstream. By the tracks, he knew there were eight riders moving at a fast clip. The trail generally followed the river, and the direction was due east. He estimated that the gang was now some seven hours ahead.

Turning in the saddle, he motioned Madsen and Thomas forward. When they joined him, he pointed out the tracks. "Sign's easy to follow," he said. "Trouble is, they're too far ahead."

"Have to stop somewheres," Thomas said. "They'd kill their horses tryin' to make a direct run for the Nations."

"Who knows?" Madsen ventured. "Maybe they've split up and Doolin headed for Dunn's place. Think it's worth a try?"

"Tend to doubt it," Tilghman told him. "Doolin's likely to stay clear of there after pullin' a job. I'd say he's headed for the Nations."

Madsen shifted in his saddle. "So what do we do now? Got any ideas?"

"If I was them," Tilghman said, "I'd swing south of Guthrie. The land's less settled down that way."

"Yeah, but where?" Thomas said with a quizzical frown. "You're talkin' about a lot of land."

"Heck, you were right about them having to rest their horses. You know where the river makes a wide horseshoe bend, about halfway between here and Guthrie?"

"Sure do," Thomas said, nodding. "There's a good ford there, too."

"That's what, maybe fifteen miles?" Tilghman remarked. "Hard as they're pushing their horses, that'd be a good rest stop. Ford the river there and that puts them south of Guthrie."

"So what's your plan?"

"We cut overland and catch them at the ford. I figure they'd rest up for four, maybe five hours."

"Sounds good to me," Thomas said. "How about you, Chris?"

Madsen shrugged. "One guess is as good as another. Let's go find out."

They crossed the river over the railroad bridge. Then, with the sun in their faces, they turned cross-country toward the distant ford. They held their horses to a steady trot.

* * *

A hot noonday sun scorched the land. The lawmen topped a low knoll on the south side of the Cimarron. Their horses were lathered with sweat, their shirts soaked. Before them, the river arced in a broad horseshoe bend.

Tilghman suddenly yanked back on the reins, brought his horse to a dust-smothered halt. Thomas and Madsen were only a beat behind, but still too late. Below, on the south side of the ford, they spotted men and horses in a grove of trees. Even as they reined to a stop, they saw that the men were in the midst of saddling their horses.

A shout of alarm went up from the trees. One of the outlaws pulled his pistol and winged three shots toward the knoll. The distance was perhaps fifty yards and the shots went wild. The other men, fighting to control their horses, scurried for cover behind the trees. The marshals bailed out of their saddles, grabbing Winchesters as they stepped down. They swatted their horses on the rump, turning them to the back side of the knoll.

The dull boom of rifles sounded from the distant trees. Slugs kicked up dirt along the crest of the knoll, forcing the lawmen onto the reverse slope. They went belly down on the ground and snaked their way back to the crest. Warily, after removing their hats, they edged their Winchesters over the top of the knoll. Madsen saw one of the outlaws still struggling with a spooked horse along the border of the treeline. He sighted quickly, allowing for the downward angle, and fired. The man staggered sideways, then dropped on the river bank.

Tilghman and Thomas waited for targets of opportunity. Whenever a gang member eased from behind a tree to fire, they peppered him with lead. Madsen joined them, turning his fire on the grove, and they hammered out a volley of shots. Bark flew off trees and slugs zinged through the woods, but none of the outlaws were hit. The return fire, with the odds now seven to three, kept the lawmen ducking as bullets raked the knoll. For every man they fired on, other men fired on them, and the snarl of slugs was constant. Their accuracy was thrown off as they were forced to sight and fire in an instant.

Yet they held the high ground. Despite the odds, it slowly became apparent that the lawmen had the advantage. Doolin was a shrewd tactician, and he gradually realized that his position was untenable. To charge the marshals over the open ground would have been tantamount to suicide. But as the gun battle raged, it was clear that his men would be picked off one at a time. Though they were behind trees, they had to expose themselves to get off a shot. The marshals, with only their heads exposed, offered much smaller targets. Time worked in their favor.

A shouted command brought all gunfire from the trees to an abrupt stop. Then, in the next instant, men were darting through the grove toward their horses. The marshals suddenly realized that the gang had been ordered to break off the fight and fall back in retreat. Without thought, they assumed solid kneeling positions on the knoll and began firing at the outlaws. A horse went down, thrashing and kicking, as they levered a barrage of shots. The rider screamed a curse, blood spurting from his hand, and scrambled aboard behind one of the other men. A second horse faltered, clearly wounded, but managed to regain its stride. The outlaws pounded east along the river at a hard gallop.

The marshals quickly collected their horses. They mounted, Winchesters laid across their saddles, and rode down to the grove. As they approached, the wounded horse kicked one last time and went slack in death. The downed outlaw lay sprawled on his back at the river's edge, a rosette of blood spread across his shirt. The lawmen reined to a halt, staring down at the body. Thomas finally broke the silence.

"Tulsa Jack Blake," he said. "You drilled him dead center, Chris."

Madsen nodded. "Wish to Christ it was Doolin."

"Look on the bright side," Thomas said. "None of us got hit, and it's a puredee wonder. I could've sworn we had a mile or so to go when we came over that rise."

"Luck was with us," Madsen agreed. "The way we stumbled onto them, they should've shot our lights out."

Tilghman was staring off downstream. "We'll play hell catching them," he said, as though thinking aloud. "They're mounted on fresh horses and ours are pretty well spent. Doolin's the one that lucked out."

Thomas looked at him. "Are you sayin' we break off the chase?"

"Not by a damnsight," Tilghman said levelly. "But we'll have to take it slow and easy. Otherwise our horses won't last."

Madsen shoved his carbine into the scabbard. "Way I see it," he said, "they're slowed down, too. One horse carrying double and another wounded. Maybe we've still got a chance."

"Hope you're right," Tilghman said. "We're long overdue a decent break."

After watering their horses, they rode out from the grove. Tilghman took the lead, following the tracks along the river bank. He thought their chances were slim, unless Doolin made a mistake. But even that seemed a remote likelihood.

So far the Wild Bunch had gotten all the breaks.

The trail looped south from the Cimarron. The outlaws were moving at a fast pace, and their course was plain to read. They would skirt Guthrie and make a run for the Nations.

The land was sparsely settled, scattered farms located along creeks. There were no towns on the line of march, and thus no way to telegraph ahead and alert the authorities. Doolin, ever the tactician, had once again selected an escape route that hampered pursuit. Hour by hour, forced to conserve the strength of their horses, the three lawmen fell farther behind.

Toward mid-afternoon Tilghman signaled a halt. Ahead, on the opposite side of a creek, the horse they'd wounded earlier lay dead. Dismounting, he searched the area on foot, and found a grisly trophy. He held up a man's forefinger crusted with blood.

"We winged somebody," he called out. "Looks like it was almost shot off and he finished the job with a knife."

"Better than nothin'," Thomas said. "Leastways we've drawn blood."

Tilghman pointed to the dead horse. "There's two of them riding double now. That'll slow them down."

"Let's pick up the pace," Madsen said. "Maybe we'll get lucky."

They rode on at a sedate trot. The trail led straight as a string on an easterly course. Tilghman had no trouble cutting sign, for the gang was still pushing their mounts. Yet two of the horses, the ones carrying double, were lagging behind the others. That meant four of the outlaws were slowly losing ground, and Tilghman was encouraged. He thought perhaps Madsen was right, after all. Maybe their luck had changed.

Late that afternoon the trail led them across a plowed field to a farmhouse. As they rode into the yard, they saw a woman and a small girl crouched over a body on the ground. The body was that of a man in bib overalls, and the woman was wailing hysterically. The girl stood sucking on her thumb, her eyes blank with shock. Flies buzzed around a splotch of blood on the farmer's overalls.

Thomas managed to separate the woman from her husband. The girl trailed along, eyes still round, as he led the woman into the house. Tilghman and Madsen inspected the body, and saw that the farmer had been shot at point-blank range. Mixed with the blood on his overalls were scorch marks from the muzzle blast of a pistol. They gently hefted the body and carried it to the front porch of the house. Inside, they heard the woman trying to talk between choked sobs.

A short while later Thomas emerged onto the porch. His features were grim. "Got most of the story," he said. "The gang rode in here and took the only two horses this man had. He went runnin' out to the barn and tried to stop them. From her description, the one that shot him was Red Buck Waightman."

"Sonovabitch," Madsen cursed in a low growl. "I'd like to get him in my sights."

"Yeah," Tilghman said, his expression wooden. "Only you'd have to beat me to him."

Thomas stared down at the farmer. "We're gonna have to bury him for the woman. She's out of her mind with grief."

"What about the gang?" Madsen said. "We've still got a couple of hours of daylight left."

"Lost cause for now." Tilghman's toneless voice underscored the words. "They're all mounted and they've got fresh horses. We'd never get close."

"Bill's right," Thomas said, shaking his head. "Sometimes things just don't work out. Today wasn't our day."

They dug a grave beneath a tree near the house. Shortly before sundown, with the farmer wrapped in a blanket, they gathered under the shadows of the tree. The woman sobbed while the girl stood clutching her legs, and Tilghman read a passage from the family Bible. Madsen and Thomas lowered the shrouded body into the hole.

Dusk fell as they began shoveling earth onto Homer Godfrey.

CHAPTER 26

The next morning they followed the trail into the Creek Nation. They felt obligated to continue the manhunt as long as there was sign to follow. All the more so since the outlaws had wantonly killed an innocent man. Still, none of them held out any great hope of cornering the Wild Bunch.

The trail ended shortly after they crossed into the Creek Nation. Tilghman found the spot where the outlaws had halted, presumably to split the loot from the train robbery. Like leaves scattered by the wind, the gang then split off in different directions. From past experience, the marshals knew there was nothing to be gained by further pursuit into the Nations. The manhunt ended where the tracks were obliterated on a heavily traveled wagon road.

The lawmen were less than a day's ride from Tilghman's ranch. Thomas decided to stay the night and then continue on to Guthrie. Though they had killed one of the gang, he was in no rush to deliver their report to Evett Nix. Madsen was determined to push on to El Reno, even though it meant spending a night on the trail. They parted at a crossroads southeast of Chandler.

Tilghman and Thomas arrived at the ranch shortly before sundown. As they rode into the compound, they saw a strange horse tied outside the corral. Neal Brown hurried from the house as they dismounted and began hitching their horses. His features were troubled.

"Wondered if you'd show up," he said by way of greeting. "There's a feller waitin' inside to see you."

Tilghman nodded. "Who is it?"

"Don't know," Brown said. "Wouldn't give me his name. But he's nervous as a whore in church."

"Why'd you let him in the house?"

"Told me it was official business. I figgered he was somebody from the marshal's office, in Guthrie."

Tilghman and Thomas exchanged a look. They followed Brown back to the house and filed through the door. George Dunn was seated in the parlor, nervously running the brim of his hat through his hands. He jumped to his feet as they entered the room. His expression was a mixture of relief and worry. Tilghman turned to Brown.

"Do me a favor, Neal. Would you unsaddle our horses? Give them some grain?"

Brown appeared offended. "Hell, I know when I'm not wanted. All you had to do was say so."

"Nothing personal," Tilghman said. "I'll explain it later."

"Don't even wanna know. Keep your damn secrets."

Brown stormed out of the house. When the door closed, Tilghman turned back to Dunn. The parlor lamps were lighted, and in the cider glow the man's features seemed pasty. He continued to twirl his hat by the brim.

"Let's have it," Tilghman said. "What brings you here?"

Dunn's throat worked. "Bee sent me to fetch you. Pierce and Newcomb are at our place."

"What about Doolin?"

"Just them two. They showed up a little after noontime."

Tilghman's look betrayed nothing. Out of the corner of his eye, he saw that Thomas's features were set in a skeptical frown. In the past, none of the gang members had stopped at Dunn's ranch except when accompanied by Doolin. The presence of Charley Pierce and Bitter Creek Newcomb—by themselves—seemed oddly out of character.

"That's a new one," Tilghman said absently. "They just turned up unannounced—without Doolin?"

"Never done it before," Dunn said in a raspy voice. "Bee thinks Doolin don't know nothin' about it. He's worried sick."

"Why would they come there alone?"

"Told us that was the last place you'd look. Figure you're still off chasin' around the Nations."

Tilghman watched him. "Bee could've brought word himself. Why'd he send you?"

"Lots safer," Dunn said earnestly. "Them boys never pay me no mind. They won't miss me."

"Where's Bee now?"

"Took 'em into Ingalls to get some poon-tang. Woman just outside town runs her own little cathouse. Just her and her daughter."

"Will they spend the night?" Thomas broke in. "Or will they come back to your place?"

"They'll come back," Dunn said. "Bee just went along to introduce 'em. This woman don't generally take in strangers. Too dangerous."

"How long you reckon they'll be there?"

"Till their peckers go limp," Dunn said with a quirky smile. "Them boys was on the rut somethin' fierce."

"So they'll be back tonight?" Tilghman asked, staring at him. "You're sure about that?"

"Don't see no reason why not. They said they was gonna stick around a couple of days, maybe more."

"And they'll sleep in the dugout?"

"Have to," Dunn said. "No place for 'em in the house."

"Here's what you do," Tilghman said in a reassuring tone. "Tell Bee we'll hit the dugout at sunrise. Take 'em by surprise."

"One last thing," Dunn said. "Bee don't want our names brought into it. You gotta make 'em think it was one of your regular raids. Just outhouse luck."

"You and Bee have held up your end of the deal. We'll keep you out of it."

Tilghman showed him to the door. Framed in the glow of lamplight, he stood there until Dunn rode out of the yard. Then he turned back into the parlor.

"Sounds all wrong," Thomas said as he closed the door. "Why would Pierce and Newcomb double back and hide out there? They'd already lost us in the Nations."

"Monkey see, monkey do," Tilghman pointed out. "Doolin's pulled the same trick before, and it worked. So they figure it'll work for them."

"Then they damn sure take the prize for dumb."

"Heck, nobody ever accused them of being bright. Doolin's the brains of that outfit."

Thomas was skeptical. "Still stinks to high heaven. I don't like it."

"Why?" Tilghman pressed him. "You think it's a trap of some sort?"

"Anything's possible with that bunch. They're all snakes, the Dunns included."

"In that case, George Dunn's a smooth liar. I got the feeling he was telling the truth."

"What if he wasn't?" Thomas persisted. "We're liable to have a reception committee when we walk in there."

"Only if we get there at sunrise."

"That's what you told him, wasn't it?"

"I was lying," Tilghman said with a wintry smile.

"We're leaving right now, on fresh horses. That'll put us there not long after midnight."

"I'll be a sonovabitch!" Thomas marveled. "That's why you asked him how long they'd be at the cathouse. You aim to lay a trap of our own."

"Good night for it, too. We'll have a full moon."

"Like I've said before, you've got a devious mind. I'm glad we're on the same side."

Outside they met Brown walking toward the porch. He waved back at the corral. "Got your horses unsaddled and grained."

"Give us a hand," Tilghman said, moving past him. "We need a couple of fast horses out of the work stock."

"Where the hell you headed now? You just got here."

"No rest for the weary, Neal. We're off again."

"Just knew it!" Brown trotted along beside them. "That jasper without a name brought you some hot news. What is it, another holdup?"

"Not exactly," Thomas said with a faint smile. "More like a surprise party."

"Party?" Brown sounded bewildered. "For who?"

"A couple of gents without invitations."

"That don't make no sense."

Thomas laughed. "They're liable to think so, too."

Brown watched them ride out a few minutes later. He turned from the corral, walking back toward the house, still at a loss. He told himself all over again that lawmen were a strange breed.

And pure hell on horses!

The moon heeled over to the west. A glow like spun silver sparkled off the waters of Council Creek. The house was dark and the horses in the corral stood immobile, statues bronzed in sleep. Somewhere in the distance an owl hooted a mournful cry.

Tilghman checked the angle of the moon. He calculated the time at somewhere around three o'clock. His position was north of the trail that led into town. Across from him, Thomas was hidden in the trees closer to the creek. They had been waiting since shortly after midnight.

Their horses were tied deep in the woods. They had approached on foot, and taken their time inspecting the compound. There was no way to tell if Charley Pierce and Bitter Creek Newcomb were already asleep in the dugout. But based on what George Dunn had told them, that was doubtful. The outlaws apparently intended a long night of celebration.

The plan, like most good plans, was flexible. Tilghman and Thomas had agreed to wait in the woods, operating on the premise that the outlaws would make a late night of it. Barring that, they could only assume that the wanted men were already in the dugout. In that event, they would await sunrise and keep on waiting. The outlaws would have to emerge from the dugout at some point, however long it took. Either way, the trail or the dugout, the result would be the same.

"Whooeee!" a voice crowed from farther down the trail. "Flushed the birds outta that little 'uns nest!"

"Charley, I still say the mama was a better lay. A broke horse is always the best ride."

"Hell, you must be gettin' old. That young 'un was just too much for you."

"That'll be the day! How come she squealed when I forked her? You tell me that."

Pierce and Newcomb rode around the bend in the creek. Still some thirty yards away, they were visible in the shaft of moonlight that lit the trail. By the tone of their voices, they had consumed copious amounts of whiskey while frolicking at the local cathouse. Their horses came on at a slow walk.

Tilghman waited until the distance had closed to ten yards. The Winchester at his shoulder, he laid the sights on Newcomb, who rode on the north side of the trail.

Across the way, he caught movement as Thomas edged from behind a tree and sighted on Pierce. His shouted command split the night.

"Federal marshals! Raise your hands!"

The outlaws reined up sharply. Pierce went for his gun while trying to wheel his horse around in the trail. Thomas fired, working the lever on his carbine, and touched off another shot. The slugs caught Pierce in the throat and the head, blowing out the back of his skull. He pitched sideways onto the trail.

The fiery muzzle blasts spooked Newcomb's horse. Instead of turning away, the crazed animal bolted straight up the trail toward Tilghman. Newcomb managed to get off one shot, which buzzed harmlessly through the woods. Tilghman fired as the range closed to five yards, and drilled the outlaw through the chest. The impact drove Newcomb backwards out of the saddle and dropped him on the ground. His horse pounded past on a beeline for the corral.

The reverberations of the gunshots slowly faded along the creek. Tilghman and Thomas moved from the trees, their carbines still cocked, and walked forward on the trail. In the moonlight, the bodies of Pierce and Newcomb lay twisted in death. Thomas grunted sharply under his breath.

"Good riddance," he said. "Gone to hell just in time for breakfast."

Tilghman nodded. "Homer Godfrey ought to rest a little easier now."

"His wife won't be happy till Red Buck Waightman's dead and buried."

"None of us will, Heck. We'd all like the honors on him."

They turned and walked toward the compound. A match flared and the glow of a lamp lighted the house. As they moved through the yard, Bee Dunn opened the front door. He stood framed against a spill of light from inside.

"I heard shots," he called out. "Did you get 'em?"

"The party's over," Thomas said with cold irony. "Your visitors got their candles snuffed."

"You just remember, I kept my part of the bargain."

"We'll remember," Tilghman said, halting outside the door. "We need to borrow a wagon and team."

"What for?"

"What d'you think?" Thomas growled. "We're gonna cart 'em back to Guthrie."

Dunn looked puzzled. "Why would you do that?"

"Our orders were to bring 'em in dead. We aim to please."

Tilghman restrained a laugh. Under normal circumstances, he wasn't much for gallows humor. But he thought it fitting in this instance.

Evett Nix was about to see his first dead outlaw.

CHAPTER 27

The crowds began gathering along Division Street. Thomas drove the wagon bearing the dead men, with his horse hitched to the rear. Tilghman rode alongside the wagon, somewhat amazed as more and more people flocked around them. By the time they reached the center of town, young boys were running ahead to spread the word.

Outside the Herriott Building, Thomas brought the wagon to a halt. Stores emptied along the street and the crush of people grew steadily larger. Tilghman dismounted, leaving Thomas with their grisly cargo, and entered the building. Upstairs, he moved along the hallway to the marshal's office. He found Nix seated behind his desk.

"Afternoon," he said. "We've got a present for you downstairs."

"A present?" Nix said, staring at him. "What are you talking about?"

"Charley Pierce and Bitter Creek Newcomb. We caught up with them early this morning."

"Are they alive?"

"Nope," Tilghman said simply. "Dead as doornails."

Nix was stunned. "You brought them here?"

"Got them outside in a wagon. Left Heck to guard the remains."

"Are they . . . presentable?"

Tilghman smiled. "The townfolks seem to think so. Quite a crowd out there."

"I—" Nix hesitated, clearly taken aback. "I got a telegram from Madsen just a few minutes ago. He told me about Jack Blake."

"And the two outside make three. You want to have a look?"

Nix seemed to shrink back in his chair. Then, as though struck by a sudden inspiration, he sat upright. "You know," he said, nodding rapidly to himself. "We might get some newspaper coverage out of this."

Tilghman feigned a concerned look. "I'd say the reporters better hurry. What with the warm weather, our boys are startin' to get a little ripe."

"Ripe?"

"Not all that good on a sensitive nose. They'd bear looking after by an undertaker."

Nix blanched. "Perhaps you should take them on to the funeral parlor."

"What about the reporters?" Tilghman fought back a smile. "Thought you were interested in the newspapers."

"Yes, of course, you're right. We need to issue a statement."

Tilghman led the way. When they emerged from the building, a mob of some five hundred people jammed the street. The press, drawn by the excitement of the crowd, was already hard at work. A camera platform, jerry-rigged with boxes from nearby stores, had been positioned at the rear of the wagon. The outlaws, arms neatly folded across their chests, were being photographed for posterity.

Nix seemed momentarily nonplussed by the enormity of the event. For his part, Tilghman was reminded that

people had a ghoulish, altogether morbid fascination
with the spectacle of death. He'd witnessed a similar
reaction at public hangings, when mobs ganged around
to watch a man step off into eternity. There was often a
festive air to such occasions.

Tilghman shouldered a path through the crowd. Nix
had no choice but to follow along and mount the wagon
seat with an assist from Thomas. His Adam's apple
bobbed when he stared down at the dead men and got a
whiff of the rank odor. For a moment, his features
colored and the taste of bile gagged his throat. But then,
ever the politician, he collected himself and looked
straight into the camera. The flash pan exploded, capturing his pose as a brave defender of the law.

Hastily avoiding another look onto the wagon bed,
Nix climbed down to the street. He was followed by
Thomas, who cast a sly wink at Tilghman. A reporter
from the Guthrie *Statesman* appeared from the throng
of people massed about the wagon. His eyes were wild
with fervor and he held a pencil poised over a notepad.
He nodded to Nix.

"A great day for the law, Mr. Nix. Would you care to
comment?"

"Indeed I would," Nix said staunchly. "In the past
four days, three of the Wild Bunch have been killed.
You may quote me as saying that we now have this murderous gang on the run."

"Three?" the reporter queried. "I only see two in the
wagon."

"Tulsa Jack Blake was slain in a vicious gun battle
four days ago. I might add, that was only one day after
the train robbery outside Dover."

"Who was responsible for tracking down these desperadoes?"

"Who else but the Three Guardsmen? Heck Thomas,
Chris Madsen, and Bill Tilghman. The people of Oklahoma Territory owe them a large debt of gratitude."

"Marshal Thomas. Marshal Tilghman," the reporter said, pointing at the wagon. "Exactly where were these men killed?"

"Outside the town of Ingalls," Thomas replied. "We surprised them after a night of revelry at a house of ill repute."

"That's really something! A house of ill repute. How did you know they were there?"

Tilghman jumped in to cover the Dunn brothers. "We tracked them there," he improvised quickly. "Tried to give us the slip in the Nations, but we stuck to their trail. Led straight to the bordello."

"First rate!" The reporter jotted it all down. "Did they resist arrest?"

"Fired on us," Thomas said. "After we ordered their surrender. So we cut loose."

"Cut loose and cut them down. That's great, just great! Now, what about Bill Doolin? Anything new on him?"

Nix reclaimed the interview. "You may quote me directly," he said. "Doolin and his Wild Bunch are not long for this world. They will be brought to justice in the most forceful manner."

Later, after delivering the bodies to the undertaker, Tilghman and Thomas paused outside the funeral parlor. The crowds had drifted away, quickly losing interest after the spate of excitement downtown. Tilghman rubbed his whiskery jaw, silent a moment. Then he chuckled softly.

"Guess the tables were turned on us. Nix got himself plastered all over the newspapers."

"Who cares?" Thomas said with a broad grin. "Did you see his face when he got a gander at them dead boys? Tell you, Bill, it was worth haulin' them in here."

"I suppose so," Tilghman said agreeably. "Likely as not, he'll skip supper tonight."

"Hell, he might not eat for a week!"

"We ought to be ashamed of ourselves, Heck."

"I'd be lyin' if I said I was. How about you?"

"Well, for me personally—" Tilghman broke out laughing. "I wouldn't have missed it for all the tea in China."

"Goddamn!" Thomas crowed. "Better'n a circus, wasn't it?"

"Yeah, it was. Even without the elephants."

On Saturday, Tilghman took Zoe into Chandler. The town square was crowded with farmers and their families, and cowhands from ranches throughout the county. Saturday was the one day of the week that everyone came to town.

Apart from laying in supplies, the attraction centered on various forms of entertainment. Every Saturday afternoon horse races were held on a flat stretch of prairie outside the town limits. During warm weather months, following the races, a dance was held that evening on the town square. Local merchants, eager for business, supplied the orchestra.

Tribesmen from the various reservations always comprised a good part of the crowd. Like the white men, they brought their wives and children early every Saturday morning. The weekly trek to town was to them a peculiarly white ritual, but one they enjoyed. Their trade was welcomed by merchants, though there was widespread prejudice toward any Indian. Still, the array of goods in the stores, and most especially the horse racing, made the white man's patronizing manner more bearable. Inveterate gamblers, the race drew them like steel to a magnet.

Moses Keokuk never missed the races. The Sac and Fox chief generally arrived with a string of fleet ponies, and a willingness to wager his last dollar. His horses were admirably suited to the racetrack, a mile-long graded oval bordered by rails. Speed, coupled with endurance, usually decided a race, and his prize stock was renowned for stamina. He invariably left the races a richer man than when he'd arrived.

The largest purse, and the wildest betting, was reserved for the last race of the afternoon. The favorites in today's final outing were a roan stallion owned by Keokuk and Steeldust, Tilghman's sorrel stud. Tilghman and Zoe, along with Keokuk, stood behind the railing at the finish line, waiting for the race to start. The friendship of a lawman and a tame Indian was still thought to be somewhat odd, and drew criticism from some quarters. Yet no one, drunk or sober, voiced their opinion within Tilghman's hearing.

The field of eight horses got off to a clean start. Steeldust jumped out to an early lead, while Keokuk's roan was mixed with the pack. The horses held their positions until the turn for home, when the roan stallion attempted to close ground by going to the rail. The stratagem failed, for the roan was boxed in by Steeldust out front and another horse on the outside. The jockey, a young tribesman, then had no choice but to pull back and pass on the outside. In the homestretch, the roan swept past the other horse, gaining ground quickly if too late. Steeldust crossed the finish line a length ahead.

"Big fool!" Keokuk, thoroughly disgruntled, shook his fist at the young jockey. "Got me robbed by them . . . mules!"

Tilghman laughed, waving to Neal Brown who was up on Steeldust. Then, with Zoe hugging his arm, he turned to the chief. "You weren't robbed, Moses. The better horse won."

Keokuk rolled his eyes. "Your horse Sac and Fox horse. Never shoulda sold 'im to you!"

The chief stormed off in a huff. Zoe wagged her head at Tilghman. "Shame on you," she said, squeezing his arm with merriment. "You've spoiled his whole day."

"Fat chance," Tilghman said, grinning. "Moses probably covered himself with a bet on Steeldust. He's a cagey old fox."

"You mean he bet on his horse *and* yours?"

"Knowing Moses, I'd say he had himself covered six ways to Sunday."

The races over, they followed the crowd into town. There, in one of Chandler's better cafes, they had a leisurely supper. Shortly after dark, the Saturday evening dance began on the courthouse square. They joined throngs of people attracted by the fiddlers and the brass section of the orchestra. Farmers and cowhands, their women held closely, swept around the enclosure to a variety of rousing tunes. On the sidelines, fascinated by yet another of the white man's curious rituals, the Indians watched with vast amusement. Children, laughing and playing, darted through the crowds of onlookers.

Tilghman and Zoe left about ten o'clock. The drive to the Stratton ranch, and then back to his place, would put him home well after midnight. As the buckboard rolled out of town, she snuggled closer, gaily chattering on about their day together. But a mile or so farther on, when she began talking about wedding plans, Tilghman fell silent, listening but not responding. She slowly realized that she was talking to herself.

"Bill?" She searched his face intently. "What's wrong? You suddenly got very quiet."

Tilghman avoided her gaze. Smiling and cheerful until a moment ago, he now seemed wrapped in gloom. "Something's been bothering me," he said at length. "Started eating on me after we dropped those boys off at the funeral parlor in Guthrie. I don't rightly know how to tell you."

"Just tell me," she said promptly. "Whatever it is, you know I'll understand."

"Well—" Tilghman stared off into the distance, as though wrestling with some inner turmoil. Then, all in a rush, he let it out. "I got to thinking we ought to post-pone the wedding."

She sat back, startled. "Why on earth—" Her voice failed her and she fought for control. "Have you changed your mind, about marrying me?"

"Not for a minute," Tilghman said quickly. "I want to marry you worse than before. That's the God's honest truth."

"Then what's wrong?" she asked. "Something has to have changed."

Tilghman looked away. "Zoe, I've got myself involved in a war. The other night, when we shot it out with those boys, I saw it for what it was." He hesitated, reluctant to put it into words. "We'll have to kill every one of them. They're not about to surrender."

She tilted her head. "And you don't want to leave me a widow. Isn't that what you're thinking?"

"Yeah, in a way." Tilghman's tone softened. "I never believed any man could kill me. Hell, I still don't. But there's always . . ."

"Always a chance," she said, finishing the thought. "Isn't that what you were going to say?"

"I'm just sayin' we ought to wait till this Doolin thing's ended. For all I know, that could be tomorrow."

"But you believe it will be longer, much longer?"

"That's my hunch," Tilghman said in a thick voice. "They'll fight to the last man."

She was suddenly caught in a crosscurrent of emo-tion. If she insisted, she had no doubt he would go through with the wedding as planned. Still, he would be worried for her sake, and in the midst of a gunfight, that concern might rob him of the edge, cause him to make a mistake. His mind needed to be on the deadly business of survival, not on her.

For a moment, she toyed with the idea of an ultima-tum. She could demand that he choose between her or the law. But then, just as quickly, she set the thought aside. She had no right to make such demands, to force a decision that they both might regret. Instead, she must somehow lessen his concern for her. Her role was to give him strength rather than an added burden.

"You're silly to worry," she said brightly, "but I think I have a solution."

"I'm open to anything that makes you happy."

"Suppose we leave our plans just as they are. But if you haven't caught Doolin by December, then we'll postpone the wedding till it's ended. I think that makes perfect sense."

"You're sure?" Tilghman said. "That's what you want?"

"Yes, on one condition."

"What's that?"

"Shoot first," she said fiercely. "Don't be noble about it."

Tilghman laughed and she snuggled again against his arm. Neither of them said anything more, for the decision had been made. A wedding was a wedding, whenever it happened.

They drove on into the night.

CHAPTER 28

A week later there was still no word on the Wild Bunch. Doolin and his men were thought to be in the Nations, but little else was known. For all practical purposes, the manhunt was at an end.

Tilghman was hardly surprised. Newspapers across the territory had trumpeted the deaths of Blake, Pierce, and Newcomb. Three of the Wild Bunch hunted down and killed made for splashy headlines and a clearcut warning to the remainder of the gang. Their vaunted record of escaping without harm had been ended on a deadly note. Far from invincible, they were now at risk.

To Tilghman, the gang's reaction was almost predictable. Whatever else Doolin was, he was a man who coolly calculated the odds, and weighed the risks. With three men dead, he had wisely opted to lie low and let time work in his favor. In effect, he operated on the old military adage that it was sometimes better to give ground, and live to fight another day. There was every likelihood that the Wild Bunch would not strike again until they ran out of money.

On that assessment, Tilghman bided his time. He arrested a few backwoods whiskey smugglers, and late one night, he paid a secret visit to the Dunn brothers. But they, too, were in the dark, having seen nothing of

Doolin or his men. For the most part, Tilghman worked around the ranch and devoted his spare time to Zoe. Tomorrow, the last Saturday in July, they planned to attend the races in town and then the evening dance. Given an even break, Steeldust would bring home yet another purse.

But late that afternoon his plans abruptly took a wrong turn. He was seated on the porch thinking of tomorrow's race when Heck Thomas rode into the yard. His first thought was to get word to Zoe that their Saturday outing was now off. For even as Thomas stepped down from the saddle, he knew that the interlude had just ended. Their manhunt was about to resume.

"Helluva note," Thomas said, walking toward the porch. "I work my butt off and you've turned into a loafer. Don't hardly seem fair."

"Grab a chair." Tilghman motioned to a nearby rocker. "I take it you've come bearing glad tidings."

Thomas took a seat in the rocker. He removed his hat and wiped sweat from his forehead with a soiled kerchief. "Got a tip this morning," he said casually. "A headman of the Osage tribe had some government business in Guthrie. He brought word from Johnny Longbone."

"Who's Johnny Longbone?"

"One of my Osage friends. Off and on, he whispers things in my ear."

Tilghman nodded. "One of your informants."

"Johnny's more than that." Thomas set the rocker in motion. "Damn good scout when it strikes his fancy."

"So what did he whisper in your ear?"

"Bill Raidler."

Raidler was one of the five remaining gang members of the Wild Bunch. Tilghman shifted in his chair. "Let me guess," he said. "Raidler's somewhere in the Nations."

"Yep," Thomas affirmed. "A cabin on Five Mile

Creek, over in the Cherokee Nation. You familiar with that country?"

"I don't recollect having been there."

"Near as I recall, it's about a two-day ride northwest of here. We'll pick up Longbone and his cousin along the way. They've scouted for me before."

Tilghman looked at him. "The Osage know Cherokee country that well?"

"Like the back of their hand," Thomas said. "They've been dealin' with the Cherokee for fifty years. Longbone will get us there."

"What about Madsen?"

"Take too long to get him here from El Reno. Nix figured you and me could handle it."

Tilghman considered a moment. "There's no moon tonight. We'd best leave at daylight."

"Sounds reasonable," Thomas said, rocking back and forth. "What's for supper?"

Tilghman arranged for one of his workhands to carry word to Zoe. After supper, with Thomas and Neal Brown seated around the table, he started collecting his gear. They were still sipping coffee when he brought oily rags and a ramrod to the kitchen.

He began cleaning his Winchester.

Three days later they forded the Caney River shortly after sunrise. They were in the heart of the Cherokee Nation, a remote stretch of wilderness as yet unsettled. On the opposite shore Five Mile Creek emptied into the river.

Their scouts led the way. According to Johnny Longbone, the creek ended five miles farther on, at a backcountry crossroads called Talala. Somewhere ahead, perhaps two or three miles, a deserted cabin was situated along the creek. There they would find Bill Raidler.

Tilghman was impressed by their Osage scouts.

Johnny Longbone and his cousin, Tom Dog Eater, were
taller than most Indians he'd met. Their features were
angular and dusky red in color, with high cheekbones
and deep-set eyes. Though they spoke passable English,
they clearly descended from a long line of warriors.
They read the sign of wild things, and men, as if it were
written in a book.

On the trail, Thomas had explained that the Osage
were one of the fiercest tribes on the Southern Plains.
Long ago, they had roamed over what was now Kansas
and Missouri, until finally being resettled in Indian Territory. At one point, they had warred constantly on the
Cherokee, who were seen as intruders on Osage land.
The two tribes had been at peace for many years, but
not without lingering hostility. The Osage still looked
upon the Cherokee as unwelcome foreigners.

In years past, operating as a marshal out of Fort
Smith, Thomas had exploited this ancient rivalry. He'd
gone out of his way to befriend the Osage, though many
of them still had no use for federal lawmen. His most
stalwart converts were Longbone and Dog Eater, who
had assisted him on several manhunts into the Nations.
Their contempt for the Cherokee was aggravated by the
fact that tribes in the Nations were quick to grant refuge
to white outlaws. The hunt for Bill Raidler was a case in
point.

For all their ancient rivalry, a certain amount of trade
went on between the Osage and the Cherokee. Johnny
Longbone, who kept his ear to the backwoods grapevine, had picked up a rumor. A white man had bought
supplies at the trading post in Talala, and word was out
that he'd taken over an old cabin on Five Mile Creek.
Further inquiry, discreetly conducted by Osage traders
with business in Talala, had identified the man as Bill
Raidler. Longbone had then arranged for the message
delivered to Thomas.

A short distance ahead, Longbone now held up his

hand. He signaled for quiet, then motioned upstream, apparently alerted to a sound not heard by the marshals. The terrain was heavily wooded, and nothing was visible to their direct front. After a moment, Longbone and Dog Eater slid off their ponies, armed with worn Winchester repeaters. Tilghman and Thomas dismounted, pulling carbines from their saddle scabbards. Longbone stood listening to a distant sound, then waved them onto a line. They advanced through the trees.

Some fifty yards ahead the woods opened onto a small clearing beside the creek. A log cabin, with one side of the roof caved in, was centered in the clearing. As they emerged from the treeline, a man on horseback, until then hidden from view, appeared on the far side of the cabin. Unaware of their presence, he reined his horse toward a narrow trail that led upstream. Tilghman and Thomas moved out front of the Osage scouts, shouldering their rifles. Thomas bellowed a command.

"Federal marshals! Halt right there!"

The man glanced over his shoulder, and they saw the face of Bill Raidler. He hunched low in the saddle, raking his horse savagely with his spurs, and took off at a lope up the trail. The lawmen fired in unison, their shots clipping bark off trees on either side of Raidler. They worked the levers on their carbines, but by then Raidler had disappeared into the woods bordering the creek. The thud of hoofbeats faded rapidly in the distance.

"Goddamn the luck!" Thomas thundered. "Sonovabitch didn't even know we were here!"

"Never had a clue," Tilghman agreed. "Looked like he was headed for the trading post. I saw a gunnysack tied to his saddlehorn."

"Well, he's not all that far ahead. Let's get after him."

A few minutes later they rode upstream. But Raidler, schooled in the tactics of the Wild Bunch, proved to be elusive. A mile or so upstream, he crossed the creek, then swung wide through the woods and doubled back to the Caney River. There he turned north along the rocky stream.

The Osage scouts clung to his trail. By early evening, as dusk fell, they were some twenty miles upriver. On a rocky stretch of shoreline, where a small creek fed into the Caney, the tracks abruptly vanished. Longbone and Dog Eater, after studying the terrain, were of the same opinion. Raidler had quit the ground and taken to the water.

One way led upriver. The other led west along the creek. Tilghman agreed with the scouts that either direction was a tossup. There was no alternative but to separate and search in both directions. With dark approaching they camped on the river bank and settled it with the toss of a coin. Thomas and Longbone would continue north, along the Caney. Tilghman and Dog Eater would take the creek.

The next morning they parted as dark turned to dawn.

Tom Dog Eater taught Tilghman a new trick. Instead of separating, and riding both banks, they stuck to the center of the creek. That way, wherever their man left the water, they would not overrun the tracks. In single file, their eyes sweeping north and south, they rode west.

Four miles upstream Dog Eater motioned a halt. Along the south bank, he spotted scuff marks on an outcropping at the water's edge. On ground beyond the outcropping, he found horse tracks and the bootprints of a man. There, as he pointed out to Tilghman, their man had made a cold camp and watched his backtrail. Anyone who had followed last night would now be dead.

The trail led southwest toward Osage country. Tom Dog Eater was no less surprised than Tilghman. As the day progressed, their surprise turned to thoughtful deliberation. The tracks were on a line straight as a string, never deviating, always headed southwest. Raidler was moving at a slow trot, with no idea that he'd been followed. He clearly had a destination in mind.

Tilghman and Dog Eater camped that night on the open prairie. The chase resumed at dawn and by noonday they were some forty miles from where they'd parted with Thomas. Toward midafternoon they topped a low rise and before them lay a great northward bend in the Arkansas River. A stand of woods wound a mile or so to the west along the shoreline, and to the east was a field of corn. Between the field and the trees, smoke spiraled from the chimney of a log farmhouse.

"I know this place," Dog Eater said in a guttural voice. "Man's name is Sam Moore."

"A white man?" Tilghman asked.

"Umm," Dog Eater grunted. "Married to Osage woman."

"Let's have a look."

The tracks led straight to the yard of the farmhouse. As they approached, Tilghman saw a stock pen beside the barn, but no sign of a saddlehorse. A man in rough work clothing moved from the barn into bright sunlight and stood waiting. They reined to a halt.

"Mr. Moore," Tilghman said bluntly, "I'm a U.S. deputy marshal."

Moore blinked, his features suddenly waxen. The reaction was all the tip-off Tilghman needed. "A man rode in here yesterday," he went on. "His name is Bill Raidler and he's wanted for murder. Hiding him makes you an accomplice to murder. You're under arrest."

Tilghman was bluffing. But the effect on Moore was immediate, and devastating. To avoid arrest, he agreed to cooperate, and began talking. He was providing Raidler with food and a place to sleep, and a stall for his horse, in exchange for payment. Yet Raidler was a wary man, and he stayed hidden deep in the woods during the day. He came to the house only at sundown, where he took his evening meal and spent the night. By sunrise, he was back in the woods.

Satisfied with the story, Tilghman ordered Moore to the house and told him to bolt the door. Then he and Dog Eater took their horses into the barn, treating them to grain and water. For the rest of the afternoon, hidden in the barn, they took turns peering through a crack in the logs on the west wall. Time weighed heavily, but the sun finally tilted over and began dropping westward. Toward sundown, Tilghman relieved Dog Eater and took his place at the spyhole.

Raidler came out of the woods shortly after dusk. He paused a moment, guardedly inspecting the layout, then headed for the house. From the barn, Tilghman watched until Raidler was closer to the house than to the woods. He wanted his man out in the open, with no place to take cover if a shootout developed. As Raidler neared the house, Tilghman cocked his Winchester, motioning Dog Eater to take a position off to one side. He stepped through the barn door.

"Raidler!" he commanded. "Get your hands up!"

In midstride, Raidler took off running for the house. He jerked his pistol, firing as he sprinted across the yard, and winged a shot toward the barn. Lamplight from the windows silhouetted him against the house, and Tilghman fired. The slug struck Raidler in the side, jarring him to a halt, and he swung around. He raised his pistol.

Tilghman shot him twice in the chest. Raidler collapsed at the knees, dropping his pistol, and pitched to the ground. He groaned, both hands clamped to his chest as Tilghman and Dog Eater hurried across the yard. His breathing was shallow, a trickle of blood leaking out of his mouth.

"Bastard," he mumbled, staring at Tilghman through a haze. "I think you've killt me."

Tilghman knelt beside him. "Get right with God, Raidler. Go out with a clean slate. Where's Doolin?"

"Stuff it up . . ."

His voice trailed off and his body went slack. Tilghman climbed to his feet, lowering the hammer on his carbine. He glanced around at Tom Dog Eater.

"Damn fool had to do it the hard way."

Dog Eater shrugged. "Only way some men know."

"Sure as hell seems like it."

Tilghman walked toward the house.

CHAPTER 29

The last week in August was sultry and humid. Late every afternoon thunderclouds rolled in from the west, threatening rain. But the hot weather held, with no rainfall for the month, and the plains slowly parched under the heat. People watched the thunderheads, fearful of the darkened skies, waiting for a tornado.

The air was stifling in Evett Nix's office. The windows were open but there was no hint of a breeze. For once, sacrificing dignity to comfort, Nix had discarded his suit jacket. He was in shirtsleeves, seated behind his desk, trying to cool himself with an oval-shaped hand fan. Before him, sweltering in the heat, were Tilghman, Thomas, and Madsen.

The marshals had been summoned to Guthrie only that day. They sat now, watching Nix fan himself, awaiting a tirade. In the month since Bill Raidler's death, there had been no word of Doolin or the Wild Bunch. Inquiries and investigation had led nowhere, and informants, as though struck dumb, had nothing to report. The lawmen fully expected to be dressed down in scathing terms.

Nix paused with the fan. He wiped a rivulet of sweat off his forehead and again set the fan in motion. Then, to their amazement, he smiled. "Wonders never cease," he said with curious good humor. "You'll be interested to know that I have been contacted by the distinguished attorney-at-law, Simon Warner. He's due here any moment."

The lawmen exchanged puzzled glances. "Don't get it," Thomas finally said. "What's this got to do with us?"

"Everything," Nix replied, enjoying himself. "Mr. Warner has formally advised me that he represents Bill Doolin."

There was a moment of stunned silence. The marshals stared at him like three owls suddenly blinded by a flare of light. Tilghman was the first to recover.

"Doolin's got a lawyer?" he said, as though the notion defied belief. "What's his game?"

"I just imagine Mr. Warner has all the particulars. We'll find out shortly."

"A deal," Madsen said in a tone of sudden discovery. "Doolin wants to make a deal of some sort."

"I suspect you're right," Nix acknowledged. "Which is precisely why I asked you gentlemen here today. You have spent how long chasing Doolin?"

"A year next month," Thomas said. "Seems like a helluva lot longer."

"No doubt," Nix agreed. "For that very reason, I felt you gentlemen should hear what Warner has to say for yourselves. I want your counsel before framing a response to whatever Doolin has in mind."

The lawmen were less surprised than skeptical. Nix was prone to issuing edicts rather than seeking advice. By now, they had him pegged as something of a gloryhound, perhaps more interested in political fortunes than in seeing justice done. A deal with Doolin might easily be his springboard to future public office. They were leery of being drawn into what smacked of personal intrigue.

Before anyone could reply, a knock sounded at the door. The man who entered was tall and beefy, with

sharp eyes and a commanding bearing. He was attired
in a well-tailored suit and a fashionable hat, and there
was not a drop of perspiration on him. Nix performed
the introductions and got him seated in a chair angled
to face the three marshals. Their immediate impression,
though unspoken, was uniformly shared. None of them
trusted a man who didn't sweat.

"Well, now," Nix said, spreading his hands. "You certainly have our interest whetted, Mr. Warner. How did
you come to represent such an infamous client?"

"Every man," Warner said in an imposing voice, "has
the right of legal counsel. I was retained to act in that
capacity on behalf of Mr. Doolin."

"So Doolin contacted you directly?"

"I believe that falls under the category of privileged
information."

Nix studied him. "Are you also privileged as to the
matter of Doolin's whereabouts?"

"Come now," Warner admonished him. "You know
I'm not about to discuss such matters."

"Then let's move right along. Why are you here, Mr.
Warner?"

"To bring an end to the bloodshed and violence. Bill
Doolin wants to surrender."

"Does he?" Nix said blandly. "To be perfectly frank,
I'm not surprised. After all, our marshals have dispatched four of his men in the last six weeks. Your client
would be wise not to risk a similar fate."

"I agree," Warner remarked. "In fact, I've advised
him to surrender at the earliest opportunity. Naturally,
that would be contingent on certain conditions."

"Such as?"

"All murder charges waived—"

Warner paused for a reaction, and Nix said, "Go on."

"All robbery charges waived, except for one of your
choice. Of course, my client would plead guilty to the
one charge. For that, he would receive a maximum sen-

tence of ten years. With assurance of early parole for good behavior."

"Anything else?"

"No, I believe not," Warner observed. "Except to say the offer merits your serious consideration. God knows the public would applaud an end to this matter."

Nix steepled his fingers. "What about the other members of the Wild Bunch?"

"I speak only for Mr. Doolin. However, with his surrender, I suspect the others would listen to reason."

"Would you excuse us?" Nix rose from his chair. "I would like to discuss your offer with my marshals. Perhaps you could wait in the hall."

Warner appeared momentarily flustered. Then, with a polite nod, he stood and crossed the room. Nix waited until the door closed.

"Your opinion, gentlemen?" he said, nodding to the three marshals. "Let's take it one at a time. Heck?"

"Horseshit," Thomas said sullenly. "I didn't work my ass off just to see Doolin get a slap on the wrist."

"Chris?"

Madsen's face hardened. "The man's a cold-blooded murderer. I say we kill him, or bring him in and hang him. Anything less would be like selling our souls."

"Bill?"

"Seems pretty cut and dried," Tilghman told him. "We're close, probably closer than we know. Otherwise Doolin wouldn't be so hot to cut a deal. I vote with Chris and Heck."

"Excellent!" Nix looked positively chipper. "Anticipating an offer of some nature, I took the liberty of telegraphing the attorney general. In so many words, I suggested that it would be a travesty of justice to dismiss even a single charge. I'm delighted to report that he concurred in full."

The lawmen stared at him with blank astonishment. For all his grandstanding, they realized that they had misjudged Evett Nix. Whatever his political maneuverings, he was, in the end, a man of some integrity. He would not barter honor.

Warner was brought back into the room. Nix made a point of not offering him a chair. "No deals," Nix said curtly. "Not now, not ever. Tell Doolin he has twenty-four hours to surrender. Barring that, we will hunt him down and kill him. Have I made myself clear?"

"Abundantly," Warner said. "You leave me no choice but to take this matter before the governor."

"Take it wherever you please and be damned! Good day, Mr. Warner."

When they were alone, Nix briskly rubbed his hands together. He looked invigorated, his eyes bright with newfound resolve. His face creased in a wide grin.

"Gentlemen, in the truest Biblical sense, I demand an eye for an eye. Go forth and do your duty."

The next evening Tilghman and Zoe came outside after supper. He was stuffed on pot roast and fresh garden vegetables and a huge chunk of chocolate cake. His belt felt one notch too tight as they seated themselves on the porch swing. He wondered if fat men were as jolly as they pretended.

Zoe saw through him like a gypsy fortune teller. Whenever he came for supper, he was normally talkative, and often related amusing anecdotes. But tonight, at the dinner table, he had been unusually quiet, as though mired in his own thoughts. She knew he was brooding on something, and that worried her. He was not the brooding sort.

After a few minutes of desultory conversation, she saw that his mind was still elsewhere. She decided on a direct approach. "Aren't you in a mood?" she said in a huffy voice. "I feel like you would rather be somewhere else."

"You know better than that," Tilghman said quietly. "Guess I'm just not good company tonight."

"Well, it's certainly not my cooking. You ate enough to founder a horse."

"Got a lot on my mind, that's all."

"Why not talk about it?" she insisted. "Keeping it bottled up inside doesn't solve anything. Unless it's a big dark secret, why not tell me?"

A jagged streak of lightning split the sky off to the west. Another bolt struck nearby and Tilghman was silent a moment, watching nature's fireworks. Then, halting at first, he told her about the meeting with Doolin's lawyer. He ended with Evett Nix's admonition to get the job done.

"I'm stumped," he said in a glum tone. "How can you get the job done when you've got no idea where to start? No leads, no rumors . . . nothing."

She sensed his bitter frustration. "What about Heck Thomas and Chris Madsen? Do they have any ideas?"

"We're all in the same fix. We've got to feeling like dunces. Doolin's fooled us at every turn."

"You shouldn't blame yourself. You've done everything humanly possible."

"Easy to say," Tilghman muttered. "Not so easy to admit you're downright baffled. It's like I hit a dead end."

"Look on the bright side," she said, catching his eye. "You've all but put the Wild Bunch out of business. Doesn't that count for something?"

"Doolin can always recruit more men. So long as he's on the loose, the Wild Bunch isn't finished."

"You've been a lawman for what, ten years? Have you ever failed to catch the man you were after?"

"Not until now."

"So there!" she said with a mischievous smile. "If you were betting on it, who would you bet on? Yourself or Doolin?"

Tilghman was forced to laugh. "Led me right into it, didn't you?"

"Let's just say my bet is on you."

A flash of lightning lit the distant sky. Tilghman put his arm around her and set the swing in motion. He told himself he was a lucky man.

She was so full of ginger it was catchy.

Late that night Tilghman rode into the ranch. A strange horse was hitched to the corral, and his every sense alerted. As he stepped out of the saddle, he saw the figure of a man on the porch. Bee Dunn moved into the yard.

"Howdy," he said, walking forward. "Wondered if you was ever comin' home."

"How long have you been here?"

"Couple of hours."

Tilghman nodded. "You met my partner, Neal Brown?"

"Crotchety, ain't he?" Dunn said. "Told me to park it on the porch and wait till you showed."

"Well, I'm here now. What's up?"

"Thought you oughta know," Dunn said stolidly. "You remember John Ellsworth? The father of Doolin's wife."

"I remember him."

"Ellsworth pulled out of town today. Way I hear it, he bought himself a new store over in Lawson. That's maybe fifteen miles northeast of Ingalls."

Tilghman sensed there was more. "And the girl?"

"Her and the baby went with him."

"She's already had the baby?"

"Just last week," Dunn said. "Doolin's got himself a boy."

Tilghman suddenly put it together. Doolin's offer to surrender was prompted by the birth of his child. A light prison sentence, rather than a hangman's rope, ultimately would have given him a normal family life. He wanted to live to see his son grow to manhood.

"Sort of sudden," Tilghman said now. "Ellsworth moving just after the baby was born."

"For a fact," Dunn affirmed. "Figured you'd wanna know right away."

"How'd you get wind of this?"

"Mary Pierce told my old woman in town today. She's the wife of Bob Pierce, runs the hotel. Come to think of it . . ."

Dunn hesitated, and Tilghman gave him a sharp look. "What is it?"

"Just occurred to me," Dunn said. "The Pierce woman and Edith Doolin got to be good friends. Lots of folks looked down on the girl for marryin' a wanted man. Mary Pierce sorta took her under wing."

"You think the Pierce woman ever met Doolin?"

"Hard to say." Dunn hawked up a wad of phlegm and spat it on the ground. "One thing's for sure, though."

"What's that?"

"Doolin won't be visitin' Ingalls any more. Not with his wife and kid over in Lawson."

Tilghman gave him a long level gaze. "Stranger things have happened, Bee. Doolin might figure your place is a safe hideout, now that his wife's moved on." He hesitated, stressing the point. "Leastways Doolin might figure the law figures that way."

Dunn grimaced. "So I'm not off the hook yet. That what your tellin' me?"

"You're off the hook when Doolin's caught. Or killed, whichever happens first."

"Like I told you one time, you must piss ice water."

"I appreciate you ridin' all this way, Bee. Keep up the good work."

"Do I have a choice?"

"Not one you'd like."

When Dunn rode out, Tilghman stood staring after

him for a moment. The information had improved his mood like a shot of elixir tonic. A new father, looking for a new lease on life, might yet make a mistake.

He thought he'd pay a quiet visit to Lawson.

CHAPTER 30

Tilghman rode into Lawson two days later. Located in Pawnee County, the town was situated some five miles south of the Arkansas River. The business district, which was fairly large, serviced the area's farmers. Shops and stores, as well as a bank and a newspaper, lined the main street.

Merchants were opening for business as Tilghman reined up before a cafe. He wore rough range clothes, and he was once again posing as Jack Curry, the horse trader. His principal concern was that he would be spotted by John Ellsworth, who knew him on sight. The storekeeper would almost certainly alert his daughter.

The cafe was all but empty. Like most small towns, people got an early start and were off to work before eight o'clock. Tilghman took a table by the window, where he had an unobstructed view of the street. A waitress, who greeted him pleasantly, bustled over with a coffeepot. He ordered a breakfast of ham and eggs.

Two nights before, following Dunn's visit, he had composed a letter to Evett Nix. He'd outlined that Doolin and the girl were now parents, and that the girl had accompanied her father to Lawson. His plan was to place the girl under surveillance, in the hope of uncovering a lead on Doolin's whereabouts. The next morning, before riding out, he had given the letter to Neal Brown. He instructed that the letter be placed in the express pouch on the noon stage.

The waitress returned with his breakfast. As Tilghman ate, he pondered the thing that concerned him most. He was convinced that Doolin's offer to surrender was directly tied to the recent birth of the baby. Yet there had been no robberies, no sign of the Wild Bunch, for six weeks. He considered the possibility that Doolin had disbanded the gang and quit Oklahoma Territory. That being the case, particularly after the offer to surrender had been rejected, Doolin might never return. Instead, in some clandestine fashion, he might try to secret his wife and child out of the territory. Which made the girl the last remaining lead to Doolin.

Still, given all that, it begged the question of why the girl had moved with her father to Lawson. If she was planning on fleeing, she could have just as easily done so from Ingalls. So maybe Doolin had some other scheme in mind. Or maybe he hadn't disbanded the Wild Bunch, after all. The possibilities were endless, and it made second-guessing Doolin an exercise in futility. The one certainty in the whole affair was the girl, and her baby, Doolin's son. She had to be located.

The waitress brought the check. Tilghman counted out money and gave her a generous tip. Local customers were usually far less generous, and by her smile, he saw that she was impressed. He thought she might be helpful.

"I'm just passing through," he said. "Where would a man mail a letter in Lawson?"

"Granby's—" She paused, correcting herself. "No, it's Ellsworth's store now. He just moved to town this week."

"Guess that makes him the new postmaster, too."

"Sure does," she said. "He even bought Ed Granby's house. Took over everything."

"Granby left town, did he?"

"Sold out lock, stock, and barrel. I heard he moved to Oklahoma City."

"That a fact?" Tilghman stood as though losing interest. "Well, I gotta be on my way. You serve a mighty fine breakfast."

"Come back and see us next time you're through."

"I'll do it."

Outside, Tilghman paused, inspecting the street. Half a block to the north, he saw a freshly painted sign over Ellsworth's store. He turned downstreet, entering a hardware store, and engaged the owner in conversation. By pretending he was passing through looking for Ed Granby, he got much the same story. But in the process, with a few offhand questions, he managed to learn the location of the Ellsworth house. He emerged from the store with a place to start.

The house was situated two streets to the west, on the south edge of town. Tilghman rode past, searching for a place where he could keep watch on the house and not be observed. He saw an older woman standing in the doorway holding a baby, as a girl in her early twenties walked to a wagon at the side of the house. Neither of them was looking his way, and he gigged his horse into a trot. Like John Ellsworth, they both knew him on sight.

The older woman was Ellsworth's wife. The girl, her daughter, was Edith Doolin. Last year, following the gun battle in Ingalls, Tilghman had met them both while questioning the family. He hadn't forgotten them, and given the circumstances, he doubted that they would have forgotten him. At the end of the block, he rounded the corner and slowed to a walk. Looking back, he saw the girl hike her skirts and climb into the wagon. She reined the horse into the street.

Tilghman watched as she turned in the opposite direction. After the older woman entered the house, he followed at a discreet distance. The girl drove to the business district, and he thought she was headed for her father's store. But she surprised him by turning right on Main Street, away from downtown. She drove south on the wagon road out of Lawson.

Tilghman trailed her by a half mile. Some distance south of town, he began to get a prickly sensation on the back of his neck. No more than a hunch, he nonetheless believed he knew her destination. He thought she was headed for Ingalls.

A noonday sun seared the land. Tilghman dismounted in the stand of woods north of town. A mile or so back, certain of her direction, he'd left the road and cut overland. He waited now for her to roll into Ingalls.

From his saddlebags, Tilghman pulled out a small telescope. He would have preferred to be closer, but his face was too well known by the townspeople. Whatever the purpose of her trip, he would have to watch from a safe distance. Any hint that she'd been followed would spoil the game.

Edith Doolin brought her wagon to a halt in front of the hotel. As she carefully stepped over the side, a woman hurried from the hotel and rushed across the boardwalk. She threw her arms around the girl, laughing with happiness, and hugged her tightly. Then, talking with great animation, they moved into the hotel entrance.

In the woods, the telescope extended, Tilghman watched them disappear through the door. There was no doubt in his mind that the woman was Mary Pierce, wife of the hotel owner. Why the girl had driven fifteen miles to see her, or to what purpose, was still a mystery. All the more so since the girl had moved from Ingalls to Lawson only three days ago. To return so soon had about it a sense of urgency. He settled down to wait.

Shortly after the noon hour a wagon rolled through town and stopped outside the store previously owned by

John Ellsworth. The driver hopped down, gathering the daily mail delivery of a postal bag and several packages, and entered the store. Within minutes, he returned to the wagon with the postal bag and a single package. As he drove out of town, Mary Pierce emerged from the hotel, waving to him as he went past. She hurried toward the store.

A few minutes later she stepped outside and rushed across the street. Through the telescope, Tilghman saw that she was holding a letter in her hand. He noted as well that her expression was curiously merry, and that the letter appeared to be unopened. She scurried along the boardwalk, skirts flying, and ran into the hotel. Somewhat puzzled, uncertain what it meant, Tilghman lowered the spyglass.

Not quite ten minutes later the Pierce woman and the girl came out of the hotel. Edith Doolin looked overcome with joy, somehow radiant. She was holding the letter clutched to her breast, laughing and talking as they stopped beside her wagon. Unexpectedly, she began crying, and pulled Mary Pierce into a fierce hug. When they separated, the Pierce woman was crying as well, and the scene had the look of two friends caught up in a moment of final parting. The girl quickly mounted the wagon and backed into the street. She drove off with a last wave.

Tilghman collapsed the telescope. He stood there a moment, all uncertainty now erased. Mary Pierce was acting as a go-between, passing letters back and forth between Doolin and his wife. The girl had clearly returned to Ingalls because a letter she'd been expecting hadn't arrived. Still more telling was her outpouring of elation at what she'd read in the letter. Added to that was her tearful farewell from the Pierce woman.

To Tilghman, the girl's obvious joy was the most telling factor. He thought she wouldn't be returning to Ingalls any time soon, if ever. But he wondered if she might be planning another trip, a longer trip. A reunion.

He followed her back to Lawson.

There was yet another tearful farewell the following morning. John Ellsworth and his wife stood waving goodbye as their daughter pulled away from the house. Beside her, in a wicker basket padded with blankets, was her baby. All her worldly possessions were loaded in the back of the wagon.

Tilghman trailed her out of town. He expected her to travel east, toward the Nations. But instead, she turned onto the farm road leading north out of Lawson. The Kansas border lay some fifty miles to the north, and in a practical sense, that seemed an even more logical destination. From there, she could catch a train to anywhere.

Toward midmorning Edith Doolin forded the Arkansas River. She continued north across the plains, pausing occasionally to tend to her baby. Tilghman followed a mile behind, using the telescope to keep her in sight. He was forced to admire her spirit, for the trail was rough and no place for a woman to be traveling alone. Her bond with her husband was clearly equal to any hardship.

By noontime she was deep in Osage country. From a knoll, Tilghman watched as she brought the wagon to a halt outside a farmer's log house. The farmer and his wife, who were both Osage, greeted her as though they were old friends. Thoroughly puzzled, Tilghman watched as they assisted her from the wagon and carried the baby inside. At first, he thought she'd stopped for the night, to rest for the journey ahead. But then, as time passed, he became aware that no one had unhitched her horse from the wagon. He took up a lookout on the knoll.

Hardly an hour later, Edith Doolin emerged from the house. Her bonnet shielded her from the harsh sun, and the Osage man walked beside her, carrying the wicker basket. She climbed into the wagon, taking the basket from the farmer, and gently positioned it beside her on the seat. When she drove out, the farmer stood watching as she forded a creek near the house. She once again set a course almost due north.

Later that afternoon the wagon rolled into Pawhuska. A trading center for Osage farmers, the small village was some twenty miles south of the Kansas border. When the girl halted outside a store, Tilghman felt certain she meant to locate a place to spend the night. After a hard day's travel, there was little doubt that she and the baby needed a good night's rest. But as she stepped down from the wagon, a vagrant breeze whipped the bonnet back over her head. Tilghman almost dropped the telescope.

The face in the lens was not Edith Doolin. Angered, cursing himself roundly, Tilghman saw instead the Osage woman, the farmer's wife. He suddenly realized that he'd been duped by a simple, yet devilishly clever, masquerade. The Osage woman had changed into Edith Doolin's gingham dress, with the sunbonnet to hide her face, and driven out of the farm. The clincher was the baby basket, which Tilghman knew beyond doubt had been empty at the farm, and was empty now. He'd been gulled into following the wrong woman.

Thinking back, Tilghman ruefully admitted that he had been outfoxed. Doolin had expected his wife to be followed, and he'd devised a plan to throw off pursuit. The only question was how much the Osage farmer and his wife had been paid to take part in the masquerade. Tilghman felt outraged that he'd taken the bait, swallowed it whole. One last look at the Osage woman as she entered the store brought the taste of bile to his throat. He swung into the saddle and rode south.

Shortly after midnight Tilghman burst through the door of the farm house. His pistol cocked, he routed the

Osage farmer out of bed and marched him into the main room. He ordered the man to light a lamp, then rammed the snout of the pistol into his belly. The Osage stared at him with a stoic expression.

"Let's have it," Tilghman said coldly. "Where's the Doolin woman?"

"You won't kill me, white man. Your law forbids it."

"Don't push your luck, mister. I want some answers."

"No," the Osage said stolidly. "Find your own answers."

"You sorry bastard," Tilghman said, his eyes glinting. "You're helping an outlaw escape."

The Osage smiled. "Why don't you arrest me?"

Tilghman knew he'd lost. He wouldn't kill the man, and he couldn't stoop to a physical beating in order to extract information. Nor was there anything to be gained in arresting the farmer. Since he was Osage, the courts were reluctant to enforce federal law. The charges would simply be dropped.

The farmer was still smiling when he walked out the door. Tilghman was angry and baffled, and infuriated that he'd been played for a fool. He mounted his horse, reining away from the farm, wondering on his next move. Then, though the admission came hard, he saw that there was little choice. The place to begin was where he'd started.

He rode toward Lawson.

CHAPTER 31

Doolin reined to a halt. He sat for a moment, studying the grove of trees ahead. A warm September sun beat down on the prairie, and birds flitted from limb to limb within the trees. He saw no other sign of activity.

The grove was located in southern Kansas. Less than a year ago, while planning a raid, Doolin had scouted it as an emergency hideout. A natural spring, deep within the trees, provided clear water for man or horse. The thick stand of timber provided cover.

Off to one side of the spring there was a lush patch of grass. Doolin dismounted, unsaddling his horse, and carried the saddle to the spring. After watering the horse, he attached hobbles to its forelegs and left it to graze. He opened his bedroll and took out a frayed shirt, a tattered pair of trousers, and a rumpled jacket. From his saddlebags, he collected a worn pair of ankle-high brogans and a battered slouch hat. He began undressing.

The idea was to convert himself into a tramp. He removed his range clothing and boots, wrapping everything into a bundle with his gunbelt. Then he donned the bedraggled outfit, and stuffed his pistol into his waistband, hidden by the threadbare jacket. When he finished, he looked like a shabby, disreputable bum who lived off of handouts. There was no need to dirty his face, or wallow about to give himself a foul body odor. He had just ridden almost seven hundred miles.

The disguise completed, Doolin surveyed his new campsite. The spring was an out of the way spot, and there was little likelihood that his horse or his gear would be discovered by anyone. He made his way through the woods and emerged from the treeline with the sun directly overhead. Some two miles to the east was a town he'd once scouted, among others in the area, as suitable for a bank holdup. But he'd never gotten around to it, and looking back, that seemed a rare stroke of luck. He walked off with a pronounced limp.

The limp was not part of his disguise. Doolin's foot had never healed properly after he'd been wounded in the running gun battle with a posse. Some eight months had passed, and in that time, the added complication of rheumatism had developed in his foot. He found it painful to walk, every step sending fiery streaks shooting from his foot to his lower leg. The worn brogans he wore today further complicated the problem, but he had no choice in the matter. A tramp could hardly ride into town on a fine-looking horse.

Far ahead, he made out the irregular shape of buildings against the skyline. A small farm town, Burden was located in the southeastern quadrant of Kansas. The state line was some twenty miles to the south, and directly across it, the land of the Osage. As he trudged along on his game foot, Doolin was reminded that the town's proximity to the border was only one of the reasons he'd chosen it. The larger reason had to do with the matter of transportation. Burden was serviced by the railroad.

Doolin's plan was at once simple and devious. In the letter to his wife, delivered through Mary Pierce, he had instructed her to meet him in Burden the week of September 4. To throw off pursuit, he had made arrangements through Dick West with the Osage farm couple outside Pawhuska. Once he and Edith were reunited, they would then take passage by train to California, and a new life. Yet, even with the elaborate planning, he had to assume a disguise and proceed with caution. His picture was still plastered on wanted dodgers throughout Oklahoma Territory and the border states.

The thought reminded him that all his grand schemes had gone to hell in a hurry. He marked the Dover train robbery as the turning point, where luck seemingly ran out for the Wild Bunch. Since then, in only two months, federal marshals had killed Jack Blake, Charley Pierce, John Newcomb, and Bill Raidler. With four men dead and the law on their heels, he'd had no choice but to disband the gang. From there it was every man for himself, and the wise ones had departed the territory. What none of them knew was that he had departed it for good. His days on the owlhoot were at an end.

In town, Doolin hobbled along the main street. His money belt, with over three thousand in cash, was cinched beneath his shirt. But he warned himself, as he entered a mercantile, that he had to play the part of a tramp. The storekeeper gave him a leery eye when he came through the door and moved to the aisle with women's goods. Finally, he found what he wanted, an inexpensive shawl. He walked back to the front counter.

"How much?" he asked.

"Two dollars," the storekeeper said. "Hard cash."

Doolin pulled a handful of coins from his pocket. He slowly counted out the correct amount, as though parting with his life's savings. The storekeeper scooped up the money, fixed him with a curious look.

"What d'you want with a ladies' shawl?"

"It's a present," Doolin said with a diffident smile. "For somebody that done me a favor."

The storekeeper sniffed. "You ought to spend it on some duds for yourself."

"Maybe next time. Could you wrap that for me?"

Outside, Doolin continued on his way uptown. A block before the main intersection, he crossed the street and entered the Royal Hotel. Though hardly royal, the place was clean and the rooms were modestly priced. As he approached the desk, the room clerk caught a whiff of his clothes. He nodded politely.

"You have a Mrs. Barry stayin' here?"

"Why?" the clerk countered, wrinkling his nose in distaste. "What business is it of yours?"

Doolin held up the parcel, wrapped in brown paper and tied with twine. "Got a package for her."

"Just leave it with me. I'll see that she gets it."

"Wish I could, but I can't. Feller that hired me, he said to give it to her personal."

The clerk considered a moment. Then, with a heavy sigh, he consulted the registration ledger. "Mrs. Will Barry," he said in an officious tone. "Room two-oh-one."

"Much obliged."

Doolin crossed the lobby. He took the stairs to the second floor, checking room numbers as he walked along the hall. He hadn't seen his wife since before the baby was born, and his pulse quickened as he stopped outside 201. He rapped softly on the door.

"Yes?"

"Package for Mrs. Barry."

Footsteps sounded on creaky floorboards. A moment later Edith Doolin opened the door. "Who—" she faltered, recognition flooding her features. "Omigod!"

Doolin shushed her with a finger to his lips. He stepped into the room, nudging the door shut with his foot, and took her in his arms. She went up on tiptoe, her arms around his neck, and gave him a long, lingering kiss. Finally, short of breath, she broke the embrace. Tears welled up in her eyes.

"Oh, Bill," she said joyously. "You're here. You're really here."

"With bells on," Doolin said, grinning. "When'd you get in?"

"Yesterday. Yesterday afternoon. I've been waiting and waiting for you to knock on that door."

"Well, I'm here now."

She suddenly became aware of his clothes. "Why are you dressed like that?"

"Just being careful," Doolin said. "Folks don't give a bum a second glance. Here, I brought you something."

"For me!"

She took the package and swiftly unwrapped it. The shawl was clearly inexpensive, but she hugged it to her breast, kissing him again. "You always were a sweet man."

"Forget me," Doolin said. "I hear I've got a son. Let me see him."

"How on earth did you hear that?"

"Honey, there's no secrets on the owlhoot grapevine. News gets around."

She led him across the room. The baby was asleep on the bed, tiny arms and legs stretched out in repose. Doolin stared down, stock-still with awe, his features oddly gentle. Several moments passed in silence, and then he let out a slow breath. His mouth creased in a wide smile.

"You've done us proud, Edie. He's a fine boy."

"Poor little thing," she said, her eyes on the baby. "The trip up here just wore him to a frazzle."

"Any trouble?" Doolin said. "Everything go like we planned?"

"I did just what you told me in your letter. Traded horses and wagons with that Osage man, and came on here. Nobody tried to follow me."

"Somebody did," Doolin said with a bitter smile. "You can bet the law's been keepin' an eye on you."

"After all this time?" She looked downcast. "Wouldn't they have given up by now?"

"Not on your tintype! Why do you think I laid low so long?"

Doolin had no doubt that his life was at risk. After the death of Jack Blake, he had decided to put distance between himself and Oklahoma Territory. Along with Dick West, he'd crossed the plains on horseback and drifted into New Mexico Territory. There, under the names of Bill Hawkins and Dick Porter, they had found work as cowhands. The rancher who had hired them, Eugene Rhodes, suspected they were operating under aliases. But men were asked few questions in that part of the country.

The ranch was located in Socorro County, deep in the San Andres Mountains. A short distance from the border of Old Mexico, the area was widely known as "Outlaws' Paradise." Wanted men from across the West came there to hide out until their trails cooled down. At times, half the cowhands in the county were thought to be on the run. But they generally behaved themselves, and the ranchers found them to be a strong deterrent against cattle rustlers. The law usually turned a blind eye, and on those occasions when men were sought, nothing came of it. They skipped across the border into Old Mexico.

The third week in August, after mailing the letter to Mary Pierce, Doolin had headed for Kansas. Dick West had tagged along, drawn by the notion that the gang would be reformed in the Nations. Doolin gave him no reason to believe otherwise, for he'd confided in no one about his plans for California. Instead, he had sent West on ahead to deal with the Osage couple, who had assisted the Wild Bunch in the past. All he'd told West was that he wanted his wife and child out of Oklahoma Territory, away from the law. Then, his destination still a secret, he had proceeded to the spring outside Burden.

"Hey, I forgot to ask," he said now. "What'd you name the boy?"

Edith smiled. "I waited till we could talk about it. But I sort of like Bill, Junior."

"I dunno," Doolin said haltingly. "We'll have to change our names in California. Let's think about it on the train."

"When were you planning on leaving?"

"Since you're here, we ought to leave tomorrow. No sense takin' chances."

"I can't," she said, not looking at him. "This morning I had to go see a doctor. I started spotting . . . bleeding."

"Bleeding?" Doolin appeared confused. "You mean from—" He hesitated, clearly embarrassed. "From having the baby?"

She nodded. "The trip in that wagon must have jarred something. The doctor said I needed bed rest." She paused, her head lowered. "Otherwise it could turn into something serious."

"How serious?"

"He wants to keep an eye on me for a few days. But if it gets any worse, he said he might have to operate."

"That settles it," Doolin said forcefully. "You're not movin' till the doc gives you the go-ahead."

Tears suddenly spilled down her cheeks. "Oh God, Bill, what about the law? I'd sooner die than have them catch you now."

"Forget the law," Doolin said with grim assurance. "I've stayed a jump ahead of them so far. We'll manage somehow."

"Will you stay here, with me?"

Doolin paced across the room, thinking. She saw his limp, the wince of pain when he put weight on his foot. He stopped at the window, staring down at the street a moment. Then he turned back to her.

"Wouldn't do for us to be seen together. This place got a back door?"

"Yes," she said. "On the alley."

"Good." Doolin moved across the room. "I'll sneak in here every night to see how you're doing. Meantime, I'll stay at a camp I've got outside town."

Her shoulders squared. "I promise you it won't be long. I just won't let anything stop us from going to California."

"You get well, that's the important thing. Don't worry about nothing else."

"What about yourself? Your foot's worse, isn't it?"

"Comes and goes," Doolin told her. "Got a touch of rheumatism just now."

"You should see the doctor," she said. "We have to stay here anyway, so why not? He might be able to help."

"Damn thing hurts something fierce. Maybe that's not a bad idea."

"I'll tell him I met a poor soul on the street with a lame foot. He'll probably treat you for free."

Doolin laughed. "He'd believe that story. I stink like a garbage wagon."

She touched his arm. "You smell sweet as candy to me. I've missed you so much."

"Been a long time." Doolin got a funny look in his eyes. "Guess you're not up to any monkey business, are you?"

"Heaven knows, I wish I was. I can't keep my hands off you."

"Tell that sawbones to get you well quick."

"I will," she promised. "Until then, we'll just suffer together."

Doolin enfolded her into his arms. His gaze went past her to the baby, and a strange look came across his face. The full impact of it hit him abruptly, that he had a son, even more reason to live. He hugged her tighter, swore an oath to himself.

Come hell or high water, they would make it to California.

CHAPTER 32

The ride to Lawson required two days. Along the way, Tilghman had considered and discarded any number of ideas. None of them were workable, and he'd finally decided that he had no option in the matter. Nor did he have anything to lose by coming out in the open. The direct approach was the only approach.

Tilghman sighted Lawson at dusk. Given the circumstances, he had no great confidence that John Ellsworth would divulge anything. The storekeeper was, after all, the father of Edith Doolin, and grandfather to her son. Yet he remembered the anonymous letter betraying Doolin's whereabouts to the U.S. marshal. That was many months ago, and the situation had now changed, but it was worth a try. He had nowhere else to turn.

Upon reflection, Tilghman decided to speak with the storekeeper in private. He thought Ellsworth would be even more reluctant to talk in front of his wife. Often as not, the women of a family were more protective than the men, and less fearful of the law. Not quite a week ago, when he'd first located the house, he had seen the Ellsworth woman holding her grandchild. Some instinct told him that she would be as hostile as a grizzly sow defending her young. He decided to stay away from the house.

The town's main street was closing for the night. Tilghman dismounted outside the store and left his horse at the hitch rack. He came through the door just as Ellsworth started to trim the wick of a lamp suspended over the front counter. The storekeeper turned, on the verge of telling a late customer that he was closed. Then, unable to hide the reaction, he recognized Tilghman. His eyes narrowed in a guarded look.

"Evening," Tilghman said, closing the door. "I'd like to talk with you."

Ellsworth's mouth set in a line. "What do you want?"

"I followed your daughter when she left here. Lost her outside of Pawhuska."

"Why would you follow Edith?"

"Don't play dumb," Tilghman said evenly. "By now, she's met up with Doolin. I figure they're somewhere in Kansas."

Ellsworth's face went ashen. "That's got nothing to do with me."

"You don't sleep good at night, do you?"

"What's that supposed to mean?"

"Well, your daughter's married to a wanted man. Your grandson's got a killer for a father. I'd say you're worried sick."

"You're wrong." Ellsworth averted his gaze. "Nothing I can do about it."

Tilghman gave him a piercing look. "You could tell me where they are. It's only a matter of time till Doolin gets himself killed." He paused, letting the storekeeper think about it. "You want your daughter there when the shooting starts?"

"I—" Ellsworth suddenly appeared stricken. "I wish to God she'd listened to reason. But she's headstrong, takes after her mother. I don't know where they are, and that's the truth."

There was a moment of silence. Tilghman examined him, slowly accepted that his words were genuine. "Too bad," he said at last. "Any idea where Doolin's headed?"

"Edith might have told her mother. But her or her mother don't tell me anything. They know I don't approve."

"Wherever they go, your daughter's bound to write home. When she does, will you let me know where they are?"

Ellsworth stared out the window into the deepening twilight. Finally, with a resigned expression, he nodded. "When she writes, I'll get word to you. She'll never have a decent life with Bill Doolin."

"No life at all," Tilghman assured him. "Doolin's living on borrowed time."

They shook hands on it. But as Tilghman walked from the store, he was struck by a wayward thought. One that had to do with an exchange of letters, and old friends. A particular friend came immediately to mind.

He decided to have a talk with another postmaster.

Early the next morning Tilghman rode into Ingalls. He reined to a halt outside the general store and dismounted. Whether or not he was seen was of no particular concern. His dealings there would be of a confidential nature.

The store had just opened for business. A heavyset man, bald with sagging jowls, stood behind the counter. There were as yet no customers, and he looked around with an alert eagerness as Tilghman came through the door. He smiled pleasantly.

"Good morning."

"Mornin'," Tilghman said. "You the new owner?"

"I am," he replied, staring at Tilghman's badge. "Joshua Burnham's the name. How can I help you?"

"I'm Bill Tilghman. Deputy U.S. marshal. I need your assistance."

"Always glad to oblige the law."

"A lady in town," Tilghman said easily. "Mary Pierce, down at the hotel. I'm interested in her mail."

Burnham looked startled. "Her mail?"

"In particular, the letters she receives. I want to know where they're from."

"I don't think I can do that. Bob and Mary Pierce are friends of mine."

"You'll do it." Tilghman's voice was cold and clear. "Otherwise I'll charge you with obstruction of justice. The Pierce woman is involved in aiding and abetting criminals."

"I don't believe you! Mary Pierce is a fine woman."

"How would you like to spend five years in federal prison on her account?"

Burnham swallowed, his jowls quivering. "You're talking about Edith Doolin, aren't you? Everybody knows her and Mary are friends."

"Good guess," Tilghman said with a slight smile. "Look, I'm not interested in Mary Pierce. You cooperate, and nobody gets hurt—including her."

"You'd let her off, not press charges?"

"You've got my word on it."

Burnham thought about it a moment. Then, as though reconciled to the situation, he shrugged. "Mary's in bed with the croup, and Bob's tendin' her along with the hotel. Guess he didn't have time to come get the mail yesterday."

Tilghman felt his scalp tingle. "There's a letter for her?"

Burnham darted a look out the windows. After inspecting the street, he led the way back to the mail cage. He took a letter from one of the bins, weighing it with a last moment of deliberation. Finally, with a heavy sigh, he slid it across the counter.

Tilghman stared down at the envelope. The writing was in a delicate hand and it was addressed to Mary

Pierce. But his attention fixed on the return address. He burned it into memory.

> MRS. WILL BARRY
> ROYAL HOTEL
> BURDEN, KANSAS

"You know," Burnham said, as though reading his mind, "it's against the law to open somebody else's mail."

Tilghman's smile darkened. "You just keep your part of the bargain. Not a word to Mary Pierce about me being here. Understood?"

"No need to worry about that."

"I'll hold you to it, Mr. Burnham."

Tilghman rode out of town calculating time and distance. He placed Burden, Kansas, some sixty miles southeast of Wichita, and perhaps thirty miles north of the state line. By horseback, he was at least four days away, and that seemed far too late. By train, he could be there tomorrow.

He rode west toward the Santa Fe depot at Perry.

The train pulled into Burden late the next afternoon. Tilghman stepped onto the platform with his warbag and walked to the end of the stationhouse. His badge was in his pocket, and his appearance was that of a grungy, bearded cowhand. He stood for a moment surveying the town.

The overnight trip had taken him north from Perry to Winfield, Kansas. There he had switched to the afternoon eastbound, which made several stops before arriving in Burden. He'd stalled his horse at a livery stable in Perry, and brought only the essentials he could cram into his warbag. He thought it would be a short stay.

Doolin and his wife were in Burden, or they were gone. Either way, Tilghman expected to be in town for no more than a day. On the train ride, he'd decided not to contact the local town marshal. His federal commission was good in Kansas, and the fewer who knew of his presence, the better. There were no secrets in small towns, and he was also unwilling to entrust his life to a lawman he'd never met. He preferred to handle it himself.

Uptown, Tilghman kept to the opposite side of the street from the Royal Hotel. A block beyond the main intersection, he checked into the town's only other hotel, and dumped his warbag. Then, outside again, he turned south as the sun dipped toward the horizon. He had no choice but to verify that Edith Doolin was still in Burden. Whether or not Doolin was staying with her at the hotel was a moot point. He had to take the risk of being seen.

The room clerk had a newspaper spread across the counter of the front desk. He glanced up as Tilghman entered the door, and an expression of distaste came over his face. His eyes were frosty.

"Help you?"

"Hope so," Tilghman said amiably. "Depends on whether we can make a deal."

The clerk frowned. "What kind of deal?"

"Information." Tilghman pulled a wad of greenbacks from his pocket. "I'm willing to pay."

"Information about what?"

"Somebody stayin' in the hotel."

The clerk quickly scanned the empty lobby. His voice lowered in a conspiratorial tone. "That kind of thing doesn't come cheap."

Tilghman peeled off several bills. He fanned them out on the counter. "Fifty dollars," he said. "For the information and your silence."

Fifty dollars represented almost a month's wages for the clerk. His eyes brightened with avarice. "What do you want to know?"

"You have a woman here by the name of Mrs. Will Barry?"

"She's in room two-oh-one."

Tilghman jerked a thumb upward. "On the second floor?"

The clerk nodded. "All the way up front. Faces the street."

"Anybody stayin' with her?"

"Just her and her baby."

"Anybody called on her?"

"No." The clerk paused, remembering. "A tramp delivered a package for her. Somebody hired him to bring it around."

Tilghman looked interested. "Describe this tramp."

"Worn-out clothes. About my height. Dark hair."

"Anything else?"

"Yeah," the clerk said, nodding. "Walked with a real bad limp. Must've hurt his foot somehow."

Tilghman pushed the bills across the counter. "Don't let me hear that you told anybody about our little talk. You'd regret it."

The cold look in his eyes unnerved the clerk. "No need for threats," he said. "I'll keep my mouth shut."

"See that you do."

Tilghman turned toward the door. Outside, he crossed the street and entered a saloon with a plate-glass window. He took a spot at the end of the bar, where he had a direct view of the hotel. Ordering a beer, he nursed it, mentally reviewing what he'd learned. He felt charged with energy.

For whatever reason, the Doolin woman was still in town. But it was the tramp, more than the woman, that kindled his interest. He recalled that Doolin had been shot in the left foot, and reports had it that the wound hadn't healed properly. Operating in disguise, Doolin might easily have passed himself off as a tramp. What he couldn't hide was the limp.

After supper at a nearby cafe, Tilghman returned to the saloon. There, with one eye on the hotel, he engaged several men in conversation. Casually, as though making small talk, he commented on the number of bums traveling the country these days. Other men picked up on the subject, and before long he learned that Burden had a new bum. The man had attracted attention because of his game leg, and the fact that he was rarely seen during the day. He was around mainly at night, and even then not for long. One moment he was on the street, and the next, he was gone.

Late that night, Tilghman walked back to his hotel. He was now fairly sure that the tramp was in fact Bill Doolin. The way it appeared, Doolin was camped somewhere outside town, out of sight. He apparently came into Burden only at night, probably to visit his wife. Which raised the question of how he got into her hotel room without being seen. Beyond that was the greater question of why they were still in town. What was holding them in Burden?

Tilghman got the answer in part the next day. Around midmorning he resumed his spot at the bar, keeping watch on the hotel. A short while later Edith Doolin emerged from the hotel, carrying her baby. He gave her a short lead, then followed as she proceeded uptown. At the main intersection, she turned east, and a block down the street, she entered a one-story frame house. He strolled past, and suddenly the last piece of the puzzle fell into place. A doctor's shingle hung on the wall beside the front door.

Downstreet, near a feed store, Tilghman waited beneath the shade of a tree. A half hour later, when Edith Doolin emerged from the doctor's office, he trailed her back to the hotel. All doubt had been erased as to why she and Doolin remained in town. Either she or her baby was ill, and required care by a physician. When care was no longer required, he felt certain they would depart Burden. Which left him with an immediate problem. He had to locate the tramp.

And positively identify him as Bill Doolin.

CHAPTER 33

The campfire smoldered, all but dead. Doolin sat with a cup of coffee, staring into the embers. Dark had fallen, and the glow of the coals lighted his features. His expression was one of troubled deliberation.

Four days had passed since he'd first made camp at the spring. Yet there had been little or no improvement in his wife's condition. The bleeding, though slight, showed no signs of stopping. The doctor had no cure, and seemingly, only the most basic of medical advice. She had to have bed rest.

Doolin was genuinely concerned. There had been many women in his life, from lusty young farm girls to cowtown whores. But Edith was the first one who had ever touched the core of emotion that lay buried deep within him. Touched him to such an extent that he had gladly married her, and been happier still when she gave him a son. He dreaded the thought that she might need an operation.

Along with the dread, there was anger. Doolin's plans for California, and a new life, were now at a standstill. Looking back, it was as though all the scheming to get her safely out of Oklahoma Territory had been for nothing. They were stranded in Kansas, and according to Dr. Bailey, the local sawbones, no idea when it might end.

Whether fate, or simple bad luck, it reaffirmed what he'd been brooding on for the past couple of days. Something always seemed to go wrong.

Mulling it over now, Doolin saw no ready solution. He was determined that he wouldn't leave without Edith and the baby, and yet the risk grew with each passing day. Sooner or later someone was bound to stumble across his camp in the grove and begin asking questions. For that matter, people in town were already curious about his strange comings and goings. He'd seen it in the faces of men he passed on the street, the regulars who frequented the saloon across from the hotel. Their curiosity would lead to idle speculation, and eventually, the kind of talk that spread. A bum who hung around too long just naturally drew attention.

Doolin tried to offset the risk by varying his schedule. He went into town after dark, and each night he'd made it a point to arrive at a different hour. Still, whether early or late, there was no way to avoid being seen. There were always people on the street, and by now, many of them had begun to recognize him on sight. He'd made only one trip during the day, to replenish food supplies for his camp. But that had been one too many times, and he grew warier each time he set out for town. Luck could be stretched just so far.

Tonight, some three hours after dark, Doolin prepared to leave. After checking that his horse was secured to the picket line, he doused the fire with water from the spring. Then he moved through the trees in what had become a nightly journey into his own personal hell. The two-mile hike into town was an exercise in torture every step of the way. His left foot felt as if thousands of barbed quills had been jabbed through nerves and flesh, and now pressed against bone. He hobbled off across the darkened prairie.

Three days ago, at his wife's insistence, Doolin had gone to see Dr. Bailey. Following a long and painful examination, the physician had told him what he already knew. The bullet wound had damaged nerves in his foot and brought on rheumatism, which was now in an advanced state. Apart from liniment, which provided fiery if temporary relief, there was little to be done. In passing, Dr. Bailey had suggested therapeutic treatment at one of the mineral bath resorts in Arkansas. The waters were famed for their soothing effect, though nothing offered a permanent cure. The best advice was simply to stay off the foot.

By the time he reached town, Doolin was acutely aware that these nightly walks were crippling him. He felt another round-trip might well reduce him to using a crutch. On the outskirts, he crossed the end of the street and limped toward the uptown area. He stayed on the boardwalks where shadows were the deepest in an effort to avoid being seen. Still, there were streetlamps at every corner, and no way to elude the light when he crossed an intersection. Tonight, with sparks shooting through his foot, he was unable to move through the lampglow as fast as usual.

A block from the hotel Doolin slowly scanned the street ahead. He normally turned right at the intersection and walked to the alley behind the hotel. But as he approached the streetlight, he saw a man step out of the saloon and pause on the boardwalk. Some visceral instinct set off a warning, and he moved into the shadows. He watched as the man stood at the edge of the boardwalk, staring up at the second story of the hotel. After a time, the man turned, and for an instant his features were framed in the spill of light from the saloon window. He slipped into the darkened doorway of a store next to the saloon.

Doolin's blood went cold. The face he'd seen in that instant was one he remembered from newspaper photographs in Oklahoma Territory. He recalled pictures of federal marshals, and suddenly he put a name to the

face: Bill Tilghman. One of the much-ballyhooed Three
Guardsmen. The marshals who had hounded the Wild
Bunch and killed four of his men. Then, so abruptly that
he took a sharp breath, he realized the full meaning of
what he'd just seen. Tilghman was watching the window
of his wife's hotel room.

For a moment Doolin was paralyzed with shock. His
mind roared with sudden comprehension. Tilghman had
somehow tracked him to Kansas. With startling clarity,
he saw that all his slippery plans and clever maneuver-
ing had been for nothing. The Osage farmer, the exchange of wagons, even the Osage woman's masquerade
to throw off pursuit, had been an exercise in folly. Tilghman hadn't tracked him anywhere, let alone to Kansas.
Instead, in a neat switch, Tilghman had turned the tables on him. His wife was being used as bait.

Doolin turned back downstreet. He moved from
doorway to doorway, hugging the shadows, fearful that
he might be spotted at any moment. Halfway along the
block, he ducked into a narrow passageway between two
buildings. A short distance ahead he emerged into the
alley and reversed directions, again heading north. At
the end of the alley, his hand on his pistol, he paused
and inspected the corner on Main Street. There was no
one in sight.

Wincing with every step, his foot on fire, Doolin scuttled across the street. He disappeared into the alley and
moved through the dark, halting behind the hotel. At
the back door, he pulled a jackknife from his pocket,
and jimmied the blade between the door and the door-
frame. There was a muted *click* as the tip of the blade
sprung the bolt. He stepped into the hallway.

A rear stairway led to the second floor. Doolin
paused at the top of the landing to check the hall. There
was no one about and he moved to the end of the corridor. He rapped gently on the door.

From inside, he heard the creak of floorboards under

quick footsteps. Edith Doolin opened the door, a welcoming smile across her face. He shushed her, a finger to his lips, warning silence as he moved into the room. He closed and locked the door.

Her eyes were now wide with fright. Doolin quickly scanned the room, saw the baby asleep on the bed. A lamp glowed on the dresser, which was positioned near the window. He nodded to his wife.

"Don't ask questions. Put out the light."

She moved to obey. At the dresser, she cupped a hand behind the lamptop and expelled a sharp breath. The flame was extinguished, casting the room into darkness. A dim ray of light seeped through the window from distant streetlamps.

"Stay away from the window," Doolin ordered. "We're being watched."

Her mouth sagged. "Who is it?"

"A federal marshal from the territory. I spotted him on the street."

"Do you think he knows you're here?"

"Has to," Doolin said. "He wouldn't be watching your room otherwise."

"Oh, my God." Her voice trembled. "How did he find us?"

"Only one way that makes any sense. He must've trailed you from the time you left home."

"What are we going to do?"

"I dunno just yet."

Doolin crossed the room. He removed his hat, tossing it on the dresser, and edged into position beside the window. Slowly, careful not to disturb the curtains, he eased his head past the drape of the cloth. He stared across the street.

The doorway of the store next to the saloon was framed in darkness. For several moments, his eyes squinted, Doolin saw nothing. Then, as his vision ad-

justed to the dim light, he uttered a low grunt. He saw
the faint outline of a man in the doorway.

"Bastard's still there," he said, turning from the window. "Wouldn't know it unless you were looking for
him."

"Just one?" she asked softly. "Maybe he hasn't called
in the town marshal."

"You might be right about that. He probably figures
to take me himself."

She moved to a chair near the washstand. As though
drained of energy, she sat down heavily. "I don't understand," she said. "Even if he followed me, how would he
know you're here? How could he be certain?"

"He's not certain," Doolin told her. "But he's got no
doubts you're here. Hell, he even knows what room
you're in. He's just waitin' for me to show up."

"And if you don't show up?"

"Then he'll stick with you till hell freezes over. He
knows you're the only link to me."

She lowered her head. In the darkness, Doolin heard
a sniffle, and then a choked sob. He moved to her and
knelt on the floor. He took her hands.

"Don't go teary-eyed on me."

"It's not that," she said miserably. "It's just so . . .
unfair."

"What d'you mean?"

"I saw the doctor today. The spotting has stopped,
Bill. We could have left for California tomorrow."

Doolin laughed ruefully. "Honey, you haven't got the
picture. We're damn lucky we didn't try boardin' that
train yesterday. Or any other day."

She looked at him. "Why do you say that?"

"Because our friend out there would've followed you
to the train station. Sure as God made little green apples, he'd have waited for me to put in an appearance.
Then it'd all be over."

"Over?"

"Yeah," Doolin muttered. "He would've collared me or killed me. Whichever come handiest."

"Sweet Jesus," she moaned. "Won't it ever end?"

Doolin rose to his feet. He began pacing the room like a trapped animal pacing a cage. His mind whirled, exploring and discarding ideas for a way out. There was no sense in sending her on to California, for Tilghman would just follow. Nor was there anything to be gained by leaving her here, hoping Tilghman would weary of his vigil and leave town. The last year had proved that Tilghman hung on like a bulldog.

For a moment he toyed with the idea of killing Tilghman. But that, too, posed a host of risks. The major one being that he might himself be killed. To leave behind a widow and a fatherless child was not an option. Not after he'd come this far, this close to a new life. Hard as it seemed, there was only one way to handle the situation.

"Hate to say it." Doolin stopped pacing, halted in front of her. "You're gonna have to go back to your folks."

She bolted from her chair. "What are you talking about?"

"Edie, I don't like it any better than you do. But we're gonna have to start all over again."

"Start where?"

"Here's the idea," Doolin explained. "Sell the wagon and horse for whatever you can get. I don't want you busted up again makin' that trip in a wagon. Then you and the boy take a train back to the territory."

"But why?" she demanded. "What does that accomplish?"

"That jaybird outside will follow you all the way back to Lawson. So we've got him off my trail and we've bought time to come up with a new plan. I'll think of something."

"You mean you'd stay here?"

"Nooo," Doolin said in a musing tone. "You know what that sawbones told me about the mineral springs over in Arkansas? I might give it a try. See if it'll help my foot."

"And then what?" she persisted. "How long do we wait?"

"Just till things cool down. Nobody'll think to look for me in Arkansas. Couple of weeks, and they'll get tired of watchin' you. Then we'll make our move."

"How will I know where to reach you?"

"I'll write you through Mary Pierce. Tell her I'll use the same name as before—Tom Wilson."

"Oh God, Bill." She slumped against him, tears flooding her eyes. "I can't bear to leave you after all this. I'm afraid I'll never see you again."

"What a way to talk." Doolin gently stroked her hair. "Have I ever let you down before?"

"No . . . never."

"Well, I won't now, either. Trust me a little longer, and you'll see. We're gonna get to California—the three of us."

She sniffed, tilted her head back. "You're proud of him, aren't you?"

"Proud as punch," Doolin assured her. "A man's naturally partial to havin' a son."

"We'll have more, won't we, Bill?"

"Have ourselves a blessed litter. You got my word."

She laid her head on his shoulder. Doolin wrapped her tighter in his arms, rocking back and forth in a snug embrace. He wanted nothing more than to take his wife and child and move on, put the past behind them. Yet, unbidden, her words of a moment ago echoed through his mind.

He too wondered where it would end.

CHAPTER 34

Tilghman was at a loss.

For three days he had tagged after Edith Doolin. Whenever she left the hotel, he had followed her around town. At night, from his lookout across the street, he'd kept watch on her room. Yet, in all that time, he had seen nothing to indicate that she was in touch with her husband. He began to wonder if Doolin somehow got messages to her.

Yesterday morning, to his surprise, the Doolin woman had not visited the doctor. The only reasonable conclusion was that she, or her baby, whichever had been ill, was now well. But it that were so, he had to ask himself why she continued to stay on in Burden. Which raised the greater question of why she'd ever come there in the first place.

Then, one surprise following another, the situation became even more murky. Yesterday afternoon Edith Doolin had emerged from the hotel with her baby and walked to a livery stable on the south edge of town. There, with a man who appeared to be the livery owner, she had inspected a wagon parked at the rear and a horse in the outside corral. The livery owner had then counted out a small stack of greenbacks.

Tilghman had no doubt that it was the horse and

wagon she'd used on the trip to Burden. He was no less
certain that he had just witnessed her selling them to
the livery owner. To confound matters even further, she
had then spent the rest of the afternoon on a shopping
spree. She'd bought herself and the baby some new
clothes, as well as a matched pair of suitcases. On her
last stop, at a novelty store, she had purchased what
appeared to be souvenirs. All of the goods had been
delivered to her hotel.

Last night, once more watching her room, Tilghman
had felt thoroughly bewildered. The sale of the horse
and wagon indicated that she planned to travel by train.
By the same token, the purchase of clothes and suitcases, not to mention souvenirs, indicated a trip was in
the offing. All that being true, the obvious question was
where she was headed and when did she plan to leave?
Perhaps more to the point, was she planning to meet
Doolin at some distant destination?

None of it made sense. She could just have easily
eluded pursuit in Oklahoma Territory, and caught a
train from one of a dozen different locations. Instead,
she had made an arduous trip by wagon through Osage
country and then on to Kansas. To presume that she'd
done all that simply to catch a train boggled the mind.
Logic dictated that she had traveled to Kansas for one
purpose only, to somehow connect with Doolin. But if
that were the case, where the hell was he?

One thing troubled Tilghman even more. From the
hotel clerk, and again with regulars in the saloon, he
had confirmed that a tramp was hanging around town.
To further his suspicions, he'd verified that the man had
a pronounced limp and fit the general description of
Doolin. The corker was that the tramp hadn't shown up
in Burden until the day after Edith Doolin's arrival. All
of that was coincidence compounding coincidence, and
to Tilghman, any coincidence was suspect. He still be-

lieved that Doolin was camped out somewhere around Burden.

But now, his fourth day in town, Tilghman was no closer to the truth than before. A late morning sun filtered through the saloon window as he stood at the bar. Inwardly, though he had no notion of what it might be, he felt certain that something would happen today. Yesterday's shopping spree, and the suitcases, seemed to him too great a tip-off to ignore. Edith Doolin was headed somewhere, and he thought today was the day. Which merely brought him full circle in a looping enigma. Where the hell was Bill Doolin?

Through the window, Tilghman saw a man wearing a porter's cap enter the hotel. Looking closer, he saw Edith Doolin holding the baby in the lobby. A moment later, the porter came out the door, carrying her suitcases, and moved off in the direction of the train station. She followed a few paces behind, attired in one of the new outfits she'd bought yesterday. She looked like a woman who knew where she was going, and how to get there.

Tilghman trailed them by a half block. Some minutes later, they rounded the corner of the train station and disappeared down the platform. He stopped at the corner, looking around the edge of the building, and saw Edith Doolin enter the depot. The porter guarding her bags remained on the platform, surrounded by a crowd of people waiting on the train. Shortly she came through the door, nodding to the porter, the baby cradled in her left arm. In her right hand, she held a train ticket.

Off in the distance a whistle sounded. Tilghman glanced to the east and saw a passenger train perhaps a quarter of a mile away. Time was short, and he felt there was no choice but to risk being seen. He stepped around the corner, aware that the Doolin woman was looking downtrack at the approaching train, and strode rapidly along the platform. He scanned the faces of the crowd, assuring himself that Doolin was not among them. As the locomotive rolled into the station, he hurried through the waiting room door.

The ticket agent was a spare man with a receding hairline. He looked up with an expression of birdlike alertness, nodding pleasantly. Tilghman pulled out his badge.

"Federal marshal," he said. "I need some information."

"What can I do for you, marshal?"

"A woman with a baby just bought a ticket. What was her destination?"

"Wearing a blue dress, was she?"

"That's the one."

"Oklahoma Territory," the agent informed him. "Final destination the town of Perry."

For a moment Tilghman was too stunned to speak. "One last thing," he finally said. "Where does she change trains?"

"Winfield," the agent replied. "Southbound from there takes her to Perry."

"Much obliged."

Tilghman walked out of the depot. The passengers were in the process of boarding, and he saw the porter follow Edith Doolin onto the train. His head was still reeling from the fact that she was headed back to Oklahoma Territory. Her trip to Kansas made even less sense now. Something about the whole affair smelled.

Still, fishy or not, Tilghman had no choice but to follow her. There was always a chance that she would change tickets at Winfield, or meet Doolin at a stop somewhere along the line. His badge would guarantee him passage, and he delayed boarding until the last moment. He watched as the porter stepped off the train.

Then, oddly, Tilghman sensed that he was being watched. He glanced around the platform and saw no one but the stationmaster. His gaze swept the passenger coaches, and abruptly stopped at the one directly in front of the depot. Edith Doolin was seated at the window, the baby cuddled in her arms. She was staring at him with a strange smile.

When their eyes locked, she suddenly turned away. But in that instant, Tilghman saw that her smile was more on the order of a gloating smirk. The realization came over him that he'd been spotted, that she knew him. Perhaps not his name, but she had no doubt that he was a lawman. Her look, the sly smile, said it all. She knew he was following her.

Tilghman made a snap decision. Some inner voice told him that the Doolin woman was bait, meant to lure him away from Burden and out of Kansas. His instincts had never played him false, even in situations when his life was on the line. Whatever the source, these sudden hunches had never failed him, and another one came over him now. He felt an eerie certainty that Doolin was somewhere close at hand.

The thought was reinforced as the locomotive belched steam and got under way. Tilghman saw Edith Doolin's head snap around, staring at him as the passenger coach pulled away from the station. Her eyes were filled with a look of disbelief and desperation, the sudden awareness that he had no intention of boarding the train. As the coach gathered speed, her face became a mask of bewildered outrage. Her expression betrayed her, and he knew he was right. She'd tried to gull him.

The train rolled out of Burden, heading west. Tilghman watched until the last coach in the string was far down the tracks. Then he turned and walked back into the depot. The ticket agent gave him a curious look.

"Find the lady you were asking about?"

"More or less," Tilghman said. "Who do I see about sending a telegram?"

"You're looking at him," the agent said with a slow

smile. "Tickets, telegraph, sweep the floor. Jack of all trades."

He pushed a telegram form across the counter, along with a pen and inkwell. Tilghman considered a moment, composing the message in his head. Then he began writing.

Evett Nix
U.S. Marshal
Guthrie, Oklahoma Territory

Edith Doolin arrives Perry on Santa
Fe tomorrow. Have her followed to
determine final destination. Heck
Thomas knows her on sight.
Believe Doolin still in Kansas.
Will keep you advised.

Tilghman

Finished, Tilghman slid the form across the counter. The agent read through it quickly, silently mouthing the words. His eyes went round and he glanced up with a questioning look.

"Bill Doolin's here in Burden?"

"Let's understand each other," Tilghman said in a low voice. "You keep your lip buttoned, or I'll have to see you in an official capacity. You get my drift?"

"Bet I do," the agent said hastily. "Don't give it another thought, marshal. You can depend on me."

"How much do I owe you?"

Tilghman paid for the telegram and walked to the door. Outside, crossing the platform, his thoughts turned again to Doolin. How he'd been spotted, or when, seemed to him a moot point. Edith Doolin's sudden departure, her return to Oklahoma Territory, spoke for itself. He'd somehow given himself away, and the result was a change in Doolin's plans. Which left him

with few options and no real choice. He had to turn up a
fresh lead.

Headed uptown, Tilghman mentally reviewed the last
few days. The Doolin woman had spoken with several
people during her stay in Burden. A short list included
the hotel clerk, the doctor, the livery stable owner, and
clerks in various stores. However smart she thought she
was, she might have dropped some telltale clue in conversation. So his first task was to talk with those who
had spoken with her at any length. From the first day,
he'd been curious about her visits to the doctor. He
decided to start there.

Some ten minutes later a nurse ushered him into the
physician's office. Phillip Bailey was in his fifties, with a
mane of white hair and an open manner. Seated at an
ancient roll-top desk, he motioned Tilghman to a
nearby chair. His smile was inquisitive.

"What seems to be the problem today?"

"Nothing medical." Tilghman showed him the badge.
"I'm a federal marshal. I'd like to ask about one of your
patients."

"You don't say?" Bailey examined the badge, nodding. "Which patient would that be?"

"A woman staying at the Royal Hotel, Mrs. Will
Barry. Or maybe her baby was the patient. I never really
knew."

"Yes indeed, a fine young woman. And you're right,
she was the patient rather than her baby. May I ask your
interest in Mrs. Barry?"

"Just routine," Tilghman said evasively. "She got herself involved with some unsavory people."

"What a shame." Bailey appeared saddened by the
news. "Well, in any event, she had complications result-
ing from childbirth. A few days' bed rest and she was
fine. The problem took care of itself."

"Did she mention anything about herself? Where she

was headed, who she was traveling with? Anything of
that sort?"

"No, not that I recall. She just said she was stopping
over in Burden for a few days."

Tilghman looked at him. "So you only talked about
her medical condition? Nothing else?"

"No, nothing—" Bailey hesitated, suddenly thoughtful. "Well, now that I think on it, there was one thing.
She asked me to see some poor fellow she'd met on the
street. A panhandler."

"A tramp?" Tilghman said quickly. "Dark hair, average height, with a lame foot?"

"Yes, that's the fellow. Told me he'd accidentally shot
himself in the foot some time ago. Developed into a bad
case of rheumatism."

"Are you still treating him?"

"I saw him only once. Four or five days ago, as I
recall. Gave him a bottle of liniment to ease the pain."

"Have you seen him around town since then?"

"No, I haven't," Bailey said. "Perhaps he took my
advice. I suggested one of the bath resorts, in Arkansas."

"Which one?" Tilghman asked. "Hot Springs or Eureka Springs?"

"Actually, I made no specific recommendation. I just
mentioned that the waters would relieve his condition."

"Did he say anything about one over the other?"

"Not that I remember."

"What name did he give you?"

"Let me see." Bailey thumbed through an index file
on his desk. "Yes, here it is. Thomas Wilson, male, advanced rheumatism of the left foot. No address, I'm
afraid."

"Out of curiosity," Tilghman said, "how old would
you say his gunshot wound was?"

"Less than a year." Bailey paused, his expression benign but his eyes inquisitive. "You seem to have taken

quite an interest in Mr. Wilson. Has he committed a crime?"

"I'll know that when I find him, doctor. But if you're a betting man, bet the farm."

Tilghman left the office at a vigorous stride. The day was half gone and there was still a great deal to be accomplished. He had to buy a horse and a saddle, camping gear and a rifle, and then start a hunt too long delayed. For while he was days behind, there was one thing he knew with dead certainty.

Bill Doolin, alias Thomas Wilson, would never take the train to Arkansas.

CHAPTER 35

Tilghman began the manhunt on a central premise. He was convinced Doolin would not take the train from Kansas to Arkansas. For one thing, the Wild Bunch had staged several robberies in the area where Kansas and Arkansas abutted Indian Territory. For another, trains were often crowded, and the risk of being recognized was simply too great. Doolin's face was widely known from wanted posters and newspapers.

So the greater likelihood was that Doolin would travel by horseback. Tilghman tried to look at it through the other man's eyes whenever he conducted a lone manhunt. There were several routes by which a man might travel from Burden to the state line of Arkansas. But he thought Doolin would take the shortest route, while at the same time hugging the border of Indian Territory. That way, were he recognized, a short hop took him into the Nations.

One other factor entered into Tilghman's thinking. From the doctor in Burden, he knew that Doolin was suffering considerable pain from his foot. Should the pain worsen, Doolin might well seek medical attention along the way. That meant entering towns—where there were doctors—and running the risk of being recognized. Whether or not Doolin would stick with his tramp's disguise was a matter of conjecture. But if he needed a doctor, it made sense that he would look for one in a small town. The chances of being spotted by the law would then be reduced by a large degree.

All these things were weighed in the balance before Tilghman departed Burden. His approach to an investigation was to think it out, rather than conduct a harum-scarum search. Studying a map of Kansas, he found what seemed the perfect route for a man with Doolin's problems. In the southeastern corner of the state, there was a string of small towns along the border of Indian Territory. The towns would have doctors, with little law enforcement, and great strategic advantage. None of them were more than five miles from refuge in the Nations.

The wild card in all this revolved around Doolin's ultimate destination. There were two notable bath resorts in Arkansas, Eureka Springs and Hot Springs. Which one Doolin might choose was a matter of pure guesswork. After pondering on it, Tilghman saw that there was no way to pick one over the other. He might have to search both, and hope that Doolin continued to use the same alias. On the other hand, any investigation was equal parts deduction and good detective work, and getting the breaks. This time out, things might fall his way.

For three days Tilghman rode steadily eastward along the border. He stopped in one town after another, pausing only long enough to question the local doctor. Though they were cooperative, none of them had been consulted by a man with a lame foot. On the fourth morning, still confident that he was on the right track, he rode into the town of Chetopa. By now he had covered some eighty miles, and all the towns had begun to look alike. But he was no less determined than when he'd set out from Burden.

Tilghman discovered that there were two doctors in

Chetopa. He learned as well that they were father and son, Harold and John Millsap. The younger Millsap, who routinely made house calls across the countryside, was out of town. Dr. Harold Millsap, who no longer made house calls, was in the office. He was a frail man, on the sundown side of sixty, stooped and hard of hearing. He greeted Tilghman with a genial warning.

"You'll have to speak up. I'm damn near stone deaf. What ails you?"

"Nothing," Tilghman said loudly, taking a chair beside the physician's desk. "I'd like to ask you some questions."

"Questions?" Millsap boomed, shouting in order to hear himself. "What sort of questions?"

Tilghman pulled out his badge. "Federal marshal," he said. "I'm looking for a fugitive."

"A what?" Millsap asked sharply. "Consarn it, you'll have to speak louder."

"A fugitive," Tilghman bellowed. "A man with a game left foot. He's got rheumatism."

"Well, why didn't you say so? I treated a man like that a couple of days ago."

Tilghman sat straighter. "Had he been gunshot in the foot?"

"Yeah, a while back," Millsap acknowledged. "Nothing to be done for that. He'd run out of liniment and wanted more. I gave him another bottle."

"Did he ask you anything about the mineral baths over in Arkansas?"

"Told him it's the closest thing to a miracle. I've got a touch of arthritis in the spine. Go over there myself once or twice a year."

"Did you recommend any particular resort?"

"Told him to go where I go. The Davidson Hotel in Eureka Springs. Has the best waters in Arkansas."

Tilghman allowed himself a smile. "Do you think he'll follow your advice?"

"Why hell, yes," Millsap trumpeted. "He'd chew nails if he thought it'd help. He was hurting bad."

"Thanks." Tilghman stood. "You've put me on the right track, doctor."

"What'd he do, anyhow? Murder somebody?"

"That and a few other things."

Millsap cackled. "By golly, I knew it! Told me he'd shot himself in the foot. Didn't believe him for a minute."

Tilghman turned at the door. "Was he using the name Tom Wilson?"

"Now that you mention it, he was. Yessir, that was it. Tom Wilson."

"How was he dressed?"

"Looked more like a cowhand than he did a desperado. Smelled like he'd been on a horse for a while, too."

"Thanks again."

Outside, Tilghman felt like clicking his heels. His assessment of Doolin had proved to be on the mark. Avoiding trains, the outlaw had taken a route along the border. Two days ago, almost by happenstance, he'd stopped to see a doctor who had definite opinions about the bath resorts in Arkansas. There was little doubt that Doolin would be found in Eureka Springs.

Tilghman saw no reason to waste time. By switching from horseback to train, he could be in Eureka Springs sometime tomorrow. A half hour later, after a short dickering session, he sold his horse and saddle to a local livestock dealer. Then, at a mercantile store, he swapped his new rifle for a black suit and a parson's white, ringed collar. The merchant, knowing he'd got the best of the deal, even threw in a black, broadbrimmed hat.

For the past few days, Tilghman had dwelled at length on having been spotted in Burden. The obvious answer was Edith Doolin, who knew him on sight. But that set him to thinking about pictures of himself and other marshals that had appeared in newspapers. The more he wondered, the more it made sense that Doolin knew him on sight as well. So he'd decided to give himself whatever edge was possible when they finally met. He would assume the guise of a preacher.

From the store, with his bundle of clothes, Tilghman proceeded to the train station. A passenger train, headed eastbound, was scheduled into Chetopa in two hours. After purchasing a ticket, he composed a telegram, worded in cryptic language, to Evett Nix. The wire stated that business affairs required his presence in Eureka Springs, and he asked for an immediate reply regarding his last telegraph message. Less than an hour later, he was handed an equally cryptic telegram from Nix. The package, Nix informed him, had arrived as scheduled, and had been delivered to Lawson.

The meaning was clear. Edith Doolin had arrived by train in Perry, and Heck Thomas had trailed her to her parents' home in Lawson. Upon reading it, Tilghman suddenly realized that all the pieces had fallen into place. Eureka Springs was some fifty miles east of the border with the Cherokee Nation. From there, Doolin planned to take the healing waters and bide his time. Then, after a suitable interval, he would again spirit his wife and child out of Oklahoma Territory. All of which dovetailed with what Tilghman had suspected from the beginning. Doolin never intended to return to the territory, or the Wild Bunch.

Tilghman boarded the train shortly after one o'clock. He placed his bundle in the overhead rack, took a seat, and stared out the window. He was reminded of the adage that time and tide waits on no man.

He thought Bill Doolin had lived on borrowed time long enough. The tide finally had ebbed.

Eureka Springs was the oldest bath resort in Arkansas. Located in the Ozark Hills, the town was a place of twisting streets and houses that clung precariously to steep slopes. People came from across the country to luxuriate in the steaming sulfur waters.

Tilghman stepped off the train early the next morning. The porter had pressed his new suit and blacked his boots, and the white dog-collar of a minister encircled his neck. He carried his range clothes and gunbelt in a warbag, and his pistol was stuffed in the waistband of his trousers. He looked like a preacher in search of miracle waters.

The Davidson Hotel was located along the town's main street. A short walk from the train depot, the hotel was situated beneath rugged hills dotted with the yawning mouths of large caves. On the street, men tipped their hats and ladies nodded pleasantly as Tilghman strolled uptown. He played the role, smiling with benign good cheer, thinking that Zoe would be amused. At last, in a manner of speaking, he'd got religion.

Entering the hotel, Tilghman walked straight to the registration desk. The lobby was crowded and he scanned faces from beneath his broad-brimmed black hat. There was always the risk that he would stumble across Doolin and be spotted, despite his disguise. Still, the parson's outfit seemed to hold people's attention, and the risk was unavoidable. He had to verify that Doolin was staying at the hotel.

"Good morning, Reverend," the desk clerk greeted him. "May I help you?"

"You're too kind," Tilghman said unctuously. "I'm looking for one of my parishioners, Thomas Wilson. I believe he's a guest at the hotel."

"Yes, of course, I know Mr. Wilson. He stopped by only a few minutes ago to mail a letter. He was on his way to the bath house."

"How would I find the bath house?"

"See that hallway, Reverend?" the clerk said, point-'

ing across the lobby. "At the end, turn right and go
down the stairs. You can't miss it."

Tilghman checked his warbag with the bell captain.
Down the hallway, he found stairs that descended to
what had once been a natural cavern. At the lower level,
he tugged his hat low and entered the door of the bath
house. There was a lounge out front, with an attendant
serving coffee, and a counter where guests were given
towels and locker keys. Beyond was an entrance to the
dressing room and the baths.

Several men waited their turn at the counter. Others
were seated around the lounge, conversing over their
morning coffee. Across the room, Doolin was seated in
a club chair, reading a newspaper. Attired in a suit and
tie that appeared to be newly purchased, he looked
much like the other hotel guests. A cup of coffee was on
a table beside his chair, and he kept glancing over the
top of his newspaper. He was apparently waiting for the
line to thin out at the counter.

Head lowered, Tilghman moved toward the men
waiting for towels. As he approached the end of the
line, he saw Doolin glance at him, then return to the
newspaper. He continued on, aware that Doolin had
been distracted by the minister's outfit rather than inspecting his face. Quickly, before he was noticed again,
he closed the distance to Doolin's chair. He halted a
step away, drawing his pistol.

"Doolin!" he ordered sharply. "Stand up and keep
your hands in sight. You're under arrest."

A flicker of recognition crossed Doolin's features. He
stared over the newspaper, his mouth set in a tight
smile. "Where'd you get the preacher's duds?"

"You heard me," Tilghman said. "On your feet."

Doolin rose from his chair. He flung the newspaper
forward with his left hand and his right hand flashed
inside his suit jacket. On the verge of firing, something
stayed Tilghman's finger on the trigger. He grabbed

Doolin's wrist with his left hand, locking it in a fierce grip only inches away from the butt of a pistol. Standing toe to toe, he jabbed his Colt into the outlaw's stomach.

"Let it go," he said in a hard voice. "Don't make me kill you."

Doolin struggled, trying to free his arm. Around the room, the other men suddenly became aware of the wrestling match. They backed away, watching in silence, confounded by the sight of a minister with a gun in his hand. The minister was bigger and stronger, but the second man continued to fight. He clawed desperately at something inside his coat.

"Give it up," Tilghman growled, shoving Doolin into the wall. "Stop now or your wife's a widow."

The warning touched a nerve. Doolin ceased to struggle, the wild look in his eyes abruptly gone. His tensed muscles went slack, and he allowed his arm to be forced aside. Tilghman pulled a pistol from his waistband, then moved back a step. They stared at each other.

"What stopped you?" Doolin said sullenly. "Why didn't you kill me?"

"Let's just say I preferred to take you alive."

"What for?"

"I doubt you'd understand, Doolin. Walk ahead of me."

Tilghman informed the crowd that he was a federal marshal. None of them moved as he marched Doolin across the room and out the door. Upstairs, his gunhand hidden inside his jacket, Tilghman reclaimed his warbag. He saw no reason to alert local law officers, or to undergo a formal extradition hearing. Outside the hotel, he ordered Doolin to lead the way to the train station.

A northbound train was scheduled in at eleven that morning. Tilghman took Doolin into the men's toilet and locked the door. He reclaimed a set of manacles from his warbag and clamped them around the outlaw's

wrists. While Doolin watched, he shed the parson's outfit and put on his regular clothes. He pinned the deputy
marshal's badge to his shirt.

"Takes the cake," Doolin said, staring at him. "Hadn't
been for that preacher's getup, I would've spotted you.
You're a lucky man."

"Your wife's the lucky one, Doolin. I almost brought
you home in a box."

In the waiting room, Tilghman seated his prisoner on
a bench against the wall. Then, after purchasing two
tickets for Guthrie, he asked about sending a telegram.
He composed a brief message to Evett Nix.

> **I HAVE HIM IN CUSTODY. ARRIVE THERE ON THE NOON
> TRAIN TOMORROW.**
>
> TILGHMAN

PART THREE

CHAPTER 36

The railway station at Guthrie was mobbed. A crowd of more than two thousand people waited around the depot and along the Santa Fe tracks. Word of Doolin's capture had spread throughout town, and there was an air of celebration among those thronged about on the warm September morning. They were there to greet the most famous outlaw in Oklahoma Territory.

In large degree, they were there as well to greet the man who had captured Doolin. Overnight, with telegraph wires humming the news, Tilghman had become a celebrity throughout the territory. All the more so because he had taken Doolin alive, rather than killing him. None among them understood why he had spared the dreaded leader of the Wild Bunch.

The train rolled into town shortly after the noon hour. The engineer throttled down, setting the brakes, and let loose several blasts with his whistle. As the locomotive ground to a halt, pandemonium erupted among the packed masses outside the depot. Shoving and jostling, they pressed closer around the passenger coaches, fighting for a better vantage point. Slowly, then gaining momentum, a chant went up from the crowd. Their voices built to a drumming roar.

"Doolin! *Doolin!* DOOLIN!"

Tilghman stood in the aisle of the last passenger coach. Doolin was still seated, his hands manacled, staring out the window with a look of raw fear. For all either of them knew, a lynch mob had gathered to perform summary execution on the outlaw leader. Under his breath, Tilghman cursed Evett Nix for allowing the news to leak out. The matter should have been kept quiet, he told himself, at least until Doolin was locked in a cell. There was no way to control a crowd that large.

The train shuddered to a halt. Through the window, Tilghman saw Nix on the depot platform, surrounded by Thomas and Madsen and several other deputies. He took Doolin by the arm, got him on his feet, and walked him to the rear of the coach. After opening the door, he moved onto the observation platform, motioning for Doolin to remain inside. Behind Doolin, he noted that the other passengers were hurrying toward the front of the coach. He leaned out across the rear steps.

Heck Thomas spotted him. Gathering Nix and the other deputies, he bulled a path through the crowd. A moment later Thomas clambered up the steps, followed closely by Nix. Madsen and the remaining deputies formed a wedge at the bottom of the steps. The mob surged toward the rear of the train, their chant now raised to a deafening beat. Thomas waved Tilghman and Doolin back inside the coach. Nix hastily slammed the door.

"You ol' scutter!" Thomas said with a wide grin. "Did it all by your lonesome, didn't you?"

Before he could answer, Nix pushed forward. "Congratulations, Bill! You're the talk of the whole territory."

Tilghman accepted his handshake. "Thanks," he said evenly, nodding out the window. "Where'd that reception party come from?"

"No way to stop the news from spreading. Those folks wouldn't have missed this for the world."

"He's right," Thomas added quickly. "You'd think it was the Fourth of July all over again."

Tilghman looked at him. "Will we have any trouble getting Doolin under lock and key?"

"From that crowd?" Thomas laughed, shook his head. "They're not gonna do anything but bust your eardrums. They're here for the show."

"Why do they keep yelling for Doolin?"

" 'Cause he's the show." Thomas glanced past him, at Doolin. "You're the luckiest feller that ever lived. If it'd been me, I'd have brought you back across a horse."

"If it'd been you," Doolin said with a sarcastic smile, "you wouldn't've brought me back. Tilghman's likely the only man that could've done it."

"You sorry sonovabitch. I'd have—"

"Enough of that," Nix broke in. "Mr. Doolin, it's a pleasure to meet you at last. I think you can rest assured of a swift and speedy trial."

"Got a rope handy, have you?"

"All in good time," Nix said jovially. "But first, we have to get you through that crowd. Heck, lead the way."

Thomas went out the door. He was followed by Nix and Doolin, with Tilghman acting as rear guard. As they came down the steps, the mob around the depot spotted Doolin and went wild with a renewed burst of excitement. Madsen and the other deputies formed a phalanx to the front, their Winchesters held at port arms. They moved forward as the chant of the crowd raised to a thunderous pitch.

The lawmen wedged a path through the massed throngs. Doolin was in the middle, protected on all sides, with people screaming and shouting and lunging forward for the chance to touch him. Slowly, often a step at a time, they shouldered their way across the platform and past the depot. On the street, other deputies waited with a buggy and several horses. Doolin was

quickly loaded onto the buggy, along with Nix and
Tilghman. Thomas swung aboard a horse and motioned
for the deputies to mount. They formed a shield around
the buggy.

On the way uptown, the crowd surged along, steadily
growing larger. Tilghman gradually realized that
Thomas was headed for the marshal's office rather than
the jailhouse. He turned to question Nix, who was
seated on the opposite side of Doolin. But the noise
from the mob was too great to be heard, and he let it go.
Some minutes later the driver brought the buggy to a
halt outside the Herriott Building. Their mounted escort swung around to block the swarms of onlookers.

Tilghman hustled Doolin from the buggy. Thomas
and Madsen dismounted, hurrying forward with Nix,
and followed them inside. Upstairs, with Tilghman guiding the prisoner, they proceeded along the hallway to
Nix's office. When they entered, a pack of reporters,
with cameras mounted on tripods, was ganged around
the desk. Tilghman stopped just inside the door.

"What's all this?" he said, looking at Nix. "You didn't
tell me anything about reporters."

"Too crowded at the depot," Nix said. "The gentlemen of the press want to interview you and Doolin."

Tilghman stifled a response. There was nothing to be
gained in airing their differences before reporters. Nix
clearly intended to reap a harvest of newsprint, and an
obstinate deputy marshal would merely result in bigger
headlines. Tilghman and Doolin were quickly positioned in front of the desk, facing the cameras. Nix
hovered about like a stage manager orchestrating a the-
atrical production.

"Mr. Doolin!" one of the reporters shouted as flash
pans fired in rapid succession. "After all this time, how
did you come to be captured?"

Doolin seemed to bask in the attention. "I practically

gave myself up," he said in a jocular tone. "High time I had a chance to prove my innocence."

"How can you prove your innocence?" another reporter demanded loudly. "There are dozens of witnesses to the robberies and murders committed by you and your Wild Bunch."

"Mistaken identity," Doolin said with a broad smile. "Nobody can eyewitness me for anything. I'm a law-abiding citizen."

That drew an appreciative laugh from the reporters. One of them prompted him further. "Are you saying you were never the leader of the Wild Bunch?"

Doolin spread his manacled hands. "Boys, I wouldn't know the Wild Bunch from a hole in the ground. I'm just a simple cowhand."

"Will you plead not guilty at your trial?"

"Why, being innocent and all, what else could I do?"

"Deputy Tilghman!" the first reporter cut in. "How do you feel about Mr. Doolin pleading not guilty?"

"That's his right," Tilghman said levelly. "A jury will decide his guilt or innocence."

"Do you think he'll get off?"

"What I think doesn't matter. He'll have his day in court like anybody else."

"How'd you capture him?" a reporter outshouted the others. "Where did you find him?"

"Eureka Springs, Arkansas," Tilghman replied. "I tracked him to a hotel there."

"What was he doing in Eureka Springs?"

"Getting ready to take a bath," Tilghman said with a slow smile. "I believe he felt in need of cleansing."

"Do you favor hanging over life in prison?"

Nix stepped on stage, sensing an opportune moment. "Gentlemen," he said, motioning for silence. "You may quote me as saying Bill Doolin will get a swift and impartial trial. All the evidence will be presented then, and we believe a jury will render the proper verdict."

The door opened and Governor William Renfrow stepped into the room with one of his aides. Everyone fell silent as the governor strode forward, nodding amiably to the reporters. Nix rapidly plucked Doolin off stage, and the aide just as quickly positioned the governor beside Tilghman. The reporters waited expectantly.

"Gentlemen," the governor said in a sonorous voice, "I would first like to commend U.S. Marshal Nix and his intrepid force of deputies for bringing law and order to Oklahoma Territory. None but the brave would have undertaken such a monumental task."

The reporters jotted furiously in their notepads. Governor Renfrow turned to Tilghman. "The bravest of the brave stands beside me here today. For apprehending Bill Doolin," he paused, took a bank check from his suit pocket, "I have the distinct pleasure of presenting Deputy U.S. Marshal William Tilghman with a reward in the amount of five thousand dollars. Our heartfelt congratulations, Deputy Tilghman."

The governor clasped Tilghman's hand, still holding the check, and faced the cameras with a nutcracker grin. The flash pans exploded and shutters clicked, freezing an image of the moment for posterity. A moment later, with his aide clearing the way, Renfrow swept out of the room. Tilghman stood there, holding the check, having never said a word. When Nix began ushering the reporters toward the door, he understood that it was curtain time. The show was over.

Outside again, with Doolin in tow, the deputies regrouped around the buggy. The crowd had diminished in numbers, but fully a thousand people trailed them to the jailhouse. There, grinning and waving his manacled hands, Doolin played to the spectators as he was escorted inside. They roared their approval at his display of grit.

"Doolin! *Doolin!* DOOLIN!"

* * *

Late the next morning Tilghman prepared to leave town. An arraignment had been held earlier, and there was nothing more for him to do until Doolin was brought to trial. He planned to take a few days off and attend to personal matters. High on the list was time alone with Zoe.

After the arraignment, he'd borrowed a horse from Heck Thomas. His horse, which was still stabled in Perry, would have to be retrieved when time allowed. But now, before departing, he had a guard escort him back to the central cell block, where prisoners were allowed to gather during the day. He wanted a last word with the man he'd captured.

Doolin was seated at a table with several other inmates. When Tilghman halted in the corridor, he stood and walked to the bars fronting the bull pen. "Just been thinkin'," he said with a wry smile. "You got yourself a real nice payday with that reward. How you gonna spend it?"

"I'll think of something." Tilghman paused, looking at him through the bars. "Wondered if you'd be interested in talking about the rest of the gang? Might work to your advantage when you come to trial."

"Never kid an old kidder, Tilghman. They're gonna hang me no matter what. We both know it."

"Courts have been known to grant leniency before. You've got nothing to lose by cooperating."

"Yeah, I do," Doolin said firmly. "All my life, I never could stomach a turncoat. Too late to start now."

Tilghman shrugged. "Well, you understand I had to try. Guess it's hard to teach an old dog new tricks."

"On that score, I was always a slow learner."

"I reckon I'll see you in court."

Doolin stuck his hand through the bars. "I owe you one for that day in the bath house. You could've shot me easy as not."

Tilghman accepted his handshake. "I didn't do you any favor. Not if you've ever seen a man hanged."

"Hell, marshal, it's not over till it's over. I take it one day at a time."

Outside the lockup, Tilghman walked back to the front office. As he came through the door, he saw Edith Doolin talking to one of the guards. She looked pale and tired, and he imagined she had driven through the night after hearing of Doolin's arrival in Guthrie. The guard motioned to Tilghman.

"This lady says she's Doolin's wife. You ever seen her before?"

"I'll vouch for the lady," Tilghman told him. "She's Mrs. Edith Doolin."

"Thank you," she said. "After all the trouble I put you to in Kansas, that's nice of you."

"You and your baby get home all right, Mrs. Doolin?"

"Just fine, though all that seems a waste now. You caught Bill anyway, didn't you?"

"Yes, ma'am," Tilghman said, nodding. "Took a while, but things have a way of working out."

"I—" She hesitated, searching for words. "I want to thank you for not killing him. I know you could have, and no questions asked."

"Just doing my job, Mrs. Doolin. No thanks necessary."

Tilghman watched the guard escort her into the hallway. He idly wondered if she knew anything about the remaining members of the Wild Bunch. But then he put the thought aside, for in her own way she was as tough as Doolin. Perhaps tougher.

She would have to watch her husband be hanged.

CHAPTER 37

Tilghman sighted the outline of Chandler late that afternoon. Over the past hour he'd become aware of a steady rise in the temperature, unseasonably hot for September. The air gradually became still and close, without so much as a hint of a breeze. Trees along the roadside stood like statues of leafy stone.

A mile or so from town the land suddenly went dark. Tilghman turned in the saddle, staring off to the southwest, and saw a massive black cloud blotting out the sun. Even as he watched, the cloud spiraled earthward in a whirling funnel and swept northeast across the plains. He knew he'd just seen the birth of a tornado.

The funnel skipped along the earth at an astonishing speed. As it approached, the roar became deafening, and in the next moment, hailstones and torrential rain pelted the ground. Tilghman reined his horse off the road, spurring hard, and galloped into the mouth of a nearby ravine. A short distance ahead, hailstones bouncing around him like white cannonballs, he spotted an outcropping of rock jutting over the gully. He brought his horse to a halt beneath the ledge.

Some moments later, as abruptly as it began, the pounding hailstorm suddenly stopped. Tilghman reined about, gigging his horse, and rode to the top of the ravine. In the distance, he saw the tornado plow into the southern outskirts of Chandler, hurling the debris of flattened houses skyward. Timber and shingles, reduced in an instant to kindling, floated downward across the path of devastation. The funnel churned north through the downtown business district. He urged his horse into a gallop.

On the outskirts of town the destruction was complete. All through the residential area, the tornado had blown off rooftops and then battered the houses to flinders. It seemed another world, somehow demonic, the streets dotted with twisted rubble and cracking flames. Fire from cookstoves had ignited homes, and charred corpses, burned beyond recognition, still smoldered within the wreckage. Survivors clawed through the debris with a look of numbed horror, one of them staring blankly at a dead dog skewered onto a tree branch. The stench of death grew stronger.

An eerie calm, without a whisper of wind, had settled across the land. Ahead, Tilghman saw tendrils of smoke drift skyward, then hang there, suspended over Chandler like a dark shroud. Worse than anything he'd imagined, the funnel had savaged the residential area and then torn a swath along the main road leading into town. The business district had simply disintegrated, transformed by titanic winds into a mass of bricks and glass and timber. Virtually every store on the square had been blown down only to be enveloped in a raging holocaust.

Tilghman slowed his horse to a walk. For a moment he couldn't comprehend the enormity of the devastation, and he had a fleeting image of a world turned topsy-turvy. The top of the hotel had been ripped off, and trees bordering the square had been stripped clean of bark and leaves, standing ghostly white against the brown earth. Only three buildings were undamaged: the mercantile emporium, the hardware store, and a saloon on the far side of the square. Throughout the wreckage, people wandered about in a stupor, their clothes in tatters. It was as though some diabolic force had left behind a blotch of scorched devastation.

A scream attracted Tilghman's attention. On the west side of the square, a bucket brigade had formed outside Wallace's Cafe. The building was engulfed in flame, and he saw men dart into the rubble only to be driven back by a wall of fire. He dismounted, hurrying forward, aware that Jane Wallace, wife of the owner, was being restrained by several women. Her eyes were wide with horror and she screamed hysterically, thrashing to break loose. A line of men desperately passed buckets of water from a pump beside a nearby horse trough.

Malcolm Kinney, the town mayor, and Albert Dale, the county judge, were directing the fire brigade. Tilghman halted beside them as they exhorted the men to work faster. Judge Dale turned to him with a desolate look.

"Bob Wallace," he said in a shaky voice. "He's trapped in there."

Tilghman followed his gaze. The roof on the cafe had collapsed, and the stove in the kitchen had set the building ablaze. Bob Wallace, in an effort to escape, had made it only halfway to the front door. A falling timber, the main beam from the roof, had landed across his legs and pinned him to the floor. He struggled to free himself from the beam.

"It's hopeless," Judge Dale muttered. "We'll never get him out."

Tilghman considered a moment. "What about wetting down a path on a straight line? We might be able to reach him."

"Tried it," Dale said. "Not enough water to douse the fire. A bucket at a time won't do it."

The trapped man screamed from inside the cafe. Flames were all around him, fueled by the jumble of timber from the roof. His hair was singed off and raw blisters covered his face and hands. His eyes were stark with terror.

"Don't lemme burn!" he wailed. "Oh God, please, somebody shoot me! *Shoot me!*"

His wife shrieked his name in a wild cry that racketed across the square. The women holding her tried to turn her away as tongues of flame lapped over her husband. Her head twisted around, fighting the women to look back, and then she fainted. She went limp in their arms.

Judge Dale took Tilghman's arm. "Marshal, I order you to shoot him. I'll take full responsibility."

"No," Tilghman said hollowly. "I can't kill a man in cold blood."

"Don't let him die like that, Bill. I beg you, give him a merciful end."

An instant slipped past. Then Tilghman nodded, his features wreathed in sadness, and walked forward. He pulled his pistol, thumbing the hammer, and stared down the sights. From inside the cafe, his face charred and his clothes afire, the doomed man looked into the bore of the pistol. His expression went from one of agony to desperate hope.

"Do it!" he pleaded in a tortured voice. *"Do it!"*

Tilghman touched the trigger. But even as he squeezed, sighting carefully for a clean shot, the walls of the cafe collapsed. The framework toppled inward, burying the trapped man beneath a roaring pyre of timber. Flames leaped skyward in a blinding inferno.

Forced to retreat, Tilghman lowered his pistol. A faint smell, harsher than woodsmoke but mingled with a sweetish odor drifted from the flames. He recognized it as the stench of burnt flesh, and turned back into the street. The men of the fire brigade moved away, some of them slumping to the ground in exhaustion. Judge Dale nodded to Tilghman with a sorrowful expression.

"Terrible thing," he said quietly. "Bob Wallace was a good man."

"Yeah, he was." Tilghman's voice was raspy. "Wish it had turned out different."

"I appreciate what you tried to do, Bill. Thank God his suffering is over."

Mayor Kinney joined them. "We have to get busy organizing a relief effort. Lots of people lost their homes and everything they owned."

"Not to mention the dead," Judge Dale added. "We'll need volunteers for a burial detail. Bill, would you take over forming—"

Tilghman wasn't listening. His gaze was fixed on the north side of the square, where all the buildings had been demolished. Beyond, the tornado had cut a swath along residential streets and then veered off to the northwest, flattening more houses. A grove of trees at the edge of town stood stripped of leaves.

"Bill?" Judge Dale asked, watching him with concern. "What's wrong?"

"Looks like that twister headed northwest."

"What are you getting at?"

"Quapaw Creek's off in that direction."

Judge Dale suddenly understood. "You're worried about the Strattons. Is that it?"

"I'll see you later, Judge."

Tilghman ran for his horse. He gathered the reins and swung into the saddle. People on the street dodged aside as he spurred from a standing start into a headlong gallop. On the outskirts of town, he turned northwest.

He rode toward Quapaw Creek.

The path of the tornado zigged and zagged across the plains. For all its whirling twists, it was nonetheless easy to follow. A swatch of grass some hundred yards in width had been ripped from the ground.

Shortly before sundown, Tilghman spotted the treeline along Quapaw Creek. The trail of the twister left
much the same sign he'd seen in town. Trees were de-
nuded of leaves and bark, and some had been torn by
their roots from the earth. A cow, its legs stiff in death,
lay sprawled on the prairie.

Tilghman forded the creek a half mile south of the
Stratton ranch. To save time he had cut cross-country,
rather than taking the road. Yet his horse was laboring
for breath, foamed with sweat from the long run. On the
opposite bank, the horse lost its footing, then recovered
as it reached the barren treeline. He slowed the gait to a
steady trot.

When he rode into the compound, Tilghman was
struck by the silence. There was no sound, no one in
sight, simply an empty stillness that pervaded the clearing. Off to the far side, he saw that the barn had been
torn from its foundation and scattered to the winds. But
closer to the road, as though the funnel had zagged at
the last instant, the house was relatively unscathed.
Other than the windows being blown out, it appeared to
be intact.

In the yard, Tilghman leaped from the saddle and hit
the ground running. He left his horse wheezing for air
as he sprinted across the yard and onto the porch. The
front door was hanging open, the windows on either
side of the house imploded in shards of glass. He
stopped in the hallway, listening a moment, straining to
catch any sound. The parlor was empty.

"Zoe!"

"Bill?"

Her voice came from the rear of the house. Tilghman
hurried along the hall as she stepped through a door at
the far end. Her face was smudged with dirt and tears,
and the sleeve of her dress was ripped at the shoulder.
She threw herself into his arms.

"Oh God, Bill!" she cried. "I've never been so happy to see anyone in my life."

"Same here," Tilghman said, holding her wrapped in his arms. "I was afraid you might've been hurt."

"No, I'm fine," she said. "I've been tending to Daddy. He was hit by flying glass."

"How bad?"

"His arm and chest."

She led him into the bedroom. Amos Stratton was bare-chested, stretched out on the bed still clothed in his work pants and boots. His right forearm was bandaged, and a blood-soaked compress was bound tightly across his chest. He managed a weak smile.

"Hello, Bill," he said. "How'd you weather the storm?"

"Not a scratch," Tilghman replied, halting at the foot of the bed. "How are you feeling?"

"Little woozy in the head."

Zoe moved to his side. "We were in the house when the funnel went past. The windows blew out just as he came through the parlor."

"How deep are the cuts?"

"His arm isn't too bad. The cut on his chest is worse, but I got the bleeding stopped. I think he'll be all right."

"Damnedest thing," Stratton said in a fuzzy voice. "That twister was headed for the house and then it spun away. Just blew the barn clean to hell."

"Barns can be rebuilt," Tilghman said. "Where were your horses?"

"Turned 'em loose when I saw it coming. I expect they pulled through."

Stratton lay back on the pillow, suddenly weary. His eyes closed, and a moment later he drifted off to sleep. Zoe checked the compress on his chest, then turned from the bed. She led Tilghman into the hall.

"He's worn out," she said, walking toward the parlor.

"More from worry about me and the horses than anything else."

"I'm just glad you're safe," Tilghman said, putting his arm around her shoulders. "Things could've been a lot worse."

"Where were you when the storm hit?"

"A mile or so out of Chandler."

She saw his features darken. "What happened?"

"Looked like hell on earth." Tilghman paused, shook his head. "Half the town's gone. Blown down or burned down."

"Good Lord," she sighed. "It must have been terrible."

"Yeah." Tilghman had a sudden image of a man trapped beneath fiery rubble. "Hope I never see anything like it again."

"There must be some way to help them. What can we do?"

"You know what I said about your pa's barn?"

"When you told him it could be rebuilt?"

Tilghman nodded. "We'll help them rebuild Chandler."

CHAPTER 38

A week later Tilghman was summoned to Guthrie. The message, sent by express pouch on the stagecoach, ordered him to report to Nix's office on September 20. There was no reason given, and the terse wording left him vaguely uneasy. He wondered what Nix was planning.

Tilghman was reluctant as well to leave Chandler. At the request of the mayor, he had assisted Sheriff Frank Gebke in restoring order to the town. The day after the tornado, special deputies had been sworn in and assigned to patrol the streets. Their primary responsibility was to maintain order in the midst of chaos.

The toll from the storm was worse than anyone had imagined. Fourteen people had been killed and more than eighty had suffered crippling injury. The Presbyterian church had been converted into a hospital, as well as a temporary morgue for the dead. Doctors from nearby towns volunteered their aid, along with donations of medicines and drugs. The dead were buried in services conducted by local ministers.

Aside from human loss, the damage to property was almost beyond reckoning. The downtown business district, for all practical purposes, was a total loss. Merchants salvaged what they could from the wreckage, and resumed business in hastily constructed board shanties. But there was no way to house the vast numbers whose homes had been destroyed by the tornado. Farmers and ranchers offered shelter to many families, and others built temporary shacks on their lots. Their personal effects were buried beneath the rubble.

Under the direction of Harry Gilstrap, editor of the *Chandler News*, a relief committee was formed. The other members of the committee were Will Schlegel, a storekeeper, and Tilghman, whose name was known throughout the territory. Within days, word went out requesting aid and hundreds of wagons began rolling into town from as far away as Guthrie and Oklahoma City. The raw essentials for survival were needed, and there was an outpouring of donations from other communities. The wagons were loaded with food provisions, bedding, and everyday clothing for the newly destitute of Chandler.

Three days after the storm, Zoe began working with the relief effort. Her father was well enough to fend for himself, and she moved into one of the undamaged rooms on the ground floor of the hotel. A warehouse near the sawmill that had escaped destruction served as headquarters for the storage of relief goods. There, working with other volunteers, she handled the distribution of food and clothing to the needy. The work was demanding, with long hours, but Zoe went at it with energetic cheerfulness and a natural talent for organization. By the end of the week, she was practically running the operation.

After receiving the message for Nix, Tilghman went by the warehouse. He found Zoe supervising a group of women volunteers who were parceling out food at one counter and clothing at another to families who had been devastated by the storm. Waiting until she could break free, he stood off to one side, admiring the way she deftly kept the operation moving. Finally, when the lines began to thin out, she came around the counter. Her dress was soiled from the dusty warehouse and her hair had come unpinned on one side.

"Whew!" she said, blowing a lock of hair off her forehead. "I must look a sight."

Tilghman grinned. "You look pretty good to me. I wouldn't change a thing."

"Why, thank you, sir." She smiled engagingly. "You know how to make a girl's day."

"How are things going?"

"Oh, the usual misery and heartbreak. All these unfortunate people with their lives turned upside down. I just don't know how they bear it."

"You forget," Tilghman said. "These are the folks that pioneered the territory. They're not quitters."

"Yes, you're right." She glanced back at a woman with two small children. "I just hope our supplies hold out."

"Don't worry yourself about that. We got word there's another shipment on the way from Oklahoma City."

"Well, that is good news! Was that what you came to tell me?"

"Not exactly," Tilghman said with a sudden frown. "I've been called to Guthrie. I'll have to leave this afternoon."

She searched his face. "Do you know what it's about?"

"Nix didn't say in his message. I'll find out when I get there."

"Then why do you look so glum?"

"Shows that much, huh?" Tilghman was silent a moment, then shrugged. "Guess I've gotten used to being around you the last week. I'm not keen on leaving."

Her eyes sparkled with laughter. "Will you miss me a little bit?"

"Yeah, I will, and that got me to thinking. Doolin's scheduled to stand trial late next month."

"I somehow missed the connection. What does that have to do with your leaving today?"

"Well, don't you see—" Tilghman knuckled his mustache, clearly fumbling for words. "Fact of the matter is, Doolin's caught and he'll likely swing before Christmas. So there's nothin' to stop us from getting married."

"Yes!" she burst out. "That was the only reason you wanted to delay. And now, there is no reason!"

"Not so far as I'm concerned."

"Oh, aren't you a sweetheart! You didn't come here to talk about a trip to Guthrie. You're here to talk about our wedding—aren't you?"

Tilghman ducked his head, and she sensed that he was somehow embarrassed. Whatever he was feeling, he found it difficult to put into words. He motioned with an offhand gesture. "I'm not much on plannin' such things. You just tell me when and where, and I'll be there."

She laughed. "You knew I planned on a church wedding—didn't you?"

"Figured as much."

"And that's all right?"

"I've got no objections." Tilghman looked at her with a wry smile. "Leastways if the parson doesn't carry on too long. Never could stand a windy preacher."

She knew they were past his moment of discomfort. He was now teasing her, and she was perfectly willing to play along. "I'll speak to the minister," she said. "A short ceremony without the hearts and flowers."

Tilghman chuckled, aware that she was gently mocking him. "Think you've got my number, don't you?"

"Why, mercy sakes, whatever gave you that idea?"

She walked him to the door of the warehouse. Several people on their way inside snickered when she stood on tip-toe and gave him a kiss. She then waved gaily and went back to work.

Tilghman thought she was the sauciest woman he'd

ever met. A kiss in broad daylight would be the talk of
the town.

Early the next morning Tilghman, Thomas, and Madsen
trooped into the Herriott Building. Like Tilghman,
Madsen had been summoned from El Reno by a cryptic
message. The three of them had spent a good deal of
time speculating on the reason for the meeting. But
nothing of any great import had occurred to them, particularly now that Doolin was in custody. They were still
in the dark when they walked into the office.

Nix greeted them with a bonhomie normally reserved
for close friends. He was positively chipper, shaking
their hands with warmth, as though delighted by their
company. Finally, after he got them seated, he took the
chair behind his desk. He made a grand motion with a
sweep of his arm.

"Gentlemen, let me first extend my thanks for a job
well done. You three deserve credit for devotion to the
law that is truly above and beyond the call of duty. You
have my utmost admiration."

The sentiment, as well as his grandiloquence, took
them by surprise. His unusually jovial manner lent even
greater mystery to the occasion. They stared back at him
with slight smiles, thoroughly baffled.

Nix fairly beamed. "I brought you here for a most
momentous occasion." He paused for dramatic effect.
"Today, I am announcing my resignation as U.S. marshal."

The three lawmen blinked in unison. Whatever else
they suspicioned, his resignation would not have made
the list. Their bafflement of a moment before had now
turned to dumbfounded astonishment. After a moment
of profound silence, Thomas was the first to recover his
wits. He shook his head.

"Why the devil would you resign?"

"For the best of all reasons," Nix said, striking a pose.

"Doolin will shortly walk the gallows and the Wild Bunch is but a distant memory. My job is done."

"Have to say," Thomas admitted, "you caught me off guard. I figured you'd stay on till there was another political shake-up."

"Timing is everything," Nix replied. "You gentlemen have afforded me the opportunity of exiting on a high note. I couldn't have asked for more."

Tilghman thought there was some honesty in the statement. With Doolin captured, all the glory had been reaped from the office of U.S. marshal. Nix was probably moving on to bigger things, with a reputation as the man who had brought law and order to Oklahoma Territory. He gave Nix an inquiring look.

"Who's been picked as your replacement?"

"Patrick Nagle," Nix said. "One of the finest legal minds in the territory. He's from Kingfisher."

"A lawyer?" Tilghman asked.

"A brilliant lawyer," Nix amended. "I gave my personal endorsement to his appointment."

"From the sound of it," Thomas said dryly, "I take it we can assume he's a Democrat."

"His politics are immaterial," Nix insisted. "Pat Nagle is a man of great integrity and high moral standards. You gentlemen are fortunate to have someone of his caliber in this post."

The three of them were of the same mind. Though unspoken, they realized that it was a matter of politics as usual. The job had gone to a man with all the right connections, and worse, to a lawyer. Based on long experience in courtrooms, none of them held lawyers in high esteem.

For Chris Madsen, who had listened quietly, the appointment forced him to a decision. "I am resigning too," he said abruptly. "Effective today."

"Hold on, Chris," Tilghman protested. "No need for

hasty decisions just because he's a lawyer. Let's give him a chance."

"Not a hasty decision," Madsen told him. "I've been offered the job of chief deputy of the Western District of Missouri. I was leaning toward taking the job, anyway. Today just decided it for me."

Tilghman and Thomas immediately grasped the reason behind his decision. General Joseph Shelby, one of the famed Confederate commanders during the Civil War, was the U.S. marshal of the western district. Madsen, a former soldier himself, would be working for a military man of the first order. Which was far preferable to working for an unknown lawyer with political connections.

"Hell's bells, Chris," Thomas muttered. "The three of us make a damn good team. Hate to see you break it up."

"An excellent point," Nix chimed in, hoping to salvage the situation. "You're the Three Guardsmen, the greatest manhunters ever! You should really reconsider all this, Chris."

"No, my mind's made up," Madsen said, glancing at Tilghman and Thomas. "We were a good team, and I'll miss working with you fellows. But it's the right decision for me."

"Look, Chris," Nix said quickly. "Pat Nagle's waiting in the governor's office right now. At least meet him before you make such a rash decision."

"No need." Madsen stood, unpinning his badge, and dropping it on the desk. "I'd rather leave before he gets here."

He gave Nix a perfunctory handshake. Then, one at a time, he clasped the hands of Tilghman and Thomas in a strong grip. Their parting was short and without sentiment, for their comradeship went beyond mere words. Without saying it, each man knew he could count on the other whenever the need might arise. Madsen went out the door without looking back.

After that, Nix moved things along swiftly. His wholesale grocery business was flourishing, and there were political opportunities on the horizon. Earlier, he'd briefed Nagle on the duties of the office, and he saw no reason to delay in the transition of power. Nor was there any reason to delay his own departure.

Excusing himself, Nix walked up to the governor's office. A few minutes later he returned with the newly appointed U.S. marshal. He performed the introductions, lavishing praise on Tilghman and Thomas, and quickly explained Madsen's abrupt resignation. Then, with a chipper farewell, he left his successor to take charge.

There was a moment of awkward silence as the door closed. Patrick Nagle was young, not yet thirty, with thick glasses and the somber manner of a professor. He was clearly uncomfortable staring across the desk at seasoned lawmen who were both older and far more experienced. Finally, nudging the glasses higher on the bridge of his nose, he attempted a confident smile.

"I'm very pleased that you gentlemen have elected to stay on. You are doubtless aware that I have no background in law enforcement, or in matters pertaining to criminals. So I will rely heavily on your advice and counsel."

"No problem there," Thomas said. "You probably already know that Nix gave Bill and me lots of leeway. We work at our own speed, and we don't always follow the rules. But we generally get the job done."

"Your record speaks for itself," Nagle observed. "With Doolin and the Wild Bunch under control, the situation appears fairly stable. How would you recommend we proceed?"

"There's some unfinished business," Tilghman informed him. "We started out to break the Wild Bunch to the last man. Clifton, West, and Waightman are still on the loose."

"Just so you understand," Thomas added. "Our main assignment was to bring down the Wild Bunch. We'd like to keep it that way."

"By all means," Nagle said agreeably. "We have adequate marshals to attend to other matters. You men are entitled to finish what you started."

"In that case," Thomas said, "we're gonna get along just fine. One way or another, we'll bring those murderin' bastards to justice."

"Gentlemen, you have my full support. Keep me advised of your progress."

After another round of handshakes, the lawmen walked from the office. Neither of them said anything on the way downstairs, seemingly lost in thought. On the street, Tilghman finally broke the silence.

"Not much like Nix, is he?"

"Amen to that," Thomas said. "So what d'you think?"

"Heck, I think we can write our own ticket. He'll go along to get along."

"By God, maybe we finally got ourselves a smart one."

They strolled off congratulating themselves on their new boss.

CHAPTER 39

A town began to emerge from the rubble. Under the constant din of hammering and sawing the framework of buildings began to take shape. Brickmasons were imported to rebuild the bank and start work at last on the county courthouse. The people of Chandler set about putting their lives in order.

Zoe stayed busy at the warehouse. Yet the number of families in need of food and clothing had gradually dwindled off. There was an independent streak about the townspeople, some vestige of the pioneer spirit that had brought them west. Nearly two weeks had passed since the tornado, and most thought that too long to accept charity. They got back to fending for themselves.

Evenings were for Zoe the best time. Tilghman joined her for supper at the hotel dining room, which had returned to full operation. Then they strolled around the square, filled with pride and amazement as the new town rapidly took shape. By now, they were a common sight on their nightly walks, and people greeted them with a mixture of warmth and respect. Everyone in town knew of their selfless efforts in the aftermath of the storm.

Tonight, they paused to admire construction on the bank. The first floor was almost completed, the smell of fresh mortar strong in the still air. After a moment, arm in arm, they strolled on toward the corner. Tilghman was unusually quiet, and Zoe sensed that his thoughts were elsewhere. For the last three days, since his return from Guthrie, she'd known he was wrestling with some inner quandary. To her, his moods were by now an open book.

"Something wrong?" she asked, aware that he might never speak unless prompted. "You're awfully quiet to-night."

Tilghman nodded vaguely. "Just thoughtful, that's all."

"Are you concerned about the rest of the Wild Bunch?"

"No more so than usual. We'll turn up a lead sooner or later."

"Well, something is bothering you." She gave him a long look of appraisal. "You haven't been yourself since you met with—what's his name?—Nagle."

"Not that," Tilghman said. "Nagle's the least of my worries. He won't be any problem."

"So what is it, then? You might as well tell me. I eventually worm it out of you anyway."

"Some things are hard to put into words. Guess it's got to do with the town, and the people. What they lost."

"Their homes and businesses, all that?"

Tilghman shook his head. "I was thinking more of their personal loss. Folks like Jane Wallace."

She glanced at him. "Are you talking about the loss of her husband?"

"Yeah, I am."

Zoe had heard the story from women at the ware-house. She shuddered inwardly, remembering their description of the cafe owner trapped beneath fiery timbers. She recalled as well the awe in their voices, their admiration, when they spoke of Tilghman. Everyone respected him for his attempt to save a man from being burned alive, even though he had never fired the shot. They thought such an act of mercy required a special brand of courage.

Tilghman had never spoken to her of the incident. She knew, after listening to the women, that he'd been dragooned into it by Judge Dale. But only after first refusing, and then with great reluctance, agreeing after it became apparent that the trapped man was doomed. She considered the courage part of his character, the willingness to act when others flinched from the task. Still, reflecting on it now, she wondered what the personal toll had been for him. Perhaps he was trying to tell her something.

"Bill?" she said at length. "Do you blame yourself for the way he died? For not shooting sooner?"

Tilghman was silent as they crossed the street to the opposite corner. Finally, not looking at her, he shrugged. "Maybe I was too concerned with a clean shot. But the walls collapsed and the chance was gone. I don't fault myself for that."

"So it wasn't him so much as his wife. You're talking about *her* loss."

"The last couple of days it put me to thinking that it doesn't matter how a woman loses her husband. She grieves the same no matter how it happens."

"I don't understand," she said in a bemused tone. "Are you talking about Jane Wallace, or someone else?"

"Someone else." Tilghman hesitated, then went on. "I've been wondering about Doolin's wife."

"What about her?"

"Doolin's sure to hang. She'll likely suffer more than he does. Lots longer, too."

Zoe looked at him in surprise. "You're worrying about Edith Doolin, aren't you?"

"Not worrying," Tilghman said uncomfortably. "Just

that she'll be a young widow with a boy to raise. That's a heavy load."

"I see," she said with sudden dawning. "So you plan to help her in some way. Is that it?"

"Figured I might," Tilghman admitted. "Thought I'd give her part of the reward money. Half of it was hers, anyway."

"How could it be?"

"Doolin was wearin' a money belt when I captured him. Had a little better than twenty-five hundred in cash. I turned it over to the office."

"Yes, but that was stolen money, wasn't it?"

"I suppose most folks would say so."

Zoe smiled. "You just want to help her, don't you?"

"That's the problem," Tilghman said, frowning. "I've been studying on a way to pull it off."

"What do you mean?"

"Some way she won't know it came from me. She might look on it as blood money . . . from the reward."

Zoe felt a lump in her throat. She thought it was so like him to take a practical approach to a compassionate act. He wanted no credit, no recognition, no thanks. He was concerned instead with Edith Doolin.

"Why do I get the feeling," she said lightly, "that you're asking for volunteers?"

Tilghman avoided her eyes. "Well, you're due a break from the warehouse. Thought you might be willin' to lend me a hand."

"In other words, you want me to give her the money."

"Figured you could just tell her it came from a friend."

"How do I find her?"

"I'll take you." Tilghman hesitated, cleared his throat. " 'Course, it'll take a couple of days by buckboard. Your pa's liable not to be too happy with that."

"Let me handle him," she said brightly. "We are betrothed, and you have no designs on my virtue . . . do you?"

Tilghman grinned. "None that I can't control."

"What a shame." She laughed, hugged his arm. "Will we be camping out along the way?"

"Tell your pa I'll bring separate bedrolls."

"Omigosh! I can't wait till he hears that!"

On the west side of the square, they turned back toward the hotel. She looked up at the sky and wondered what it would be like to camp with him under starlight. Not the same as being married and snug together in their own bed. Still, she told herself, it was a start.

Two bedrolls were better than nothing.

Tilghman halted the buckboard on the outskirts of Lawson. The trip had taken a day and a night, and he'd timed it to arrive early the second morning. He handed Zoe the reins, then moved to the rear of the buckboard, where his horse was hitched. He planned to wait while she called on Edith Doolin.

"All set?" he said, returning with his horse. "You remember how to find the house?"

"Stop worrying," she said, a glint of amusement in her eyes. "Your instructions were quite clear. I'm sure I'll have no problem."

"Just give her the money and leave. Don't let her get you into a conversation."

"Honestly, Bill, you've told me a dozen times. I know what to do."

She gave him a quick kiss, and drove off. Last night, camped beside a creek, he had behaved like a perfect gentleman. She'd been ambivalent then, and still had mixed emotions, for she wanted him as much as he wanted her. But she had no ambivalence, no reservations whatever about today's mission. She thought of it as a pleasant conspiracy, their own little secret.

Some minutes later Zoe reined up before the house. She stepped down, securing the horse to a hitching post, and proceeded along the pathway. On the front porch, she quickly checked her gaily feathered hat, then knocked on the door. The woman who opened it was her own age, though shorter and plumper. Zoe nodded with an engaging smile.

"May I speak with Mrs. Edith Doolin?"

"I'm Edith Doolin."

"I wonder if we might have a word in private?"

"Who are you?"

"A friend, Mrs. Doolin. My name is Zoe Stratton."

Edith Doolin hesitated a moment, then held the door open. Zoe entered, moving into the parlor as an older woman came out of the kitchen. After closing the door, the girl motioned Zoe toward a sofa. Then she looked at the older woman.

"It's all right, mama," she said in a dull voice. "Would you check on the baby for me? He probably needs changing."

She turned back to the parlor. Zoe noticed that she had dark smudges under her eyes as if she had not slept well, and there was a haunted, fearful cast to her features. She gave Zoe a veiled look.

"What can I do for you, Miss—Mrs.?—Stratton?"

"Miss," Zoe clarified. "Won't you call me Zoe? And may I call you Edith? I feel like I know you already."

Edith seemed disarmed by her open manner. She took a seat beside Zoe on the sofa. "How is it you know about me?"

"A mutual friend asked me to call on you."

"What for?"

Zoe took an envelope from her purse. "I was asked to give you this."

Edith accepted the envelope. She opened the flap and her mouth ovaled with a sharp intake of breath. After a moment, she riffled through the stack of greenbacks.

"God," she said softly, glancing at Zoe. "That's a lot of money."

"Twenty-five hundred dollars."

"Who's it from?"

Zoe smiled. "An anonymous friend."

"Anonymous?" Edith repeated, as though testing the word. "Someone who doesn't want their name known?"

"Yes, that's right."

"Well, it wouldn't be too hard to guess. It's from one of Bill's men, isn't it? Clifton or West."

Zoe realized she was being drawn into conversation. Her instructions were to deliver the money and leave. Yet she couldn't bring herself to allow a false impression. "I'm sorry," she said with some conviction. "The money isn't from any of your husband's men."

Edith tilted her head. "Who's it from, then?"

"I really wish I could tell you. But the donor wants to remain anonymous."

"What do you mean *donor*? Is this some kind of charity?"

"No, no," Zoe said quickly. "It's a gift from someone who has your best interests at heart. A gift for you and your son."

Edith studied her a moment. "Where are you from?"

"What difference does that make?"

"Are you afraid to tell me for some reason?"

"Chandler," Zoe said, not willing to lie. "I live outside Chandler with my father."

Edith sat straighter, staring at her. "The marshal that caught Bill—the one named Tilghman—he's from Chandler, isn't he?"

"What makes you think that?"

"Stop treating me like a fool! I read it in one of those newspaper stories. He's from Chandler, isn't he?"

"Yes, I believe he is," Zoe said evasively. "But what does that have to do with anything?"

"I get it now." Edith's voice sounded brittle. "My husband's going to hang and Tilghman's feeling guilty about the reward." Her gaze dropped to the money in her lap. "This is half the reward, isn't it?"

"Edith, listen to me," Zoe said earnestly. "Your husband had that exact amount on him when he was captured. Marshal Tilghman just thought you should have it, that's all. He feels compassion for you, not guilt."

"Who are you, anyway? What's Tilghman to you?"

"I—" Zoe hesitated, unable to avoid the truth. "I'm engaged to him. We're going to be married."

"I met him," Edith said distantly. "When I went to the jail at Guthrie, he was there. I thanked him for not killing Bill."

"Funny that both of our men are named Bill. We have something in common."

"I suppose you could look at it that way. Do you think I ought to keep this money?"

"Of course you should," Zoe said firmly. "If not for yourself, then for your boy. Your husband would want you to have it."

"Maybe he would." Edith smiled wanly. "When you see your Bill, thank him for me. You've got yourself a good man."

On the way out, Zoe saw the older woman standing in the hall. She assumed the woman had been listening to their conversation. At the door, she impulsively kissed Edith Doolin on the cheek. Tears welled up in their eyes, but neither of them could say anything. She hurried toward the buckboard.

A few minutes later, at the edge of town, she saw Tilghman waiting by the roadside. Her first inclination was to tell him nothing of the conversation that had taken place. But then she thought it only right that he hear everything said by the woman he'd helped.

Edith Doolin would want him to know.

CHAPTER 40

The train chuffed to a halt outside the Guthrie depot. Thomas stepped through the rear door of the last passenger coach, and stopped on the observation platform. He watched as passengers hurried off the train, and those headed north waited to board. His eyes scanned the stationhouse for any sign of reporters.

After a moment, he turned back to the coach and motioned an all-clear signal. Tilghman herded their prisoner through the door, pausing on the observation platform. Dynamite Dick Clifton was bearded, hat pulled low over his forehead, his hands manacled. A short man, wiry in build, his clothes were dirty and wrinkled, and he smelled. He looked like a vagabond in chains.

Thomas led the way to the north end of the depot. Clifton followed close behind, with Tilghman bringing up the rear. Unless someone looked closely, it would have been difficult to identify the man in the middle as a prisoner. A buggy, arranged by telegram earlier, waited for them on the street. The driver was a town deputy who had no idea as to why he was there. Clifton was assisted into the rear seat, positioned between Tilghman and Thomas. They drove toward the jailhouse.

Earlier in the week Clifton had been apprehended in

Paris, Texas. The town was some twenty miles south of the Nations, and Clifton was using the alias Dan Wiley. Arrested for drunk and disorderly, he was quickly identified by local police from wanted posters. Federal marshals in the Eastern District of Texas were notified, and they in turn wired Patrick Nagle, U.S. marshal for Oklahoma Territory. A day later, on October 17, Nagle met with Tilghman and Thomas.

A murder warrant was outstanding on Clifton, and the marshals were ordered to hop a train to Texas. Before leaving, they persuaded Nagle to delay any announcement to the public or the press until Clifton was safely behind bars in Guthrie. Their argument, which Nagle accepted, was to avoid a repeat of the circus atmosphere surrounding Doolin's capture. The following day, after presenting the murder warrant in Texas, Clifton was surrendered into their custody. Late that afternoon, they boarded a train bound for Oklahoma Territory.

On the train, Tilghman and Thomas took turns grilling the prisoner. They were seated at the rear of the coach, with empty seats around them, and no one to overhear the interrogation. Alternating shifts, one sleeping while the other asked questions, they kept Clifton awake throughout the night. At first, he denied any knowledge as to the whereabouts of the last two members of the Wild Bunch, Dick West and Red Buck Waightman. But as the night wore on, the relentless grilling left him in an exhausted state. He eventually admitted that the gang had gone their separate ways, and the last he'd heard, West and Waightman were somewhere in the Nations. Toward dawn, he was finally permitted to sleep.

Today, approaching the jailhouse, Tilghman was not encouraged. The information on West and Waightman was a month old, and they might have skipped the territory by now. His thoughts turned instead to the upcoming elections in Lincoln County, scheduled for November 4.

A week ago, at the ranch, he had been offered the job of sheriff by Judge Albert Dale and Mayor Malcolm Kinney. If he accepted, they promised their support, which virtually guaranteed he would win. After talking it over with Zoe, he decided that it was time he began thinking about their future. As sheriff, he would be home every night rather than tracking outlaws through-out the Nations. There was much to be said for that when a man was contemplating marriage, not to mention his expansion plans for the ranch. Before leaving Chandler, he had informed Dale and Kinney that he would run for sheriff.

But with the urgency of the trip to Texas, he had de-layed saying anything to Patrick Nagle. After jailing Clifton, he knew he could delay no longer in breaking the news. He would have to meet with Nagle, and advise him of his decision. He planned to resign his federal commission, effective November 1.

Upon entering the jailhouse, Tilghman and Thomas surrendered their prisoner to the chief jailor. Clifton's manacles were removed, and his arrival was duly noted in the log book. A guard then led them along a corridor to the steel door fronting the cell block. To the left of the door, a row of metal bars rose from floor to ceiling and extended to the far wall. Directly inside was a large bull pen, where prisoners were allowed freedom from their cells in the daytime. At the rear of the cell block, built one atop the other, were two tiers of barred cages, with stairs leading to the upper tier. After the evening meal, the prisoners were locked in their cells for the night.

Doolin was seated at a table in the bull pen, playing checkers with another inmate. For the most part, the prisoners were a motley collection of whiskey smugglers and bandits who preyed on backcountry stagecoaches.

To them, Doolin was a celebrity, leader of the Wild Bunch and a man who had achieved national notoriety. They accorded him the respect due an outlaw whose picture had made the front page of the *Police Gazette*. One of them interrupted the checkers game, directing his attention to the door.

Clifton stepped into the bull pen as the door slammed shut. Doolin rose from the table, moving forward with a sorrowful look. He clasped Clifton's hand in a firm grip. "Too bad, Dick," he said with genuine concern. "I figured you'd got away for good."

"Yeah, me too," Clifton grumped. "Bastards caught me across the line in Texas."

"Hold on a minute. I want a word with Tilghman."

Doolin walked to the front of the bull pen. He stopped at the bars, ignoring Thomas and nodding to Tilghman. "How's tricks?" he said amiably. "Got a line on the rest of my boys?"

"Only a matter of time," Tilghman observed. "They're not bright enough to beat the law."

"You never know." Doolin paused, lowered his voice. "My wife was by to visit last week. I'm obliged for the way you treated her."

Tilghman sensed that the statement was purposely cryptic. With Thomas listening, there would be no direct mention of the money he'd sent to Edith Doolin. "No thanks necessary," he said. "Your wife strikes me as a good woman. She deserves whatever luck comes her way."

"For a lawdog, you're all right." Doolin flicked a glance at Thomas. "Not like some buttholes I could mention."

Thomas bristled. "You smart-aleck sonovabitch. I'm gonna dance on your grave after you're hung."

Tilghman moved between them. The last week in October he and Thomas were scheduled to testify at Doolin's trial. The charges were cut and dried, with an

army of witnesses, and the verdict would result in a
death sentence. Doolin's fate was sealed, and he saw no
reason to push the matter further.

"C'mon, Heck," he said forcefully. "Let's get out of
here. We've finished our business."

Thomas seared the outlaw with a look. Then, muttering a curse, he strode off along the corridor. Tilghman
followed him out, trailed by the guard. Doolin waited
until they were gone before turning back into the bull
pen. He clapped an arm over Dick Clifton's shoulders.

"Don't look so down at the mouth, sport."

Clifton grunted. "Why the hell not? They're gonna
string me up alongside you."

"Trust me," Doolin said in a conspiratorial tone. "It'll
never get that far."

"What's that supposed to mean?"

"Dick, if you had to pick a day to get caught, you
couldn't have done better. You played into luck."

"Quit talkin' riddles, will you?"

Doolin walked him off to one side. "How'd you like
to bust out of here?"

"What?" Clifton gaped at him. "You figgered a way
to escape?"

"Took a while, but it's all set. Tonight's the night."

"Tonight?"

"You lucky dog. You got here just in time."

Doolin, ever the strategist, laid out the plan.

In the evening, after supper was finished, the dirty
dishes were collected. Inmates were required to stack
their dishes in an open cart, which was mounted on
wheels. While three armed guards watched, one of the
prisoners rolled the cart to the door where it was taken
by a fourth guard. The door was then closed and locked.

After supper, the prisoners were allowed the freedom
of the bull pen. Some played checkers or dominoes,
while others lounged around, talking of better days.

There were thirty-five inmates, only a few of them hardened criminals, and they were permitted to stay in the bull pen until eight o'clock. Four men to a cell, they were then locked up for the night.

There was seldom any official activity during the night hours. Shortly after supper, the chief jailor and the daytime guards were relieved of their duties. The night guards, a skeleton staff of two men, then assumed responsibility for the jail. The head guard at night, Jack Tull, was a man of few words and cold nerves. He was assisted by Joe Miller, one of the youngest guards on the staff.

A few minutes before eight Tull halted outside the bars. "Awright, boys," he rumbled in a sing-song voice. "Time for bed."

The prisoners slowly stood, grumbling among themselves, resigned to the nightly routine. Doolin and Clifton, absorbed in a game of checkers, remained seated at the table nearest the door. George Lane, a burly whiskey smuggler, ambled toward the bars with a tin cup. Outside the bars, to the left of the door, was a water bucket on a wooden stand. Inmates were allowed to take a cup of water to their cells for the night.

Tull, the key in hand, waited at the steel door. Following regulations, which permitted no armed guards in the cell block, Miller unholstered his pistol and placed it in a box mounted on the wall. Watching him, Tull turned, unlocking the door, and swung it open. Miller entered the bull pen with a master key for the cells, motioning the prisoners toward the tiered cages. His job was to lock them away.

Lane, who was reaching through the bars for the water bucket, dropped his cup just as Tull began to close the door. The cup bounced off the floor with a metallic clang, and Tull looked down, momentarily distracted. In the instant his eyes were on the floor, Lane lowered his shoulder and charged the half-open door. The impact drove the heavy steel door into Tull's face, smashing his nose. He staggered backward, dazed, blood pouring out of his nostrils.

On cue, Doolin spun out of his chair and raced for the door. Clifton and another prisoner jumped Miller, hitting him high and low, and took him to the floor. Lane hurtled through the door, grabbing Tull in an iron bear hug, and pinned his arms to his sides. Only a beat behind, Doolin stepped through the door and snatched Tull's pistol from the holster. With no hesitation, he moved to the box on the wall and grabbed Miller's pistol. He turned with a gun in either hand.

"Well now!" he said, grinning broadly. "How's that for teamwork?"

Tull, still struggling to break free from Lane's grip, glowered at him. Clifton climbed to his feet, the master key in his hand, while other inmates hauled Miller off the floor. The majority of the prisoners, stunned by the flurry of action, crowded together along the rear of the bull pen. Doolin motioned with his pistols.

"You boys know the drill. Let's get to it!"

Lane wrestled Tull to the door and hurled him into the bull pen. Under Clifton's direction, several prisoners collared Tull while others manhandled Miller, and marched them to cells on the lower tier. There, Clifton locked the guards into separate cells and hurried toward the door, still carrying the master key. When he stepped out of the bull pen, Doolin handed him one of the pistols. With Lane at their side, they faced the other inmates.

"Here's the story," Doolin called out. "Anybody that wants to run has five seconds to get moving. After that, I lock the door."

There was a rush as ten prisoners crowded through the door. The others, now reduced to twenty-two in number, remained where they were. Doolin slammed the door, locking it, and stuck the key in his pocket. He nodded to Clifton, then led the way along the corridor to the empty front office. The prisoners followed him across the room and abruptly jarred to a halt as he stopped at the street door. Before anyone could react, he and Clifton suddenly turned on them with pistols leveled.

"Listen close," Doolin said with an ominous smile. "You boys are gonna give me and Dick a five-minute head start. Anybody pokes his head out this door beforehand is liable to get it shot off."

"Like hell!" Lane bellowed. "You and me worked all this out before Clifton ever showed up. You're not leavin' me behind."

"Count your blessings, George." Doolin gave him a hard stare. "I sprung you and the rest of these boys, and you're free to run. Try to follow me and I'll kill you."

None of the prisoners, Lane included, doubted his word. While Clifton kept them covered, Doolin cracked the door open and peeked outside. The street was deserted for a block in either direction; farther downtown he saw the usual evening traffic. He stepped through the door, followed closely by Clifton. They walked west along Second Street.

Doolin's original plan had been to jump the evening freight train. Every night shortly after being locked in his cell, he'd heard the whistle as the train rolled through Guthrie. But as they approached the rail yards, he made a spur of the moment decision. George Lane, who'd been his new partner until Clifton appeared, was aware of the plan. Should Lane be caught, there was no question that he would betray them. His decision was influenced as well by unexpected opportunity.

Ahead, Doolin saw a buggy slow for the Second Street rail crossing. There was no one else about, and he quickly explained the new plan to Clifton. They separated, Doolin moving to the other side of the street, and approached from opposite directions. As the buggy cleared the rail crossing, Clifton scurried forward and grabbed the horse's bridle. The driver hauled back on the reins, and the woman beside him uttered a startled shriek. Doolin stuck a cocked pistol in the driver's face.

"Keep quiet and you won't get hurt. Climb down out of there."

The man obeyed with alacrity, and the woman, her eyes filled with terror, clambered out the other side. Doolin took the reins, hefting himself into the driver's seat, and waited for Clifton to scramble aboard. Lowering the hammer on his pistol, he stuffed it into his waistband and reined onto the road beside the railroad tracks. The man and the woman heard the reins pop, and the horse broke into a run. The buggy rattled south out of town.

"Shoulda shot 'em," Clifton muttered. "They'll hightail it to the law."

"Don't matter," Doolin told him. "First farm we spot, we'll steal ourselves some horses."

"You aim to head for the Nations?"

"Straight as a string."

"Then what?"

"Dunno yet. I'm thinkin' on it."

They drove on into the night.

CHAPTER 41

The press treated Doolin's escape with more sensationalism than had been devoted to his capture. The chief jailor, along with guards Jack Tull and Joe Miller, were crucified in front-page articles. Doolin was portrayed as a mastermind who had engineered a daring getaway.

Patrick Nagle emerged relatively unscathed. On the job less than a month, his performance as U.S. marshal drew little criticism from the newspapers. Yet enormous pressure was brought to bear by Governor Renfrow personally, and by way of stinging telegrams from the attorney general in Washington. Additional rewards were posted, and Nagle was ordered to find and kill the remaining members of the Wild Bunch. Failure would not be tolerated.

Nagle had anticipated the firestorm. On the night of the breakout, he had summoned Tilghman and Thomas to his office. In total, thirteen prisoners had escaped, and he sought their counsel in organizing a manhunt. Federal marshals, working with county sheriffs, were ordered into the field. By late the following morning, squads of lawmen were raiding known outlaw haunts throughout the territory. The heaviest concentration of peace officers was positioned along the border with the

Nations. There was general consensus that Doolin and
Clifton would make a run for their old sanctuary.

Tilghman and Thomas spent a full day interrogating
witnesses around Guthrie. Their first session was with
the couple whose buggy had been stolen at gunpoint the
previous night. From the description, the lawmen felt
reasonably certain that the thieves were Doolin and
Clifton. But then, late that morning, George Lane and
three other inmates were returned to jail after being
caught near the railroad tracks outside town. Lane, who
was furious at Doolin, readily agreed to cooperate. The
story he told merely muddied the waters.

According to Lane, Doolin had planned to hop the
southbound freight train the night before. Yet that in no
way gibed with the theft of the buggy just minutes before the train passed through Guthrie. The lawmen
hardly thought Doolin would attempt flight in a buggy,
which confined travel to roads and could be easily spotted. They were left to ponder if he'd ditched the buggy
and hopped the train somewhere south of town. That
seemed the more likely prospect.

Wires went out alerting officers at stops along the
train line. But then, shortly after the noon hour, a
farmer added a new twist to the manhunt. His farm was
three miles south of Guthrie, and he reported that two
saddle horses had been stolen from the barn sometime
during the night. Further, the thieves had left behind a
buggy and horse, found not far down the road from the
farmhouse. The farmer, who fancied himself a deer
hunter, had tracked the horses east from the barn. He'd
lost the trail where it crossed a wilderness stream.

For Tilghman and Thomas, the farmer's story removed all doubt. It was now apparent that Doolin, fearing Lane would be captured and talk, had hastily
improvised a new plan. The stolen buggy had been
dumped, and the fugitives had switched to saddle
mounts capable of traveling overland. There was no

question in the lawmen's minds that their first hunch had been dead on the mark. Doolin and Clifton were headed on a beeline for the safety of the Nations. With a head start of some sixteen hours, the outcome seemed a foregone conclusion. They had probably already crossed into Indian Territory.

Thomas was all for a manhunt centered on the Nations. He wanted to alert his informants and put the backwoods grapevine to work. But Tilghman had been down that road several times over the last year. Though they had caught gang members in the Nations, they had never once gotten a lead on Doolin. To the contrary, he argued, Doolin was a will-o'-the-wisp who left no trail. Instead, virtually every time, the outlaw leader had doubled back, usually picking a hideout far removed from other members of the Wild Bunch. There was no reason to believe he would do otherwise this time.

Tilghman thought their search should be centered around Ingalls and Lawson. He was convinced that Doolin's primary concern was his wife and child, rather than an attempt to resurrect the Wild Bunch. There was a remote likelihood that the outlaw would contact the Dunn brothers. The ranch was a known hideout, but he was wily as a fox, and often relied on the unpredictable to throw off pursuit. The greater likelihood was that Doolin would somehow spirit his wife and child out of Oklahoma Territory. All the more so since he'd tried once before to take off with his family. The high probability was that he would run and keep on running.

Thomas was finally persuaded. He found it hard to differ with the only man who had caught Doolin, and one who clearly understood how the gang leader thought. They rode out the next morning, and arrived at the Dunn ranch late that evening. A quick check confirmed that Doolin was nowhere around, and they sat down with the Dunn brothers. The Dunns were cooperative, reminded that the charges against them would be

dropped only when Doolin was imprisoned or hanged.
But they knew nothing of his whereabouts, and swore
they hadn't seen him since his escape. Nor had they
heard anything on the grapevine from their horse-thief
friends. There was simply no word on Doolin.

They stayed the night with the Dunns. The following
morning over breakfast, Tilghman casually asked Bee
Dunn if he knew anyone in Lawson. To his amazement,
Dunn remarked just as casually that his sister lived
there. Dunn went on to say that she was married to
Charlie Noble, who had settled in Lawson rather than
Ingalls during the territory's first land rush. Noble was a
blacksmith and operated a shop jointly owned with his
brother, Tom. Under questioning, Dunn grudgingly admitted that the Noble brothers frowned upon their in-
laws' dealings in stolen horses—their major reason for
settling in another town.

Upon riding out that morning, Tilghman and Thomas
were still astonished at the turn of fortune. They agreed
that a simple, off-the-cuff question often resulted in a
payoff far larger than expected. Tilghman was prompted
to ask the question in the unlikely hope that Dunn had
shady business dealings with a livestock dealer in Lawson. A thief turned informant sometimes led to another
thief who could be persuaded to turn informant. What
neither of them ever expected was that the Dunns had a
sister, and two brothers-in-law, living in Lawson. The
joker in the development was that the brothers-in-law
were honest men. They decided to appeal to greed.

Early that afternoon they rode into Lawson. The Noble brothers' blacksmith shop was located at the south
edge of town, on the west side of the street. As they
dismounted, Tilghman and Thomas noted that the back
window of the shop afforded a clear view of John Ellsworth's home. The Ellsworth house was two streets over
on a corner lot that jutted southward farther than the

houses in between. The window was a perfect spyhole on the activities of Edith Doolin.

The Noble brothers were busy shoeing a plow horse. No one else was in sight, and the lawmen assumed the horse's owner had stepped uptown. Tilghman quickly took the lead, explaining that they were there at the suggestion of Bee Dunn. The brothers paused, frowning at the mention of the name. Tilghman related in a confidential voice that the Dunns were informants for the government. The revelation seemed to shock Tom, the younger brother, whose shoulders bulged with muscle. Charlie, married to the Dunns' sister, was apparently beyond being shocked by his in-laws. A man of some girth, heavier than his brother, he seemed unfazed by the news. He appointed himself spokesman for the family.

"Why you tellin' us all this?" he said, when Tilghman finished. "We don't have no truck with the Dunns."

"They're still your wife's brothers," Tilghman observed. "Would you want them to go to jail?"

"Don't make no never mind to me. Jail's where they belong."

"Unless you assist us, they might still wind up in jail. Or maybe you'd be more interested in the reward."

Noble's brow wrinkled. "What reward?"

"We're after Bill Doolin," Tilghman said. "His wife lives here with her father. John Ellsworth."

"Whole town knows about Edith Doolin. Saw her on the street with her baby only this mornin'. So what?"

"There's a five-thousand-dollar reward on Doolin. You lend a hand and we'll split it with you."

"Twenty-five hundred dollars?" Noble squinted, head cocked to one side. "Whadda we have to do?"

Tilghman pointed through the rear window. "Keep your eye on the Ellsworth house. Let us know when it looks like Edith Doolin's headed on a trip."

"That's all, jest get word to you? Nothin' else?"

"Tip us in time to catch Doolin and that's the end of it. You get the money."

Noble's mouth curled in an ugly smile. He glanced at his brother. "What you think, Tom? The Dunn boys're family of sorts. Wanna help 'em stay outta jail?"

The younger Noble grinned. "Hell, Charlie, you know me. Family always comes first."

"Thought you'd think so," Noble said, turning back to Tilghman. "We'll keep an eye peeled, marshal. Anything happens, you'll get the word."

Tilghman explained where they could contact him, and how to get hold of Thomas. They shook hands on the deal, and the lawmen walked from the smithy. After they were mounted, they rode south on the wagon road. Thomas was silent for a long while, then he grunted.

"Bet those boys never saw twenty-five hundred all at once."

"Let's hope they get the chance this time."

"Amen to that, Brother Tilghman. Amen."

The men were hidden in tall weeds beside the tracks. Their horses were tied in a grove of trees fifty yards west of the Edmond depot. Across from them, outside the Santa Fe stationhouse, the agent waited with a mail sack for the midnight train. He paced the platform to warm himself against a brisk wind.

Dick Clifton kept his hands stuffed in the pockets of his mackinaw. Beside him, stiff from squatting in the weeds, were Dick West and Red Buck Waightman. On his other side were Al and Frank Jennings, and beyond them, Pat and Morris O'Malley. They waited, watching the station agent, wondering if the train would be on time.

A week ago, after busting out of jail, Clifton had thought it would be like the old days. He knew where West and Waightman were hiding out in the Creek Nation, and he'd assumed Doolin would reform the gang.

But shortly after crossing into the Nations, it became apparent that Doolin had other plans. With hardly more than a handshake, Doolin had left him at trailside and turned north into the Cherokee Nation. There was no invitation to come along, and no mention of future jobs for the Wild Bunch. Clifton knew then that he would never return.

A day later Clifton had rejoined West and Waightman. He found that they had long since given up hope of Doolin's return. Instead, they had been recruited into a new gang, formed by Al Jennings. Short and wiry with a thatch of red hair, Jennings was a man with grandiose ideas. Over the past month, he'd led the gang in a series of holdups on backcountry general stores. The raids, according to him, were a training ground for their first big job, a train robbery. He meant for them to become the new Wild Bunch of Oklahoma Territory.

Clifton immediately pegged him as a penny-ante bandit. But West and Waightman, who were short on brains, had accepted him as their leader. To compound matters, Jennings was backed by his brother and the O'Malleys, who were none too bright themselves. With the odds stacked against him, Clifton saw no choice but to fall in line. A train holdup was already laid on at Edmond, which was some fifteen miles north of Oklahoma City. He planned to go along, collect his share of the loot, and then strike off on his own. He thought Al Jennings would sooner or later get them all killed.

But now, waiting in the weeds beside the tracks, Clifton was intent on the job at hand. He watched as the train approached from the north and ground to a stop before the depot. On signal from Jennings, the O'Malleys boarded the locomotive and covered the engineer. The rest of the gang followed Jennings around the front of the locomotive, rushing toward the stationhouse. The guard opened the door of the express car, leaning out to collect the mail bag, just as they scattered across the depot platform. West, Waightman and Frank Jennings, their guns drawn, spread out to cover the passenger coaches. Clifton and Al Jennings halted in front of the express car.

"Don't try nothin'," Jennings barked, waving his pistol back and forth between the station agent and the guard. "I'd as soon shoot you as not."

Clifton vaulted into the express car. He disarmed the guard, motioning to the safe. "Get it open and be damn quick about it."

"I can't," the guard said in a shaky voice. "They stopped givin' us the combination back in July. Nobody can open it till we get to Oklahoma City."

"You lyin' sonovabitch! Open it or I'll kill you where you stand."

"Honest to God, mister, I'm tellin' you the truth. The Santa Fe wires the combination on ahead to the stations. Only Guthrie and Oklahoma City get it any more."

Clifton suddenly realized that it had been three months since he'd pulled a holdup. He thought the guard's story made sense, particularly from the Santa Fe's standpoint. An express guard without the combination was of no use to train robbers.

"Climb down outside," he ordered, waiting until the guard jumped from the car before he nodded to Jennings. "I'm gonna have to blow the safe."

"Holy shit!" Jennings protested. "That'll wake up the whole gawddamn town."

"Told you a town wasn't no place to rob a train. You should've listened."

"Stop sayin' I told you so and get it done. We're not leavin' empty-handed."

Clifton pulled two sticks of dynamite from inside his mackinaw. He found twine inside the express car and used it to tie the dynamite to the safe door. Then he struck a match, held the flame to the fuse until it sputtered. He bolted from the door.

The explosion rocked the train. Debris and dust drifted through the open door as the conductor popped out of one of the coaches. The gang drove him back inside with a flurry of shots, and began peppering the coaches to keep the passengers inside. Clifton hefted himself into the express car.

The safe door was scorched but otherwise undamaged. A section of the floor was buckled and tongues of flame leaped along the wall opposite the safe. Clifton tried the handle on the safe door, then stepped back and kicked it in frustration. After a moment, muttering to himself, he turned away. He hopped down beside Jennings.

"No soap," he said glumly. "Hardly touched the damn thing."

Jennings glared at him. "How the hell'd you ever get the name Dynamite Dick?"

"Never blowed a safe!" Clifton said sharply. "Just used it for express car doors."

"Some sorry state of affairs, you ask me. Let's get outta here before the town throws us a necktie party."

The gang beat a hasty retreat across the tracks. The men cursed and grumbled as they ran toward the distant treeline. There, after swinging aboard their horses, their leader set a course for the Nations. Clifton brought up the rear as they thundered off into the night.

He told himself it was time to get far away from Al Jennings.

CHAPTER 42

The aborted robbery made headlines. Not as large and not as bold, but nonetheless a front-page story in the Guthrie *Statesman*. Though unsuccessful, in many ways laughable, the raid was still hot news. There had not been a train holdup in more than three months.

Tilghman and Thomas had returned from Lawson the night of the holdup. At first, when they met with Nagle, there was some speculation that Doolin had given fresh life to the Wild Bunch. But by early morning, details of the raid began filtering in over the telegraph. They were somewhat mystified by the reports.

The express car guard positively identified Dick Clifton. The Edmond station agent was equally positive in his identification of Dick West and Red Buck Waightman. Wanted posters on the three outlaws were plastered on the walls of train stations across the territory. Yet the witnesses were no less familiar with Bill Doolin, whose image still decorated wanted dodgers. None of them could place him at the scene of the holdup.

Their descriptions of the other gang members added still more confusion. Three of them were nondescript in appearance, the type of men who would blend in with a crowd. But the fourth man, according to witnesses, would be a standout in any crowd. He was described as short and slight of build, a bantam of a man with flaming red hair. The witnesses reported as well that he was the leader of the gang.

Thomas and Tilghman were of the same opinion. With the demise of the Wild Bunch, someone had stepped into the breach and forged a new gang. In the process, the man had somehow recruited Clifton, West, and Red Buck Waightman. Which meant that Clifton had joined the gang within days of his escape from jail. In turn, that meant Clifton had known all along where to contact West and Waightman.

Hard as it was to admit, the lawmen had to conclude that Clifton was a skilled liar. On the train from Texas, when they'd interrogated him throughout the night, he had convincingly denied any knowledge of West and Waightman. For Tilghman, the fact that he'd been fooled was of no great consequence. He was intrigued, instead, that Doolin was no part of the Edmond holdup, or the new gang. All of which seemed to bear out his original hunch. The key to Doolin was his wife and child.

Thomas was more intrigued by the new gangleader. Something about the man's description bothered him, tickled his memory. He began rummaging through a stack of field reports from marshals around the territory. At last, he came across a report about a pint-sized bandit with bright red hair, who led a band of misfits in looting general stores. The man had been identified as Al Jennings, and the band he led included his brother Frank and the O'Malley brothers, Pat and Morris. They operated out of the Creek Nation.

When Thomas and Tilghman put their heads together, the conclusion was obvious. West and Waightman had apparently taken refuge in the Creek Nation, and somehow run across Al Jennings. Clifton, after his escape, had joined them and fallen in with the new gang. With Doolin out of the mix, the whole thing made perfect sense. Jennings had absorbed the dregs of the Wild Bunch into his own gang, and gone from looting stores to robbing trains. The question that remained was where Jennings and his men might be found.

A wire late that afternoon brought the answer. Federal Marshal George Bussy, who was stationed at Chickasha, had been contacted by one of his own informants. For the reward money involved, Clifton, West, and Waightman had been betrayed by a Creek tribesman. Al Jennings, along with his brother and the O'Malleys, had been betrayed as well. The gang was scattered throughout the Creek Nation, but their locations were known. Marshal Bussy requested instructions.

Patrick Nagle wired him that Tilghman and Thomas were on the way.

Deputy marshals George Bussy and Andy White tied their horses in a stand of trees. Armed with Winchesters, they moved forward through the timber and halted at the edge of a clearing. Their position overlooked a farmhouse.

The farm, according to Bussy's informant, belonged to Wallis Brooks. A white man, Brooks had married a Creek woman and thus gained the right to property in Indian Territory. Located outside the town of Eufaula, the farm was a couple of miles north of the Canadian River. Dynamite Dick Clifton was reported to be staying with Brooks.

Bussy had met yesterday with Tilghman and Thomas, and several other federal marshals. There were ten lawmen in all, and Nagle had ordered that Tilghman and Thomas were to direct the operation. Three raiding parties were formed, with Tilghman and Thomas in one, and the largest party, with six marshals, under the command of Bud Ledbetter. Bussy and White were assigned to capture, or kill, Dick Clifton.

Their information was that Clifton had a Creek lady

friend in Eufaula. He apparently spent his nights in town and returned to the farm every morning. Bussy and White, traveling through the night, had timed their arrival with sunrise. There was no way to determine if Clifton was in the house or still with his lady friend. They settled down to wait beside a wagon road at the edge of the clearing.

Bussy was a large man with a handlebar mustache. He shook his head, watching the house. "Way Thomas talked, we ought to kill him and have done with it. Tilghman tended to favor taking him alive. Funny the way men think different."

"Not so different," White remarked. "I recollect Tilghman's killed his share. Doolin's the only one he ever brought in alive."

"Wonder what the hell's the score with Doolin. They didn't say nothin' about him."

"Doolin's like their own private grudge match. You can tell, they want him real bad."

"I'll bet you one thing," Bussy said. "Next time, they'll stop Doolin's clock."

"Yeah, he's already dead and just don't know it."

The conversation dwindled off and the lawmen waited as the sun rose steadily higher. Toward midmorning Bussy nudged White with his elbow, nodding in the direction of the farmhouse. Clifton, mounted on a horse, had taken a shortcut through a cornfield to the north. He was broadside to them, already halfway across the clearing.

"Clifton!" Bussy yelled, shouldering his Winchester. "Hold it right there!"

Clifton reined his horse about, drawing his pistol. He winged a shot at the trees as he booted his horse into a gallop. The lawmen fired an instant apart, the reports of their carbines blending into one. White's shot struck the horse, and it plowed nose first into the ground. The slug from Bussy's carbine broke Clifton's left arm as he was thrown from the saddle. He hit the dirt with a hard thud.

Bussy and White stepped from the trees, levering fresh rounds into their Winchesters. Clifton scrambled awkwardly to his feet, his left arm dangling at a grotesque angle. He hobbled toward the cornfield, triggering two wayward snap-shots as he moved. The lawmen fired simultaneously, one slug drilling Clifton through the chest and the other shattering his shoulder. He dropped three steps short of the cornfield.

White spun around, leveling his carbine as Wallis Brooks ran out of the house. He kept the farmer covered while Bussy walked forward to inspect the body. After a moment, Bussy waved his Winchester overhead.

"Dynamite Dick won't dynamite no more!"

Shortly before noon Bud Ledbetter and his squad of five marshals were in position. Throughout the morning, he had waited in the woods while the lawmen, one by one, took their assigned posts around the clearing. They now had the farmhouse surrounded.

The farm belonged to Sam Baker, brother-in-law by marriage to Wallis Brooks. Located some five miles farther along the Canadian, the house overlooked the river. George Bussy's informant had reported that the house was occupied by Al and Frank Jennings and the O'Malley brothers. So many outlaws were difficult to conceal, particularly when they made nightly trips into Eufaula. Their presence was apparently known to everyone in town.

Bud Ledbetter had saved the most critical task for himself. The gang had posted a lookout, armed with a rifle, seated in a wagon near the barn. Ledbetter surmised that the outlaws' horses were stalled in the barn, for there was no outside corral. He stepped out of the woods, on line with the back of the barn, which screened his movements from anyone in the house, or from the lookout. A few moments later he paused at the corner of the barn, less than five yards from the wagon. He shouldered a 10-gauge double-barrel shotgun.

"Hey, mister," he called out in a low voice. "Over here."

Morris O'Malley looked around. He found himself staring into the twin bores of a scattergun. The man behind the gun stared back with a grim expression. "Climb down off that wagon," Ledbetter ordered. "Walk over here slow and easy. You open your mouth and I'll kill you."

O'Malley gingerly moved off the wagon. For a moment, staring into the shotgun, he thought he would wet his pants. But he made it to the corner of the barn, where he was yanked out of sight, quickly disarmed, and his hands manacled behind his back. Ledbetter motioned with his hat toward the woods west of the clearing. In turn the marshal posted there signaled a marshal covering the front of the house.

"Al Jennings!" the marshal out front shouted. "This is a federal marshal speaking. I order you and your men to surrender!"

The back door burst open. The Jennings brothers and Pat O'Malley boiled out of the house in a headlong rush for the barn. Their pistols were drawn, and in their panic to escape, they failed to notice that their lookout had disappeared. Ledbetter moved around the corner of the barn, his shotgun leveled.

"Halt or be killed!"

Al Jennings and his brother fired in what sounded like a single report. Ledbetter triggered both barrels of his shotgun in a thunderous roar. From either side of the house, marshals cut loose with a rolling volley from their carbines. Jennings went down with a slug in his shoulder, and O'Malley collapsed, his legs shredded by buckshot. Frank Jennings froze, dropping his pistol, somehow unscathed in the hail of lead. He raised his hands.

The marshals converged on the house. Ledbetter shifted the shotgun to his left hand and drew his pistol as he moved forward. Al Jennings clutched at his shoulder, his eyes watering with pain. O'Malley writhed about on the ground, his trousers soaked with blood. Frank Jennings stood as though struck by sudden paralysis.

"Helluva note," Ledbetter grunted, inspecting them with a bemused look. "I think you boys are gonna live."

The grass was crisp underfoot. A glazy afternoon sun shed splinters of light over the swift-running stream. Tilghman and Thomas ghosted through the woods, halting deep within the treeline. To their front was a dugout at the bottom of a stunted hill.

The dugout bordered a creek that fed into the Canadian. A battered wooden door was framed as an entrance, and smoke drifted from a stovepipe protruding through the roof. Off to one side was a log corral, with two horses standing hip-shot in the sunlight. There was no sound, no one in sight.

Tilghman and Thomas had elected to raid the dugout themselves. So far as they were concerned, the other marshals were fully capable of handling the rest of the gang. But the informant had reported that Dick West and Red Buck Waightman could be found at an abandoned dugout burrowed from the side of a hill. They hadn't forgotten the farmer gunned down by Waightman some three months ago. Nor had they forgotten burying the farmer while his grief-stricken wife and little girl looked on. Waightman was theirs, and West was icing on the cake.

The congregation of outlaws around Eufaula was to them a matter of blind luck. According to the informant, who had finally let greed overshadow prudence, West and Waightman had used the dugout off and on for over a year. Clifton, whose Creek girlfriend lived in town, was a frequent visitor as well. Jennings and his men were apparently regular guests at the farms of two white men married to Creek sisters. By whatever quirk of fate, the demise of the Wild Bunch had brought them all together. Their mistake, the blind luck, was that they'd opted to stick with hideouts around Eufaula. Old habits had played into the hands of the law.

Thomas hadn't taken his eyes off the door of the dugout. "What d'you think?" he said in a graveled whisper. "Do we call 'em out or do we wait?"

"We wait," Tilghman replied. "They can't stay in there forever. Let's catch 'em in the open."

Looking back, they would remember the words as somehow foreordained. The door opened and Red Buck Waightman stepped from the dugout, followed by West. They were freshly shaved, their hair slicked down, apparently set for a night in Eufaula. Waightman still in the lead, they turned toward the corral.

"Federal marshals!" Tilghman yelled. "Don't move!"

Waightman whirled, pulling his pistol, and fired. West crouched and ran, dodging back toward the dugout, snapping off a hurried shot. The slugs whistled through the trees an instant before the lawmen opened fire with their carbines. Thomas levered two rounds and Waightman fell spread-eagled, his shirt splotched with blood. Tilghman let off only one shot, dusting West front to back, and the outlaw dropped just as he reached the door. His right leg kicked in a spasm of death.

The lawmen walked forward, their carbines at the ready. They inspected the bodies, satisfying themselves that both men were dead. At length, Thomas looked around, his eyes still cold with anger. A hard smile touched the corners of his mouth.

"Scratch Red Buck Waightman off the rolls. Sorry bastard won't kill any more farmers."

"No, he won't," Tilghman observed. "We've done a good day's work here."

"Still got one to go. The he-dog himself."

"Heck, I just suspect we'll get our chance."

They both wondered where they might next meet Bill Doolin.

CHAPTER 43

The washed blue of the plains sky grew smoky along about dusk. A stiff breeze fell off, but there was a lingering nip in the sharp, crisp air. The lawmen rode into the ranch as twilight slowly gave way to dark. Neal Brown helped them unsaddle their horses.

Tilghman had convinced Thomas that they should make another scout around Lawson. Two days past, at a prearranged site on the Canadian, they had rendezvoused with Bussy and the other marshals. The time and place of the meeting had been part of their overall plan for the raids. Any of the gang who had slipped through the net would be pursued from there.

Yet, after everyone arrived at the rendezvous, pursuit proved to be unnecessary. The last three members of the Wild Bunch had been killed, and the Jennings gang had been taken alive. Wagons confiscated at the farms providing refuge had been loaded with the dead and the wounded. Bussy and Ledbetter, both senior marshals, had escorted the wagons on to Guthrie.

Thomas and Tilghman had then turned their attention to the unresolved matter of Bill Doolin. From the Canadian, they had angled northwest through the Creek Nation, headed for the ranch. News of the raids rushed ahead of them, spreading along the grapevine from town to town. Tilghman became increasingly concerned, for newspapers were certain to headline the violent end of the Wild Bunch. He was worried that Doolin would take it as an omen and run.

Their two days on the trail had cost them precious time. Tonight, walking toward the house, Thomas was no less concerned that they might be too late. For all they knew, Doolin might already have heard the news, and made arrangements to flee the territory with his family. But they were weary from the grueling manhunt, and they both felt it would be a mistake to push on without rest. They needed a hot meal and a good night's sleep, as well as fresh mounts. They agreed to leave at dawn.

Brown got busy in the kitchen. While they washed and shaved, he fired up the cookstove and began slinging together a meal. By the time they were finished, he had the table laid out with charred beefsteak, fried potatoes, and warmed-over biscuits. They wolfed it down while he peppered them with questions, whooping loudly about the last of the Wild Bunch. When their plates were clean, he served them large wedges of Dutch apple pie. Their bellies full, they lingered over a final cup of coffee.

Finally, thinking about sleep, they rose from the table. As they walked from the kitchen, they heard hoofbeats, the sound of a horse being ridden hard. Tilghman moved through the parlor to the door, and saw a man dismount outside. His features were revealed in a spill of lamplight as he stepped onto the porch. Tilghman realized it was the young blacksmith from Lawson, Tom Noble. He held the door open.

"Way you pushed that horse, you've got news. What's up?"

"Charlie told me not to spare the whip." Noble entered the parlor, nodding to Thomas. "We think Doolin's about to make his move."

Tilghman looked at him. "Why so?"

"Edith Doolin bought a wagon and horse from the livery stable this mornin'. She's got it parked out beside her dad's house."

"How'd you get wind of it?"

"Saw her drive by in the new rig," Noble said. "Last time she left town, we remembered she'd done the same thing. So Charlie talked to the feller that owns the livery."

"Yeah?" Thomas coaxed. "What'd he find out?"

"She didn't dicker none a'tall about price. Agreed right off, like she's in a powerful hurry."

"Tell me," Tilghman said casually. "Has the news hit Lawson about the Wild Bunch?"

"Has it ever!" Noble wagged his head. "Everybody in town's been talkin' about it 'cause there was no word on Doolin. We heard the others was all killed."

Tilghman and Thomas exchanged a glance. Their fears were confirmed that the news would goad Doolin into hasty action. The fact that Edith Doolin had bought a wagon was all the corroboration they needed. She was planning on leaving town.

"Let's get back to the wagon," Tilghman said. "Has she loaded it, or is it just sitting there?"

"Just sittin' there." Noble paused, then went on. " 'Course, I lit out to bring you the word. She could've started loadin' up after I left."

Tilghman considered a moment. "Where's a good place to keep watch on the Ellsworth house? Your smithy won't do, not for us. Too much chance we'd be spotted."

"Lemme think." Noble studied on it, scratching his jaw. Finally, with a quick smile, he bobbed his head. "There's a big patch of woods off to the west of town. Starts maybe a quarter-mile behind Ellsworth's place."

"Yeah, I remember," Tilghman said, nodding. "I was checking on the Doolin woman at the time and didn't pay much attention. Do I recollect a trail leading into the woods?"

"You sure do," Noble affirmed. "Old logging road that cuts through there to Eagle Creek. Anyplace in them woods, you'd be lookin' right at Ellsworth's back door."

"No rest for the weary," Tilghman said, glancing at Thomas. "We'll have to leave tonight."

"Suits me," Thomas agreed. "I've done without sleep before."

An hour later, mounted on fresh horses, the lawmen and Tom Noble reined away from the corral. They rode north under a star-studded sky.

John Ellsworth looked stricken. Seated in the parlor, he nervously clasped and unclasped his hands. He stared blankly at the wall, avoiding his wife's steely gaze. She glowered at him from the sofa.

A plain dumpling of a woman, Sarah Ellsworth was stout, with sharp, beady eyes. She had the formidable manner of a drill sergeant, and she ruled her household with an iron hand. Tonight, watching her husband, she was incensed by his attack of nerves.

"Stop twitching," she said angrily. "Any minute you'll start having conniption fits."

Ellsworth winced. "Sadie, you know the law's not far behind whenever he shows up. How'd you expect me to act?"

"You've got no spine, never did. Edith loves him and he's the father of our grandson. Now, let's hear no more about it!"

Doolin had appeared at the back door late last night. The word was out that his gang had been eliminated, and Ellsworth knew what his sudden arrival meant. All the more so when Edith had gone out this morning and bought a horse and wagon. Yet he wasn't able to summon the strength to contact the federal marshals. Nor was he able to defy his wife.

"How did it come to this?" Ellsworth said heavily. "When he showed up again tonight, that was the beginning of the end. You know he plans to take Edith and the boy . . . don't you?"

"What did you expect?" she said with a nettled look. "They're man and wife, and they want to be together. You just keep your nose out of it."

Ellsworth slumped down in resignation. At the end of the hall, a bedroom door opened and Edith walked to the kitchen. She filled a glass with water, then paused in the dining room, looking into the parlor. She smiled at her father.

"Don't act so glum, Daddy. The world's not coming to an end."

She disappeared down the hall into the bedroom. Doolin was seated at the foot of the bed, holding the baby. She gave him the glass, then took the baby from his arms. As he drank the water, she gently nestled the baby between pillows at the head of the bed. She laughed softly.

"Daddy's such a fussbudget. He can't bear the thought that you've finally come for me."

"Don't worry about it," Doolin said, placing the glass on the floor. "Your ma will bring him around."

"I'm sure," she said, seating herself beside him on the bed. "Whatever tune Mama plays, Daddy hums along."

"Well, let's let them work it out for themselves. We've got plans of our own to think about."

She hugged herself with merriment. "I still can't believe it! We're really on our way this time, aren't we?"

"For a fact," Doolin said earnestly. "Come tomorrow night, we're Californey bound."

"And we'll make it." She took his hand, pressed it to her cheek. "Nothing's going to stop us this time."

"Nothing or nobody," Doolin said with a determined

edge to his voice. "We're gonna get there come hell or high water."

"You're sure the law has no idea you're here?"

"Honey, they don't have the least notion of where I'm at."

Doolin had spent almost two weeks covering his trail. He'd stuck to the backwoods, living off the land, as he slowly made his way from the Cherokee Nation to Lawson. After scouting the area, he had made camp on Eagle Creek, some three miles west of town. Then, certain his wife wasn't being watched, he'd left his horse in the woods last night and approached the house. Walking still bothered him, but he was happy to endure the pain. By tomorrow night, they would be long gone. On their way at last.

"Bill, would you tell me something? It's been on my mind."

"I've got no secrets from you."

She lowered her eyes. "Why didn't you just send for me . . . like you did last time?"

"Last time you was followed." Doolin smiled indulgently. "I aim to make sure you're not followed this time. That way nobody'll ever know where to find us."

"Oh, I love the sound of it! No more worrying whether we're being spied on. Just the three of us—a new life!"

"But we gotta do it right. You don't start loadin' that wagon till it gets dark. No sense tippin' our hand."

"I'll remember," she said with a vigorous nod. "We've got supplies enough to last till we're out of the territory. Won't take long to load."

Doolin patted her hand. "Don't worry if you don't see me right away. I'll be waitin' somewhere on the trail to Eagle Creek. Anybody tries to follow you, I'll take care of it."

"I know you will." She paused, her voice suddenly

husky. "Couldn't you stay the night? It's been so long since we . . . were together."

"Plenty of time for that later. Better safe than sorry, and I'm lots safer back at my camp. One more night won't matter."

She walked him through the hall. Doolin waved to the Ellsworths and followed her into the kitchen. At the back door, she melted into his arms, gave him a long, passionate kiss. He gently stroked her hair, then stepped into the night.

After closing the door, she danced across the kitchen, her skirts flying. John and Sarah Ellsworth looked up as she hurried into the parlor. Her eyes were bright with happiness, her smile radiant.

"Only one more day! We leave tomorrow night!"

Shortly after sunrise the lawmen parted with Tom Noble south of Lawson. They skirted west a mile, then entered the woods and worked their way back in the direction of town. A half hour later they found the old logging road.

The Ellsworth house was visible from the trees. Outside, they saw the wagon, the horse loosely tied to the rear. After scouting the area, they picketed their own horses deep in the woods, away from the road. At the edge of the treeline, they settled down to wait.

Throughout the day, one slept while the other kept watch. The telescope from Tilghman's saddlebags brought the house into sharp focus. They saw John Ellsworth depart for work shortly before eight o'clock, and later, Edith Doolin came out with a bucket of oats for the horse. The morning passed uneventfully, and as the afternoon dragged on, there was still no sign of activity. They continued to watch.

Tilghman and Thomas were both of the opinion that Edith Doolin would head for the Nations. Once there, knowing she'd been trailed the last time, she would probably attempt some new dodge to throw off pursuit.

They surmised that she would not turn north toward
Kansas, for Doolin never used the same plan twice. Instead, they thought she would meet Doolin at some
backwoods whistle stop, where the Katy railroad bisected Indian Territory. A train from there could take
them north or south, possibly Missouri or Texas. Where
they planned to travel after that was pure conjecture,
and of no great importance. The lawmen intended to
waylay Doolin in the Nations.

Late that afternoon Tilghman was on watch. As the
sun dropped below the horizon, he saw Ellsworth return
home from the store. Lamps glowed in the house, and
within minutes twilight faded into darkness. The night
was crisp and clear, the sky brilliant with the glimmer of
stars. Another hour passed, and when Thomas came to
relieve him, he suggested that they pitch camp by their
horses, fix a pot of coffee. There seemed little likelihood
of anything happening tonight. Thomas agreed.

But then, as they started to turn away, Tilghman
caught a flicker of movement outside the house. He extended the telescope, training it on the wagon, which
was dimly visible in a spill of lamplight from the windows. Looking closer, he saw Edith Doolin, assisted by
her father, loading bundles into the wagon. When they
finished, her father went to hitch the horse as her
mother came out the back door with the baby. Finally,
after a quick round of hugs, she climbed into the wagon
seat. Her mother handed up the baby.

Tilghman was on the verge of sending Thomas to
fetch their horses. But he hesitated, somewhat astounded, watching as Edith Doolin swung the wagon
around and headed in their direction. Taken off guard,
he and Thomas discussed their options, and quickly for-
mulated a plan. They retreated roughly a mile deeper
into the woods, and posted themselves on either side of
the road. When the Doolin woman passed by, Tilghman
would trail her on foot and Thomas would follow along

with their horses. The logging road ended at Eagle Creek, some two miles farther on, and beyond that were open plains. They would have to trail her at a distance.

Some while later, hidden behind a tree, Tilghman watched as the wagon approached their positions. He readied himself to follow along, but suddenly froze, listening. From the opposite direction, toward Eagle Creek, he heard the slow clop of hoofbeats on hard earth. He craned around, looking over his shoulder, and saw a man on foot leading a horse. A shaft of starlight flooded the road, and as the distance closed to less than ten yards, the man's features became visible. Directly across from his position, he picked up a blurred shadow out of the corner of his eye. Thomas stepped into the road.

"Doolin! Surrender or be killed!"

Doolin's pistol appeared in his hand as though by magic. He fired from the hip, and the slug thunked into a tree behind Thomas. A split-second later, the carbine at Thomas's shoulder spat a streak of flame. Doolin staggered backward, arms windmilling, and his horse bolted down the road. His knees buckled and he dropped to the ground, the pistol skittering from his hand. His chest rose and fell with a last shuddering breath. Then he lay still.

"Ooo God no!"

Edith Doolin's scream echoed through the woods. Tilghman moved into the road and saw her tumble over the side of the wagon. He hurried forward as Thomas levered a fresh round and walked toward the body. She scrambled off the ground, her eyes wild with terror, and Tilghman caught her in his arms. She struggled to break free, wailing a low, keening moan, but he held her tighter. Her mouth opened in a tormented cry.

"I have to see him! Please, God, let me see him!"

"Later, Mrs. Doolin," Tilghman said in a quiet voice. "There'll be time for that later."

Her features sagged, tears spilling down her cheeks. She went limp in his arms, her body shuddering with soft, mewling sobs. Tilghman held her close, saddened by her grief, knowing it could have ended no other way. Unbidden, a wayward thought came to him, something out of the past. A remark once made by Heck Thomas, and now come true.

One of them would be renowned as the man who killed Bill Doolin.

EPILOGUE

The Wild Bunch was no more, and Bill Doolin was dead. A mood of celebration prevailed, and the Three Guardsmen were once again summoned to Guthrie. The Capitol Building was at last under construction, and on November 14 a crowd of some five thousand people gathered before the capitol grounds.

The capitol was located at the east end of Oklahoma Avenue. A tall speaker's platform had been erected in front of the construction site, the railings and stanchions festooned with bunting in patriotic colors. Behind the podium there were rows of chairs, occupied by legislators, judges and other dignitaries. Seated among them were Bill Tilghman, Heck Thomas, and Chris Madsen.

Governor William Renfrow had proclaimed it Marshal's Day. His proclamation, circulated throughout the territory, had set aside a day to honor the men who had brought law and order to a new frontier. Foremost among that number were the three men seated on the dais today. Their names were household words across Oklahoma Territory, and people had traveled by train and buggy and horseback to be there for the occasion. Men sat children on their shoulders so that they could one day say they had seen the greatest lawmen of an era.

Zoe stood with her father in the front rank of spectators. The crowd stretched westward along Oklahoma Avenue and spilled out onto sidestreets. Newspapers from throughout the territory were represented by reporters and cameramen positioned directly before the speaker's platform. Off to one side, a uniformed band played rousing tunes made popular by John Philip Sousa, bandmaster for the U.S. Marine Corps. The music and the patriotic trappings lent a holiday atmosphere to the occasion.

On the platform, Governor Renfrow and U.S. Marshal Patrick Nagle were seated beside the three lawmen. The governor nodded to one of his aides, who in turn signaled the bandleader. The air filled with the blare of trumpets as the band segued into ruffles and flourishes to open the ceremonies. The crowd broke into lusty cheers as the governor made his way to the podium. A consummate politician, he spread his arms high and looked out over the throng with his trademark nutcracker grin. Finally, lowering his arms, he motioned for silence.

"Good people of Oklahoma Territory!" he boomed in a resonant voice. "We gather today to honor the men who brought law and order to our great land. We commend in particular the three men who again and again risked their lives in stamping out that infamous gang of killers, the Wild Bunch." He paused, an arm thrust out in dramatic gesture toward the lawmen. "I speak of peace officers whose deeds have made their names legend across this land—the Three Guardsmen!"

The crowd burst out in a spontaneous roar. After a moment, the governor quieted them with outstretched arms, and went on with his speech. Thomas glanced at Tilghman, then at Madsen, who had returned from his post in Missouri for the occasion. They exchanged the slight smiles of men unaccustomed to the fanfare and hyperbole of public acclamation. The governor's rich baritone continued to extol their deeds, playing on the theme of good versus evil, lawman against outlaw. The spectators stood as though mesmerized by his words.

Tilghman listened with only mild interest. His mind drifted back over the people and events that had brought him to this point in time. He recalled every manhunt, every shootout, all the death and suffering that littered the past. His most vivid memory was of Bill Doolin, who somehow seemed the last of a breed. Far more clever, and deadly, than the likes of Al Jennings, who awaited trial in federal court. He saw it as the end of an era, horseback marshals pitted against outlaws who ran in packs. Oklahoma Territory would soon absorb Indian Territory, and the sanctuary of the Nations would be gone forever. The outlaw days were finished, and with it, a moment in time. A new era, far different from the old, lay ahead.

Watching from the crowd, Zoe was overcome with pride. Only ten days ago, Tilghman had been elected sheriff of Lincoln County by a landslide vote. Yet she knew, looking at him now, that he would be remembered most for his work in eliminating the Wild Bunch. Historians would one day write of him and Heck Thomas and Chris Madsen, and all the other men who had worn the federal badge. Their courage and dedication, their iron determination, would be recorded for future generations. She thought the record would accord them their due, their rightful place in history. They were, indeed, the stuff of legend.

"So I say to you," Governor Renfrow told the crowd. "Never before in the annals of crime have peace officers faced such a daunting and bloody challenge. These men fought a war, a long and unrelentless war for the rule of law in Oklahoma Territory. And they won!"

Hands upraised, the governor stilled the crowd, promising more. "These are valiant men, each one by any measure, a man of valor. Accordingly, we are here today to recognize their devotion to duty with a special award. The Medal of Valor!"

The band broke out in a stirring tune and the crowd went wild with cheers and applause. Aides got Tilghman, Thomas, and Madsen positioned beside the podium, on line with the cameras. The governor moved from man to man, pinning a beribboned gold medal to the breasts of their suit coats. Flashpans exploded as he paused before each of the lawmen, shaking hands, smiling broadly for the cameras. Then, with a final word of praise, the governor was whisked away by his aides. The band played on as the crowd raised a last, rousing cheer.

"How 'bout that?" Thomas said, fingering the medal on his chest. "You boys ever expect to be heroes?"

"I don't know about heroes," Madsen said in a wry tone. "But the governor was right about one thing. We took on a dirty job and we got it done. That goes for you and Bill, especially."

Tilghman laughed. "Truth be known, none of us deserve medals. Nobody forced us to wear a badge."

"Nobody but ourselves," Thomas said, grinning. "Otherwise you wouldn't have run for sheriff. Told you once, you're a born lawman."

"You should talk," Madsen heckled. "All the badges you've worn, you've lost count by now."

"Chris, I found my calling, that's all. Took the gospel to the heathens."

Patrick Nagle interrupted their bantering to offer his congratulations. He wished Tilghman well in his new job, and thanked Madsen for having made the trip from Missouri. They chatted for a while and after a final round of handshakes, he drifted off. Thomas suddenly looked somber.

"Just hit me," he grunted. "You boys are leavin' me all by my lonesome. Don't know what I'll do for laughs."

"Door's always open," Tilghman said. "Come visit me

over at Chandler. Maybe we could catch ourselves some whiskey smugglers."

"Jesus, I don't know as I need laughs that bad."

Their good-natured joshing continued as they moved off the platform. Zoe and her father joined them, and Tilghman introduced the other two lawmen to Amos Stratton. Thomas shook his hand with an expression of mock concern.

"Guess you know your daughter's marryin' a drifter."

"Drifter?" Stratton repeated, missing the humor. "Bill Tilghman?"

Thomas nodded solemnly. "Drifts from one job to another real regular. One day a marshal, the next day a sheriff. Never know where he'll end up."

"Oh yes, I do!" Zoe interjected gaily. "He'll end up at home every night, right where he belongs. No more wild chases with you, Heck Thomas."

"With me?" Thomas sounded hurt. "Bill's the one that was always draggin' me off to the Nations and such. I'm strictly a stay-at-home sort."

Zoe laughed, taking Tilghman's arm. "Well, I've removed temptation from your path. You can stay at home all you care to."

"Yeah, I know," Thomas said sadly. "Gonna be awful dull around here."

Tilghman said his goodbyes there. He and the Strattons had a long drive, and Madsen was scheduled out on the evening train. The lawmen were kindred spirits, and there was a strong sense of loss when they shook hands. They realized they would probably never work together again, and their parting was all the more difficult. As Thomas and Madsen walked away, Tilghman felt an inward tug of regret. He would miss them.

Later, on the road out of town, Tilghman was in a quiet mood. Stratton was driving, and Tilghman and Zoe sat close together in the back seat of the buggy. Zoe sensed that his thoughts were on the parting with Thomas and Madsen. Yet her thoughts were on an altogether different matter, one she had never before put into words. She understood that a lawman's work was often cold and hard, sometimes brutal. Today, watching the three marshals shake hands, she was reminded that a badge brought with it a burden. She wondered how it affected the man she was about to marry.

"Bill?" she said, unable to resist curiosity. "Would you tell me something if I ask?"

"I'll do my best."

"When you face someone like Doolin, a killer? Does it change you—inside?"

"Never thought about it." Tilghman was reflective a moment. "Guess I've been at it so long, it's like second nature. I do what needs doing to get the job done. What makes you ask?"

"Well—" She hesitated, selecting her words. "I've never seen that side of you, and I'm curious. What you're like when you . . ."

"Zoe, I'm just me," Tilghman said with a crooked smile. "Told you before, I'm only good at two things. One's raising horses and the other's enforcing the law."

She was silent a moment. His statement was his way of telling her that however things might appear, in the end he was simply himself. She snuggled closer, hugging his arm.

"Let's hope you're good at one other thing."

"What's that?"

"Oh, you know," she said in a throaty voice ". . . being a husband."

Tilghman burst out laughing. "We'll know soon enough."

"No," she whispered in his ear. "Not nearly soon enough."

Amos Stratton strained to hear her reply. Then he

realized that he wasn't meant to hear, even if she was his daughter. Some things, and rightfully so, were between a man and a woman.

He drove on toward Chandler.